The GATE of SORROWS

MIYUKI MIYABE

The GATE of SORROWS

Miyuki Miyabe

Translated by Jim Hubbert

HAIKASORU
SAN FRANCISCO

The Gate of Sorrows
HITAN NO MON
by MIYABE Miyuki

Originally published in Japan by Mainichi Shimbun Publishing Inc., Tokyo.
English translation rights arranged with RACCOON AGENCY INC., Japan
through THE SAKAI AGENCY.

Cover Illustration by Dan May
Interior Design by Sam Elzway

HAIKASORU
Published by VIZ Media, LLC
P.O. Box 77010
San Francisco, CA 94107

www.haikasoru.com

Library of Congress Cataloging-in-Publication Data

Names: Miyabe, Miyuki, 1960– author. | Hubbert, Jim, translator.
Title: The gate of sorrows / Miyuki Miyabe ; translated by Jim Hubbert.
Other titles: Hikan no mon. English
Description: San Francisco : Haikasoru, 2016. | "Originally published in Japan by Mainichi Shimbun Publishing Inc., Tokyo" — Verso title page.
Identifiers: LCCN 2016021706 | ISBN 9781421586526 (hardback)
Subjects: LCSH: College students—Fiction. | Serial murder investigation—Fiction. | Monsters—Fiction. | Tokyo (Japan)—Fiction. | BISAC: FICTION / Fantasy / General. | FICTION / Fantasy / Contemporary. | GSAFD: Fantasy fiction. | Mystery fiction.
Classification: LCC PL856.I856 H5513 2016 | DDC 895.63/5
LC record available at https://lccn.loc.gov/2016021706

Printed in the U.S.A.
First printing, August 2016

Also by
Miyuki Miyabe
from VIZ Media/Haikasoru

Brave Story
The Book of Heroes
ICO: Castle in the Mist
Apparitions

Table of Contents

BOOK I:

Grains of Sand in the Desert

Prologue

The rain drummed against the window—a winter storm. The clouds hung heavy and low in the sky. Wind moaned between the buildings.

The drumming had a rhythm like anxious knocking, millions of tiny fists pummeling the windowpane that sagged in its weathered wooden frame, the putty crumbling with age. The little girl rested her elbows on the sill with her chin in her hands. Her forehead and the bridge of her nose almost touched the glass. The wind blowing through the gaps in the frame puffed her ragged bangs upward.

The apartment was a single room, just six tatami mats. The girl's mother was sleeping on the floor behind her, back to the window under a thin blanket. With each big gust, the old two-story wood-frame apartment, built twenty years before her mother was born, trembled to its foundations.

The room was freezing. The girl wore her mother's coat over her head. Less than an hour earlier, when her mother had gotten up to go to the toilet, she had wrapped it around her daughter like that. The fabric was ripped and worn, but the thick wool was heavy. The girl was buried in the coat. Only her face peeked out.

It had been two days since the little girl's fifth birthday. That was the day they turned the electricity off. Seeing her desperate situation, the man from the power company had gone easy on the mother for as long as he could, but he'd finally been forced to give up.

"You're ten months behind, you know. I've got no choice but to shut the power off. If you can get a month's payment together somehow, I'll switch it back on right away."

The man had given her mother lots of advice. *Get some help from the city. I bet the landlord would be willing to introduce you to the Welfare Bureau. Anyway, you can't go on like this. You don't look well and your little girl needs looking after.*

Yes, thank you, her mother had said. *I'll do that. Thanks for your concern. I'm sure I can put together enough to pay for a month at least. Yes, I'll ask a friend for help. I can pay at the local office, then?*

Call me, the man had said. *I'll come right away. Does your phone work? Do you have money for a pay phone?*

Oh yes, money for the phone. I haven't had a mobile for ages, but I'll call you from a pay phone.

But after the man was gone, her mother had gone to bed and stayed there. She wasn't well, just as the man had said. Indeed, she was far sicker than he could have guessed. She crawled more than walked the distance between her bed and the toilet.

The little girl wanted to cling to her mother because Mama was warm with fever. But her mother pushed her away. *Don't be mad at me. I just don't want you to catch my cold. Be a good girl. I'll be fine soon. I just need some rest.*

She stayed in bed after that. She was always warm. She was almost hot. But when the girl touched her mother, she could feel her shivering. When the coughing fits came, her mother's wasted body twisted in a strange way.

The girl wondered what time it was. *Outside is black, so it must be nighttime*, she thought. The only light in the room came from the little battery-powered alarm clock, but the girl wasn't good at reading its hands yet.

The wind blasted the building again, shaking it from top to bottom.

The girl tried more than once to turn on the television, but none of the switches worked. She didn't understand that without electricity, she couldn't watch TV.

Mother and child had faced many problems. This was not the first time they'd had to make do without power. Still, the little girl was too young to understand the nature of the problems her mother had faced and overcome, or their causes.

Yet she still had an uneasy feeling that at long last, a problem had come that they might not be able to fix.

At least it's cold. The food in the fridge won't spoil. That's what her mother had said after the electricity man had gone away.

Eat something if you get hungry, Mana-chan. There's some of that bear bread you like.

The bear bread had been eaten up a long time ago. The food in the refrigerator didn't spoil, not because it was cold but because there wasn't any. The refrigerator was empty.

The little girl was faint with hunger. She was cold. Her mother, wracked with fever and nodding off into dreams between fits of coughing, didn't feel the cold and emptiness the way her daughter did.

The rain battered the windowpanes. Millions of tiny fists beat insistently on the glass. *Come out, come out, come out. You have to get out of there. Mama is sick. You have to tell someone. Mama is sick and you're cold and hungry. You have to tell someone!*

The little girl didn't know the right way to say the thoughts in her head. Her mother had had to struggle hard to make ends meet, and her daughter had never been to nursery school or kindergarten.

A big, cold spoon had come down from the sky and scooped the little girl and her mother up off the big cake called Society. The spoon just floated in the air. It didn't take them anywhere, and it wouldn't put them down.

The girl exhaled on the windowpane. Her stomach was empty but her breath still came out. The little cloud on the window bloomed and went away. Sheets of silver rain sluiced from the bloated clouds.

The little girl liked the apartment because she could see the forest of tall buildings in the distance with their windows upon windows that lit up every night, just like Christmas trees.

Her mother had told her about the buildings when they moved in. *Those buildings are all about forty stories high. They're very, very tall. The elevators are very fast, otherwise it would take forever to get to the top.*

The forest of buildings wasn't so far from this neighborhood of old apartment houses and narrow streets. A grown-up could walk there and back again. The little girl saw lots of people walking toward the buildings every morning.

There were lots of other buildings between the skyscrapers and the apartment. The whole city was packed with buildings. Some were like the Christmas trees but looked smaller from so far away. Others were wide and gray. Some had steep red roofs and others had gray roofs with stuff sticking out. Most of them had colorful signs that lit up at night. Some of the signs were small and some were big. Some of them were pretty, but others looked old and dirty.

There were different colors and shapes and sizes, but the most important thing to the little girl was whether or not a building had lights at night. The little girl loved the lights in the neighborhood. The lights from the buildings were all different colors. They were like so many Christmas trees. Every night was Christmas.

But the girl was afraid of one building, the only one that never had any lights, ever. It was right in front of her, out the window. She could see it in the rain-smoked light from the other buildings. Hulking, dark, alone.

Mama had taught her how to count. One, two, curl your fingers. Or stick them out and count out loud. Counting that way, the scary building was a little more than three traffic lights from the apartment. The girl wanted to count the buildings between, but she ran out of fingers and didn't know what to do next. So she counted the traffic lights.

The building was peculiar. Mama had told her it was for business, but it had a different shape from the forest ones, and it was different from the nearer ones that seemed to be made of glass.

To the little girl, the building looked just like the can of cookies one of Mama's customers had given her a long time ago. There was a picture of Mickey Mouse on the outside, and cookies that tasted like cocoa nestled beneath the lid.

This shape is called a cylinder. They don't always have cookies. They hold all kinds of things. Tea, or candy.

The little girl could see the round building whenever she looked out the window, like a dark pillar between her and the sparkling buildings in the distance.

One, two, three. She had counted the number of stories on her fingers, with Mama's help. The building had four stories.

It looks like no one is using it. Mama had told her no one was living there, probably.

The building was empty. That's why the lights didn't go on. No one was going in and out. The little girl had never seen anyone open or close the windows in the daytime.

The roof of the building was a little bit funny. There was no railing. Instead, it was surrounded by a notched wall. There was a gap in the wall, at the left edge of the roof. There was something in the gap.

At first she thought it was a somebody. That was the afternoon of the day they had moved to this apartment, before she found out the building was dark at night. *Mama! Mama! Look, somebody is sitting up there!*

At first her mother was surprised too. She scrunched her eyes up and tilted her head this way and that.

That's not a person. It's some kind of statue, Mana. It must be a roof decoration.

A statue. A decoration.

Like the ones in the park, remember? That one's a little funny though, isn't it?

It was funny. The little girl had never seen anything like it. She had said somebody was sitting up there because that's just how it looked. But it wasn't a somebody. It couldn't be, because it had wings.

What was it, this something squatting on huge legs, hunched over, brooding on the roof of that black pillar?

In the girl's eyes, that something was a monster out of the darkness, like in movies on TV or a picture in a book, a monster that spread its wings and rose into the air, slashing people with hooked claws. She wanted to take a closer look, even climb up to that roof. But maybe it would move if she got too close. It was a monster, after all.

The girl looked at the monster every day. She wanted to be sure it hadn't moved, that it wasn't getting closer, that monster brooding in the center of the view she loved to look at from the window.

The girl looked out the window, wrapped in her mother's coat. The only trace of warmth in the freezing room was the fog of her breath. The monster was there now, in the winter storm and silver rain. Sometimes it disappeared in the sheeting downpour. Whenever that happened, the girl squinted to make sure it was still there.

The monster is there. It's just a statue. It's not scary or anything.

On the floor behind the little girl, her mother—the only person in the world she could rely on, and who herself was desperately in need of someone to rely on—was dying of pneumonia. Her five-year-old mind did not understand that death was near. She was too young to understand what death was.

But instinctively, as a living creature, she knew death was close. It was coming for her mother, coming to take away her single mother, worn out by years of toil and hard luck, to leave her only child—who had only ever heard her name spoken by her mother—alone in the darkness of this tiny room.

Death was coming. She could feel it. She wanted to snuggle up to Mama, but it was forbidden. All she could do was look out the window. But she could be a sentinel. She could watch to see how close death was. The monster would show her. If it moved, if it spread its wings, if it kicked off into the sky from that gap-toothed rampart, she would know.

Maybe she had been wrong to stare at it every day. Maybe looking at it so much made it notice her and Mama.

Her mother was wracked by another violent coughing fit. Then her throat made a different sound. It was like the wind blowing through the gap in the window frame. A creaking hiss.

The rain poured down the glass. Everything was blurred. The girl wiped the glass with a little hand. The freezing window raised goose bumps on her arms.

The monster would come. It would start to move. What would be scarier, to watch or turn away? She would hide in Mama's bed, put her back close against her mother's back.

Mama, the monster is coming!

In vain, her mother gasped for air.

That was when she saw it.

An enormous darkness descended onto the roof of the black pillar. It seemed to drop from the sky and alight by the hulking statue.

Yes, it moved. It didn't just appear, like pushing a switch. It didn't come out of the shadows. It came down from the sky.

It came from the sky!

Out of the swollen clouds, beyond the sheets of silver rain.

This new darkness was bigger than the squatting monster. The inky silhouette was shaped like a person. Its hair was long. Its arms and legs were long too.

And like the monster, it had wings.

1

Kotaro Mishima bit back a yawn and yanked his bike out of its spot in front of the house. He was about to jump on when he heard a shrill voice behind him.

"Ko-chan, we need to talk!"

She came running toward him, her thick wooden clogs clattering. Her voice wasn't the only thing that was dynamic about her. Her hair was bleached blond. She was wearing a crimson apron, a flower-pattern sweater, and striped pants. Pure Aunt Hanako.

"Bright-eyed and bushy-tailed this morning, aren't you, Auntie?"

Hanako raised a precisely drawn reddish eyebrow. "At my age, it's the only time I can be." This was ironic, because Hanako had likely never thought of herself as old for a single moment.

"The morning's half-gone anyway. But I bet you're running late."

"I don't have class till after noon."

"And you call that a school!"

"Hey, it's a good school," Kotaro said. "When Mika starts going to college you'll understand, Auntie."

"You know, I wanted to talk to you about Mika. Mind you, it's very hush-hush."

Kotaro sighed inwardly. Hush-hush? Aunt Hanako was so loud the whole neighborhood could hear her.

Then again, it was already five past ten. Mika had left for school hours ago. She was a freshman in middle school. Had Hanako not cornered him, Kotaro would've been burning rubber for the station now. Jump on the express, change at Tokyo Station, get off at Ochanomizu. The whole trip took under an hour.

Kotaro's neighborhood was a picture-perfect housing development in the Tokyo suburbs—constructed as a unit, neat as a pin, pretty in a mathematical way, with multicolored sidewalks lined with streetlamps on either side of roads just big enough for two cars to pass, lined with tract houses that were only saved from being utterly identical because of the little vanity options the owners had chosen. Someone looking first at the developer's plans, then the real estate company brochures, and later the finished houses with people in them, would hardly have seen a difference.

But things *were* different, under the façade. The development was just as neat, orderly, and pretty as its designers intended, in a physical sense. When you added people to the mix, things instantly get chaotic. Kotaro's neighbor Hanako Sonoi was the embodiment of that chaos.

Not that she noticed. Aunt Hanako lived in her own dimension of time. Among other things, this meant that hanging out with her posed grave dangers to Kotaro's schedule. Normally he would've begged off, but at the mention of Mika he hesitated. He put the kickstand down.

Mika Sonoi was Hanako's granddaughter. She went to the same middle school as Kotaro's sister, Kazumi, and was a year her junior. Both girls belonged to the soft tennis club. Kazumi was the one who had originally invited Mika to join.

The girls had known each other since kindergarten and were as close as sisters. Kotaro regarded Mika almost as his little sister.

"What's up with Mika?"

"You're a computer wiz, right, Kotaro?"

Aunt Hanako liked to talk, and like most people who enjoy the sound of their own voice, she didn't get right to the point. Problem was, if you got impatient and tried to cut to the chase, it only made things worse. Kotaro had known the Sonois since before both families had moved to this cookie-cutter housing development. They went way back. Kotaro was an expert at dealing with Aunt Hanako.

"I'm no wiz. I know as much as most people."

"But you've got a part-time job at a computer company. Mama said so."

"Mama" was Kotaro's mother, Asako. Kotaro's father, Takayuki, was of course "Papa" to Aunt Hanako. Yet she addressed her own daughter, Mika's mother, as Takako-*san*. She "san"-ed her own daughter. It was bizarre.

"It's not a computer company. It's not like I'm coding and stuff like that."

"But 'computer' means 'program,' doesn't it?"

"PCs won't run without a program, but they're not the same thing. What I'm trying to say is, I'm not working at the kind of company you think I am. So what's going on with Mika anyway?" Kotaro knew that without regular prompting, Aunt Hanako was liable to forget what she set out to say in the first place.

Hanako's eyes narrowed, as though what she was about to say next were dangerous information. "Someone's been writing things about Mika in the dark."

If Kotaro's parents had been listening in, they probably would've thought Hanako was talking about graffiti someone was leaving at night.

But Kotaro was a 21st-century boy. The Internet had been part of his life since he could remember. He knew instantly what Aunt Hanako was trying to say.

"On a dark website?"

Her eyes opened wide with excitement. "Yes, that's right. What you said."

"Was it something mean? Aunty, did you hear this from Mika?"

"Oh no, she hasn't said a thing to me. But the school called Takako-san yesterday afternoon. She gave me the short version after she got back. I'm not sure I understood it."

So it had something to do with computers, and that's why she came to me.

Kotaro stood for a moment, thinking. He'd definitely be late if he hung around much longer.

"Listen Auntie, I have to get going, but here's some advice. I don't think Mika will say anything to you about this, so it would be better if you play dumb."

"But the school called Takako-san in for a conference. It sounds very serious to me."

"Schools are scared to handle stuff by themselves these days. They call parents about every little thing, just to cover their rears. Did Mika go to school today?"

"Yes, she did."

"Then you don't have to worry. Maybe Kazumi knows what's going on. I'll ask her when I get home. Confidentially, of course."

"Oh? But...I don't know..."

Hanako hated loose ends. She didn't seem keen on this course of action. Kotaro gave her his biggest smile.

"She'll be fine, I'm telling you. Mika's training hard. Kazumi told me she might even play in the regionals. Not many first-year players are that good."

"Yes, she's just like Takeshi. Sports were always his strong point."

Takeshi was Mika's father. He and Takako had divorced soon after Mika was born. Hanako, however, had been very partial to him and never missed a chance to bring him up.

"Well, I better get going."

"Take care. Study hard."

Kotaro mounted his bike and took off. Just before he reached the corner he turned to see Hanako going into the house. He wondered why she insisted on wearing heavy clogs when all she could talk about was how bad her knees were. What if she fell down, broke a bone, and ended up bedridden?

It was the 15th of December. The year was practically gone. The wind cut like a knife out of a clear blue sky. Winter was Kotaro's favorite season. It was perfect for a bike sprint, much better than spring or autumn.

But the morning's mood had turned a little heavy. Aunt Hanako had been wrong in thinking Kotaro worked at a computer company. But if someone was spreading rumors about Mika online, Hanako was right to bring the problem to him.

Was someone bullying Mika on a dark site?

He had to find out. Seigo would know what to do.

▼

Kotaro was nineteen years and three months old. He was a freshman education major at a so-so university in central Tokyo.

Neither the university nor the major had been Kotaro's choice. His school was the only one that had accepted him; he'd failed his other entrance exams. The heavy hand of fate had gone ahead and decided things for him.

He had no plans to become a teacher. Tokyo was awash with would-be teachers anyway. There were no jobs—none at all.

"Ko-chan, what are you going to do? You don't have a chance," Kazumi would say.

"I'll make it somehow."

He had more than two years before he had to start thinking seriously about where he might find a job. Now was the time for him to congratulate himself on at least getting in somewhere. Now was the time to enjoy his student life.

That's what he'd thought, at first.

Much to his surprise, student life wasn't much fun after all. This rude awakening took place soon after the term started. Why was everything so boring? He had to admit, he'd never thought things would be this bad. Why was school so lame?

He was surrounded by students who'd drifted into university with no goal, no purpose. People just like him. They were all having a great time. They were enjoying this one best time of their lives to the max, and they acted like their goal was to enjoy it even more, if that were possible.

Somehow Kotaro couldn't go along. He didn't even know what it was he was supposed to be enjoying. He'd joined a few of the clubs, but aside from their activities and names, they were mainly about parties and drinking. The "serious" clubs were so serious that Kotaro was put off. Why did everyone tell him university clubs would be fun?

Then again, who *was* "everyone," exactly? Who had told him that being a college student was a nonstop party? Who had told him the clubs were totally cool?

For Kotaro, it was the lectures—the one thing in school that bored the kids around him to tears—that somehow seemed interesting. His general education courses were mostly tedious, but every now and then he'd stumble across something new in one of his classes, something fascinating. The clubs, with their nonstop partying and drinking, offered nothing new. The basic difference between high school and this university that fate had chosen for him was that now he could openly do things that before he'd had to do in secret.

Maybe I chose the wrong path, he told himself. *Maybe I should've thought about college more carefully. Maybe I should've chosen my major more carefully, even if it meant taking a year or two off.*

Was he having some kind of psychological letdown? No, letdowns were for people who were serious about school. He hadn't burned with motivation while he'd been studying for exams. Making it into this school didn't feel like an accomplishment. He was just glad he'd got in somewhere.

Kotaro's father was a salaryman who worked in a credit union. His mother Asako was a homemaker, but she'd always had some kind of job since she married. For the last two years or so she'd been working the register at a big retailer not far from their house.

Both of his parents were model citizens. They had worked diligently to raise Kotaro and Kazumi, setting aside their own enjoyment to pay for their children's education, which wasn't coming cheap. Pretty much everyone would probably say that was what parents were supposed to do. But Kotaro wasn't remotely sure he could sacrifice as much and as patiently as his parents had, were he called on to do the same. They had him beat on that one, as someone his age might say.

It would be awful enough to confess to his father and mother that it looked like he'd screwed up his choice of school and major because he hadn't taken the whole thing very seriously, that he found nothing rewarding about student life. Maybe they'd worry about his mental stability. He knew he wasn't going crazy, though he couldn't put his finger on what he felt.

In fact, that was the problem. He didn't know what he was feeling. He hadn't felt motivated studying for his exams. He wasn't feeling a letdown after getting admitted. It wasn't because he was disappointed that so far he hadn't met any guys he could really talk to, or girls who were his type. He knew something was missing in his life. He just didn't know what.

That was then. But in the middle of summer break—his first, unbearably long college break—something happened.

He parked his bicycle at the station and sprinted up to the platform. The express had come and gone. *Better send a message to Kaname.* She'd have to wait ten minutes longer than usual for their handoff.

Kotaro mulled Aunt Hanako's request while he waited for the next express. She had asked the right person to help her based on a misunderstanding. Explaining that would be practically impossible. The Internet jargon would sail clear through her nets.

Listen, Aunty. I'm not working for a computer company. But it has something to do with computers.

Yes. It had a lot to do with them.

See, what I'm doing is called cyber patrolling.

He had found the missing piece.

2

Kumar Corporation was in a compact office building not far from Ochanomizu Station. The staff lounge offered a nice view of the dome of the Holy Resurrection Cathedral.

Kotaro had first stepped through these doors in early July. The rainy season had just ended, and the sprawling used book district at Jinbocho, not far from the station, was sweltering in the muggy heat. Kotaro was hitting the bookstores when he ran straight into Seigo Maki.

Seigo was an alum of Kotaro's high school. Like Kotaro, he'd been on the futsal club. Kotaro left the club to study for exams when he became a senior, but until then he'd seen Seigo almost every week.

Seigo was mad about futsal. Ostensibly he was donating time to coach the team, but his main motivation was the chance to play. At the time he'd been thirty. He didn't look like much of an athlete. He was five-foot-four and pudgy, but a tenacious player and an outstanding coach.

Since they'd met in front of Sanseido Books, they decided to head upstairs to the coffee shop for a chat. As he was bringing Seigo up to speed on what he'd been doing, Kotaro made the mistake of mentioning how uninspiring school was.

Seigo wasn't at all surprised. "I could see you were bored from a long way off. Why don't you start a futsal club?"

"They've got one. Thing is, they hardly ever play. All they do is party."

"So that happy, free, stimulating campus life doesn't suit you, Ko-Prime?"

Back in the day, there'd been another club member named Kotaro Inoue. Seigo was the first to start calling Inoue "Ko." Since "I" came before "M," that made Kotaro "Ko-Prime." Using Kotaro's name would've been simpler, but for some reason the nickname stuck. It was a sign of how much the team trusted Seigo.

Kotaro hadn't heard this nickname in a while. *High school was pretty cool after all*, he thought wistfully.

"In fact, I'm thinking about making a switch," he told Seigo.

"You mean changing schools? Don't do that. If you're not going for senior civil servant or law school, you'll face the same problem wherever you go. If you can't stand your school, try the police academy. Or join the Self-Defense Forces."

Kotaro's iced coffee almost shot out his nose. "Me? A cop? Or a soldier?"

"What's wrong with that?"

"No way. My father's just a salaryman."

"What does that have to do with it? Sure you're not interested?"

Going into law enforcement or the military had never even remotely occurred to Kotaro. "I mean, both of those jobs are pretty tough, right? Taking orders from superiors and stuff like that?"

Seigo put a hand on his head and rubbed his summer haircut, which was cropped almost to the skin.

"Hmm. Okay, so you don't like ranks and orders and so on."

"Hey, I didn't say I couldn't handle it."

"Seriously, I think you'd make a good cop, Ko-Prime. Haven't you noticed? I always thought you were looking for a way to help people. Help the world, you know? At least a little."

Kotaro had to laugh at that. "You gotta be joking."

"Really? You were always up for the chores no one else wanted to handle. Cleaning the court, stowing the gear. You know? That time you negotiated with those jerks on the soccer team to get us some field time. You were good at mediating when people disagreed."

"If those are qualifications, I'd feel sorry for the cops who had to work with me."

"You think so? I don't know, maybe I'm wrong."

Kotaro watched with amusement as Seigo sucked the last of his iced coffee noisily up the straw. He just didn't get it.

If Kotaro had indeed been so conscientious in high school, it was mostly thanks to the man sitting across from him. Seigo led by example. Whether current members or alumni, Kotaro's seniors in the futsal club had always loved to throw their weight around for no reason at all. Things had been even worse on Kotaro's middle school basketball team. At least that was what he thought, until Seigo showed him things could be different.

People just can't see themselves the way they are.

"Listen, Ko-Prime…" Seigo set his glass of melting ice on the table sharply. "If you're that bored, why not get a job?"

"Doing what?"

"Feel like some part-time work?"

Now that was more like it. Kotaro already had several hooks in the water. "I was thinking about applying to a convenience store. The pay on the late shift is sweet."

"So you can work nights?"

"Sure, I can juggle my schedule."

"Are you sure you could do that and not neglect your studies? Your parents would worry. You're still a minor." Seigo was pretty levelheaded when it came to this sort of thing.

"Don't worry. The homework will get done."

"Then let's go. It's right around the corner." Seigo picked the check off the table and smiled. He took Kotaro to Kumar Corporation, not far from the Holy Resurrection Cathedral.

"This is where I work," he said as they stood in the lobby. "Our headquarters is down in Nagoya. This is the Tokyo office. We've got the third and fourth floors."

The lobby was nice enough. The building looked brand new. Reception was on the third floor, but it was unmanned—just a counter and a phone. There was a glass disk on the wall behind the counter with the company name and logo etched into it with a kind of 3-D effect.

"Kumar is a funny name for a company."

"Yamashina has had this book since childhood, about a monster named Kumar."

"Yamashina?"

"The founder. We went to college together. I'm an executive director. I also basically run the Tokyo office."

Kotaro goggled at him in surprise. Seigo had attended all their after-school practices on weekdays and worked with them on Saturdays and during summer breaks. Kotaro remembered asking him about it.

Are you taking time off from work?

We've got flextime.

You're not busy on weekends?

No family, no girlfriend, no problem.

That was it, though; he'd never asked Seigo for more details about his private and professional lives. Somehow it had never seemed necessary.

Seigo and the founder were classmates? Executive director? Maybe this Yamashina, president or CEO or whatever, founded the company as a student? It was more than possible, considering how old Seigo was.

The door to the offices had an electronic lock. There was a small panel next to the door. Seigo dug around in his chinos and pulled out a key card on a strap. He put the card against the panel. There was a low tone as the door unlocked.

"Here we are. After you."

Kotaro bowed reflexively and went inside. A short corridor led off to the left and right with a door at each end. The wall in front of him was glass from about waist height. The floor beyond was spread out before him.

"Wow..." Kotaro couldn't hide his surprise.

The office was packed with rows of tables and swivel chairs. Most were occupied. The people were dressed as casually as Seigo—T-shirts, polo shirts, jeans, chinos. There was a loud aloha shirt. Everyone had cards dangling from their necks like the one Seigo had used to open the door. Most looked younger than Seigo, maybe a bit older than Kotaro.

The periphery of the room was dotted with file cabinets and big whiteboards on casters. The boards were crammed with writing that was too small to read from the corridor. There were also smaller blackboards at the end of the rows of desks, the kind that bars and restaurants used to announce the day's specials, with writing in white and pink chalk.

None of this was out of the ordinary for an office. But two things were unusual. For one, the blinds were tightly closed in the middle of the day. There were also two flat-screen monitors on every desk. Everyone in the office—mostly men, but there were a few women too—was looking back and forth between their two monitors. They had multiple windows open on each one, with information scrolling upward. Once in a while a user would touch his mouse or keyboard, but not often. No one was punching a calculator. There were no papers on the desks. No one was in a meeting.

It was quiet. There were no ringing phones.

"What are they all doing?"

Seigo looked at Kotaro intently.

"Kumar is a security firm. We keep cyber society safe."

▼

As Kotaro had told Aunt Hanako, he wasn't a PC expert. The net-surfing bug had never bitten him. He'd never started a blog and didn't read them. For everyday things—looking for a shop, checking a map—he usually used his phone, but he couldn't even use half the apps it came loaded with. He'd never tried to hide his lack of interest in the net. Kazumi probably knew a lot more than he did. She was always chasing down gossip about her favorite celebrities.

Still, this wasn't the first time he'd encountered the term "cyber patrol"—people who monitored the web, investigated, and when necessary took action when they turned up something against the law, or something harmful or dangerous, or likely to encourage people to commit a crime.

But until he'd seen it with his own eyes, Kotaro never thought cyber patrolling could be a job. He'd had this idea it was something PC maniacs did. Either that or volunteers, which didn't sound too interesting.

"You're right, Kotaro. There are people who volunteer to do it, like registered members of a website who patrol the site in their free time."

"I didn't know that. I just saw a bit about it on TV."

The news spot Kotaro had seen reported that the Internet was the place to go for illegal drugs, guns, and child pornography. There were people who recruited friends to help commit shocking crimes. Mass murderers proclaimed their intentions on the web before taking action. After spotlighting a few examples, the program showed how cyber patrols monitored the flow of information on the web and worked to prevent crime.

"It was on in the evening, I think," said Kotaro. "Some kind of special report."

"Right. We've gotten some attention from the media ourselves."

Seigo gave Kotaro a quick tour of the office, then brought him to the lounge. It reminded Kotaro of his campus cafeteria in miniature. Everything was tidy and new. A bookcase bulged with graphic novels and other kinds of fiction. There was a vending machine with soft drinks, candy, and instant noodles. Kotaro was surprised to see there was no TV.

The lounge was empty. Everyone at Kumar was hard at it, except for one employee Kotaro noticed, out cold in the nap room.

"So what did you think of that news show? Did it pique your interest?"

"Why? Not much to do with me."

Seigo laughed and turned to the window. The cathedral dome baked in the summer sun.

"True, our regular employees and contractors all have degrees, a lot of them in computer science." Seigo reeled off some big-name universities. "We have a lot of midcareer hires too." He ticked off the names of several major tech companies.

Kotaro was hard put to hide his surprise. Everyone looked so young, so informal, so *into* it. They didn't look like they had elite credentials.

He'd missed it by a mile. He laughed to cover his embarrassment. "I knew it. They sure look like pros."

"They are. They've got the background and the chops, otherwise they couldn't do their jobs. That's why we've never hired students part time. But recently I've been trying to get Yamashina to rethink the policy. We need more diversity.

"You saw the people in the office. There's not much of an age spread. I'm thirty-three and I'm the oldest. Our youngest full-timer joined us last spring. She's twenty-two. Everyone's in the peak generation for net users. But as time goes by, the user population is going to get older and younger at the same time. We have to be ready."

Seigo explained that with more people of all ages joining web society, the kinds of trouble that could occur and the types of difficult and dangerous information circulating would also change. If the patrollers were all in their twenties and thirties, they would start to miss things.

"The web is a world of its own, full of secret signs and double meanings. A lot of words are used to mean something else. Some of the jargon is based on punning, and if you don't get it, you don't, even if you share the same language and culture. What we do know is that different generations use words differently, and we have to understand those differences if we're going to patrol web society effectively."

Kotaro had never heard Seigo talk this passionately about anything other than futsal.

"We thought we'd start by hiring some older people. There are more people than you'd think who are getting up there, but are really into computers."

Kotaro found that hard to picture. The only really old member of the Mishima family was his paternal grandfather, who lived near Osaka, and even figuring out how to return messages on his phone was a challenge for him.

"Problem is, most people that age have problems with their eyesight. They can't pull long shifts either, so we'd have to have a lot of them, and they'd all need training.

"That leaves us with students. In a way, they're the opposite of seniors. They don't know how society works yet, or where they're going. They haven't developed the skills to navigate the adult world. But without their point of view, there are things we might miss."

Kotaro wondered what that "point of view" actually was.

"Of course, we'll also get publicity from hiring college and high school students. Recruiting people from that age group would generate a lot of word-of-mouth. Young people are getting bored chasing information that's hot for just a day or two. They want something more, like the lowdown on the occupations of the future. Life hacks."

Kotaro could picture that.

"So listen, Ko-Prime. Want to try working here?" Seigo grinned. "To cure that boredom of yours. You don't have to think about it too hard. I'll show you the ropes myself. We'll figure out a schedule that works for you."

Kotaro had to admit that it sounded fascinating. He was definitely interested. Still...

"What you're saying is, I'll be guinea pig number one for Kumar Corporation's part-time hiring experiment."

This brought a burst of laughter from Seigo. "That's a great way to put it. You're exactly right. Maybe instead of 'guinea pig' you should say 'prototype model.' "

Guinea pig it is.

"So if I screw up, you might decide it's not a good idea to hire people like me. I'm not sure I want to that responsibility."

"You always were a straight-up kind of guy, Ko-Prime."

"It's not that at all."

"Don't sweat it. No one's going to put success or failure on your shoulders. And there's something else I haven't told you." Seigo lowered his voice and leaned forward. Kotaro found himself doing the same.

"We're closing the Tokyo office a year from now. This city's just too expensive."

When Kumar was starting out, the Tokyo office was essential to get the word to clients. Now that the business was on track and growing, things were different.

"If you close down, what happens to all those people I saw? What happens to you?"

"We're moving to Sapporo. We'll have our own building there—well, it'll be pretty small, but we're moving ahead with construction. I'm looking forward to getting out of here. I'm sick of Tokyo's sticky summer nights."

Services like Kumar's could be delivered from anywhere. Still, finding the right people would be tough unless the company set up shop in at least a medium-size city. Kumar could put the best hardware money could buy on a remote island or in the mountains, but the software—people—would be missing. Big regional cities like Nagoya, where Kumar was based, were the perfect solution.

"My family lived in Sendai for a while after my father transferred there. It's a great place. I tried to sell Yamashina on moving up there, but one of our competitors—we don't have very many—is already based there. It seemed like a good idea to keep our distance."

Kotaro knew that Sendai and Sapporo were both home to some of the best science schools in Japan.

"If you're interested in what we do, this is your chance, Ko-Prime. Try it for a year. I mean, even if you end up feeling like you got pulled into a weird job just because we're friends and you ran into me, you'll still have a year's worth of work experience. All you have to do is stick it out."

"Come on Seigo, it's not like I'm saying no."

"Look, I can't force you to answer right away. Think about it, okay?"

Seigo showed him to the lobby. Kotaro watched him head back to work with a spring in his step.

Kotaro hadn't come to Jinbocho for any particular book. His father, Takayuki, loved to stroll from one used bookstore to another. He often brought Kotaro with him, and the used-book bug had bitten him too. When he had time on his hands and nothing special to do, Kotaro still went there out of habit.

He checked his smartphone. There was a mail from Kazumi with a long list of celebrity photo collections and manga with maximum prices, asking him to pick them up if he "just happened" to run across them. Kazumi's suggested prices were unbelievably optimistic. "The bookstores aren't that stupid," Kotaro muttered.

Then again, he'd never hear the end of it if he didn't at least try to find something. Along the way he turned Seigo's offer over in his mind.

Kumar Corporation interested him, but one thing made him hesitate, though Seigo kept telling him not to worry. How could he measure up to the people there? Compared to them he was nothing.

As he went from shop to shop looking for the titles on Kazumi's list, he found one that specialized in children's books. The sign in the window said THOUSANDS OF TITLES, NEW AND OLD.

Kumar. Wasn't that a name from a children's book? A book about a monster that the founder of the company loved as a kid.

Kotaro knew he couldn't expect to find it just like that. Still, it would be fun if he could. From the look of the shop, "thousands of titles" was probably an understatement.

He went inside. The shop was pleasantly cool. He walked around on the creaking floorboards, surveying the shelves. All he had to go on was the name Kumar. He didn't even know the title of the book. He was probably wasting his time.

I must be nuts, he was about to conclude, when a section of shelves caught his eye. A sign read PERENNIAL FAVORITES. And there it was: *Kumar of Jore*, its big cover at eye level amid a collection of colorful children's books.

It was a translation of a foreign book. The author's name was long and unpronounceable. The artwork and colors were charming, but somehow different from Japanese books for children.

Kotaro glanced furtively up and down the aisle, took the book from the shelf, and opened it.

Kumar was a monster.

That was the opening sentence. It was the only text on a double-page spread. The artwork showed a fjord framed by mountains under a blue sky. There was a little waterfront town in the distance with tall, peaked roofs and a church with a steeple. Kotaro turned the page.

Kumar had always lived in these mountains. He loved the mountains that rose above the fjord.

Right, got it. So what kind of monster is this? What's he look like? Kotaro riffled the pages, but there wasn't a single picture of Kumar. Then his eye fell on a line that told him why.

The people in the town could not see Kumar, because he was invisible.

Kumar was a monster who had lived for uncounted years in the mountains overlooking the fjord. In fact, he had lived there for so long that he couldn't remember living anywhere else.

If this had been a Japanese tale, Kumar would have been the guardian spirit of the mountains. He'd have protected the mountains and the fjord and the little town of Jore from bad monsters, and lived happily ever after.

Kumar loved the town and the people who lived there. He loved the songs they sang at festivals and the music they made. He loved the smell of pancakes that wafted up from the town. He loved the sound of people's laughter, too, and the church bells.

Kumar was born invisible. That's the sort of monster he was. But he didn't suffer; on the contrary, it made him a more formidable opponent for the bad monsters. He could sneak right up on them before they knew it.

But one day, while Kumar was fighting a cunning lizard monster trying to sneak into the town, he miscalculated and let his opponent strike a blow. The wound was deep and painful, and Kumar's blood poured out. Worse, the precious horn on the top of his head was broken. Long ago his father and mother had warned him that his horn was almost as important as his life.

That was when Kumar saw it. What was this? His body was invisible no more. He could see his arms and legs. He was astonished to see, for the first time, the sharp, curved claws that grew from his fingers and toes.

Without his horn, Kumar was visible. Until it grew back again, everyone could see him.

Oh no!

Then something worse happened. The old belfry keeper and his little granddaughter, up in the tower, caught sight of Kumar.

In an instant, the whole town was in an uproar. A monster! A monster is here! In great pain, Kumar staggered into the mountains. The townspeople kept the lights on all night, and some went into the mountains with torches to search for Kumar. Find the monster! Find him, kill him!

I'm not a bad monster. I'm a monster, but I'm still Kumar.

Kumar shed bitter tears as he fled deeper into the mountains. But no matter how far he went, his pursuers would not give up. Day after day, they harried him and gave him no rest.

Kumar was tired and hungry. He wanted to eat a fish from the fjord.

Just before dawn, Kumar came out of the mountains and went to the shore of the fjord. He could see Jore in the distance. He watched the sun rise above the town.

Lit by the sun, Kumar saw his face and body for the first time in the water.

He looked just like the bad monsters he had been fighting all his life.

My face is no different from the bad monsters. I'm the same color. I have the same tail. That's why people are so afraid of me. That's why they harry me and give me no rest.

Kumar walked into the water. He dove in and began to swim. He had to go somewhere far away.

Goodbye, good people of Jore. May we meet again.

Kumar could hear the church bells in the town ringing as he swam away. He never returned. The waters of the fjord were deep and cold, and Kumar was wounded and weary. The waters swallowed him up.

But the story of Kumar was told ever after in Jore, the legend of a terrible monster who came out of the fjord and attacked the town.

There was a brief profile of the author with the unpronounceable name at the end of the book. He was from Norway.

Kotaro closed the book and put it carefully back on the shelf.

He thought he'd like to meet this person named Yamashina, who had loved this book, founded a company, grown it into something real, and named it after Kumar.

Kumar Corporation. I think I'll give it a try.

3

Kotaro didn't wait for the elevator. He sprinted up the stairs to the fourth floor. On the way he pulled his key card out of his backpack and slipped the strap over his head.

Today's shift was eleven to two. It was now 11:12. He stashed his pack and jacket in the hall locker, touched the pad by the door with his card, and pushed it open. Toward the back of the room, in the far left row, Kaname Ashiya was already eyeballing him with a fierce look of disapproval.

Kotaro put both palms together, dipped his head quickly, and called good morning to the rest of the room. The office was two-thirds full, and around half of those present gave scattered responses ranging from grunts to a clipped "morning." Greetings weren't required; many of the employees never gave or responded to them because it didn't contribute to efficiency, and no one took it amiss. Most of the people who did respond never took their eyes off their monitors.

Kotaro paused by the time clock to punch in his ID code, then hurried over the soundproof (and odor-eating) carpet toward his work station.

"Sorry, my bad. Someone cornered me on the way out the door. I missed my express."

Kaname put on her scariest face. "You owe me big time."

"Yeah, I know. I'll buy you a Big Mac."

"Get out of here. Italian."

Kaname was twenty. Her women's university was in the Tokyo suburbs, within biking distance of Kotaro's house. She was from Nagoya.

First impressions would have been of a reserved young woman. Her clothes were quiet and refined. Before sitting down for her shift, she would sweep her long, lustrous black hair into an attractive ponytail. Seigo's nickname for Kaname, "The Lady," was inspired by the upscale town of Ashiya near Osaka whose name she shared.

Kaname and Kotaro were shift buddies, covering each other's schedules to ensure there were no gaps in patrolling. Kaname lived in her university dorm and couldn't take night shifts, but other than that, she and Kotaro would review their schedules against the shifts they needed to cover and trade off flexibly, which was convenient. If one of them missed a shift, it would fall on the other to cover it. This system was effective in making sure that both took their schedules more seriously than the average student part-timer—another of Seigo's innovations for the "Kumar Corporation Part-Timer Employment Experiment."

The risk with the buddy system was that if you and your buddy didn't get along, life could be hell. But Kotaro had been lucky. Kaname was a levelheaded, serious student. Her major was Japanese literature. From time to time she'd throw out a reference to some early modern author that went clear over Kotaro's head. She also ate like a horse, belying her figure. Kotaro had joined Kumar about a month ahead of her, and in the beginning he'd had to teach her everything, but by now she'd learned to manage without help. She had a fine sense for the nuances of language, which made sense given her choice of major. It wasn't long before she was patrolling like a veteran.

"I pass the patrol to you." Kaname yielded her chair to Kotaro.

"The island's deserted," Kotaro said as he took the chair. The rest of the seats on their island were empty.

"Island" was Kumar-speak. Each team was an "island" named after their patrol "beat" on the web. Kaname and Kotaro were members of Drug Island, the fourth-floor team patrolling for transactions involving illegal drugs and dangerous substances that weren't yet illegal. The next row over was Suicide Island, which monitored sites where people looking to form suicide pacts with others could make contact. The team on the other side of the row was Adult Island, and patrolled for child pornography. Most islands had five or six members, but because of the amount of drug-related activity on the web, Drug Island had eight members, plus Kotaro and Kaname.

"It's some kind of meeting." Kaname unbundled her long hair and shook it out over her shoulders. "Yamashina's here." Kumar's president came up from Nagoya to visit the Tokyo office once or twice a month.

"Did something happen?"

"I don't think so. Everyone from Adult Island got called in half an hour ago. They're probably calling people island by island to talk about Sapporo."

Closing the Tokyo office was a done deal. All the regular and contract employees had to decide whether to move to Hokkaido or find another job. It would be a tough decision, especially for those with families. They also might earn less in Sapporo.

"So it doesn't have anything to do with us."

"I guess. Listen, take a look at this." Kaname pointed to a Post-it stuck to the bottom edge of the monitor. "I finished processing this, but you might get a reaction. A high school student uploaded this video of himself jamming along the Tama River on his bike after scoring some herb last night." The Post-it had a list of handles in Kaname's rounded script.

"Pretty stupid."

"I haven't seen these handles before, but they look like friends of the biker who showed up here after he asked them to watch his video. They might get mixed up in something here. Seigo said we should keep an eye on it."

Every island had its chief, usually a veteran employee, but Drug Island was headed by Seigo, partly because it was often the destination for new employees and staff on short-term contracts.

Kaname glanced at her watch. "Gotta catch my express. See you," she said and hurried out. Kotaro gave her a big wave without taking his eyes from the monitor.

As Kotaro scanned his inbox, the other residents of Drug Island filed back from the meeting. Seigo was with them.

"Morning, Ko-Prime," he tossed out a greeting as he sauntered back to his desk, which occupied a central position in the office. The rest of the team went back to work.

A few days before, Kotaro had come across a site that was bothering him. The administrator's handle was Alice's Rabbit. At first glance it looked like a site for gardening tips. The admin's blog talked about growing spices and herbs for tea, but there was something about his (her?) "lemongrass" and "mint" and "basil" that didn't seem quite right. Kotaro suspected these names were euphemisms for potentially dangerous if not illegal plants. He dug around for information on cultivating lemongrass, mint, and basil, and what he found matched nothing that Alice's Rabbit blogged about.

If that weren't enough, the blog sometimes contained cryptic, "those who know will know" remarks that seemed aimed at insiders. Alice's Rabbit urged his readers to get into herb cultivation. He invited them to trade seeds and seedlings, and offered free seedlings he had crossbred himself. These were the kinds of clues Seigo called "omens"—ominous signs that would pop up and disappear on websites that otherwise seemed innocuous.

Still, he didn't have proof. Alice's Rabbit had been busy; there were a lot of updates. Less than an hour earlier, he'd told his readers that he had just returned from a trip to the land of dreams, enveloped in the aroma of a new type of lemongrass.

Another blog Kotaro had recently discovered was written by an art student. Each day seemed to bring a new post wailing about how behind schedule his projects were. Recently he'd written, "To liberate my high-level creative power, I need an external assist." This entry drew a comment from someone recommending that the blogger use drugs. Kotaro hadn't decided yet if the person was actually selling something, but he did have a pitch: he claimed he was a musician and had found something that saved him when he was in a creative slump. The anxious art student's site had a lot of visitors, and the musician's sales talk started a minor debate. Some comments warned the blogger not to get mixed up with the musician, but most urged him to give it a try: "I have the same problem. Why don't we try it together?" Perhaps the people commenting were just as bogus as the "musician," or maybe the "musician" was posing as different people.

Today's entry found the art student still struggling: his graduation project was never going to be finished in time, he went to a friend's exhibition and was devastated because it was so good, now he couldn't get any sleep. Nothing but doom and gloom. This last entry was posted at 3:40 a.m. *Why doesn't he just go to bed?* thought Kotaro. Things always look different in the morning.

Suddenly there was a commotion. Several people had left their desks and were crowded around Seigo, peering at his monitors and talking excitedly.

"Here we go," said a fellow islander named Maeda, who sat next to Kotaro. He was looking at his work monitor, not his patrol monitor. There was a browser window open to a news feed.

"Seigo nailed it. This is the third one."

Kotaro went to the same feed. It was a news flash marked NEW.

BODY FOUND IN FOREST NEAR MISHIMA, SHIZUOKA PREFECTURE, WITH MIDDLE TOE OF RIGHT FOOT SEVERED

Kotaro glanced at Maeda, a rumpled man of about thirty. There were rumors that his hobby was Brazilian jiu-jitsu. His muscles bulged beneath his T-shirt.

"The third one?"

"Didn't you hear him talking about it? Started in Hokkaido. Kushiro, was it? They find this dead guy in a refrigerator dumped by the road. Head bashed in, strangled with some kind of rope. His left big toe was missing."

"When did that happen?"

"Maybe six months ago. Hold on."

Maeda grabbed his mouse and clicked on a file. Hardly anyone bothered with paper at Kumar. Kaname was one of the few people in the office who actually used Post-its.

"Here it is. June first. Not Kushiro. Tomakomai. The victim ran an *izakaya*. Forty-one. Named Shiro Nakanome. Weird last name."

"June? That was before my time," said Kotaro.

"Really? You look like you've been here ten years."

"Ten years ago I was nine."

"Wow, you must've been a prodigy." Maeda laughed. "This is going to be a tough one. That's what Seigo said after the news broke. I mean, chopping off the guy's toe? Come on."

"It does sound bizarre."

"I didn't agree with him at the time. Maybe he's watching too many murder mysteries, okay? They figured out who the guy was right away, and I figured when they caught the killer, it'd be the usual motive—money or some kind of sex thing. So he's minus a toe. I didn't think it meant much."

"Maybe the victim was mixed up with gangsters or something."

"Yeah, but the yakuza don't collect toes."

Since the police identified the Tomakomai victim there had been no further progress on the case. This hadn't seemed odd to Maeda, but—

"Next one's Akita. September 22. Found in a dumpster behind some public housing. Female, dead two days. Cause of death was strangulation. The fourth toe on the right foot was missing. Sliced off cleanly with some kind of sharp tool. When Seigo saw the news he jumped out of his chair. 'Serial killer!' he yells. It takes a lot to shake Seigo, okay? He actually smelled it coming. I was blown away."

Seigo had sensed what was coming, like a fisherman looking out across the vast ocean of the web spotting a flock of seabirds circling something beneath the surface.

"Did they identify the victim?"

Maeda shook his head with a pained expression, almost as though he'd known the victim personally. "Her age was twenties to forties. The body was pretty badly decomposed. No clues at all. No personal effects. The tags on the clothes were snipped off. Even the linings of her shoes were ripped out."

Kotaro felt a real chill run down his spine. Severing a toe was ghastly. Going to such lengths to obliterate any trace of the victim's identity was highly calculated. Taken together, they didn't just add to the horror. They multiplied it.

"I guess the cops must be checking the missing-persons lists."

"Prefectural police would, sure, but you can't assume the victim's from Akita. Fact is, there are a whole lot of people no one would bother filing a report on if they dropped out of sight tomorrow. You do this job, you know what I'm talking about, okay? You hear their voices out there in cyberspace."

Kotaro nodded. People who were so isolated they couldn't even ask for help. People so lonely they'd given up on anyone ever listening to them. Yes, he knew what Maeda was talking about.

"Do you think the police know they're dealing with a serial killer?"

"I wish I could tell you." Maeda frowned. "Cops are bureaucrats too, and each department protects its turf—which means if something isn't on it, they ignore it. Not their turf, not their responsibility. I like to think they'll wake up, though."

The circle of people around Seigo's desk had dispersed. Everyone had gone back to work. Seigo picked up the phone and started punching in a number.

Kotaro went back to work too. The patrollers on the previous shift had added two new search terms, "parlor" and "malt." Naturally the second term had nothing to do with whiskey.

Someone clapped him on the shoulder. Kotaro looked up. It was Seigo.

"Sorry," he said to Maeda. "I need to borrow Ko-Prime."

Seigo pointed to the exit. Kotaro rushed to square away his desktop before running to catch up with Seigo, who was almost out the door. In the corridor he headed for the opposite door, which led to the third floor.

"We're dredging the textboards. I need your help on BB Island," Seigo said.

Dredging was different from crawling, which involved searching on multiple terms simultaneously and gathering hits for later analysis. Dredging meant reading through everything the search terms returned, page by page.

BB stood for Black Box. The island specialized in monitoring sites for information about crimes already committed, or people looking for accomplices in murder, kidnapping, and robbery. BB Island also handled sites used by people looking for ways to take revenge for one reason or another.

"You and Maeda were talking. Did he tell you about Mishima?"

They walked down the stairs side by side. "Yeah, he told me. The victim was missing a toe."

"The police haven't confirmed it." Seigo sounded cautious, but he looked like a dog on a scent.

"Maeda told me you thought this was a serial killer after the first victim was killed."

"I did. I hoped I was wrong, though. Anyway, there should be a lot of stuff going up about this today and tomorrow, so I'm putting more people on it. We're going to dredge this sucker good."

"I'm game."

They went through the security door into the third floor. The room was buzzing. Kotaro noticed a few other faces he usually saw on the fourth floor. People were rearranging PCs and monitors and allocating positions. The whiteboard near the wall already showed a list of bullet points relating to the latest murder.

"Hey Ino, say hi to Kotaro from DI."

Seigo jerked a thumb at Kotaro. Shinya Inose was the chief of BB Island. "Ino" was one of the brightest people in the company; he had taken a PhD in information engineering last year, just before joining Kumar. Small stature, round face, narrow eyes, gentle-looking, usually smiling. Kaname said he looked like her neighborhood tofu maker.

"Here's another body."

"Very good," said Shinya and waved a hand toward the desks along the window. "That row's open."

Kenji Morinaga, another part-timer, was already there. He was a junior majoring in civil engineering. They knew each other well. Shinya and Kotaro had joined Kumar together, and they'd trained together for the first few days.

"Hey," said Kenji.

Kotaro took the seat next to him. "Looks like we're buddies."

"Welcome."

This was a stroke of luck. Kenji was a member of School Island—in fact, his job was to monitor unofficial school sites on the deep web. Kotaro had been waiting for a chance to talk to Seigo about Mika's problem, but if he was going to be working with Kenji today, he could talk to him directly.

Kenji was into eyewear in a big way. He had a whole collection of gaming glasses just for working on his PC. Today's pick had emerald-green frames.

"How's Kaname?"

Kenji had a thing for Kaname. As soon as she joined Kumar he couldn't stop raving about how cute she was. He was a naïve boy from a well-to-do family; a girl like Kaname was perfect for him. Unfortunately, he didn't seem to be perfect for her. She'd never shown any interest in him at all.

"I was late for the handoff today. I had to promise to buy her lunch."

"I can handle that for you if you want."

"All right, listen up!" Shinya clapped his hands. "We've got help now. Row Two and guests, I want you all over this thing. Check your search terms."

A list of terms popped up in a window on their work monitors. *Tomakomai. Akita. Mishima. Shiro Nakanome. Profiling. Corpse mutilation. Dismemberment. Psycho killer....* Terms kept being added. There were titles from movies and novels.

"Rows One and Three, business as usual. If you come across anything, pass it on immediately. We'll be dredging this till the end of shift three tomorrow. Good luck."

Kumar operated around the clock on three shifts, starting at 8 a.m.: eight to three, three to eleven, and eleven to eight. Part-timers coordinated their shifts, but in emergencies like this, all bets were off.

"When were you supposed to get off today?" asked Kenji.

"I was on eleven to two, but I'm fine. I can blow off class." Kotaro had two classes today, the first starting at three, but he could always copy someone's notes later.

"You still have class? I'm on winter vacation. I was going to stay late anyway."

As a third-year student, Kenji would normally have been busy setting up job interviews for after graduation, but he was planning to go on to graduate school, so his schedule was flexible.

"I'm off the twentieth," said Kotaro. "But I don't have anything major till then. I could start winter break right now."

"I don't know. Don't make a habit of cutting class. Wait a minute—coming from me that's not very convincing, is it?"

"No. It's not. Well, when it comes time to knuckle down, I'll do what I have to."

Seigo and Shinya stood in front of the whiteboard talking. They turned to the room.

"I think we're going to be working on this case for a while. We'll need a name, so here you go: The Toe-Fetish Killer."

A quiet laugh rippled around the room. Seigo smiled wryly. "It's not a great case name, but maybe that's better. We don't want it to sound cool."

"I don't need to remind you," Shinya added, "that other people will be naming it too. As soon as you run across a name for the case, add it to the term list. If you run across someone with an unusual *interest* in naming the case, better look into it."

"Kumar is counting on you," said Seigo as he left the floor. Shinya went back to his desk. Kenji pulled up his chair and prepared to get down to work.

"Listen, Kenji," Kotaro whispered. "This has nothing to do with work, but in case I forget, I need your advice about something during the break."

"What's going on?"

"It's about somebody close to the family. I think she's having problems with an unofficial school site."

Kenji pushed his emerald-green glasses up the bridge of his nose and cocked his head. "You have a sister in middle school, right?"

Kotaro couldn't even remember if he'd mentioned Kazumi, but Kenji hadn't forgotten. A good memory seemed to be a common trait among Kumar employees.

"Yeah. Luckily it's not her. It's a friend of hers from the neighborhood. It looks like somebody's bullying her."

"Got it. More later."

They settled down to work.

▼

Kotaro had no experience dredging textboards, but he had a vague notion that there would be a fair number of threads devoted to criminal activity. He found many more than he expected, and the threads were constantly being updated.

Seigo had suspected from the beginning that there would be more murders, but Kotaro overrated his nose for criminal activity. The textboard threads were full of posts from people with noses even more sensitive. They were more passionate about the case than Seigo was, and had been following the Toe-Fetish Killer closely from the start, debating their own theories and hypotheses.

Before the second killing, in Akita, people were arguing intensely about where the next murder would occur. They were even trying to profile the next victim. Profiling victims before they were killed was something Kotaro hadn't heard of, but he soon discovered that it was a recurring theme in American crime dramas.

The identity of the first victim was quickly established, but one victim was not much of a basis for profiling. Some of the posters seized on the man's unusual name and insisted that the killer would go on to claim another victim with a rare last name.

There were also aggregators who summarized the gist of these exchanges, the leading hypotheses, and other points that had to be considered. The killer had been christened Toe-Cutter Bill, after the psychopath in a popular crime novel that probably every one of these amateur detectives had read.

Indeed, most of them were like fans waiting for the next installment of a novel or a TV series. Before the second murder, they'd debated whether it would be committed in Hokkaido or, like a burning spark, jump to somewhere else in Japan. When the second killing was announced, there was a huge response. As he scrolled down the dozens of excited messages and emojis, Kotaro couldn't help picturing the scene at the end of a horse race, where bettors throw their losing tickets to the ground and the winners jump and cheer with excitement.

Dredging also meant reading through masses of content that would turn out to have nothing to do with the case. That was the nature of textboards. At first Kotaro found it challenging to stay alert when reading something he knew would probably not be relevant. But then again, after hours reading debates between profilers and criminal psychologists, it was a relief to turn to something that had nothing to do with murder. Criticism of politicians, celebrity scandals, book and movie reviews, etc., etc.

He checked his phone. Two hours until the dinner break. He decided to send his mother a message. He wouldn't need dinner, and he might pull an all-nighter, but she shouldn't worry about his classes for today and tomorrow. SEND. He hesitated, then decided to text Kazumi too.

This might sound weird, but has Mika mentioned any problems recently? Her grandmother mentioned something might be going on.

As Kotaro and the rest of the team kept dredging, more news flashes appeared about the killing in Mishima, but there were no new details. The victim was still unidentified, and there was no information about the mutilations.

The Internet and TV news programs, on the other hand, were starting to put the pieces together. The media hadn't made the connection between the first two murders, but they were having a field day now that there were three killings to talk about.

People who post frequently watch a lot of television. Kotaro hadn't realized this until he started working at Kumar. Anything on television became an instant subject for comment on the web. Thanks to this there was no need to watch TV at all. Just by following the comments, it was easy to find out what each announcer was saying on which channel, what the talk show guests were saying, and which reporters were where, all in near-real time.

People who should've known better were saying that the Internet would sooner or later make broadcasting obsolete, but this was a huge miscalculation. The citizens of cyber society relied on television for most of their information, whether they knew it or not. Sometimes important news first appeared and spread on the Internet, with TV playing catch-up, but there were very few players on the web who could match the reach and the muscle that the broadcasters wielded to sift and analyze information. Most people were just posting about something they saw on TV, or adding a comment or two to something someone else said. It didn't matter what the subject was, the bounce of information from TV to the web was always the same.

Shinya Inose dropped by at seven. "You guys get dinner too," he told Kenji and Kotaro. "Fifty minutes. The president is buying. It's in the lounge. One meal per person," he laughed. Though no one could outdo Kaname, there were more than a few big eaters at Kumar.

"Let's eat and go for coffee," Kenji said as they headed for the lounge.

They finished eating quickly and grabbed their jackets from the lockers. Kenji pulled out his laptop case and slung it over his shoulder. Outside, the cold cut like a knife. The two men walked down the street exhaling clouds of steam.

On the way to the self-service coffee shop, Kotaro explained his problem. When they reached the shop, he went to pick up two cups of coffee while Kenji grabbed a table in the back and started setting up his laptop.

"Thanks," Kenji said as he took the coffee. "Two hundred, right?"

"It's on me. Consulting fee."

Kenji laughed. "I'm not sure if that's gonna turn out to be cheap or expensive."

Kenji's laptop was loaded with Kumar's security software. Employees who wanted to work from home had to get Seigo's approval to load the software, and submit their laptop to a thorough check for file-sharing software. Users also had to change their passwords every week and report the change to their chief. In spite of the inconvenience, more than a few employees put up with it to be able to patrol outside work hours, less out of a feeling of obligation or responsibility than because it had become an ingrained habit. That's what Maeda had told Kotaro once. He hadn't quite gotten to that point, but the bug had already bitten Kenji.

"We look for basically the same thing you DI guys do, so you could probably do this yourself." Kenji wiped his hands with a wet tissue and turned to the keyboard. "Then again, if you're really close to this person, it would be better for me to handle it. We see a lot of people libeling each other in this job. If it's aimed at someone you know, it can be pretty shocking."

Kenji opened two windows on his desktop—work window on the right, watch window on the left.

"What's the school name?"

"Aoba Middle School."

"That's a pretty common name."

"Oh, right. It's Ikuno Municipal Aoba Middle School. In Niban. I live in Oto, same as Mika."

Kenji input the terms and scanned the hits. " 'Cherry Town?' That's a pretty name."

"It's one of those tract housing developments."

"Hmm. And Mika's a freshman. Okay. Does she have a nickname?"

"I'm not sure. My sister just calls her Mika."

"Has she ever sent you an email?"

"Mails, sure."

"Do you remember how she signed them?"

"No. Sorry, I left the phone at the office. But you know, I think she just calls herself Mika."

Kenji hit the return key. In a few moments, a single line of text appeared in the left window.

YOUR SEARCH RETURNED TOO MANY RESULTS

"Hey, that's unusual for a middle school. Okay, let me explain what's going on here. Sites like this are part of the deep web. Some people call it the deep net. Deep net sites aren't indexed by search engines. Officially, this site has nothing to do with Aoba Middle School. You can't get on a forum like this without special software and an access code. Kids can talk about whatever's on their minds without worrying about teachers or the school looking over their shoulder."

Kotaro and Kenji had joined Kumar at the same time, but Kenji already sounded like a veteran.

"Aoba Middle School's dark social site is pretty hot right now. High school kids are way more likely to have smartphones and PCs than middle-schoolers, but I still got so many hits off the search terms that our software couldn't display them. It's like there are ten freshmen named Mika and they're all using the site to spend tons of time chatting with their friends."

"Are things out of control?"

Kenji took a sip of coffee. "I wouldn't say that. They're just hot. I can think of two reasons. One is, whatever's going on, there are a lot of people participating. The other is that a small number of students are spending all their time posting about something, whatever it is. Well then," Kenji steepled his fingers. "Let's narrow it down. Is Mika in any clubs?"

Kotaro nodded. "She's on the soft tennis team." He was about to say more, but stopped. Kenji raised an eyebrow.

"I don't know who would want to bully her," Kotaro continued, "but I can think of one thing people might be calling her."

"And that would be?"

"Aborigine."

Kenji looked at him with blank incomprehension.

"I know it sounds stupid, but it's true." Kotaro gave a pained chuckle. "You said the neighborhood had a pretty name. It is pretty, but it's artificial too. The next block of houses over is called 'Dappled Sunshine Town.' "

Kenji didn't laugh.

"See, the whole area used to be farmland and scattered patches of woods. A developer came in and kind of conjured up the town whole. It's only been there since around the time I was born.

"My father's from Himeji, but my mother grew up near where we live. Her parents were farmers. They grew tomatoes and other stuff in big greenhouses. My mother was an only child and she wasn't interested in taking over the business. Her father died kind of young, so the family got out of farming. I don't have any memories of this, but I heard a lot about it. A lot of farms in Ikuno closed down the same way."

"The farms go away, and developers turn the land into tract housing."

"Right. So, the thing is—" Kotaro had never spoken to anyone outside his immediate friends and family about this—"there are basically two types of people living in Cherry Town and Dappled Sunshine Town and the other tracts in Ikuno: people who've lived there for generations—they almost all used to be farmers—and people who moved from somewhere else after the houses were built."

Kenji nodded thoughtfully.

"The first group, the people from Ikuno, got a special deal, like low-interest loans or subsidies from the city. Some of them traded land for a house of equal value."

"Interesting."

"People who moved in from outside didn't get that. My neighborhood—it's kind of embarrassing to say this—it has this image as sort of an upscale district."

"I had that impression. Just now I thought, 'This guy seems like he's from a good background.' " Kenji's tone didn't betray a hint of irony.

"The subway to Shibuya opened four years ago. That raised property prices. So there's this image that a lot of rich people live there. It's kind of true, I guess. A lot of residents work for elite companies in downtown Tokyo. There are self-made businesspeople too, and people who are just rich."

"I'm starting to get the picture. So we have some middle school girls from well-off households—and maybe their parents too—who are proud of their wealth, and they think they're on a different level from people who've been living in Ikuno for generations."

"I think they're right. About being richer, I mean."

"So they call the 'native' residents aborigines. With prejudice, of course."

"Yeah. They do. Mika's family used to farm too. They still have a little land in the city, growing vegetables and such."

Kenji shook his head with resignation, entered "aborigine" in the search term box and hit ENTER. The left window overflowed with hits.

"Okay, let me look at this first," said Kenji. He turned the laptop slightly away as Kotaro craned his neck to see. With nothing to do, Kotaro sipped his tepid coffee and listened to the background music.

Finally Kenji spoke. He kept his eyes on the screen as he scrolled through the messages. "Did Mika mention anything about a boyfriend recently?"

Kotaro had no idea.

"Maybe someone said he liked her?"

"I haven't heard. Kazumi might know something."

"Has she ever called herself 'Mikarin'?"

Kotaro was surprised. "She's pretty quiet. I don't think she'd give herself a cute nickname. She's so shy, she practically hides behind Kazumi. My sister is the outgoing one."

"There's a lot here." Kenji kept the screen turned away. "Just scrolling through this, it doesn't look like a lot of people are involved. But they all seem to be members of the soft tennis club. Some of them are third-year—there are comments here about high school entrance exams. Your sister is a second-year student?"

"Yes."

"Her name is in some of these posts." Kenji waved a hand reassuringly. "The comments aren't negative. In fact, the posters seem a little worried your sister might find out."

Kotaro was so nervous about what Kenji was seeing that he bit his lip reflexively.

"I'd have to backtrack to be sure, but it sounds like some third-year guy is the cause of all this. Somebody who used to be in the club."

"Is he the one bullying Mika?"

"No. He's interested in her. The other girls aren't too happy about that. They keep bitching about it."

Kotaro couldn't help but lean forward for a look at the screen. "What are they saying?"

Kenji scrolled down the posts. "They're being pretty rough on her." He turned the screen so Kotaro could see for himself.

Raw language is perfect for expressing raw emotions. Kotaro was astonished at what he was seeing.

I can't believe that slut keeps showing up for class.

Aborigines don't know their place.

Mikarin doesn't have nerves. If you killed her, she might not even die.

I hope she dies quick, she's seriously getting on mine.

Kotaro looked up from the screen. His eyes met Kenji's.

"This is bad." Kotaro was in a cold sweat. "I mean, 'slut'? Do these people know what they're saying?" The surface of Kotaro's now-cold coffee had a skin of creamer. The aroma was gone.

"I'll get some water." Kenji returned with two glasses. The two men drank it silently, thinking.

"You told me the school called Mika's mother?" Kenji kept his voice low. Kotaro nodded, still holding his glass.

"That would mean they know about the site. I wonder what they told her mother."

It hit Kotaro suddenly that things might be the other way round. "Mika's grandmother told me the school called Mika's mom, but that doesn't mean she was right. Maybe Mika's mother contacted the school."

"She would've done that only if Mika went to her for help."

"Which means her mother knows about this site too."

"Not necessarily. The girls posting here have got to be treating her pretty badly in class and at practice. Something's sure to be going on. Mika would know how they feel, but we don't know if she told her mother or your sister."

Kenji set his empty glass on the table and shut down the laptop. The clock on the wall read 7:45.

"Don't do anything for the time being," Kenji said. "There's nothing you can do anyway." He closed the laptop and sighed as he packed it away. "At least the school is taking action. I'd tell her grandmother not to worry. Tell her parents too."

"Her mother's divorced. It's just her and Mika."

Kenji looked pained. "I see. Well, what's the mother like? Would this kind of thing bother her?"

"Takako Sonoi? No, she's not the type. She has bigger stones than the average guy. She's good at what she does, I hear. Work keeps her busy."

"So why don't you tell her about your work? Tell her Kumar can help. We don't have an official channel for this kind of thing, but we consult for people who're having problems with unofficial school sites."

"Maybe that'd just complicate things."

"Schools protect themselves in cases like this. You can't just assume they'll be on Mika's side. What her mother needs is someone who can give her useful advice, kind of like a lawyer."

Kenji hoisted his bag onto his shoulder. "Listen, Kotaro. Don't try to handle this yourself. Neither of us has enough experience. Okay?"

"Sure, okay."

Walking back to work, Kotaro felt a great weight on his shoulders.

Fresh news on the murder in Mishima was waiting when he got back to his desk. Now he knew why the first reports hadn't mentioned the victim's gender. The corpse, which was missing the third toe of the right foot, was that of a transsexual woman. The victim had undergone breast augmentation surgery.

4

"Wouldn't you like to take a short walk?"

Toshiko bent down to close the little dust window that faced the balcony. This floor-level fixture was a sign of how old the apartment was. The south-facing balcony was flooded with sunlight. Newly hung laundry swayed gently in the breeze.

"It's too cold."

Shigenori Tsuzuki sat on the sofa in front of the television, clipping his toenails. A sheet of newspaper spread over the faux wood floor caught the clippings. The breeze that blew in when Toshiko opened the dust window had caught the paper and scattered some of the fresh clippings.

"Well, it's December. Of course it's cold. But the weather's so nice today." Toshiko looked up into the cobalt-blue winter sky and squinted against the sunlight.

The five-story apartment building had stood for thirty years in this quiet corner of Shinjuku's Wakaba district. The Tsuzukis' apartment, on the southeast corner of the third floor, looked out over an elementary school and a small park. The couple had always loved the southern exposure and fresh breezes.

"The doctor said you ought to be walking as long as it doesn't tire you. It's good for the circulation in your legs."

"Not today." Shigenori pushed his reading glasses up the bridge of his nose.

"Is it bothering you much?"

"It hurts even to stand and brush my teeth."

Toshiko sighed. "Then you'd better not lean forward like that to trim your toenails. I can do it for you."

Yeah, that would be great, Shigenori thought. *Just like a doddering old basket case. I'm only sixty-three.*

"Well, I'm going shopping. Are you sure you wouldn't like me to do that for you first?"

"I'll do it myself."

"What would you like for lunch?"

"Anything."

"What about dinner?"

"No special requests."

"Requests that aren't special are the hardest to deal with," muttered Toshiko. Shigenori heard her putting her arms into her coat sleeves, then the front door opening and closing behind her.

The two-hour news shows every morning at eight mostly covered celebrity scandals. It was almost ten now, but the program coming up would be similar, with a different name and a different panel of experts. Still, there might be some new developments in the case. Shigenori left the television on.

The first reports of a corpse dumped in the woods in Mishima had aired in the early afternoon the day before. By late evening, the victim was confirmed to be a transsexual female. She had had her breasts augmented. One toe from the right foot had been severed. Those were the only details. The morning paper had nothing to add, but the eight o'clock news had the victim's identity, adding that she'd been strangled, likely with a belt. The third toe of the right foot had been severed after death with a sharp implement, probably shears.

The deceased was now officially a victim. Not only that, she was the "third" victim.

Every day was Sunday for Shigenori, and he devoured the morning and evening papers front to back. He'd been following the murders since the one on June 1 in Tomakomai, Hokkaido. He was thoroughly familiar with the second murder, in Akita on September 22; after the murder, he'd started a scrapbook. He knew instinctively that the two killings were related, and that there would be more.

His instincts had proven correct, though this hadn't given him any satisfaction. The first two killings had been buried in the back pages of the newspapers. Now the same papers, and the news shows that specialized in celebrity love affairs and political scandals, had given themselves over totally to the story, hooting about serial psycho killers. Shigenori was appalled.

The latest victim was Masami Tono, thirty-five. She'd owned a small bar near Hamamatsu Station called Misty. Masami was popular with her customers, who called her Mama. Regulars knew about her transition—the cosmetic surgery and female hormone replacement therapy she was undergoing. Masami also belonged to a group that advised young people coping with gender dysphoria.

A local news team sought out a handful of regulars at Misty. All of them reacted to the news of Mama Masami's death with shock and sadness. One young woman broke down as she spoke. "She was a wonderful person." "Always so cheerful and full of energy." "She could drink you under the table, and her cooking was amazing." "Mama wasn't the kind of person anyone would want to hurt..."

▼

The interviews were off-camera, but after years of sizing people up for a living, Shigenori could tell that the emotions were genuine. Masami Tono had been surrounded by people who loved and needed her. She was part of their lives. She hadn't been in a relationship when she died, but she'd often said she was "dreaming of finding the right person."

She had last been seen outside Misty on December 14, just past 1 a.m., as she waved goodbye to the last two customers of the evening. A college student helped out at the bar, but only until ten. Every night, Masami closed up the bar alone and drove home. The old rented house where she lived with a pair of cats was about ten minutes away.

From then until the next morning at just past ten, when her body was found in a storage trunk in the woods outside Mishima, her movements were unknown. The prefectural police had assembled a special investigation unit and were searching her house and bar. She was probably killed in one of these locations, or in her beloved yellow Volkswagen, her pride and joy. She'd always referred to it as her "yellow submarine," and told everyone it was her good luck charm. Now it was missing.

Masami was a native of Mishima. Her parents still lived there. She'd moved to Tokyo after graduating from the local high school, but returned to Shizuoka just before her thirtieth birthday to open Misty. Her decision to live and work in her home prefecture, but not her hometown, seemed connected to a lingering conflict with her parents, who refused to have anything to do with the media. When a reporter leaned on the intercom call button at their front door, her father snapped in a gravelly voice, "We've had nothing to do with Masayoshi for a long time." That was his first and last comment on the murder of his child.

Did the killer who stuffed Masami's body into a trunk know about this family conflict? Shigenori suspected he did. That would be why the body was dumped in Mishima. Masami was born and raised there; she'd probably left because she had no choice. When her parents cut her off, she'd had no home to return to. Stuffing her corpse in a trunk and dumping it in the forest near her old home like a load of worn-out clothes seemed an act of spiteful mockery.

As he put the clipper away and balled up the newspaper, Shigenori shook his head. He was thinking too much again. Reading too much into things. It was a habit he'd had as a professional, and his bosses and colleagues had often warned him about it.

Shigenori had been a cop all his working life. Born in Tokyo's old town, he'd joined the Tokyo Metropolitan Police Department straight out of high school. After more than twenty years in uniform, patrolling neighborhoods out of one of Tokyo's hundreds of police boxes, he'd became a detective at the Osaki Police Station in Shinagawa.

That was the start of a new period in his life, years of almost pure detective work, transferring every few years from one station to another. Just before his fiftieth birthday he was transferred to Section One of the Criminal Investigation Division at MPD headquarters. It was another step up, but not because of his performance as a detective. The section chief knew Shigenori as a man who never lost his cool, even in the tensest situations. He also had a genius for dealing with people and looking after young patrol officers, who sometimes struggled with the pressures and regimentation of police work.

With the new century, Tokyo's violent crime rate started falling, yet this only made people more sensitive to perceived threats to their safety. The face of violent crime—shameless, cruel, and callous, often senseless and absurd—stoked the public's worst fears. The general atmosphere of media-stoked hysteria made investigating such crimes even more trying for law enforcement and tended to put the detectives on edge about everything. To Shigenori, the younger men on the force seemed to need more psychological support than had the men of his own generation. This was why the section chief had reached out to him. His job was to be a mentor and role model.

Shigenori was assigned to Division One, Section Three, Squad Two. Everyone called it the Edano Squad, after its leader. He expected to be rotated to another squad in due course, but he never dreamed that, in the end, he would be the one to request the transfer.

In his sixth year on the Edano Squad, Shigenori started noticing occasional tingling and numbness in his legs. At first it only happened when the seasons changed or when there was a marked difference between the day's high and low temperatures. But over time it became a constant problem. Eventually the tingling became a stabbing pain in the back of his left thigh that made it hard to walk.

Shigenori's annual police physical didn't cover orthopedic problems. He hated hospitals anyway, and didn't have time to fool with doctors. He chalked his symptoms up to advancing age. Many of his fellow detectives were suffering from herniated disks. Lower back and knee pain were part of life for men who spent hours on their feet. There wasn't a man on the force who wasn't coping with, or more often ignoring, some kind of physical complaint. Shigenori visited a massage therapist whenever he could. Otherwise he made do by plastering his legs with medicated patches.

Gradually the pain increased to the point where massages and patches didn't help. When winter's cold deepened toward the end of each December, Shigenori could barely climb out of bed in the morning. Now the pain was constant, not only when he walked, but even while standing.

It was hard enough for Toshiko to watch her husband cover his legs with medicated patches every day. Eventually she'd had enough. She made an appointment with a nearby hospital. When the day came, she'd almost had to drag him to the examination.

The verdict: a minor disk herniation. Shigenori was treated with a nerve block and had to spend a night in the hospital. Afterward the numbness remained but the pain was gone, almost miraculously. He passed the holidays in an upbeat mood, but by early spring the pain was back. Another injection and the pain lessened—then a few months later it was back, worse than ever.

After the third nerve block had worn off and the pain and numbness again made it hard to use his leg, he saw the writing on the wall. He would just be a burden to the Edano Squad if he hung around longer. He wrote out a summary of his medical history and attached it to his transfer request. His new posting was back to Osaki Police Station, where he'd started his career as a plainclothes detective. He was assigned to the crime prevention section and served three years as an advisor. At fifty-nine, with retirement near, they sent him to the records section. By then he needed a cane to get around.

It was just bad luck. This was the body he was born with. His mother had had a bad back and ended her life bedridden. His father had also struggled with lower back pain. Shigenori accepted his fate stoically, but Toshiko refused to give up. She started pestering him to see a specialist. He pretended not to hear.

On his retirement, the Metro Police found Shigenori a position as a security supervisor at a supermarket. The job was a thank-you for decades of service; he showed up three days a week, read the papers, and occasionally met with the rep from the security company. He could take it easy and there was no stress. Even the pain was not as bad as before, or at least it seemed that way, which made him even less inclined to pay attention to Toshiko's suggestions that he see a specialist. He hated anything having to do with doctors and hospitals.

Shigenori had purchased the apartment for his retirement. It was only 650 square feet, with two bedrooms, a kitchen and a dining room. The building was old but solidly built, and the price was affordable despite the location near the center of Tokyo. Shigenori had spent his younger years as a foot patrolman out of a police box not far from the apartment. Somehow it felt like coming home.

The Tsuzukis were childless. Neither had wanted to own a home, but they'd worried that landlords would be reluctant to rent to pensioners. The apartment would be their final residence. Shigenori thought he would live out his days here, always depending on a cane.

But in mid-May he'd caught a cold, which was unusual. After a night with a temperature of 100.4, both legs were so numb he couldn't make it to the toilet in the morning. He'd been able to sit up with Toshiko's help, but couldn't stand; his left bicep femoris was so swollen, it felt like an iron plate was embedded in his leg.

"I need another nerve block," Shigenori had said. Toshiko didn't listen. She got on the Internet, found an orthopedic surgeon with a stellar reputation, and dragged her husband to an examination. The diagnosis: yes, he had a slightly herniated disk, but that was not the cause of his numbness and pain.

Shigenori had spinal stenosis. His lumbar vertebrae were out of alignment and pressing on one of his spinal nerves.

"It's common in postmenopausal women, but we see it in men from time to time. Athletes and orchestra conductors are prone to it too," the surgeon had told him. Toshiko remembered a television personality who'd had an operation for the same thing years before.

"We still don't understand what causes it, but it's treatable," the surgeon had told him. "We can adjust your spine and stabilize it with an implant. If you'd come to me sooner, you could've avoided years of unnecessary pain. The longer you leave this untreated, the longer it will take your nerves to recover after the operation."

What kind of medical condition is this? thought Shigenori. *My legs are killing me but the problem's in my back.* He had never had back pain. He never dreamed that was where the problem might lie.

There was another reason the surgeon had admonished him for not having a proper examination sooner. The hospital Toshiko had found after a determined search was indeed one of the top centers for treating spinal stenosis. To prove it, there was a long waiting list for the operation.

"You'll have to wait three to six months before a bed opens up," the surgeon had told him.

Now it was December and Shigenori was still waiting. He'd already quit his job with the supermarket. For the first time in his adult life, he was unemployed.

Shigenori had had a job as long as he could remember. Now he had to find a different way of life, and he attacked the problem with the same tenacity he'd brought to his work. Housework, he discovered, was something he could get lost in. He found new hobbies. In the final years of his career, he'd spent a lot of time thinking about what he would do after leaving the force. He wanted to make life easier for Toshiko, who hadn't had an easy time of it all these years. Maybe they should travel all over Japan. He could learn to cook, give her a chance to relax. He wasn't allergic to the kitchen. He just hadn't had a chance to cook since he was young.

Now all these plans, or maybe dreams, were on hold. In police work, and not just detective work, patience was the number one requirement. Stamina and tenacity were no less important than courage. In that sense, Shigenori was an exceptional cop. He knew it, and the men he worked with knew it too.

One more time.

That was his motto during his years on the Edano Squad. It even became a byword for detectives in other units. When investigations were going nowhere and the search for witnesses couldn't get off the ground, when there was no way to trace a piece of evidence back to the criminal, when everyone was ready to give up because further effort seemed pointless, Shigenori would say: *One more time. Let's interview the witnesses one more time. Let's visit the crime scene one more time.*

And yet, and yet. Waiting endlessly like this, in his condition, was genuinely hard to bear. One more day. Hold on for one more day. Day after day, the accumulated weight of time pressed on his emotions like the displacement in his spine pressing on his nerves, gradually leaving him numb. Day after day, that look of impassive suffering began to wear on Toshiko too. Maybe things had been easier for her when he'd been busy and hardly ever home. The thought only made Shigenori more frustrated.

With nothing to do all day, even minor tasks like cutting his nails were becoming tiresome. He listlessly tossed the balled-up newspaper in the trash, sat down heavily on the sofa and stared at the blue December sky outside the sliding doors to the balcony. Just as he was thinking that perhaps he should've gone for a walk after all, the wireless extension for the video intercom chimed. Toshiko had had the intercom installed so she could see who was at the door without getting up.

Shigenori peered at the tiny screen. It was Shigeru Noro.

"Good morning," Shigeru said politely when Shigenori opened the door. "Sorry to trouble you this early. Something's come up."

Shigeru was seventy-eight. He had been born and raised in Wakaba. Other than a few years of school in northern Japan, keeping out of harm's way during the Pacific War, he'd been a fixture in the neighborhood. For many years he'd also been the head of the district association.

"Come in, then." Shigenori bent to get the guest slippers.

"That's all right, this will just take a minute," said Shigeru cheerfully.

"Please sit down." Shigenori kept a stool in the entryway to help him put on his shoes. "There's something I want you to take a look at."

Shigeru ran a little tobacco stand out of his house. Business had been bad enough, he said, as more and more people insisted on smoke-free environments, but it nosedived when even vending machines started requiring electronic cards with proof of age. But he also managed an apartment building and was comfortably well-off.

Shigeru looked warm and chic in his trademark multicolor alpaca coat and hood. His brand-name sneakers were emblazoned with a flashy logo. He pulled a new-looking digital camera from his coat pocket and started scrolling through the images with a practiced hand.

"You remember the tea caddy building in Ida, don't you?"

Ida was a district of Shinjuku just north of Wakaba. Not far from one of Tokyo's biggest shopping areas, Wakaba and Ida were islands that time seemed to have passed by, with houses dating from before the war still occupied by the same families, and "modern" apartment blocks built just after the war. In the bubble economy of the mid-eighties to early nineties, both districts were roiled by speculators whose tactics for persuading owners to part with their property ranged from persistent to unscrupulous. Many old buildings disappeared, replaced by condominiums and apartment buildings—but before the empty lots were filled the bubble collapsed, the speculators disappeared, and many orphaned lots stood empty, like missing teeth. This didn't make the neighborhood safer from crime.

Twenty years out from the implosion of the bubble, the neighborhoods had gradually recovered. The empty lots had mostly filled in with apartments, tiny condominiums, and metered parking lots. Things had returned to normal, more or less. The bubble had been a dream, after all, and a foolish one at that. No one expected things to change much in the future, because a bubble like that wasn't going to come again anytime soon. Just as disease progresses more slowly in the aged, an aging town changes slowly too.

The tea caddy building was built on the site of a parking lot in Ida during the tech bubble that got rolling early in the new century. Its four cylindrical stories looked for all the world like one of those everyday containers of green tea. The name caught on quickly.

The tech bubble was different from the stock and real estate bubble of the 1980s and 1990s. That one had raged like a typhoon; this was like a summer downpour that drenched one street but left the next one over dry. It didn't last long, and the benefit—or damage—was limited to certain people and companies and locations. The people who made money made it in buckets, and one of them was a young founder of a software company who decided he needed a building shaped like a tea caddy in Ida.

Shigeru had dug around and discovered that no one was living there. It had been used more like a club where the owner and his tech industry friends could throw lavish parties. It seemed astonishing that someone would erect an entire building for such a purpose. It definitely didn't seem designed as a commercial property. The owner had probably planned to find someone to live there once he tired of it.

The proportions were indeed like a tea caddy, but the details were ornate, with projecting bay windows adorned with fancy ironwork, reliefs on the outer walls, and a rooftop encircled by a crenellated wall like the turret of a medieval castle. To Shigenori, the building looked like a cheap imitation of an old European castle, or perhaps a monastery. In the building's heyday, the entrance had actually been flanked by stone statues—a knight in a suit of armor and a robed goddess.

When the tech bubble popped and the young tycoon's business sense proved to be a myth, the building was left to its fate. Perhaps because it was a tax dodge, the building had multiple layers of ownership, and multiple people came forward claiming to own it, with each denouncing the others as imposters. A civil suit ensued, and the trustee sealed the building temporarily; then, when a resolution had seemed to be in sight, the building was reopened, gutted and remodeled several times by a series of commercial tenants—a beauty salon, a bar, a restaurant—with each new business going bust almost as soon as it opened its doors. Then another hasty renovation would follow, with another grand opening and another business failure.

Around the time Shigenori moved to Wakaba, these attempts to do business at the tea caddy building came to an end, and it stood abandoned and empty. Rumor had it that the ex-wife of the original owner had managed to capture half the rights to the building, but without the other half she couldn't sell it. It wasn't close to any station, and its history seemed to put potential tenants off. The building's doors were locked, but it was empty and unwatched, and it soon became a hangout for local teenagers, who seemed to have a talent for spotting opportunities of this kind. A year earlier there had been a minor panic over a small fire that had broken out. Since then the Ida District Association and associations from neighboring districts had taken to regularly patrolling the building, though all they could do was check the outside.

"Is there something wrong with the building?" Shigenori asked. "Did the patrol run across something?"

"It's not easy to explain, actually," said Shigeru. "In fact, it's rather odd."

He found the image he had been searching for and held the camera out so Shigenori could see the screen. "Take a look."

It was a photo of the building, but not from the ground. It had been taken at roof height, from about ten yards away. "I took this from Tae's living room window," Shigeru said. Tae Chigusa was the vice-chair of the Ida District Association. She was in her seventies and lived alone.

Shigenori blinked, puzzled. "Am I supposed to see something?" Without a doubt, the image was odd, but not in a way anyone familiar with the building would've thought surprising. "It's just that bizarre statue."

A monster out of European legend perched on the edge of the roof. It had astonished Shigenori when he saw it for the first time.

It was a gargoyle, a demonic creature with wings sprouting from its back. The face and ears were not those a Japanese demon would've had. It looked more like an evil bat. Shigenori had looked it up; gargoyles were a decorative element of Gothic architecture. They usually decorated drain spouts that kept rainwater from flowing down the sides of buildings.

The tea caddy building's gargoyle was pure decoration. It sat almost directly above the entrance, and there were no visible rainspouts or gutters anywhere near it. If it had been a drain spout, people using the building entrance would've been soaked.

Shigeru smiled like a mischievous child. If his manner of dressing belied his age, so did his youthful vigor. It was a smile that suited him perfectly.

"It's the statue, but can you spot the problem? It's not quite like the one I'm used to seeing."

Shigenori took the camera for a closer look.

"Tae noticed it. She can see it from her window, whether she likes it or not."

There it was. Shigenori nodded and kept looking at the monitor. "He's holding something, isn't he?"

"Very good," said Shigeru brightly. "Holding, or maybe shouldering it. It looks like a pole." The long object projected backward at an angle from the right shoulder of the crouching form. It hadn't been there before.

"A pole, or maybe the handle of something," Shigenori said. "How long has this been here?"

"About a week, according to Tae. Remember the big storm?"

Shigenori nodded. A tropical storm had hit Tokyo in the middle of December, but the rain had been cold as ice.

"Next morning she's brushing her teeth and looking out the window. That's when she sees this thing sticking out over the statue's shoulder. At first she thought there was something wrong with her eyes. Tae is old and her eyes are none too good, but when she looked the next day, there it was again. She thought it was odd, so I dropped by and took the picture."

Shigeru chuckled a bit uncomfortably. "The thing is, that's not all. It gets stranger still. The statue is moving. Just a little, but it moves every day. Tae was so surprised by the pole that she's been watching it like a hawk. There's no mistake, she says."

The gargoyle, which originally faced away from her, would be facing slightly to the right the next day. Or the wings would be folded a bit differently, or it would be in a slightly different spot. The position of the head would be different. Sometimes the pole would be nearly vertical. On other days it would be at a forty-five-degree angle.

"I guess it's alive after all." Shigenori smiled. Shigeru laughed and Shigenori joined him.

"I know. I laughed too. Tae gave me a piece of her mind."

The statue was bronze, or perhaps stone. Neither of them knew for sure. Whoever placed it there had very strange tastes, as Tae put it. A statue would not move around or get a pole from somewhere and put it over its shoulder. Someone was playing a prank on the neighborhood.

"Tae says the neighborhood isn't safe."

"Well, it is strange, I suppose."

If someone were trespassing, that would be hazard enough, but if they also attached that pole to the statue, it wasn't likely to have been done professionally. It might fall into the street.

Since the building was empty, some members of the district association had questioned whether it was safe to leave the statue there at all. It was exposed to the elements and might be developing cracks. It was an irregular object, and some part of it could fall off. That was danger enough.

"Tae went to Goro for advice, but he's in the hospital at the moment."

Shigeru scratched his head. Goro Ito was the head of the Ida association. He was elderly too, and had a chronic illness that put him in the hospital regularly.

"So that's why she came to you," said Shigenori.

"Well, we go back a long way." Tae had come to him yesterday morning. That was when he'd taken the photo.

"I'm guessing that she's making too much of this, but I'm a bit concerned myself, so I decided to look into it. I spent half a day trying to discover who I needed to talk to if I wanted to get in there. It wasn't easy. I finally found out that the original owner's ex-wife remarried. Her new husband's company is looking after the building. I got their permission to go inside."

Shigenori shifted in his chair, slightly impatient. "So you're going to check it out?"

"Yes. Someone from the company is meeting me outside with the key this morning. Now, I wanted to ask you..." Shigenori lowered his voice. "In a case like this, do you think I could get a policeman to go with me?"

Shigenori couldn't serve on the association, since it would mean a lot of walking around. But when Shigeru discovered his background, he began consulting him frequently on keeping the district safe, and Shigenori had tried his best to help out.

"A police officer." Shigenori folded his arms. "What does the company say?"

"They're treating it as a joke. They also said it wouldn't look good to call the police until we know more."

"I'm not surprised they're worried about their image, but if that's what they say, I guess you have to go along with them."

"I was afraid you'd say that. Well, we don't know for sure whether anything's been stolen or damaged. I didn't really expect to have the police along. But this whole thing has got me a little spooked."

Shigeru ran the association with energy and vigor, but he was old, and that was a fact. Shigenori could see that venturing into an empty building with a stranger might worry him.

"Shall I come along?"

Shigeru was startled. "You can't do that. In your condition?"

"I'll be fine as long as we keep the pace slow."

"The power's off. We won't be using the elevator. You'd have to climb all the way to the roof."

"If you can do it, so can I." Shigenori smiled. "I'm quite a bit younger than you."

"Of course, but still—"

"You need to go now, don't you?"

Shigeru checked his watch. "Yes, we're meeting in front of the building."

"Then I'll get my cane."

Shigenori went to the living room, wrote a short note to Toshiko and left it pinned to the refrigerator with a magnet.

Going for a walk with Shigeru.

He got his threadbare down jacket and threw a muffler around his neck. He put his phone in his pocket, paused to think, then gathered a few extra things and stuffed them in his pockets too.

"Sorry to trouble you," said Shigeru.

Next to Shigeru with his alpaca coat, Shigenori with his walking stick looked much the older of the two.

The tea caddy building was officially named the West Shinjuku Central Round Building. The name was still there, etched in fancy script on a brass plaque by the front entrance. When the two men arrived they found a tall young man in a new trench coat, carrying a black briefcase and standing near the plaque with a bored expression. Shigenori could only walk slowly, and they were almost ten minutes late.

"Hello. Sorry to keep you waiting," Shigeru greeted him.

As the young man introduced himself—his last name was Aizawa—and traded cards with Shigeru, Shigenori sized him up. Late twenties, just under six feet, probably 175 pounds. He wasn't just tall, he had muscles, the kind you get from working out. If something happened, he would be good to have along.

And what might that "something" be?

To justify his presence, Shigeru introduced Shigenori as a security consultant for the district association. Shigenori tried to look appropriately serious.

"I handle sales for Labbra Technofusion," Aizawa said. "We're terribly sorry the building is causing you concern." He was surprisingly polite. "I just joined the company, so I don't know much about it, except that it's been in this state for quite a while. My boss has been telling me to get out and apologize to the association."

Aizawa was still wet behind the ears, but his sincerity came through. Shigenori hoped Labbra Technofusion was a legitimate operation.

"We're just glad you came so quickly," said Shigeru. "Shall we go inside?"

The main entrance was a large double door faced with heavy planks of wood. It had a pair of iron door handles that looked like they could serve as boat anchors in a pinch. A heavy chain had been wound around them, secured by a fat padlock. Aizawa opened his briefcase and took out a large key ring with a metallic jangle.

"I can open this padlock, but I'm told the door can only be unlocked from the inside. There's a service entrance around the back."

Aizawa turned toward the walkway that ran between the building and a low cinder block wall. Before he could set off, Shigenori spoke up.

"Just a minute. Mr. Chairman, I'd like you to take a picture of this lock and chain."

Shigeru pulled out his camera. "You want a picture of that?"

"Yes. We'll need it for evidence." Shigenori was being a little dramatic, but who knew what they might find? He examined the chain with its padlock. There didn't seem to be any evidence of tampering. There were tiny cobwebs between the chain links.

"Does this path go all the way around the building?" he asked Aizawa.

"Yes, it should."

"It's a tight fit, but let's circle the building first."

Shigeru was still holding the camera. He smiled at Aizawa. "Shigenori used to be a detective."

Aizawa's eyes widened. "That's cool! I've never met a real detective."

"I'm just an unemployed old codger now."

"Why do you want to go all the way around? Are you looking for signs of a break-in? Or traces of a ladder or footprints? The windows on the first floor don't open. All the windows from the second floor up are covered with grilles."

He seemed to be enjoying himself now. If his employers had been skittish about getting the police involved, they'd sent the wrong guy.

"I'd just like to have a look. By the way, when businesses were operating in this building, did the staff have to use this path to reach the service entrance?"

Shigeru spoke up. "No, there's a little walkway that leads to the back door from the street behind the building. But the association blocked it off. That was after the break-in."

The gap between the building and the wall was not much more than a foot wide. The passage was filled with leaves and scraps of trash. The first-floor wall was pierced here and there with ventilation slits of different sizes. These too were dusty and full of cobwebs.

The walk from the street behind the building to the service entrance went through a gap in the cinder block wall. The entrance was only a few feet from the street. The walk was flanked with plots of soil that had once been flowerbeds. Now they were choked with weeds.

The walk was blocked by a barricade of stamped metal chairs bound securely with rope. The chairs were stacked in a matrix, like gymnasts in a human pyramid with legs sticking out here and there. It looked far too heavy to push over.

"We found these chairs in the employee lounge. The design is unusual, so I guess they couldn't unload them. They just left them there."

"That's amazing." Aizawa grasped the legs of a chair that pointed to the sky and tried unsuccessfully to move the barricade. "Solid as a rock. Whoever did these knots knew his stuff."

"One of the guys from a shipping company in the neighborhood put this together," said Shigeru with a touch of pride. "The patrols make sure the ropes are tight and in good shape. It's very sturdy."

Shigeru told them the service door had been replaced after the fire. "Someone pried it open with a crowbar. We don't know if it was the same person who started the fire. Without the fire, no one would've noticed the break-in."

A crowbar was a violent way to get inside. Professional thieves often used them to strip empty buildings of valuable materials like wiring and plumbing fixtures. The kids partying here probably came along after the lock was broken.

Aizawa jingled his keys and unlocked the door. He pulled a long flashlight from his black briefcase. "I thought we might need this."

"You came prepared." Shigeru nodded approvingly.

The first floor of the West Shinjuku Central Round Building was cavernous and empty. There were no partition walls. From the service entrance they could see nearly the entire expanse of round floor. There were no traces of the fire. Someone had been in to repair the damage.

"Looks like it's in pretty good shape," said Aizawa. The flashlight was needed after all; the sun was shining, but the windows were too small to shed much light. "This used to be a gallery. I heard the owner was into pop art. Gothic art outside, pop art inside."

On the opposite side of the floor, they could see a stairway that followed the curve of the north wall. Aizawa started toward it, but Shigenori stopped him.

"Sorry...I need you to put these on over your shoes." He pulled out a stack of plastic shopping bags that Toshiko had carefully folded, along with a small roll of scotch tape. "Tape them around your ankles. They'll make it harder to keep your footing, so be careful."

Aizawa had another attack of excitement. "This is just like *CSI*."

Shigeru noticed Shigenori's puzzled look. "It's an American TV series. My grandchildren can't get enough of it."

They slipped the bags over their shoes. Shigenori helped his two companions tape their feet. He put a bag around the tip of his cane, but took it off because it seemed likely to slip.

"Even with these bags, we should be careful where we walk, right?" Aizawa asked.

"Don't worry. You don't have to be that careful."

After Shigeru took several shots of the first floor, they headed toward the stairs. Shigenori naturally took the lead, with Aizawa bringing up the rear.

"The fire was a year ago?" Shigenori asked.

"Middle of last November, I think," said Shigeru.

Close to thirteen months had passed since the firefighters were in the building. Dust accumulates even in tightly closed spaces. Shigenori squatted and ran a finger along the stair. The surface was grainy. There were no footprints.

There was a bar counter on the second floor, with two round tables. The windows here were larger, and the light poured in. Aizawa turned off the flashlight. Shigeru took pictures of everything.

"How's your leg holding up?"

"I'm fine. Thanks for asking," Shigeru said. Luckily the stairs ascended at a shallow angle.

"Everything seems okay here too," Aizawa said.

Perhaps in consideration of the older men, Aizawa took the lead to the third floor. He stayed close to the wall as he went up so as not to disturb any evidence, but here too there were no footprints or other signs that anyone had been here for months.

The third floor was divided by a partition wall. The door in the wall was open. The area beyond looked like a bedroom.

Aizawa rubbed his cheeks nervously. "This floor was supposed to be an apartment."

Shigenori leaned through the door and looked around. He saw the remains of a once-fancy bathroom. The toilet was missing.

"So the building had tenants?" Shigeru was huffing slightly. The stairs were starting to tell on him.

"Only on the first and second floors," Aizawa replied. "Whenever a tenant left, they tore out the interior fixtures. That's why the toilets are missing."

Aizawa looked from Shigeru to Shigenori uneasily. "Wasn't the district association notified? Someone died on this floor."

The two men gaped at him in surprise.

"Not recently," he added anxiously. "It was about six months after the building was finished. Under the original owner."

That would have been during the building's nightclub phase, yet the news never reached the ears of people in the neighborhood.

"Who was it?" asked Shigeru.

Aizawa shook his head. "A young woman. There was a party. She had too much to drink and collapsed. They brought her up here to sleep it off. When they checked on her later, she was dead."

It sounded like acute alcohol poisoning. Maybe she'd been mixing something with her alcohol. The tea caddy party scene was notorious.

"I wonder why the news never got out," said Shigeru. He was leaning against the wall. Shigenori took the opportunity to sit down and rest his leg.

"Well, it's not like someone killed her." Aizawa was growing increasingly nervous.

Shigeru chuckled teasingly. "Mr. Aizawa, you're in the real estate business and you're scared by a building where someone died?"

He shook his head vigorously. "I'm not scared. And Labbra Technofusion isn't a real estate company. We manage talent."

Shigenori was also surprised. Shigeru had given him the impression they were dealing with a real estate agent. The young man had certainly come across that way.

"The owner's ex-wife was a model. Popular too, for a while. She was on TV all the time."

And her new husband managed talent. It made sense.

"But this place still scares you." Shigeru wouldn't let it go.

"Okay, it's creepy, I guess." Aizawa sounded embarrassed as he peered anxiously around the empty floor. "There were rumors that the woman who died was having an affair with the owner. My boss said it was pretty obvious."

"Rumors are rumors," said Shigenori.

"True. You know, she must've had a grudge against the owner and his wife—"

"And that means there'll be a ghost. Did your boss tell you that too?" Shigeru laughed. He waved the camera casually. "What do we do if there's something strange in these photos?"

"Don't even say that. I wouldn't be surprised if there is a ghost. That's why no one ever rented this floor, probably."

Shigenori smiled. "The layout up here isn't very practical, and the building itself is rumored to be cursed as it is."

"You don't believe in ghosts? With all the things you must've seen on the job?"

"I'd be more worried about the people behind the owner. Young wheelers and dealers often have underworld connections."

"Is that your detective's sixth sense?"

"It's common sense. Somebody gets very rich very fast. It attracts the wrong kind of people. Otherwise why would selling the building be so complicated?"

They climbed to the fourth floor. Again the stairs were covered with a thick layer of dust.

"If someone was here, they didn't come up these stairs," said Shigenori. He couldn't walk for long with his bad leg, but the pain was bearable with frequent pauses to rest. That's how it was with spinal stenosis. Shigeru was having a harder time. His legs were getting heavy and he was panting nonstop.

"Sorry, can I give you a hand?"

Aizawa offered his hand and Shigeru took it without hesitation. "Thank you."

Half of the fourth floor was empty. The other half was taken up by a machine room housing the elevator motor, water pump, circuit breakers and other electrical equipment.

"Why did they put all this up here? Why spoil the view?" Shigeru asked.

"I think they were going to put it in the basement, but they couldn't get the permit," Aizawa said.

"This wasn't built as a residence. Maybe they didn't care," Shigenori said. "Anyway, the fourth floor isn't exactly high up."

The owner was evidently more interested in having a place to do things away from prying eyes. If he'd wanted a good view, Shinjuku was full of high-rise condominiums. He would've had his pick of places to live.

There was no stairway to the roof. Instead there was a trap door in the ceiling above a ladder that folded up and away when not in use. Pulling the cord attached to the ladder unfolded it down to the floor.

"Is this how they got the statue up there?" Shigeru said. He put a hand to his lower back and looked up at the ladder doubtfully.

"Shigeru, you should stay here," Shigenori said. "I'll go up with Mr. Aizawa."

"Are you sure? What about your leg?"

"I'll be careful. Sorry, I'll need your camera."

Aizawa climbed first. At the top of the ladder, he turned to give Shigenori a hand up.

The sunlight on the roof was dazzling. The panoramic view was unimpeded and impressive, belying the building's height.

"Would you look at that!" Aizawa didn't mean the view. "What is that, anyway?" Shigenori saw what he was looking at and tensed.

The gargoyle at the edge of the roof was surrounded by a ring of broken fragments. Aizawa went closer to pick one up. It was a pointed ear. There was a hand with talonlike nails and part of the edge of a wing. The largest piece must have been the torso.

Shigenori took a deep breath.

The gargoyle that had been placed here as the building's finishing touch, glowering down at the neighborhood, upsetting some and fascinating others, had been shattered into hundreds of pieces.

Now a different gargoyle sat in its place. A rod like the handle of a mop was balanced on its shoulder, projecting up and back.

Someone had installed a new statue here to replace the original. If Tai Chigusa was to be believed, it had happened a week ago, during the night of the big storm.

Aizawa squatted down and hefted a fragment. "This is some kind of plastic. It's not metal or stone." He sounded disappointed. "Cheap material. Was there a pair of these things up here? Somebody smashed one of them, I guess. But why did they leave all this up here?"

Shigenori walked cautiously across the roof to the gargoyle and peered at it closely. It seemed to be the same shape and color as the first statue. He'd never seen it up close before and couldn't be sure, but they seemed very similar.

"No, there was only the one statue. Someone's made a switch."

"What?" Aizawa tossed the fragment aside and came closer. Shigenori went around to the other side of the statue and started in surprise.

There was a large crescent blade at the end of the pole. It was close to the statue's body, as if the squatting gargoyle were trying to conceal it.

A sickle. The new statue was holding a weapon.

Shigenori touched the gargoyle's right shoulder with his palm. He jerked his hand away.

It was warm.

The winter sun shone down out of a clear sky. It was almost noon. The statue would naturally be warm. Logic dictated that. But there was something different about the warmth under Shigenori's hand. It pulsed from inside, like the heat of blood.

"What's this made of?" Aizawa tapped the top of the statue's head a few times. It made a dull sound. "Metal, maybe? It doesn't sound like plastic."

"It seems very heavy," said Shigenori. He indicated the broken pieces around the statue with his jaw. "Not like those fragments."

"Yeah." Aizawa gave the statue a few more taps. "It's warm. I guess it's the sun." He looked at the fragments and narrowed his eyes. "Anyway, if people are going to smash things, they should clean up afterward. Shall we collect these pieces?"

"No. Let's leave this the way we found it. I don't think there's any danger. They're not going to blow off the roof."

Shigenori took a few photos. He took a close-up of the gargoyle's hand on the sickle. Fingers and handle seemed to be bonded together, or all of a piece; there was no visible join. The sickle didn't look very likely to fall into the street.

The gargoyle itself was baffling. It wasn't mounted on a visible base. It didn't seem fixed to the roof, yet it was absolutely stable. The two men tried to move it, but it wouldn't budge.

"Mr. Aizawa, let's go back down. I'd like to take a look at the elevator."

They climbed carefully down the ladder. Shigeru was waiting at the bottom.

"What did you see?"

"Let's just say things are a little strange." Shigenori gave him an "I'll tell you later" look. The three men descended to the first floor.

The elevator doors opened onto an alcove behind the stairs. With the power off, they had to pull the doors apart by hand.

"Leave this to me," said Aizawa. "I might be afraid of ghosts, but not of a little heavy lifting."

He started pulling the doors apart, grunting with the effort. The doors were covered with dust. His palms and fingers left smudges on the polished metal surface.

When he got the doors open about a foot, the older men helped by pulling from either side. The doors quickly slid open onto a dark void.

"Give me your flashlight," Shigenori said to Aizawa. Still holding the door open, he leaned in and shined the flashlight upward.

"Careful, now," said Shigeru.

Shigenori was astonished. The shaft was empty. Someone had removed the car. Now there was nothing but cables dangling from the top of the shaft.

"What in the world—?" Aizawa craned his neck upward, baffled. "How did they get the statue onto the roof?"

"Who knows?" was all Shigenori could answer. He felt his leg going numb again.

The two men parted with Aizawa in front of the building and went to Shigeru's tobacco stand for coffee. Shigenori walked Shigeru through the scene he'd found on the roof of the building. Shigeru looked at the photos carefully.

"It's makes no sense. I wish I'd seen it with my own eyes." He looked intrigued. "It's like some kind of setup. Like those reality things they do for TV."

But if someone wanted to shoot an episode of television on the roof, they would've notified Labbra Technofusion. Even if the plan was to do it without telling anyone in advance, that didn't explain how the statue was transported to the roof. A crane? That was impossible; the whole neighborhood would've noticed.

"Well, what do you think we should do?" Shigeru asked.

"Watch and wait. That's all we can do. If someone's planning a location shoot, as you suggested, there'll be more activity soon enough."

"I guess you're right. No harm done so far."

"Tell Tae what's going on and not to worry."

"I will. There's a new statue, that's all. I'll tell her not to worry about that pole falling. She told me she's too scared of the building to walk past it. When she goes shopping she takes the long way around. But—" Shigeru looked thoughtful. "She said the statue moves sometimes. What about that? She keeps saying it's not her imagination."

"People's eyes play tricks on them," Shigenori was quick to answer. "Even when they're completely confident, they still make mistakes. I've seen it happen hundreds of times."

"Really? I'll tell her, then." They both chuckled as Shigenori got up to go. But as he walked home alone, supported by his cane, he didn't feel like laughing.

Tae said the statue moved. Sometimes it even changed its pose. And it was warm. Shigenori was certain it hadn't been heat from the sun.

Oh, what a crock. Tae's eyes *were* playing tricks on her. And the heat he'd felt *was* warmth from the sun.

Okay, if we're going to think foolish thoughts, how about this? If the statue can move by itself, we don't need to worry about how it got to the roof. It got there by itself. All it had to do was spread its wings. Shigenori slapped his forehead with his free hand.

Toshiko was waiting when he got back. "What did Shigeru want?"

"Oh, nothing much."

Shigenori didn't want to get into details. Instead he sat down at his laptop. He'd only been using a PC on a daily basis since his retirement. He was still learning. Searches were tricky; he had a hard time thinking of the most efficient search terms.

Still, he managed to call up a selection of gargoyle images from around the world. The statue on the tea caddy building didn't seem too special. It was an ordinary gargoyle.

The sickle gave him more trouble. Entering the Japanese term returned a succession of fantasy weapons and tools. It took some effort before he found what he was looking for.

Scythe. So that's what it was called in English.

A long-handled tool with a crescent-shaped blade. Originally the scythe was used for cutting grass or reaping crops, but sometimes also as a weapon. It became widespread among European peasant farmers in the late sixteenth century, and served them as a weapon when they were mobilized as soldiers. The scythe was never used as a weapon by regular troops.

Shigenori's eye stopped on the last sentence of the entry.

The skeletal Grim Reaper, the personification of death, is never without his scythe.

The gargoyle was armed with Death's weapon of choice.

5

After three days dredging textboards for Black Box Island, Kotaro took a day off to deal with classes he'd been skipping. When he got to work on the afternoon of the fifth day, Seigo told him he could go back to Drug Island. It was business as usual.

"The police aren't making progress and the net has quieted down." The patrollers had come up empty. The media had moved on.

"If you need help again, just let me know," Kotaro said.

"Will do." Seigo nodded and peered at Kotaro, slightly concerned. "But forget that. Listen, Ko-Prime. Don't get into this stuff too deep, okay?"

"Do I look obsessed?"

"Not exactly, but you look gloomy. Maybe all this depressing content is getting under your skin."

Perhaps the poison was having an effect after all. But it wasn't coming from the Toe-Fetish Killer. It was the students badmouthing Mika Sonoi.

The day after Kenji advised him not to try fixing the problem himself, Kotaro asked for permission to run Kumar's web-spider software on his laptop. Seigo didn't ask him why. He just walked him through the procedure for using the software outside the office and approved his request. He probably thought Kotaro wanted to put in extra time patrolling for clues to the Toe-Fetish case.

Kotaro had a different goal. He didn't exactly plan to ignore Kenji's advice, but he wanted to help Mika.

The attacks had started at the beginning of summer break, with an update to a personal page on a mobile-access deep net site for students at Aoba Middle School. The owner of the page was a girl with the handle Glitter Kitty.

"I love it that Gaku is nice enough to come to practice, but the way Mika throws herself at him really ticks me off."

It looked like Gaku was a third-year student, a former star member of the soft tennis club and general heartthrob. He was "nice enough to come to practice" because he was taking time to coach the first- and second-year students during summer break, though as a third-year student he'd already ended his extracurricular activities and was focused on high school entrance exams.

Glitter Kitty had erupted sporadically throughout the break. "Everyone else is so devoted to Gaku." "Mika's so phony-cute."

Aoba's soft tennis team had its own clearnet social networking page. Glitter Kitty didn't post comments like that to the team page, nor did anyone else. The posts were always wholesome and pure, maybe awkwardly so. "Let's work hard and make the top four in the fall nationals!" "Today's practice was great! Everyone worked so hard!" "Our doubles are totally in sync. We're in the zone for the nationals!"

Glitter Kitty was making her jealous comments outside official channels. No one on the team posted reactions to her comments during the summer. Maybe they weren't even aware of them at that point. Had Glitter Kitty deliberately kept her page secret?

She wrote that Gaku had also taken part in the team's summer camp. He'd paid a lot of attention to coaching Mika, Glitter Kitty fumed. "She totally drives me crazy. I'm so ticked I might actually barf."

Still, the comments were Glitter Kitty's personal vendetta. She was still at it when the second term began in September.

Things changed completely at the end of October. Other members of the club—most of them girls—started posting frequently to Glitter Kitty's page, and most had something negative to say about Mika. She was stuck-up. She was a showoff. Veiled references to the Mika thread even popped up on the team's clearnet site. "Recently one of our members is violating team etiquette. She should reflect on her behavior carefully." "People who join for reasons other than tennis are bad for the club."

What had happened? The darknet thread didn't point to anything definite. One of the comments was "It's not Gaku's fault." That meant he was involved, but since "how" was common knowledge, there was no need to say it. *Why don't they set up a wiki or something*, thought Kotaro. *Just to keep the details straight.* But these girls didn't know anything about the web. They were just following the herd and yapping away at each other.

The end of October was also when they started referring to Mika Sonoi as "Mikarin." Nicknames for girls that ended in -rin were common enough, but in this case the nickname was spiteful; *rinrin* was the sound a tiny bell made, and Mika was "like a tiny bell screaming for attention."

Kotaro in his wildest dreams couldn't imagine Mika trying to get attention from anyone. If she had, she would've been very bad at it.

I wouldn't be surprised if someone—their advisor or senior members—warned them about the comments on the team page, thought Kotaro. Posting unsubstantiated complaints was the last thing that page was for. If they had a problem with Mika, the best thing to do was talk it out with her directly.

Normally that would've been the correct advice, but it just added fuel to the fire. The attacks on Glitter Kitty's page got more aggressive, and several girls started posting attacks on Mika on their own pages, as though they were trying to outdo each other. Kotaro had seen how much venom they'd been spewing when he looked over Kenji's shoulder in the coffee shop.

How in the world did Mika get sucked into this in the first place? Who was Gaku, and what was his relationship with Mika?

Kotaro had had enough. Obviously he wasn't going to get anywhere until he talked to Kazumi. But just because they were siblings living under the same roof, that didn't mean getting information out of her was going to be easy.

Kazumi hadn't answered Kotaro's mail. In fact, she acted like she'd never even gotten it. That too was a kind of answer, and it didn't bode well.

There was something that Kazumi didn't want to talk about with her brother. They may have been siblings, but he was a college freshman, five years ahead of her in school, and Kazumi was crossing the line from little girl to young woman with the usual drama and fuss. She refused to let her clothes be washed with her brother's and father's. She used a separate toilet and washbasin. She had to be first into the bath. If Kotaro or Takayuki were careless enough to use the water first, she threw a fit. She would drain the water and scrub the tub so single-mindedly before filling it up again that Kotaro almost wanted to ask her if she thought men were genetically unclean. Takayuki was a bit messy at home, and if Kazumi discovered his shirt and socks on the sofa, she acted like she'd been exposed to a biological agent. If Takayuki used her drinking glass by accident, she never touched it again.

Kazumi didn't hate her father and brother. "She's just going through a phase all girls go through," said Asako. Kotaro was used to her hot buttons, but when he had something he needed to talk about, her sensitive antennae were a pain in the butt.

It was four days before he found a chance to corner her. Coming home well after sundown after a long day of classes, he opened the front door to find Kazumi tugging on her sneakers.

"Going somewhere?"

"Convenience store."

"I'll go with you."

Her displeasure was all over her face. "What do you want? I'll pick it up."

"I want to check it out myself."

He stood aside so she could go first, scowl and all. As soon as they started off he got to the point.

"You blew off my mail."

Kazumi walked quickly ahead. The ends of her favorite checked muffler flapped in time with her stride.

"You saw it, didn't you?"

"Don't know what you're talking about."

"Liar. You check your inbox fifty times a day."

She stopped suddenly. Kotaro almost walked right into her.

"I don't want to talk about it." She glared at Kotaro.

"Really? I do. And I'm not the only one. Aunt Hanako is worried sick."

Aunt Hanako talked too much and was too excitable, and she dressed too young for her age. She had lots of quirks, but she'd always been very kind to Kotaro and Kazumi. Both of them had a weak spot for her.

"Ko-chan, that's cheating." Kazumi's shoulders slumped in defeat. She turned and kept walking, more slowly now. Haltingly, she began to tell the story.

"So, you want to know about Mika? I know what's going on."

Glitter Kitty and her pals had tried to keep their back-and-forth secret from Kazumi, but obviously they hadn't succeeded.

"Mika asked me to keep it a secret. She doesn't want people worrying about her."

So the one being bullied ends up protecting her tormentors. Why am I not surprised?

"Everything is Gaku's fault." Kazumi sounded bitter. "He's so immature."

Immature? In middle school? Wow, that sounds unbelievable.

"What's he like? What's his last name?"

"Shimakawa. Gaku Shimakawa. Third year."

"I guess he's pretty popular."

"Girls like him. Good looks, good at sports. His grades are good too."

Maybe he wasn't Kazumi's type, or maybe she started disliking him after the attacks on Mika started. It was hard to tell.

"You know what kind of work I'm doing. I know what's going on, just not as much as you do." As Kotaro filled her in on how he'd discovered Mika's problem, they walked right past the convenience store.

"The school called her mother," he added. Kazumi looked genuinely surprised.

"You didn't know?"

"No, it's news to me."

"Mika wouldn't tell you, I guess. She wouldn't want you to worry."

"But I mean, if her mother and the school know, they'll do something, right?"

"I hope so." Kotaro put his hands in the pockets of his coat. "What happened at the end of October?"

Kazumi sighed. "What day was it? The last Sunday. After practice. Gaku confessed to Mika. You know what I mean, right?"

"Said he was in love with her? Asked her to be his girl?"

"Right. He said he had to start studying for exams, and he wanted to get his feelings out in the open before then. But it was totally obvious that he liked her way before that."

"I read it on the site. She was his favorite."

"Mika was completely trapped. All he did was get her in trouble."

"She doesn't like him?"

"What are you talking about? She's still a child."

And you're only a year older.

"So she blew him off?"

"How could she? I said she was trapped."

"Trapped? How?"

Kazumi wheeled on him, furious. "He didn't tell her in private! He did it in front of the whole club! 'I love you, Mika. I want to apologize to the club for not making it official till now.' "

Kotaro was so surprised, he almost walked straight into a telephone pole. "What a jackass!"

"You think? He didn't consider her feelings or how she'd look."

Confessing his love got a load off Gaku's chest. He never dreamed he might be making trouble for Mika. He took it for granted that she'd feel the same way. His confession would put all his ducks in a row: smooth exam prep, smooth dating.

"Then he tells us he can't come to practice anymore and wishes us luck. He hasn't been back since."

And Mika was stranded in the club. Her enemies wasted no time turning on her.

"How did she handle it? She doesn't want to date him?"

"You're joking, right? Of course she doesn't."

"Did she tell him?"

"She wrote to him, she said. But I bet he didn't believe her. He probably just thinks she's shy. That's Gaku. Everything goes his way. Plus he's really selfish. Mika told me he wants them to start dating *after* he gets into high school. So right now nothing's changed—for *him*."

Selfish indeed, and very smooth. He wasn't the type to show off, but in the end he would arrange everything to suit himself. A little prince.

Kotaro pulled up short and looked at his sister. "Do you know who Glitter Kitty is?"

Kazumi's expression turned darker before she switched to poker face mode, which only made it more obvious.

"You know, don't you?" Kotaro said. Kazumi frowned.

"Okay, that means Mika knows too. She knows who the ringleader of the bullies is. Am I wrong?"

Kazumi just kept frowning. Kotaro wasn't going to get an answer.

"I won't force you to tell me. But I think I'm going to tell her mother to get some advice from Kumar. They're the pros when it comes to this kind of problem."

For a moment, Kazumi looked puzzled. Then she nodded. "I can never remember that name. It's so weird."

"Hey, come on. There's a reason they call it that."

Kotaro didn't tell his sister that Kenji had given him the idea of having Mika's mother consult Kumar. It wasn't that he wanted her to think it was his idea, but he knew Mika and her mother would hate hearing that he'd been talking about her to someone they'd never met. They'd be upset enough when they found out Kotaro knew.

"I don't know how I can bring this up with Takako. I don't know what the school's told her either. But now that I know there's a problem, I can't pretend I don't."

Kazumi said nothing.

"If she says anything to you after I talk to her, tell her everything you know, even if there's something you don't want to tell me. At least do that for me."

"Okay." Kazumi stopped and looked at her brother. "Just make sure you take care of this personally."

"Personally how?"

"Don't get Mom involved."

"Mom? I wasn't planning to. I'll talk to Takako myself. Why are you telling me this?"

"She and Mom get along, but..." Kazumi looked like something was stuck in her throat and she wanted to spit it out.

"She's always trying to act big around Mom. I know maybe men don't understand." She turned and started for home. Kotaro stood stunned for a moment, then hurried after her.

"Hey, what's that supposed to mean?"

"You don't need to know."

"Yes I do."

Kazumi sighed even as she hurried along. A gush of white vapor blew into the cold and trailed back toward Kotaro.

"Mom's a housewife. Takako got divorced. She's a single mother. Maybe they're friends, but it's complicated."

"Complicated?"

Kazumi's voice was sharp with impatience. "Takako. Doesn't. Want. To look. Weak. In front of. Mom. She doesn't want anyone to think her being single means she can't manage. It's obvious that's how she feels. That's why I want you to keep this whole thing with Mika a secret from Mom. Get it now?"

Kotaro was astonished. *Do women really worry about such piddling stuff?*

"Okay, I get it." Kotaro walked by his sister's side. They'd ended up doing a circle of the neighborhood. When they could see the lights of home, Kotaro spoke again. "Don't give Mom a hard time, okay?"

"You don't need to tell me that," she snapped. "Stupid brother."

▾

The next day, while Kotaro was having lunch in the cafeteria, his phone rang. It was Takako Sonoi. He hurried outside and found a quiet spot in the shade of the building.

"Sorry to call you suddenly. Kazumi gave me your number." Takako's manner of speaking was clipped and efficient as usual. She didn't sound worried about anything. "Kazumi sent me a mail last night. I hear Mika's problems are causing trouble for you too."

Before Kotaro could find the right timing to reach out to Takako, his sister had taken it out of his hands. She'd certainly made sure that he started off on the wrong foot.

"Um, no. Sorry to butt in."

"It's perfectly all right. I appreciate it."

Takako laid out the situation without further ado. About a week before, she'd received a call from Mika's homeroom teacher, who told her Mika was being attacked on an unofficial school website. Mika herself hadn't said a thing about it.

"I changed my schedule and saw the teacher right away. I'd already noticed Mika seemed a little down."

"I see."

"Her homeroom teacher—his name's Soejima, he's about my age—apologized and told me he's not that familiar with the Internet, and he's not very sensitive to the issues his girls get into conflicts about. He said he didn't even know about the site until one of his students told him."

She must've told him so he'd do something to help Mika.

"He was surprised to find out what was happening, so after he discussed it with the club advisor, he called me. He told me the bullying is only happening on the site. She's not having any problems in class."

Kotaro didn't believe that. The teachers just didn't notice it, or everyone involved was doing a good job hiding it.

"Did you talk to Mika about it?"

"Yes, right after I got back from Aoba."

"What did she say?"

"She knew about the site but she didn't think it was anything to make a fuss about. She gave me a hard time for worrying about it, to be honest."

Right, because she doesn't want *you to worry about it.*

"She told me everything would die down naturally as long she doesn't do anything. She doesn't want to date this Gaku fellow. Anyway, he's busy studying for exams, isn't he? I mean, that's that, don't you think?"

This sounded way too optimistic. Maybe Mika and Gaku weren't a happening thing, but the girls on the team didn't see it that way. They could make things a lot worse for Mika if it suited them.

"I'm not really sure that's the end of it, Mrs. Sonoi."

"You're still in school too." Takako laughed gently. "It makes sense you'd be sensitive to things that go on between students. So listen, Mika says she's fine now. You don't need to worry."

"But—"

"I know the comments on the site are terrible, but it's hard to tell how seriously they mean them. When I was young, we put our feelings in our diaries and that was the end of it. But kids today put their frustrations online. They haven't figured out that everyone can see what they write."

She was right. Kotaro had witnessed this up close at Kumar. People were putting their personal feelings out there without understanding that the Internet *is* society, and that they were participants in that society.

"If you believe the things teenage girls say to let off steam, and criticize them for it, it could make the situation worse," Takako said.

"Is that what their homeroom teacher says?"

"Yes, but I feel the same way. We had a similar problem here at work. This isn't the first time I've had to deal with this sort of thing."

Okay. All right. But adults and kids are different. They react to things differently.

"Mika goes off to school day after day in a great mood. She's practicing hard too. True, she seemed kind of down for a bit, but that was when the comments were hot and heavy on the site. Things have quieted down."

If what I saw was the quiet version, what were things like when it was hot?

"The comments still seem pretty bad to me."

"They are bad, aren't they? Very vulgar. But it's just teenage name-calling."

Takako, come on. Kotaro gripped his phone. *You're putting up a front.*

Kazumi had nailed it. Takako was trying to put herself in the best light, not just to his mother but before the whole Mishima family. Or maybe for Takako, the Mishima family was a symbol of something bigger called "society."

On the other hand, maybe Takako was actually frightened. Maybe she was so scared that she was forcing herself to dismiss what was happening.

"I hope you'll let this drop. If Mika knows it's not just Kazumi, but you who're worried about her, she'll feel so bad that she'll probably hide under her desk."

"Well... if you're asking me to do that, I'll do it."

"Thank you."

Is that it? Was I just wasting my time? Then why can't I breathe? Why do I feel so awful?

"Mrs. Sonoi?"

"Yes?"

"Let me know if you need any help."

"Of course. I'll do that."

"I'm hoping you won't need to, but anyway."

"Um, sorry Ko-chan, my lunch break is over."

She ended the call. To Kotaro, it sounded like she was running away. Was she really that optimistic, or was she covering something up? Protecting her reputation or secretly scared?

Let it go. Did that mean turn a blind eye?

The call left a strange taste, as though Takako had blown bitter grains of sand into his mouth.

▼

He had the five to eleven shift at Kumar that night. Kaname stared as he took over from her.

"What's up? You look weird."

"How?"

"Your eyebrows are practically touching."

Kotaro put a fingertip between his eyebrows and rubbed hard as he sat down.

"The media came to see the president today." Kaname ducked behind the monitor and whispered. The rule at Kumar was no chatting on patrol.

"The media?"

"A TV crew. They've been following Yamashina around for a month, for a TV show."

Kotaro hadn't seen Kumar's president on this latest visit to Tokyo, though it had started over a week ago.

"What kind of show?"

"It's called *Movers and Shakers*. Ever see it? It's on late. They do in-depth profiles. Yamashina's going to be covered as one of Japan's outstanding young company founders."

"Did they shoot here?"

"Not Drug Island. I think they were down filming BB Island at work."

"Bet you wanted to be on TV."

"Ugh, don't say that. No interest at all. I'm a serious student."

The president had never struck Kotaro as having any interest in media exposure. Seigo once mentioned that more than one magazine had asked for an interview, but they'd always been refused. "A company in our business doesn't need publicity," he had added.

Maybe there was a reason for the change in policy. Maybe it had something to do with the move to Sapporo? Kotaro was thinking about the president again. He had to get to work.

There was a forty-minute break at eight. Kotaro didn't feel like inviting anyone to eat with him. As he walked down the stairs to the front door, he ran directly into the person he couldn't stop thinking about.

"Hello, Mishima."

Ayuko Yamashina was wearing a white polo-neck shirt under a black business suit and matching three-inch stiletto heels. She was carrying a large briefcase and a fawn-colored coat over her arm.

"Oh, hi." Kotaro still didn't know how to address her properly. "So, um, heading home? Take care."

"Is this your dinner break?"

"Yes."

She nodded and cocked her head curiously. Her raven hair was braided and gathered on top of her head. Loose, it reached to the middle of her back. The source of this intelligence was Kaname.

Ayuko Yamashina was thirty-five years old, five-foot-eight and slender, with long, shapely legs. During her days at one of the top prefectural high schools in Nagoya, she'd been captain of the women's ballet club. She still loved to exercise and made it to the gym whenever she could. She always used the stairs except when she was with clients.

"I was just leaving, but..." She smiled. "Are you a soba guy, Mishima?"

"A what?"

"*Ehh*, wrong answer. 'Yes, Ms. President, I love soba.' That's what you say. Let's go." She gave Kotaro a hearty slap on the shoulder and led him to the basement of a building just behind the office.

Instead of the simple eatery he'd expected, Kotaro found himself in an elegant, expensive-looking restaurant. The room was half full. The atmosphere was relaxed and quiet. Classical music played softly in the background.

Ayuko glanced at the menu and ordered from the chef, whom she seemed to know, without consulting Kotaro. "We'll be here an hour," she told the chef. She took her smartphone out and wrote a quick mail.

"I let Sei-chan know you're in an interview with the president. Don't worry about the time." She certainly was efficient.

"Oh. Uh, thanks."

Ayuko looked across the table at Kotaro, a cup of soba tea in one hand. "Sei-chan tells me you're working hard for us."

She calls him Sei-chan, as if they're still in school. Kotaro had never heard Seigo call her anything other than Yamashina. What was their relationship? Business partners? Friends?

"I think it's more than that," Kaname had told him once. She didn't usually show much interest in people's private lives, but she made an exception for Ayuko, whom she admired in every way.

Were Seigo and Ayuko lovers? They didn't seem to be living together, but from the way Seigo talked, it sounded like they were in and out of each other's homes fairly often.

Kotaro thought a lot more about Seigo and Ayuko's relationship than Kaname did. It wasn't mere curiosity. It had reached the level of an obsession.

Kotaro was struggling with his feelings. He certainly admired Ayuko, but he was in a different position than Kaname. Ayuko was much older, and their relationship was that of company president and part-time employee. In his own mind, Kotaro wasn't enough of a male to have the right to say he was in love with anyone...yet.

But he was in love. That hot summer day, standing in the bookstore reading *Kumar of Jore*, he'd been moved; he wanted to know more about the person who cherished that story. When he met her at his employment interview, he was startled to discover that the company founder was a woman. Moreover, he'd never met a woman so beautiful, so masterful. *No wonder I feel the way I do*, he thought, though it wasn't as if anyone had asked him to explain.

Kotaro's hands were trembling now. He sat stiffly at attention, hoping to hide them. He also hoped Ayuko would attribute his flushed cheeks to the warmth of the room. Here he was, having dinner with the president. He doubted the chance would come again.

"I'm still learning the ropes."

"Really? Sei-chan says you're an asset to the team."

The first course arrived, several small dishes on tiny individual trays. "Let's eat. You must be hungry."

She took up her chopsticks smoothly. Kotaro's hands wouldn't work; he almost dropped his chopsticks, which made his cheeks burn even hotter.

"It must be hard, balancing the kind of work we do with your studies. Is everything all right?"

"It's okay. Kaname covers for me."

"She's smart, like you." Ayuko began to laugh, her eyes sparkling at the memory. "She eats a lot, doesn't she? I couldn't believe it. Where does she pack it away with that slim figure of hers?"

"So you knew?"

"I found out six months ago. We went to an all-you-can-eat Korean restaurant."

That must've been her interview. Ayuko was vetting each part-timer herself.

And that's all this is. An interview. It wasn't special treatment. The only reason he was sitting here was because he'd run into Ayuko on the stairs.

Kotaro was crestfallen. It was stupid, but he was still disappointed. What had he expected?

"I hear Sei-chan had you working with BB Island on the Toe-Cutter Bill case. He has this thing about serial killers."

How can she eat, talk, and look so beautiful at the same time?

"I'm concerned about him. He's been worrying for ten years now that serial killings like the ones in America are going to start happening in Japan."

"There are some strange things going on."

"But the circumstances are different. The scale is different too. They say there are maybe thirty serial killers at work in America at any given time, killers no one knows about yet."

After only three days on the case, Kotaro suspected there were at least that many people in Japan with the potential to become serial killers. Some of the amateur detectives posting to the forums obviously derived intense pleasure from visualizing the killer's point of view.

"I don't think it's just the serial killers we don't know about," Kotaro ventured.

"You mean people with the potential to kill who haven't acted on it yet?" Ayuko asked. Kotaro chewed his soba sushi and nodded.

"Unfortunately, I agree," she said. "That's why I try not to think about it." Chopsticks in midair, she gracefully placed a slender elbow on the table. "If people think about something long enough, sooner or later they'll do it."

Can thinking make things real?

"I haven't studied psychology," she continued, "so I don't know if this fits, but have you heard of the collective unconscious? It's like everyone having the same software installed in their subconscious minds. I think serial killers all have the same MO. How they operate, what motivates them. Information comes across the ocean and affects certain people, triggers something in their minds. If people in Japan were isolated from the world, they might never end up committing certain types of crime. But with outside influence, it can happen."

Sashimi was followed by the main course, cold soba noodles with shrimp tempura. The rich aroma of sesame oil rose invitingly to Kotaro's nostrils. His stomach rumbled.

"Things happening elsewhere in the world will happen here sooner or later. We've been saturated with American culture." Ayuko sighed as she moved their empty dishes to the side.

"That's why we need to be prepared. But the information we collect could uncover patterns that become self-fulfilling. It's like two sides of a coin, or chicken and egg. I don't want to dismiss Sei-chan's concerns out of hand, but I also think we could end up causing exactly what we're trying to prevent."

Kotaro's stomach rumbled again despite the serious tone of the discussion. He was perspiring with embarrassment. If that weren't enough, he was also feeling giddy over something he knew was surely trivial. Ayuko was using the familiar "I," *atashi*, with him. In their few exchanges until now, she had always used *watashi*, the formal first person.

"Don't you care for tempura?"

"What?" Kotaro was startled from his reverie.

"It's better when it's hot."

"Yes. You're right. Thank you."

I'm blushing big time. This is so stupid. What's happening to me?

Ayuko laughed cheerfully. "Sorry for going on and on about this." Little laugh lines spread out from the corners of her eyes. Kotaro had never imagined wrinkles could make a woman look so captivating.

"I was actually talking to Sei-chan about this just before I ran into you. Things got kind of heated. He sent me packing," she added indignantly. "Said he was too busy to talk more about it."

"I guess you needed to talk to someone."

"Right. Maybe it's not fair to you, but just listen anyway. Sei-chan actually laughed and said *I* was the one thinking about it too seriously." She gracefully inhaled a mouthful of noodles. "Do you know why they're calling the killer Toe-Cutter Bill?"

Kotaro had wondered about this. The name was already a fixture on the textboards, but he hadn't found an explanation.

"There's this novel called *The Silence of the Lambs*. They made a movie out of it."

"A murder mystery? I've never been that interested in mysteries."

"Really? It's about a serial killer. Every time he kills a woman—" Ayuko glanced around the room and lowered her voice. "He flays his victims and sews the skins together to make a kind of girl suit. His nickname is Buffalo Bill. That's how they came up with Toe-Cutter Bill, except this killer is real, and he doesn't kill women only. I guess it was inevitable."

That's not much of a similarity....

"The villain in the novel was inspired by a real killer, named Ed Gein." Ayuko looked at Kotaro solemnly. "Toe-Cutter Bill is the nickname of a real killer based on a fictional killer who was based on a real killer. Real incidents give birth to stories. The stories are incorporated into real events, and they snowball. If an observer can grasp the underlying theme of the story, he might be able to predict the killer's next move."

Ayuko forgot to keep her voice down as she warmed to her subject. "Serial killers in the United States almost always start out as copycats. First they imitate, then they try to go their model one better—claim more victims, cook up fancier MOs. They're looking for attention. Without attention they can't get the satisfaction they crave. If the crimes don't tell a story, no one will pay attention.

"The whole phenomenon is about acting out a story. To catch a serial killer, professionals look at the crimes he's committed, deduce motivations and behavior patterns, and build up a profile."

All Kotaro could do was nod.

"The thing is, the whole profiling thing strikes me as basically unhealthy. Killing is fundamentally *un*healthy, however you look at it. How should I put this—I can't help feeling that trying to understand something like murder in terms of stories is causing murders that never would've happened." She suddenly clapped a hand over her eyes.

"What's wrong?" Kotaro stared at her with surprise.

"See? I'm doing it again. Lecturing," she said in a small voice. "That's why Sei-chan laughs at me."

"No, I thought it was really interesting. I never thought of it that way."

You really did need to talk to someone about it.

Kotaro hesitated. "Is that what you talked about to the media?"

Ayuko took her hand from her eyes and shook her head with surprise. "Not at all. That was something completely different." She sat up straight in her chair. She was the president of Kumar again. "I want to start something new, but to do that I need investors. I'm just working with the media to generate buzz."

Kotaro's skeptical expression prompted her to laugh reassuringly.

"Don't worry. It doesn't have anything to do with Kumar. It's completely separate, just my personal project. I can't talk about it yet, but I'll announce it soon." She was back to the formal first person.

"Oh, look at the time." She glanced at her watch and signaled to the chef.

"I'm sorry you didn't have more time to eat."

"No, it's okay. The food was great. Thanks for inviting me."

The manager brought the check. Ayuko handed him her credit card. She signed the slip and turned to Kotaro.

"Seigo told me you're using our spider software."

"Yes."

"Be careful about patrolling too much outside office hours. You should concentrate on your studies."

"Seigo says the same thing. I'll be careful."

"How's the work? Is it affecting your outlook?"

Kotaro considered carefully before answering. "Until I started this job I never spent much time on the web. I don't know if what I think is really valid. I'm still a beginner."

"That's all right. Tell me."

"There's so much information, or maybe knowledge on the web. So much that's important. But it's scattered around, like islands."

Ayuko nodded. "I know what you mean."

"The rest of the web—the part that's like the ocean—is for killing time and blowing off steam. Not that it's all bad, of course."

Chatting idly with friends. Encountering people who share your interests, but who are so far away that you'd never have had the chance to meet them otherwise. The chance to complain and be comforted, confess your fears and get advice, exchange opinions about your favorite movies and comics, gossip about celebrities and their scandals.

"There's not much truly useful stuff on the web, and not a lot that's really dangerous. The web ocean is rough and chaotic, but it's full of energy. That's how it seems, anyway."

"Interesting." Ayuko smiled. "Do you post on textboards to blow off steam?"

"Oh, no. Seigo's always reminding us about confidentiality."

"That's not what I meant." Ayuko rested her chin in her hand and looked at him closely. "Some people are really aggressive all the time."

"You mean they like to pick fights?"

"Not exactly pick fights. Maybe it's a film you saw or an actor you're sizing up. What you have to say is right on target, but you put it in an edgy, aggressive way. Everything you say comes out sounding aggressive."

Kotaro nodded. "I know what you mean. When I was dredging the textboards for BB Island, most of the people posting used this kind of nasty tone."

"I have friends like that—very straightforward and responsible, good at what they do, good home life. But they get stressed, and they blow off steam by posting aggressive comments on the web. Their web personality is different from their real personality. They keep them separate. They just laugh and say it's okay to write whatever you can't say in the real world, no matter how critical or negative it is. That does seem to be one purpose of the Internet for a lot of people."

Kotaro nodded.

"But I think my friends are wrong. Their posts will never disappear. They think they're just putting opinions out there. They don't use real names. They say what they think. They assume no one pays attention for more than a few moments. That's a big mistake."

"Most of what goes on the net, stays on the net—somewhere."

"That's not what I mean. No matter how carefully they choose their words, whatever they say, the words they use stay inside them. Everything is cumulative. Words don't 'disappear.'

"Maybe they post a comment saying a certain actress should just die. They think they've blown off steam by criticizing someone no one likes anyway. But those words—'I hope she dies'—stay inside the writer, along with the feeling that it's acceptable to write things like that. All that negativity accumulates, and someday the weight of it will change the writer.

"That's what words do. However they're expressed, there's no way people can separate their words from themselves. They can't escape the influence of their own thoughts. They can divide their comments among different handles and successfully hide their identity, but they can't hide from themselves. They know who they are. You can't run from yourself."

Mom would say, "What goes around, comes around."

"So be careful, Kotaro. If the real world is stressing you out, deal with your stress in the real world, no matter how dumb you think it makes you look. Okay?"

"I'll remember," said Kotaro.

▼

A day that began like any other had ended amazingly. It had been wonderful, but it had also left Kotaro feeling exhausted. He punched his ID code and departure time into the clock. It was just past eleven, and it was all he could do to suppress a giant yawn.

Somehow his dinner with Ayuko had left him feeling hungry for more. He headed for the lounge to pick up something from the vending machines and found Kenji at a table by the wall, scarfing instant ramen out of a Styrofoam cup.

"Hey Kotaro. Working late?"

"Just getting off. How about you?"

"Graveyard shift. I'm not off till morning."

Kotaro bought a can of coffee and sat down across from Kenji, who started talking about the day's visit from the media. The camera crew had also visited School Island, and the reporter from the TV station had been quite hot.

After rambling on for a bit, Kenji asked, "By the way, how's that problem of yours?"

"Thanks for the advice. I'm starting to understand what's going on, but I'm still in the dark about some things." Kotaro gave him a brief rundown.

"I see. So it was all about matters of the heart," Kenji said solemnly. "Hopefully the whole thing will die down naturally." He noticed Kotaro's look of unease. "But you don't seem satisfied."

"It keeps bugging me."

"These problems are never cut-and-dried," Kenji agreed. Then, almost as if to himself: "Sometimes they just get worse."

"I saw some statistics that say 49 percent of middle school students have smartphones," he continued. "The figure for high school students is 98 percent, but no one's teaching them net literacy. It's scary to think about the future."

"That's the second time I've heard that today."

Kenji laughed. "Then I'll leave it at that." He stood his chopsticks in the empty cup. "Listen, do you know much about the area along the Seibu-Shinjuku commuter line?"

Kotaro stared at him uncomprehendingly. "Why?"

"Well…I mean, I'm not from Tokyo." Kotaro remembered that Kenji's hometown faced the Sea of Japan.

"Google Street View doesn't give you a good feel for the environment in a city like Tokyo, even though the area along the Seibu-Shinjuku is mostly residential."

"It's a lot more urban and busier than where I live," said Kotaro. "There's a large student population, too."

Kenji nodded. "One of the cases I'm handling for the island involves middle school kids attacking homeless people. Maybe they think it's fun, or maybe they're just bored. These kids go out in groups of a few members to a whole gang, attacking homeless people. Sometimes they injure them. Sometimes the victims die. The police have investigated dozens of incidents. Newspapers run articles now and then. Sometimes even elementary school kids are involved. It makes you wonder what the world is coming to."

"I know."

"A lot of these idiots are active members of the net society. They keep in close touch, share information and try to top each other. Sometimes they upload videos of their attacks." Kenji sounded truly disgusted. "These attacks are a big part of our work with the Hotline Center."

Several years earlier, the National Police Agency had launched an Internet Hotline Center. Citizens could call with information about illegal or dangerous web content. The Center would notify local police and work with Internet providers to remove the offending content. In effect, the Center was Japan's highest-level cyber patrol. Sometimes the Center also subcontracted patrol work to companies like Kumar, which bid for one-year contracts. The year before last, Kumar had been awarded one of those contracts.

Kotaro hoped Kumar would win another contract while he was working there. He knew it wouldn't affect his day-to-day work, and corporate consulting contracts were much more profitable, but working for the NPA sounded cool.

"I've been monitoring this for a while," Kenji said. "Sometimes the kids just make fun of the homeless, or kick down their cardboard shelters. Steal their stuff. But you never know when things will escalate. They have a way of egging each other on, on the textboards."

He paused. "The thing is, there've been some strange rumors recently. Homeless people seem to be disappearing."

"What do you mean?"

"They're just gone. The people these kids were having so much fun mocking and harassing aren't around, at least along the Seibu-Shinjuku Line. Kids are saying 'There's no game to hunt,' and other kids along the line are reporting the same thing."

"That's a densely populated area. You're talking about a lot of kids."

"Yep. And a lot of them report the same thing."

Kotaro looked out the window. He could see the streetlights outside. He thought for a moment and turned back to Kenji.

"So? They went somewhere else. They got tired of the harassment."

"But they wouldn't go far. These people have their territories and they stick to them. How far can they go? They don't have cars."

Kotaro mulled that over. "Maybe they went into shelters and the kids just haven't heard. The district associations might be tightening up on people living in the streets, trying to get them into shelters where it's safer."

"That's what I thought. I called a few of the ward offices. They told me nothing like that was going on. I looked through their websites and newsletters. Nothing. No new shelters have been built in and around the area. I did my homework."

"How many people are we talking about?"

"These kid gangs usually give 'their' homeless people nicknames. It looks like at least five have vanished."

That was enough to be significant. It was more than Toe-Cutter Bill's victims.

"When did this start happening?"

"Maybe two weeks ago." Kenji scowled. "It's not just the five who disappeared. Something else happened on the fifth."

Kotaro took out his phone and called up a calendar.

"This was in the Hyakunin district of Shinjuku, near a Seibu-Shinjuku Line station. A seventy-two-year-old man named Kozaburo Ino was reported missing.

"Now, this guy is no homeless person. He has an apartment in the district and is registered as a Shinjuku resident, but he makes a living collecting empty cans and cardboard for recycling. He might be mistaken for a homeless person. He disappeared suddenly. His apartment was untouched, and the cart he used to haul his stuff around in was found along the route he always took. It was piled with recyclable trash."

"Were the kids targeting him too?"

"No. There are no 'homeless hunting' groups in that area. But I ran across him when I was dredging the boards. A middle-school student who lives in Hyakunin said a dirty old homeless man in the neighborhood had disappeared."

Kenji used this clue to do more digging, and ran across the website of a local FM station. The owner of a coffee shop that Ino had patronized nearly every day ran an announcement on the station saying that he'd disappeared on the fifth, and asking anyone with information to come forward.

Kotaro thought back. The fifth of December...

"There was a big storm the day before. Wind and rain like you wouldn't believe." Kotaro remembered it well, because Kazumi had been thoroughly freaked out about it. "The water got above floor level in some parts of Tokyo. A few power poles even fell over. There was a lot of damage."

"Yeah. The street by my apartment was flooded. It was a mess."

"Then Ino must've had his accident the day of the storm. Maybe he was out with his cart, even in the bad weather."

Kenji shook his head. "What kind of accident? You mean like falling into a river? There are no rivers anywhere near there."

Kotaro tried to think of some other explanation. "Maybe the wind blew something on top of him and he couldn't get up."

"With that many people in the area, someone would've noticed and taken him to a hospital. He has a place to live. Someone would've reported it—his landlord, or someone at the hospital. The police. Somebody."

Kenji had clearly thought things through. Kotaro was stumped. "Maybe he disappeared like the others, then."

"That's what I think. In fact, he was the first to vanish. Someone mistook him for a homeless person, the same person who's responsible for these other disappearances."

"Did you tell your chief?"

"Sure. This isn't like the other cases we're monitoring, but he reported it to the Hotline Center anyway. He knows one of the people there, from the time we had that contract. But you know, I doubt the police will do anything right away." Kenji sighed. He sat back in his chair and put his hands behind his head.

"Why wouldn't the police do something? You've got six people missing," Kotaro said.

"Except for Kozaburo, everyone who's gone missing was already missing, in a sense."

Kotaro felt a stab of pity, not only because of what Kenji said, but because of the uneasy—no, clearly worried—look on his face.

"These guys do things by the book. They're not going to swing into action because of a few rumors on the Internet. I'm thinking of doing a little investigation of my own."

"How? Starting with what?"

"With the first person to vanish: Kozaburo Ino. And the rest in order, one by one. How about it? Do you think a rank amateur like me could come up with something?"

Kotaro wondered how he could talk Kenji out of this idea. "You must be kidding, it's impossible" wouldn't stop him. Still, he was likely to end up getting in over his head. There was no reason for him to go from patrolling the net to investigating a real incident. They weren't responsible for that kind of thing. Contacting the Hotline Center was what they were supposed to do. It was more than enough.

Before Kotaro could lay out his reasoning, Kenji seemed to have read it in his face. He took his hands from behind his head and sat up straight.

"This one's personal. I know what it's like to lose your home. When I was in fifth grade, my family had to sneak away in the middle of the night.

"My father's business failed. We took what we could and left. It was the only way we could escape the collection agencies. I was just a kid. It was scary and frustrating. I was miserable and embarrassed all the time. I pretty much wished I was dead."

"I can't imagine what that must've been like."

"We kept moving around. We'd stay with relatives or friends of the family. It took almost two years to get back on our feet. I'll never forget that time.

"A place to live. Electricity, gas, water. Three meals a day. The parents have jobs and the kids go to school. You can lose all of that so easily. One or two poor decisions topped off with a bit of bad luck and the whole thing can fall apart very quickly.

"Even now, when I see people living under a bridge, or in a shelter made of cardboard and blue plastic sheeting in a park, something hurts right here." He tapped his chest.

"People are like grains of sand. Society is a desert of millions of tiny grains. The desert doesn't care about a single grain of sand. It's pointless to expect that. Still..." Kenji laughed shyly. "Grains of sand can care about each other. I want to care. When I think of people who've disappeared with no one to search for them, I can't bear it."

Kotaro gave up. He knew he couldn't change Kenji's mind. "Then you should give it a try."

Kenji's face lit up. "I knew you'd say that, Ko-chan."

"But this is the worst time of the year to find out anything. There's Christmas, then the New Year holidays. Are you sure you can find out much before next year?"

Kotaro had heard his mother and Kazumi just that morning, talking about what they should plan for Christmas dinner. A little Christmas tree already adorned the living room, and a wreath was hanging in the entryway.

Yes, Christmas would be here soon. Suddenly Kotaro knew that his dinner with Ayuko was an early Christmas present dropped on him from heaven. Just as suddenly, his regrets dissolved—regrets about not being a brilliant conversationalist, or having more time to be with her, and many others besides. When you get a present without expecting it, all you can do is be grateful.

"What's wrong? Did you just think of something?" Kenji looked at him doubtfully. Kotaro snapped to attention.

"No, nothing. So anyway, it's, um, it's not a good time of year for detective stuff. A lot of people are going to be gone, back to their hometowns or on vacation."

"I'm going to go for it anyway. People must be worried about Kozaburo Ino right now. If I can find his landlord, I might learn something. The only thing is—"

Kenji knitted his brows. "Judging from Street View, I'm surprised his apartment building didn't get blown away in the storm. It's falling apart. The area probably has a lot of poor residents. Worst case, they might be victims of the poverty industry."

"Whoa. Then you better stay away from them."

"Poverty businesses" offered shelter and meals to the poor in exchange for a cut—or all—of their welfare payments. Many of these operators had ties to criminal organizations and preyed on the poor while pretending to help them.

"Kenji, if you think that's a possibility, then it's way too dangerous for an amateur sleuth to be poking around in."

"It's a possibility. Just my guess. I told you, the police aren't going to lift a finger based on what I have so far."

"I know, but—"

"If I sense danger, I'll get out fast. Anyway, I wanted to talk to you for insurance, just in case it *is* dangerous."

"Insurance?"

"If something happens to me, I'm counting on you to fill in Seigo and the police."

"What are you talking about? In that case I'll help you."

"No, that doesn't work. It would defeat the whole purpose of having you as insurance. You have to stay out of it." He stood up and clapped Kotaro on the shoulder. "Quit worrying. I'm just preparing for the worst case. It's how I work. Details. Caution."

Kotaro was in a cold sweat. Kenji was taking this too lightly. He remembered what Seigo told him when he invited him to join Kumar.

I always thought you were looking for a way to help people. Help the world, you know?

Kotaro wasn't the only person with this aspiration. Kenji wanted to help people too. Ayuko and Seigo had gathered many people like them at Kumar. The warnings they gave Kotaro, in different words but with the same meaning—*Don't get too involved*—were because they knew Kotaro was that kind of person.

"I'll be your insurance, but on one condition," said Kotaro. "Tell your island chief about your investigation."

Kenji waved a hand. "Of course, I get it. I might not see you again till next year. Just get ready for some juicy information in the new year."

"Watch your back, okay?"

"Sure. I will."

Kenji went back to work and Kotaro went home.

It was the last time he saw Kenji Morinaga alive.

BOOK II:

GRIM REAPER

1

Shigenori Tsuzuki wasn't surprised to find that his little investigation of the tea caddy building had put a strain on his spine. The pain and numbness in his leg was back with a vengeance. Even sitting was briefly painful. His ankles were swollen and his feet looked like misshapen turnips.

"That's what you get for pushing yourself too hard," Toshiko scolded him. Shigeru Noro was worried enough to call him and apologize.

"I'm really sorry to have put you out, Shigenori."

"Oh, don't worry. I'll get that operation and be fit in no time."

Just before the end of the year, he'd been to see his surgeon, who was just as hard on him as Toshiko had been. "I'm telling you, you've got to take it easy," he said. As he wrote out a prescription for a painkiller, he told Shigenori that a bed would open up sometime around the twentieth of January.

"You'll be with us for about a month, you know. As long as your pre-op is clean, we'll go in right away. Try not to catch a cold."

Shigenori had had to wait far longer than he'd expected. Now the day was finally approaching. His body was in poor shape but his spirits were improving. The future was looking bright.

He woke on January 1 feeling much better, and spent a leisurely morning with Toshiko over a traditional New Year's meal. As a detective, Shigenori had been known among his colleagues as a big drinker, but he'd dropped alcohol without a second thought when his leg started bothering him. He thought it would be better if he avoided relying on drink for relief from the pain and frustration. It had been so long since he'd given it up that the few tiny cups of sake with the meal were enough to make his face flush red.

Television was back-to-back New Year specials and variety shows. There was hardly any focus on news. The newspaper was fat with holiday supplements, but crime reporting was minimal. There were no updates on the serial killer. A New Year's Eve special on the biggest stories of the year had given the case a passing nod, but since then there'd been nothing new. The identity of the second victim, in Akita, was still a mystery.

Shigenori knew from experience that the lack of fresh news didn't mean the investigation was stalled, but he was certain that the latest murder would be giving the police a lot of trouble. Still, in the end he decided it was a waste of time to think about it, though many details of the case struck him as suggestions for potential leads. He wasn't in a position to help the investigation, and in any case he had another problem closer to home: the moving gargoyle atop the tea caddy building. He realized there might be information about it on the Internet.

A statue on the roof of an empty building appears to move. Is it alive? The story was interesting. If there were other witnesses who were as sure of what they'd seen as Tae Chigusa was, there should also be something on the web, given the way things worked these days.

But he found nothing. His skills weren't up to the task.

Mindful that haste just makes for slower progress, Shigenori stopped searching and started studying. He already had some books about the Internet that he'd asked Toshiko to buy, but as he struggled with his searches, he discovered that the web was its own best source of information on how to use it. If he had a question, someone had already found an answer or was willing to give one. For the first time, his eyes were opened to the potential of the Internet as a tool for communication with dynamic access to knowledge, not the static access of reference books and dictionaries. His searches improved. He took another run at the gargoyle in Ida and started discovering things.

Each nugget of information was brief and inconspicuous, and none contained enough to know where the witness had been located. There were no photos. "I can see it from my office window." "I was on the roof of the school when I noticed it." Comments like this made it easy to deduce the general age of the witness, but little more. People were seeing the statue move, yet it wasn't generating excitement.

Somehow the mystery was eluding his grasp. These were sites where fans of urban legends gathered, forums where they discussed the mysterious and bizarre. For regular visitors, Shigenori realized with surprise, a story about a moving gargoyle on the roof of an empty building caused hardly a ripple of interest.

Urban legends had a stronger flavor of the bizarre. They were fascinating. Moving statue stories, on the other hand, were a dime a dozen. The statue not only had to move, it had to talk, or attack people, or put a curse on someone that turned the victim to stone. Shigenori found version after version. The tea caddy building's story was so simple it was boring. There had to be more—something that triggered the gargoyle's movement, or something it did when it moved. The story had to have a logical flow.

But give it time. Even a few reports could trigger the embellishing process. That was how urban legends got started. Shigenori was well aware of this from his years as a cop. Simple movement wasn't very interesting, but add something more, such as the statue suddenly acquiring an object it hadn't possessed before, and public interest might soar. Once that happened, it would be impossible to tell the difference between corroborating evidence and fabrication.

He needed to be up and doing. He knew there were multiple witnesses besides Tae Chigusa. He needed to hear unembellished stories before the information was contaminated by imagination and rumors. He decided to use his proven technique: shoe leather and face-to-face interviews. If his leg started to go again, well, he'd be having that operation soon enough. Until then he wanted to do as much as he could.

Just as he settled on this plan, the phone rang. It was Shigeru. After a formulaic exchange of New Year greetings, Shigeru said: "So how are you feeling? Can you make it today?"

"What's happening today?"

"The party with the Ida District Association. Would you be up to it?"

Shigenori looked at the calendar on the wall next to him. There it was, in his own handwriting, for January 4: *NY party, Ida Assn. office, 2 p.m.*

"No worries, I'm fine. Looking forward to it."

"I'm glad to hear that."

"Listen, Shigeru—has there been any new information about the tea caddy building?"

"Not a thing. Aren't we done with that?" He sounded fed up with the topic. "I told Tae not to worry, someone's just screwing around." Which was not exactly untrue, but left out a lot.

"That kid—what was his name, Aizawa? Nice guy, but he's probably too junior to know what his bosses are up to. We can drop it. The statue and the sickle aren't going anywhere, right? No danger of anything falling into the street?"

"It's all right, I checked."

No new information. Shigeru had moved on. Well, Shigenori could apologize for digging around for witnesses when Shigeru found out. And he would definitely find out.

Shigenori took up his cane and walked over to the Ida association office. Low tables were spread with simple fare: beer, sake, snacks, and cooked food from the nearby supermarket. After a toast and brief, formal greetings from the association bigwigs, the party got under way. Tae Chigusa was there, sitting next to Shigeru. Shigenori wanted to hear the story directly from her, but he didn't want to be the one to bring it up.

Shigenori was not a member of the Ida District Association. He'd been invited to the party because of his friendship with Shigeru and the respect accorded him as a former police detective. Glass in hand, he visited each table, chatting with people he knew and refilling their drinks. The captain of the crime prevention patrol, pleasantly inebriated, made a show of humility at having his glass refilled by a real detective. After the first toast, Shigenori switched from beer to oolong tea.

Shigeru was in fine form, enjoying his sake. Shigenori tried his best to relax and enjoy himself, though he didn't feel entirely at home. He did make a point of staying alert, hoping the topic of the tea caddy building might come up naturally.

After the party had been going for about an hour, the knot of women looking after the food supply near the entrance turned to look curiously toward the door. One said "Coming!" and went to open it. She stood there talking to someone for a few moments, then turned and called out, "Excuse me, we have a visitor."

A young man in a black down jacket, jeans and sneakers, wearing black-frame glasses, stepped inside. Shigenori put him at around five feet eight inches, maybe a hundred and fifty pounds. Probably a student. Twenty, twenty-one. Pale skin, slight build under the big down coat. Not an athlete.

"Sorry to disturb you."

The young man bobbed his head apologetically. Definitely not an athlete. His voice betrayed a lack of guts. His mouth was twitching with nervousness or perhaps embarrassment.

"Who are you, anyway?" Shigeru called out from his place at the table. Even in this relaxed atmosphere, Shigeru was alert. He got right to the point.

"My name is Kenji Morinaga." The young man bowed again. "Sorry to drop in like this. I was walking by and saw the flier on the notice board. It said there was a party for the association today."

And? thought Shigenori.

"That's right. As you see," the head of the association said. His speech was already a bit slurred. "What do you want?"

The young man swallowed nervously. Yes, um, it's.... Is the chairman of the Hyakunin association here? I've been looking for him. There's something I wanted to ask him."

People exchanged glances. Shigeru spoke up.

"Look, I'm sorry, this is the Ida association. You want to talk to the Hyakunin association, go look them up."

Kenji's face was blank. "Then, you mean...."

"I told you, he's not here. If it's about Hyakunin, you're in the wrong place."

Shigenori stood with effort and approached the entrance with Shigeru close behind, holding his vending-machine portion of sake.

"Maybe I can help you," Shigenori said. He took a closer look at the visitor, who was blinking continuously but did not have the characteristic smell of the bad egg.

"Mr. Morinaga, was it? You don't live around here, do you?"

"No, I don't."

"Why are you looking for the head of the Hyakunin association?"

"I'm—" The young man looked from Shigenori to Shigeru. Behind them, the party got going again. Obviously things were being handled.

Perhaps because Shigenori—unlike Shigeru—seemed completely sober, the youth turned to him. "There's an apartment house in Hyakunin. It's called Asahi House. It's pretty run-down, actually."

"I know it," Shigeru said. He nodded to Shigenori. "Built right after the war. All-wood construction."

The young man became excited. "Do you know the landlord? I talked to some of the residents but I couldn't get anything out of them. I don't know why."

"It's full of old people," Shigeru said. "They keep to themselves. They wouldn't answer questions from a stranger."

Shigenori peered levelly at the youth. "Why do you need to see the landlord?"

"Um, I...."

Shigenori's gaze still had the power to box people in. The young man's nervousness increased.

"I'm looking for someone who lives there. His name is Kozaburo Ino. He's seventy-two. He's been missing since December 5. I thought his landlord might know something about it."

Shigeru frowned suspiciously and set his sake on a table. "That's Cart Man. Are you a relative of his?"

"Shigeru, do you know this person?" asked Shigenori, startled.

"Yeah. He's this old guy who collects cans and old newspapers and loads them onto a cart he hauls around. Right?" He looked at Kenji.

Kenji nodded vigorously. "That's the one."

"He's old, but I'm even older," Shigeru said with a chuckle. "I've seen him myself and heard about him from my customers. He goes around the neighborhood and collects anything he can sell for recycling. He's not shy about taking what he wants, either. There've been complaints." Shigeru frowned. "You say he's missing?"

"It's been a month already. His landlord must be worried."

"Of course. The rent."

"Hold on," Shigenori broke in. "You haven't answered my question, Mr. Morinaga. Are you a relative of his?"

Shigenori's voice was quiet. The voice of a detective. The young man flinched. "Y-yes. I'm a relative. That's why I'm worried."

He's lying, thought Shigenori.

"Well, of course you would be," Shigeru said gently. "But you won't get any information about Asahi House from the people here. As far as I know, the landlord doesn't live in the neighborhood. The head of the Hyakunin association chairs the residents' committee in that big condominium, I forget what it's called. He probably wouldn't know anything about a run-down apartment house. But listen, I know someone who sees Cart Man more often than I do. He runs a liquor store. You should ask him. He might be able to help."

Shigeru explained how to find the store. The young man kept nodding and saying, "Okay, okay." He avoided eye contact with Shigenori, whose eyes never left him.

"Thank you," the young man said finally and left in a hurry. The door banged shut.

"What was all that about?" murmured Shigeru. "Why would Cart Man disappear?"

Something else bothered Shigenori more. Why would a rank amateur search for an old man and leave a trail of transparent lies?

If it isn't one thing, it's something else.

What was this feeling? Why was his heart pounding?

2

For the elderly living alone, money makes all the difference. Tae Chigusa lived very comfortably. That was immediately obvious.

"Sorry to drop by on such short notice," Shigenori said.

Tae ushered him into an immaculate living room. She chatted about the party the day before, moved on to the topic of her son, whose elite trading-company employer had posted him to Bangladesh, and followed up with a round of complaints about her daughter, who was disturbingly headstrong. Shigenori sat drinking her aromatic green tea and listening as she covered her current events before bringing the topic around to the gargoyle next door.

"I have to thank you. Shigeru told me the two of you checked the building."

"I thought there might be others who saw the statue move. After we visited the building, I did a little research. You're not the only one."

The fourth floor and the roof of the tea caddy building dominated the view from the large bay window. From this distance, the gargoyle crouching on the roof was about the size of Shigenori's palm.

"It moved again this morning."

"What did you notice that was different?"

"It's about four inches to the left of where it was yesterday."

The gargoyle faced away from the window. Tae was very confident about this new development, though given the distance it was hard to say if such a small movement would be visible even to someone next to the statue.

"Shigeru thinks I'm seeing things, doesn't he? You told him people's eyes often deceive them."

"That's true. Still, I'm not completely comfortable that's the case here. I'm sorry to bring it up again. Let's not mention this to Shigeru. It's just a little preoccupation of mine."

"That's fine with me." Tae didn't seem to have any reservations. "Shigeru is a kind man, but he's also a businessman. He's a realist. He doesn't pay attention to things that aren't concrete. Still, there's no one else nearby to consult. I could tell the woman from home nursing care, but she'd think I was getting senile."

Tae had little to add to what she'd already told Shigeru. The decorative wall surrounding the roof had kept her from noticing the scattered fragments of the previous gargoyle. Still, her memory of when she first noticed something out of place was as clear as ever.

"There was a huge storm the night of December 4. I noticed that the gargoyle was different the next day, though not until late afternoon. After I consulted Shigeru, I felt hesitant to look at it too often. It seemed like it might be bad luck. I usually keep these curtains drawn, but I happened to look outside. That statue has always seemed sinister to me. Ominous."

"Well, it's a statue of a monster. Not exactly cheerful."

She gazed at the statue. "I don't know why, but when the New Year came, my feelings changed, somehow. Now it seems more lonely than sinister.

"The weather's been so nice, as it always is this time of year. The sky is so blue. The skyscrapers near Shinjuku Station seem close enough to touch. They're lit up at night. It's almost too bright, really. But the tea caddy building is always dark, with that monster on the roof. I thought, 'You're all alone.' "

Somehow Shigenori wasn't surprised. No matter how comfortably she lived or how successful her son was, Tae was an elderly woman who had to spend the New Year holidays by herself.

"After that the statue didn't seem ominous anymore. Now I greet him every morning and say goodnight to him before I go to bed."

Something about this bothered Shigenori. "So you never look at the statue at night?"

"No. I close the curtains after sunset. If I left them open, people in the neighborhood could see right into this living room. I don't need to advertise that there's an older woman living here alone."

"True. Keeping them closed is a good idea, for your security as well as your privacy. But then you haven't seen the statue at night? Not once?"

"Should I be watching it? If it will help your investigation, I will."

"Oh no, this isn't an investigation. Nothing so serious. It's just—if the statue can actually move, it seems to me it would be more likely to do so under cover of darkness."

For a fleeting moment, Shigenori pictured the monster spreading its wings and rising to its full height, holding the Reaper's scythe.

"I see. All right, then I should take a look at the statue when it's dark. In the middle of the night?"

"That would be perfect, if you wouldn't mind."

"I'll set the alarm to wake me."

Tae seemed very game. Daily life probably didn't offer much variety. Something different would be welcome.

As Shigenori was leaving, she remembered something suddenly. "By the way, that young man said that Cart Man is missing."

"Yes. The circumstances aren't clear. So you heard us talking at the party?"

"Shigeru told me afterward."

"You haven't met him yourself, have you? This Mr. Ino?"

"I only saw him now and then. But he was living alone too, I hear. For someone like that to suddenly vanish hits close to home."

Tae's earnest tone suddenly made Shigenori sad. "Don't worry about a thing, Mrs. Chigusa. You have a lot of friends in the neighborhood, especially Shigeru. If it would make you feel better, I'll give you my mobile number. We'll be speaking about the gargoyle too."

"Let me get my phone," she said excitedly. "It's easier that way." The two of them donned reading glasses and swapped contact information by infrared link.

"I almost never have a chance to do this," she said. "Now we're mail friends." She seemed genuinely happy.

Shigenori went home and sat at his computer to rest his leg. He'd already sent feelers by email and through the forums to witnesses of the gargoyle.

I live near the building in question. I've always been interested in strange tales and urban legends, and I'm collecting information. Would anyone be willing to share their story in a bit more detail? I would prefer to interview you in person if possible.

The responses were all over the map, including no response at all. "It's not really important enough to talk about." "Sorry, I actually heard about it from a friend." "It's just a rumor going around the office." Others made pointless comments like "Are you a writing a book?" or "Aren't you actually _____, the urban legend researcher?"

Then there was the person, apparently a middle school student, who wrote back, "If we meet, will you pay me an interview fee?" That was the kind of thing people thought of first.

No one seemed willing to just come forward and tell his story. People seemed to think Shigenori was making too much of something minor, or perhaps his polite tone had put people on their guard. It was a problem he understood well. Dealing with people at a distance is difficult.

There were no notable responses today either. The Internet had already been well established when Shigenori retired from his work as a detective, but bloggers and social media services like Twitter were much more prevalent now. The police still failed to pay much attention to activities that were limited to the web. His impression from his colleagues was that the web was an incubator for drug dealing and child pornography. But then how in the world did people trust each other enough to deal with others whom they'd never met?

Maybe the only way to catch a thief was to use a thief. Shigenori glanced at his watch. Noon. *He has to be out of bed by now*, he thought.

He picked up the phone and dialed. He still knew the number by heart. A voice like a stone Buddha came on the line.

"Hello. What's this about?"

"It's been a long time, Yamacho."

Silence, then a friendly response: "Is that Detective Tsuzuki?"

"You remembered."

"How could I forget? I'm forever in your debt."

"Don't exaggerate. How've you been?"

"Not bad. Keeping busy. What about you? How's the arthritis?" The last time they'd spoken, Shigenori had dismissed the pain and numbness in his leg as arthritis.

"Actually I'm going under the knife soon."

"What? That bad, huh? When?"

"Maybe the end of the month."

"Let me know when you go in. I'll send flowers. Or maybe you'd rather have a fruit basket?"

"Thanks. I'll think about it."

Veteran locksmith Choichi Yamabe, a.k.a. Yamacho, was close to Shigenori's age. He'd run a shop out of a converted room in his home in Tokyo's Suginami ward. Upon turning sixty, he'd handed the running of the business over to his apprentice and devoted himself to collecting and researching old locks.

A locksmith's business never sleeps. When the customer calls, he has to be willing to get out of bed and work through the night if needed. Yamacho was a big drinker with a case of cirrhosis, and the irregular hours had finally become too much for him.

He also had another side, a clandestine side. Shigenori's call was about that side.

"Listen, Yamacho. I need a favor."

Here it comes, the laugh on the other end of the line seemed to say. "What do you need to get into? On the QT from the boys upstairs, I assume?"

Shigenori smiled. Yamacho was so wrapped up in the Way of the Locksmith, as he liked to call it, that time had apparently stopped for him completely.

"I'm out, Yamacho. Been retired a long time."

"You're kidding!" His voice was shrill with surprise. "Say it ain't so, detective. You're that old?"

"Only two years older than you. We're both old as far as society's concerned."

"You're unemployed, then?"

"Yeah. I've got time on my hands. I'm doing a little investigation, just keeping myself entertained. I need a key so I can come and go as I please."

Yamacho was a precious commodity, a locksmith willing to help out on black-bag jobs when you couldn't get a warrant, or when you needed to see the inside of a place that just smelled wrong, even without signs of criminal activity. He'd never met a lock he couldn't open, and he could make keys to match.

If he was going to follow his nose, Shigenori had to be able to get in and out of the tea caddy building freely. He'd decided to get in touch with Yamacho after his first visit with Shigeru.

"It's a service door. I watched someone open it. It was one of those—I don't know what you call that kind of key. The new type. It has little pits all over the surface."

"A dimple key. Is that all? No pass code? What about an alarm system?"

"There probably was one, but the place is empty now. You won't have to deal with anything sticky."

"Sounds simple, then. Where?"

"Shinjuku. When can you get started?"

"Tonight, if you want. Just send me the address and the layout and I'll take care of it myself."

Yamacho always worked alone, preferably at night. He said the darkness helped him concentrate.

"It might get a little messy if someone sees you. I'll go with you."

"That would complicate things. If it's just me, I can say I'm a lock researcher doing fieldwork."

Shigenori laughed. Yamacho hadn't changed a bit.

"How many keys we talking?"

"One's enough. You can give it to me at—wait, I didn't tell you I've moved."

"Really? Give me your new address, then. Fax the whole thing. Unless the customer is tough, you'll have a key in your mailbox tomorrow morning." Yamacho always referred to locks as "customers."

"The building's empty, so there's no power. It's pitch-dark. Be careful, okay?"

"Sure, sure."

"What's the charge?"

"I'll leave the bill with the key. How's the wife?"

"In a lot better shape than me."

"Same here. Are all women like that? The older they get, the more energy they have."

"They're stealing it from us old men."

Yamacho laughed. "You got that right."

Shigenori hung up with a pleasant feeling he hadn't had in a long time. Toshiko had heard the whole conversation and was staring at him. "It's lunchtime."

Shigenori hadn't noticed the aroma of soba noodles.

"What've you been up to recently? You seem so energetic. It's strange."

"You think so? Maybe I'm just less grouchy now that I've got a date for the operation."

After lunch, Shigenori picked up his cane and small shoulder bag and left for the tea caddy building. If Yamacho was going to be there tonight, he wanted to walk the site again first.

He made his way to the narrow street that ran behind the building. The barrier of piled-up chairs, tied firmly with rope, was just as before.

No—it wasn't. Someone had moved it.

The concrete walkway was faintly scored. Someone had pushed, or pulled, the heavy barrier slightly out of position. The last time he'd been here, Shigeru had watched Aizawa, who was fairly strong, try and fail to budge the barrier. Someone had apparently tried a lot harder since then.

He looked up at the building. Nothing seemed to have changed. No one had done any maintenance. The tea caddy building was as silent and deserted as ever.

He peered through the barrier at the service entrance. The keyhole was in the locked position. The door had acquired a fresh coat of windblown dust.

He carefully paced the perimeter of the building. The main entrance was locked tight, but here and there, the cobwebs in the padlocked chain were missing. Someone had touched it.

For several minutes he stood in front of the entrance, arms folded, thinking. He sat down on the low cinder-block wall that surrounded the building and drew an access map and a sketch of the site, with a warning. *Someone was here. Watch your back.*

He went to a nearby convenience store and faxed the map to Yamacho. He'd decided this was the perfect location to begin a clockwise sweep of the neighborhood. He would go in a circle, moving outward gradually. Working alone, this was the most efficient strategy.

Shigenori had been living in Wakaba long enough that most of the shop owners in the neighborhood recognized him. He would tell them his doctor had said he should get out and walk. He could strike up a conversation and try to steer it to the tea caddy building. "It's bad for the neighborhood to leave that building empty." "Someone should open up a business there." "Mr. Tsuzuki, no one's going to do that in this economy."

Many of the buildings in the neighborhood were apartment houses with businesses on the ground floor. The restaurants and bars opened in the evening. Now was the time of day for beauty shops and clinics, and clean massage parlors that would treat stiff shoulders in fifteen minutes. These businesses had usually been operating for a relatively short time and had shallow roots in the area. Some of them had no view to the street and probably wouldn't be a good source of eyewitness testimony. "Someone broke into the tea caddy building again, not too long ago. Did you notice anything suspicious? I'm the crime prevention rep for the district association." "I see, thanks for keeping an eye on things, but we didn't see anything." And so it went.

Commercial buildings had security guards. Condominiums had building supervisors. Shigenori used his security rep cover story, but came up empty here too. When he asked a building supervisor if there had been complaints by residents about suspicious events, he got an earful. Why was the district association running around digging into stuff like that?

He missed having his police incident notebook. When he pulled it out, somehow it always commanded respect. At the same time, he realized that he missed the notebook more than he missed his old job.

He walked on, stopping now and then to rest his leg. At the end of his second circuit, someone called him by name. A woman in an apron was bowing from the front door of a florist on the first floor of a condominium. Shigenori recognized her from the party: Mrs. Yamada. She was one of the rotating subdistrict reps.

"Thanks for coming the other day," she said.

Shigenori returned the bow. "I had a very nice time."

"On your way somewhere?"

"No, just taking a walk."

"Maybe you're looking for that old man and his cart?"

Shigenori was surprised by this direct question. "The one who lives in Hyakunin?"

Mrs. Yamada nodded. "They say he's been missing quite a while."

"Someone claiming to be a relative was asking after him at the party."

"Yes, I heard about it afterward."

"Do you know this Mr. Ino?"

Mrs. Yamada glanced around furtively and took a step closer. "The thing is, we have to separate all of our recyclable garbage. It's a city rule. The old man used to come around like clockwork and pick it up from us. It was his only source of income, and, well, I don't think he was doing any harm."

It made sense. Florists take many deliveries every day. They would have a lot of cardboard boxes, and having someone take them off their hands more often than the regular trash collection would be convenient. Although he lived alone, Kozaburo's trash-collecting efforts created ties with the community.

"He lives like a pauper, but some people say he's really quite wealthy," Mrs. Yamada added.

"Is that so?"

"Maybe some shady person was stalking him."

The possibility had occurred to Shigenori. In fact, it was all too possible.

"But you could see he was growing weaker recently. Somehow you had to feel sorry for him." She touched her temple. "He talked to himself constantly. He was seeing and saying strange things. My husband was worried about him too. 'That man shouldn't be living alone,' he said."

"Strange things? What sort of things?"

"You know, like he was dreaming or something. He was strangely excited. 'Mrs. Yamada'—he tells me—'early this morning a giant bird, like some kind of monster, swooped right over my head and flew away.' "

Shigenori's heart thumped once, hard.

She smiled. "He used to go around to condos and apartment houses before the garbage truck came and grab the trash he was looking for. He had to be up early to collect as much as he could. He was already on the streets before dawn, sometimes starting in the middle of the night.

"I'm not surprised he thought he saw something. In the dark a person can see all kinds of things. At the beginning of last spring, I think it was, he was running around telling people he saw the ghost of a little girl at that intersection up the street, right where there was a hit-and-run."

A ghost could be a trick of vision, or an overactive imagination. Maybe a hallucination. What about a giant monster bird?

"When did he tell you about the bird?" Shigenori asked.

"Wait—you're not serious, are you?"

"Of course not. It's just that there might a little bit of a coincidence."

Mrs. Yamada scrutinized Shigenori warily.

"When was it? Could you recall the date?"

"Well...early December. Yes. There was something like a typhoon, do you remember? I saw him the next morning.

"As soon as the weather clears, here comes Mr. Ino pulling his cart. He told me once that the day after a storm is a good time to pick up things that blow into the street. He said he made good money then."

Shigenori took his notebook out of his bag. He didn't keep a diary, but he never failed to note the weather each day. It was a habit from his days as a detective.

"The typhoon arrived at four in the afternoon. It was stormy all night."

The storm had died down around five in the morning. The sky suddenly cleared and the temperature rose, typical for a typhoon.

Mrs. Yamada, early this morning a giant bird, like some kind of monster, swooped right over my head and flew away!

On the morning of the fifth, as soon as the weather cleared, Kozaburo Ino had gone out with his cart, not waiting for December's late sunrise, and seen—what? Whatever it was, it had made enough of an impression for him to collar the florist and tell her about it.

And the same day, he'd vanished. At least that was what the young man calling himself Morinaga had said when he interrupted the New Year's party.

"Mrs. Yamada, did you notice when Mr. Ino stopped coming by?"

"No. It's not like he came every day. I thought he might've changed his route. I found out from someone at the party that he'd disappeared."

Shigenori had to determine when Kozaburo had gone missing and under what circumstances. He thanked Mrs. Yamada quickly and walked on.

Shigeru had told Kenji to find his friend the liquor-store owner. Shigenori had listened and remembered them. He had no trouble finding the store. It was small and somewhat fancy, on the first floor of a small condominium building.

The owner was young, probably thirty or so. The shop seemed to have a history; there was a row of framed sepia-toned portrait photos on the wall behind the register. Shigenori asked about them and learned that the owner's family had been running the shop for four generations. As soon as he mentioned Shigeru's name, the owner was ready to share any information he had.

"Yes, a young man named Morinaga was here. A university student."

"Did he say that's what he was?"

"He seemed very nervous, which made me a little suspicious. You never know these days. I asked for proof. He showed me his student ID. He said he was related to Ino through his maternal grandfather."

That's got to be a lie, Shigenori thought. *But at least he's using his real name. Have to give him credit for that.*

"What sort of questions did he ask?"

"Lots. Problem was, I don't know much about that old man. I didn't even know his name. I see him go by now and then with his cart, that's all."

"So you didn't give him any of your trash for recycling?"

"It's against city regulations." Strictly speaking, he was right. "Morinaga was asking about Asahi House. He was pretty nosy, actually. Wanted to know what kind of person the landlord was, what kind of people lived there, that sort of thing."

"What kind of place is it? I hear the landlord doesn't live in the neighborhood."

"No, but he's a reputable person. Sort of a philanthropist. The tenants are all old people living alone, with nowhere else to go. The rent is practically free. It's the zoning laws. Even if they tear the place down, the owner won't be able to build anything there anyway."

"Yes, I hear the building dates back to the occupation."

"By the way, that student told me he heard from the radio that the old man was missing."

"It was on the radio?" Shigenori was startled.

"We have a little local FM station. I listen to it sometimes myself. He told me someone was appealing for information about where the old man might be."

"Do you know where I can find it?"

"No need to go there. Just look at the website. They keep a log of the announcements."

The owner obligingly pulled up the station website on the laptop behind the register. There was a chronological list of requests for music and on-air announcements. Shigenori backtracked through the list until he found it. The appeal for information about Ino's whereabouts came from Yasushi Kadoma, the owner of a local coffee shop.

"Is this shop nearby?"

"Go out, turn right, then left at the first corner. Straight on from there, second corner on the right."

Shigenori had already overextended himself. His leg was beyond the pain and tingling stage; it was almost completely numb. It was difficult even to lift his foot off the ground. Leaning heavily on his cane, he trudged unsteadily until he could see the sign for Kadoma Coffee. By then he was drenched in cold sweat.

But he hit the jackpot. The owner was nattily turned out with a small mustache, slicked-back hair, and a red vest that was fashionable in some bygone era. Shigenori took a seat inside. After he'd caught his breath, the owner told him his story.

"The morning of the fifth—it was still dark—Kozaburo told me he was sure he'd seen a birdlike monster. A huge, black bird, this big"—Kadoma spread his arms wide—"flew over his head."

As soon as the weather cleared before dawn on December 5, Kozaburo Ino had left his apartment to collect trash for recycling. Along his route, he stopped at the florist, told Mrs. Yamada he'd seen a huge bird, and then presented himself at Kadoma Coffee at six thirty, as he did every day.

Kozaburo was a regular customer. The shop opened at seven, but perhaps because he knew other customers would be put off by his appearance—and because being gawked at was unpleasant for him as well—he showed up every morning before business hours and took a wrapped breakfast home. He'd never eaten inside the shop.

Kadoma agreed that the old man seemed strangely excited that morning. "He said he'd seen something fantastic. He could hardly wait to tell me about it."

Like the florist, he had noticed Kozaburo acting increasingly oddly of late, and he hadn't paid much attention to this latest episode. Kozaburo had been wearing several layers of clothing against the cold, but they were damp from the wind and rain. Concerned that the old man might catch cold, Kadoma had given him a towel and invited him to sit by the kerosene stove. Kozaburo did not go into the shop. Though he looked cold, he was excited.

" 'I saw such a strange thing early this morning,' he told me. 'Today will be a good day. I might strike it rich.' And off he went with his cart. I wished him luck, the way I always do."

And that was the last time he had seen the old man. "When he didn't come for his breakfast on the sixth, I thought he must be laid up with a cold. But..."

A bit past two that afternoon, a local salaryman who was a regular at the shop told him Kozaburo's cart was parked in an empty lot not far away. Surprised, Kadoma closed the shop and went to investigate. It was indeed Kozaburo's cart, piled high with cardboard, empty cans and old newspapers.

"At first I thought the police might've picked him up. But they would've impounded the cart. They wouldn't just leave it next to an intersection."

At the time, Kadoma had not known where Kozaburo lived. The old man had told him only that he had an apartment in central Shinjuku and lived alone. "I wasn't convinced, to be honest. I suspected he might be homeless."

There was nowhere to begin a search. The lot where the cart was found was hardly bigger than a postage stamp. There was no fence around it; it was full of trash and detritus. If the old man had wanted to leave his cart unattended for a few minutes, it was the perfect spot. "But I couldn't shake the feeling that something terrible had happened."

Kozaburo depended on his cart. It was how he earned his livelihood. He never would have left it unattended for more than a short time.

"Then I remembered I could put a message out on the local station. If he was being cared for somewhere, or was in the hospital, I was sure someone would hear the message and contact me."

Shigenori had to agree that the coffee shop owner's approach was more efficient than a search with no leads.

"I said I hadn't seen him since the morning of the fifth, and asked people to contact me if they had any news. About three days later, his next-door neighbor at the apartment house got in touch with me. She told me he hadn't come home. But it was true—he did have a place to live.

"His neighbor heard my message on the radio and started to worry, so she went out onto her balcony and looked through his windows. It's a first-floor apartment. The curtains were wide open. She could see right into the room."

The room was almost bare of furniture. There was a bed, a TV, and a small table with a few dishes. It looked undisturbed. The door and windows were securely locked.

"That was all she could tell me. I'd run into a wall. Nothing further happened until close to New Year, when that young man came around asking questions. When was it...I'd just put away the Christmas tree, so it must have been the twenty-sixth or seventh. He told me he'd seen my message on the station website. He was very interested in Kozaburo, but unfortunately all he had for me were questions, not answers.

"I told him what I knew. There was nothing else I could do. He told me he'd ask around the neighborhood and visit Asahi House."

Kenji's actions seemed natural enough. First he visited the coffee shop, then the surrounding neighborhood and Asahi House. He probably hadn't learned anything, so he kept asking around. On January 4 he saw the notice for the party in Ida and rushed there to see if he could get more information. He probably wanted to find the landlord to get into Kozaburo's room. He'd need permission for that.

Kadoma did have one piece of interesting information about Kenji.

"He told me his name was Narita. Said he was Kozaburo's grand-nephew on his mother's side. I didn't ask for proof."

Why did he start using his real name? His cover story was probably blown when he was canvassing the neighborhood for information. After that he had decided he'd better stick to the truth. It was the kind of blunder only amateurs make.

Who is this guy? Shigenori was puzzled.

Was he really a relative of Kozaburo? That didn't seem likely. He'd started his search too long after Kozaburo went missing, for one thing, and his approach was scattershot. When Kadoma urged "Narita" to file a missing-persons report, the young man suddenly became flustered and insisted that the police never made much effort to investigate such reports.

What was his real relationship with the old man? Why did Kozaburo Ino vanish? What happened to him? Where was he now?

An old man living alone, eking out a living by selling trash for recycling. What could someone like that encounter that would cause him to disappear?

The florist had suggested Kozaburo might be sitting on a lot of money. That would be a plausible reason for his disappearance. But he said he'd seen a birdlike monster.

As a detective, Shigenori had always had a habit of speculating too much. It was pointed out to him frequently, and he himself was aware of it. But his speculations were always rooted in reality. He never fantasized. Still, he couldn't put the image of the giant bird out of his mind.

Kozaburo Ito sees a giant bird flying overhead. The next day he's gone, as abruptly and completely as if he'd been snatched up into the sky.

His cart had been discovered the afternoon of the sixth, but exactly when he'd left it there was an open question. It seemed unlikely that he'd parked it on the fifth, otherwise it would have been discovered sooner.

His apartment was locked, the curtains left open. That suggested he'd gotten up as usual on the sixth and set out before sunrise. Before the city was awake, while it was still dark, he had disappeared in the vicinity of that traffic light.

Why before sunrise? Because a giant bird would find it easier to move about freely under cover of darkness? The distance from the tea caddy building to the empty lot where the cart was found was around five hundred meters in a straight line.

The distance a bird of prey might cover in a single glide.

▼

A low hum. Shigenori's eyes snapped open. The call light on the phone next to his pillow was flashing as the phone vibrated. The caller ID was TAE CHIGUSA.

3:22. The numbers leapt into his eyes. He pressed TALK. "Is that you, Tae? What's going on?"

He heard a coarse rustling, like someone blundering through undergrowth. He sat up. Toshiko was deep asleep on the futon next to him.

"Hello, Tae? It's Shigenori. Has something happened?"

As he spoke, he realized the sound on the end of the line was ragged breathing.

"I'm…I'm sorry…"

It was Tae. Shigenori was so relieved that he put a hand on the floor to support himself.

"I'm sorry to call you this late." She was sobbing.

"No, I'm the one who should apologize. What are you doing up at this hour? You must be cold. Are you all right?"

No answer. More ragged breathing.

"Tae, it sounds like you're having trouble breathing. Do you feel ill?" *Am I going to have to call an ambulance?*

"I'm afraid to look outside," she said finally. Shigenori was at a loss. Toshiko stirred restlessly.

"I'm afraid. I can't open the curtains," she whimpered. "It knows what I'm doing. I'm sure of it."

"Are you all right, Tae?"

"It doesn't want me to see."

Shigenori wondered if he was actually awake. Was this a dream?

"Tae—you mean the monster, right? The gargoyle?"

Silence.

"Tae?"

"It's outside my window. I can feel it," she whispered. The tension in her voice was contagious. Shigenori shivered with fear.

"I'm sorry. I'm just too scared to look out the window. I have to hide."

This had gone too far. "Tae, listen to me. You're not in any danger—"

"I'm sorry." She ended the call.

For the next hour, Shigenori lay on his side, unable to sleep, his mind filled with regret.

Tae was an old woman living alone, cut off for the most part from the everyday world. Because of him, she had suffered a shock. His high spirits—excessive spirits, maybe—had infected her.

Since his diagnosis of spinal stenosis, every day had been a struggle as he waited for a bed to open at the hospital. A struggle with pain and boredom.

In the tea caddy building, he had discovered something to pull him out of his boredom, something that made him feel alive. A statue of a gargoyle, come to life? It was utter nonsense. If he investigated, he'd find a rational explanation.

Maybe "mysterious gargoyle" was just an excuse. Maybe he would've been happy with anything that allowed him to walk, investigate, think. Toshiko had said it herself.

You seem so energetic. It's strange.

Shigeru might've looked grim as he scrutinized his notes, but he'd been enjoying himself. Still, this investigation was something he should've handled himself. He shouldn't have gotten others involved.

I'll visit Tae first thing in the morning and apologize, he decided. *I've got to soothe her and get her back to her quiet routine.*

At last he fell into a fitful sleep that lasted till dawn. When he woke, Toshiko was already up. He went to retrieve the newspaper from the box inside the front door and sat down. The morning edition was thick with ads and fliers. And there was an envelope.

Yamacho. *When was he here?* Shigeru wondered. He had hoped he'd gotten away from the tea caddy building before Tae called.

A shiny new dimple key fell from the envelope. So the "customer" hadn't been difficult, just as Yamacho had guessed. There was a bill for services rendered. He'd also stuffed Shigeru's fax into the envelope. He was always very careful about the details.

There was a Post-it stuck to the fax.

Work start 02:15, end 04:05. Pitch-dark, as advised.

There was a gap, as if he'd hesitated, then a hasty scribble.

Strange noises several times during visit. From overhead. Like the beating of giant wings. Saw nothing. Alone the whole time. Your "intruder" isn't a bird, is it?

The newspaper slid off Shigeru's lap into a heap on the floor.

3

"What do you mean, you can't reach him?"

Kotaro knew he sounded aggressive, but he couldn't help it. Seigo and Narita, the chief of School Island, exchanged glances but said nothing.

It was ten past nine on January 6, Kotaro's first day of work since the year began. He'd actually hoped to begin on the fourth, as soon as the holidays ended, and was itching to start work. School was still out for winter break. He was ready for a full day of patrolling. But as soon as he'd hit his chair, Seigo had called him over and Narita had joined them.

"How long have you been trying? When did he stop responding?"

Narita chuckled soothingly, trying to keep things light. "Hold on, you're jumping the gun. We don't know if he's disappeared."

Narita was a former high school teacher, past forty. His move to Kumar had been unusual even compared to some of the other employees, but he was capable, easy to get along with, and highly rated by Seigo. At the moment, however, Kotaro couldn't have cared less.

"How can you be so calm? You knew what he was up to. He was investigating missing persons. Not one but several. Now he's out of contact too. Wouldn't it be natural to worry that something's happened to him?"

Seigo and Narita exchanged glances again. They looked more worried than before.

"Ko-Prime, calm down, please." In other words, lower your voice. Narita looked pained. They were getting anxious glances from people at their desks.

"He was keeping me posted." Narita held up his smartphone. "I reacted the same way you did. I wasn't thrilled by the idea of his going off on his own. I told him to keep me informed of everything. He sent me a lot of messages. Called, too, a few times."

So Kenji updated Narita but not me. I guess insurance is all I'm good for.

"He's not a professional at this kind of thing. Of course he couldn't solve it just like that. After he tracked down his first lead—the coffee shop—he took the twenty-fourth and twenty-fifth off. Then he went to the apartment house. He knocked on every door and got no response. He even laughed about his lack of progress. Said it never happens like this on TV."

Kenji had also visited the neighborhoods where other disappearances had taken place, but the story was the same: finding out anything was much harder than he'd expected. The homeless people he'd approached had been less than helpful.

"Not only were they not used to being interrogated by strangers, the questions he was asking were unsettling. 'Has anyone you know suddenly vanished?' That kind of thing. It probably sounded like an accusation.

"By the end of the year, he basically had nothing to show for all the time he'd put in. He told me he was taking an overnight bus back home and planned to spend the first and second there."

Kenji was back in Tokyo on the afternoon of the third. He decided to return to Asahi House and go from there to see what he might be able to learn. Still, not much in the way of results was likely with such a haphazard approach, especially when he came across as an amateur, which would immediately put people on their guard.

"He told me he'd underestimated the difficulty. I advised him to drop the whole thing." Narita looked at Seigo and winced in discomfort. "I couldn't get him to quit. He wanted to keep going until he decided it was hopeless."

"Kenji's the quiet, serious type. I'm not surprised, really." Seigo sighed. He might've been thinking of himself as a young man.

"His last message was the day before yesterday, the fourth." Narita said. "At 9:34 p.m." He held out the phone so Kotaro could see.

Something's been bugging me. I'm going to check it out tonight.

Kotaro read the message twice. "He went somewhere after he sent this message."

Narita nodded. Seigo frowned. "I asked him where he was going. No answer," Narita said. "That definitely bothered me. I called him several times that night but couldn't connect. He might've turned his phone off. If he did, it's still off."

"Did you try his apartment?" Kotaro asked.

"He's not home. The door's locked."

"Do his parents know anything?"

"I called them last night," Seigo said. "We'd been out of touch with him for a full day. His parents were surprised to hear from me."

Kenji's parents hadn't noticed anything unusual during his visit home. He'd eaten a lot, drank a lot, and had a good time. The day he left for Tokyo, he told them that both school and work were keeping him busy, and that both were fascinating.

"Are you going to file a missing-persons report?" Kotaro asked.

"I'd like to wait another day. If he doesn't show up, we'll take the next step."

"If you file a report, you'll tell the police everything, right? About his investigation and the missing homeless people?"

"Of course."

"Let me know if you need help. Any time of the day or night. I remember everything he told me. The police have to understand that he was serious about finding those people."

Seigo nodded vigorously.

"Did Kenji contact you at all?" Narita asked.

"No. Maybe he thought you were the only one he needed to keep in the loop."

"I'm not talking about the investigation. You guys are friends. Don't you ever shoot the breeze?" Narita's eyes widened as he remembered something. "Wait a minute—"

He pulled out his phone again and scrolled through his messages. His thumb stopped. "He sent me this."

He held the phone out again. Seigo peered at the screen too.

"He didn't tell me every detail of what he was doing, just where he'd been that day, things like that. But then I got this." It was a mail with an attached image. The timestamp read 3:03 p.m. on December 30.

"He gave me a call right after he sent this. He said he thought it was fascinating. He asked me if I could figure out what it was."

"What—it's a drawing," Seigo said.

"It looks like a child did it," Kotaro said.

A giant gray bird filled the screen, crayon on drawing paper. The drawing was crude, obviously the work of a child.

Narita's phone had a retinal screen. Kotaro could see how the young artist's hand had trembled as he drew the image.

"It's a bird," Seigo said.

Narita smiled. "That's a pretty odd bird."

"It has wings like a bird," Kotaro said, "but legs like a human."

"Correct. There's no face, but you can see it doesn't have a beak. Again, more human than bird."

"Come on, it's a kid's drawing," Seigo objected. "It's a mix of reality and imagination."

"Kenji was excited by this picture. If you look closely, it's actually very well executed. It's Mothman."

"I don't get it."

"An imaginary being. An urban legend. You've never heard of Mothman, Seigo?"

"I've heard of MOS Burger."

Kotaro was still peering at the smartphone screen. "Did Kenji say anything else about this?"

"No, nothing. He didn't send it to you?"

"No. Could you send it to me? I want to take a closer look at it."

Narita blinked in surprise. Kotaro's eyes were burning with determination.

"Sure, but I don't see how it has anything to do with his investigation. It must be something he just happened to stumble across."

As Kotaro turned to go, Seigo warned him again not to lose his cool over Kenji's unexplained absence.

Back at his desk, Kotaro found it hard to concentrate. It was all he could do to keep from surfing the web. He couldn't track what has happening in front of him. Text flowed past on the monitor, but he couldn't follow it. It was like looking at a foreign language.

For two hours he worked, or at least tried to. When he glanced up, Seigo was frowning and beckoning.

"You're thinking about things you shouldn't."

There was no use denying it.

"You're thinking about contacting that FM station, or searching their site?"

"Of course not!"

"Well, you didn't. That's admirable." Seigo had been watching him.

"The first person to go looking after that old guy with the cart was a coffee shop owner, right? Kenji must've talked to him. And you're planning the same thing. I thought of talking to him too. So did Narita. We were going to go there yesterday, but in the end we decided not to. It wouldn't have led to anything."

Kotaro had to speak up. "What makes you so sure? We should be trying to find Kenji right now."

"No, we should be quietly watching and waiting. If he doesn't show up, any investigation should be left to the police." Seigo's expression softened. "Look, Ko-Prime. As far as we know, we could all be laughing about this someday."

"But Kenji's gone. That's reality."

"Maybe he just can't contact us. Maybe he can't get back to his apartment right now, for some reason that has nothing to do with his investigation."

Sure. Just a coincidence.

"Kenji's an adult. He's been out of contact for less than two days."

"More than twenty-four hours."

Kotaro wouldn't budge. Seigo sighed.

"That's enough. Go home. Right now, you're less use to me than an old man in a PC course who just learned how to turn the computer on."

"What? Why? I'm doing my job."

"Don't BS me. Your reputation will suffer." Kotaro had never heard Seigo talk this way.

"Go home and cool off. Got it? Go straight home and sit tight till you hear from me or Narita. There must be a thing or two you can do for fun besides work. Do something different for a change."

He finally smiled and clapped Kotaro on the shoulder. "The Lady is up in Gunma or Niigata skiing, you know. You ought to call her and go on up there."

"She's in Nagano," Kotaro said in a small voice. "And she's snowboarding, not skiing."

And like a kid defying his father, Kotaro turned his back on Seigo and stalked off.

Kotaro was glad he'd brought his laptop to work. With the case over his shoulder, he headed to the coffee shop where Kenji had briefed him about darknet school sites.

It was close to lunchtime and seats were filling up. Kotaro managed to grab an empty spot in the corner. As soon as he sat down, he became an unwilling audience to the conversation of four young women at the next table.

"It's so awful. I didn't worry because until now it's been happening in the sticks, but I mean, Yokohama..."

"Yeah, but it's Totsuka. Not a very fashionable part of Yokohama."

"It's still close to Tokyo. I live in Musashi Kosugi. That's practically next door."

The women's winter outfits were trendy, with makeup to match. Kotaro guessed they were students from a nearby polytechnic. What were they afraid of?

He opened the image file that Kenji had sent to Narita. He quickly realized that he'd missed some important details on the phone's small screen.

The sketch was innocent and crude. Anyone could see that the artist was a very young child, but children usually preferred bright colors. Whoever drew this picture had used three colors only: gray, black, and dark green.

"This is the sickest one yet."

"They're all sick."

"I know, but this time he took off a leg at the knee. A leg, not a toe."

Kotaro froze with one elbow on the table. The women looked disgusted. They leaned in with their shoulders scrunched up, talking animatedly about something dreadful. Yet they seemed excited.

Kotaro clicked on his news feed. There it was at the top. The conversation next door continued in whispers.

"They can't call him Toe-Cutter Bill anymore." The Toe-Fetish Killer had claimed his fourth victim.

"Who cares what they call him? He's a murderer." The woman sounded angry. Her three companions exchanged uncomfortable glances.

"Of course, you're right."

"But everyone's going nuts about it."

"I don't want to be like other people. This is serious. People are dying."

"I know, but won't they find the killer faster the more it's on the news and stuff? Like that time when they captured a killer by searching through surveillance camera pictures."

"I remember! You could see his face close-up. It was gross."

Kotaro kept one ear on the conversation as he paged through the news sites. The fourth victim was a woman in her thirties or forties. Cause of death was undetermined, as was the victim's identity. The body had been discovered in the restroom of a gas station in Yokohama's Totsuka Ward. The right leg had been severed at the knee. The information was only ten minutes old. None of the news feeds had further details.

Things must be hot back at Kumar, thought Kotaro. Seigo would be putting together another special team. Dredging textboards was hard work, but it had made Kotaro feel like a true cyber patroller.

He immediately shook his head. Something had occurred to him for the first time since he started following the Toe-Fetish Killer. The discovery of each new victim must be traumatic for people with missing relatives or loved ones. It was something that had never occurred to him.

But now Kenji was missing. It was a minor incident compared to the murders, but for Kotaro, it was more than enough to bring home how unforgiving reality could be.

A person vanishes. Her life is taken and the corpse is discovered. It was a terrible, terrible thing. Kotaro's mind was so preoccupied with concern for Kenji that he could hardly concentrate.

The group at the next table got up and left, still talking animatedly. Two businessmen quickly took their place. They started talking about money as soon as they sat down.

Kotaro left the news site and returned to Kenji's drawing. Gray, black, and dark green. Somber colors. The figure of the creature was blurred at the edges, obviously crayon. Kotaro could picture the child working on the drawing with a box of crayons at his side.

The creature was winged but without a beak. The legs were humanoid. Narita had thought the creature was more human than bird, but it was missing something that was essentially human: a pair of arms.

There was something even more distinctive, something that made Kotaro even more unsure of what he was looking at: long hair.

He hadn't noticed it before. The smartphone screen was small, and the background was filled with slanting lines, as if the figure were in flight. That was why the hair had been hard to see at first.

Still, it was definitely hair. It swept back at an angle, perhaps windblown. At rest, it would've hung all the way down the creature's back.

This meant something else. The face wasn't missing, because there was no need to draw it. The figure was facing away.

Kotaro blinked. The arms. It was the same thing. They weren't missing, they just weren't visible in this pose. But would a child be this skilled? Whether the subject was real or imaginary, depicting it from behind seemed odd. Kotaro had been taught that a child's sketches could reflect their psychological state.

Or did the child see this in a book somewhere and simply copy it? Kotaro had seen images of centaurs with long hair, but centaurs had four legs and no wings. Pegasus? It had wings, but was clearly a horse. It was neither birdlike nor human.

Narita had said the sketch was of Mothman, but that was an American urban legend, an eerie cross between human and moth.

Chief, what do you think this is?

Kenji had been fascinated by the sketch. He'd not only sent it to Narita, he had called him up about it afterward.

I don't think it has anything to do with his investigation. It must be something he just happened to stumble across.

No. It had to mean something.

Resting his chin in his hand, Kotaro tinkered with the image, zooming in, rotating the image, reversing it, trying to organize what it was about it that bothered him.

First of all, where did Kenji find this?

A child's drawing, on public display. There weren't too many possibilities. A classroom in a kindergarten or a nursery school? Those weren't places a stranger could just stroll into. What about an exhibition of children's drawings? Again, not too many possibilities.

Kotaro looked at the image again. He'd been scrutinizing it from close range. Now he pulled back. He had to examine what else the camera had caught besides the sketch itself.

The problem was, he didn't know how to enhance the small amount of extra information the image contained at the edges. Go to the web. He entered a query.

The information he needed accumulated as he sipped his tepid coffee. He found a suitable free image-analysis package. The software was basic, but that was all he needed.

Top edge, right edge, bottom edge, left edge. He navigated clockwise around the image, looking for clues. In the center of the right edge was a beige object of some sort, blurred. It took him a split second to realize it was Kenji's finger, holding the smartphone.

He could see parts of clothing. The tip of someone's jaw a short distance away. Part of a finger, all in the part of the image on either side of the sketch. Kotaro was puzzled. How had the sketch been displayed? It was unframed. It wasn't mounted on a panel or pinned to a wall. He could see people behind it. Maybe some sort of transparent sheet, or—

Glass. Window glass. The sketch was taped to a window, with people in the room beyond it.

That meant the picture hadn't been taken at a school. The date stamp was December 30. School was out for vacation.

So it was some kind of public facility. City hall? Closed that day too. A community center? Possible. They sometimes exhibited children's art.

Kotaro zoomed in on the left edge. The image outside the sketch was wider here than on the other side. Kenji had been holding the phone in his right hand, standing slightly to the right of the picture when he tripped the shutter.

The left edge of the image contained something important—part of a red box, with something like a poster affixed to it. Kotaro could make out the words NEW YEAR'S CARDS.

It was a postal delivery scooter. The full text probably said something like "Mail your New Year's cards early" or "Mail New Year's cards before December 25."

A post office!

Kenji had walked all over the area, but he was searching for information about Kozaburo Ino. Kotaro called up a list of post offices in Hyakunin and surrounding neighborhoods. He was surprised how many there were.

The coffee shop was packed and getting louder. He decided to move. There was a bus stop out front for a bus that only came once an hour or so. He could sit there and keep working.

The day had started badly with the warning from Seigo, but Kotaro's luck was with him. The soft-spoken woman who picked up at the third number he called told him what he needed to know.

"Yes, that's correct. We had an exhibition of children's art here last month."

Gotcha!

"Excuse me, where are you located?"

"Sakae, in West Shinjuku."

Sakae. Kotaro zoomed in on his map. It was right next to Hyakunin.

"The exhibition is over, I guess?"

"Yes, we're doing a different one now."

"I was really impressed with that artwork. I'd like to see it again. I don't know which school the kids were from. Would you happen to know?"

Silence, then: "We can't release the children's names..."

"Of course. I just need the name of the school. I'll ask them about the artwork."

"But it wasn't a school exhibit."

"Sorry?"

"Didn't you notice? The title of the exhibit was 'Little Artists from the House of Light.' "

Now it was Kotaro's turn to fall silent.

"You should probably ask the person in charge of their children's association."

"I see. Okay then, thanks for your help."

Search: House of Light. Children's association?

The results came back. "You gotta be kidding," Kotaro said out loud. A passerby glanced at him warily and walked on quickly.

House of Light was a nonprofit religious organization.

Not far from Shinjuku National Garden was a small neighborhood of old apartment houses built of reinforced concrete. House of Light occupied the first floor of what was probably the oldest building in the area. Perhaps it had once been a large shop. The listing on the residents' directory simply said HOUSE OF LIGHT CHILDREN'S ASSOCIATION.

Kotaro had expected House of Light to have security. Religious groups often did. He was wrong. The doors were wide open. Outside on the step, a tall, heavyset man was smiling and talking to an older man in a windbreaker and cap. A battered pickup was parked at the curb. The cargo bed had a canopy and was piled high with vegetables in cardboard boxes. The old man was selling them out of his truck.

"See you soon, then." The old man touched his cap and got into the truck. The heavyset man called to him from the steps.

"Everyone's looking forward to it. Give my regards to your family."

The old man waved. Kotaro watched from the other side of the narrow street as the truck pulled away. When he looked back at the man standing on the step, their eyes met.

"Hello there," he said amiably. "Are you a student? Live around here? We're having a little neighborhood get-together here tomorrow. If you have time, why don't you join us?" That must've been what he was chatting about with the greengrocer.

Kotaro felt a sudden inspiration. Kenji had been here. If that sketch was important to him, he must have found his way here. And he must have spoken to this same man.

It's a lead. I have a real lead. It reached out and found me.

"Sorry to trouble you." Kotaro bowed and crossed the street. "I'm actually looking for someone, a friend of mine. He seems to be missing."

He had to show the man Kenji's sketch. He took his laptop out of its case. "Let me show you something. My friend sent this last month on the thirtieth. Right now this is the only clue I have to go on."

The man interrupted him. "Let's not stand out here. Come on in."

"You don't mind?"

"Not at all. Please."

He seemed genuinely friendly. Kotaro should have been grateful, but then again he wondered if it was smart for the man to welcome a stranger. Kotaro might have been a pedophile. He had a younger sister, which made him sensitive to things like this.

The first-floor office was spacious. There was an area with office furniture and cabinets, but the center of the floor was empty. It was big enough to hold a small gathering.

Kotaro peered around the room and saw an array of twenty or more sketches on the wall. The pictures were colorful and full of life, except for one.

It was gray and black, with a touch of dark green. There was no mistake.

"I should introduce myself. I'm responsible for the association. My name is Masao Ohba." The man offered Kotaro his card. Kotaro hastily retrieved his student ID.

"Kotaro Mishima, is it? I'm pleased to meet you." He bowed. Coming from him it was a big bow. His card was simple and unadorned:

MASAO OHBA
CHAIRMAN, CHILDREN'S ASSOCIATION
HOUSE OF LIGHT

House of Light was one of the newest of the Buddhist sects in Japan. Kotaro had checked out their web page; it seemed like a legitimate organization with a gentle, friendly feel. Its three thousand members probably made it a medium-size group of its type.

"I'm sorry to show up suddenly like this," Kotaro said. "There wasn't much about the association on your web page. I was in the area, so I decided to just come over."

Masao nodded. "We try to put as much information as possible on the site, but we have to be careful when it comes to the children."

"I totally understand," Kotaro said. "Please don't worry about me. I'm just interested in that picture over there of the winged figure—that birdman, or whatever you call it."

Kotaro pointed to the sketch. Masao strode over to the wall and stood close to it, almost protectively. "This was one of the pictures in our Little Artists exhibit at the post office. It ran for ten days from the twentieth."

Masao furrowed his brow slightly. "Another young man about your age was here, asking about this picture. A week ago, maybe. Is he the friend you're looking for?"

Yes!

"I think so. Did he tell you his name?"

"Kenji Morinaga."

Everything was falling into place. Kotaro could barely control his excitement. "He must've been here on the thirtieth," he said. "He took the picture at three, so it would've been after that."

"Yes. Now that you remind me, I think it was around four."

The post office had closed at five on the thirtieth. After that, someone from the post office arrived with the pictures. Kenji had waited and examined it himself before leaving. By then it was almost seven in the evening.

"The Sakae Post Office lends out their front windows for exhibits like this. It's free—if your application gets picked. A lot of people want to exhibit during the Christmas season, so we were lucky this time."

Masao must have noticed that Kotaro was itching to talk about more important things. He turned to the picture and detached it from the wall. "Be careful with this." Kotaro accepted it reverently.

He began examining it closely. It was certainly the sketch Kenji had seen. The long hair was easier to see, and the fact that the figure was facing away.

"You're devouring that picture with your eyes just like your friend did," Masao said.

"This is supposed to be hair, isn't it? A human with the wings of a bird. The lines in the background are probably the wind blowing by."

"I think it's rain."

Kotaro looked up from the sketch. "Is that what the artist said?"

"No, that was Kenji's theory. He thought it looked like a downpour."

As though he realized he didn't have to keep standing, Masao pulled up a chair and clasped his hands in his lap. He peered at Kotaro.

"Let me ask you something. Are you and your friend really students?"

What's this, all of a sudden?

"Sure—I mean, of course we are."

"Is that all you are? Kenji said he worked at Kumar."

Kotaro was surprised that Kenji would have disclosed that much. "You've heard of Kumar?"

"It's well-known in its industry. The president is a woman. That's unusual."

"Yes. Kenji was there when I joined."

Masao kept staring at Kotaro thoughtfully. "What is your real purpose here? Are you sure someone didn't ask you to get information about us?"

Kotaro blinked in confusion. "I don't understand."

Masao lowered his gaze and frowned. "If you two really have the skills to work at Kumar, you could dig up anything if you really wanted. Couldn't you?" His tone implied that Kotaro knew exactly what he was talking about. "We work with a company like Kumar. They monitor what people say about us on the web. Religious organizations are easily misunderstood. We try to be careful, but if someone with an ax to grind wants to spread lies, there's not a lot we can do."

"I think you misunderstand, Mr. Ohba. Kenji and I do work for Kumar. Kenji's specialty is unofficial school websites. We're part-timers, but we get the same strict training as full-time employees."

Masao was silent.

"I'm not surprised you're suspicious about the way we suddenly showed up here, but neither of us are looking for skeletons in your closet. We're not that kind of people."

Masao's expression was still wary. "I wonder why your friend is missing?"

"I don't know. That's why I'm looking for him."

"Maybe because he had something juicy and took off with it? Took it to a higher bidder?"

"Something...juicy?"

Kotaro was stuck. This was not going well. He'd have to tell Masao everything. If Kenji gave him a hard time later for being loose-lipped, he'd just have to deal with it. He'd had enough of going in circles trying to gain this man's trust.

"Mr. Ohba, I'm going to tell you everything. Could you just listen?"

Kotaro told Masao everything that had happened so far. The office was quiet. The phone didn't ring. No one came to the door.

"I don't know..."

Masao drew his hand slowly down over his face and looked at it for a long moment, as if he were expecting to find something there. Finally he dropped it into his lap. "All those people vanishing...it's eerie, isn't it?" He looked genuinely unsettled. "I hope nothing's happened to your friend."

He finally seemed to understand. He was more in tune with Kotaro's feelings than Seigo or Narita had been.

"I apologize for being so suspicious. It's just that I have my own reasons for being cautious. Religious organizations often find it difficult to gain people's trust. If we step out of line for any reason, the media is right there to beat us up. House of Light is not a big organization, and we do have some internal differences of opinion."

"Still, you seem pretty open," Kotaro said. "You had that exhibit at the post office. And that greengrocer just now. You're having an open house for the neighborhood."

Masao laughed wryly. "We try. We have to stay very close to the local community." He scratched his head awkwardly. "So when your friend Kenji came to the door, he seemed very sincere. Lots of students live around here. I thought he might've had an apartment in the neighborhood."

Masao had been friendly to Kotaro from the start, too. He was trying to be friendly to everyone.

"I understand why you'd be suspicious, with me and Kenji showing up like this, asking strange questions about this picture. This was done by a child of one of your members, I guess. Could I meet this child? If I can't talk to him directly, could you introduce me to his guardian? I really need to get more information. It may give me a hint, even a small one, about where Kenji is. Please." Kotaro placed his palms flat on the table and bowed deeply.

"I'm sorry," Masao said, nonplussed by this request. "I'm afraid that's impossible."

Kotaro looked up. Masao's face was contorted into an expression of genuine discomfort. "The artist is a little girl. She's only five."

So the sketch was by a preschooler after all.

"She lived with her mother, just the two of them. They were very poor. The mother died of pneumonia without ever seeing a doctor. To make things worse, their utilities were cut off. The girl didn't even know her mother had died. They found her hungry and cold in an apartment without gas, electricity, or water."

Kotaro was stunned. "When did this happen?"

"They found her on December 6. They think her mother passed away sometime early on the fifth."

The little girl had spent the night of the fifth huddled next to her mother, not realizing she was dead, in a room without light or heat.

"The power was off. The meter reader was worried about them. When he went round to check, no one answered the door."

The meter reader contacted the landlord. When they entered the apartment, they found the little girl.

That is the way of the world. No matter how much you might worry about someone, without the right or the qualifications to help them, you can't go breaking down the locked doors of cheap apartments. Yet without the formalities that stand in the way of rescuing someone, people can't be safe. That's life in the city.

"Where's the child now? Is someone taking care of her?"

Masao looked uncomfortable again. "Fortunately they were able to contact her father. But he's unwilling to take the child back. It's not surprising. He runs a busy bar—" As if it sufficed to answer Kotaro's question, Masao finished the sentence by scrunching up his round nose.

"If things end there, the child will end up in an orphanage. But the landlord took pity on her. He probably feels guilty that he didn't realize what was going on. He could've done something." The only thing to do was for the landlord to care for the little girl until her father could be persuaded to take responsibility for her. "The apartment is in Ida, but the landlord lives near here. He's one of our members."

So that's why you know so much about the little girl.

"So if I ask the landlord, can I meet her?"

"I'm sorry, I told you. It's impossible." His face darkened. "You see, she hasn't uttered a word since she was found."

The little girl was being taken care of and her health had improved. But she was mute—and most of the time, expressionless.

"Is that because of the shock of losing her mother?"

"Well, that has to be part of it, but apparently that's not the only reason. She never attended nursery school or kindergarten. She had no contact at all with the outside world, so her communication skills never developed. She should be much more communicative for a five-year-old. But she loves to draw. Give her crayons and a sketchbook and she'll draw all day."

Kotaro looked at the sketch of the birdman with its long hair and imagined the little girl drawing.

"She keeps drawing the same thing, over and over."

"What?" Kotaro looked up.

"It's all she draws. I've seen four or five of these pictures myself."

"She must've seen something that made an impression on her. Or something that frightened her. She's only five. Something on television, or in a picture book."

"No one knows. She won't say a word."

The children's association was working with the landlord to get the child to start speaking, but so far nothing they'd tried had been successful.

"Did you tell all this to Kenji?"

"He was very inquisitive, but no, I didn't tell him. All I said was that a child of one of our members had drawn it."

So Kenji had left empty-handed.

"He said something interesting, though." Masao touched the edge of the sketch gently with a fingertip. "He said he thought this was a straightforward depiction of something the girl had actually seen."

Kotaro's eyes opened wide. "She saw this?"

"I was surprised too. But once he mentioned it, I have to say I tend to agree. Look at the pose. Five-year-old children always draw facing figures."

"But don't they say that if children suffer some kind of trauma, it might be reflected in what they draw? A child like that might draw anything."

Masao looked at him with surprise. "I see you know a lot about this. You're absolutely right. But traumatized children don't draw accurately proportioned human figures in this sort of pose. They draw distorted figures, or people without faces, like a Japanese monster."

"Is this well done, for a five-year-old?"

"Extremely. That's why I think there's something to be said for Kenji's opinion. The girl saw it and it made a strong impression on her. That's why she was able to draw it so well."

Was that what Kenji meant when he'd said the sketch was fascinating? But where was the connection with Kozaburo Ino and the others who were missing? Such creatures didn't actually exist. She had obviously seen it somewhere, in a painting or as a sculpture. Was the place where such artwork could be found the key to solving the mystery?

"Her name is Mana." Masao traced the Chinese characters on the tabletop. "Ma" from the character for true. "Na" from the character for blossom.

"Mother and child lived in desperate poverty, but they seem to have been very close. Even now, Mana sometimes seems to be searching for her mother. She doesn't understand that her mother is dead."

"That's so sad," Kotaro murmured.

The phone buzzed in his jacket pocket. It was Seigo. Not a mail; a voice call.

"Hello, it's Kotaro." He waved "sorry" to Masao and went outside to take the call. It was lucky that he did. Seigo got right to the point.

"They found his phone. It wasn't off—it was smashed. That's why we couldn't get through to him."

"Where did they find it?"

"At the bottom of a gap between an apartment house and another building in Ida. The gap was only about a foot wide. There's a gas meter back there. The meter reader found it and turned it in at a police box.

"It was completely crushed. Not working at all. But the police were able to read the data. They called his parents and the office."

"I'm surprised they were able to do that."

"Some of the younger cops are pretty handy at that kind of thing. Apparently it didn't look like it was just dropped. And it was found in a strange place. That's probably why they investigated. Anyway, we'll be filing a missing-persons report today. I contacted his parents and they asked us to proceed. His father's coming to Tokyo."

"Okay. Thanks for keeping me in the loop."

"Listen Ko-Prime, I don't know where you are right now, but—"

"Don't worry, I won't do anything rash. I'm leaving it to the police." He pressed END and went back inside.

"Is Ida nearby?" he asked Masao.

He looked puzzled. "No, it's a subway stop away from here. I think Ida is near the west exit of Shinjuku Station."

"They found Kenji's smartphone there." As Kotaro gave him the details, Masao went pale.

"Mana and her mother lived in Ida. It's an old section of town. Years and years ago it was nothing but low-rent apartments and little shops, but it's mostly built up now. There are still a few old apartment houses that for one reason or another were never torn down. There are pockets of the past all around the west side of Shinjuku Station."

"Mr. Ohba." Kotaro sat up straight. "My request still stands. Please let me talk to Mana. I promise not to say anything to frighten her. I give you my word."

Masao looked at Kotaro for a long time and said nothing. He stood up.

❖

The landlord of Asahi House lived in a rambling old mansion that was rare in modern Tokyo, especially so close to Shinjuku's Imperial Gardens.

"Kotaro, this is Mr. Nagasaki and his sister, Hatsuko."

The landlord was a small, silver-haired old man. He and his sister shared a strong family likeness. Hatsuko's hair was frosted light purple.

"Somehow we just can't seem to turn down a request from you, Mr. Ohba," Hatsuko Nagasaki said in a slightly sharp tone. She scrutinized Kotaro from behind lenses tinted the color of her hair. "If this means Mana-chan might actually speak, then I suppose there's nothing we can do but try."

"Thank you. I'm grateful," Masao sounded just as eager as Kotaro to find out if something could be done, if not more.

"Our little angel artist is drawing right now," Hatsuko said.

They left the entryway and walked down a long, winding corridor past a bank of windows that looked out over a sere winter garden. The landlord led the way, slippers flapping on the wood floor.

If these people are this rich, why didn't they do something for an impoverished young mother and her child before it was too late? She was your tenant. She was in trouble. Aren't landlords obliged to do more than just collect rent?

Kotaro struggled to swallow his anger before it burst into the open. The corridor snaked on interminably, making him feel even worse.

He knew it wasn't simple. There was a limit to how much one person can help another. Once you start, you can't stop. Whom do you help and whom do you abandon? The whole purpose of a social welfare system was to relieve individuals of the need to make those decisions.

At the end of the corridor was a small room, bright with sunshine. As Nagasaki entered, he clapped his hands lightly and said, "Mana-chan, you have visitors."

It was the ideal room for a child, like something out of a childcare magazine. Mana sat on the floor at a little round table, gripping a crayon. The table was scattered with sheets of drawing paper. A woman dressed casually in sweater and jeans sat next to her, also holding a crayon. They were both drawing flowers. The pictures were colorful and full of life.

"This is Ms. Sato. She's a childcare specialist."

Kotaro bowed slightly to the woman, who acknowledged him with a nod. She looked about thirty. She was plump and gentle-looking, but her eyes followed Kotaro with watchful alertness.

Kotaro knew that the only reason someone as green as he was had gotten this far was the landlord's trust in Masao. That trust was based on a special relationship between an officer of a religious organization and a believer. The smallest misstep would put an end to the visit. He had to proceed carefully.

"Hello," he said to Mana. The little girl showed no sign of having heard him. She kept drawing. Her fine, bowl-cut hair was pretty. She had an angel's whorl on the top of her head.

Her body was tiny. Kotaro wasn't used to being around children this young, but even he could see she was smaller than the average five-year-old. She wore a pastel pink sweater and soft jeans with the cuffs rolled up. Her socks were white with red polka dots.

"This is how she always is," Nagasaki said. "We can't even get her attention."

"But Mana can hear you just fine." Ms. Sato smiled.

Mana had her own room and a dedicated caregiver. Maybe this drastic change in her situation had actually been stressful for her.

"Will she be going to kindergarten?"

Kotaro's question was for Ms. Sato, but Nagasaki answered.

"She doesn't seem to be taking to it, and the school said they can't admit her until she starts talking."

"There's no need to rush her," Masao said. Perhaps because he didn't want to crowd the girl, he motioned Nagasaki to join him on the sofa against the wall. It was a small sofa, low to the floor, built for a child.

Kotaro learned forward and spoke quietly. "Hello, Mana-chan."

Mana was drawing leaves with a red crayon and carefully filling them in. She kept her eyes on the paper.

"Sorry to bother her while she's drawing," he said to Ms. Sato in a friendly tone. "Those pictures are very colorful." Ms. Sato nodded but said nothing.

"The picture I saw used fewer colors. They were colder colors. If she's drawing this kind of picture, does that mean she's starting to recover?"

"Excuse me. You're a college student, aren't you?" The woman addressed him directly for the first time.

"Yes."

"Are you majoring in child psychology?"

"No. Education."

Masao chimed in supportively. "Mr. Mishima isn't here to do research. He simply wants to know where Mana got the inspiration for those drawings of hers."

Ms. Sato raised an eyebrow primly. "And what drawings might those be?"

Masao had the picture with him. He rose from the sofa and quietly handed it to Ms. Sato. She knitted her brows with a studied expression. "Oh, this…"

"I understand she draws a lot of pictures like that," Kotaro said.

Ms. Sato studied the drawing and gave a small nod. "She's done nothing like this recently."

"Could you show it to her?"

Ms. Sato turned to Nagasaki and Masao. "Is this really necessary?"

Nagasaki looked at Masao, who lobbed the question back at her. "Do you think showing it to the child will hurt her?"

"I don't know. But I'd like to avoid it." She turned back to Kotaro. "It took so long for her to start drawing cheerful pictures."

But something unexpected happened. Mana reached out and touched the picture.

"Mana-chan?" Ms. Sato said to the child.

Mana's fingers brushed the edge of the birdman's wings. She stared wide-eyed at the image she had drawn. Kotaro looked at her steadily. "Please give it to her." The woman hesitated. "Please."

Mana grasped the edge of the sketch. Her fist was tiny, but her grip was resolute. To Kotaro, it looked like she was asking for it.

"That's right, you drew this picture, didn't you?" Ms. Sato humored the child as she tried to tug the drawing out of her hand. But the girl just grasped it more tightly.

"Ms. Sato wasn't happy when we included this picture in the exhibit," Nagasaki said, "but it seemed to me this was the one Mana liked the best. Hatsuko said so too. We all went to see it when it was at the post office."

"How did she react?" asked Kotaro.

"She didn't say a thing, so we weren't sure, but she reached out to touch it, just like she's doing now."

Kotaro sensed that something had entered Mana's eyes and buried itself in her heart. By drawing what she'd seen, over and over, she had freed her heart. Now that something was outside her again. It had left her. Confirming this by looking at the picture made her feel safe. Wasn't that it?

Kenji, I think you were right. Mana had seen it with her own eyes.

"Mana-chan?" Kotaro whispered softly. He pointed to the birdman and spoke slowly. "What is that?"

Her eyes gazed at the picture, two pure orbs of deep brown crystal. Kotaro had never seen a child with such unblinking eyes.

Her lips trembled. "Is a monster."

Everyone in the room started in astonishment. Kotaro's palms were damp with excitement.

"Yes, that's a monster. You must've been scared." Mana didn't answer. She stared at the picture.

"Where is the monster?"

No answer.

"Can you tell me where it came from?"

Mana blinked. Her eyes shone. Now they were fixed on Kotaro. Her gaze struck him like an arrow. He nearly gasped.

She opened her right hand, dropped the crayon and raised her index finger. The tiny nail was a healthy pink. She thrust the finger toward the ceiling.

"Sky."

▼

The six-mat apartment where Mana lived with her mother was vacant, but when Hatsuko loaned Kotaro the key, she grumbled about having to show the apartment to a "stranger." The gap between her luxurious living conditions and the rathole that was Asahi House probably had her feeling a bit guilty.

"Managing rental units can be very trying," Masao mumbled apologetically, trying to cover for sentiments he certainly didn't share.

Kotaro stood at the window. The winter sun streamed into the room. It was already low. The putty around the windowpanes was old and broken in spots. Frigid wind whistled through the gaps. Mana had stood here while her mother lay behind her on the floor, hurrying toward death.

She had been here when she saw it. Kotaro saw it too.

"What is that?"

He pointed to a four-story building with a shape like a truncated tower. Asahi House stood on a small rise, and the round building was squarely in the center of the window.

"Is that in Ida too?"

"Yes. Let's see, what is that..." Masao shaded his eyes and peered at the building. "There's a statue on the roof," he said. "A gargoyle, maybe. I hear it's well-known in the neighborhood. The owner must've had strange tastes."

"Is it an office building?"

"No. It's empty now."

A winged monster crouched on the roof of the deserted tower.

Is a monster.

This was what Mana saw. This was what Kenji had gone looking for.

4

Shigenori Tsuzuki sat near the emergency room admissions desk at West Shinjuku General Hospital. Tae Chigusa's niece sat next to him. She was a beautiful woman with the same eyes and gaze as Tae, but her symmetrical features were lined with fatigue. Shigenori was not surprised; it was 10:30 a.m. and she had been here since early morning, beset with worry and tension.

That morning, just after the note from Yamacho, Shigenori had sent Tae a message. After an hour with no answer, he sent her another. He was anxious to make sure she was okay.

Thirty minutes passed with no response. He telephoned. No answer. Perhaps she didn't feel like reading messages or using her phone just now. Shigenori could understand that, but he needed to hear her voice.

He decided to visit her. It would be enough to speak to her through the lobby intercom. He was putting his arms through the sleeves of his jacket when he got a call from Shigeru Noro.

"Shigenori, I thought you ought to know that Tae was taken to the emergency room this morning around five o'clock."

Shigenori froze.

"Luckily she was conscious when the medical team got to her. She used her emergency call button and they came right away. Her building has a contract with a security company. I'm on the list of people to contact if something happens to her."

"What's her condition?"

"I don't know the details. I was about to go over there myself."

"I'd like to go too."

Shigeru swung by Shigenori's apartment and the two men hurried to the emergency room. A man with the security company logo on his jacket was talking to a nurse.

"She's in the operating room," he told them. "It looks like she had a heart attack."

Tae had a number of medical conditions. One of them was hardening of the arteries. According to the security rep, her home caregiver had gone to her condo to pick up her collection of medications.

"We got in touch with her niece in Yokohama. She's on the way."

"Thanks for all your help. You've done a wonderful job." Shigeru bowed gratefully. "If you hadn't come right away, she might not have made it."

"When the team arrived, she was conscious and talking, but her speech was slurred. They weren't sure what she was trying to say."

"Did she seem frightened at all?" Shigenori asked. "Like she'd had a shock of some kind?"

The security rep and Shigeru exchanged curious glances.

"For someone her age, any kind of shock or surprise could put a strain on the heart. A loud noise, for example. Or maybe she stumbled and fell."

"Sure, that must be what happened," Shigeru said.

Shigeru was a kind man and eager to help, but digging for information and connecting the dots was not his strong point. The fact that Tae's condo looked directly out onto the gargoyle seemed to have completely slipped his mind. Half out of guilt, half with relief, Shigenori averted his eyes.

About an hour later, after the security rep had gone, Tae's niece Shizuko had arrived. Once the introductions were over, Shigeru left to tend to his shop. Now Shigenori and Shizuko were waiting for the operation to end.

Perhaps she found the silence uncomfortable; though Shigenori hadn't asked, she kept talking about her relatives. She was the eldest daughter of Tae's late husband's younger brother, and worked at a large trading company. Her last name was also Chigusa, and from what she said, Shigenori inferred that she was unmarried.

"My father is gone too. My mother doesn't get along with Tae. She never has."

"Have you contacted her son?"

"He told me to 'look after her.'" Shizuko sounded bitter. "I'm sure he's busy. He won't come back to Japan—unless there's a funeral."

For a moment, Shigenori saw vividly why Tae seemed so lonely.

"I guess that means you're the relative she's closest to."

"I wouldn't say we're close."

"Did you notice anything different about her recently?"

"Different? How do you mean?"

"Just that—different. Did she mention anything to you that seemed odd, for example?"

Shizuko cocked her head and looked at him as though the question were utterly absurd. For Shigenori, that was answer enough.

What had happened to Tae this morning?

I'm afraid to look outside.

She had called at 3:22 a.m. and collapsed roughly two hours later.

At 5 a.m. in early January, it would still have been dark outside her windows. Perhaps there'd been a faint line of dawn on the eastern horizon, but that would've been all.

Still, five o'clock was morning. It was not the middle of the night. Tae would have decided she couldn't be afraid forever, remembered her promise to Shigenori, calmed down, forced herself to put a hand on the blackout curtains. She wouldn't have had the courage to fling them open. Just part them a tiny bit, take a quick peek outside—

And she saw something. It was enough to make her collapse with shock. Her heart attack must have been caused by that shock.

What did she see? Was the gargoyle actually moving? Flapping its wings? Dancing in the predawn darkness?

It might have been a hallucination. She hadn't been in a normal state of mind. People see all kinds of things when they're afraid. They see what they fear to see.

It didn't matter. However things actually happened, Shigenori's responsibility was no less.

The operation wasn't over until after noon. Tae's life had been saved, but her condition was serious. She would be in intensive care for some time.

While Shizuko went to see her aunt, Shigeru dropped by again. When he heard Shigenori's description of Tae's condition, his shoulders sagged with disappointment. "It's hard, you know. She's younger than I am. I hate to see this happen to younger people."

Shizuko returned from the ICU. Her face was streaked with tears. "She looked so small lying there. It's like she suddenly shrank."

Shigenori's guilt sank like poison into his bones.

"Did the security rep give you the key to Tae's condo?" Shigeru's voice was gentle.

"Yes..."

"You should go there and take a rest. I'll stay here while you're gone. If anything happens, I'll call you."

"I'll take her over there," Shigenori said. Shizuko demurred, but Shigenori was insistent. Together they left the hospital.

"There's something I have to tell you," he said along the way. "It's somewhat unpleasant, so I'll speak quietly."

Shizuko blinked her swollen eyes in puzzlement.

"I'd appreciate it if you could let me take a look around your aunt's condo. You see—"

Shigenori explained his background as a detective, and that he was helping Shigeru, the chairman of the district association, with crime prevention.

"Maybe she saw someone on her balcony. Or perhaps there was a strange noise outside her window. I just can't shake the feeling that something startled your aunt."

Shizuko was visibly perturbed. "Should I notify the police?"

"I'd like to take a look first, if I might. I could be wrong, after all."

"All right, then. Please have a look."

Shigenori regretted deceiving this woman who had no idea what was going on. But he had to stand at that window one more time. What sort of pose would the monster show him today? Would anything be different?

What he'd just told Shizuko was not totally false. Tae *had* been frightened. And she'd sensed something outside her window.

The security company had locked the condo door securely. To get in, they'd had to cut the chain. There was a notice pasted on the inside of the door confirming that they had been there and cut the chain. *Very professional*, thought Shigenori.

"Please, come in." Shizuko offered him a pair of slippers and took her smartphone out of her bag. She'd turned it off at the hospital; she probably had mails and messages to attend to. Shigenori left her peering intently at her phone and approached the living room window.

The blackout curtains were open. He pulled the lace curtains aside.

The tea caddy building stood under a bright blue winter sky, framed by the West Shinjuku skyline. There was the gargoyle. To Shigenori's eye, the statue hadn't moved an inch since yesterday. Even the angle of the great scythe handle projecting above the statue's right shoulder was the same.

It's outside my window. It doesn't want me to see.

It was just a statue. A decoration.

Strange noises several times while working.

He said a huge, black bird flew over his head.

Your "intruder" isn't a bird, is it?

Now it looked like a monster.

I've got no choice. I've got to go back up there, Shigenori thought. His mind made up, he was about to turn away from the window when he saw something on the glass.

It was low down on one of the panes on the right, at about waist height. There was a built-in shelf under the window that Tae had decorated with a large flower vase. Shigenori hadn't noticed that part of the window at first because the vase partially obscured it.

He doubted his eyes. He blinked several times and rubbed them with his fists, but it was still there. It hadn't disappeared. It would not go away.

A handprint.

A hand had pressed against the outside of the pane. At this height off the ground. In that place.

How could anyone explain the size of that hand? The length of the fingers? A hand twice as large as Shigenori's.

The hand of a monster.

Suddenly Shigenori knew. He could read the sign.

I am here. I am not a dream. Not one of your hallucinations, not a trick of the eye. I am here.

It's outside my window.

It had been indeed. Tae had spoken the truth.

▼

"Well, this is rather sudden."

Toshiko looked skeptical as she watched Shigenori pack a small Boston bag. It was a prize possession from his days as a detective and always accompanied him on trips or when he had to spend a night on stakeout duty. It was great to have it out again.

"Someone had to cancel. It would be a shame to waste the reservation."

"But can you travel? Your leg—"

"That's why they didn't invite me in the first place. But someone canceled, so they contacted me. I don't think they expected me to say yes."

To discover the truth, Shigenori would have to stake out the roof under cover of darkness. When night fell, he would use Yamacho's key to enter the building, and find a good spot to stand watch until morning.

He didn't want to think about tomorrow, when he'd have to return with stories about a trip that never took place, but there was no alternative. A group of former colleagues was planning a hot-springs jaunt to Hakone. Someone had fallen ill and had to cancel. That's how he got the invitation at the last minute. A likely cover story.

"Well, a spa wouldn't be bad for your leg," Toshiko said with a distinct lack of cheer. "I wonder how long it's been since I—"

"When my leg is healed, I promise I'll take you."

"All right, whatever you say. I'll look forward to it in the meantime."

"One more thing. It might not look good for me to be traipsing off to a spa with Tae laid up in the hospital. I'd be embarrassed to have Shigeru find out. Let's keep this a secret. I'll tell him when I get back."

"I don't think you need to feel so obligated to the association."

"I just want to observe the niceties."

Toshiko was channel surfing as they spoke. Shigenori couldn't see the screen from where he was, but every program sounded like it was covering the same news. The announcers sounded tense.

"What are you watching?"

"It's the same on every channel. They found the fourth victim."

Shigenori straightened up in surprise. "The fourth—you mean the serial killer who's been cutting people's toes off?"

"Yes. But this time it's not a toe, it's the whole leg below the right knee. It's just terrible." Toshiko frowned in disgust. Even as the wife of a policeman, her reaction to something like this was the same as anyone else's.

Shigenori closed his bag and shuffled on his tingling leg into the living room. The TV camera was focused on a small, run-down gas station.

"This time it's Totsuka. He keeps getting closer to Tokyo."

"When did they start reporting this?"

"About noon I think. At first they didn't know who it was. Now they're saying it was a pharmacist from Kawasaki. She had a three-year-old son," Toshiko said with a pained look. "They'd better capture the killer soon. I remember you once said the prefectural police in Kanagawa were top-notch."

Shigenori grunted absentmindedly. His eyes were fixed on the TV, which now showed a long shot of a detached restroom screened by blue sheeting, with forensics team members going in and out.

"The restroom is beyond that blue sheeting," the announcer said. "We can't see what's going on, but it's a separate structure behind the gas station."

The camera moved slightly to bring a reporter with a microphone into the frame. He was so excited that little drops of spittle flew out of his mouth occasionally.

"It's a single restroom for men and women. The entrance isn't visible from the gas station, which seems unsafe. The key has to be borrowed from the station attendant."

Someone on the studio panel broke in. "Do we know whether or not the door was locked when the body was found?"

"The door was locked. The station opens at nine, but the attendant arrived around eight thirty to clean the restroom. That's when he found the body."

"In other words, the victim was killed in the restroom, or the body was dumped there, before eight thirty?"

"That's right! You're correct."

Shigenori stood next to the living room table, listening. He slowly began to feel a chill. *Who on earth is behind this?*

"Dear?" Toshiko was trying to get his attention. She looked worried.

"Hmm?"

"Are you all right? Your face..."

Shigenori grunted dismissively again. "The Metro and Kanagawa police are like cats and dogs. I don't know if Kanagawa's competent or not."

He tore his eyes away from the screen, but the chill crawling up his spine refused to go away. He shivered.

▼

With the laptop, the Boston bag was quite heavy. Shigenori hailed a taxi as soon as he got out onto the sidewalk. The hotel room he'd reserved on the Internet was in Yoyogi, one station from Shinjuku. Staying in Shinjuku itself would've been risky; he might run into someone who knew him. One station away was safer. Once evening came, he'd take a taxi to the tea caddy building as well. His leg wouldn't stand much walking with the weight of that bag.

The first thing he did after checking into his small, spare room was lie down on the bed. He put the laptop beside him on the mattress and booted it up to see if anything new had come in, especially on the urban legends site.

There was nothing new, or at least nothing interesting. The seed he'd planted hadn't grown. No one was adding information and embellishment. Instead the seed seemed to have died a natural death. He did find different versions of the gossip surrounding the tech mogul who built the building, including rumors about the death of a certain model, but there seemed to be much more interest in the scandal than in the gargoyle the owner left behind on the roof.

There was no news from Shigeru either. Shigenori decided to call him. He was at home. Tae hadn't woken up yet.

"I'm out taking care of something," Shigenori said. "I'm not at home."

"I wouldn't worry. There's nothing we can do anyway." Shigeru's voice turned irritated. "But that son of hers. He doesn't have any feelings."

"Her niece was crying."

Shigenori had a long night ahead and had to catch some sleep. When he was a detective, especially on the Edano Squad, he could fall asleep and wake up as easily as flipping a switch, even in the middle of the day if he'd had to. But today he could do neither. He had a hard time going under, and even when he did, the slightest noise had him awake again and glancing at the window.

Looking for a huge handprint.

Just to be able to lie down was magic for his leg; the tingling went away. He sat up and turned on the TV. It was time for the news. Nothing had changed: every channel was devoted to the fourth victim and new developments in the serial killer case.

The victim's name was Saeko Komiya. She had lived with her husband and son in a large condo building in Kawasaki. The pharmacy where she'd worked was twenty minutes by bus from her home.

At five o'clock the evening before, Komiya had said goodbye to her colleagues and left the pharmacy as usual. Her hours were eight thirty to five. Her three-year-old son went to the day care center in her building. She often mentioned her luck in getting a slot at the center to her coworkers. It was convenient and she never had to worry.

She had set off for the bus stop, but she never boarded the bus. The drivers knew her by sight and were used to seeing her around the same time each day. She had even filled prescriptions for one of them. But yesterday she hadn't gotten on the bus, nor had anyone seen her at the bus stop.

By eight that evening, when Komiya had still not appeared at the day care center and failed to answer her phone, the worried staff called her spouse. The astonished husband immediately left the office to pick up his son. When he returned to their apartment, it was cold and dark.

As soon as he called the pharmacy to confirm that his wife had left as usual, the husband called the police. The murders in Tomakomai, Akita, and Mishima were nowhere in his mind, but for his wife to change her daily routine without contacting anyone was unthinkable. It could only mean something unusual had happened.

That was the husband's story. He emerged from his interview at the police station to find a crowd of waiting reporters. Trembling with anxiety, he retold his story for the cameras. They did not show his face, but his voice and gestures eloquently conveyed his agitation, anguish, and fear.

Komiya's husband had searched the condo with the police. Toshiko might've thought this was "just terrible" too, but Shigenori wouldn't have done it differently. The possibility that Saeko Komiya—alive or dead—was somewhere in the apartment had to be eliminated.

They found nothing, and Saeko's husband asked the police to locate his wife. The day care center looked after his son. He called everyone he could think of who might've seen or heard from Saeko, while the police canvassed the emergency rooms of hospitals in the area. They walked her route from work to home, searching for witnesses.

The next morning, her body was discovered at the gas station. The cause of death was strangulation with some sort of cord, probably a rope, like all the previous victims. The mutilation had been carried out after death, again like the other victims.

At first, suspicion was focused on the station manager and his assistant, because they had access to the restroom keys. But Saeko Komiya had never visited this gas station. Her family didn't even own a car, and she didn't have a license. The manager and his assistant both denied ever seeing her.

The gas station stood along a prefectural road and had operated in the same location long enough to become fairly dilapidated. Thousands of people must have used that restroom over the years, yet there was no other choice but to try to contact them one by one. One of them must have made a duplicate key before committing the crime. One of them knew in advance where he planned to dump the body.

Shigenori was feeling sick to his stomach with shock and irritation. He either needed to see something uplifting or turn off the TV; otherwise he would be thinking about the murders through the long night ahead.

He switched off the set and lay down again. At seven he left the hotel and went looking for a convenience store. He bought a packaged meal and a few disposable hand warmers and went back to his room.

Nine o'clock. Preparations complete, Shigenori was ready to leave the room when something occurred to him. He called Yamacho.

"Thanks for the key."

"Ah, Detective Tsuzuki."

"I'm about to go use it right now."

"It wasn't a very tough customer, but the building was impressive. It's going to be dark as the grave with the power off."

Tsuzuki glanced at his flashlight.

"Cold as hell, too. Hope you're dressed for it."

No questions about what Shigenori was planning to do once he was inside the building. Good old Yamacho.

"I'm bundled up. Look, about that note you wrote—the huge bird beating its wings?"

"Sorry about that. You must've thought I was crazy. But I did hear something."

"Not crazy at all. Let me ask *you* something crazy, Yamacho. When you heard that sound, did you think at any point that you were in any danger?"

Yamacho was silent.

"I mean, in your line of business, you do have to be careful, don't you?"

"You and me both, detective."

"I'm finished with all that. I don't have the same reflexes now." Shigenori could tell Yamacho was stalling.

"Well," he said finally. "It did seem odd. I wasn't scared, though. A lot of things in the world are worse."

"You speak the truth, Yamacho."

"Sometimes you guys were pretty scary too."

"Come on, now. We always worked hand in glove."

"Then let's leave it at that." Yamacho chuckled.

"I hate to trouble you, but I have one more request, Yamacho." Shigenori had made up his mind. "I'll be more than happy if we can both laugh about this tomorrow. I'll even buy you a drink. So just bear with me."

"What gives?"

"Tomorrow, if you don't hear from me—oh, say by around noon—I want you to call my wife. Tell her I'm in that building in West Shinjuku."

"Is that all you want me to say?"

"Yes. Toshiko knows who to call if something happens to me. We've discussed it before."

"Just what is it you're planning to do there, Tsuzuki?"

"Just a little stakeout of my own."

"You're up to something dangerous, I can tell."

Shigenori laughed. His voice sounded unnatural even to him, but he needed to laugh right now.

"Dangerous? I don't know. Maybe I'm on a wild goose chase, or I'm so bored with life that I'm having a strange dream." He waited for Yamacho to laugh, but there was only silence.

"An old man said he saw a huge bird near that building. Then he up and vanishes, and no one's seen him since. He was gone as suddenly as if he'd been snatched up into the sky by the bird he saw."

Yamacho was silent again. Then: "As far as I know, most birds are night-blind. So maybe this bird of yours isn't really a bird. It just looks like one. Better watch your back, detective."

"I will, Yamacho. I will."

He hit END and stood there, thinking. Something that flies, but not a bird. Yamacho was right. Birds don't leave huge handprints.

▼

Shigenori flicked the beam of his flashlight around the base of the barricade. No good—it wasn't bright enough to tell whether or not the mountain of chairs had been moved again.

Yamacho's key was smooth as silk. *He always does good work*, thought Shigenori. He'd even oiled the lock. The stale air of the tea caddy building was waiting for him.

The streetlamps and buildings in the neighborhood were still bright at this hour. The space just inside the doorway was dimly visible, but toward the center of the floor, where the light petered out, there was an inky blackness so clotted that it almost looked moist. Shigenori half expected it to stick to him.

He stood inside the door, thinking. He ought to lock it behind him.

No. Just shut it. Don't lock it.

Maybe—just maybe—something might happen. If it did, he'd have to get out of there fast. He needed an escape route.

No plastic bags this time. He walked straight up the center of the stairs, keeping the flashlight pointed at his feet so it wouldn't be noticed from outside. Years of experience had taught him to memorize the layout of a building with a single visit.

There was nothing frightening about the darkness. Many things in society were far more terrifying.

He climbed to the fourth floor, set down his bag and went into the machine room. He remembered seeing some soiled cardboard boxes with the logo of a moving company, flattened and piled up in a corner.

He grabbed a few boxes by the edge, dragged them out into the room, and layered them around the ladder that led up to the hatch on the roof. He was alone here with a bad leg. He might slip, or fall trying to get away. He couldn't be sure it wouldn't happen. The cardboard would cushion his fall at least a little.

He pulled the ladder down and looked up at the hatch. The hinges were rusty and probably tight. He'd have to hold on to the ladder and push the hatch open with one hand. He cracked his knuckles, did a few quick knee bends, and climbed the ladder. He had to push hard to open the hatch.

The cold hit him in the face. It wasn't wind, just a hard wall of freezing air that stung his eyes, making them water.

The sky looked like all the stars in the Milky Way had been scooped up and thrown down again. Humanity had no way of reaching the stars yet, he thought, but they had long ago re-created the heavens on earth, in colors far more gaudy and vulgar.

Shigenori peered around the roof and froze.

The gargoyle was gone.

5

Kotaro watched as the seven o'clock news came on. The announcer started speaking excitedly. It was the same on every channel. Dinnertime in the Mishima household started at seven sharp, and if the news was grim, Asako usually switched the channel to something more pleasant. But today her eyes were glued to the set. Hearing that the fourth victim was a young mother seemed to hit her especially hard.

"Why haven't they caught him yet? Doesn't Kumar work with the police on this kind of thing? Hurry up, do something!"

"Kumar isn't working *for* the police. We can't do anything right away about something like this."

"Was there anything on the Internet? Like an announcement by the killer or something?"

"Nothing so far."

"Well, you should do something anyway. Someone needs to catch this guy now."

As Kotaro watched his mother out of the corner of his eye and listened to her complaints, his pulse was racing.

That empty building in Ida with a gargoyle on the roof—he knew now that the locals called it the tea caddy building. A building constructed at the height of the tech bubble by a rich CEO. A building with a history.

He was going to sneak in there tonight. He was almost ready.

He'd already cased the premises. In the afternoon, after he left the dilapidated apartment that had been home to Mana and her mother, he had gone straight for the tea caddy building. Masao had been reluctant to let him go by himself.

"Both entrances are locked and the windows are barred. Without a key, there's no way you could get in here." When he saw the building up close, Masao had looked a bit relieved.

Even if Kenji had come here, Kotaro thought, *he couldn't have gotten in*. He could only have looked at the outside of the building. There had to be a connection between Mana's picture and Kenji dropping out of sight.

"Yeah, you'd need a key," Kotaro said. But in his mind, he was calculating furiously.

Kenji's disappearance, this building, Mana's picture, the homeless people Kenji was investigating—no way these were unconnected. On January 4—two days ago—Kenji had sent a mail to Narita at 9:34 p.m.

Something's been bugging me. I'm going to investigate it tonight.

After he'd sent that mail, Kenji had gone somewhere. It had to have been here.

Maybe the building is used at night? Maybe if I come back at night, someone will be here, or I can get in somehow, Kotaro thought. That would explain why Kenji decided it would be better to investigate after dark.

He had to get ready. He'd decided to go home first. Sitting in his gently swaying seat on the train, he had used his laptop to search for anything on the tea caddy building. What he found was astonishing.

Kotaro put the photos he took of the building and the gargoyle on his desktop. The shots of the statue were taken from a distance, but they were sharp and clear. He entered a raft of search terms, hit ENTER, and got a gusher of information.

The statue moved at night. Its pose and location were different from day to day. It was holding something that looked like a weapon, something that had not been there when it was first placed on the roof.

The tea caddy building was definitely on people's radar screens, though not in a huge way. Urban legend websites were awash with these kinds of rumors. A moving statue was not going to surprise anyone. In fact, comments about the gargoyle were outnumbered by posts about the building's history and how it ended up empty and abandoned.

Still, information about the "moving gargoyle" would've been gold for Kenji. It must have been enough to drive him to seek further answers from the building under cover of darkness.

The monster came from the sky, and it moved by night. It beat its wings.

Mana saw it.

Kotaro gaped suddenly with surprise. The background Mana drew, the dozens of slanting lines. Kenji had thought they looked like rain. He was right.

Mana's mother had died of pneumonia early on December 5, so she must have been bedridden before that. The night before, Tokyo had been struck by a violent winter storm. The lines Mana had drawn behind the monster must be the slanting downpour.

Kotaro could see it in his mind's eye—Mana looking out the window of the tumbledown apartment, her bedridden mother behind her on the floor. The monster descending from the sky as she watched. That was the night of the fourth. Kozaburo Ino had vanished the next day.

Kotaro called up a map. The Ida and Hyakunin districts were practically next to each other.

Then homeless people started going missing. One after another, along the Seibu-Shinjuku commuter line.

Kotaro had to get into the building and find out what was inside. Maybe he would find Kenji—hopefully unharmed, but who knew what sort of shape he might be in? Maybe he got in and found himself trapped. Without his phone he'd have no way of calling for help. No one would hear his cries, or maybe he'd be in no shape to use his voice. He didn't have his phone, that was definite—it had been found in a narrow space between two buildings, smashed and nonfunctional.

How had it gotten there? Why was it so badly damaged? Maybe Kenji had been running for his life. From a monster out of the sky?

Or maybe the monster grabbed him and carried him skyward? Kenji dropped his phone and the impact pulverized it.

It was time to stop thinking and start doing.

Kotaro's first task on returning home was to give Asako his cover story. He'd told her in the morning that he'd be home late, but with this new murder by the Toe-Fetish Killer, his schedule had changed suddenly. He'd have to be back at the office by ten, and he'd be there all night.

Then, in the privacy of his room, he had stuffed his backpack with everything he thought he might need, including his flashlight and digital camera.

He'd be watching the statue until morning. It would be freezing. A sleeping bag would've been perfect, but he didn't have one. He'd just have to dress as warmly as he could.

The real problem was—what if he couldn't get inside? He needed a tool to open the back door.

A crowbar. He'd once seen a news special about a ring of burglars that used them to lever open locked doors. He could borrow the crowbar that was sitting in the garage on his way out. At this time of year, his father was out every evening at New Year's parties. He wouldn't miss it for one night.

Kotaro's mind kept flitting from one thought to another. There was no way a monster like the one Mana had drawn could be real. If so, someone was pretending to be a monster. Why such an elaborate deception? Abducting homeless people—if that was the goal—wouldn't be much more difficult than what the kids Kenji had been monitoring were doing.

It was a strangely elaborate piece of performance art. If it weren't for the missing people, it could easily be a reality TV prank.

Kotaro's research suggested that the tea caddy building had been abandoned because it couldn't be sold. There was a conflict of ownership. Maybe someone was staging this whole thing to drive the building's value down and force another party to relinquish their claim. But in that case, it would make sense to do something more conspicuous, more outrageous. Maybe the abductions were a warning of some kind? If so, it was a very roundabout way of sending a warning.

Or perhaps it was some kind of copycat thing, re-creating or restaging some story. Kotaro had searched for something similar on a website devoted to summaries of serialized comics and movies dealing with winged monsters that terrorized cities by night, attacking people. His search returned—sure enough—Mothman and even pterodactyls, but no gargoyles. A humanoid creature with wings? That would be vampires.

Vampires?

Kotaro felt a flicker of fear. What if he got inside the building and found the corpses of the homeless people piled up and sucked dry of blood?

C'mon, man, get a grip.

He went downstairs at seven. Kazumi was just getting home. The tournament was approaching, and she was practicing every day before the new term began.

On New Year's Day, Kotaro had visited the Sonois to offer his greetings. Mika had seemed cheerful and happy. The feeling in the household had been warm, and Aunt Hanako had been in a good mood. Kotaro half-thought he might be able to pick up some fresh information about Mika's problem, but what he saw put him at ease. Just as her mother had predicted, the worst seemed to be past and the problem was dying down. Which basically meant it was solved.

"Hey, you're home," Kotaro said. Kazumi ignored him. For a girl of her age, an older brother ranked lower than an insect.

"How's Mika?"

Kazumi padded off toward the bathroom, radiating an aura that declared, *Can't you see I'm tired and in a bad mood?* As she went down the hall she half-turned and spat out, "You saw her at New Year's."

"That was then."

"It was last week. What day is it, anyway?"

"Fine, forget it."

Asako didn't take her eyes off the TV all through dinner. She kept talking about what a terrible crime it was and how the world was getting worse and worse, but for all that she seemed to have a terrific appetite.

The crime absorbed her attention. She worried about the victim's family and hoped for a solution as soon as possible. Most people watching the news right now were probably feeling the same thing, and like most of them, Asako Mishima wasn't unusually curious about homicides, nor was she impetuous or unusually tenderhearted.

Yet to Kotaro—preoccupied as he was with Kenji's whereabouts—there was something ugly about his mother's interest in the crime. She might feel sympathy for the victims, but there was something about the crime that was intoxicating. And she was enjoying it.

Kazumi had showered before dinner. Now she ate in sullen silence with a towel wrapped around her head.

"Your father will be home tomorrow. I'll be making something special. When are you planning to come home, Ko-chan?"

Kotaro wasn't sure what condition he'd be in at this time the next day, but it was no time to spoil his mother's mood.

"I'll probably be home by dinner."

"You're going to stay up all night and then go straight to class? Well, your studies are more important than that job of yours," Asako said pointedly and stared at Kotaro. "Making a student work all night? I can't say I appreciate what Kumar is doing."

"Come on, Mom. Cyberspace doesn't go to bed when the sun goes down."

"I don't have the faintest idea what you mean."

"We're like security guards. Sometimes we have night duty. What's the problem? I'm getting some good experience."

Kazumi pushed her empty plate away and left the table. After she went upstairs, Asako lowered her voice. "Do you think something happened at practice?"

"She's got a competition coming up. She's just on edge."

"Are you going to take a bath before you stay up all night?"

"No. I'd probably just catch a cold."

"Well at least change your underwear, for heaven's sake."

For a moment Kotaro felt a pang of guilt about lying to his mother. He also found himself thinking she was a pain in the neck.

With his bulging backpack slung over his shoulder, he crept into the garage and opened the toolbox. The straight crowbar was right on top. If he tried walking around Shinjuku at night with this thing in his hand—or sticking out of his backpack—he'd have company very quickly in the form of an officer of the law. He vacillated, wondering what to do, and finally decided to slip it into an umbrella case his mother had picked up for a hundred yen at a thrift store.

He rode his bicycle to the station with the case bungeed to the frame. The train into the city had few passengers and was cozily warm. The heat coming up from the vents below the seats made him sleepy. As he sat half-drowsing, Kotaro almost wondered if his plan to break into the building was just a dream.

A monster with wings...

Mana's upraised finger...

He got off in Shinjuku and navigated his way to the ticket gate through the throngs of people who packed the station every day of the week, night and day, rain or shine.

Shinjuku. Bright lights, dark corners, trendy and vulgar, vibrant and decrepit, throbbing with life and on its last legs. This entertainment district of entertainment districts, with everything ever found in any entertainment district anywhere, was impossible to categorize.

Kotaro's path from the station to the tea caddy building was in the opposite direction from the one he'd taken yesterday from Asashi House. Away from the bustle of the station, Shinjuku's quiet neighborhoods were packed with residences along narrow streets. Kotaro could feel the life of the city pulsing around him.

The power was still off at the tea caddy building. The blackness around the building was complete. An island of darkness like this was hard to find in the city.

Kotaro's heart beat faster. He was walking faster now, too, with the same rhythm.

When he'd checked out the building in daylight with Masao, they'd both been astonished by the strange barricade blocking street access to the service entrance. Masao had conjectured that it might have something to do with a suspicious fire some time before.

There was no barrier facing the main entrance. The double doors were easy enough to approach, though not to go through. They were locked and secured with a thick padlocked chain.

By walking between the building and a low cinder-block wall, Kotaro had been able to reach the back of the building and the service entrance, but the path was so narrow he'd had to traverse it by walking half-sideways. Masao didn't even try. He was not only too large, his paunch was too big.

The service entrance had also been locked. At least there'd been no security cameras or visible alarm systems.

He took the same route around the side of the building to the back door. It was five past ten, slightly later than he'd planned.

The street beyond the barricade was quiet. Many of the eateries were already closed for the evening. Still, it would be hard to explain what he was doing here if someone noticed him. He crouched low and breathed with his mouth open.

The break-in technique he'd seen on the news required brute force. At the end of the process, the door would be twisted completely out of shape.

Am I strong enough to pry this open?

Kotaro suddenly remembered what his father used to say about people who tried to replicate things they saw on television: that they were idiots. Kotaro wasn't here to steal anything, but the thought of what he was about to do made him feel scared, and guilty too.

He pulled the crowbar from the umbrella case and gripped it with both hands. It felt cold and hard even through his gloved hands. Which side of the door was he supposed to attack? The one with the hinges? Or the knob side? The door had looked fairly strong in daylight—

It was unlocked.

Kotaro felt his heart shrink, climb up his throat into the top of his skull, take over from his brain, and begin pounding like a drum.

He'd guessed right. People were using the building at night.

He gave the door an exploratory push. It opened about eight inches. He could see the darkness within.

A car approached on the road behind him. He ducked quickly. The car seemed to have its windows open in the middle of winter. The sound system was playing music with a heavy beat. The car passed and the beat faded.

Kotaro could hardly breathe. He was sure someone would see him if he stood up. He got on his hands and knees, poked his head through the door, and pushed it open with his shoulder.

The tea caddy building. Officially known as the West Shinjuku Central Round Building. Current tenants: darkness, dust, and mold. The smell was sharp in his nostrils.

Inside, he rose to his knees and shoved the door closed with his shoulder. It shut with a metallic bang.

The first floor was round like the building itself. Small windows ran along the wall near the ceiling, letting in just enough light to see. Few neighborhoods in Tokyo were without streetlamps. Funny how one never noticed them in the daytime, but they were indispensable at night.

From the outside, the building had looked like it would be pitch-black inside. Kotaro was relieved to find it wasn't quite that dark, but the dimness was more than a little spooky. The broad round space seemed empty of furniture and fixtures. It was clean. Maybe the room had been stripped of damaged items after the fire.

A stairway followed the curve of the north wall to the upper floor. Very convenient. He wouldn't have to waste time looking for a way up.

He adjusted the pack on his back and shoved his flashlight into the pocket of his down jacket. With the crowbar in his right hand, he headed toward the stairs.

Up the steps—a gentle gradient. The smell of mold was so strong that he started breathing through his mouth. Even inside the building, he could see his exhalations steaming out before him.

Was there a draft? He sensed cold air flowing over the tip of his nose. There was a window open somewhere. That meant someone was upstairs.

Second floor. The windows here were larger than on the first floor, yet it was darker. Why? Maybe the streetlamps outside were in the wrong location to shine in?

He switched the bar to his left hand, got his flashlight out and clicked it on. A circle of light fell on the floor. He saw someone's leg and panicked, then quickly realized it was the leg of a table. He almost laughed out loud. A round table. Two, in fact. Toward the back wall, a counter. It almost looked like a café.

He leaned against the wall and tried to calm his breathing. He opened his ears. Maybe he could catch a clue—something moving, a person's voice, the sound of the wind.

He felt the same draft moving past the tip of his nose. It was coming down from above.

He switched off the flashlight and kept climbing. Until now he'd been walking up the center of the stairs. Too risky. He moved to the left, close to the wall, his back half-rubbing against it as he moved upward, one careful step at a time.

The third floor was even darker. Nothing was visible beyond the landing. The darkness was a solid mass. *It's because I'm above the streetlights*, he thought. *Or maybe it's something else?*

His heart still occupied the space where his brain was supposed to be, and it was starting to hammer again. With each beat, he flashed back to the scene he'd pictured earlier—mounds of bloodless corpses. White faces. Legs and arms sprawled in all directions.

His imagination was working overtime. He toggled the flashlight on and saw why the floor was so dark. A partition wall divided it, cutting off any light from that side of the building. The area beyond looked like it was designed to be lived in.

This is the floor where somebody died.

The lover, or ex-lover, of the young mogul who owned the building had died here under strange circumstances. There was something on the web about how she may have killed herself, but someone had managed to block any investigation.

He played the circle of light around the room and saw nothing of special interest on the floor or the walls or the ceiling. Just an empty building. An empty, unused room—

Were those footsteps over his head?

He stepped into the lee of the nearby door, killed the flashlight, and stood there rooted to the floor.

Four floors. One more to go. *If I don't keep going, this whole visit is wasted.*

He climbed stiffly, flashlight pointed at his feet, dragging his back against the wall so hard that it was difficult to move forward.

Fourth floor and more darkness. The cold was deep here. Outdoor air was clearly coming in from somewhere.

The first thing he saw in the beam of his flashlight was a heavy door. Another living area? No, the area behind the wall was too small for that.

He traversed the room with the beam. His breath caught in his throat.

A ladder. It led to a hatch in the ceiling. The hatch was closed, but not all the way. The ladder was designed to fold out and down from the ceiling at the pull of a cord.

The draft was gone. *That hatch must've been open.* He slipped the backpack off and set it down slowly by his feet.

Well, guess it's time to climb up there. That's where someone—

No. He's here.

Kotaro turned. Something struck his left wrist. The crowbar clattered to the floor. The next instant his right arm seemed to vanish and then reappear, twisted behind his back. He flew face-first into the nearest wall, flattening his nose.

"Ow!"

He felt like a fool, but it was the only thing he could think to say. No one had manhandled Kotaro like this before, ever.

"Ow! Cut it out!"

Not only was his right arm twisted up behind his back, something long and hard was pressing down on both shoulder blades, keeping him from moving his left arm. All he could do was flop it uselessly. The side of his face was trying to merge with the wall. His left cheekbone and the bridge of his nose ground against the concrete.

"What the hell are you doing? You're hurting me!" It's hard to yell out of one side of your mouth, but Kotaro did his best.

He sensed the surprise of the person behind him.

"What...you're just a kid." A gruff old voice. "Okay, who are you? What are you doing here?"

I haven't done anything wrong. Kotaro decided to take the good-offense route.

"Tell me who *you* are first!"

The voice over his shoulder was calm and unhurried. "I asked you first. What were you planning to do with this thing?" The bar pressed even harder against his back. Kotaro groaned. *He's got the crowbar.*

"Look, I'd really like to tell you. It would help if you'd back off a bit."

This was a good time to be polite. The man didn't seem all that dangerous. Or maybe that was just wishful thinking.

"I'm not a kid, by the way. Well, I'm sort of a minor."

The man actually laughed. "Sort of? What kind of sort of?"

"I mean, I—I'm a college student. I'm not a kid anymore. Maybe I'm one of those people who still needs a legal guardian or something."

"Where's your ID?"

"In my backpack."

"That doesn't work for either of us."

"No, that doesn't work at all. So, could you let me go?"

"Why were you carrying this?"

"I thought I'd pry the door open. The back door. But it was open already."

The man sighed. "I should've locked it."

I knew it. This guy has a key.

"I wasn't going to steal anything. I'm looking for someone."

"In here?"

"Yes, another student. Like me." It was hard for Kotaro to talk with his face and chest mashed against the wall. He paused to get some oxygen, but before he could go on, the man came back with a question.

"Would his name be Morinaga?"

Kotaro gagged with astonishment. "Yes!" he croaked.

This old geezer knows Kenji!

The pressure of the bar against his back went away. His right arm was free. He slid to a squatting position and gasped for breath between attacks of coughing.

His flashlight lay on the floor near the foot of the ladder, spreading a cone of light across the floor. Maybe the man didn't have a flashlight.

"Damn, my leg hurts." The shape behind Kotaro collapsed into a crouch, as though he'd been holding back the pain. "I'm getting too old for the rough stuff."

Kotaro's breathing finally calmed down, but he stayed leaning against the wall as he examined the old man. He was bundled up in a down jacket, gloves, and several layers of clothes. Medium height, once of medium build but tending to chubbiness now. A formidable man, but maybe older than he looked by the way he was doubled up with pain.

"Are you okay?"

The old man was supporting himself with the crowbar, but he still seemed about to topple over. He was groaning.

"Did you hurt yourself? I didn't do anything."

"Help me up." The man held out his hand. "See the cardboard around the base of the ladder? Help me over there."

It was only now that Kotaro noticed the layers of cardboard spread beneath the ladder.

"Is this where you live?"

"Oh, for—knock it off. Would you give me a hand, please?" The man was almost shouting at him.

Kotaro anxiously detached himself from the wall to help the old man, who clung to him as he stood up, using the crowbar as a cane. The point of the bar made a metallic scraping sound on the floor.

"Where'd you learn about opening doors with things like this?"

"I saw it on TV."

The distance from the wall to the foot of the ladder was only a few yards, but the man could only manage one shuffling step at a time. Together they weaved across the floor.

"But I've never done it before. That's the truth."

"The things you can learn on TV these days."

Despite his shuffling gait, Kotaro revised his opinion of the man clutching him by the shoulder. He wasn't weak at all. His voice was strong and his body was thickly muscled.

"That's far enough. Help me sit down."

The man groaned again. Kotaro helped him into a sitting position. From there he toppled over onto his side.

He'd been quite heavy. This was no old man after all. He didn't seem to be injured, but he was still in a lot of pain. *Maybe he's sick or something.*

"Um..." Kotaro felt uncomfortable talking down to him, so he squatted beside him. His forehead glistened with sweat. "Do you have arthritis? Or like, a herniated disc?"

The man frowned but said nothing. Maybe he didn't want to talk about it. His eyes were almost closed.

"Shall I call an ambulance?"

"No! That would just be more trouble for me. You too. We're breaking and entering, you and me both."

"All I did was walk through an unlocked door."

The man sighed deeply. He raised a gloved hand and wiggled his fingers. "ID."

"Oh, right." Kotaro quickly pulled his student ID from his backpack and handed it over.

"Light."

Kotaro shined his light on the card. The man peered at it with one eye. He was still in pain. Back pain? Maybe it was his knees.

"Kotaro Mishima."

"That's me."

"What's your relationship with Morinaga?"

"So you actually know him?"

"*Relationship*." This man could corner people with his voice alone.

"We work at the same place."

"What kind of work?"

"It's a company called Kumar."

The man made a face. Kumar wasn't a real informative name in situations like this. "We do cyber patrol work."

"Internet security. Okay." He actually knew what Kotaro was talking about. "You said you were looking for this guy. Where is he?"

"How do I know? That's why I'm here. He's missing."

The man opened both eyes in surprise. "What did you say?"

"He's been missing since the night of the fourth. Listen, um..." The fierce expression was getting a little scary. Why did he look so grim? "They found his smartphone near here. It was completely smashed."

"Did you file a missing-persons report?"

"I'm sure one was submitted. His hometown is near Niigata. His father's concerned enough that he's already on his way."

Instead of looking convinced, the man eyed Kotaro even more fiercely.

"There's a machine room over there. See?" Still on his side, the man waved Kotaro's ID in the direction of the door. "There's a bag with my gear just inside. Bring it here."

Kotaro did as he was told. He found the old Boston bag inside the door. It was fairly heavy.

"Here's your ID. Put it away. Now help me up."

Kotaro gave the man his hand and pulled him to a sitting position on the cardboard. He exhaled slowly, unlatched the bag and drew out a Thermos bottle.

Kotaro could see a laptop in the bag. Another surprise. It was unusual to see people this age carrying laptops. In that case, it might not be surprising that he knew right away what Kumar did.

"Mishima."

Kotaro glanced up. The man was taking pills with water from the Thermos.

"Painkiller. It takes about ten minutes to kick in." He put the sheet of pills back in the bag. "When that happens, my brain will start working better. Until then, I want to hear your story. Tell me about this Morinaga."

"He's an engineering major, third year. A very serious guy. He's planning to go straight to graduate school."

The man nodded and held the Thermos out. "Water? It's hot."

Kotaro must've looked like he needed some. He was very tempted. The cold was starting to get to him.

"No, I'm fine. Thanks anyway."

The man put the Thermos back in the bag. "As far as I know," he said, "Morinaga was looking for an old man who disappeared."

How does he know all this?

"When did you see Kenji?" Kotaro asked. "Where—"

"Not yet. My ten minutes aren't up yet. Sorry, brain's still off."

He was like a teacher correcting a slow student. In the beam of light, his pale face and muscular voice suddenly reminded Kotaro of the PTA chairman from his grade school days. The man was the president of a local construction firm and more impressive-looking than the principal. He always had a stern expression when he talked.

The man shoved a driver's license at the tip of Kotaro's nose.

"This is me."

Kotaro took the license and shined the light on it. Shigenori Tsuzuki. The man in the picture was trimmer than the one in front of him.

"I live in the neighborhood."

Kotaro nodded. The address was in Wakaba.

"See the DOB? I'm sixty-three. I could be your grandfather. Show some respect."

I think I've been doing that.

"It's spinal stenosis."

"What?"

"Not arthritis, not a disc problem. No other health issues. If I have to, I can go at it with you again before the night's over. Unless you want to kiss that wall all over again, tell me how you found this place—fast. I handle security for the district association," he added, seeing Kotaro's look of confusion.

Do district associations have security people this aggressive?

"See, I'm an ex-cop. I even worked at MPD headquarters for a while."

Kotaro could believe it. Now he knew why this man was so intimidating. His old PTA chairman couldn't hold a candle to this guy.

"Maybe you believe me, maybe you don't, but I'll tell you something: I've dealt with armed robbers and murderers and arsonists longer than you've been alive. Know what they all have in common?"

Kotaro said nothing. He just shook his head.

"They lie. I know how to handle liars. If you lie to me, I'll know. Understand?"

Kotaro nodded. "Yes, I understand. But I'm not lying. It's just a really strange story."

Shigenori Tsuzuki, ex-detective, gave Kotaro a skeptical look through narrowed eyelids.

"First I want to show you something." Kotaro pulled his backpack closer and brought out his laptop. He pulled off his gloves, booted up, clicked on the photo of Mana's sketch and turned the screen toward Shigenori.

His face was lit by the ghostly light from the screen. He seemed surprised, then dumbfounded.

"I think this picture and the gargoyle up on the roof here are connected," Kotaro said.

Shigenori's eyes were glued to the screen. "Who drew this?"

Interest mingled with astonishment. Kotaro suddenly relaxed. He didn't know why, but this man and he were pursuing the same riddle.

He told Shigenori everything that had happened, in chronological order—from Kenji asking him to act as insurance until his first sighting, earlier today, of the tea caddy building, including every person he'd met and every rumor he'd heard. Partway through his account he started shivering and wrapped his arms around himself. The hand warmers he'd brought along weren't good for more than temporary relief from the cold.

When he finished, Shigenori brought out the Thermos again. This time Kotaro accepted the steaming water gratefully. His hands were shaking so much that he almost dropped the cup.

"So Cart Man isn't the only missing person." Shigenori said pensively. "That's what people in the neighborhood called Kozaburo Ino."

The heat of the water spread pleasantly in Kotaro's stomach. "Kenji said the police wouldn't do anything in a case like this."

"He was probably right," Shigenori said with a touch of remorse. He was sitting more comfortably now. Maybe the painkiller was finally working.

"So after all this, you didn't visit the FM station? Or Kadoma Coffee?"

"My boss told me to stop looking for Kenji."

"He has good judgment. Too much digging could complicate things once the real investigation starts. You could even end up as a suspect."

Kotaro shrugged, trying to look nonchalant.

"You found your way here with nothing but this picture for a clue." Shigenori stared at the laptop screen. "You've got a good nose."

That sounds like praise.

"Okay, let me show *you* something interesting. Climb up that ladder and take a look around the roof."

Kotaro looked up at the hatch in the ceiling.

"When you let the hatch down, don't shut it tight. If you shut it all the way, you'll make a lot of noise getting it open again." That would explain why it was so freezing cold. "Be quiet and be careful. There's a lot of light from the buildings and neon. You won't need the flashlight."

Kotaro stood up. He blew on his hands and rubbed them together before picking his gloves off the floor and putting them back on. He took a firm grip on the ladder rail, climbed up and lifted the hatch. It was lighter than he expected. It looked like you could put a dent in it with your fist, but the latch was strong.

He raised his head quietly above the level of the roof.

"The gargoyle is to your left," Shigenori called from below. Kotaro shifted his gaze left.

The lights of West Shinjuku fell dimly across the roof of the building. The air stabbed icily into his nostrils, making his eyes water.

There was no statue. Kotaro held the hatch open with one hand and scanned the whole roof. It was definitely gone. There was nothing to be seen anywhere on that round platform.

"It's gone. But what's all that stuff spread across the roof?

"Pieces of the statue."

"Did someone smash it?"

Kotaro started to climb up, but Shigenori tugged on his jeans. "Get down here."

He lowered the hatch, climbed halfway down the ladder and jumped to the floor. "I just saw that statue a few hours ago. I even took pictures."

"I believe it. In the daytime it's right where it's supposed to be."

"When was it shattered?"

"I'm not sure. When I was here last year, before Christmas, the fragments were already there."

Now it was Kotaro's turn to furrow his brow.

"Fascinating, isn't it?" Shigenori used the same expression that Kenji had. "Truly curious. The original statue was smashed to pieces somehow. The statue you saw is the replacement. In the daytime, anyway. After dark it has a habit of disappearing. Tonight's no different. I got here less than an hour ago and it was already gone. I didn't think it would make its move so soon."

A monster from the sky. It descended to this building, wings spread. And at night, using its wings again, it moved about the city.

"I thought about this and came up with a logical explanation," Kotaro said, "but now and then I step back and look at it, and it makes me laugh. I mean, a statue that flies around? It's total BS."

Shigenori stared at him. "I agree with you. Completely. Here's what I know."

When the ex-detective got to the end of his account, Kotaro was thoroughly chilled. "I need to find a restroom."

"No toilets here."

"I know. I'll be right back."

Kotaro picked up the flashlight and trotted downstairs. At first his legs were so numb from the cold that he almost stumbled.

He'd seen a coffee chain outlet on the way. Luckily, it was still open. *That's Shinjuku for you.* He ordered two coffees, paid with loose change, and headed for the restroom.

He hadn't left the tea caddy building just to answer nature's call. He wanted to think. The ex-detective was intimidating, but he had a reassuring aura. His words were convincing. But would it be wise to trust him?

Maybe we're both crazy. That was a possibility. *But I don't see how we could be.*

Even alone, with time to think, surrounded by the city in all its mundane reality, it didn't seem possible that they were sharing a hallucination.

He left the shop with the coffees in a paper bag and retraced his steps to the front of the tea caddy building. He took a moment to stand on the other side of the street and look up at it. For some reason it looked brighter from a distance. The closer he got to the foot of the building, the thicker the darkness became.

When he got back to the fourth floor, Shigenori was on the ladder, peering out the hatch. He heard Kotaro's footsteps, lowered the latch and clambered down. "No change."

Shigenori sat cross-legged on the cardboard and chuckled. "Feel better? Get a chance to cool off?" He'd known what Kotaro was thinking.

"Yeah, sorry about that."

"I know how you feel. I was regretting it myself, spilling all that information to a kid."

Kotaro was silent a moment before he pointed out, "Maybe we both needed someone to talk to about this."

"You're probably right." Shigenori chuckled wryly. Kotaro felt suddenly relieved.

"Mr. Tsuzuki? At the very least, I think both of us have done the right thing so far."

"Maybe. We'll find out. Coffee, huh? How much?"

"It's okay."

"I'm not letting someone young enough to be my grandson buy me coffee." Shigenori accepted the cup happily.

"When you're on stakeout, don't you try to avoid too much fluid?"

"Not me. I have a huge bladder. That's what happens to most cops." The light steam and aroma from their cups spread out into the freezing air.

"Why don't we just sit on the roof?"

"There's no place to hide. Whatever we can see will see us too."

"Maybe we could hide under some of this cardboard."

"We'd stick out like a sore thumb. If that gargoyle, or someone pretending to be a gargoyle, sees us, that's the end of the stakeout."

"Why don't you ask somebody in the neighborhood to let you set up a telescope in the window? That way you wouldn't run the risk of being seen. Or attacked."

"Why don't you do it yourself, then?"

"I don't have connections. You live around here."

"I don't want to get other people involved." Shigenori's tone was brusque. Kotaro felt a stab of regret. Shigenori had told him about the elderly woman who'd ended up in the hospital after he asked her to get involved.

"That woman—in your local association—"

"Mrs. Chigusa?"

"How's she doing? Why don't you call the head of the association and find out?"

Shigenori pressed a button on his watch. The face lit up. It was past 11:30. "He went to bed a long time ago. Old people turn in early."

"I hope she's okay."

"You've got a phone too, don't you?"

Kotaro showed him.

"I thought young people all had smartphones now."

"Somehow I never get around to getting one."

Kotaro was one of the few people at Kumar, or on campus, who still used a simple flip phone, though it did offer limited web access. A lot of people thought this was fairly strange.

"Anyway, I can do whatever I want with the laptop."

"That's what real net jockeys do, or so I hear. Okay, let's synchronize our watches. We'll take turns checking the roof every half hour."

"Once an hour for each of us, then. Until six?"

"Yeah. No alarm."

"Naturally. Set for vibe."

Shigenori watched carefully as Kotaro set his alert. "Set it for me," he said awkwardly, handing him his phone.

"Sure." He couldn't help chuckling. He set Shigenori's alert. "So I guess we just wait."

"That's what stakeouts are like."

"If I don't talk, I'm going to freeze to death. Do you mind?"

"Keep your voice down."

"Of course. Could I get a spot on the cardboard too?"

Shigenori made a show of grunting with effort as he moved over. Kotaro's buttocks were almost numb from the cold, hard floor. He sat on the cardboard and rubbed himself all over, trying to warm up.

"There's a lot of stuff I wanted to ask you about. I need a professional opinion." His voice was shaking from the cold. "Let's see...okay, first off, what do you think of those homeless people going missing? Isn't it a stretch to connect those disappearances with Kozaburo Ino?"

"A do-gooder, huh? Is Morinaga like you?" Shigenori's voice was calm and impervious to the cold. His breath was white in the air.

"Am I a do-gooder?"

"You haven't noticed?"

No one had ever called him that before. True, Kazumi sometimes complained that her older brother was an acute pain.

"When did you get addicted to the Internet?"

"I don't like it that much, really. A graduate of my high school invited me to take the job."

"You seem pretty involved with it."

"It turned out to be interesting."

"Is that what Morinaga thought?"

"Probably, yes."

"I see. So it's fun playing detective." Shigenori sounded a bit sarcastic, but Kotaro forged ahead.

"Kenji told me when he was a child, his father's company went bankrupt. The whole family had to skip town in the middle of the night to get away from their creditors. The experience made it impossible for him to ignore the poor and defenseless. He told me he thought it was sad that people were vanishing and nobody was even looking for them."

Shigenori was silent a moment before grunting in agreement. He uncrossed his arms and rubbed his hands together, blowing into them.

"You're right. I don't see anything that ties Kozaburo Ino to those homeless people. But I noticed something on the roof just now."

"You went up there?"

"I wanted to see how visible the station and the tracks are. From where the gargoyle sits, the Chuo Line cuts diagonally across your field of vision from left to right. The Seibu-Shinjuku Line runs off to the left—west-northwest—from Shinjuku Station. It's not so conspicuous in the daytime, but the tracks are lit up at night. You can easily see the line, even when there's no train. You can see the stations and estimate distances along the tracks. They make good landmarks."

"For what?"

Shigenori didn't answer immediately. He wasn't looking at Kotaro now.

"Today—no, yesterday. Until I saw that handprint on Mrs. Chigusa's window, I thought I was dealing with some kind of animal. A huge nonnative species of bird. Carnivorous. What do they call them?"

"I don't know. Raptors?"

"That's it. They're native to certain countries."

"But how could a bird like that get to Japan?"

"Someone could've imported it. Go to any pet shop. Snakes and iguanas. Alligator snapping turtles. Not long ago people were screaming about an alligator in the lake at Inokashira Park." Kotaro had never heard of it.

"When they caught the thing, it turned out to be a gar with a head like an alligator. Anyway, it wasn't native to Japan. Somebody released it. Maybe they couldn't keep it and couldn't sell it, or they just got tired of it."

Shigenori thought a raptor might have taken up residence in Shinjuku after having escaped, or been released, under similar circumstances. "It's a reasonable conjecture, don't you think?"

"Maybe, but are there really raptors in other countries big enough to grab a man and fly off with him? I mean, we're not taking about a dinosaur."

"No, I wasn't suggesting that." Shigenori sounded slightly embarrassed. He scratched the bridge of his nose. "I'm thinking Kozaburo wasn't carried away. He saw some huge bird, panicked and hid someplace where no one could find him, but he couldn't move because he was hurt."

Kotaro was silent.

"Does that sound ridiculous?"

"I was wondering why he'd hide someplace no one could find him."

"You'd do the same if a predator chased you. Get under cover. Hide."

"Hmm...it seems like a stretch."

"Okay, what do you think happened?"

"I don't know. But I don't think it was a bird."

Shigenori nodded. "Neither do I. Not anymore, not after seeing the picture that child drew. We're not talking about a bird here. It's clearly human, or something that's at least partially human."

It was so cold now that Kotaro's eyes were starting to water. He narrowed them and peered at Shigenori. "So a human dressed like a bird flies—glides, let's say—through the air. He comes down out of the sky and commits crimes?"

"At this point, that's the second reasonable hypothesis."

"Like Spider-Man."

"That's a movie."

"No, there are people who can do that kind of thing. I heard about a guy who can dress up like Spidey and climb right up the side of a building. He's not in Japan, though."

Kotaro's phone started vibrating inside his down jacket. He stood up, climbed the ladder, and quietly raised the hatch. No change.

He decided to climb onto the roof. As he stood up, a gust of freezing wind almost made him lose his balance. Shielding his eyes with one hand, he took a quick look around, then climbed back down. For several minutes his teeth were chattering so hard he couldn't close his mouth.

"You were right. The tracks make a g-good landmark. They run straight out from the station. Some insane person pretending to be a bird is using this b-building as a base to go after homeless people along that commuter line. He's hunting people."

Shigenori's voice was firm. "I wouldn't push Reasonable Conjecture Two that far."

"But you said—the landmarks—"

"Conjecture Two doesn't explain why the gargoyle's here in the daytime. Why would your crazy birdman go to the trouble of sitting up there all day without moving a muscle, pretending to be a statue?"

"You've got a point."

"Let's just sit tight until we figure out what this thing is."

Kotaro nodded and looked around for the crowbar. With his eyes adjusted to the dimness, he quickly found it. He picked it up and put it on the floor beside him. *Good thing I brought this. It might come in handy as a weapon.*

"I don't think you need to worry." Shigenori laughed. He'd seen through Kotaro's fear. Were all detectives like this? It suddenly hit him that Shigenori hadn't given a straight answer to any of his questions. Instead, he'd answered with a different question. It wasn't unlike the detectives he'd seen on television.

"You must have friends or coworkers who stay up late. Is there someone you can contact? Maybe they have news about Morinaga."

Kotaro should've thought of it himself. He quickly sent Seigo a message. As though he'd been waiting, Seigo responded immediately.

Still missing. No news. Get some sleep. Kotaro looked at Shigenori and shook his head.

An hour passed. They each climbed the ladder once. Nothing changed. Between trips, Shigenori nodded off. After checking the roof a second time, he climbed down, covered his nose with both hands and sneezed violently.

"You were right. It's even colder if we don't talk."

Kotaro's mouth was frozen shut.

"Hey, are you still alive?"

"I'm about to freeze to death."

"We should keep talking. The president of Kumar is a woman, I think. What was her name, Ms. Ayuko Yamashina?"

"Ms.?" He hasn't even met her. Is this how detectives talk?

"I'm surprised you've heard of her."

"Saw her on TV. *Movers and Shakers*, something like that."

The TV crew that visited the office. So it had already aired.

"Now she's starting a nonprofit? Do you and Morinaga have anything to do with that?"

Kotaro pictured himself at the soba restaurant, gazing at Ayuko. She'd said she wouldn't get Kumar involved.

"We're not involved with that one. What you saw on TV was basically PR. She wants to attract sponsors. What kind of nonprofit was it?"

"Don't you know?"

"I missed it."

In the dim light, Shigenori seemed a little uncomfortable. "It's a support organization."

"For who?"

"Victims of sexual violence."

Kotaro's surprise came with a sudden picture of Ayuko's smile.

"The police can't give those victims the attention they deserve. There've been organizations like that in America for a long time. Rape crisis centers, I think they call them." Again, Shigenori looked uncomfortable. "They'll take the victim to a hospital, handle notifications to law enforcement and generally help out with a lot of things."

"Take care of them, you mean."

"Right. I thought you didn't know about it," Shigenori said mildly.

"That's the kind of person our president is."

Working for the benefit of society and helping those in need. Pure and gentle, with the persistence and push to get things done. *So that's what her new project was about. She could've told me,* Kotaro thought. Everyone in Kumar would've been willing to help if she'd asked. Seigo must feel the same way.

"She's a wonderful person," Kotaro said.

"A real looker, too." Shigenori's tone was playful. Kotaro had the feeling he'd been read again.

"When I started doing cyber patrol work, I found out how vulnerable women are to that kind of abuse online. There's a lot of it. I think she must've felt like she had to do something."

Shigenori looked at him thoughtfully. "You respect her, don't you?"

"Of course, but the police don't like that kind of organization much, I guess."

"What makes you think that?"

"You know—amateurs getting involved in your work."

"I don't agree at all. That's my personal opinion. There's a limit to what the police can do. If leaving something to the private sector works better and it's more effective, fine. Business or nonprofit, whatever works."

"That's a pretty progressive way to look at things."

"If you think that's progressive, you're behind the times." Kotaro had just taken a hit.

"Especially with sexual violence, society doesn't always sympathize with the victims. People tend to think the victim was partially responsible. They let their guard down. Or they were careless. If the government tried to do what your president wants to do, there'd be people screaming about using the public's hard-earned taxes for the wrong thing."

Kotaro had had enough of people who were against everything, but he took the point, especially after seeing the number of people on the web who disclosed personal information in the course of trying to find someone to date, or put out ads soliciting "dates" for money.

"In a democracy," Shigenori said, "you can't ignore those opinions. I used to be paid by taxpayers myself, so my hands were tied. That's why I appreciate what private support groups can do."

"I never looked at it that way."

"It goes for you too, you know. Cyber patrolling falls into the same category. If the government tried it, people would say it was censorship and an attack on freedom of speech and expression, the freedom to think and believe."

"I hear Kumar gets complaints like that too. I haven't seen them myself, though." He'd heard Seigo mention it casually.

Some people just can't stand us. They call us a stalking horse for the authorities but they still use pseudonyms, the stupid cowards.

"But that Ayuko Yamashina. What a beauty. People who attract attention attract opposition too. I think she's in for a rough ride."

"We'll protect her."

Shigenori laughed. At least it sounded friendly.

For the next several hours they waited quietly, each occasionally checking to make sure the other hadn't frozen to death. Nothing changed on the roof. Kotaro suspected that their stakeout had been detected from the sky, but he was afraid that saying so might make it true. He held his tongue.

Half past four. Kotaro climbed down the ladder to find Shigenori on his feet, limbering up his shoulders.

"How's it look?"

"No change."

"Maybe it got away."

"I don't think we've done much to be seen."

"I don't know. Mrs. Chigusa didn't even open—" Shigenori shook his head, canceling that last statement. "Let's keep at it till dawn. I took a little nap. I'm feeling better."

He rubbed his face with his gloved hands and sat down with his back against the edge of the ladder. Kotaro sat back against on the opposite side.

"If these disappearances turn out to be murders, there'll be more victims than Toe-Cutter Bill."

Kotaro was about to explain, but Shigenori already knew. "They're calling him Buffalo Bill the Toe Cutter on the web." He sounded chagrined. "The Toe-Fetish Killer too."

"What kind of person would do this?"

There was no answer. *Maybe he doesn't think he should be talking about it,* Kotaro thought. *Even though he is retired. Maybe I shouldn't have asked.*

But then Shigenori said quietly, "Not person. People."

"What?"

"There's more than one killer. I can't believe this is the work of one person."

"But all the victims were strangled. And each one was mutilated—"

"That might just mean the killers have an understanding."

"What motive could there be?"

"I don't know." Shigenori's tone was heavy, as though he thought he was supposed to know.

"What makes you think there's more than one killer?"

Still with his back to Kotaro, Shigenori sighed deeply. "Someone's going to come to the same conclusion and say it on television, tomorrow if not today. There are a lot of ex-detectives who appear on TV as analysts these days." His voice didn't betray whether he approved of this or not.

"The victim in Tomakomai managed an izakaya. Mishima was running a bar. She was popular with her customers. Totsuka was a pharmacist. Each victim was kidnapped and killed, but not by a stranger. They each knew their killer.

"The victims in Hokkaido and Mishima were both taken soon after closing up shop but before returning home. The pharmacist met her killer on the way home after work, that much seems certain. She dropped out of sight before she reached her regular bus stop. No one noticed anything out of the ordinary. That means she probably got into someone's car."

Each killer knew the victim's daily routine. Each killer could approach and greet the victim without arousing suspicion.

Kotaro pictured how it might've happened. The killer smiles, says hello. *How's everything? Just getting off work? Can I give you a lift?* Or maybe, *Can you give me a lift?* The car door opens...Mama Masami had probably been killed in her beloved Volkswagen.

"Do you really think a single person could've committed a murder in Tomakomai and then, in the space of six months, moved a considerable distance—twice—to strike up relationships with two more victims?" Shigenori asked. "People in different lines of work, not even the same gender? That's not how serial killers operate."

"But all three victims worked with customers. It would be easy to get to know them."

"Customers, yes, but in an izakaya, a bar, and a pharmacy. Those are very different settings. The degree of familiarity is different. If you're running a bar, you might get to know customers well enough to give them a ride home after you close up. Now let's take the Totsuka murder: Saeko Komiya. She had a three-year-old son. She was on her way to pick him up from his nursery school. She meets someone she recognizes by sight from the pharmacy. A customer—a patient, in this case. This person offers to give her a lift. Do you really think she'd accept? It'd have to be someone living in the same building, or someone whose child was in the same school, at least."

Let's go home together.

"The Akita victim is unidentified, but that in itself is a clue. Maybe she was traveling, or someone who just moved to the area, someone in a special situation."

"Like what?"

"Maybe she had something she wanted to hide. If she owned a bar, maybe she was on a trip with a customer. There's no way a single person could've set up all those relationships at short notice."

Kotaro hugged his knees to his chest and thought about it. "Maybe they met up on the Internet?"

Shigenori turned to look at him and shook his head. "There's no connection between the victims. Internet friends? Maybe they read the same blog or had a mutual friend? Rule it out. Any police department worth its salt could tie them together immediately, if there was a connection like that. All they'd have to do is find the victim's PC, or their mobile."

"No, I don't mean that. I'm talking about the killer."

Shigenori looked at him sharply.

"The victims are unconnected," Kotaro continued. "But each one could have a connection to the killer through the Internet. It would be easy enough. Distance is irrelevant on the net. The kind of work the victims did would be too. Someone could make friends with each of them in a short period."

I just happened to be in town on business. Would you like to get together?

"The killer could use any kind of excuse. No need to get together somewhere fancy. It would just be an offline meeting. I'm not sure about the Akita victim, but it seems to me the other three could easily have gotten to know the killer on the web."

"People in Hokkaido and Shizuoka and Kanagawa?"

"They're all in Japan. Okay, Tomakomai is a bit far away, but the problem isn't real distance. It's perceived distance. Net friends can get very close. One person could've killed them all."

Shigenori looked at him in disgust. "If the killer and his victims were communicating by Internet or smartphone, there'd be a trail."

"Trails can be erased. With the right skills and software, the killer could even do it remotely."

Shigenori was about to answer, but stopped. He held up a hand for silence. He looked up at the hatch in the ceiling. Kotaro did the same. "What is it?" he whispered.

"I heard movement. Something's up there. It passed overhead."

Kotaro held his breath for a moment, then grabbed the ladder and hoisted himself to his feet. "I'll take a look."

"I'll do it."

"You can't move as fast as I can." Kotaro picked up the crowbar and put his foot on the first rung.

"Leave that here," Shigenori said.

"Just in case."

Kotaro climbed up and raised the hatch cautiously to look out. The sky was still black, with the faintest premonition of morning. It was just past five.

The roof was deserted. There was nothing but the fragments of the original statue. The wind was blowing hard now.

Kotaro tipped the hatch back and climbed halfway, then all the way out. He stood next to the hatch, tense with anticipation, and peered all around. There was nothing to see. The north wind was keening. The colors of the neon signs were starting to fade as the darkness showed the first signs of retreating.

Shigenori put his head out of the hatch and looked up at Kotaro. "Come on, get back in here."

"It's all right. There's no one here."

"But—" Shigenori's voice caught in his throat. His eyes widened and his jaw dropped. He stared at Kotaro. His face was pale with shock.

No, he wasn't staring at Kotaro. He was looking into the sky behind him.

Very slowly—slowly enough to hear the bones in his neck creaking—Kotaro turned his head and looked over his shoulder.

BOOK III:

The Circle and the Warrior

1

It was Mana's monster. It was not a drawing. It was real, and it was descending toward them.

Even with its feet higher than Kotaro's head, the monster's outspread wings filled his field of vision. Its wingspan was—twelve feet?

And its height—seven feet?

Maybe more.

It descended in excruciating slow motion. The air beaten down by those enormous wings struck Kotaro full in the face.

The monster fixed its eyes on him. He was paralyzed, yet the first thought that entered his mind was wildly at odds with his predicament.

She's beautiful.

The creature was definitely female. Mana's sketch was faithful. She had a good eye. A winged woman, with long black hair streaming in the wind. Her wings were a deeper black, a muted obsidian sheen, yet her skin was almost translucent in its whiteness. Her bare right shoulder and arms were covered with an intricate network of black, tattoo-like arabesques.

The first word to cross Kotaro's mind was *warrior*. The woman wore leather leggings and tough leather boots reaching almost to the knee. A broad strap crossed her torso from left shoulder to waist. The thick leather belt was studded with metal that glinted in the dimness. Well-worn creases slanted across the surface of her black leather battle gear.

Intense surprise can make a person burst into laughter. Kotaro was laughing, though his vocal chords were paralyzed. His mouth and eyes were locked open in silent hysteria.

The warrior's face was an unblinking mask. Her black pupils drilled into him. He felt as though they were sucking him in.

He couldn't speak. He couldn't move. Even his lungs were paralyzed.

Her feet touched the roof. She flexed her knees slightly touching down, proof that she was a living being. She flapped her wings once more and extended them to their full reach.

Her right arm moved swiftly to her shoulder and grasped something. Kotaro heard a slicing sound as his body was blown sidewise. His shoulder slammed against the low rampart encircling the roof. There was a hard metallic crash and a spray of sparks.

For an instant he blacked out. When he came to, he found himself splayed on his back, head and shoulders jammed upright against the wall. It was an unnatural position and his neck hurt. He was trapped.

A sharp blade was embedded in the wall inches from his neck, a crescent-shaped blade longer than his arm, bound to a stout handle by thick strips of hide.

A scythe.

Shigenori had told him about the blade. The Grim Reaper. He was its prey. She had paralyzed him. Now she would kill him.

Shigenori's head was just visible above the open hatch. He was frozen in place, and not only out of surprise. The fingers of the warrior's left hand were leveled at his face. Parallel with her fingers, four needle-sharp darts extended from the leather gauntlet that sheathed the back of her hand. Her eyes remained fixed on Kotaro. She cocked her head slightly in puzzlement, or perhaps derision.

The tips of the darts and the crescent blade glimmered in the darkness.

A creature of fantastic appearance, a monster. Yet a woman, so beautiful one could scarcely look away. A mythical race of giants might have had women warriors such as this.

The bloodless lips moved. "Who are you?"

That's what I want to ask you.

Kotaro didn't answer. He couldn't move a muscle. His eyes were fixed and unblinking, watering from the cold. He was paralyzed and trembling. No laughter now. He trembled to his very bones from cold and terror.

He stared deep into the creature's eyes. Those pupils—something was wrong. He wasn't sure what it was.

Head still cocked, the warrior spoke again. "Who are you?"

She speaks our language. She can communicate with us.

The voice had a curious resonance; her words lingered like the vibration of a tuning fork, each with its individual pitch. The vibration was inaudible, but it penetrated to the center of Kotaro's heart, where it sought and found an answer from his body, a sympathetic resonance that moved outward in response like ripples in a pond.

She was scanning him. He knew it instantly. He needed no explanation. She was probing.

"He's a child." Shigenori's face above the hatch was deathly pale. His voice was inflected with fear. "He's just a kid. Please don't hurt him."

The leonine head pivoted smoothly over and down, taking in Shigenori whole.

"Rise up."

A violent tremor passed through him.

"Show me," the warrior said. Kotaro couldn't grasp the meaning, but Shigenori did.

"All right! I'm not armed."

Kotaro heard Shigenori's feet slipping on the metal rungs as he climbed. *I almost forgot. His leg. Can he make it?*

Shigenori hauled himself up onto the roof and knelt on the concrete, shoulders heaving with exertion. He held up his hands, palms outward, fingers spread, before clasping them behind his head. The black mantle and its needles never wavered from the center of his forehead.

"I have a question." He squeezed the words out between ragged breaths, yet his face was fierce. "Who are *you*?"

There was no answer. The three figures on the roof were motionless. Kotaro's crowbar lay useless, out of reach.

The ebony wings folded behind the warrior's back without a sound. She lowered the hand that was pointed at Shigenori.

Kotaro was still paralyzed. He was chilled through, but the glint of the scythe buried in the wall inches from his neck was colder still.

The woman spoke to Shigenori. "I am sorry."

This was the last thing Kotaro expected to hear. An apology?

"I am not of this...region. Once my mission is fulfilled, I will be gone."

Whenever she spoke, the strange resonance lingered, but now the sensation of being scanned was gone.

Shigenori and Kotaro would've been hard-pressed to describe that voice. The pitch was neither high nor low, its texture neither gentle nor coarse. It was characteristically female, but with a faintly metallic timbre. There was also something of raw nature in her voice, like the sighing of the wind.

"What do you mean, region?" Shigenori's expression was still fierce. His voice was stronger now.

"What you call a world."

"This world?" Kotaro had somehow found his voice, though his neck was bent up against the wall. "The world we're from?"

Her head swiveled to gaze at him once more. His breath caught in his throat. She truly was beautiful, too beautiful even for the word. It was the beauty of something beyond earthbound reality, almost celestial, like a solitary nebula of stars.

Something seemed to jostle his shoulders. In an instant the scythe was back in her hand. She spun its handle with practiced ease and anchored it behind her back before the zephyr from its motion died away. The crescent glowed like ice above her head.

With a single giant stride and a soft clashing of metal fittings, she closed the distance to Kotaro, leaned toward him, thrust out a gauntleted hand and held it there, waiting.

Later, whenever he remembered this moment, Kotaro Mishima was so filled with shame and embarrassment that he wanted to dig a hole and hide in it. For the first time since childhood, he almost lost control of his bladder.

Still sprawled on his back, he looked up into those black pupils. Now he knew why her eyes had bothered him.

The left eye had a double pupil, two black windows side by side, overlapping like an illustration of set theory in a textbook. A circle and a crescent.

"Can you rise?"

The outstretched hand was enormous, at least twice as large as his own, its back sheathed with thick black leather. But the white fingers were slender, the nails long and regular. A woman's hand and a woman's fingers.

Teeth chattering, holding his breath, and without taking his eyes away from hers, Kotaro reached out a hand.

Instead of pulling him to his feet, she pulled him completely *off* his feet, as if he weighed nothing. She turned smoothly and flung him toward the hatch. Shigenori made a brave attempt to catch him, but they both went sprawling.

"Oh, my."

The creature's reaction was so bizarrely human that Kotaro almost laughed. She was seven feet tall and had wings, she was immensely strong and armed to the teeth—and yet, bizarrely human.

A random thought crossed his mind. *I wonder if she ever laughs?*

The woman's face remained an impassive mask. Again he heard that bloodless voice with its strange resonance. "Interesting. So you know nothing of the Circle."

Both men struggled to their feet. Still leaning against each other for support, they exchanged glances and looked up at her.

"The Circle?" Shigenori said angrily. "Come again? You know our language but you speak in riddles."

"Then riddles they shall remain to you." She paused to gaze out at the city spread beyond the roof. "I am sorry I disturbed you. I will leave this place. I was already weighing the merits of a new base."

The resonance of her voice was not unpleasant. In fact, it was almost delightful. If dappled sunlight or a cool breeze on a late summer afternoon were transformed into sound that reverberated in the heart, it might have felt something like this.

"A base for what?" Shigenori asked. His tone was aggressive. Kotaro gasped. Didn't he feel the resonance?

"An old man disappeared near here. He's gone and no one can find him. What do you know?" he insisted.

Man, would you please chill out? She's packing, okay?

"Someone else is missing too—a young man, about this one's age."

He gripped Kotaro by the shoulder, stared at the creature and stood his ground. He was a detective interrogating a suspect.

"What are you doing here? You said you had a mission. What kind of mission would bring you here?"

The warrior gazed down at them. She threw her head back lightly, tossing her hair away from her face.

Kazumi and Mika were both growing their hair long. They said it saved them time, despite their constant grumbling about split ends. They often made precisely the same movement of the head. Kotaro again had the strange feeling that he was in the presence of a human female.

"I am sorry." The resonance that lingered after her apologies was somehow unique. It was silky and pleasing. "You shall forget this encounter."

"That doesn't work for me." Shigenori started to take a step forward. Kotaro had to restrain him.

"That young guy who disappeared is a friend of mine. His name is Kenji," Kotaro said.

For the first time the creature blinked. Her pupils—one on the right, two on the left—darted once, uncertainly.

"He's a nice, straight-arrow guy. I'm very worried about him. If you could just—"

Light glinted from the crescent blade above her head. It was not the light of dawn. The sky was still dark; first light was far off. The eastern horizon was a curtain of black, fringed with the faintest gray.

The light came from the blade itself. Something moved inside it.

Kotaro's eyes widened in astonishment. Shigenori groaned as Kotaro involuntarily gripped his arm.

It was Kenji. His eyes peered out of the blade. Kotaro knew those eyes. There was no mistake.

"Kenji!" He was shocked at how high-pitched his voice was.

Kenji's eyes, visible in the blade. It was as though the crescent were a window and he was looking through it. The eyes reacted to Kotaro's voice and blinked with surprise. They moved away and out of sight, as if he wanted to hide.

"Kenji!"

Kotaro screamed again and charged the warrior. She flexed her knees and sprang away, alighting on the edge of the roof. Kotaro tripped head over heels and pitched onto the concrete.

Dazed, he rose halfway and looked toward the scythe. Another pair of eyes was looking out at him. He saw the faces of strangers. They disappeared quickly.

Kotaro called over his shoulder. "Did you see? Did you see that just now?"

Shigenori's reply was a groan. He'd seen it too. "Was that Morinaga?

"Yes!"

"What did you do to him?" Shigenori growled at the warrior. He was struggling to remain standing.

The giant figure perched lightly at the edge of the roof. The parapet was only six inches wide, but she stood there with ease, looking down at them. There was flicker of emotion in those three improbable pupils. Was it compassion? Kotaro couldn't be certain.

"I came to this region to gather power. I have my mission." The voice seemed to radiate sympathy. Kotaro felt the resonance again in his heart. Each word was enunciated precisely, for the benefit of children. With each word, there was a wave of vibration.

"I know what it is to lose a compatriot. I am sorry. But I did not harvest them."

Kenji's alive.

"What did you do to Morinaga? Is Kozaburo there too? In your—inside that blade?" Shigenori said.

How could a flesh-and-blood person be trapped in a weapon?

"Enough. No more questions." The woman shook her head slowly. "Do not pursue me." She peered at Shigenori. "You were once a fisher on an ocean of evil."

Shigenori's face went slack with surprise. "What do you mean?"

Did the warrior know he'd been a detective?

"You have turned your back on its sin-tainted breakers. You are old and sick."

Shigenori dropped to his knees again and pitched forward. He put a hand on the concrete for support, gasped for breath, and clutched his chest with his free hand. His fingertips jammed into his ribs.

It was the resonance. She was scanning him. He was in agony.

"Stop it! Stop, please!" Kotaro tried to charge her again. His knees were like water. She kicked off lightly from the wall and evaded him easily. Shigenori was frozen in the same position but turned his head to watch, breathing raggedly.

"Old man," the creature said. "You understand the virtue of prudence. Do not pursue me. Nor allow this little one to pursue me." She nodded at Kotaro. "I am not in this region to harvest lives. That is not my mission. But if you pursue me, if you hinder me, I will harvest yours."

Harvest. With one swing of her scythe. Like cutting grain.

"I—" For a moment, the warrior hesitated. "My region is the birthplace of the souls of words. Just as you know friends by their voices or their form and face, I will know you when you speak. I will read the flow of your words and seek you out wherever you are, even as you seek to conceal yourself from me."

Kotaro's mind was racing. His heart was beating so hard that he couldn't concentrate. What was she saying?

"To be born in the Circle is to live as a heap of words, spawned by the souls of words."

What is she talking about?

"Pursue me and I will know. Scheme to hinder me and I will know. I will find your words and trace them. I will hunt them down. I will find you and harvest you. I am a warrior. Whoever challenges me must fall." The scythe glinted coldly with each word. "Do not pursue me." And then, more softly: "I am sorry."

"Yes. I understand," Shigenori rasped. His face was ashen. He wasn't getting enough oxygen. His right hand clutched his chest as if he were trying to rip his heart out. "I won't come after you. I won't tell a soul."

The creature jerked her head lightly, swinging her windblown hair away from her eyes and over her shoulder. Shigenori gasped and coughed convulsively, like someone pulled to the surface of the ocean at the point of drowning.

"You have gathered too much sin, old man."

In a single stride she was beside him. Her gauntleted right hand reached for him as he gasped on his hands and knees.

"To seal our covenant, I will end your pain." She placed her hand on his head.

Kotaro felt a surge of desperate strength. He could only growl like a beast as he charged. The warrior's left hand shot out, palm up. He froze in midcharge in a pose that defied the laws of physics, though she hadn't touched him.

Her other hand lay on Shigenori's head. Its huge palm and white, slender fingers cupped his head from the base of his skull to his forehead. She moved her lips in a lilting song with a gentle resonance.

"I am Galla the Warrior, Guardian of the Third Pillar of the Tower of Inception. In the Name of the Tower, I purify you."

She'll crush his skull. Or break his neck!

Kotaro's eyes were locked open. His tears welled up. Though he couldn't move his fingers, the tears streamed down his cheeks.

Galla's lips moved again, but he couldn't hear the words. She seemed to be saying something to Shigenori. Her hand stroked his head.

Shigenori's head dropped limply against his chest. He toppled forward in a fetal position.

"No!" Kotaro screamed.

He could use his voice. He could move.

Galla drew herself to her full height and unfurled her wings. The sable feathers filled Kotaro's field of vision again.

Her wings stroked powerfully downward. A wind sprang up. As the two men watched, she wrapped her wings around herself and unfurled them in a single slashing motion as she whorled into the air. The wingtips flashed close by Kotaro's face.

He was blown bodily into darkness.

▼

Pain.

Kotaro's entire body ached. He was frozen to the marrow.

He lay crumpled on his side against the parapet. The left side of his face was jammed against the concrete. He tried to stand, but felt a wave of nausea and stabbing pain in his hands when he tried to move them.

Shigenori was crumpled next to the open hatch facedown, with his knees folded neatly under him and his arms thrown out, as though in prostration.

Kotaro groaned and struggled again to stand. His legs refused to work. He tried bending his knees but fell flat on his back. He gave up finally and started edging toward Shigenori like a crab, on his feet and elbows. A thin dawn suffused the sky.

Shigenori's face was hidden. His ears and even his earlobes seemed drained of blood.

"Detective?"

He reached out and gripped Shigenori's shoulder. He wanted to shake him, but he had no strength.

"Mr. Tsuzuki? Are you alive?"

No. He's dead. That thing killed him.

Shigenori sat up as abruptly as if he'd received an electric shock. Now instead of prostrating, he was sitting on his heels like a Zen monk. He blinked furiously. His eyes were utterly bloodshot, almost hemorrhaging.

"Detective . . . ?"

Shigenori spasmed again, as though struck by another jolt of electricity. His eyes finally focused on Kotaro.

"Mishi . . . ma . . ." They stared at each other in wonder. "Are you all right?" Shigenori finally moved. He tried stiffly to help Kotaro sit up.

"Wha—what about you, detective?"

I will end your pain.

She hadn't meant to kill him after all.

"You're a mess, Mishima. Sure nothing's broken?" With help from Shigenori, Kotaro managed to sit up.

"Don't try to move right away. Just stay there and breathe deeply."

Kotaro did as he was told. The right side of his chest hurt. His cheek stung; his fingers came away with blood when he touched it. He'd gotten a bad scrape.

The two men could see each other clearly. It was dawn. Another midwinter morning had come to Shinjuku.

"Do you think you can get up?"

Kotaro felt himself all over cautiously. He rotated his ankles. That hurt. In fact, he hurt all over, but all he had were bruises, nothing he couldn't put up with.

"I guess I'm okay."

"Then let's get the hell off this roof." But Shigenori's leg was uncooperative. "I can't feel my leg. Damn it, I think it's finally gone out on me."

"I'll support you. Can you hang on?"

"I'll try."

"You have to go down that ladder."

Kotaro helped, but Shigenori had to descend the ladder using his arms only. He half-climbed, half-fell onto the cardboard, where he remained motionless for many minutes.

"Shall I call an ambulance?" Kotaro said finally.

"No, wait. We've got to get out of here first."

"But—"

"I'll put my arm around your shoulder. We'll take our time. Be careful, okay? It won't be funny if we both fall down the stairs."

"At least we're going down and not up."

Reaching the first floor seemed to take forever. Shigenori sat down heavily on the staircase.

"Sorry, would you bring my bag down? While you're taking care of that, I need to think."

As Kotaro climbed the stairs, he wondered what Shigenori needed time to think about. When he returned, the ex-detective was holding his head in his hands. Kotaro sat next to him on the step.

"Are you all right?"

Shigenori's gaze was piercing. "Listen to me carefully. We never met." His tone was imperative. "You were never here."

"What are you talking about? Have you lost your memory?"

"I haven't lost anything, that's why I'm telling you. Don't you remember what that thing said to us?"

Do not pursue me.

"It was a warning. No, a covenant. That's what she called it."

"Are you going to abide by it?"

"We don't have a choice, at least for now." Kotaro thought he saw tears welling up in Shigenori's bloodshot eyes. "I screwed up. I should've thrown you out instead of letting you stay."

"Thanks a lot."

"But it's too late now. Are you listening? Pay attention!" He grabbed Kotaro's wrist. His grip was like iron. "Tell no one what happened here last night. I won't. You won't."

"But what about Kenji?"

"Leave it to the cops. Stay out of it." He sounded as though he were trying to convince himself as well as Kotaro.

"Have you lost your nerve, detective?"

Shigenori gave a short, desperate laugh. "After something like that? You're damn right I have!"

"I don't want to give up."

"I don't care. This time you do what I tell you. It's the only way. Nobody's going to believe you. I don't care who you tell or how you tell it—no one will believe you. If you tell someone, it'll just make things worse."

They tried to stare each other down. In the end Kotaro lost, and not because of a difference in age or maturity. It was a difference in resolve.

"Leave my bag by the main entrance. Once I'm out of here I'll call an ambulance. Go ahead and go. Just disappear."

Kotaro was intimidated by this fierce urgency, but he thought of a way to push back. "Do you have your phone?"

Shigenori dug around in his down jacket. "I've got it." He held up the phone and Kotaro grabbed it. Shigenori started in surprise. "What are you doing?"

"Address swap." He pulled out his own phone. "Let's keep in touch. Don't think this is the last time I'm going to see you."

"You're pretty uppity. Did you know that?"

"Yeah."

Kotaro exchanged addresses via infrared link and pocketed his phone. He held on to Shigenori's and peered at him.

"What?" Shigenori said. "Got something else to say?"

"Are you all right, detective?"

"What's that supposed to mean? I can't walk."

"I meant in the head." The warrior woman named Galla had said it on the roof.

You have gathered too much sin, old man. I will end your pain.

She had put her hand on his head.

I will purify you.

He looked the same. *She must've done something to his mind. Or his heart,* Kotaro thought. But his memory didn't seem to have been tampered with.

What did she do to you, detective?

"Give me my phone and get out of here, now." Shigenori was getting irritated. Kotaro took a step back and thrust out his other hand.

"Give me the key."

"Huh?"

"The key to this building. You've got it, right?"

Shigenori rolled his eyes in disgust. "What do you need that for?"

"I'll hold on to it for you."

"You don't have to do that. Give me my phone."

"Trade you for the key." Kotaro held the phone out of reach. "Please."

Shigenori snorted angrily. He searched in his pocket and withdrew the shiny new key.

"You don't have any use for this, you know."

"Maybe, maybe not."

They made the trade. Kotaro stood up, put a thumb under the strap of his backpack and headed for the door. Shigenori called after him almost despondently.

"Leave it alone. You heard what she said."

Kotaro didn't answer. His right ankle throbbed as he walked.

"There's nothing we can do about what we saw." Shigenori's voice was hoarse. "Don't do anything stupid!"

Kotaro pushed the door open with his shoulder. Morning sunshine poured into the first floor of the tea caddy building.

"Don't hang around too long, detective," Kotaro called over his shoulder.

He put distance between himself and the building, walking as fast as he could with his sore ankle, still clutching the key to the back door. The sensation of it in his hand was the only tangible proof of the events he had witnessed.

2

All day, Kotaro tried his best to think of nothing.

He discovered that was easy. Not *remembering* anything, though, was the hard part. Even with his eyes open, if his attention shifted away from his immediate reality, he could see the events of the night before as vividly as if they were being projected onto the back of his eyelids. The voice of the woman warrior with the raven wings kept echoing with a strange resonance deep in his ears and throughout his entire body.

Each time the resonance came back to him, his confidence grew. It really had happened. He hadn't been hallucinating. The warrior was real. And Kenji was trapped in the blade of her great scythe. No matter how stupid it sounded or how hard it was to believe, what he'd experienced at the tea caddy building had been real. He couldn't deny it to himself. He wasn't crazy.

There were no more doubts. Kotaro shut himself up in his room and started furiously searching the web for clues. He missed classes and put Kumar off with excuses. He was on the hunt.

Searching for "Galla" as a personal or place name returned too many hits. "Winged human" was a staple of fantasy fiction and, sure enough, it produced too much information as well.

What about "circle"? An ordinary word, but the way Galla had used it, it sounded like it had some special meaning. So did "region."

He decided to attack the problem from a different angle and search for information on sympathetic resonance. Was it possible for an organism to physically affect other creatures with sound and cause them to share emotions? If so, would it be possible to investigate what made that possible?

Kotaro waded through an ocean of information but found nothing to explain his experience. He visited libraries and bookstores and came up empty.

During his search, he sent Shigenori a message asking about his health and where they could meet, if he wanted to meet. There was no reply. Kotaro hadn't been expecting one right away in any case.

Shigenori had seemed to have a steel backbone even before Kotaro learned he was an ex-cop. But when confronted by Galla, he'd given up without a fight and agreed to her terms. It made sense; there was an overwhelming difference in strength, and refusing to cooperate might've gotten them both killed.

Of course they'd both been scared. Frightened out of their wits. What had Shigenori said? Who wouldn't have lost his nerve after seeing something like that?

Yet even allowing for their fears, Kotaro was disturbed by how diminished Shigenori had been even after Galla departed. *Do not pursue me.* Okay, sure. We made a promise, so you better not go after her either, Mishima. Was that really how a hardboiled detective would behave after experiencing something that astonishing?

Kotaro was beginning to suspect that Galla had "purified" Shigenori of his nerve and backbone. She had stolen his mettle and broken his spirit.

Galla said Shigenori had gathered too many sins. That was a baroque way of putting it, but it meant his life had been devoted to fighting crime. Could Galla extract that sort of information with her scan, with its strange resonance? Judging from her attitude toward Shigenori before and after the scan, that seemed the only conclusion.

If so, she must've figured out Kotaro too. Just a run-of-the-mill student with no fighting ability whatsoever. He couldn't even pick up the crowbar and use it as a weapon. Shigenori had tried to protect him.

He's just a kid. Please don't hurt him.

Galla had known Shigenori was the one in command, the one who might pose more of a problem. That was why she'd forced him to promise not to go after her. It would be enough to take care of them both; Kotaro, the weak child, wasn't worth her attention. *Do not pursue me.* Okay, we won't. Simple.

If she thought that, she was wrong. "I'm coming after you," Kotaro said aloud. Working on his PC in the middle of the night, pedaling his bike to the station against the winter wind, spending a few minutes in the kitchen to eat with the family—the thought drummed in his head every waking moment. Sometimes he said it out loud; maybe she could hear him.

"I'm coming after you. I'm going to find out what happened to Kenji, and what you're trying to do. I'll never give up."

I will know when you speak. I will read the flow of your words and seek you out, no matter where you are.

Pretty cool. *Then do it. Find me. We've got business to transact, Galla. No way*—no way—*am I going to blow all this off just because you say so.*

If what Kotaro was feeling was anger, it was reckless anger. He knew it wasn't courage. It was righteous anger, a thirst for justice.

He had to avoid getting anyone else involved. He couldn't speak a word of what he was doing. It had to remain his secret and his alone. No matter how hotheaded he became, he kept his head concerning this one point. At least here, Shigenori's judgment was correct. Who would believe it if he told them?

Two more days passed with little to show. That evening his phone buzzed. It was Kaname Ashiya.

"Kotaro, where have you been?"

He was in his room, still working at his PC. Her voice brought him back to the real world; he realized suddenly how tired he was.

"I sent you like a million messages. Didn't you see them?"

He'd been checking his mail every day in case Shigenori had responded, but he hadn't been reading his other messages. He knew his inbox was practically overflowing.

"Kaname, I'm sorry."

"Well thanks a lot. You practically disappeared. I feel completely abandoned."

That was a little over-the-top. He'd only been out a few days. Still, her words made him happy. He felt like a part of his heart he hadn't used for too long was working again.

"You've got mail from Seigo too, I'm pretty sure. And the police want to talk to you about Kenji."

"Did they start looking for him?"

Kaname paused slightly before answering. "Yeah. I guess so."

"What do they want to talk to me for?"

"Kenji told you something, didn't he? They even asked *me* to let them know when you come to work."

So that was it. They hadn't even tried to contact him at home. They were just waiting for him to show up at the office.

"What do the cops think about his vanishing like that?"

"I'm not sure. I think they think he got mixed up in some kind of trouble. You better ask Seigo. Kotaro, you're not going to quit or anything like that, are you?"

"I'll be in tomorrow morning early."

It was pointless to hope the police would be able to do anything. But it wouldn't be right to ignore them either.

"Seigo's mad at you. He wants to know why you picked a time like this to take a vacation. You need to contact him and apologize."

"Okay, sure. Sorry for the hassle." He ended the call and sighed.

So Kenji had gotten mixed up in some kind of trouble? Well, they were right about that. Kenji had gotten involved in some frighteningly bizarre trouble, the kind the police couldn't even touch.

I am not of this region.

How could they track down a being from another world?

Kotaro arrived at Kumar the next morning at eight. Seigo was already at his desk.

"Over here, Mishima."

Kotaro was braced for a reprimand but got a briefing instead. Kumar had submitted a missing person's report to the police division responsible for Seigo's neighborhood. The Metro Police didn't think it very likely that a crime had been committed, and they weren't devoting much attention to the case. Kenji's smashed phone bothered them a bit, but that was all.

"It's almost too bad he's not a woman. Things would be a lot different." Seigo couldn't conceal his dissatisfaction. "Narita told them Kenji was investigating something. That's why they want to talk to you."

"Okay, I understand."

"His father was anxious to meet you while he was here."

"Oh. I'm sorry I couldn't make it."

"Why did you take time off, anyway?"

Kotaro was ready with a cover story. "It was a family thing. It's kind of private. I'm really sorry if I messed anything up." He bowed his head deeply.

When he looked up again, Seigo was eying him with deep suspicion. "Something's wrong with this picture." Kotaro looked away.

"You're too calm. Aren't you worried about Kenji?"

"Of course I am."

"You don't look like it."

Kotaro didn't answer, and Seigo didn't press the point.

"Work out a new schedule with The Lady. She had to work pretty hard to cover for you while you were gone."

"Okay, will do."

The conversation lapsed into uncomfortable silence. Kotaro was turning to go when Seigo said, "I put together a new Toe-Cutter Bill team."

Kotaro blinked impassively.

"He's getting a lot of attention now. It's not about toes anymore. The next one may be even worse."

"Okay."

"That's it? You don't want to join?" Seigo was beyond suspicion. Now he was plainly upset. "You've lost your mojo. What happened, Ko-Prime?"

Kotaro fought to suppress the emotion that boiled up suddenly. "Nothing happened."

He wanted to tell Seigo. He wanted to tell him everything. *I can't think about work, Seigo. I had an experience I can't explain. It was totally out of this world. You might think I'm crazy, but it's true. Something unbelievable happened to Kenji. I think I know where he is—*

No, no, *no*. He mustn't involve anyone. Shigenori said it himself. He'd gotten Mrs. Chigusa involved. Now he wished he never had.

That was what it meant to be trapped with a secret. It wasn't just his heavy heart. It wasn't just the pain. It was the way he felt cut off from everyone around him.

He went back to work and did his job. It was routine for him now. A policeman came and interviewed him. The middle-aged detective was polite, but didn't seem all that interested in the case.

Kaname came in the afternoon. At first she joked about Kotaro taking her to a *very* expensive restaurant to make up for his absence. But gradually she started to get truly worried.

"Kotaro, what happened? You can tell me."

"I told you. Nothing happened."

"You're different."

"Take some time off. I owe you."

"That's not the point."

Just then Ayuko Yamashina poked her head in the office door. She looked like she'd just stepped off the bullet train. She was wearing a long coat and carrying a small suitcase. She waved at Seigo. "Sei-chan!" Seigo nodded and stood up.

Ayuko held the heavy glass door open with her shoulder and smiled at Kaname and Kotaro. "Hey, you're back."

"Finally, right?" Kaname said.

"I'm sure you're worried about Kenji, but don't let it get you down."

"We won't." Kaname gave her a big nod and elbowed Kotaro in the ribs. He wasn't responding at all. Ayuko peered at him.

"Kenji's disappearance was quite a shock, wasn't it?" She smiled at Kaname. "Men can be quite fragile when things like this happen. Take care of him."

"Don't worry, I've got his back."

"Who're you calling fragile?" Seigo said as he walked up to her.

"Look who's talking," Ayuko said. "You're so worried about Kenji you can hardly sleep at night."

"You talk too much." Seigo put his hand on the small of her back and guided her out the door. It closed behind them.

The way Seigo touched her was natural and intimate. Kotaro felt a stab of jealousy that was no less painful for being immature.

"Come on, Kotaro. Cheer up."

Kaname patted him lightly on the head, as though he were a child. The spontaneous kindness of her touch drew him back to the present moment.

These people are so important to me. They're depending on me too. I've got to bring Kenji back to them.

▼

After turning things over in his mind for days, Kotaro came to a conclusion.

Galla had said she could find her prey by sensing their words. If that was true, then all he had to do was send out as many words as possible—words that would anger her enough to come and "harvest" him.

The Internet was a vast, tossing ocean of words with countless rivers flowing into it. *Circle. Region. Galla. The souls of words. Does anyone know what these words mean? Does anyone remember seeing or hearing these words used together?* Kotaro posted his questions on every likely forum he could find.

And what else did she mention? Something about a tower? The third Pillar of the tower of something or other?

Kotaro's questions drew many responses, some serious, some not. Some were kind and others mocked him. It didn't matter. The point was to keep at it.

Galla, you made a mistake by underestimating me. I am pursuing you.

He would've been lying if he'd pretended he was being brave. He was still as frightened of Galla as he'd been on that rooftop. Who knew when she might appear? As he input more bait and hit ENTER, thinking this might be what finally did it, he'd suddenly have the feeling that if he turned he would see her standing there, bringing down that huge curved blade.

As he pondered his dilemma, he realized something else important about Galla: she could be persuaded with words. He was sure there would be a way to make her understand.

Of course he could never best her in a fight, but if he could make her understand that he was genuinely worried about Kenji and wanted to understand her mission, he felt sure he could get through to her.

Maybe he was just fooling himself. But he was surprised it had taken him so long to realize how many times Galla had said it.

I am sorry.

There was something about the focus and the sincerity of those words. She was not an evil being.

I am gathering power in this region. I have my mission.

Galla had a goal. She had come to this world on a mission. Perhaps she was like a knight in the service of someone, or something.

Another day of posting to the web, and still Galla did not appear. Maybe it was time to go back to the tea caddy building.

There was still no response from Shigenori, but even if Kotaro couldn't consult a pro, he could always do what he saw on police dramas: when you hit a dead end, revisit the crime scene.

Ten days after that fateful night, Kotaro stood once again, alone, on the roof of the tea caddy building. The darkness inside was no longer frightening. He stood there in the freezing air, surrounded by the fragments of the smashed statue, staring patiently at the night sky, waiting.

He waited in vain. Galla was as good as her word. She had moved on.

Early the next morning, half-frozen, shouldering his backpack and his disappointment, he returned home and nearly collided with Kazumi as she rushed out the front door. She wore her team jersey under her coat and was lugging her racket case.

"Finally decide to come home?" She narrowed her eyes and inspected him disapprovingly. Her breath was white in the chill. "I've got practice."

"Oh, okay." Kotaro stepped aside to let her pass, but she stood there with her back to the door.

"You were out all night again. This is the second time."

Kotaro stared at her blankly. Had he come home to get a tongue-lashing?

"Mom says she's gonna make you quit that stupid job." That was Kotaro's cover story: another all-nighter at Kumar. "You're working on that serial killer thing, aren't you?"

The latest mutilations had prompted the media to switch from Toe-Cutter Bill to the somewhat unimaginative Serial Amputator. Cross-jurisdiction investigations were the police's Achilles' heel, and as usual, there had been no new developments the day before. TV served up the same warmed-over details every evening. But if Kotaro's family thought he was holed up in his room or staying out all night to work on the case, so much the better.

"I'm not quitting. I'm keeping up with class just fine. I'll explain to Mom."

"Is that so?" Kazumi said coldly. She brushed her bangs out of her eyes with a gloved hand. "I don't think you've been staying out all night 'cause of your job. You're dating somebody."

Kotaro burst out laughing. Dating someone. Staying out all night. *Sorry, that's a little too simple, middle-schooler.* "That's it. You're right. You nailed it." Kotaro thought sarcasm would be effective, but Kazumi didn't take the bait. She thought he was being serious. Her eyes flashed with anger.

"I don't know what kind of woman she is, but you'd better dump her. Have you seen yourself in the mirror? You look terrible. If that's what she's doing to you, she's one to stay away from."

I've been outside all night. I'm frozen to the marrow. I'm exhausted. I'm about to die of hunger, and all I get is a sermon.

He looked at his sister's face, the picture of seriousness. He started laughing again. He wanted to pat her on the head the way Kaname had done to him. In fact, he wanted to hug her, though if he had she probably would've knocked him down.

"Just don't worry about it." What he really wanted to say was, *Thanks for worrying about me.* But he had his position as big brother to consider. "Still practicing hard? How's Mika these days?"

Kazumi looked at him as though she'd volleyed a tennis ball over the net and he'd passed a football back to her. "What are you talking about? Don't change the subject."

"I'm not trying to. If she's fine, then fine." He ducked past her and started to open the door.

"The bullying is over," she whispered quickly. "It stopped. Just like that, like it never happened. It's almost kind of wei—" She caught herself, as though she were worried about bad luck.

"Weird, you mean?"

She nodded.

"Stuff on the web can be like that, like a typhoon," Kotaro said. "Of course it doesn't exactly disappear, because it stays on the web somewhere. But when people calm down, it just goes away. You almost wouldn't believe it ever happened."

"Really?"

"Really. I'm still a beginner, but I'm working with the pros. You can believe it."

Kazumi shouldered her bulky racket case and walked down the steps. Kotaro watched as she crossed the street and rang the Sonois' doorbell. Mika appeared with an identical jersey and racket case.

"Ko-chan? Good morning!" She looked and sounded happy. Kotaro waved.

"Hey."

Kazumi leaned close and whispered something. Mika started laughing. "Oh my God. Be careful, Ko-chan!"

"What's that supposed to mean?"

"See you!"

As Kotaro watched his official and unofficial little sisters bounce off to practice, the thought hit him. *I've got to see Shigenori.*

The feeling came out of the blue. His partner in crime was the only person who could share what he was struggling with. If he couldn't see him, Kotaro wasn't sure he could go on anymore.

Before he went inside, he sent Shigenori another mail. That was just as well, because when he finally went inside, his mother was waiting.

"Kotaro!"

Breakfast lasted long enough for him to get chewed out, defend himself, and negotiate a compromise. By the time he got out of the bath, he was ready pass out from exhaustion. No class until two today. He went to his bedroom, set his alarm and hit the sack. When he woke up, there was a message waiting for him.

KOYO HOSPITAL. NEW WING, ROOM 302.

▼

"What is that?"

"Haven't you ever seen one of these?"

When Kotaro got off the elevator at the third-floor lobby, Shigenori was waiting for him. He was wearing a cardigan sweater over his pajamas and supporting himself with a walker.

"I'm up and down this corridor every day, training myself to walk again."

After they'd split up, Shigenori had called an ambulance and had himself taken to the hospital where his procedure was scheduled. Two days later, he'd had his spinal operation.

"You're walking already?"

"I was up the day after the operation."

Shigenori's lower back was still in a cast. "It hurts where they went in. I'll be here for another three weeks or so. But my legs don't hurt, not anymore. All the tingling and numbness are gone. It's like it never happened." Shigenori looked like a hostage who'd just been rescued. "Let's go back to my room. Don't worry, we can talk there. I've got a private room."

Shigenori slowly turned the walker around. Kotaro was relieved. He was so cheerful that Kotaro thought he might've forgotten the events of that night.

"They weren't expecting me that soon, so the only thing open was a single. I think they're transferring me to a four-bed room next week."

Room 302 was comfortable and bright. The northwest corner of the Imperial Palace moat was visible from the window. Shigenori got himself comfortable in bed. "What have you been up to?"

Kotaro was thankful that he was making it easier to get down to business. "I just can't forget what happened."

He pulled up a folding chair and fought back the tears. He finally had someone to talk to. Now he could get some relief from the constant stress of keeping his secret, at least briefly.

"What did you end up telling your wife?"

"Something plausible. It's all right. I was supposed to be at a hot spring with some old friends. She didn't believe me anyway. She'd already figured out I was up to something else."

Were all wives as sharp as that? Or was it because Shigenori's wife was married to a police detective?

"The one thing she was sure I wasn't doing was cheating on her. On that one point, she trusts me completely. It's a little disappointing, to be honest." Shigenori seemed truly happy. Kotaro felt a twinge of apprehension.

"I've been doing a lot of research since that night," he said.

Haltingly, he recounted the events of the last ten days, though he left out the visit to the tea caddy building. Shigenori's face made the decision for him. Lying on his back with his head turned toward Kotaro, it reflected pity and concern.

He finished his story. The sunny room was enveloped in silence.

"So, no new developments, eh?" Shigenori said finally. He sounded only half-interested.

"Um, no."

"And Galla hasn't shown up again?"

Kotaro nodded. His chair squeaked. It was a lonely sound.

"Look, Mishima..." With a groan that was more frustration than pain, Shigenori twisted over onto one shoulder to face him. "Can't we just chalk up what we saw to a bad dream?"

Kotaro couldn't find an answer. Shigenori didn't seem to want one. He went on in the same dry tone.

"That thing threatened to kill us. She told us not to go after her—several times, in fact. She said she was a warrior. That's what she does."

Kotaro could only nod in agreement. The chair squeaked again.

"But after everything you've done over the past ten days, she didn't show up, even though you broke our promise with all that posting you did. What that means—" For the first time, his expression softened. "What that means is that it never happened. There is no Galla. What we experienced was some kind of extreme, bizarre dream."

Kotaro still couldn't bring himself to say anything, but now it wasn't because he couldn't find the words. There was something he wanted to say, but he couldn't summon up the will to say it.

There is something wrong with him. Now he knew how Kaname felt when she saw him at Kumar. Something about Shigenori was definitely different. Galla had done something to him.

What was it that Galla had "purified"? She'd said she would take away his pain. What did she take away?

Backbone. Guts. His pride as a detective. It didn't matter what you called it. Whatever it was, the man in this hospital room was not the same person who had roughed up Kotaro in the tea caddy building. That ex-detective, the one who was determined to solve the riddle of the moving statue? That was somebody else.

"Yeah, I guess you're right." Kotaro heard himself speaking in someone else's voice, flat and expressionless. "I'll chalk it up to a bad dream. I don't have a choice anyway. I've hit a dead end."

"Yes, that's the way it is." Shigenori's eyes shone dully with tranquility and release.

"I'm glad your operation went okay."

"I couldn't sleep at all the first night, it hurt so much. They repositioned my vertebrae and fixed them in place with titanium bolts—four of them, this big." Shigenori made a circle with thumb and forefinger. "That's probably it for me as far as airplanes go. I'll trigger the metal detectors every time."

"You'll have to carry X-rays to prove you're not dangerous." Kotaro laughed, and Shigenori laughed too, with a painful expression.

The nurses were beautiful, but they expected you to mend quickly. The pre-op examination was agonizing. The food was surprisingly good. If it were spring, the cherry trees around the moat would be blooming. After walking through the usual topics between a hospital visitor and a patient, Kotaro stood up.

"It was good to see you, detective. Take care of yourself."

"Thanks, Mishima."

Kotaro was almost out the door when he paused. There was one loose end he felt compelled to tie up.

"That neighbor of yours—Mrs. Chigusa, was it? The one who collapsed and had to be taken to a hospital. How is she? Have you heard anything?

"Things didn't turn out well, I'm afraid. She died three days ago without regaining consciousness."

"I see. That's really too bad."

"Thanks for asking, anyway." That was all he had to say.

Out in the corridor, Kotaro thought his legs were about to give way. He was close to tears again, but for a different reason.

He couldn't rely on the detective anymore. He really was alone now.

▼

Kotaro was at a dead end. All he could do was wait.

But for what? For Galla to return? For someone completely new, someone he'd never met, to appear suddenly with new information?

He attended classes. He worked his shifts at Kumar, monitoring for drug-related activity. He gave Kaname a muffler in thanks for covering for him. He'd never seen her happier.

He returned to everyday life. He stopped posting about Galla, circles, and regions. He'd run out of things to say anyway.

February came, and the first day of spring according to the old lunar calendar. Kenji was gone. There was no news from the police about their investigation.

Galla was missing in action. On waking, Kotaro always checked his window for a huge handprint. But there was nothing.

It had all been a dream. A hallucination. Maybe Shigenori was right. Maybe leaving it at that was the best thing.

The key to the tea caddy building that Kotaro had received—confiscated—from Shigenori stayed tucked in a pocket of his backpack. Shigenori hadn't even asked about it.

The TV news programs kept up their coverage of the serial amputator, milking it for everything it was worth, but the story was getting stale. If some new scandal broke or a disaster loomed, the media would lose interest in a heartbeat.

It had just been a bad dream. A hallucination.

Sure, that's it. Just go with the flow. You can't beat it anyway. Give up. That's a lot easier.

But a small, intractable voice always pushed back whenever he tried to see things that way. He could never quite stamp out that resistance.

His Saturday class was canceled for the long National Foundation Day weekend. His shift at Kumar started at six.

Suddenly, Kotaro remembered Mana. He wanted to see her one more time. Why not today? They'd thought she was mute, but the last time he'd seen her, she'd spoken to him and no one else.

Is a monster.

The sky.

What was she doing now? If he could see her one last time, if he could see she was getting along well, he'd be ready to consign his experience on that rooftop to the crazy bin, just as Shigenori had. If Mana had broken out of her silence, that would be enough. If he could see her laughing happily, the weight on his mind would finally be lifted.

He decided to dispense with formalities and go straight to the Nagasaki mansion without calling. He gave his name through the intercom at the front door, and in moments Hatsuko appeared.

"You're that student who visited before. Come in, then. Come in, come in." She kept talking as he went inside.

"I'm so glad you came. It would've seemed odd for us to ask you here. My brother and I were wondering what we should do."

"Did something happen?"

"No. That's what we're worried about. She still won't speak to anyone. We consulted a child psychologist. He told us cases like this don't usually improve quickly. He said we shouldn't push her.

"Then we told him about you, that Mana did speak once, just to you. He said we should try to get your help if possible. But you're not a specialist in anything, are you? Just a college student. You're not a friend of the family. We couldn't make up our minds. We asked Mr. Ohba for his opinion, but he said it wouldn't be good for us to depend on someone without special qualifications. Or good for you, for that matter." This was commonsense advice, but it just made the Nagasakis' dilemma worse.

"Mana is alone right now. She's drawing pictures again."

Just as they had that first time, Hatsuko and Kotaro padded down the long corridor in house slippers.

"My brother and Ms. Sato are meeting her father today. They're trying to work out when he can take over custody. The man simply refuses to make up his mind. My brother hasn't been able to make any headway with him, so we decided to see if Ms. Sato might be more persuasive."

The nursery door was open. As before, the room was filled with sunlight. Hatsuko called to Mana in a friendly voice.

"Mana-chan, you have a visitor. It's that young man who came before. You remember him, don't you?"

Mana sat at the little round table with a sketchbook in front of her. Crayons were scattered over the table. Everything was the same as when Kotaro first met her, other than the clothes she was wearing. The hand holding the crayon stopped as soon as Kotaro stepped into the room. She turned to look at him.

Hatsuko whispered in his ear. "She hasn't drawn a picture of that strange creature since the day she met you."

"Hello, Mana-chan." Kotaro sat down on the floor across from her and looked closer at the sketchbook. She was drawing a colorful picture, a procession of baby chicks. There was a book open on the table with the same picture. She was using it as her model.

"Those chicks are very pretty."

Mana peered steadily at him and nodded once. "Um-hm."

Hatsuko gave an exclamation of surprise.

The girl's pupils were clear pools of black. Those eyes had seen Galla. A woman warrior descending onto the roof of the tea caddy building at the height of a storm.

"Did you stop drawing that monster?"

She nodded once, again. "Umm."

"That makes sense. You drew it so many times, you must be tired of it now." At this, her gaze wavered slightly. Kotaro looked up at Hatsuko. "Do you think I could be alone with her for a few minutes?"

She seemed ready to leap into the air with astonishment. "But of course, of course. It's three, time for her snack. I'll fix it. We're having pudding today, Mana. You love pudding, don't you?" She motioned to Kotaro to keep talking and padded out of the room.

He slid over next to Mana. She cocked her head toward him trustingly.

"Mana?" Kotaro lowered his head and whispered against her smooth cheek. "I saw the monster too. I met her."

She blinked once, hard. Her tiny nostrils flared slightly. Her lips began to move. She whispered back to him. "Were you scared?"

They shared the same secret now. They could communicate.

"At first." Kotaro nodded. Mana nodded back. "She came down from the sky again. She had big black wings."

Mana kept on nodding. When he touched her cheek lightly, she stopped.

"But you know what I found out? The monster can talk. I talked to her, just like we're talking now." He pointed to Mana, then to himself. "And you know what? She apologized."

Mana was five. Kotaro decided he'd better rephrase that. "She said she was sorry for making you feel scared."

Mana looked down at the table. The skin of her eyelids was so thin he could almost see through them to the eyes beneath. Her eyelids and fine, tiny lashes were trembling. She leaned closer to him and whispered in his ear.

"Did the monster take Mama?"

When Mana saw the monster, her mother had been hurrying toward death. Death had been in the room with them. For Mana, the terror and foreboding she had felt were wrapped up in her mind with that extraordinary being descending from the sky. That being must have taken her mother away from her.

Mother and child had been cut off from society. There'd been no one to help them. They'd been living in that apartment with only each other to rely on. Mana had never attended nursery school or kindergarten.

But her mother did a splendid job of raising her, showering her with love and teaching her everything she could. Mana's heart would grow tall and strong.

Then how should Kotaro answer her question? He looked into her eyes and wondered.

"It wasn't the monster's fault that your mother went away."

Her mother had died of pneumonia. She was not like Morinaga or the homeless people who disappeared. Kotaro didn't know what Galla had done to them, but she'd had nothing to do with Mana's mother. That was the all he could say with certainty.

"The monster didn't take your mother."

She blinked and looked up at him. He nodded back at her. "She won't do anything to frighten you ever again. She won't come and take you away. You don't have to be afraid anymore."

This didn't seem to reassure her. Instead, her tiny face relaxed into sadness.

"Where's Mama?" She pointed a tiny index finger toward the ceiling. "Is she in the sky?"

"Why do you think that?"

"Auntie and Uncle said so. Uncle Ohba too."

"They're right, Mana. Your mother is in the sky. But she's not where the monster is. The sky is a very big place, you know."

Kotaro was suddenly seized by doubt. Could he really be sure that the place Galla was from—"the birthplace of the souls of words"—was not the afterlife as human beings conceived of it? After all, no one knew anything about the world of the dead. No one could say he knew anything about an afterlife.

Of course, some said they did. They said they had traveled there and seen it. But the words they used to make their claims were the only foundation those claims had. Wasn't that what Galla meant by the birthplace of the souls of words? That the world of the dead brought the words of living human beings into existence?

No, he had it backward. The world of the dead existed because of the words of the living. It was not the source of those words.

But if Galla could imprison people in the blade of her scythe, it meant she could manipulate not only their bodies but their souls. And a place where the soul existed separately from the body—wouldn't that be the world of the dead?

"Is Mama coming back?"

Kotaro opened his eyes wide. It was the only way he could keep from averting them.

"I don't know." It was a gutless answer, with no value other than being honest. "But if I find out, I'll tell you. I promise."

He presented an upraised little finger. Mana instantly did the same. Her tiny, slender, warm finger hooked around his.

Kotaro sensed someone at the door. He turned to see Hatsuko peeking in. She was holding a tray with cups and bowls.

"May I come in?"

Kotaro smiled at Mana. "See? It's snack time."

Mana looked from Kotaro to Hatsuko. She blinked once and said, "Pudding."

Hatsuko burst into tears.

▼

Later, Kotaro realized that for the first time in his life, he had sealed a promise with a pinky swear. He had never done it before, even as a child. Maybe boys just didn't do it. Or maybe his parents had never cared for hocus-pocus customs like that.

If I find out, I'll tell you.

He'd made an unbreakable promise.

I've got to find Galla. I have to know where she came from, what kind of world her "region" is. Is it in another dimension? A parallel world? The world of the dead?

And what is the Circle?

3

The lecture was over. Kotaro had joined the crowd walking up the aisle in the lecture hall when he made eye contact with a girl sitting in the top row.

For a split second he thought it might be Kaname. She had the same pale complexion and long ponytail. But Kaname had bangs cut evenly across her forehead, almost hiding her eyebrows. She was self-conscious about her slightly protruding forehead.

The girl in the back row didn't try to hide her forehead. Kaname would never have done that. Kotaro blinked once and looked away.

The class just ended was part of the required course load and had a huge lecture section. With everyone trying to leave at once, the hall was like a crowded theater after a movie. The audience moving up the aisles slowed to a crawl.

Kotaro glanced around casually. Once again his eyes met those of the girl in the back row.

This time he made a calculated effort to look away casually, then surreptitiously glanced back at her out of the corner of his eye. She hadn't moved. He could see her staring straight at him.

He looked down at his beat-up sneakers, then at the sneakers of the student just ahead of him, who wore them with the backs crushed under his heels. Kotaro wore Nikes, the other guy wore Adidas. Kotaro's mother washed his sneakers in special sneaker soap. She insisted on it, because she didn't want the smell lingering in the entryway. The guy ahead didn't seem to have ever washed his sneakers.

By the time Kotaro was finished with his sneaker analysis, he'd reached the last row of seats. He looked up. The girl was nowhere to be seen.

No big deal. He'd been thinking too much.

He emerged from the building onto the quadrangle. The sun was warm. The quad was bordered on one side by a compact grove of plum trees. He'd heard the trees were pretty when they bloomed. Winter had been exceptionally cold, and the blossoms were not quite ready to open.

He had half an hour to kill before the next lecture. It was a class in the history of science, an elective that counted toward the general education requirement. Kotaro had hoped it would be interesting, but the lectures were straight out of the textbook; he could've found something more intriguing in any bookstore. The class was pure boredom, but he didn't have to make a special effort to attend. *Oh well, may as well blow it off and get to Kumar early.* First he would pick up a sandwich or something at the cafeteria—

"Are you the guy who wants to know about circles?"

Kotaro spun around. He was almost into the plum grove on a path that led to the cafeteria and the library.

The girl from the lecture was a yard away from him. He pretended he'd never seen her before. "Are you talking to me?"

"Why do you want to know about circles?"

She peered at him fixedly and came a step closer. Kotaro reflexively took a step back. He felt suddenly flustered.

Up close she was even prettier than he'd thought. Kaname was pretty too, of course, but this girl's "pretty" was more like "hot," his ideal type but refined to a higher degree, with the addition of a certain something, some sort of essence Kotaro couldn't quite put his finger on. With apologies to Kaname, but it was true.

"Why are you asking me?" he pointed to himself.

The girl laughed lightly, dissolving his wariness and suspicion instantly. It was like a spring breeze.

"Why else? You're the one who keeps telling everyone you're desperate to learn about circles. That *was* you, wasn't it?"

Kotaro went from flustered to heart-pounding mode.

"I did a web search," the girl said. With a trace of a smile, she came and stood next to him. She was a head shorter, with narrow shoulders and a graceful figure.

"You're not a student here," Kotaro said. She was clearly still in high school, probably on the cusp of her first and second years.

"Yep," the girl said crisply. "Universities have such big campuses!"

She was wearing jeans and a parka under an oversize fake leather jacket, topped by a crossover body bag. Her thick-soled boots were leather and must have been fake as well. The classic style was long out of date and the material had a fetching patina of age. *They can't be real,* Kotaro guessed. Otherwise they'd be unbelievably expensive.

"What are you doing here? It's not orientation season."

"I'm here to meet you."

"You? You personally?"

The girl looked away for a moment, as though trying to hide how hilarious this was. "Yes, me *personally*. I thought bringing my associates along might be a little much."

Before Kotaro could ask what this meant, she added, "Not playmates. And not, you know, bad people. Not friends either. Collaborators might be the best way to put it."

That didn't explain anything.

As he was struggling to figure out what she meant, Kotaro noticed the girl's pendant. It was a strange, curved object on a heavy silver chain. The end was sharp.

A fang. It had to be. An animal fang.

Knew it. She's some kind of delinquent. She's in a gang or something.

The girl must've followed his gaze, because she touched the pendant lightly with a fingertip. "This is my amulet."

"Not many girls have something like that."

"I'm not like many girls," she said casually. Kotaro's heart-pounding mode shifted to something more like anxious arrhythmic mode.

"Listen, um, I've got to—"

He was about to beat a hasty retreat when she touched his arm lightly—or at least that's how it seemed at first, until he felt her grip. She was strong!

"I came here because I had to see for myself what kind of person you are. I'm glad I came. I can see you've had contact with a being from another region."

Kotaro was paralyzed. The girl suddenly leaned in close and stared into his eyes, almost the way Kotaro had peered at Mana, but without the gentleness. Instead, her eyes communicated intense curiosity and wary urgency.

"I know what the Circle is, and what regions are. That's how I know they're not something to mess around with casually. But you want to know, too. That means you might be a threat. Or something terrible might end up threatening you."

The words came in a rush, clear and dancing, in the same cute, high school-girl tone.

"Maybe I can help you, or maybe I'll have to eliminate you. I'm asking so I can decide which one it is. Why are you looking for information about the Circle? What kind of creature from another region did you contact?"

To his utter embarrassment, Kotaro was trembling. "Before that..."

"Before what?"

"Before that, let's go someplace we can sit down."

▼

Conveniently, the cafeteria wasn't crowded this time of day.

"This is really nice."

One side of the room was floor-to-ceiling glass. The big sun blinds were halfway up. Kotaro and the girl sat facing each other across a round table. She had a chocolate cappuccino in front of her—so sweet, it made Kotaro sick just thinking about it—and looked as if she couldn't be more satisfied.

"University students get to hang out in places like this between classes? I can't wait." She looked and talked like any high school student.

Once they were seated, she reached into her pack and pulled out her student ID. She was a tenth grader after all, at a first-rate private high school. She'd be about two rungs up the ladder from Kotaro in terms of smarts if she was going to that kind of school. Her name was Yuriko Morisaki.

"So you're Kotaro Mishima." She perused his ID. Her tone was slightly patronizing.

"And you would be Yuri-chan." Kotaro countered with the Big Brother card. "Do your friends call you Yuri-chan?"

"The call me Morisaki-san, actually." She didn't smile. "But my associates call me U-ri. That's the name I usually use. It's who I really am."

Kotaro was beginning to suspect he was in the presence of a classic head case. *This is what I get for posting all those questions on the web. If I'm not careful, she might turn out to be a real pain in the butt.*

"Kotaro." She peered at him intently. "Before you start worrying that I might be some kind of oddball, there's something else you need to worry about first."

"Um...What?"

"I said I did a web search and found your questions."

"That's what you said."

"Doesn't that seem a bit odd to you?"

She had the looks, the style, the aura. Yuriko Morisaki was a head turner. There were only a few people in the cafeteria, but she was getting looks from everybody. Kotaro could feel it. The student who'd just walked past their table made no effort to conceal his interest.

"How do you mean, 'odd'?"

"How did I just up and find you? How did I go from reading your posts to sitting here talking to you?" She looked at him steadily. Her eyes were not large, but her pupils seemed dilated. "I'm not a hacker. I'm not even good at web searches. Finding you here just with your handle and mail address would be way over my head."

Kotaro had to work hard to generate a carefree smile. "So maybe your brother or father's the hacker. Or your boyfriend."

Her expression didn't change, except for a slight smile at the corners of her mouth. "You're logical. I like that."

"Thanks for the vote of confidence."

The student who had passed by earlier was back. He was holding his smartphone to his ear and talking in a loud voice. The performance wasn't convincing. He had bleached blond hair and pierced ears, and a large backpack with a camouflage pattern.

"Sorry to tell you this, but my brother and father aren't hackers. My brother—" She glanced away and paused. "I had a brother, but he's not here anymore."

Kotaro was startled. "Hey, I'm sorry to hear that."

"No, it's all right. He's not dead or anything. He's just not in this world."

Sorry Yuri-chan, but in my book, you are a stone head case.

As Kotaro took a sip of water, he heard the faint but unmistakable sound of a shutter. He turned quickly to see Blondie grinning and pointing his smartphone at Yuriko. He had a sidekick with the same smile and taste in clothes, and a big bag under one arm with the strap slung over the opposite shoulder.

"Hey, knock it off!" Kotaro's voice was sharp as he stood up.

"It's okay." Yuriko's fingers brushed his wrist. "Don't get upset. They can't take my picture."

She smiled when she saw Kotaro's eyes start from his head. "Don't be scared. I'm not a ghost. I cast a barrier spell. No pictures."

Kotaro eyes wouldn't bulge any further, and since there didn't seem to be anything he could do, he sat down.

"You don't like rule breakers, do you?" Yuriko's voice was gentle. "You hate it when people cheat, even when it doesn't matter. My brother was like you."

Maybe Blondie and his sidekick thought Kotaro had bowed out. They walked up to Yuriko, bold as brass.

"Hey, babe. 'Sup?"

"Wanna join our club? It's dope." Blondie's sidekick used too much men's cologne. "The Computer Communication Club. You'll love it."

Blondie's grin turned upside down as he paged through his photos. "What the hell?" he muttered and turned to his friend. "She's not there."

He showed the phone to Sidekick, who peered at the screen and frowned too. "Can't you even take a picture?"

"I'm telling you, I nailed it!"

Yuriko watched this exchange with a smile. She turned away and moved her lips quickly, murmuring. She wasn't talking to Kotaro, or to anyone, in fact.

"Hey, quit yanking!"

Sidekick was bewildered and angry. His bag had twisted itself behind his back and was expanding like a balloon, straining against the straps as though it were trying to escape upward. Blondie shouted with fright. Kotaro almost had the same reaction.

Sidekick's bag hung in midair, tugging hard and pulling its owner backward, like a headstrong dog tugging at its leash and yanking its owner off-balance.

Scattered gasps of surprise rose from the room. Outside, people stopped to watch through the windows.

Blondie's scream prompted Sidekick to throw up his arms. His bag slipped up and away, but instead of falling to the floor, it flew across the room as if thrown by an invisible hand. It thudded onto the floor near the entrance.

"What the hell are you doing?" Sidekick's eyes flashed with anger as he stepped quickly toward Kotaro, but Blondie body checked him and they fell to the floor in a heap.

"Ow!"

"It's not me! I'm not doing anything!" Blondie yelled.

"Quit acting like an idiot and get off me!"

"I told you, it's not me. Something's holding me down!"

Blondie's camouflage backpack was expanding crazily. It kept rising and slamming down on its owner. Then it rose violently, bending Blondie's spine backward. Over by the door, Sidekick's bag started to move again, as though something alive were inside it, and righted itself so abruptly that the straps flew up in the air. Before they could fall again, it hurtled out the door.

Seemingly determined not to be left behind, Blondie's backpack began dragging its howling owner toward the door. Sidekick brought up the rear, close to tears and wailing just as loud.

Almost everyone was on their feet now, along with Kotaro. Everyone except Yuriko Morisaki. She put her chocolate cappuccino on its saucer and shrugged her shoulders. "I guess they had to go."

"How far?"

"Until they run into something." She stood up, looking as if nothing special had happened. "Let's get out of here while everyone's distracted. Come on."

Kotaro had no objections. They left quickly by the opposite door.

"Is there somewhere quiet around here where we can talk?" Yuriko said.

They crossed the street at the edge of campus to the municipal library and a large park that doubled as a disaster evacuation area. Kotaro reflexively broke into a trot and headed into the park.

"You don't have to hurry, you know."

"What did you do back there?"

"Just a little parlor trick." Yuriko was diminutive, but she had no trouble keeping up with him.

"You mumbled something right before it happened. It looked like—I don't know what it looked like. Were you casting a spell or something?"

She raised a shapely eyebrow. "You're a good observer."

So I was right. But how could I be?

Kotaro didn't slow down until he reached the first bench along the path. He was out of breath.

"If a little run like that is enough to make you huff and puff, you must be spending too much time in front of your PC. You ought to get some exercise," Yuriko said.

"I'm huffing and puffing from emotional shock."

"Oh, well. Better sit down, then."

She planted herself on the bench and crossed her legs as though she were quite used to sitting there. "You've never seen that kind of thing before, have you? The being you encountered didn't use spells."

Kotaro still hadn't caught his breath. He stood looking at her. "I still don't understand what you did."

She shrugged her shoulders lightly under the baggy jacket. "I borrowed the power of the books they were carrying."

He gaped at her.

"Both those guys've been ignoring their textbooks for too long. The books were pretty ticked off about it."

Come on. What is this?

"Books have power, you know. They all have a basic power that's the same. They each have their own individual powers too, depending on what they're about."

Kotaro just shook his head.

"They had natural science textbooks. Probably introductory texts, maybe study guides. All I did was borrow the books' power to move on their own. You saw the rest."

The books ran away?

"Books like the ones those guys carry are very young, or babies. It's a sure bet."

"Time out. Hold it a second."

Yuriko wouldn't wait. She glanced through the trees at the glass-enclosed main floor of the library. "There are a lot of young books over there, but one of the Elders is there too. Maybe I should pay my respects on the way home."

Kotaro's head was spinning. He put a hand on the back of the bench for support and sat down unsteadily.

" 'I come from the birthplace of the souls of words.' " Yuriko was abruptly solemn. "That's what the warrior told you. Am I right?"

Kotaro put a hand to his head to steady it. "Did I put that on the web too?"

"Yeah, you did. Was it human?"

Kotaro jerked his hand away from his forehead and stared at her. "Why are you asking that?"

"Because a being that would've used those words wouldn't really look human at all."

Kotaro gulped, loudly.

"Its true form is a terrible monster. You would've been so scared, I doubt you could've exchanged words with it. Still, I guess you must have."

He nodded once, twice. He felt like someone was moving his head. "It was…It had wings."

"A woman with wings sprouting from her back?"

"Yeah. And she was big. She must've been seven feet tall. And she was… She was beautiful."

Yuriko looked very serious. "Ah, yes. The beautiful woman."

"She said she was a warrior."

Yuriko nodded slowly. "She guards the Tower of Inception. She probably told you she was the Guardian of the Third Pillar."

"That's right."

"The guardians of the first nine Pillars are especially powerful. A being like that would never leave its post except in the direst emergency." She whispered to herself, "It's just as Ash feared."

"Ash?"

"An associate of mine." For the first time, her eyes were smiling too. "Someone who helped me once. He's my wolf master."

Kotaro almost said "time out" again, but by now he could see that was pointless. "A wolf. Right. Is that an animal wolf? Or a man with the spirit of a wolf?"

Yuriko looked puzzled. "A man…with the spirit of a wolf. I never looked at it that way. You *are* interesting, Mr. Mishima."

Under different circumstances, this sort of comment from a pretty girl would've been welcome, but not now.

"What is the Circle, *Miss* Morisaki?"

"I'm asking the questions. Why do you want to know?"

Kotaro was losing patience. "Why don't you just cast a spell on me like you did with those guys back there? You're a sorcerer, right? Use your magic. Make me tell you everything."

She shook her head. "Some wolves are powerful wizards. Not me. I can't do just anything. I'm still new at this."

"Oh, okay. That explains it."

"But I can read your words." She cocked her head and looked at him as though sizing him up whole, for the first time.

"You live with your parents and two sisters. Are they twins?"

She didn't wait for an answer. Instead, she blinked once and shifted her pupils, still looking at him. "And there's an older person. A woman. Not a relative. Oh—"

She raised an index finger and wagged it gently. "Correction. You have one sister. Not twins. Your sister has a good friend. You know her very well too."

Yuriko's eyes kept flicking here and there across Kotaro's face. "You have teachers, or mentors. People with a lot of influence over you. A man and a woman. They're married, or lovers. You're very worried about someone too. A friend, or maybe someone you look up to. I can't see him clearly... He's not your older brother."

Kotaro almost swallowed his tongue with astonishment.

Yuriko's wandering gaze stopped. Her eyes narrowed. She almost seemed to be listening for a distant sound.

"That girl, the one who's friends with your sister. Is something happening to her?"

Kotaro was speechless. All he could do was goggle at her.

"Seriously. Something bad, or strange, is happening to her, I think."

"What— How—"

"Complete sentences, please. You want to know how I know." He nodded stiffly.

"The book in your backpack is telling me everything. It's really worried about her. About Mika. That's her book, right? You borrowed it from her, or she gave it to you."

Kotaro dragged his backpack onto his lap and unzipped it. It was filled with a jumble of stuff. He upended it and dumped everything on the bench—textbooks and notebooks and dictionaries. Half-buried in the pile was a slender paperback.

LAND OF THE SUN: ANCIENT EGYPT AND THE RIDDLE OF THE PYRAMIDS

Yes, this book definitely belonged to Mika Sonoi. Kazumi had borrowed it from her, and it had been sitting on a shelf in the living room for some time before he'd stuffed it in his backpack, thinking it might be a good way to kill time.

"Your friend Mika likes this kind of thing." Yuriko's gaze was gentle. "Does she like to read?"

Kotaro finally managed a natural reaction. "Yeah, she does. Me and Kazumi—my sister—don't read much, but Mika loves books."

"Did you read that?"

"No. I was going to, but...I don't even remember when I stuck it in there. I haven't felt like reading much of anything recently. I've had a lot on my mind. Is this—is this book worried about Mika?"

"It's very, very worried about her. She chose it herself and read it cover to cover. They have a connection. But that's not the only reason, it seems." She reached for the book, but stopped.

"It's better if you check it. There's a note in it."

Kotaro opened the book and riffled the pages slowly. It was still practically new. Nothing was written in the margins.

"Look again." Yuriko sounded impatient.

"I looked."

He froze. There was something between the cover of the paperback and the binding—a thin, tiny, light-pink Post-it. He might've read the whole book and never noticed it. There was a message in small, rounded script.

If you touch Gaku, I'm going to kill you.

Kotaro sat paralyzed with astonishment for a full ten seconds with the tiny note in his hand.

"Girls use those little stickers all the time to pass notes in class."

Kotaro knew. He'd seen girls using them all through middle school and high school.

Yuriko plucked the note from his fingers. "Don't rip it up." He had been about to do just that. "You borrowed this from her, then?"

"Kazumi borrowed it from Mika, and I borrowed it from Kazumi."

"Kazumi's your sister, then. Anyway, Mika didn't know about the note. If she had, she wouldn't have lent the book to someone. Would you agree?"

"Sure, I guess so."

"This is an important piece of evidence about what's happening to her. You can't throw it away."

"But I can't put it back where it was."

"Of course. I'm not saying you should. It wouldn't be fair to the book. You should put it somewhere safe."

Kotaro felt faintly defensive for some reason. "I know what this is about, but the trouble's blown over already."

The bad blood over Gaku and the soft tennis club had ended. Kazumi had said so herself. It had ended so suddenly that it almost seemed strange. Glitter Kitty had gone quiet.

"Things were bad at the end of last year—at least, that's when I found out about it, but it'd been going on for a while before that. That's probably when someone put that note in the book."

"When did you borrow it?"

Kotaro's mind was blank. He couldn't even remember the last time he'd checked his pack.

"Look at the colophon."

"The what?"

"The last page. It shows the publication date. The book looks new."

The publication date was October 25 of the previous year. Kotaro was relieved.

"See? Mika's a fast reader. If she read this first and lent it to Kazumi, that would be the middle of November at the latest. That was when things were boiling over, supposedly. But everything's settled down now."

"Looks like some kind of conflict over a guy."

"I guess so, yeah."

"What year are the girls?" Yuriko asked.

"Kazumi will be a ninth grader in April. Mika's a year behind her."

"I wouldn't be too complacent then. You have no idea what girls of that age can get up to."

This struck Kotaro as a little condescending—after all, Yuriko wasn't much older than Kazumi and Mika.

"It's because they're young. They don't have the capacity for judgment. Girls can get pretty extreme."

"Well, 'I'm going to kill you' *is* pretty extreme."

"Not if it's just words. The problem is the story behind the words." Her expression was suddenly intensely focused, like a child who loves to observe insects and has just found a colorful, poisonous bug on the underside of a leaf.

"The story?" Kotaro thought he understood what she meant, but her choice of words was puzzling. "I think you mean the motivation, right? The reason?"

"No." She shook her head. "The story. Everything is a story. Human beings live their stories as they create them. Each person spins a story, and their words come out of those stories."

That's backward. Words come first, then stories. I mean, come on.

"I just read your story, Kotaro." She leaned toward him. "I read the flow of the story you're submerged in, even now. How else could I have known about your family? Or your friends?"

"The flow of my *story*?"

"It's like a flow of energy. But it's hard to explain in words." She stroked her cheek impatiently with a fingertip. The gesture had a girlish freshness.

"I'd almost like to call it an 'aura,' but everybody uses that word. It makes it sound phony."

"Yup, it's phony all right," Kotaro said.

"Still, my reading was on the mark, don't you think?"

He didn't answer. Yuriko took a deep breath and scanned his face carefully.

"You're a very smart person."

"What—"

"You've had a very strange, dangerous experience. Way more than what you saw with me today. Yet your feet are still on the ground. Most people are different. If they have even one experience that's totally outside their world, they go off the deep end. But you're not like that. You're onto a big mystery and you're hungry for the truth. Yet when the truth finds you, you don't just swallow it whole."

I think *she's praising me.*

"I can solve your mystery for you. But to do that—to do it the right way, in a way that's true for you—I've got to know more. So could you tell me? How did you end up meeting this winged warrior? I need to know everything, from beginning to end, with nothing left out."

Kotaro gave her another sidelong look. "What happened to the ESP?"

"You and I are from the same region. I *can* read your story. But where you made contact with something from another region, that I can't read. I know something happened to you. I can see how it's influencing you, but I can't see what actually happened. And that's probably a good thing. If I made a stab at reading the part of your story that overlaps with another region, things could get...messy."

Kotaro's disorientation was starting to turn into a headache.

"That person you're so worried about—he's involved with another region too, isn't he?"

"You read that?"

"No. It's just a logical assumption."

"We work at the same place. His name's Kenji Morinaga."

"So he's around the same age. Then that other person, he's older than you—way older than you, from your point of view. You feel close to him too, I think. He's involved with the being you encountered, just like your friend from work. That makes it hard for me to read him clearly."

Kotaro hung his head. He was drained. Emotionally, he was on his knees. "Okay, but I warn you, it's a long story."

He told her everything, truthfully and concisely. Yuriko barely moved during the entire account. She only interrupted him a few times to confirm a name.

When his story was finally over, she turned her head to gaze at the library. The glass exterior glowed golden in the late afternoon sun.

"All right, first things first," she said finally and smiled. "Don't worry about your friend Kenji. He's alive. He's just not in our region now. Those other people who disappeared, they're in that other region too."

"Can they get back?"

"Probably."

"But not for sure?"

"It's not a hundred percent certain. It depends on what they want."

"What they *want*?" Kotaro couldn't help but frown.

"Kenji and the others—they weren't kidnapped. They aren't trapped in Galla's weapon. It's like they're making a deal with her. At least that's my guess."

"Do you really expect me to believe that?"

"It's the best I can offer. I've never dealt with a Tower guardian. All I can do is judge based on precedent."

And you wouldn't take a test without studying the sample answers first, I bet.

"If it's a deal, that means Kenji gets something out of it," he said.

"You'd think. Except in this case, his reward is what he's giving up."

"Could you please start making sense?"

"Galla is gathering something from this region, something people have. She's gathering desire. Or craving. Yearning."

"She said she was gathering power."

"That was the truth. Desire is power. It's the most fundamental power human beings have. The flip side of desire is inhibition. These two drives are always competing to find some kind of balance in people's hearts."

"That's too simple by half. Desire isn't a source of power."

"Then what is?"

"Stuff like love, or creativity."

"But isn't desire behind everything? You desire what pulls at your heart. You have a desire to create something. You do what you do because you want to. Am I wrong?"

"But some people love without being loved in return."

"All that means is that their desire for love can be satisfied just by giving it."

"You're not totally convincing me. But how is inhibition just as important?"

"Of course it's important. If you loved someone and couldn't control your love, things would end badly. Same for creativity. If people couldn't put the brakes on their creativity—if they just created without concern for others—society would be in chaos."

"Why? How?"

"You meet people like that every now and then. People who make their own rules." She shrugged. "Like that guy who tried to pick me up back there. If he sees a girl he likes, he takes her picture without even asking. It's rotten manners and totally outrageous, and ignores the other person's feelings. But guys like that have already decided it's okay. He's okay with it, so that makes it okay."

"Is that really an example of creativity?"

"Sure it is. Everything people do is creation."

Kotaro couldn't think of a comeback.

"Kenji and those other people who disappeared had a supreme desire, and they lived with it every day without it consuming them. But the effort it took to hold back that desire was making them suffer. I think Galla came to this region looking for people like that, people whose hearts were out of balance, so she could harvest their desires."

"So what's in it for the people who disappeared?"

"She took away their burden, the thing that was making them suffer because their hearts were out of balance. She gave them relief, even if the relief is only temporary. She gets the desire, they get relief. That's the exchange."

Kotaro shook his head vigorously. "But look what happened to them! Is that worth it? What kind of desire could make them suffer enough to want to do that?"

"There are lots of possibilities. If you're homeless, maybe you want to see your family again or rejoin society. Or have a real job."

"What about Kenji? He had a family and a job and school. Friends. He had everything."

"Then there was probably something else he desired with all his heart. Some thing, or some result. He just didn't tell you about it, that's all. Also, this older guy you look up to? He changed after Galla purified him. It's the same thing. You said he was a retired detective?"

"Yeah. He still looks the part."

"He probably wants a job. He can still work. He can contribute to society. He needs a goal in life. A purpose."

Shigenori had devoted himself to solving the riddle of the gargoyle. To him, it had been a "case." Kotaro felt a chill as he remembered. "Galla told him he'd harvested too much evil."

"He was like a fisherman, driven to gather evil with his net. He couldn't stop himself. The weight of all that evil—no, the satisfaction he got when he trapped another sinner—was something he couldn't let go of. That must be what Galla meant."

Her expression softened. "It's not forever, you know. In time, your friend will return to the way he was. As long as the heart is alive, desire always blooms again."

"Why didn't she just take us, then? Like she did Kenji and the others."

"You can answer that yourself. It would've been dangerous. If she'd taken you both, that wouldn't have been the end of it, especially since you and Kenji were friends."

"So she took away the thing that made Shigenori a threat to her and left him behind."

"And she only threatened you. She probably assumed that was more than enough."

Hearing this from a tenth grader made Kotaro feel more miserable than ever.

"Galla said she was sorry, didn't she?"

"Yeah. A few times."

"I think she was telling the truth there too. She knew both of you were worried about Kenji. She felt bad about it, and that's why she dealt with you mercifully."

"I don't know. I still can't shake the feeling that Galla didn't think I was worth worrying about."

"Listen to me, Kotaro. The guardians of the tower aren't evil. Galla wouldn't go out and harvest people without a reason. You've got to understand that."

Kotaro was no longer sure what was evil and what wasn't. He wasn't even sure if he understood what evil was.

"Why do you think Galla needs to gather power?"

Yuriko shook her head. "No idea. Only Galla can answer that."

"But it must be something important."

"I think it must be something so important, it affects the very stability of her region. That would explain why Ash is worried." She smiled. "Now it's my turn to answer *your* questions. Like, what the Circle is."

Kotaro unconsciously sat up straight.

"The Circle is the sum total of all the stories that make up this world."

"*Stories?*"

"The world is right here. Isn't it?" Yuriko spread her fingers and gazed up at the sky. "The universe is here. We can't see it, but we know it's there. Science proves it. But we can't live our lives based on science alone.

"Human beings live in a world of objects and phenomena, but those are not the only things we need to live. We *interpret* our world, and we project our desires and beliefs on that interpreted world. Only then can we live as human beings. Those desires and beliefs are stories, and the Circle is the sum of all of them—all the stories we tell about the world we subjectively experience. Because everyone in the world creates his or her own story, the Circle is much larger than the world of things that exist. It encompasses regions beyond counting.

"This reality we live in—this is a region. Japan is a region. Regions can be big, or they can be tiny. The Earth itself is a region—a region made up of all the stories of all the people who live here."

"Ti...ti—"

"Time out?

"Um, yeah. Listen, Yuriko. You're wrong."

"How so?"

"Nationalities and countries don't exist because of shared stories. They exist because of shared history."

She smiled confidently. "That's true. Except that history is just another story."

"Oh, come on! What do you think historians do? They don't make stuff up."

"Are you sure? Can they go back in time and check? Historians give us their conjectures about what happened and why. Conjectures, stories—it's all the same thing."

He wanted to disagree, but he was floundering.

"Scientists never say 'Now we know everything about such-and-such' or 'Our knowledge is pure, 100 percent truth.' If they did, that *would* be a lie."

Kotaro was ready to throw up his hands. *I'm losing a debate to a high school hottie.*

"The further scientists push back the boundaries of the unknown," she continued, "the longer that perimeter gets. The more we know, the more we don't know. That's what scientists do. It's their job. They're always formulating theories and conjectures about what lies beyond the boundary. It's a creative process, and all those explanations they're creating are stories too. Just because a theory turns out to 'work' doesn't change the fact that it's a story.

"A good scientist knows where the border with the unknown lies, at least in his own field. He never blurs the line between known and unknown—they have to be kept separate at all costs. But for people who aren't scientists, the line between known and unknown isn't all that clean and sharp. The same even goes for scientists, when it's outside their field. Then they're just as likely as the next person to blur the line. So the stories keep multiplying and spreading out farther and farther.

"Now this," she added carefully, "is not a problem, in itself. Stories are not evil. After all, they're made up of people's hopes and their joy in being alive. Or they can make people feel better. Teach them something useful, like justice or compassion.

"Yet ultimately, stories contain the seeds of evil, because they represent their own reality. Even stories that people generate out of compassion have an intimate connection with the karma of their weavers."

Kotaro's mouth was ahead of his brain. "That sounds like religion to me."

Yuriko's eyes sparkled. She nodded. "Religion is a story too. So is God. That's the greatest story humanity ever told."

"That kind of thinking could get you in trouble in some parts of the world."

"Sure it could. You make one story the basis for everything. If people don't agree with you, attack them. Like the Inquisition during Europe's Middle Ages. Or terrorism spread by fundamentalists. All of these are evils spawned by stories. They happen when stories bring out the evil in people. It's a simple concept, but it has big implications.

"The two of us sitting here now, talking. That's a story. It's us, interpreting the world together. People can't live without their interpretations of the world. That gives birth to the Circle, and from there it keeps growing."

She suddenly leaned toward Kotaro. "Where do you think stories come from?"

He drew back in surprise. "Where else? From people's heads." *Or maybe their hearts.*

"No. That's wrong. All stories come from a single source. They flow out of the source and return to it. That source is called the Nameless Land.

"In the Nameless Land, there is a pair of huge wheels called the Great Wheels of Inculpation. The turning of those wheels sends stories out into the Circle and draws them back again. The Nameless Land is the source that keeps stories circulating in the Circle."

Kotaro rolled his eyes in aggravation. "How would you even know such a thing?"

"I've seen it. I went there to save my brother. He went there too." A cloud seemed to pass over her face.

"Inculpation...Are you talking about accusation? For crimes?"

"That's right. People create stories, and their stories devour them."

"But you just said stories aren't evil!"

"They're not. But karma is karma. Sin is sin."

"I give up. This is nonsense. Listen, can I point something out to you?"

"Feel free."

"If our talking to each other here is a story, then this Nameless Land thing is a story too. You know that, right?"

"Of course."

Just like that. Kotaro felt the wind leaking from his sails.

"The Nameless Land is another region, another story," she said. "I wouldn't argue with that. The only 'real' thing is the Circle itself. No one can escape from it...And no one needs to," she murmured.

He took a deep breath. This was going nowhere. She was running him in circles. He had to bring her down to earth.

"Are the Nameless Land and the Tower of Inception different regions?"

Yuriko nodded firmly, yes.

"Okay, the Nameless Land is the source of all stories. What is the Tower of Inception?"

"The source of all words. It's the region where the souls of words are born. The Nameless Land and the Tower of Inception are a dyad. Stories and words, words and stories. It's impossible to say which comes first. They're like a circle—two snakes, each with the other's tail in its mouth."

Kotaro burst out laughing. "Words come first! That's obvious."

"Why is that?"

"Can't tell a story without words."

"But stories about the origins of words *are* stories. How could people use words if they never appeared in a story before?"

Kotaro stared at her open-mouthed for a few seconds before he could answer. "I feel like I'm talking to the Cheshire Cat."

Yuriko laughed joyously and clapped her hands. "Kotaro, you're so *interesting*!"

It's not a joke, kid. I don't care how cute you are. Not every guy is going to let you lead him around by the nose.

"I've been sitting here listening to you mixing actual places with imaginary ones, like they were both part of the same reality," Kotaro said. "Nameless Land, Tower of Inception—they're just imaginary locations. You know that."

She gazed back at him, cool and unruffled. "They *are* part of the same reality. They're all regions."

"Quit talking nonsense!"

"Why is it nonsense? The world exists and it's real. Other worlds are real, but they don't exist. That's the only difference. But as regions, they're on the same footing. Wouldn't you agree?"

"Sorry. No."

"What about *The Chronicles of Narnia*?"

Mika loved this series of fantasy novels. She'd bought the books after seeing the movies. She'd said the books were even more fascinating.

"Lots of people are familiar with the Kingdom of Narnia. They know about the things that happen there and the creatures who live there. They talk to each other about the stories and reinforce each other's interest."

"But they don't exist."

"They're still real."

"There's a huge difference."

"Are you sure? Can you dismiss something that doesn't exist as meaningless? Or say nonexistent things don't affect us? Are things that don't exist just for enjoyment or killing time in this world of ours? Are you ready to say they're just illusions we consume when and as we feel like it?"

I'm talking to the Cheshire Cat again.

"That's not what I meant. Of course things that don't exist can affect us. Sometimes even physically," Kotaro said.

"Like Galla." Yuriko's gaze was level. "I can see why an encounter like that would be so confusing. But you didn't run and tell your friends about your strange experience and have fun with it and leave it at that. You didn't write it off as some hallucination. You want to understand what happened to you. You want to know more. That's dangerous. That's why I had to find you."

"You said you might have to eliminate me. Is curiosity a crime?"

"It is in this case. It's childish."

"I don't need to hear that from you." He looked grim. "I want to bring Kenji back."

"He's not dead. He made a deal with Galla of his own free will and he's satisfied. Do you still want to bring him back?"

"You don't know what he was thinking. You're just guessing."

"You accept statements like that from people all the time without demanding proof. Can't you accept my explanation this once?"

Can't we just chalk up what we saw to a bad dream?

"Kotaro, you told me you made eye contact with Kenji when you saw him that night."

"Yes. From within the scythe."

"Did he look like he wanted you to save him? Could you feel him saying 'Save me, get me out of here'?"

"I don't know. I still couldn't believe everything that was happening."

"That's a tricky answer." She was right. Kotaro looked away at the grass beneath his feet.

"What would make Kenji do a deal with a creature like that?" he murmured.

"It would've been his secret. Something only he knew."

"He didn't look like he was carrying around a secret that big."

"If he had, it wouldn't have been a secret, would it?" She'd scored a point.

"If I really, really, wanted to know why Galla's here and what Kenji's doing right now, do you think Galla would appear before me?"

Yuriko's shoulders sagged. She sighed. "*That* would be like crossing a minefield wearing snowshoes. Is that what you want?"

Kotaro laughed at the simile, but Yuriko wasn't smiling.

"You say I'm acting like things that exist and things that don't are the same," she said. "How are you any different? You're treating Galla and the region she comes from as if it exists, but it doesn't, even though it's still real."

Another point scored.

"...What is a wolf?" Kotaro asked.

"What's this? Are you trying to change the subject?"

"Are you trying to dodge the question by answering a question with a question?"

Now she looked genuinely irritated. Kotaro scratched his head. "I'm only asking because I really want to know. What are wolves? People who get mixed up with regions that are real but don't exist?"

Yuriko didn't answer immediately. She seemed to be pondering an answer.

"No, that's not right. Not everyone who has that experience becomes a wolf." She paused again, as though searching for the right words.

"In stories, people sometimes encounter a power so strong that it changes them completely. Whether it changes them for the better or the worse depends on time and circumstance. They can go either way, because good and evil are two sides of the same coin. But if they change for the worse, it leads to a great tragedy. To conflict."

"Conflict? You mean war?"

"People oppose each other. Or one group of people subjugates another and oppresses them. There is no form of conflict that doesn't manifest.

"The source of these dangerous stories is sealed in the Nameless Land, the origin of all stories. But sometimes the seal is broken. Even if the source is sealed, the countless stories that branched off from the source when it was unbound take the form of copies. We wolves search for copies of those dangerous stories. There are many of us here in our world, in this region. This is our mission—to hunt the dangerous stories that infest the Circle, and their copies."

Kotaro looked so astonished that Yuriko was forced to laugh. "Oh come on, it's not that bad."

"That's book burning. Hunting for books? Isn't that an attack on freedom of speech?"

"No one's suppressing anybody's freedom of speech. All we do is let others know about these dangerous copies and try to keep them out of their hands as best we can. If people are infected with the poison in one of these books, we find them and help them understand that they're not weaving their own lives. They're living a story that has obsessed them. We try to bring them back to the real world. That's all we do. That's all we *can* do.

"But sometimes," she murmured, "we're too late." The black of her pupils seemed to deepen into a profound darkness.

"The Nameless Land and the Tower of Inception are immensely old regions, so old that it's impossible to say when they were created. It's not like someone—a specific weaver—created them. They arose from the hearts of countless people, from a vague sense that stories and language originated in worlds like that. People are in awe of them, though they don't have a definite image of them. Those feelings spawned the Nameless Land and the Tower of Inception. They didn't become history, or religion, or superstition. They remain as they were when they were created, from time out of memory.

"It's a simple allegory, nothing more, nothing less. That's why it's so powerful. It's not dangerous, but it has tremendous power."

Kotaro looked at her closely. "If these regions are so old, is that where the dead are? Could that be where people go when they die?"

Yuriko stared at him blankly. "That's a strange question. What would make you think dead people go to the sources of stories and words?"

"There's this little girl. She thinks Galla is the god of death because of those huge black wings."

Kotaro told her about the girl named Mana. He told her everything, including the idea about the world of the dead that Mana had planted in his mind.

Partway through his story, Yuriko closed her eyes. When he finished, she opened them. "Explaining a mother's death to a five-year-old must be the hardest thing in the world," she said gently.

"You're right."

"But you told her just what she needed to hear. And you were right when you decided that the world of the dead is real because of the words of the living."

"So . . . ?"

"Tell her about the world of the dead in your own words."

Your mother is a star. She's in heaven. She's always looking down on you. You can't see her anymore, but she's right beside you, even now.

"Tell her whatever makes sense to you. What matters is what is in your heart. That's what makes it a story.

"Since I became a wolf, I've come to see it this way: stories came into being so people could resist death." Her voice had the strength of conviction. "Life is limited. It's once only. Death comes to everyone without exception, fair or not. Humanity created stories to triumph over the terror of death and help them overcome the pain of loss, telling and retelling them from generation to generation. Stories of all kinds, stories about individuals, about the history of nations. Short stories and epic sagas. They all have the same function.

"Now, many of these stories talk about the land of the dead. People die, but that's not the end. There is a next life. Maybe they're reincarnated, or they live on in heaven. The point of the stories is that death is not the end. The people we love don't cease to exist. That's what the stories tell us. But they're not true." Her voice slowly took on quiet strength.

"Death is final. It is the end. Everything that lives dies, and the dead exist nowhere and will never return. But stories are the struggle against that truth. They deny the truth. They comfort the living, encourage them, and give them the light and the hope to go on living. That is the significance, the meaning, of why there are stories—to give us the creativity and imagination to resist the truth that life is once only.

"Fight death. That's what stories tell us. They shout it in the face of naked reality. We will *not* disappear. That's why we tell them. They're the best way to say that. So tell Mana your story in your own words. 'Mama's in heaven. She's always with you.' Whatever fits. Tell her what you hope is true. But if your story gives her hope, you must watch over her after that. If you can't be with her all the time, then at least pray for her."

"Pray? Why?"

"Pray that when she's a healthy adult, she'll be able to understand that the story you told her was not true. Her mother is dead and gone. The death of another is terribly hard to bear, and very sad. But pray that she'll realize that her mother is gone and will never, ever come back to her again."

She looked steadily at Kotaro. The darkness that had flitted across her pupils was gone now, or perhaps veiled.

"But she'll also understand that the story you told her was the truth, for her. 'My mother is still here, in my heart.' That's enough.

"The dead live in our hearts. That *is* the afterlife. The living cherish this thought. Pray that she becomes someone who can believe that."

"Pray that when she grows up, she can understand?"

Yuriko nodded. "Adults live by weaving stories. They also live by escaping them. When they get trapped in a story, they end up the way you are now." Yuriko suppressed a chuckle. "You're funny, Kotaro. You understand things perfectly, but you don't know you understand, so you're confused. Have you noticed?"

How can I notice what doesn't make sense?

"Your trying to find Galla is no different from telling a five-year-old girl a story about the afterlife to give her strength, then trying to go and actually find it."

"But I *met* Galla!"

"You encountered something real that doesn't exist, that's all." She reached out and touched his arm. "Do you understand? It was an accident. It wasn't your fault. It's not because you're special or anything. It was just an accident, that's all. The mistake would be to take it further.

"Those desires Galla is harvesting—those cravings. They don't have anything to do with you. You should be thankful for that."

Kotaro frowned. "There are things I want. I have a few complexes too."

"I'm not talking about those kinds of desires. You didn't lose your home. You're not dying of hunger or thirst. You haven't been stripped of your dignity as a person."

He brought his face closer to hers and answered between clenched teeth. "Are you talking about the homeless? Are you saying I can't understand what they want?"

Yuriko looked at him with gentle eyes and smiled. "Do you think you can?"

Kotaro felt like a boxer whose best punch just connected with empty space. His mouth was open, but his voice wouldn't come.

"Are you really so unimaginably unhappy?" she asked.

"Well... not exactly."

"Maybe you have some cravings that are more dramatic. Getting revenge, say. Something you want so bad you'd be willing to give up a few years of life to get it." She peered at him closely. "How about raising someone from the dead?"

For the first time, Kotaro felt something dreadful emanating from the attractive young girl on the bench next to him.

It wasn't that he was alarmed by what she said. It was how her eyes looked when she said it, as if she were seeing something. Whatever it was, it was something in her memory. She was seeing something in the past.

When Kotaro had been a junior in high school, he'd dated a girl who had lost her younger sister in a fire when they were both very young. Now and then her eyes would take on the same look. Even when the subject was totally unrelated, or when they were watching a movie or getting a burger and fries at McDonald's, she'd suddenly get that look, and it had always chilled him to the marrow. *She's remembering.* He'd never know what triggered it, but there she'd be, remembering what she'd seen and heard the night of the fire—what she'd had to see and had to hear.

It happened too often, and after half a year they'd broken up, though she'd been a pretty girl and very gentle.

"Listen, um, Yuriko..." He spoke softly. She blinked again, returning to reality, and turned to look at him. Her eyes were normal now. But before he could say more, she stood up.

"Anyway, that's my advice to you," she said crisply. "Mind your business and don't do anything reckless. That company you work for? Aren't they helping the police catch that serial amputator?"

Kotaro wasn't sure whether he cared to hear that sort of advice from this particular girl. "We don't work for the police."

"But you do monitor what goes on, on the net."

"We have lots of other things to cover."

"Then cover them. Please."

That was when it hit him. "Aren't you wolves supposed to be hunting killers like that too?"

Yuriko was already turning to go, but she spun round so fast her ponytail slapped her cheek. "What do you mean?"

"We're talking about a serial killer. The evidence indicates he didn't have a particular grudge against his victims. He's in the grip of his own personal obsession. To satisfy it, he's killing people. It doesn't matter who. His victims were unlucky enough to cross his path at a time and place of his choosing. Doesn't that mean the killer is weaving his own story? One he can't escape from? It's a story that makes sense from the killer's point of view. A very dangerous story. Isn't that the kind of story you wolves are supposed to be hunting?"

She shook her head so hard her ponytail flipped from side to side. "The killer's living a story, but he's not being influenced by a copy. As long as the story is his alone, there's nothing we can do about it."

"You just don't want to."

She snorted dismissively. "You don't know anything about us. We're not concerned about whether or not the police catch serial killers. It's the stories these crimes generate afterward. We have to watch them very carefully to see if the stories take on a life of their own, or wither away with time, or get established as strong stories because people's intelligence and common sense aren't strong enough to resist them."

She peered at him suddenly with narrowed eyes. "But I think you're right. Whether there's one killer or more than one, someone is being driven by desire."

"You think? A psycho killer with psycho lust."

"Those desires are Galla's prey, not ours. If she felt like it, she could probably do a deal with the killer and put an end to the murders. I don't know if that would be the right thing, though. Goodbye, Kotaro." She waved a hand and set off down the path leading deeper into the park.

"Hey, do you know where you're going?" Kotaro looked around quickly for a board with a map of the park. When he looked down the path again, she was already out of sight. How had she gotten away so fast?

"One more thing."

Her voice was right behind him. He stood up so fast he nearly leapt into the air. "Don't scare me like that!"

She was scarcely a yard away, arms folded. "Keep a careful eye on Mika. Her troubles aren't over. This is no time to relax."

"H-how do you know that?"

"Because her book is worried. I told you. Books have power. They have wisdom. They have hearts, too. Promise me!" She thrust a finger in his face. "Keep her safe!"

Kotaro was shaking with astonishment. He gave her a jerky nod. "Okay, okay."

She turned and walked away, not hurrying, as though she had nothing on her mind at all.

4

Mind your business and don't do anything reckless.

Kotaro decided to take Yuriko's advice to heart. It seemed like the best thing to do given the situation.

With no resolution for the loose ends he was holding, all he could do was wait for the next development, just as Yuriko Morisaki, a beautiful young girl with a preachy attitude, showing up out of nowhere had been a development.

On the other hand, if nothing at all happened, it would be best to let things drop. Kotaro would wait to see which way they went.

Before the new term started, he made one more visit to Shigenori in the hospital, and to the Nagasakis. At the hospital, Shigenori was off somewhere getting X-rayed, but his wife was in his room. Kotaro had the feeling that this smartly dressed, genial woman was almost wasted on Shigenori.

"I got to know your husband online," he said, which at least sounded plausible.

"Really? All he seems to think about since the end of last year is that computer of his."

"When I heard he was a detective, I was so fascinated that I pestered him into meeting."

"You must've been disappointed then. He's just a regular old guy. Not very approachable, I'm afraid."

Kotaro didn't know what story Shigenori had cooked up to explain that night at the tea caddy building, followed by his sudden admission to the hospital. But he had the feeling that whatever it was, Toshiko had seen right through it. She was a very smart lady.

After half an hour chatting with no sign of Shigenori, he excused himself. Toshiko cheerfully invited him to drop by once her husband was out of the hospital.

At the Nagasaki mansion, Mana greeted him like any little girl. Her face was still not as animated as other children's her age, and she didn't speak much, but Hatsuko said she was opening up more and more each day.

"We owe everything to you. I don't know how to thank you."

After he had untangled himself from Hatsuko's weepy embrace, he spent an hour or so in the big garden playing ball with Mana. Kotaro loved her throaty giggling; it sounded like someone was tickling her. For the first time in a long while, he relaxed and enjoyed himself. Seeing how far Mana had come since their first meeting, the mysteries and strange happenings of life hardly seemed to matter.

April came. Kotaro was a sophomore. Kazumi was in ninth grade; her high school entrance exams lay ahead. Mika was an eighth grader.

Spurred by Yuriko's final warning, Kotaro managed—after the usual struggle—to get some face time alone with his sister so he could ask how Mika was doing. Kazumi was flatly irritated at having to deal with the same topic again, but her reaction eased Kotaro's mind.

"Why do you keep bringing that up? It's all over. Completely. I mean, you're the one who said problems like that blow over all of a sudden."

"Okay, I know I said that. But if the problem dies down too suddenly, you know, something minor might set it off again or something. What about this guy Gaku? The one who started it all? Did he get into the school he was aiming for?"

"No. He didn't." Kazumi was caustic. "He was totally sure he'd make the cut, then he goes and blows it just like that. He had to scramble to come up with Plan B. He finally got in someplace else. Not as good, obviously. But they have a strong tennis team. He's been blabbing to everyone that he'll come out of this even more on top."

She laughed coldly. Kotaro had never heard her so dismissive.

"So, what about Mika?"

"She blew him off completely. So much for the big confession of love. I'm sure he's a lot more worried about his future right now.

"Glitter Kitty stopped posting, and all those girls who were kissing up to Gaku are devastated. I mean, he didn't even come close to getting in. Now he looks even worse 'cause he was acting so stuck-up before. His reputation is toast."

"Serves him right."

"It sure does, but that sounds a little childish coming from you."

Kazumi had a sharp tongue. If that was how things stood, then they must really be okay, Kotaro thought.

Becoming a sophomore didn't bring much new to his college life, but things at Kumar were changing. Kaname and Kotaro had a new workmate named Makoto Miyama. With a last name that began with the same letter as Kotaro's, they would have sat near each other in middle school and high school. That would have suited Kotaro, because he liked Makoto. He and Kaname quickly became friends too. She called him Mako-chan.

Makoto wasn't in college. He'd just completed a year of study in computer science at a technical school. In this industry it helped to be young, and what was most important was hands-on experience, not classroom study—which is what he said when he showed up one day at Kumar, résumé in hand, and asked for a job. Seigo must've liked his boldness, because he hired him on the spot.

"But Mako-chan, they're closing this office pretty soon," Kaname said.

"I know. It's okay. I'm from Sapporo. Kumar needs people like me. Seigo told me working here would show me there are some things you need to learn in school. If he's right, I might think about going to college in Sapporo."

"You're a very forward-thinking young guy," Kaname enthused.

"We're young too, you know," Kotaro said.

"But Mako-chan's more, you know, pure and innocent. It's blowing my mind."

Kaname was a sophomore too. She had a heavier class load and her seminars were taking up more of her time. Having a third member of the team was more than welcome. Makoto learned the ropes quickly.

The serial murder case had stalled completely. The news had reported everything there was to report too many times. The lack of fresh information was becoming embarrassing.

Could crimes that were so flagrant and reprehensible, so lurid and shocking to the public, really just peter out unsolved? Kotaro asked his father this over dinner one evening when Takayuki, unusually, arrived home in time to join them.

"Sure, it's happened before," he said as he tucked into the food. Kotaro was taken by surprise.

"I didn't know you followed that stuff, Dad."

"I don't. One of the weeklies had a special feature. Some of the journalists covering this story are starting to think it may never be solved. If we're lucky, just when people have forgotten it happened, the killer will screw up and get arrested for something minor. Then when they check his fingerprints or DNA, they'll find out he's the killer."

"That sounds pretty optimistic."

"That's how they caught Tsutomu Miyazaki. Most serial killers in the States are picked up for something minor too."

That's no way to solve a case, though Kotaro. He sent Kaname and Makoto a mail asking if they'd heard anything from the team that Seigo had formed to work on the case.

Pulled the plug, Kaname wrote back, copying Makoto.

I heard it was disbanded, Makoto added, copying Kaname. *Are you going to try to solve it yourself?*

This left Kotaro even more irritated. If only the Serial Amputator case could be solved, it would make the other mysteries weighing on him a little easier to bear.

The search for Kenji Morinaga was going nowhere. Everyone's interest and concern seemed to be dwindling. The detective in charge of the investigation stopped visiting Kumar. Seigo and Narita didn't mention it, and as for Kaname, pretty much all she could talk about was Mako-chan this, Mako-chan that. *Are they dating or something? Does she have a crush on him?*

Ayuko Yamashina was different too, and that had a certain influence on Kumar. Her search for sponsors for her new nonprofit venture had transformed her into an aggressive media promoter. She even landed a spot on a weekly national news program as a commentator.

Ayuko was attractive and knew how to dress the part. She was brilliant, in fact, and eloquent enough to beat Seigo in a debate if she had a mind to. She immediately captured the spotlight, but this also made her a target of gossip and slander on the Internet. Ninety-five percent of it was ridiculous, but the rest was viciously hostile threats or the twisted, obsessive comments of stalkers. Security at Kumar was tightened and Ayuko avoided going anywhere alone. She and Seigo stopped visiting each other's homes and finally moved in together.

Kotaro felt a little lonely, but things were clear now, which had its advantages. He genuinely felt good in a way. He wasn't just putting up a front.

▼

"Kota*roh*, please take me to your campus!"

"For what?"

"Ooh, that's so antisocial."

It was the end of April, just before the Golden Week holidays. Summer was ahead of schedule, and Kotaro was wearing a T-shirt under his thin parka. Kaname's sleeveless one-piece had drawn a tart "Isn't it a little early for that?" from him.

With only the two of them to cover the shifts, Kotaro and Kaname had hardly had any chance to socialize outside Kumar. But with Makoto on the island, things were different.

"I just wanted to visit a nice city campus." Kaname pouted.

"Sure, if you say so. Don't you want to invite Mako-chan too?"

"Why?"

This was a difficult question to tackle head-on. Kotaro couldn't think of an answer.

"Are you jealous, Ko-chan?"

Is it okay to ask me that outright? And what's with "Ko-chan"? It sounds a little weird.

"I'm surprised. I thought you only had eyes for our president." Kaname grinned.

"Time out—what's that supposed to mean?" Asking women for time out seemed to be the story of Kotaro's life.

"It means what it means. You're smitten with her, aren't you?" Kaname was a true lit major. Women her age never used "smitten."

"I *admire* her. Get it straight."

"It's not very masculine if you can't even admit your real feelings."

And so it went from there. They decided to visit Kotaro's campus on May Day, in the middle of the vacation.

"I want to visit the library. And have lunch in the cafeteria, definitely."

"Who's paying?"

"Who do you think?"

Kumar never slept, not during Golden Week or any other holiday, but the company was humane enough to let members arrange their shifts so they could spend more than a day or two with their loved ones. As it happened, Makoto also ended up with a day off on May 1.

"Would you mind if I joined you guys? It looks like we're off on the same day. I want to try the cafeteria." A recent TV program had featured a tour of campus cafeterias known for their food. Kotaro's school had rated near the top.

"Are you kidding? So that's the real reason," Kotaro said to Kaname.

"I heard you're one of those people who can pig out and stay thin," Makoto chimed in.

"Why don't the two of you just make a date of it?" Kotaro said sarcastically.

"What?" Makoto said. "I've got a girlfriend."

I don't understand kids these days. Kotaro threw in the towel.

▼

They rendezvoused on campus at ten that morning and audited a lecture on the history of science. Attendance wasn't taken, and the lecture hall was mostly empty because of the holiday. It almost helped that Makoto and Kaname were there.

"I heard your professor is famous in his field," Kaname said.

"You're joking. This class is super boring."

"Teaching isn't his main job. He's an academic," Makoto said. "That's the basic contradiction of higher education. Students come to learn, but academics don't come to teach."

In the library, Kaname and Makoto flitted among the shelves, entranced. They had different interests, but both loved books. Kotaro settled in a corner of the reading room, booted up his laptop and surfed the web to kill the hour before lunch.

"Can we come back after?" Kaname said. "For like, another hour."

"Is it really that interesting?"

"They have everything here. I could stay all day."

"I've got a shift at two."

"Then you and me better have a big lunch," she said to Makoto.

"You're on!"

The menu was shorter than usual because of the holidays, but the cafeteria was still fairly crowded. The TV coverage seemed to have had an effect.

"There are whole families here. They're not even students." Kaname exempted herself and Makoto from her stern judgment. "Hey, the fried chicken lunch is sold out!"

"Don't get mad. The ground meat croquettes are great," Kotaro said.

They ordered three different lunch sets and sides of macaroni gratin, pizza toast, crab croquettes, and miso soup with pork.

"Anything going on?" Kaname asked Kotaro as she dived into the food. She'd noticed him using his laptop in the library.

"Nothing new."

"Things sure were noisy in my neighborhood this morning," Makoto said. "I live near Yoyogi Park. It's always like this on May Day. I heard they used to have union riots in the old days."

"That's a pretty nice neighborhood, though. You're lucky."

"It's a rooming house. A really old residence, the kind with mortar on the walls outside. The son grew up and moved out, so the husband and wife rent the extra space to students. Comes with breakfast and dinner."

"But you eat at Kumar sometimes, don't you?"

"Sure, but I eat again when I get home." Makoto was another avid eater. It was one of his biggest pleasures. "The landlord makes way better food than I can get in a convenience store. Healthier too. Sometimes I go to the market with the family and help bring the groceries back."

"Hmm. Do your trips to the supermarket include West Shinjuku?" Kotaro asked.

"Sometimes. Not always."

"Do you know that religious organization there? House of Light?"

"Are they in that neighborhood? Okay, that explains why there's pamphlets in the mailbox sometimes."

"Well, I advise you to stay away from them. Your parents would flip."

"Who knows? Maybe they're the real deal."

"He's right, Ko-chan. Maybe you should do some patrolling and find out," Kaname said.

"Have you ever patrolled any cult sites?"

"Ayuko had me try it when I came to interview. Once was enough."

"I didn't even know we did that. Did you, Makoto?"

"Don't ask me. I haven't even met the president yet."

"That's right, she was already working on her new thing when you joined."

"Maybe she was worried about me because I'm a woman," Kaname said. "Some cults are pitching stuff girls like, like diet plans and yoga and aromatherapy, as a front."

"You're not attracted to stuff like that."

"Who knows? If I was depressed, I might think about it."

"Don't worry. I'm sure you'll always make the rational decision."

Makoto had just placed an entire jumbo crab croquette in his mouth and was reaching for his water when it happened.

Everyone's phone rang at the same time—a doorbell for Kotaro, classical music for Kaname, and the sound of a car crash for Makoto.

"Mako-chan, you can do better than that," Kaname laughed. They all stared at their phones and exchanged glances as if to say, *I knew it.*

They had all received the same mail. Everyone else in Kumar must have as well.

TO: ALL EMPLOYEES

CODE BLUE. REPORT TO THE TOKYO OFFICE IMMEDIATELY.

"What do you think it is?" Kaname buckled down on the last of the gratin. "Maybe there was a break in the amputator case?"

Makoto was already scanning the news. "I don't see anything. Yet."

"Was there another murder?" Kotaro loaded the empty plates onto a tray with a clatter. "Maeda told me there was a Code Blue when that guy with a knife went nuts in Akihabara."

"Is this the first time for you guys?" Makoto asked.

"Yeah. It's kind of a shock."

Afterward, everything they said and did, every gesture and facial expression, remained vividly in Kotaro's memory. Their silly jokes. Kaname blowing on the gratin so she could eat faster. The way Makoto slathered sauce on everything deep-fried. How everything seemed so funny, and how he almost dropped his chopsticks laughing. How they competed to see who could cram the most food in their mouth. How Kaname pointed to a grain of rice stuck to Makoto's lip and said *You've got lunch on your face*. How hard Makoto laughed. *That's great! Never heard that one before.*

How they stared at each other open-mouthed when Kotaro's phone went off.

Because that instant marked the borderline between light and darkness, between fullness and loss. A bright line that could never be erased, a border they could never cross again. The rupture between what lay on the near side of that line and what lay beyond was so deep that everything was utterly transformed. The world as it was just before the line was crossed was burned into Kotaro's memory.

He looked at his phone. "It's Maeda." Maeda was the senior member of Drug Island, after Seigo. "Speak of the devil. I hope there wasn't a murder for real."

Kaname's face clouded. Makoto was still glancing at his news feed as he ate. Kotaro exchanged glances with both of them and hit TALK.

"It's Kotaro."

"Where are you?"

Maeda was into martial arts and could be a bit scary, but Kotaro had never heard him sound like this.

"I'm on campus. With Kaname and Makoto."

"Ah, right. I heard you guys talking about the cafeteria. Well, it's good that you're out and about." He lowered his voice and spoke hurriedly. "Have you heard?"

"Heard what?"

Makoto's scrolling thumb stopped.

"I'm glad you said that. Just get back here right now."

Makoto's face stiffened. Kaname noticed. She leaned over to peer at his phone and gasped.

Kotaro felt something cold on his neck. *What's wrong with her eyes?*

"Kotaro? Are you listening?"

Kaname covered her mouth with both hands. Wide-eyed, Makoto scrolled quickly down.

"Maeda-san, what's going on?"

Makoto answered before Maeda could. "The amputator just claimed his fifth victim."

Maeda heard this. His voice went up an octave and tightened. "Don't check the news! Just get over here, all three of you!"

Kaname's face was bloodless now, her voice trembling. "Ko-chan, there's a video. Someone shared it."

Makoto was about to say something, but he stopped when he saw Kaname's expression. He put his smartphone in the pocket of his jeans. "Let's get going."

Maeda was calling to Kotaro. Shouting at him. He'd taken his phone away from his ear without noticing.

"Kotaro! Kotaro!"

"We're leaving now."

Kaname burst into sobs and squatted on the floor. Makoto sat in front of her and hugged her.

"Is that Ashiya?" Maeda's voice was breaking too.

Kaname wasn't just crying. She had begun to gag. She was about to lose her lunch. Makoto rubbed her back.

"Oh my God. *Oh my God.*" Her face was creased with pain as she gagged and sobbed. Makoto was nearly as pale.

"Take care of her," Maeda said.

"We'll get there somehow," Kotaro answered.

He hung up, squatted next to them and pulled Makoto's smartphone out of his back pocket.

"I'm gonna be sick." Kaname's eyes widened and she gagged deep in her throat. She was right on the edge. She covered her mouth with both hands.

Makoto pulled her to her feet. "It's over there." They stumbled quickly toward the RESTROOM sign.

Makoto had paused the video before he put the phone in his pocket, but the frozen image alone was enough to make Kotaro go limp. He toppled over into a sitting position.

It was the upper half of a woman's body. She was lying in thick weeds, face up, torso twisted slightly to the right, eyes open, lips parted. Her long hair was spread in a halo around her head. Some of it lay across one cheek. There was no mistaking the face.

It was Ayuko Yamashina.

Her black suit was off one shoulder. Her blouse had been ripped open at the neck, which was ringed with purple bruises. A fly perched on one of her eyeballs.

Kotaro hit play. The camera shook badly as it moved across the body. Her skirt had been pushed all the way up, leaving her completely exposed. She was barefoot. Her limbs were splayed in all directions, like a broken doll.

Who the hell took this? Why'd he upload it? Why's the host letting people see this?

There was an edit and the camera focused in on the right hand, then the left.

All ten fingers were missing.

The shot went on forever. Kotaro dropped the phone, threw back his head and howled again, and again, and again.

▼

"Don't worry. The police already have the kid who took the video."

This was the first thing Maeda said to Kaname. Her face was a mask. She'd exhausted herself crying.

When they'd arrived at Kumar, three-quarters of the Drug Island team were already there. The rest were outside Tokyo and couldn't get back right away.

Most people from other teams were there too, but Seigo was nowhere to be seen. The island chiefs were handling things, with each one briefing his team. Maeda had stepped in for Seigo.

Before they arrived at the office, Kaname had been so upset that she'd collapsed on the sidewalk. Makoto had carried her the rest of the way on his back. Now she was leaning on him for support. Many women on the other teams were clinging to each other and crying. There were suppressed tears among the men too. When he opened the door, Maeda's eyes were red and swollen. Narita, the chief of School Island, daubed at his eyes with a tissue as he walked by.

But anger was stronger than sadness. Those who were crying now would soon be just as furious as the rest. How could this have happened? How could their president, loved by all, giving her all for society, become the victim of such an outrageous crime, her body mutilated grotesquely and left for everyone to see?

"Maybe the bastard who shot the video is the killer."

"It's completely perverted."

Maeda raised a thickly muscled arm, as though pushing back the wave of anger that was about to crest.

"The killer didn't shoot the video. It's disgraceful, but the perp is just a kid. He's in the eighth grade."

Kotaro shook his head. That hit close to home. What a dumbass thing to do. Makoto was shaking his head too. There were no words.

"I'm sure the cops have him turning blue right now," Maeda added.

Ayuko's body had been dumped in a corner of a vacant lot in a dense residential area of southern Meguro Ward. The old residence that once stood there had recently been torn down, and the lot was for sale. Over the months the weeds had grown thick on the property.

"The crime scene is a typical old Tokyo neighborhood. Lots of narrow streets packed with houses and wood-frame apartment buildings."

The body had been discovered that morning around five thirty, when a woman living next door took out her trash.

"She started yelling and a lot of people heard her. A crowd formed pretty quickly. It took about five minutes for the police to get there. That was long enough for the kid to make his damn video."

The teenager had probably been beside himself with excitement. *Awesome! If I upload this, I'll get a million page views. Everyone will watch it. I'll be famous! No, I'll be a god!* He'd been so excited that he hadn't actually seen the horror in front of him. He'd been too busy videoing.

The Internet is an open space where everyone can express themselves, but it's also a playground for idiots with a thirst for attention. Kotaro suddenly began to feel nauseated.

"Why didn't someone stop him?" Makoto asked.

"They probably didn't know what he was doing. Everyone was confused and distracted. There were a lot of people milling around in that empty lot."

"Didn't they know enough to leave a crime scene alone? They might've destroyed some evidence," another member muttered bitterly.

"Still, I have to admit...It's hard to say this, but..." Maeda grimaced. "One of our patrollers found the video. That's how we knew it was Ayuko. We notified the police immediately. I hoped it was just a mis— A mis—" Maeda's tongue stopped working for a moment.

"A mistake," he said, his voice breaking. "Someone who just looked like her. Without the video, we might not even know something'd happened to her yet."

Ayuko's favorite black bag, her smartphone and laptop, her purse with her business cards—everything that might have helped identify her was missing. All the police would've reported initially was the discovery of a corpse in an empty lot.

The senior woman on the team spoke up sharply. "Wasn't anyone keeping track of her? When did she come to Tokyo? Why was she alone? Wasn't anyone managing her schedule?"

The question was on everyone's mind. Maeda winced and nodded.

"She was supposed to be in Nagoya all this week. I got that straight from Seigo. But something must've come up. She arrived at Tokyo Station at eight last night and went to her condo in Azabu. She was supposed to be here at noon."

"She took the bullet train alone?"

"No, Morohashi was with her as usual. He put her in a taxi at Tokyo Station." Morohashi was Ayuko's personal assistant in the Nagoya office. He was around thirty and fairly athletic.

Before she'd entered the public eye, Ayuko usually traveled alone, unless there was some need to bring Morohashi along. People in Tokyo rarely saw him. But things had changed, and recently Morohashi was always with Ayuko when she traveled. If he saw Morohashi, Kotaro knew she was in the office even if he hadn't seen her. Kaname called him the "president's bodyguard."

No one had seen Ayuko from the time she parted with her "bodyguard" at Tokyo Station until she was found that morning in Meguro Ward.

"I think most of you know, or probably suspected, that Seigo and Ayuko have been very close for a long time," Maeda said, looking around the room.

For the past year they'd been living together. They just hadn't made it official yet. Ayuko spent a lot of time traveling between Nagoya and Tokyo, but they were planning to marry and live in Nagoya after the Tokyo office closed.

"Ayuko was planning to have Seigo take over as president so she could concentrate on her nonprofit. He wasn't too keen on that, but since he mentioned it at one of our meetings, I guess it was a done deal.

"So there was a lot going on," he added, again sounding apologetic, as though he shared some portion of responsibility for Ayuko's death. "She had to wear different hats and juggle a huge amount of work, and she'd started planning her wedding. Morohashi told me recently that he sometimes had trouble keeping track of her. But how was she supposed to travel absolutely everywhere with him?"

"Where is he now?" someone asked.

"With Seigo, talking to the police. I think her parents are coming up from Nagoya as we speak."

Her *parents*. The room fell silent. Everyone was thinking the same thing. It was like a slap in the face.

"Where *was* Seigo this whole time?"

It was Kaname. She was standing straight and no longer hanging her head, but she wasn't looking at anyone. She was staring into space.

"He of all people should've been protecting her. What on earth could he have been doing last night?" Her tone made the question sound like an incantation—or maybe a curse. Everyone on the team except Makoto and Maeda averted their eyes from her empty stare.

"Ashiya." Maeda leaned toward her, hands flat on his desk. "I know how you feel. To lose Ayuko this way is devastating for all of us. But don't talk that way. Seigo is suffering more, and feeling more grief and guilt, than anyone." A few of the team members nodded.

"He was in the office all last night." The senior woman on the team spoke up. Her voice had lost its edge. "I was here till four, so I know. He even told me not to work too hard." Her voice faltered and she began to cry.

"My mother's in the hospital. I need money. That's why he told me not to work too hard, but he was up all night too. He said he had to catch up on the paperwork for the move to Sapporo, that he couldn't focus on it in the daytime." She glanced at Kaname and added reproachfully, "He was working all night. He wasn't goofing off somewhere. He didn't desert Ayuko."

Kaname wailed in despair and started weeping.

Maeda looked down at his desk. His eyes were reddening again. "We still don't know much about what happened. Let's do what we do best and leave the police work to the professionals. We can't let this affect our mission.

"We're also calling for two volunteers from each island to patrol for information about the case. Are there any takers?"

Kotaro didn't raise his hand. Makoto glanced sidelong at him and blinked in surprise as he raised his own.

The president of a company specializing in net-based risk management had been murdered. Soon—no, surely it was happening already—countless pieces of information about Kumar, useless and useful, harmless and harmful, would be flooding the web, along with thousands of comments from spectators and voyeurs.

"Can we assume this is the fifth murder by the Serial Amputator?" asked another team member.

"The police aren't saying. In fact, they never officially said the other four killings were by the same person."

"Yeah," said another member, "but this one's on Metro Police turf. It's a whole new ballgame."

The exchange of opinions grew more heated. Kotaro reached out and squeezed Kaname's hand. She squeezed back.

▾

I'm a machine.

I'm fast. I process of what's in front of me. I have a mind but no heart. I don't feel doubt, I don't cry, and I don't get angry.

That is what Kotaro told himself. He fulfilled his regular tasks in the regular way. He monitored it all: people looking to sell drugs, inviting others to use drugs, whining endlessly that drugs were destroying them psychologically, that they wanted to quit but couldn't.

Ayuko Yamashina was dead.

Someone had stolen her life and left her body sprawled among the weeds of a vacant lot.

For Kotaro, Ayuko would have always been out of reach. Yet she possessed something wonderful. The simple fact of her existence had been enough for him to believe that life had meaning and value.

They may as well have killed an angel.

I'm a machine. I don't feel. At least not yet. I don't feel and I don't think. Otherwise there's no way I could be here.

Kumar was besieged by journalists and reporters. Kotaro could hear the commotion beyond the glass. Maeda had conferred with Kumar's corporate communications rep in Nagoya on Skype and worked out how to deal with them. Someone from headquarters in a suit, with beads of sweat on his forehead, went into a closed-door meeting with the island chiefs.

"That guy's a lawyer," Kaname said.

Everyone's phone was ringing. Family and friends called as soon as they heard the news. Kotaro got mails from his father and mother. Even Aunt Hanako sent him a message. Kotaro hadn't the bandwidth to answer, so they kept sending them over and over. *"Ko-chan, are you all right?" "Kumar's on the news. Are you safe?" "You work at Kumar, don't you son? Or did I get that wrong?"*

He didn't see the mails until his break. As he gulped down a can of coffee from the vending machine, they brought tears to his eyes.

Kumar, Kumar, Kumar…

A gentle monster who loved the little town on the fjord, and the people in the town and the sound of the church bells ringing. A monster who quietly protected the town, though no one knew.

The angel who loved Kumar was gone.

Goodbye. May we meet again.

There would be no "again."

Kotaro clutched his phone and sobbed.

5

Three days later, at ten in morning, Kotaro was dozing in a reclining chair in the lounge after an all-night shift when Maeda, the new chief of Drug Island, shook him awake.

"The killer's made a statement."

They rushed back to the office. Everyone's eyes were glued to their monitors. Every monitor showed a TV channel.

So it had finally come to this. It was really happening.

"What's it on? NHK?" Kotaro's voice was shaking.

"Everywhere. All the networks."

He sat down at his monitor. Maeda was right. Every channel had started a special news report. News sites on the web were taking their cues from the broadcasters.

"The killer sent a letter to all five networks."

Snail mail, Kotaro thought dully, still not fully awake. A letter. *Was the killer old? Or a child? Maybe a kid who wasn't sophisticated enough to send an email?*

"He's a smart one." Maeda watched over Kotaro's shoulder, arms folded. He was drawn up to his full height with a fierce expression, like one of those huge statues of guardians that flank the gates of temples.

"Smart how?"

"Smart enough to know there's no way to hide forever if you send something like that over the net."

"He's not that stupid," someone chimed in.

"If he was one of those nut cases who 'confess' to crimes they didn't commit, he wouldn't have used the post office."

People had started posting fake confessions just hours after the murder in Mishima, but they were clearly pranks or the work of unbalanced minds.

"The killer must've figured the networks were the best way to get attention," Makoto said. He was peering over Kotaro's shoulder now too. He looked exhausted. His hair was damp; he'd gone to wash up after working through the night. Kotaro nodded to him.

"Murder in Tokyo," Makoto added with a venomous tone that was not at all like him. "It's like he's reached the big time, and TV's the best way to make that big debut."

"And this time he killed a celebrity."

It was Seigo. He was standing in the door. He looked like a ghost. His shirt and trousers looked slept in. He face was covered with stubble.

"Seigo, you're here!" Maeda rushed over to him, but Seigo waved him away impatiently.

"I've got to go back to the police station."

"What, again?" Maeda was surprised.

"Keep monitoring the news. I have to be there when Ayuko's mother arrives." He turned and weaved unsteadily toward the restroom, like someone with a fever. "I have to show her her daughter, goddamn it!" His voice was tight with grief. Maeda hurried out after him.

Kotaro and Makoto sat side by side, monitoring the news. They split the work to cover all five networks. None of them had said anything specific about the killer's statement. They wouldn't even confirm whether each station had received the same letter, yet the announcers seemed to know more than they were letting on.

"It's like they've got something stuck in their craws," Makoto said.

It was true. Apparently the networks had received more than letters in the mail, but none of them would say what that might be. Maybe it was too shocking to disclose, or perhaps announcing it now would complicate the investigation. It was impossible to tell.

Noon came and regular programming was canceled. The picture was starting to come into sharper focus at last.

All five networks had received identical letters. The lettering was squared off, as if the writer had used a template. The text was a single sentence in the center of a small sheet of plain paper:

I'M ONLY TRYING TO PUT MY BODY BACK TOGETHER

The letters were all composed in the same script, on a brand of office stationery that was distributed throughout Japan. Forensics would be checking for prints and DNA as well as where each letter was posted, but Kotaro had no interest in these details. All he cared about was whether or not the letters were genuine.

They were. The sender had enclosed something extra with three of them.

One envelope held a platinum engagement ring with a three-quarter carat Russian diamond that Seigo had given to Ayuko the month before. Their initials and the date were engraved on the inside of the band. In another envelope was a single diamond earring that matched the one on Ayuko's right ear when she was found. The third envelope contained her leather card case with her train pass and a single photograph of her with Seigo.

Other than the earring and her clothes, none of Ayuko's belongings had been found with her body. Her handbag, smartphone and laptop had vanished, presumably taken by her killer.

Now some of her belongings had surfaced. It wasn't surprising that the networks had held back the information at first. Only the killer could have sent them.

I'M ONLY TRYING TO PUT MY BODY BACK TOGETHER

Was this the killer's real motive? The newscasters traced the history of the murders repeatedly.

Shiro Nakanome was the first victim. His left big toe was severed.

The second, unidentified victim was missing her right fourth toe.

"Mama" Masami Tono had had her right middle toe severed before being stuffed into a clothes trunk.

Pharmacist Saeko Komiya, the fourth victim, had lost her right leg below the knee.

And Ayuko Yamashina had had all ten fingers amputated.

I'M ONLY TRYING TO PUT MY BODY BACK TOGETHER

Kotaro wasn't interested in TV's analysis of the case. He wanted the killer's words.

Late that afternoon the networks finally showed the letter, written on a single sheet of paper. Kotaro took a screenshot and printed out a copy. The situation in the office was so confused that no one noticed him doing it. The island chiefs were too busy putting out fires to ask what he was doing.

When he heard that a major newspaper was handing out a special edition in front of the train station, he ran to get one. There was a photo of the letter from the killer.

These were the words the killer had strung together.

Would an image of the letter be enough? Would he need to say the words aloud? Did he need one of the originals?

He didn't know. All he could do was try.

Kaname arrived for her shift that evening. Because of the emergency, she had pulled the graveyard shift.

"I can't concentrate. All I can do is cry. It doesn't matter whether I'm in my room or in class. I feel better here." She had dark shadows under her eyes. Even her cheeks had hollowed out over the last few days. "Ko-chan, you should get some rest."

"Sure, I'll do that."

"Not just a nap. Go home."

"I will. Not quite yet."

In the lounge, Kotaro took a bite out of a sweet roll and booted up his laptop.

He would try again. He would throw another stone into the vast ocean of cyberspace and wait for the ripples to find their target.

His last attempt to reach Galla had found Yuriko Morisaki instead. What she had told him was very strange, especially the scolding she gave him for meddling in things he didn't understand.

He hoped this time would be different. He didn't need Yuriko now. *I'm not the person I was.*

His fingers raced over the keys. He posted his summons again and again.

GALLA THE GUARDIAN! I HAVE SOMETHING I KNOW YOU WANT.

He didn't care who saw his message. If they laughed, that was fine. If they wanted to think he was crazy, they were more than welcome.

I have what you want.

Show yourself, Galla.

▼

Midnight.

For the third time, Kotaro stood on the roof of the tea caddy building.

The night he'd encountered Shigenori here, the freezing wind had cut to the bone. Now the night breeze felt good. It damped the heat in his breast and calmed his burning heart.

The sky looked just as it had that first night. The skyscrapers loomed like vast starships. Looking down he could see the pulsing life of the city, the vibrant lights and pockets of darkness, the haze rising from kitchen vents, filled with the smells of food.

He dropped his backpack next to the hatch and sat on it, arms around his knees. He rested his head there.

Kenji's disappearance was quite a shock, wasn't it?

He remembered what Ayuko had said after he'd returned to Kumar.

Men can be surprisingly fragile when things like this happen.

That lovely voice. Those gentle eyes.

Words don't disappear.

No one can run from the words they leave online.

Be careful, Kotaro. If the real world is stressing you out, deal with your stress in the real world. Okay?

Forgive me, Ayuko, he thought. *I have to ignore your advice. In fact, I'm going to do the opposite of what you told me. I can't handle the world as it is without help from a power that's real but doesn't exist. I need that warrior. I need her black wings and the cold light of her crescent blade.*

An entity that was real yet didn't exist had entered Kotaro's world. Now he was reaching out to her to create a bond that was real—

A puff of air caressed his ear. It was not the wind. It came again stronger, tousling his hair.

He turned around and rose to his feet like a puppet on strings.

The warrior in black stood before him, wings peaked and half-folded, head cocked slightly, arms crossed on her chest. Galla had answered Kotaro's call; it had been triflingly simple. There she stood, as real and as unreal as a dream. He hadn't even heard her touch down.

"Speak."

He took a deep breath. "I want you to hunt someone for me, Galla."

Maybe I am *hallucinating.*

Kotaro was dreaming with eyes open. He was stepping off the borderline between dream and reality and was about to plummet into the world of dreams.

Then let it be so.

"You offer me prey? In return for what?"

Her voice resonated deep in his chest. She was scanning him; she had to be sure.

"When two strike a bargain, each must have something of value to offer." She uncrossed her arms and raised an index finger. The long, sharp nail was as black as her wings. "You summon me to a hunt. Yet you come empty-handed. You would have me act on your behalf." She wagged her finger lightly, as though admonishing a child. "One does not negotiate in this way."

Kotaro stood his ground, but he was shivering so violently that the creature before his eyes almost seemed to shimmer.

She answered my call. We're communicating. I can actually negotiate with this warrior.

"What I'm asking is selfish. I know that as well as you do." He took a step forward. "But my request has something in it for you too. The prey I'm offering you is a slave to a craving greater than anything you've gathered before."

Galla gazed at him and placed a finger on her lips.

"Unbelievable craving. It's why you came to this world, isn't it? To absorb craving into that weapon—"

Finger still on her lips, she shook her head slowly, like a mother gently shushing a fussing child.

"Be silent."

Kotaro's vocal chords were already paralyzed. Her scan spread from his chest throughout his body. There was no pain or sense of suffering, but he felt as though she'd plunged a hand into his body and was about to turn him inside out.

"So? Do you understand?" He ground out the words from a corner of his mouth. His jaw was trembling. "My offer is real. I'm not lying. I called you here because I want to do a deal. You—"

The sensation of being scanned ceased abruptly and he was thrown backward onto his buttocks. He sprawled on the roof, gasping. His heart was pounding irregularly, but he kept talking.

"You must've thought you'd get something out of this meeting, otherwise you wouldn't have shown up."

A wave of nausea enveloped him suddenly. He clapped a hand over his mouth, but it was too late. He vomited. Bitter acid spewed from his mouth. He groaned.

"You never...paid attention to my messages. Why are you here now?"

Galla took her finger from her lips and tossed her head lightly, swinging her hair behind her shoulder. She approached Kotaro with deliberate steps and began to circle him slowly.

How was it possible for a creature so large, encumbered with such heavy battle gear, to move so silently? Was it because she was unreal?

"You summoned me before?" She circled to his left.

"I posted all over the web. I was looking for someone, anyone who knew something about you."

She moved behind him. "I did not know."

She seemed to stop. Kotaro tried to turn around, but he was too dizzy. It was all he could do to turn his head.

"Then why did you come?" His pulse was starting to settle down. He was breathing easier.

The answer came over his shoulder. "I sensed your craving."

You sensed my *craving.*

"You do not ask why I gather desire, or why I use my blade to gather souls in this region. Nor do you question whether I am good, or evil." She moved around to his right. "You seek only to use me, as one uses a tool." She circled until she faced him again. "Must you truly avenge that woman?"

She can read my story. She doesn't need an explanation. She sees right through me.

She sees that *woman.*

"Yes. I have to." Kotaro nodded. His faced was cold; his chin was covered with drool. He wiped his mouth with his sleeve.

"I want the piece of shit who killed Ayuko—Ayuko Yamashina. He's a serial killer. He's killed five times so far. He cuts off part of each victim's body. He sent a statement—some crap about putting his body back together. Who knows whether it's real. Maybe he's sincere, which means he's insane. Or maybe it's just a gimmick, something to torture the public. I don't care. I'm not interested in what he has to say. I don't even care why he's killing people.

"But the killer's craving has got to be huge, way beyond the despair or sadness or grief that the average person would feel. It doesn't matter if he's crazy or not. The craving of someone who would do what this guy's done has got to be priceless to you. Am I wrong?"

The wind whipped Galla's hair. She flexed her obsidian wings and folded them quickly again, the way a person might shrug his shoulders.

"You are still a child."

"What the hell is that supposed to mean?"

"You weep like a baby."

Kotaro hadn't even noticed he'd been crying. That was why his face was cold. He hurriedly wiped the tears away with his jacket sleeve. His nose was running.

When he looked up at Galla again, there was a faint smile on her lips. "You met a wolf."

She sees that too.

"Yeah. She told me to stay away from you."

"The counsel of wolves is ever in vain." Her tone was not dismissive; instead she sounded sorrowful. "Wisdom is wasted on the passionate."

"Do you know this wolf who found me? She seemed to know a lot about you."

Galla drew closer to Kotaro. She knelt down on one knee. Even then she towered over him.

"The shadow of revenge is despair. The souls of *revenge* and *despair* are an eternal dyad. Spawned by rage, begetters of sorrow."

Her gaze was penetrating. Her pupils opened onto a void beyond Kotaro's imagination, a darkness with the power to smother the brightest light. Yet it was neither cold nor frightening. This was darkness to enfold a child crying in pain, darkness to conceal and heal.

"Would you still avenge that woman's death?"

Kotaro brought his legs underneath him and sat on his heels.

"Yes. I don't just want revenge. I want justice. I want to protect this region. I don't want the killer to kill again."

Galla shook her head, never taking her eyes off him. "Revenge is not justice, though they may seem alike, as a statue to a living person."

"How can you be so sure?"

"Because my region is the birthplace of the souls of words."

"It doesn't exist!" Kotaro cried out in anguish, though he did not know why. "*You* don't exist! You and your region and words—everything was created by people of flesh and blood! You're just a shadow conjured up by people who are real!"

A shadow must follow its maker. It must do as its maker wishes. It must go where its maker goes.

I'm begging you.

Galla lowered her gaze and considered her answer.

"You are naïve," she murmured finally. "You do not know what you have to fear."

Kotaro was crying again. *It's the wind. It's been in my eyes this whole time.*

"I brought a clue with me, Galla. It's the killer's statement. The words of the killer. You can find people by tracking their words. That's what you said before."

He made to open his backpack, but Galla stretched out a hand and stopped him. Her gaze struck him like an arrow.

"Then let me take away *your* craving—for revenge. The craving that drove you to summon me. I will take your burden here and now. Would you not be satisfied with that?"

Kotaro spoke through clenched teeth.

"Never. I'm sorry, but I never want to end up like Shigenori. I want the man who murdered Ayuko. I want the serial killer. Find him for me. I want to see his face. You can have his craving. You won't kill him, right? Empty his mind and leave his body to me."

"And what would you do with it?"

"I'll give it the treatment it deserves."

He'll probably be like a tame cat. Smiling and peaceful. That's what happened to Shigenori.

But she's right—what happens to a serial killer without a motive to kill? Would his conscience awaken and torture him for his sins? Would his personality collapse? Would he even remember what he'd done?

It doesn't matter. I want to see this wretch lose his humanity with my own eyes.

"You do not grasp the value of what you stand to lose."

Bathed in the radiance of the skyscrapers, on the roof of a lonely island in the night of the city, the skinny young man and the black-clad warrior locked eyes.

"You will regret this." Galla's eyes narrowed. Kotaro watched her pupils morph into the vertical slits of a cat.

The eyes of a demon.

"You shall have what you seek. Show me the words."

Her wings spread like a black banner in the wind and engulfed him.

A back street in West Shinjuku.

Kotaro's legs were sound. He could stand. His lungs worked and he could move his arms. He had his backpack.

There was a gap. He'd left Galla, left the tea caddy building—

Something was wrong with his eyes. His field of vision was too narrow.

He started walking. The light from the street lamps flickered. A few places were still open. Steam billowed into the street from a ramen shop.

He felt suddenly famished. He parted the half-curtain at the door and went inside. A beefy man behind the counter welcomed him. His head was crowned by a twisted white towel.

The shop was crowded and hot. There were salarymen in suits and women in loud outfits. An old man read the newspaper.

A TV blared behind the counter. It was long past midnight, but the station was still running a news show. An announcer stood next to a large chart with text boxes and photos, talking with a panel of celebrities. Now and then she peeled off a section of the chart to reveal more information. Everyone in the shop was watching. The sound bounced off the hard plastic tables.

"The killer's MO is truly sickening, but at least he wasn't the one who took the video."

"It must not have occurred to him to make his point that way. Maybe he's not Internet-savvy enough to upload a video," one of the celebrities said.

"I don't think it was that. He would've worried about someone tracing him."

Kotaro took a seat at the end of the counter, next to the wall. He rested his elbows on the counter and rubbed his face tiredly. He took his hands away from his face, looked at them, and rubbed his face again. His left eye was blind. Closed or open, he couldn't perceive even a glimmer of light. The darkness was as profound as the void in the warrior's eyes.

Their agreement was sealed. His left eye was his link to Galla.

BOOK IV:

The Hunt

1

"*Kotaro?* Are you okay?"

Kazumi was sprawled in front of the TV. Kotaro sat at the kitchen table, clenching his fists and opening them again slowly, trying to see if he could detect anything with his left eye.

Nothing seemed wrong with the eye. It wasn't watering or dry or painful. He could blink. He just couldn't see. It was as though thick black paper had been pasted over his retina. He had the sensation of seeing, but all he could perceive was darkness.

"Ko-chan! Aren't you even listening?"

Kazumi wouldn't leave him alone. He glanced over at her. In his narrowed field of vision, he could see she'd twisted her head toward him. She looked irritated.

"What?"

"I mean, this program. It doesn't bother you?"

It was variety show that pretended to be serious news. The lead segment was an "exposé" of Ayuko Yamashina's private life, with a panel of guests speculating about the killer's identity. Every detail was sensationalized. The real point seemed to be to strip Ayuko's friends and family of their last shred of privacy.

"How come you're not in school?" Kotaro said.

"It's Sunday. Is something wrong with your head? You got back in the middle of the night. Since then you've been totally out of it."

Kotaro wasn't out of it, but losing his vision in one eye had made him cautious about moving around. If he wasn't careful he immediately tripped over things, or knocked them over when he reached for them.

"Haven't you got practice Sundays?"

"We're off 'cause of midterms."

"Then you better go study."

"Speak for yourself. You ought to go to class instead of spending all your time at that stupid job!" Kazumi boiled over suddenly and punched the remote, switching off the TV. "It's time to quit." She scowled at him. "You've been acting weird since New Year's. All you do is work. It's like you're out of control or something."

Kotaro turned away from her. He put his elbows on the table and rested his chin in his palms.

Something crossed the inky void of his left eye. It looked like a faintly glowing golden thread. He started in surprise and the thread disappeared.

"Listen to me!"

Kazumi's voice was shrill. Kotaro looked over at her. Swarms of golden threads were boiling out of her mouth and floating slowly toward him. He stared at them, fascinated.

What's happening?

He reached out and tried to grasp one between thumb and forefinger. It disappeared instantly, almost as if the pulse of air from his fingers had been enough to extinguish it. It was mystifying.

His sister was still talking. Kotaro realized she was crying.

"You were in love with her, weren't you? With that woman who got killed," she sobbed. "I know you were. Mom does too."

Golden threads poured from her trembling lips. Now they were much shorter. They wriggled like something alive, but instead of swimming toward him, they circled her head and flowed into her right ear. Kotaro watched all of this in amazement.

"Why are you looking at me like that? Can't you see how worried we are? Mom's so anxious she can barely sleep at night, but she's out buying you a suit for the funeral. She wants you to dress right when you say goodbye to that woman."

Kotaro finally focused his right eye on his sister. "Why are you looking at *me* like that?"

"Something's wrong with you," she said in a warning tone. She got up off the floor and came into the kitchen.

"She's not coming back, you know, so quit brooding. It was all in your head.

She didn't care about you. She was a grown-up. She had a fiancée. You're just a college kid, but you're wallowing and feeling sorry for yourself like you lost a sweetheart." She pounded the table with her fist. "Come back to reality!"

He waited for the reverberations to die away before answering. "You don't know the first thing about how I feel."

She shrank back, looking as though she'd been slapped. "What's gotten into you, Ko-chan?" she said softly. Her voice trembled and caught in a sob. The threads coming out of her mouth drooped and plunged downward in tiny whirlpools before winking out.

Are those things her feelings?

Feelings. They were like ghosts, or hallucinations. They were real, but not part of the real world. Now Kotaro could see them as ephemeral golden threads.

This is how Galla sees words.

"I'm only trying to help—"

"Yeah? Then butt out," he cut in brusquely. Kazumi gulped and stood for a moment, frozen, before running out of the kitchen. Kotaro heard her pounding up the stairs.

I've never talked to her like that before.

Kotaro and Kazumi had always had an unspoken agreement. He let her put him on the defensive; he would apologize and hear her out. He was always the gentle, caring older sibling. Whether the topic was silly or serious, he'd always been the first to yield when they disagreed. But today, though he'd known she was worried and trying to comfort him in her own way, somehow he couldn't respond the way he usually did.

Why? Was it because he could see those golden threads?

She's barfing all those wriggling worms, and she thinks she can lecture me?

He put his elbows on the table and rubbed his face tiredly. Had he given up more than just the vision in his left eye when he made his deal with Galla? He could see people's words, but what had it cost him?

He went into the living room, grabbed the remote from the sofa where Kazumi had tossed it, and switched on the TV. The panel of guests was excitedly discussing another short-lived celebrity romance. He sat close to the screen and examined it carefully.

What he saw made him blink hard and rub his eyes with his fists. He squeezed his eyes shut and snapped them open again.

He saw threads glimmering faintly. If he'd been farther away, he might not have noticed them.

They almost looked like the scanning lines on an analog TV. They crossed the screen in both directions, vacillating up and down in enmeshed waves. They were different lengths and thicknesses.

Words!

He pounded up the stairs almost as fast as Kazumi had earlier and rushed to boot up his laptop. He tried a textboard called 2channel first.

Sure enough, the monitor was crawling with threads, seemingly thousands of them, far too many to distinguish lengths and sizes. It looked like a nest of worms. The effect was slightly sickening.

Out of these millions of threads, Galla had to find the words of the serial amputator. Would she be able to match something from a swarm like this to the words in the killer's letter? It was like comparing fingerprints from a crime scene to a database of thousands of sets, waiting for MATCH FOUND to appear.

The hues and density of the threads seemed different from site to site. Kotaro moved busily from keyboard to mouse and back again in a state of near-intoxication, gazing at millions of wriggling threads on textboard after textboard.

He logged on to a news aggregator and searched for articles about the murders. Here the threads weren't wriggling. Instead they shot quickly across the screen like long, straight needles. They were also much brighter—in fact almost dazzlingly beautiful.

The words of the articles about the serial amputator reflected good sense, logic, and a strong desire to solve the case. That was apparently why they were straight and beautiful.

Like a school of barracuda.

Wait, why barracuda? What made me think that?

His head was spinning. He'd seen too many threads. *I'm too new at this. I'd better take a break.*

Coverage of the murder had started focusing on why Ayuko hadn't gone straight to her apartment after Morohashi saw her off at the train station. The taxi driver had come forward with testimony that shed more light on the case.

As the taxi was passing through the Ginza district, Ayuko's smartphone had buzzed. She'd said "excuse me" to the driver and answered the call.

Why, this is a surprise. What are you up to? Yes, I just got here. I'm in a taxi.

She'd obviously known the caller. After chatting for a few minutes, she'd rung off and asked the driver to take her to the scramble crossing in Shibuya. She'd seemed in a hurry; when the driver asked whether she had a business appointment, Ayuko smiled.

No, I'm meeting a friend.

After dropping her off, he'd watched her disappear into the crowds along the sidewalk.

Whoever called her was probably the last person to see her alive. Her phone was missing, but there would be a record of the call. It had been someone Ayuko looked forward to hearing from, someone she'd be willing to change her busy schedule to meet.

And her friend had murdered her.

That was the only conclusion. Otherwise the caller would've come forward in astonishment and fear and grief to testify that he'd seen her the night she died. Or he would've contacted Seigo to tell him they'd met the night before, where they'd gone and what time they'd said goodnight. Keeping silent at a time like this was not the way friends behaved.

Could the serial amputator be a close friend of Ayuko?

There was nothing to do but wait for Galla to find the answer.

2

Kotaro faced his nightmare in new mourning clothes.

The temple in Nagoya was every bit as imposing as the renowned temples of Kyoto and Nara. The memorial hall was designed in the traditional style, with a heavy tiled roof. A signboard with black characters on a stark white background stood outside the hall. The sign read: WAKE FOR THE LATE AYUKO YAMASHINA.

The flagstone path from the main gate to the memorial hall was crowded with mourners. Even from his post at the outdoor reception table facing the hall, Kotaro could smell the incense offerings and flowers heaped on the stage.

Makoto and Kaname were there too. They bowed mechanically to the mourners, just as they had been instructed. They gave them a registry card to fill in, received their condolence donations, and thanked them again. Many of the female mourners were in tears as they handed over the formal black and white envelopes with their donations.

After twenty minutes, Kaname surrendered to her grief. "I'm sorry," she murmured, and fled in tears. Makoto and Kotaro had to soldier on without her help.

Narita was overseeing the reception table. He stood to one side, surveying the mourners and checking his smartphone, coordinating operations at the Nagoya and Tokyo offices. Kumar's cyber patrolling never stopped. Maeda would take over from Narita tomorrow, when the funeral was held. Kotaro, Kaname and Makoto would return to Tokyo and other Kumar staff would take over for the funeral proper.

The chanting of a sutra sounded faintly from the hall. Mourners kept arriving. Kotaro spent more time staring at the tabletop from a bowing position than he did looking at people's faces. Kumar's employees would be last to offer incense for the repose of Ayuko's soul.

Not that they wanted to. No one wanted to accept what had happened, least of all Kotaro. It was a horrible dream. When he woke up he would go back to Kumar. He would see Ayuko. "How're you holding up, Mishima?" she'd say, and she'd invite him to dinner, something delicious. They'd talk for hours, laughing and never noticing the time passing. Finally he would see her to a taxi, admiring her legs as she climbed in, and stand there in seventh heaven, wreathed in clouds of exhaust as the taxi drove off.

Seigo sat with Ayuko's parents next to the altar, which was covered with floral arrangements around a large, framed photograph of the deceased. He looked lifeless, as did most of the mourners. The only one full of life was Ayuko herself, looking down on everyone with the face of an angel.

Someone clapped him lightly on the shoulder. It was Narita.

"Go ahead, you guys. You can offer incense now. When you're finished, help out at the information desk."

The flow of mourners had thinned. Those who had made their offerings moved slowly toward the mourner's lounge along a wooden gangway a few feet off the ground that extended from the hall off toward the right.

"You okay, Kotaro?" Narita said. His face was pale, like everyone else.

Ayuko is dead, and now our world is dying too.

Kotaro stepped out from under the awning that sheltered the reception table. His legs were so unsteady that he almost lost his footing. Makoto grabbed his arm to steady him.

"I wonder how Kaname's doing? I'll see if I can find her," he said and walked off.

The path from the reception table to the memorial hall was paved with stone and lined on either side with neatly clipped bushes and trees pruned to equal heights. Stone lanterns cast a soft glow. The tiled roofline of the hall rose above the black-clad mourners. Through the open doors Kotaro could see the brightly lit altar and the multicolored heaps of flowers, a vivid contrast with the bereft world of the grieving. It truly looked like heaven.

The heaven that was waiting for Ayuko.

He forced himself to look up at the roofline silhouetted against the night sky instead. A few scattered stars shone above it.

There was something on the roofline, blacker than the sky.

A darkness shaped like a person, but far larger.

It was Galla.

Her scythe was a crescent above her head. She stood with wings folded, one hand on her hip, the other raised toward him.

Kotaro saw the black gauntlet. He could see her long fingernails. She raised a finger to her face. Her translucent white skin glowed faintly in the darkness.

Silence!

Even at this distance, he could see her as clearly as if she'd been standing next to him. He saw every detail with his left eye. It was the link between them.

She turned her palm outward and spread her fingers wide. Her hand moved slowly and gracefully, almost floating, until her outstretched fingers aimed at a point on the ground.

The gauntlet held an array of darts. When Kotaro had first encountered her, she'd pointed those needles at him and at Shigenori. They'd been completely paralyzed.

Her arm tensed as she aimed.

A dart flew along the line of her index finger, straight and silent, piercing the night air, slicing through the incense and the voices chanting sutras, through the sobbing and murmuring.

Kotaro followed its flight with his left eye. The dart was forged from darkness, honed and polished like obsidian, flying toward—

The mourners on the gangway. A single individual. A face in profile, clearly visible with his left eye. A woman. She was crying, holding a handkerchief to her face, arm linked with another mourner for support. Her lips trembled as she spoke to her companion.

The dart plunged into her back and disappeared.

Kotaro gasped. A syrupy blob began spreading out around the woman's feet, growing rapidly larger, rising and morphing into her exact likeness. It was no shadow; she was much too far from the lights of the hall now.

Her doppelgänger.

A silver arrow cut from left to right across the darkness in Kotaro's left eye and disappeared.

It is the keeper of her words.

Kotaro could *see* Galla's voice. He stood rooted to the spot and blinked slowly.

The mourners moved solemnly, heads bowed, but Galla's target was different from the others. Only she had a doppelgänger. No matter where the light fell, and even in shadow, her doppelgänger never faded, never changed.

Now Kotaro would know her even if she tried to disappear among the other mourners. A woman with a white face, dressed in black, followed by a black doppelgänger.

That is your quarry.

He saw the voice again, a silver arrow.

"I understand," he said. Galla turned away and disappeared. At the same time, he felt something soft touch his back.

"What is it, Kotaro?"

It was Kaname. Her eyes were swollen. She held a crumpled handkerchief to her nose. Makoto stood beside her, one arm around her shoulders.

"Nothing," said Kotaro. He smiled. "Come on, let's make the offering."

▼

The killer was a woman.

A woman about the same age as Ayuko had murdered her, and brutally.

If the news had come from God himself, Kotaro still would not have believed it—if not for Galla.

Still, how could he be certain Galla was speaking the truth? He had every reason to doubt it. Hesitation, confusion, denial—all would've been sensible reactions.

Yet he was certain this woman was the killer, and his confidence didn't surprise him.

He followed her to the mourner's lounge, observing her as he went through the motions of tidying up glassware and beer bottles. She sat with several men and women, all about the same age. There were many tears; the women in the group clung to each other for support. Now and then there was a wan smile.

They must be Ayuko's friends from school.

He approached them casually. For the first time he saw the doppelgänger up close, the Shadow that Galla had summoned. He almost cried out in surprise.

It was moving. No—it was wriggling.

The Shadow looked like a black body bag—stuffed not with a corpse, but with writhing, wriggling animals. Disgusting creatures, rotting food, and sour-smelling old clothes combined to form this image of a woman, faithful to the last detail, a thing she dragged behind her wherever she went.

What was writhing inside the black form? It seemed ready to rip itself apart. Kotaro sensed suddenly that he might be able to see through the surface and catch a glimpse of what was inside if he focused his left eye.

He was right. He saw what moved inside the body bag: thousands of wriggling threads.

Her words.

Millions of tiny threads, undulating and colliding and intertwining, in all the colors of the spectrum, from red hot to frozen indigo. The accumulated words of a lifetime.

"Do you want something?"

Everyone at the table was eying him with suspicion. The face of the woman with the doppelgänger was startlingly near. She was twisting in her chair, trying to get away from him.

"Is he a friend of yours, Kei?" a woman at the table asked.

"I've never seen him before." The woman named Kei kept pushing her chair back, trying to get away from Kotaro. She was clearly upset.

He straightened quickly and bowed. "I'm sorry, I'm afraid I've been rude."

He looked at the woman again. She was very attractive, but her makeup was over the top. Her face was a mask.

"I believe I've made a mistake. You wouldn't be seminar classmates of our late president...?"

"No, not at all," everyone at the table said at once.

"We were in the same club with Ayuko."

"The bicycle touring club."

"Ah, I see," Kotaro said with an exaggerated nod. "Then I *have* made a mistake. I was looking for Keiko Sato. She was in a seminar with Ayuko."

"Kei's last name is Tashiro, not Sato." The woman sitting next to Kei pointed to her. "Keiko and Ayuko were the stars of the club. Who knows how many men with no interest in cycling were desperate to join because of those two?"

The rest of the table chuckled quietly. Keiko Tashiro lowered her eyes and tried to look suitably modest.

"Thank you. Every memory of Ayuko is precious." Kotaro bowed again and hurried away, bottles and glasses clinking. His heart was pounding.

Keiko Tashiro. A member of Ayuko's college cycling club. That was more than enough information. Finding out the rest would be simple.

But he'd made a bigger discovery.

I can read people's words.

The first threads he'd seen belonged to Kazumi. He'd heard her words and seen the threads. With Galla, he had seen her words, like silver arrows, and heard them directly.

Now he'd reached another level. He'd been able to read the meaning of the wriggling threads inside Keiko Tashiro's doppelgänger.

Of course, he hadn't read everything perfectly. The Shadow contained all the words that a woman in her early thirties had said and accumulated during her life. Kotaro was still clumsy at using the borrowed abilities of his left eye, and naturally he couldn't read all the words at a glance. It was like listening to a radio broadcast through a thick layer of static, and he had been able to catch only scattered fragments. But what he'd heard was more than enough.

From the Shadow of the woman whose friends called her Kei, Kotaro had heard one word more clearly than any other: *Sei-chan*. Kotaro wasn't sure whether she was calling out to him, or if he was hearing echoes of the name spoken to others. *Sei-chan*. Seigo Maki. That had been Ayuko's nickname for him too.

marriage love me what about me liar what else can I do greedy serves her right never again

The words kept coming together among the writhing threads, forming a tangled mass, pulsating, intertwining, flying apart. Whispering, importuning, reaching out to Kotaro's eye.

Sei-chan Sei-chan Sei-chan Sei-chan Sei-chan Sei-chan Sei-chan

Everything was falling into place. He would extract her story from her words and read it the way Yuriko Morisaki read his story, the way Galla read Shigenori's story.

She was the killer.

His heart wouldn't stop pounding. His left eye burned.

⌄

The day after the funeral, a small team of people got together at Kumar to compile a database of the mourners and thank them for their contributions.

Kotaro volunteered to help. Keiko Tashiro had written her address and contact number on her registry card. The bold handwriting slanted upward to the right. The address was in Adachi Ward. She'd included the name of her building and her apartment number. In the telephone field, she'd entered a mobile number.

The night of the wake, Kotaro had noticed she wasn't wearing a wedding band. That and the fact that she'd left a mobile number not only suggested she was single, but that she was living alone.

As he hurried to compile the database, the coroner released details of the autopsy. Ayuko had been strangled with something like an electrical cord. Her blood contained traces of a sedative. She had been knocked out and strangled before her fingers were severed. The police were checking the record of calls to her mobile phone and searching for video footage of her after she left the taxi in Shibuya. The whole area was a commercial district with hundreds of security cameras. If any of them had captured images of Ayuko with someone else, it would be a major break in the case.

He had no time to lose.

Before he made his move, he had to talk to Seigo. He had to know more about his relationship with Keiko.

For three days Seigo was nowhere to be seen. Ayuko had been his business partner and fiancée. He would be extremely busy coping with the aftermath of her death.

The aftermath of her death. The killer had murdered an angel and destroyed her world. Now that world had to be put back together, piece by piece, without her.

On the fourth day, Kotaro decided he'd have to go ahead with his plan even if Seigo didn't show at the office. But as he input his ID at the terminal near the door, he felt a hand on his shoulder.

"Morning. Thanks for all your help."

It was Seigo. He was wearing a suit. His cheeks were hollow. Half of him had died with Ayuko, and what was left was perishing slowly. With each passing moment a little piece of his soul expired, yet he still took the trouble to thank each of his employees personally. He might be dying, but he was still Seigo Maki.

"Good morning," Kotaro answered, not knowing what to say.

"You must be worn out. Are you holding up okay?"

"I should be asking you that."

As Kotaro groped for the right words, Seigo input his ID. "You've been sleeping here, haven't you? You must've missed a lot of class. I hope your parents aren't upset. If it helps, I'm happy to talk to them anytime. Just let me know. I'll apologize for keeping you from your studies."

Come on, Seigo. Give me a break.

"It's okay. My parents know what's going on."

"Really? Okay, then." Seigo frowned and loosened his tie. "Today's bank day. This has got to be the first time ever that I've worn a suit every day for a week." He forced a smile—a miserable smile, it seemed to Kotaro—and turned to go.

"Seigo?" Kotaro was surprised at how shrill his voice sounded. "Um—this woman approached me at the wake. She said she was a friend of you and Ayuko."

Seigo stopped and looked at him curiously. He shifted his bulging briefcase from one hand to the other.

"She said you guys were in the same club. The bicycle touring club."

Seigo's thick eyebrows rose as if to say, *Oh, her...*

"Were you good friends with the members?"

"They were Ayuko's friends."

"So you weren't a member?"

"I went on a few rides with them. She dragged me along."

Kotaro watched his face closely. "Do you remember someone named Keiko Tashiro?"

Seigo looked genuinely doubtful. "Tashiro?" He shifted the briefcase back to his other hand. "That must be Kei. She and Ayuko were friends all through college. Kei, that was her nickname." He nodded. "We all went out for drinks a few times. Good-looking, kind of a narrow face?"

"Yes. Her eyes weren't real friendly. She was wearing a lot of makeup."

"That's the one. She was into makeup big time."

"She came up to me while I was clearing tables in the lounge and asked if I worked at Kumar. She wanted to know how you were doing."

"Really?" Seigo glanced at the floor. "I've got a lot of people worrying about me." He waved thanks and turned to go, but Kotaro wasn't finished.

"What kind of person was she? Were she and Ayuko close?"

Seigo eyed him somewhat suspiciously. "I said they were."

"Does she work in the same industry?"

"I don't know that much about her."

His phone started ringing. He took the phone out, nodded to Kotaro and walked over to his desk.

Keiko and Seigo were connected through their relationship with Ayuko, and only casually at that.

Sei-chan Sei-chan Sei-chan Sei-chan Sei-chan Sei-chan Sei-chan...

But then why were so many of her words about him?

It was all in her head. He didn't even know.

He heard a sigh. "That's the saddest thing I've ever heard." A member of Drug Island, a woman Kotaro had been working with a lot recently, was standing next to him.

"He's finally calling her 'Ayuko.' I wish he hadn't waited until she died. I just hope they find who did it." She never wore makeup; the skin around her eyes was raw from rubbing away the tears.

"But then there'll be a trial, and the killer will have lots of excuses. And a lawyer to defend him. They'll do a psychiatric evaluation. The lawyer will challenge the psychologists, and they'll do another evaluation, maybe more than one. Different doctors will have different opinions. It's practically guaranteed."

Kotaro could only nod, but he had an unspoken answer: *Don't worry. It's not gonna work out that way.*

Keiko Tashiro wouldn't get a chance to make excuses. She wouldn't have the strength after her craving—a craving strong enough to drive her to murder—was sucked out of her. She'd never again be the person she was. No, she would confess willingly. And be sentenced to death.

When he got home, just before midnight, Asako was waiting. She dragged him into the kitchen and hit him with a nonstop lecture as she heated his dinner. He stared at the tabletop and accepted the criticism meekly as he ate.

"Kotaro! Are you listening?"

She pounded the table. He couldn't remember when his mother had last scolded him this way. Was it in middle school? He'd been too well-behaved to need much monitoring.

"You keep saying 'uh-huh' but your brain is somewhere else. Everyone's worried about you. We're mad because we're worried!"

She leaned across the table until her face was inches away. Blood-red threads dangled from her mouth. One of her elbows was on the table. Kotaro could see something wriggling in the shadow it cast on the tabletop.

He could read it.

"You had a fight with Aunt Hanako today, didn't you?"

Asako's eyes opened wide with surprise.

"She doesn't mean any harm. She just thought you could put that stuff out with the regular garbage. She didn't think you needed to call the city to come take it away. She doesn't like being corrected, that's all. She always thinks she's right."

Asako sat down with a thump, her eyes fixed on Kotaro. "Did Kazumi tell you that?"

He didn't answer. He just looked away and munched on the last of his tea over rice.

"No, that's impossible. She went to bed before you got home," Asako said. She sounded like she was talking to herself.

"Thanks for dinner." Kotaro piled his empty dishes and stood up. "Don't worry about classes, Mom. Now that the funeral's over, my schedule will go back to normal. I've got everything covered. Just relax, okay?"

He carried the dishes to the sink and put them in the water. When he turned around, she was standing right in front of him.

"Hey, don't sneak up on me," he joked.

She was still peering at him, eyes wide, watching him.

"Do you know what's happening?" Her voice was faint. Kotaro could smell coffee on her breath. "Sometimes your left eye has this strange glitter, like molten metal." She put a hand on his arm cautiously, as if she thought it might burn her. "Do you feel all right?"

He looked into her eyes, smiled slowly and put a hand over hers.

She snatched it away reflexively, as if in self-defense. Kotaro was her child, but Asako Mishima instinctively recoiled at his touch.

The touch of her son, who was mixed up with something not of this world.

"I feel fine, Mom."

A single drop of water fell from the faucet into the water. The sound seemed to bring Asako back to reality. She took a step back.

"Gotta hit the sack," Kotaro said.

He climbed the stairs, shut the door to his room, and stood there in the dark with eyes closed, waiting.

A blob of light swept across his left eye. He looked up. Where was she?

He crossed the room to the window and opened it. The street outside was wrapped in stillness. The streetlights glowed sleepily. A few stars twinkled overhead. It was the nicest season of the year, just before the early-summer rains.

Are you resolved to do this? asked the voice in his head.

"Yes," he murmured. "I'm ready. I'll make my move tomorrow."

Then I am with you. Do not seek me out.

Silvery granules of light. Galla's voice. The sound of words in light. Light from the heart, the energy of the will.

I am your shadow. I am with you.

He would be helped by an entity that was real but did not exist. A region that was real but did not exist would extend itself into his reality.

"I understand." Then, *Thanks for helping me*, he thought at her.

Silence. He waited.

Lure your prey into darkness.

"Is that all I have to do?"

Again, silence. Kotaro nodded.

Finally the voice came again, but not as particles of light. It was like an inky mist, condensed from darkness.

You will regret this.

3

Vendôme Adachi Castle II was too grand a name for such a tawdry-looking collection of apartments. It just made the building seem cheaper. Keiko lived in apartment 201.

The glass doors to the lobby needed a security code. The building manager was not on duty round the clock, which suited Kotaro. The little office windows that opened on the lobby were curtained. There was a sign on the wall with the manager's number.

Kotaro could make out TASHIRO on one of the mailboxes. He tried her apartment from the intercom. There was no answer.

He had started the day with classes followed by lunch on campus. He then went straight to Keiko's apartment. It was twenty minutes on foot from the nearest subway station. The area was mixed residential and commercial, with houses, apartments, and the occasional convenience store. It seemed heavily populated, yet there were few people on the streets. The neighborhood was somehow lifeless.

He left his backpack in a locker at the station and stuffed what he needed in his pockets. He donned a pair of gaudy glasses picked up at a hundred-yen store, and a black cap from a big-box outlet near campus. Then he went for a stroll, scouting out public phones for the call he would make later and checking the route for security cameras.

He would make his move after nightfall and lure his prey into darkness, just as Galla had said. He would get her to leave her apartment and lead her to a spot that was shielded from the lights of the neighborhood. That would be no mean feat in the middle of Tokyo, but it was his mission.

Once she's in darkness, Galla will do the rest.

Had this been an ordinary crime, the entire plan would've been laughably slipshod. But there was nothing ordinary about Kotaro's backup.

Luckily there was a construction site just fifty yards from Vendôme Adachi Castle II. A placard announced plans to build another condominium. The site was still being prepared; the piles of construction materials would come later. A prefab operations shack stood ready at the edge of the site with two portable toilets alongside. The area was enclosed by a rope on stakes. Most of it was exposed to anyone passing by, but someone in the darkness beyond the shack would be invisible to people on the street just a few yards away. Better still, there was a big metalworking shop in the next lot, close to the shack, with an old zinc-plated roof that cast deeper shadows onto the site. A workshop like that in a residential area would be deserted in the evening.

This was the place, then. His decision made, Kotaro walked back to the station and retrieved his backpack. He found a coffee shop, took a seat inside and opened his laptop. Maybe his target had posted something new on her blog.

Security on the social network site she used was hard to punch through; he didn't know how to use his web-crawling software to get inside. Even if he did, he'd have to explain to Maeda why he was monitoring a site that Kumar had never targeted before.

But he had an idea. He opened the official memorial homepage for Ayuko—he'd helped set it up during his shift the day before—and entered the following message in the condolences area.

> *I am a Kumar employee. At the memorial service, I encountered a few members of our late president's university cycling club. I'd like to thank you for attending the funeral and giving me a glimpse of Ayuko Yamashina before she became president. I feel her loss even more keenly now.*
>
> *M*

His ruse elicited an immediate response—from Keiko Tashiro herself.

I am a former member of the cycling club. Thank you for your message. If you visit my page, you can read more memories of Ayuko. I've also posted some photos from back in the day. Please enter KUMAR to get access.

I welcome everyone at Kumar to take a look.

Kei

He couldn't have hoped for more. He sent mails to his Drug Island colleagues, including Kaname. She and Makoto were on shift together and instantly started reading the blog.

"Ayuko was very cute back then, but she turned into a beautiful woman." Makoto was choking up as he texted Kotaro. "The older she got, the more beautiful she became. It shows what an upstanding life she led."

Kotaro played along with their messages as he sniffed out Keiko's lies and embellishments. Her memories of Ayuko were so full of false sentiment, it ought to have been clear to anyone. *I'm not as naïve as Makoto, that's for sure.*

Kotaro's message had drawn an instant response because it offered Keiko a chance to get closer to Kumar, and that meant Seigo. At the same time, she was afraid.

No matter how shameless she was, Keiko had murdered someone. She had to be under stress. She'd probably be sensitive to anything strange or out of the ordinary, any sign that she was under suspicion. Criminals are always looking over their shoulders to see if they're being followed, even when they are alone.

If Kotaro dangled some kind of bait in front of her—something that pandered to her need to feel safe, to be confident that everyone saw her as just another friend and mourner of Ayuko—she'd be sure to swallow it.

He didn't stay more than an hour in any one place. He even got back on the subway and went a few stations down the line, hanging out in coffee shops and getting gradually fed up with the self-absorption that ran through Keiko's sentimental entries. He killed time until past five, then headed for the public phone he'd picked out near the station.

A sensible woman living alone would be certain to ignore a PUBLIC PHONE caller ID, especially if the caller was persistent. But Keiko was not in a sensible state of mind. She would be no more sensible than Kotaro's strategy to snare her was sensible.

She had succeeded in erasing her rival. She would be drunk with victory, but afraid as well. What if she'd overlooked something important?

Her vigilance and suspicion would make it hard for her to ignore an anonymous call. In fact, an anonymous caller ID would only make her more likely to answer.

Kotaro heard the ringtone.

If Keiko was as busy with her career as Ayuko had been, she'd be sure to check her phone at least once this late in the day. If she got off work every day at the same time, she'd be even more likely to keep an eye on her phone. It's the evening that makes the day worthwhile.

She picked up after three rings. Kotaro held his breath.

"Hello?" The voice was quiet, wary. She'd taken the bait. Kotaro gritted his teeth and steadied himself.

"I'm sorry to call so suddenly. My name is Mishima. From Kumar's Tokyo office."

▼

Kotaro was waiting for her near the corner of the construction site. He bowed deeply. "I apologize for disturbing you this late."

It was 10:20 p.m. The stars and moon were invisible. Kotaro could feel the chill north wind through his thin jacket.

Keiko wore a boldly patterned monochrome one-piece dress and black enamel high heels. If she'd worked that day, this wasn't what she'd worn to the office. Her pearl earrings matched her pearl necklace. Perhaps her restrained outfit was meant to suggest that she was still in mourning for Ayuko. Her makeup was a mask, skillfully applied. She wore more than a little perfume.

"It's this way. Please." Kotaro gestured lightly toward the operations shack. "We're sorry to put you out like this." He stepped forward to meet her as her heels clicked on the sidewalk. With the three inches they added to her height, she was a bit taller than Kotaro.

"It's quite all right. If Sei-chan—Seigo—was kind enough to drive all the way out here..."

"He feels it would be rude to ask you to let him in at this hour."

"Why not? He's a friend."

Her loose sleeves cast shadows around her waist. When she said "friend," the shadows writhed.

"That's very kind of you," Kotaro said and turned toward the shack.

"Why did he park in such a dark spot?" she asked, calling him to wait.

"We're sorry."

"Why doesn't he park in front of my building?"

"You see, it's just..." Kotaro scratched his head, pretending to be perplexed. He was worried that if he didn't use body language, his real feelings would burst through. *Shut up and do what I tell you, murderer.*

"The media are dogging him, as I'm sure you can imagine. He wanted to make sure he didn't inconvenience you, in case he was followed here by paparazzi."

The whites of her eyes flashed in the dim light. "Dogged by the media? What do you mean?" She pretended to be flustered. "He's not under any suspicion, is he?"

Kotaro had only said that the media was trailing Seigo, yet she couldn't resist touching on the murder. Her guilt practically oozed out of her.

"Oh no, of course not. You misunderstand me." Kotaro waved both hands in an exaggerated gesture. "Ms. Yamashina was on TV quite often. She had a high profile. Reporters are chasing her parents and Mr. Maki for interviews."

"Oh, so that's what you meant." Her shoulders sagged. "I guess it can't be helped. But you know, I really don't mind if he comes up." She gave a warped smile. Her lipstick was opalescent; in the dim light it seemed to be melting. Kotaro was reminded of a vampire.

"Mr. Maki is parked on the other side of the shack." He started walking. The click of her heels was right behind him.

Earlier that evening, Kotaro had set the trap.

My name is Kotaro Mishima. I'm calling on behalf of our new president, Seigo Maki. Mr. Maki is distributing some of the late Ayuko Yamashina's possessions to select people who had a close relationship to the deceased. He'd like to deliver something to you personally. Would that be possible? He's quite busy, as you can imagine, and he wouldn't be free until later this evening. Still, he'd like to meet you as soon as possible. If it's convenient, he'll park near your residence around 10:00 p.m.

You will? Thank you! Then shall we agree on the location? Mr. Maki regrets having to ask you to leave your residence, but I believe there is a vacant lot nearby? Yes, the one with the rope around it...Yes, about fifty meters in the direction of the station. He can park off the street there.

Yes, it'll be late, but if you can make time, he'd like to go somewhere more comfortable. He'd enjoy the chance to see you, however briefly. As I'm sure you'll understand, he's quite depressed.

Seigo, Seigo, Seigo. For Keiko Tashiro, no bait would be more enticing. Sei-chan was coming to see her. Who cared what he was bringing? He was coming to see her. Maybe the part about a memento was just a ruse. After all, if he wanted her to have something, he could've sent someone else. He could've mailed it. But he was coming to see her.

The shadows around her were full of dancing threads. Kotaro realized he wasn't seeing just the words she had spoken throughout her life. Desires, hopes, prayers, fantasies, jealousy, doubts, fear—every silent thought and emotion also leaves a trace, as words.

It made sense, once he thought about it. Without language, thinking is nearly impossible.

"I wonder what he's brought me?"

Perhaps she didn't notice how she sounded, or maybe she just couldn't keep up the facade. Keiko sounded happy.

"Ayuko had such good taste. Clothes, jewelry—I'd be happy with anything."

The night was deeper beyond the shack. Against the faint light from the street, its silhouette seemed cut from pure darkness. Kotaro walked into the shadows and turned.

She stopped behind him, surprised. Her white skin and the luster of her pearls still shone faintly. But closer to the shack, the blackness was utter, the color of sin.

"What—?"

Galla's giant form rose up silently behind her. At first Kotaro thought he had hallucinated her; she seemed to have emerged from the earth itself.

"Where's the car?"

Kotaro spoke, but not in answer. "It's time."

The coal-dark wings engulfed them.

▼

Where are we?

Darkness. His knees ached. His hands felt gritty. The ground was—no, not ground. Extruded concrete. He'd seen that dull gray many times.

The roof of the tea caddy building. The skyscrapers glowed above West Shinjuku. The sky was heavy with clouds, cloaking the familiar, shining nightscape in a smoky blur.

The north wind swept over the roof. He rubbed his arms and stood up. Keiko lay on her side in a fetal position a few feet away, her hands covering her face. That was her first impulse when Galla's wings closed around her.

But where was Galla? Kotaro looked this way and that, blinking to sharpen his vision.

The black-clad warrior crouched at the edge of the roof on the gargoyle's perch. She held her scythe by the handle, with its ominous blade high above her head.

There was no moon, no stars. There were no lights on the roof of the tea caddy building, and no lights nearby high enough to shine directly on it.

But night in the city is never truly dark. Galla, Keiko, and Kotaro stood out from the darkness as dim silhouettes.

The woman groaned faintly and opened her eyes. Before Kotaro could speak, she leapt to her feet.

"What's going on? Where am I?" She sounded half-delirious. Trembling violently, she peered anxiously around her. Her eyes were wild and unfocused. "Where the hell is this? Help! Somebody help me!"

She dashed toward the edge of the roof. With no time to react, Kotaro put a foot forward to block her. She stumbled and crashed into him.

Tall women can be surprisingly heavy. For a moment, they both seemed in danger of tumbling over the edge. Limbs entangled, they struggled to regain their footing. The heel of her shoe ground into Kotaro's instep.

"Oh, it's you—"

"Are you all right?" Kotaro was surprised at how calm his voice sounded. "Please be careful. Try to breathe slowly and don't panic. You'd better sit down, away from the edge. The wind is cold. You could get a chill."

Still half-leaning on him, she stared in confusion and disbelief.

"You're that kid from Kumar. Where's Sei-chan? He's waiting in his car, right?"

"If you'll just be patient, I'll explain everything. First you'd better sit down."

There was nothing to sit on, other than the fragments of the original gargoyle. Keiko squatted next to the largest one with a look of disgust.

Kotaro was mystified; she didn't seem to notice Galla. *How could she overlook such a huge—*

He glanced toward Galla and nearly shouted with surprise.

She was gone. The gargoyle was back.

Camouflage. No, it was mimicry. Kotaro blinked. When that didn't work, he ground his fists into his eyes. The gargoyle didn't disappear. Galla had transformed herself. This was the gargoyle that had started it all, the monster that had sent Shigenori off on his investigation. Morphing into the gargoyle seemed to be Galla's way of saying that she'd fulfilled her part of the bargain. The rest was up to Kotaro.

"Listen, what am I doing here?" Keiko looked up at him, arms clasped around her knees. "Where's Sei-chan? You promised he'd give me some of Ayuko's things."

Her initial panic seemed to have passed. Now she was simply complaining. There was no anger or fear in her voice. Either Kotaro had done a stellar job of deceiving her, or she was mocking him.

"You're the errand boy, right? Let's get going then. Take me to Seigo." Her voice betrayed a flash of irritation, but she suddenly brightened. "Or maybe this is all a surprise? He's coming here, isn't he?" She batted her eyelashes in coquettish embarrassment.

"He hasn't changed a bit. He used to love giving surprise parties in college—for people's birthdays or anything, really. He was so good at it."

Kotaro looked down at her, a dim silhouette squatting on the roof with her arms around her knees. A dim shadow slowly growing darker, from dark gray to a black deeper than night.

Keiko Tashiro was turning into her own Shadow, a squatting body bag. Inside it, a wriggling mass of words, like maggots swarming over a corpse.

Kotaro closed his right eye. Nothing changed. He tried closing his left eye. Everything was dark; he couldn't see at all.

"But if we don't get going soon, I'm going to catch a cold. Where's Sei-chan hiding?"

"Keiko Tashiro."

At the sound of Kotaro's voice, the body bag stopped chirping and fell silent.

"You murdered Ayuko Yamashina."

A Shadow in the form of a statuesque woman. Darkness made solid. Its long hair hung motionless in the wind.

"Why did you do it? Was it because you couldn't stand to see her marry Seigo? You're in love with him, aren't you?"

The maggots writhed violently. Kotaro heard what he saw and saw what he heard.

why why why why how does he know what did I do did I make a mistake why does this kid know what I did to Ayuko I Sei-chan I Sei-chan Sei-chan Sei-chan Sei-chan

Kotaro squeezed his eyes shut, trying to block the words from his mind. Otherwise he was sure he would vomit where he stood.

"Are you *crazy?*"

The Shadow, the word-gorged body bag that was Keiko Tashiro, rose to a half crouch, leaning forward with her head cocked. She was ready to flee.

he can't know why does he know he's dangerous why

"There's proof. You can't talk your way out of this."

The Shadow froze, still half-crouched.

no he doesn't know I'm safe no one suspects no one knows I'll never let them I couldn't help it couldn't help it help it help it

Eyes opened suddenly in the Shadow. The whites were the color of a maggot's belly. The pupils were black voids yawning in soft maggot flesh. They bored into Kotaro defiantly.

"There's no proof. I'm not that stupid. I thought of everything."

Kotaro started in shock. She had confessed.

No. She had not confessed. Her words had confessed; they knew her crime. Word maggots gorged on dead flesh, the incarnation of her sin, had opened her mouth and testified.

"You called her while she was in the taxi. Where did you go after you met her in Shibuya?"

The writhing maggots were silent.

"Where did you murder her?" Kotaro peered at her questioningly. "It must've been a challenge, disposing of the body by yourself. But you didn't have an accomplice. You used a car, then. Was it yours?"

no one knows I washed everything it's gone I got rid of it

"Thank you. So you killed her in the car. The same car you drove to Shibuya. You said you'd pick her up. How did you kill her?" His tone was matter-of-fact. He was asking about a mundane administrative detail.

The Shadow's hand went reflexively to its throat.

"You strangled her."

Ayuko goes to meet a friend from college. The friend picks her up in her car. She suspects nothing. She gets in the car willingly, feels welcome and at home. How about something to drink? She accepts the refreshment with thanks and puts it to her lips...

"Did you cut her fingers off to make it look like the work of the serial killer?"

I got rid of everything her phone her purse no one will find them there no one will look for them there I should've hidden her too that face that bitch

"But cutting off her fingers wasn't enough. You sent letters with Ayuko's belongings. That's right, isn't it?"

The Shadow finally withdrew its hand from its throat. The hand disappeared into darkness.

"Or maybe you really are the Serial Amputator? Tomakomai and Akita and Mishima and Totsuka? Did you kill those other people too?"

The Shadow became suddenly human. Keiko Tashiro had returned, a fashionably dressed woman in high heels on the roof of an empty building at the edge of West Shinjuku. Her perfume filled the air.

"You have got to be crazy." It was her voice. Kotaro heard rather than saw it. "Stop talking nonsense. Why am I standing here listening to someone accuse me of being a serial killer?"

Kotaro was stunned. What had just happened?

"I don't know anything about those murders out in the sticks. I just put them to good use."

Keiko Tashiro, the real Keiko Tashiro, had just confessed. She had murdered Ayuko Yamashina.

But she wasn't finished. Perhaps he had touched a nerve, or maybe she was just cold; she wrapped her arms around herself and paced back and forth in irritation.

"He's killed four people already," she said, almost spitting the words. "Ayuko's just another notch on his belt, you know? If you're gonna do something, may as well do it with style. The public loves it."

The public loves it? Yeah, they do. Everyone's eating it up. TV. Internet. Good people and bad people. Smart people and stupid people. Everybody loves murder.

"Still, sending those letters to the media was going too far."

At the sound of his voice, she stopped pacing and looked at him with doubt in her eyes.

"Why? What was going too far?"

"The Serial Amputator might not be too pleased. He could just as easily contact the media and tell them you're a fake. You didn't consider that possibility?"

She stared back at him in the dimness. It struck Kotaro that the whites of her eyes were not very white. The maggot-belly eyes he'd seen moments ago—the eyes of the Shadow—were they the eyes of her soul?

"Why should I care what some pervert thinks? I wanted the letters to look like he wrote them, that's all. He hasn't made any statements. He's never sent any letters. So I thought I'd spice things up a little. Why would that upset him?"

Kotaro couldn't speak. He was dumbfounded.

"Ayuko was going around like this big celebrity. The Serial Amputator was killing people out in the sticks. He'd jump at the chance to kill someone like her. I actually went out of my way to make him look good."

Kotaro found it hard to speak. It was like she was throttling him, too. Finally, he asked the question.

"Why did you have to cut off all of her fingers? The Serial Amputator has never done anything like that. You must've had a reason."

The woman was crazy. Her actions were perverse. Yet Kotaro felt like praying. *Please, tell me you had a reason. Anything logical. Tell me you thought it would fool the police. Please.*

"I *told* you. I wanted to make a big splash. You know, I think I actually got kind of carried away. The more fingers I chopped off, the more fun it was."

Kotaro felt something in the deepest part of his being, something at his very core, slowly cracking off.

"You won't get away with this."

His voice rang in his ears with a metallic tone. Something distinctively human in that voice was missing. It was as if his mind itself had broken off and fallen into the deepest chasms of his personality, crashing from wall to wall as it plunged into the abyss.

"It's strange the police haven't taken an interest in you yet," he added.

Or maybe they already had. This bimbo simply hadn't noticed it. He'd been wise to take precautions before he approached her.

"Why do you say that?" she said with a sneer. "I took care of everything. I was really careful not to leave fingerprints or anything. Nobody can trace those letters. I even posted them from places neither of us ever went to."

Her sassy tone and sneering expression belied her crime: murder and mutilation.

"You were in Shibuya. Someone must've seen the two of you together. There are cameras all over that part of town."

Kotaro wasn't so much trying to convince her as he was trying to keep his balance emotionally. He had to keep talking.

"You must've been seen with her. Somewhere there's got to be footage of you."

"So what? I changed my hair and clothes. I rented the car—"

"Then you had to show your driver's license. Or did you whip up a fake ID? I think that's a little out of your league."

She flinched and fell silent.

"You're a fool, you know. Rental cars can be traced too, by model and license plate number. The police will know you rented it."

"Did I screw up?" Her face contorted with anxiety.

Kotaro was beyond rage and amazement. He felt something close to despair. The woman was an idiot, with a hot air balloon for a brain and the conscience of an ant.

This scum murdered my angel.

"But I haven't done anything to attract suspicion." She seemed genuinely perplexed. "I was always nice to Ayuko, and I never let *anyone* know about me and Seigo."

Kotaro almost staggered with surprise. "What about you and Seigo?"

"I was the one he really loved," she declared, thrusting her chin out proudly. "Right from the beginning. But Ayuko got her hooks into him and wouldn't let go. Seigo was too nice a guy to cut her off. So we had to break up. I got married, but Seigo didn't, for me. But getting married just made me realize I was lying to myself. Seigo Maki is the only man I ever loved. So I got a divorce. That was three years ago. After that, I started seeing Seigo again.

"Of course Ayuko tried to come between us. She went and set up a company with Seigo. It was her way of making sure he'd never get away from her. But he was in love with me. That's why he never married her, no matter how hard she pushed him."

"Then why were they engaged?"

"That's a lie!" Her voice was shrill. She stared daggers at him. "That whole thing was Ayuko's plot. Sei-chan had nowhere to turn. He needed my help. That's why I decided we had to stop putting up with her."

She spoke with conviction. The cold didn't seem to bother her now. She was full of vitality, with a faint aura that surrounded her with light.

"We had to stop being nice to her. It was time for her to face reality."

I'd like to throw those words right back in your face.

The aura that surrounded her was the color of madness. She had lost her ability to stay grounded in the real world. Instead, she'd spent years cultivating her craving until it became a delusion. This delusion, always bubbling and fermenting in her mind, finally penetrated her heart, becoming—for her—the sweetest fantasy imaginable. But for others who refused to share her fantasy, it was deadly poison.

Her craving was an illusion. That was the sickening truth.

Seigo almost certainly hadn't taken much notice of her feelings. Even if he'd realized how she felt, he would have intentionally ignored it. That would've been the appropriate response, and it should've been enough. He'd been with Ayuko since college; everyone knew they were a couple.

There was no room between them for Keiko. That was why she had practiced deception. But what she'd hidden was not a relationship with Seigo, but her real feelings. She had deceived all of her friends. Above all, she could never reveal her feelings to Ayuko.

And she had succeeded, cruelly so, for years on end.

I'm meeting a friend, Ayuko had said.

Ayuko had suspected nothing. She'd been happy to get the call, happy to change her plans for the evening. She was Keiko's friend.

At the wake, in the mourner's lounge, Keiko had seemed like a normal adult woman. Without Galla's eye, Kotaro would have perceived her only as good friend of Ayuko.

So many men had joined the touring club just to get close to Ayuko and Keiko. Two beautiful college friends. How could anyone have sensed the darkness in the heart of one of them, a darkness that would grow like a tumor?

Keiko herself probably didn't know when her obsession had become a delusion. When did she fall in love with him? Why did she love him? Why couldn't she give up her dream of being with him? What was it she really wanted from him?

It doesn't matter. Sei-chan, please want me. Not Ayuko.

Craving.

Kotaro understood. Craving was the maggot that had burrowed into her heart. Irresistible craving, more powerful than conscience or morals.

Keiko was an empty husk. Her craving had consumed her completely.

She squatted down again with her arms around her knees. Perhaps her own words had shocked her. She gazed up at him with a strangely demure expression.

"Galla." Kotaro spoke with his back to the gargoyle. "Did you hear her?"

Keiko blinked with incomprehension. "Who are you talking to?"

He ignored her. "I can see her aura."

As Keiko looked around, bewildered, Kotaro saw Galla's answer.

It is craving's glow.

"So that's the energy you've been gathering."

The glow was powerful. It pulsed with pure power.

Kotaro glanced over his shoulder. Galla hadn't moved. She was still the gargoyle.

"Look, Galla. The police are going to catch her sooner or later. In my country—my region—there's no way a criminal this stupid can avoid getting caught for long."

Keiko came to a kneeling position on the concrete with her back straight. She eyed Kotaro with suspicion and disgust. "Look, are you okay?"

I'm okay. You're not okay.

"So—Galla. One thing worries me. What if she forgets why she killed Ayuko after you harvest her craving? Won't that make it impossible for her to explain her motivation? It's going to make the investigation a lot harder."

What do you ask of me? Galla was matter-of-fact.

Kotaro shrugged. "I know I shouldn't expect you to wait, but it might be the best thing. I think we should wait till the police have so much evidence, so much proof that she killed Ayuko and mutilated her, that she has no choice but to confess.

"I want her to tell the cops exactly what she told me. After that you can turn her into a zombie. Do what you did to Shigenori—draw her fangs. Once she's confessed, that might be the best thing for her."

Is that truly your heart's desire?

"Yes. I want her to experience what the cops do to her, just the way she is now."

"Hello? Anyone home?" Keiko was almost shouting. "Your name is Mishima, right? Are you in a trance or something? You're creeping me out."

Kotaro smiled at the murderer on her knees before him. "I'm finished. You can go. Your time's up. I don't have to do a thing."

She eyed him doubtfully. "What do you expect me to do?"

He laughed. "Anything. Nothing. I don't care. Just be the idiot you are. You're perfect."

"You're not going to feed me to the police?"

"I'm not going to do anything. Listen carefully, Keiko Tashiro. I don't have to do anything. The police will find you soon enough without my help."

"But how? Where did I screw up?"

That was enough. Kotaro finally lost his head.

"Everywhere! From start to finish! Your whole life is one big fucking screwup! Even if you were a hundred times better than you are, you'd be worth less than the dirt under Ayuko's fingernails. I hope you live a long time. You're going to be an empty shell while you rot in prison." He glared at her furiously.

Suddenly she burst out laughing. She covered her mouth. Her shoulders shook with mirth. Finally, she caught her breath. "Oh, Mr. Mishima. You do need help."

She stood up and came closer, looking cheeky. She nudged him coquettishly.

"Are you all mad about Ayuko? Did you bring me here to get revenge? Or are you angry I made poor little Seigo suffer? Is that it?"

What—so you knew he was in love with her!

"Yeah, that's right." Kotaro was grim. "Ayuko and Seigo, they're good people. You'll never be anywhere near as good—"

"Ooh, very impressive. Well done." She clapped her hands and laughed. "I just want you to know that everything I said is true. I don't know why. Maybe you just talk a good game. It doesn't make you any less stupid. Or maybe you're just shortsighted.

"You think the police are going to catch me, and I'll tell them all about why and how I killed her." She moved closer, so he could feel her breath. "Now, how do you think that's going to make your beloved Seigo feel? *I* think he's going to blame himself for everything. For her death, and for the way she died."

Kotaro saw dark flames of joy in her eyes.

"That's just the man he is, you know. I know him well. That's why he couldn't bring himself to cut things off with Ayuko."

Sincere and warmhearted. A keen judge of character who never failed to consider the needs of others. Always encouraging people to make the best of their strengths.

I always thought you wanted to make the world a better place, Ko-Prime.

"I wouldn't be surprised if Sei-chan thinks even my screwups were his fault."

Kotaro couldn't hear her now. His ears were roaring.

Keiko's delusion was hers alone. But when it came to Seigo's likely reaction,

Kotaro knew she was right. No matter how much he might hate to admit it, her intuition was spot-on. When the truth came out, Seigo was certain to blame himself. He should've noticed the danger. He should've done something to stop Keiko. If he hadn't delayed marrying Ayuko for so long, none of this might've happened. That's how he'd see it.

Keiko kept on grinning and talking as the blood raged and boiled in Kotaro's veins, flooding away from where it was needed most—his heart.

Bereft of the heat of blood, his heart grew colder second by second, yet he could feel it racing, as if it were trying desperately to keep from freezing solid.

"Are you sure you want to make your beloved Seigo suffer *that* much? You look up to him, I can tell. Don't you think you ought to help me? If you want him to be happy, you'd better protect me. I thought I'd committed the perfect crime, but it looks like I messed up. I'm in trouble, aren't I? If that's really what you think—"

"Galla!"

Kotaro's scream was primal, a child calling its mother to protect it from the terror of things that hide in the dark. His voice was shrill. He was begging for help.

"Take her, Galla! She's yours now. Use your blade. It's time to rid the world of this bitch!"

The concrete beneath their feet vibrated from a giant footfall. The gargoyle had risen.

It changed color slowly, as if new blood were rising from the soles of its feet toward its heart. From ashen gray its color changed to a bilious dark green. The smooth surface took on the texture of reptile skin. As it changed, it grew.

From inorganic to organic. From a statue to a living being.

When the wave of blood reached its waist, a long tail uncoiled from around its legs and rose like a cobra. The blood began to rise from its fingers toward the shoulders; when it reached the creature's elbows, it raised its fists.

When the blood reached its shoulders, the creature shifted its grip on the scythe. It raised the weapon high and began to swing it in bold flourishes, like a sword dance. A pair of giant wings spread out behind it. The pulse of air was so strong that Kotaro reflexively shielded his face with his arm.

The creature had enormous bat wings with sheer green webbing over immense, spidery finger bones. The wings spread and the bones flexed, as though groping for a victim with the touch of death.

The creature's hideous face and pointed ears gleamed wetly in the dimness. It was nearly ten feet tall.

Kotaro and Keiko were struck dumb. They could only watch, spellbound, as the demon emerged.

Another tremor. The demon took a huge step forward and thrust its horrible face toward Keiko. Its eyes were golden. The crescent pupils were the shape of the blade that shone white in its claws.

An instant later, it opened its mouth and roared. Its four huge tusks gleamed.

Keiko gave a shriek of astonishment and turned to flee, but her legs would not move. She toppled backward and tried desperately to scuttle away, still facing the monster, screaming continuously, no words, just wave after wave of piercing screams. Kotaro saw them with this left eye.

no no no my god please help me scared scared scared scared Sei-chan help me what is it why am I no no no no

The demon spun lightly, leaping closer. Its scythe was a whirlwind.

Kotaro saw what happened with both eyes. He saw the blade pass through Keiko's waist in one smooth motion, slicing her slender torso in two. There was no sound and no gout of blood.

Her eyes met his. They were wide open, as though she were planning to flee the next moment. There was no pain or fear, only surprise.

For hardly more than a second she sat there, cut in two. The upper half of her body twisted back to look in wonder at the demon, still trying to move its arms and scuttle away. The lower half was stretched out on the concrete. Her shoes were half off. Kotaro could see her right calf spasm violently.

The next instant, she began to disappear, her body dissolving into tiny grains of sand—no, more like mist—from the cut that divided her in two. The mist, like sparkling ice particles, flowed toward the scythe. Kotaro saw this clearly, yet it took no more than an eyeblink for her to disappear.

He suddenly remembered a book Kazumi loved when she was little. It had a picture of a mother sucking up ghosts with a vacuum cleaner. Kazumi had kept asking Asako if ghosts were really burnable trash.

Keiko had been sucked into the demon's scythe like a ghost sucked up by a vacuum cleaner...

A blue-white gleam flashed across the crescent blade. The scythe laughed like a living thing—once, then again and again. With each laugh, light flashed across the blade from one end to the other, like a chemical reaction in progress. Or—

Like something being ripped apart and consumed.

Keiko Tashiro's craving.

The gleam died away. The demon examined the blade curiously, then swung it again in great arcs that completely encircled it.

The tip of the scythe flashed inches from the end of his nose. Kotaro's legs gave way. He landed on his buttocks on the concrete. An arabesque of cold, blue-white light, like an intense fluorescent glow, seemed to hang in the air as the blade dipped and soared.

As she swung her scythe, Galla began to emerge again. Long hair the color of obsidian. The huge finger bones webbed with thin green membrane shape-shifted into the proud wings of a black raptor, fitting for a warrior whose kingdom was the night.

Kotaro's breath came in juddering gasps. He couldn't seem to get enough air. He rotated his shoulders and rounded and stretched his back again and again. Slowly he stopped wheezing and regained his breath.

He was soaked in cold sweat. His face was dripping, not just with perspiration but with tears and drool.

Galla's transformation was complete. She drew the blade close and studied it in wonder.

"Her craving was strong."

Kotaro could see it had grown larger. He sensed it was sharper as well. The tip glowed with a pale light, like the North Star.

"The craving of a killer." He spat the words and tried to stand. His legs trembled. Somehow the muscles wouldn't work.

Galla stowed the scythe behind her. She stepped toward Kotaro without a sound and extended a hand. He took it and stood up, but after a moment fell to his knees, toppled backward and sat down again. He needed time to recover.

"Sorry. Guess I'm a little shaky. That was pretty shocking."

Galla nodded. "That was my true form." Her voice was gentle.

"I know. That wolf I met told me about it. I was more or less prepared, I guess. That wasn't what shocked me, though. I didn't think your true form would be a gargoyle. In our region, gargoyles are legendary demons from Europe. How did a mythical creature from our region end up in the birthplace of the souls of words? It makes your region seem like, I don't know, something out of a fantasy novel, or a movie about the Middle Ages."

Galla smiled—a full, warm smile. "You have it backward."

"How?"

"Before your legends arose, there was the birthplace of the souls of words. The creatures you call gargoyles are a pale reflection of the guardians of the Tower of Inception. So it is for your other creatures of legend. The amazement and fear and dread inspired by contact with beings from other regions fired the imaginations of people in this region. From those contacts came a multitude of strange creatures. Those you regard as benevolent are called gods and spirits and fairies. Those you fear are demons and monsters."

"Are you sure about that?"

Wasn't Galla's world a legend, a product of the imagination? A place that was real, but not in the real world? How could such a place be older than human culture?

Kotaro was turning his neck this way and that, trying to get out the kinks, when he saw something sickening on the concrete nearby. At first his brain refused to recognize it.

It was a human fingernail—a cheap shade of pink the color of Keiko's nail polish. She had ripped it off when she was trying to scuttle away from the demon.

"Take it with you," Galla said. Kotaro looked up. She towered over him, leaning forward to peer at the grisly keepsake. "A prize for the hunter."

"You've got to be kidding. I don't even want to touch it. I don't need a trophy. I'll never need anything to remind me of what I saw tonight." He paused for a moment. "She *was* evil, wasn't she, Galla?"

Her strong craving led her to kill. In Kotaro's region, a person like that was called evil.

"It is not for me to decide what is and what is not evil," Galla said coldly. "You chose this path, now you wear the look of guilt. If guilt is what you feel, return the eye to me. You have had your vengeance."

She reached out to him. The pointed tips of her fingernails closed in on his left eye.

"You have done enough. You found your killer. The woman is avenged. You have good reason to be content."

Kotaro shrank back and clapped a hand over his left eye. Galla was right. He had achieved his aim. But...but...he'd only begun to explore his new abilities. He still didn't know what he might learn from a world where words could be seen.

He slid anxiously backward on the concrete. Galla's long fingers stopped in midair, motionless.

"Keiko Tashiro wasn't the Serial Amputator. She was using his crimes for her own purpose. When I came to you with my deal, I said I wanted you to harvest the real killer's craving. Keiko was a fluke."

The killer was still at large. He might be closing in on his next victim at this very moment.

"We made a deal. I want to hunt down the Serial Amputator. I swear I'll find him. If we work together, anything's possible. Don't you agree, Galla?"

The warrior towered over him like a dark wall filling his field of view. Her skin was pale as starlight and seemed just as far away.

"Galla, please. I can help you."

She stared down at him. "Why do you wish to help me?"

"Because I promised to."

"I see." Far above his head, Galla smiled faintly. "So your craving is to fulfill your covenant."

"Why not? We're gonna catch a serial killer! That's gotta be good."

"Desire is neither good nor evil. That is why questions of right and wrong are not my concern. Are you truly ready to follow me?"

The black wings engulfed him. He plummeted into the abyss, spiraling downward on cataracts of darkness...

The street in front of his house.

A radio was playing somewhere near an open window. Four bell-like tones announced the arrival of midnight on this night in late May.

Kotaro stood rooted to the spot, breathing quietly. He had a feeling he'd fall over from dizziness if he took a step forward.

As he stood quietly, he noticed a movement in the shadow of a power pole down the other side of the street, in front of the Sonoi house. Someone was there.

Aunt Hanako? If she was putting out the trash this early, there'd be more trouble in the neighborhood. Kotaro focused his eyes, trying to see better. Reflexively, he took a step forward.

Whoever it was, the figure reacted instantly. It dashed out of the shadows and raced off down the street.

It happened too fast; all Kotaro could do was watch the figure run away. Judging from the build, it was probably a young male. He looked like he had something in his hand. What was he doing when Kotaro saw him?

Maybe it was Gaku? Gaku Shimakawa? BMOC at Aoba Middle School, until he blew his high school entrance exam. Was he trying to see Mika?

Suddenly he remembered Yuriko Morisaki's final words: *Keep a careful eye on Mika. The trouble she's dealing with isn't over.*

He approached the power pole and examined it with his left eye. It was flecked with silvery grains that looked like sand. As he watched, they dissolved into the night.

Are those traces of words?

But Kotaro was too tired to tackle another mystery this night. He turned toward his house on unsteady feet. He was faint from hunger.

He had to get a grip. His quest wasn't over. He had to get strong.

Kotaro Mishima was on the hunt for a serial killer.

4

Kumar returned to business as usual. Seigo came to the office every day. On the first day of normal operations after the funeral, it rained without letup—a rain of tears, someone said, but the tears for Ayuko had already dried. This was June rain, seasonal rain, nothing more. The rains of early summer had arrived.

A week had passed since Kotaro had hunted down Ayuko's killer. He'd held his breath, but nothing he'd read or heard during that week, at Kumar or anywhere else, suggested that anyone might have noticed her absence. Seigo seemed the same as ever. Maybe Kotaro had been expecting something big. He felt let down.

Had the police simply overlooked Keiko Tashiro? Wouldn't they at least be able to tell, from those silly letters she'd sent, that Ayuko's murder was a copycat crime? If so, Kotaro had been right to deal with her himself. If he'd waited for the police to find her, he'd be feeling like a fool about now.

His shift started at three, with a break at seven. When evening came, he decided to pick up something at a convenience store, but when he got on the elevator, a stray impulse made him touch B2.

Kumar's heart—the server room—was on B2. That was where the mainframe lived.

He stepped off the elevator into a dimly lit, featureless lobby. His ID card wouldn't even get him past the first security level, a gunmetal-gray steel door. There was a login terminal next to it; otherwise the tiny lobby was empty. The air conditioning was cranked way past comfort level, though Kotaro had heard the server room was a sauna. Kumar used a lot of computing power, and it put out a lot of heat.

There must be hundreds of millions—no, trillions of words flowing behind that door...

But there were no words from the Serial Amputator. Even if he hadn't broken his silence before, it seemed strange that he would keep quiet once Keiko stole his thunder. People who commit sensational crimes crave attention. That was one of the basic rules of profiling.

Everyone in Kumar was searching determinedly for clues. They'd already found hundreds, maybe thousands of posts that looked like potential leads, and passed them to the National Police Agency.

But every one was a bust. "I did it." "I know who did it." All the intriguing posts were bogus, people looking for attention or supposed eyewitness information that turned out to be completely off target. However well-intentioned, people couldn't help dressing up what they thought they'd seen with false details.

It is hopeless. Galla's silver threads flowed suddenly across Kotaro's left field of vision. He almost cried out in surprise.

"Give me some warning, will you? Are you watching me or something?"

The voice of the one you seek may be hiding in this vast river of words, but so too are the voices of countless other sinners.

Voices. Thoughts. Individual stories. Black body bags full of writhing maggots.

Even I cannot hear a single drop in a waterfall. This hunt is futile.

A multitude of sins. That was how much evil, or attempted evil, was flowing in that endless river. Evil as fashion statement; evil as entertainment.

"You just need something to go on, right? Like with the woman," Kotaro muttered. He eyed the steel door. "We could search for people with a connection to one of the victims. Look for any that seem suspicious and read their stories. Even without a confession, if we work together, we'll know the bad guy when we find him."

That was Shigenori's theory, anyway. The victims knew the killer. They had to have known him. The question was—how did he get close to four people in locations all over Japan?

"I've got to do what Kenji did—get out and use some shoe leather."

That is the way of the hunter. Trace the spoor of your prey, however faint.

The silver threads disappeared.

It was time to get to work. Kotaro turned to the elevator, but before he could punch the button, it started downward from the first floor. Someone was coming. He dashed into the stairwell.

He'd been avoiding the stairs since Ayuko died. The memory of her high heels clicking as she went from floor to floor was too strong. But this was no time for nostalgia.

He was dashing up the stairs to the lobby when his smartphone chimed. Speak of the devil. It was Shigenori Tsuzuki.

❦

"Sorry to drag you out this early. But you're a student. I guess you've got the time."

It was 9 a.m. the next day, at Kadoma Coffee Shop. A few salarymen were finishing off their breakfasts.

"I'm busy, actually," Kotaro said. "I ditched a class to be here. You said it was urgent."

"You didn't have to play hooky."

Kotaro had classes all day. His shift at Kumar started at six. Shigenori had insisted on meeting early—before his next shift, if at all possible.

"You're looking well, detective."

"Yep. It's almost like being young again. I've just about forgotten the bolts are there."

After the owner brought their iced coffees, Shigenori pulled his chair close to the table. There were open seats along the windows, but he'd chosen this spot at the rear of the shop. Something was up. Kotaro leaned forward and spoke quietly. "What's going on?"

Shigenori furrowed his brows slightly. "Tell me if I've got this wrong. Seigo Maki is Kumar's vice president. He hired you, right? He convinced you that cyber patrolling would be perfect for you."

Kotaro couldn't remember telling Shigenori about that first conversation with Seigo about his future. Maybe he'd told him in the hospital, after the operation? He'd been so depressed by the change that had come over the ex-detective that he might've said anything to cover his disappointment.

"Yeah, that's right."

"He graduated from your high school. You think of him as a mentor."

"I wouldn't go that far. But I guess he's a major influence on me."

At that, Shigenori's brows furrowed even more. He lifted his glass and drank a third of it off.

"I shouldn't tell you this," he said in a low voice. "But you're a good kid and pretty mature for your age. My wife likes you too. I'm going to do you a favor."

Kotaro could only stare, nonplussed. *What's coming?*

"Yesterday afternoon, an ex-colleague of mine dropped by. He said he was 'in the neighborhood' and thought he'd see how I was doing. He's working on a case—working so hard that he hasn't been home for days. He's camping out at Sumida Police Station."

Kotaro's eyes widened slightly. "Is this about what I think he is?"

Shigenori nodded. "Ayuko Yamashina. They've made quite a bit of progress. It looks like they're about to crack it, in fact."

The rest came in a rush, as if Shigenori had uncorked a bottle. "He was a new detective around the time I retired. He's still one of the younger guys in the violent crimes unit. What he found, though, was eating at him. He knew the brass wouldn't give him a hearing. Anyway, he got the itch to talk it over with an old fox like me, so he dropped by. It wasn't like him. He's not in the habit of gossiping." He looked Kotaro in the eye. "And neither are you. Am I right?"

"Sure, of course."

"Can you keep what I tell you absolutely confidential? It's just that...I thought it might be hard on you if you got this off the web. Or TV. They're going to have a field day."

"What, then? What's going to be hard?"

"Whoever killed the first four victims didn't kill Yamashina. The letters were a hoax. The killer wanted to make it look like she was killed by the Serial Amputator."

Kotaro didn't even try to look surprised, but Shigenori thought his lack of response was a sign of shock.

"I'm sorry, I know this is a bolt from the blue. It must seem unbelievable."

What's to believe? I already know.

"Do they have any idea who did it?"

Shigenori glanced away for a moment and took another gulp of coffee. Still holding the glass, he nodded once.

"Ayuko Yamashina was killed by a friend."

Looks like I underestimated the cops after all.

"Listen, Mishima... Your president's murder was a crime of pa—" Shigenori stopped. He took a moment to reboot. "There was a romance angle to it."

Kotaro didn't miss a beat. "A crime of passion? You mean like a triangle between Seigo and Ayuko and the woman who killed her?"

Shigenori's voice was a low growl. "That's exactly what I mean."

But there was no triangle. Seigo and Keiko didn't have a romantic connection of any kind. It was all her private fantasy.

"Information like that can really hurt the bereaved," Shigenori said. He sounded genuinely pained, as if he were involved personally. "It will hurt Seigo Maki more than anyone, but the truth will be unbearable for a lot of other people too. You and he are good friends, and you seemed to respect Yamashina. She was beautiful and brilliant. If you had feelings for her, I'd certainly understand."

Did I tell him that too?

"I knew it would be hard on you—people you respect so much being mixed up in a triangle. Yamashina lost her life because of it. That's why—"

He's leaking police information to soften the blow. Well, I don't need his help.

Kotaro smiled. Shigenori's face changed from awkward to suspicious.

"What's so funny?"

"Nothing. I'm not laughing. I'm grateful."

Shigenori blinked slowly. Moment by moment, his eyes cooled.

"Let me ask you something. You said Maki and Yamashina and the woman who killed her might've been involved in a triangle."

Kotaro nodded. *Very good. You haven't lost your edge, detective.*

"I only said there was a triangle," Shigenori continued. "How did you guess the third person was a woman?"

"Because I know." Kotaro had confessed.

It was Shigenori's turn to lose his poker face. The needle on his surprise meter was stuck on peak.

Kotaro went ahead and brought him up to date on everything that had happened since that night at the tea caddy building. When he finished, Shigenori was silent for nearly a minute. He'd forgotten how to blink; his eyes were fixed on Kotaro. Finally his Adam's apple moved, once. He frowned.

"Keiko Tashiro. Yes, that was the suspect. She's been missing for a week. The phone company can't trace her GPS smartphone."

Of course they can't. She's no longer in this world. She's in Galla's scythe. Where would that be? Another dimension, maybe. Or maybe she's in Galla's region…

"She hasn't shown up for work. Hasn't contacted her parents. She's dropped out of sight."

Just like Kenji.

"How did they figure out it was her?" Kotaro asked.

Shigenori finally recovered his blink reflex. He needed a moment to make sure the conversation was real. He squeezed his eyes shut and rubbed his face.

"Detective, what was it that made this person a suspect?"

"What?"

"Now I'm asking *you* a question. Please, try to get a grip."

Shigenori let his hand drop. He'd finally decided the conversation was real.

"The night of the murder, a gas station security camera in Shibuya caught her with the victim. They were in a car. Tashiro was driving."

"A gas station?" Kotaro was so appalled at Keiko's stupidity, his voice cracked. "She stopped for gas after she picked up Ayuko?"

"No. The gas station is next to an intersection. The camera caught them waiting for the light to change."

"Man, I told her she was gonna get caught. Shibuya has cameras everywhere. But she didn't get it. She actually asked me how she screwed up."

Shigenori shook his head slowly. Kotaro couldn't tell what he wasn't liking. Maybe Keiko's stupidity? Or maybe it was Kotaro's tone.

"I might've handled things differently if I'd known the cops were onto her. I guess it can't be helped. In my situation, I think you would've lost your temper too, along with your self-control."

An arrogant, overbearing, self-absorbed woman wallowing in a romantic delusion. She behaved like a spoiled child.

"Now that I think about it, I should've asked her how she lured Ayuko to Shibuya. But so much was happening. The timing was never right."

Shigenori finally stopped shaking his head and stared at him coldly.

"Tashiro was one of the wedding planners."

"Then she could've used that. Said she wanted to talk to Ayuko about something. Ayuko had plans for the evening, but she was happy to meet up with Keiko. It was a happy subject. She was totally in the dark about Keiko's delusion. She was defenseless. I can't believe she asked her to help with the wedding. Ayuko was way too trusting."

And luck had been against her. If she had just reacted differently that night—*Sorry, I'm busy*, or *I'm tired, let's do it another time*, or *If it's about the wedding, Sei-chan should be there*—Ayuko would still be alive, still be walking the stairs between floors at Kumar, her high heels clicking on the steps. Keiko would surely have kept watching and waiting for her chance, but still...Ayuko was alone that night, with no one to see until the next morning and nothing urgent to make her turn Keiko down. It was as though the devil himself had been in the saddle.

Kotaro felt emotions boiling up inside that he thought he'd sealed away. Memories of Ayuko gripped his heart.

He realized suddenly that Shigenori was talking to him.

"What?"

The ex-detective's eyes were nearly iced over. "No regrets, then? You don't think what you did was a mistake?"

"Why would I?"

"You passed judgment on another human being. You took life and death into your hands. You carried out the sentence."

Kotaro shrugged. "I didn't sentence anyone. I took revenge for Ayuko."

"Oh, that's it. Did someone ask for that? Someone who wanted you to avenge their grief?" A pale light flickered in his eyes. "No. Everything was in your hands. You took care of her personally. You wanted payback and you got it."

Shigenori frowned, and a spasm of pain passed over his face. "Did you ever think she might've had something to say in her own defense?"

"In her *defense*?" Kotaro gaped at him.

"You decided her relationship with Seigo Maki was a fantasy. Who gave you the right to do that without investigating carefully and weighing the evidence?"

"Of course it was a fantasy. It couldn't have been anything else."

"In your opinion."

"I asked him, detective. He said he barely remembered her. He couldn't even remember her name at first."

Good-looking, kind of a narrow face? As Kotaro recounted his exchange with Seigo, Shigenori smiled, but not with his eyes.

"Maybe that was just for you. No matter how close two men are, one can never tell what the other might do behind closed doors. The same goes for women. It's very hard to predict how people will behave when it comes to the opposite sex. Even harder for *you*. You're young.

"In fact, you're a child. There's no way a man who knows you look up to him, that you respect him, is going to come right out and say, 'Now that you mention it, I do have a little something going with her on the side.' No man I know would do that."

For a few moments, Kotaro couldn't quite grasp what Shigenori was driving at. But as he caught on, his anger rose so fast that it almost blotted out his hearing.

"He's not that kind of guy!"

Shigenori pushed back, hard. "Oh, sure. He's sincere. A good mentor. That's how you see him. But how he treats women? That's a different question."

"He was in love with Ayuko. You don't know, that's all. They depended on each other for years. They shared their sorrows and happiness. Just look what they accomplished—"

"A man doesn't have to love a woman to sleep with her. Even a deep relationship can become a liability. A man might cut a woman off cold in a situation like that. Sometimes kindness just gets in the way."

Kotaro's vision was shimmering from the heat of his anger, like air over a desert road. "You don't know a goddamn thing!"

Shigenori didn't bat an eyelid. "Maybe he and Tashiro really were in a relationship. It's easy to keep a woman on tap if you know how to sweet-talk her. But when he had to choose a wife, he chose Yamashina. Maybe he told Tashiro it wasn't his fault because Yamashina wouldn't leave him. Tashiro might've been so hurt, she lost her head. Everything was Yamashina's fault. She was evil. If only she'd let him go."

Ayuko got her hooks into him and wouldn't let go. Keiko's words echoed in Kotaro's head.

"She wouldn't be likely to blame the man she loves. At least part of what she told you about Ayuko could've come straight from Maki. That doesn't justify murder, but still, she had her side of the story. You didn't even consider it. You sentenced her to death because you couldn't be bothered to give her a hearing. What if you were wrong?"

"Shut up!"

Kotaro suddenly found himself gripping Shigenori by the collar. The owner stared in astonishment from behind the counter. "I'm sorry. Is something wrong?"

Shigenori gave Kotaro a cool stare and answered in a strong, firm voice. "Everything's fine. Sorry for the disturbance."

Kotaro let go. His hands were shaking. Shigenori rose out of his chair slightly and turned toward the counter. "I'm afraid I don't know when to stop preaching. I'm guess I went too far. We'll have two more coffees."

The owner smiled and nodded. The breakfast hour was over; the shop was empty.

Kotaro sat looking at his lap in silence until the refills arrived. The owner took their empty glasses. Kotaro could feel his slightly bitter smile as he turned to go.

"It's time to end this." Shigeru sat up straight. "You've done something terrible. You can't let it go any further."

Galla had said the same thing: *You have done enough. You have good reason to be content.*

No!

Kotaro was not content. He wanted to use the power of his left eye for good. He didn't want to lose it. He wanted to keep hunting. That was the most important thing. It meant something. No one could do it but him.

"I promised Galla I'd find the Serial Amputator so she could harvest his craving."

Shigenori sighed tiredly. "Give it up, kiddo. It's a pipe dream."

Kotaro raised his chin defiantly. "What is? Galla? Her scythe getting stronger with every craving she harvests? Is that a pipe dream? The regions beyond our own, are they pipe dreams?

"None of this is a delusion. I witnessed everything myself. So did you. You met her. She harvested your craving but not your memory. You've got to remember what happened. How could you forget?"

Kotaro covered his right eye and peered at Shigenori. He saw a Shadow, a bedlam of words, sitting across from him.

Faintly glowing threads. Hazy, blurred threads. Thick, writhing threads like inky black ropes. A Shadow in the shape of a man, filled with an infinity of dancing words, the words and thoughts and feelings of an iron-willed detective. Memories. Experiences. The sum total of a life, crying out from the darkness.

Kotaro read his story.

"You saw her niece again, didn't you? The older woman who lived near you, the one who died. She was terrified of the gargoyle."

Shigenori stiffened. "Tae Chigusa." His voice rasped with surprise and fear.

"Right, I remember. She had a niece. You saw her again and you apologized. You told her that her aunt's death was your fault. You shouldn't have—"

"Okay. That's enough."

"—gotten her involved."

"I said cut it out!"

Kotaro uncovered his right eye. Shigenori looked suddenly older. His shoulders sagged wearily.

"Galla gave me the power to read people's stories. You can't deny what you just heard. You heard it in reality, in this world, where we live and breathe. Some things are real but they don't exist in our world. Don't run away from them. Help me. Your craving is coming back. I can see it."

It *was* coming back, otherwise Kotaro wouldn't have asked for Shigenori's help. Bereft of his craving, he'd been like a cat curled up on a sunny windowsill without a care in the world.

"If you think I'm making a mistake, if you want to stop me, then help me." Kotaro wasn't making sense. He had to laugh. "I need you, detective. If I go it alone, I might screw up again. Do you really want that?"

Shigenori gave him a level stare. Kotaro stared right back.

The ice in their coffee melted slowly.

"Take me to Galla," Shigenori said at last. "There's something I've got to know."

5

Kotaro looked out at the lights of Shinjuku from the roof of the tea caddy building.

Shigenori's operation had been a success. He'd scrambled up the ladder ahead of Kotaro without a trace of that shambling gait he'd had when they first met. His shortness of breath after he reached the roof was almost reassuring.

This time there was no need to hunch their shoulders against the cold. The night was humid, almost sultry, but Shigenori still wrapped his arms around himself, as though secretly regretting ever coming here.

Earlier, as Kotaro unlocked the service entrance, Shigenori had muttered, "If I'd been smart enough not to give you that key, we could've avoided this whole mess."

Kotaro was tired of this refrain, but didn't reply. The tea caddy building was deeply symbolic for both of them. But if he called to her, Kotaro knew Galla would come to him anywhere.

Galla, we have things to talk about.

A silver thread as slender as a hair drifted lazily across his left field of vision. He turned just as the warrior touched down gracefully on the edge of the roof.

He motioned toward her with a jerk of his head. Shigenori saw her too and shrank back a few steps. The warrior's eyes were fixed on him as she silently folded her wings.

"Why are you here, old man?"

Shigenori trembled, not from fear, but because Galla was real. He had almost managed to convince himself that everything that had happened on this rooftop was a dream induced by the anesthetic they gave him during the operation. He was fighting the truth, but his memory wouldn't let him win.

"The boy told me what happened," he said, sounding slightly intimidated. He motioned to Kotaro. "He said you took something from me. I want it back. Then we'll talk."

Galla's eyes narrowed. She glanced at Kotaro.

He was caught off-balance. He hadn't expected Shigenori to play his first piece this way. "He wants his craving back, Galla," he said finally.

"I *see* what he desires." She tossed her head and swept her long black hair off her shoulders. "But I do not understand. Listen, old man. You relinquished your craving and found peace. Yet now you seek more suffering. Why?"

Shigenori flushed with anger. "Because it makes us human! No matter how hard they are to bear, we guard our feelings and our memories and cling to them and live with them. That's what it means to be a person."

His breathing was ragged. He was wheezing like a winded sprinter. Kotaro had never seen him this upset.

"I never asked for peace. I don't remember asking *you*. I'm a docile old fool, thanks to your meddling."

So he knows it after all.

Did he see the tranquil expression on his face in the mirror? Was he shocked by the emptiness in his heart? Yet Shigenori was gradually recovering, just as Yuriko had said he would. His anger was proof of it.

"Then you shall have your craving," Galla said. She thrust her right hand toward Shigenori with the sure, swift motion she used to aim her darts. Kotaro closed his right eye quickly.

Bolts of blinding light leapt from her outstretched fingers, each one a different color—a rainbow hurled like a knife at Shigenori's Shadow. The blade of light plunged into its heart, melting and mingling with the whirlpool of words.

The words jostling inside the Shadow came into focus and stood out sharply, coalescing into streams with similar forms and hues, flowing in new directions. Not all flowed smoothly or in the same direction. Some of the flows clashed or oscillated up and down. Everything throbbed with energy. The Shadow that was Shigenori Tsutsuki stood with feet planted firmly, shoulders thrown back, head held high.

Desire makes people human. People aren't body bags stuffed with accumulated experiences and thoughts in the form of words. They are living beings with a will and intentions.

Shigeru staggered back suddenly, as though he'd received a body blow. He dropped to his knees, shaking and gasping.

"Give me a hand. Help me up," he said to Kotaro. He looked fiercely at Galla.

"Are you all right?" Kotaro asked.

"Just give me a hand."

He stood up, stamped the concrete a few times and inhaled deeply. Then he turned on his heel and punched Kotaro in the face.

Kotaro's vision flashed red. He stumbled and fell to one knee. "What the hell was that for?"

Shigenori rounded on Galla, face twisted with fury, and said in a commanding voice, "Bring me Keiko Tashiro. This punk took it on himself to sacrifice a murder suspect. He had no right."

Galla gazed back at him impassively, arms folded.

Kotaro was astonished. *What's wrong with giving a murderer the punishment she deserves? You spent your life doing that. Aren't you the fisher who gathers people's sins?*

Almost as if he'd heard his thoughts, Shigenori gave him a steely glance. "You defied the rule of law. Why can't you see that, punk?"

Kotaro didn't appreciate this new nickname. "Rule of law, my ass. All you're saying is she didn't get a chance to tell her side of the story. Give the devil his due, huh? You sound like a human rights lawyer."

Shigenori sagged with disappointment. He gazed sadly at Kotaro. "You've changed," he said softly.

Kotaro frowned defiantly. If he'd been a genuine punk, he would've flipped the bird.

"It looks like you've had a bad influence on Mishima," Shigenori said to Galla. She was still gazing at him, stone-faced. He shook his head. "Maybe it can't be helped. But you're dealing with the law now. Bring her back. In our world, suspects get due process. There are no kangaroo courts."

Galla's symmetrical features made her face hard to read at the best of times, but now the faintest flicker of pity and regret passed across it.

"True, I can bring the woman back—" she began.

"Then get on with it."

"—but not as she was."

"What do you mean?"

"Craving gnawed at her for years. It became her."

Kotaro flashed back to the maggots writhing in Keiko's Shadow.

"After too many years, there was hardly a person left. Once I harvested her—" Galla hesitated, seeking the right words. "Strong craving is like acid. It eats away at the vessel that holds it. The vessel that was Keiko Tashiro was badly damaged when I took her. Without its craving, the vessel collapsed. That is all I can tell you."

"Is she dead?" Shigenori said.

"Not dead. Her craving and her will became one, and they live on in my blade. Together their energy is terrible. But embodiment is forever beyond her grasp. Were I to bring her here, you would see only a lump of protoplasm, like that from which you evolved. A primitive slime."

She turned to Kotaro. "Would you see her once again? See her, and know what she has become? Perhaps you would tread on her? Grind her beneath your heel?"

Kotaro held a hand to his throbbing cheek. "Is that what happened to Kenji?"

"No. His craving was a burden, but it did not usurp his mind."

Kotaro sighed with relief. "Can he come back? If he wanted to?"

"Yes. If that is his wish."

Kotaro wasn't sure whether he should ask the next question. He wasn't confident that he wanted to know the answer, but he had to ask.

"Did Kenji do something, Galla? Did he...hurt someone? Like Keiko did?"

Instead of answering, Galla stepped off the edge of the roof and sat down on the wall. Kotaro had never seen her sit as an ordinary person would. Her legs were so long that her knees pointed to the sky.

"I mean, maybe he did something bad a long time ago—I think it must've been long ago—and he couldn't forget it and it kept tormenting him. Was that why he asked you to take him out of this world? Did he want to erase his past, or go back and fix what he'd done, or get forgiveness? Was that it?"

"Is that what you believe?" Galla asked finally.

"The Kenji Morinaga I know didn't have a desirous bone in his body. He was calm and logical, and never anything but kind. But something was burning inside him. He had to find out why those homeless people were disappearing without anyone caring."

Kotaro had always assumed that compassion had driven Kenji's search for the missing homeless. But what if he was wrong? Maybe it had been guilt. Maybe Kenji had needed to repay some sort of debt.

Shigenori cut in roughly. "Only Morinaga can answer that. If he didn't tell you, don't waste time speculating. If he doesn't want to come back, there's nothing we can do. But Tashiro—"

"Give it up, man. She's not coming back. She can't."

"Stay out of this, punk."

"You have no regrets?" Galla said to Kotaro.

"None whatsoever."

"I see." She gazed at him thoughtfully. "It is not as I thought. It is difficult to read the stories in this region."

"What stories? Read them how? This is all nonsense," Shigenori spat the words angrily.

Galla crossed her long legs and said crisply, "Then I am sorry."

For one astonished moment, Kotaro thought he was seeing Ayuko. Galla had the same slender legs, the same haunting profile, the same long hair. His breath caught as the sensation of being in her presence came rushing back.

Shigenori took a step toward her and folded his arms defiantly. "Galla. Is that your real name? Or maybe 'real' isn't the right word?"

"It is not my name. But in the language of this region, 'Galla' is close enough."

Shigenori looked up at her suspiciously. "The place you come from—where words are born. Do you have your own language?"

"An excellent question," Galla said. "We have no words. We *are* words."

"Blowing smoke won't work with me, Galla."

"Then you'd best keep it out of your eyes." She almost seemed to be enjoying this back and forth, but her smile evaporated at Shigenori's next question.

"Why are you gathering our cravings? You say that weapon of yours gets more powerful by absorbing our energy. What are you planning to do with it?" He was in his element. The interrogation had begun.

"Mishima was an ordinary young man. Because of you, he conspired to murder someone. It's all your doing." He jabbed a finger at her.

"That's not true," Kotaro said. "She didn't trick me. I made my own—"

"Stand down, Mishima." Shigenori turned back to Galla. "You asked him if he had any regrets. When he said no, you acted surprised. Don't play me the fool. He took a life and has no regrets. You made him what he is."

"Yes. I used him. I had need of him," the warrior said finally. Her tone was matter of fact.

Galla's need. Galla's mission. Kotaro had never questioned them. There hadn't been time. All he'd cared about was how her power could help him.

"I must face my enemy. At all costs, I must prevail. That is why I fortify my blade."

Shigenori kept the pressure on. "What enemy? Are you at war?"

"My enemy is the Sentinel. He guards the Nameless Land."

Shigenori had said blowing smoke wouldn't work, but now he was lost in it. "What the hell is that?"

"It's where stories are born and return," Kotaro said.

"Who told you that?" Shigenori swung on him.

"Hey, I'm just the messenger. I heard it from a 'wolf.' Cute, too. She showed up at school and told me all kinds of interesting stuff."

Shigenori stared blankly. "Are you on something?"

"Of course not. What he says is true," a new voice said.

A girl's voice! Kotaro recognized it instantly. "Yuriko-chan!"

Her arrival was even stranger this time. It was as though she'd walked through an imaginary door and out of the shadows at the edge of the roof opposite Galla—not as a hologram or a vision, but by folding time and space.

Galla looked at her impassively. Shigenori staggered backward and fell on his buttocks.

"Is that a ghost? People say this place is haunted by a young woman. No, it can't be..."

Though it was early summer, Yuriko was dressed just as when Kotaro first met her, in a heavy leather jacket and retro boots. Her glossy black hair was tied in a ponytail. The peculiar pendant gleamed around her neck. She flashed a pretty smile at Shigenori.

"I'm no ghost. I'm a living human being."

"But no ordinary human," Galla said slowly. She rose to her feet and took a long step forward. Her eyes rested on Yuriko, measuring her, searching her. "You are a wolf."

"That's right."

"Yet no more than a child."

Yuriko nodded awkwardly. "Yes. This is my fate."

Shigenori was having a rough time. His eyes bulged. Kotaro squatted next to him and put a hand on his shoulder.

"Do you really have to show up like that? It's hard on people's hearts. How did you get here, anyway?" Kotaro said to the girl.

Yuriko answered breezily. "With the power of that book in your pack. You showed it to me last time. You're still carrying it around."

The book was in the bottom of his pack—Mika's book, *Land of the Sun*, with its anonymous note on a tiny Post-it that Yuriko had warned him not to throw away.

"I called to it and it told me where you were. It made a hole in space-time so I could get here quickly."

This was too much for Shigenori. Eyes still bulging, he shook his head slowly from side to side.

"Steady there, old man," Kotaro said.

"Ah...Huh? 'Old man?' Who're you calling an old man?" Kotaro's shock treatment seemed to work.

"Hey, you keep calling *me* a punk."

Yuriko chuckled, then assumed a serious expression. She walked slowly up to Galla, straightened her spine and bowed.

"My name is U-ri. My master is the Man of Ash. Galla the Warrior, Guardian of the Third Pillar of the Tower of Inception, I greet you!"

Galla gazed down at her and said nothing.

"I know my place. We wolves must never interfere with a guardian of the Tower. My master has always made this very clear to me."

"Then why are you here?" Kotaro was astonished at Galla's regal, imperious tone.

"I came to warn Kotaro." Yuriko held her ground. Her voice was firm. "Mistress Galla! I care nothing for why you are here, but I beg you, don't involve a young man who knows nothing of your world. Surely such conduct is unbefitting a guardian of the sacred Tower?"

"Yuriko-chan—I mean, U-ri—it's not what you think," Kotaro said. "I'm here by choice. I asked Galla for help and she agreed. We have a covenant."

U-ri seemed suddenly disheartened. "I know that. But your request has trapped you within her mission. It's put you under the control of something real that doesn't exist. Now that you know her destination is the Nameless Land, you should be even more wary.

"Kotaro, listen to me. An ordinary person like you can't have anything to do with that place. If you do, something bad will definitely happen. Some kind of tragedy."

Kotaro remembered that the first time they met, U-ri had talked about going to the Nameless Land to rescue her brother.

He went there too.

"Something bad—you mean like what happened to your brother?"

U-ri shuddered and winced sidelong at Galla. The warrior leaned down until their faces were close. Her eyes narrowed.

"Your brother is a nameless devout?"

U-ri flinched and looked away.

"Speak, wolf."

The girl bowed her head and nodded. "Yes. My brother is one of the nameless devout now." Then, in a softer voice: "That means he's not my brother anymore." She looked up at Galla. "His soul has found peace in the great cycling of stories. All I have left are my memories. So my brother and I...we no longer suffer."

Galla drew herself up to her full height and gazed at U-ri, weighing her words. "You have had your say," she said finally. "Now go, wolf. You have no part to play here."

"But—"

"Go."

U-ri flipped her ponytail resolutely and strode quickly over to Kotaro and Shigenori. She dropped to her knees, took Kotaro's hand and looked into his eyes.

"I'm begging you. Please go with me. Stay away from Galla and forget everything you've seen."

Kotaro's eyes sought Galla. The warrior had turned away and was gazing out over the city. She seemed to have withdrawn into herself.

"You still have time, Kotaro. Please?"

"Yuriko-chan, what is a nameless devout?"

The shadow of pain fell across her face. "The nameless devout turn the Great Wheels of Inculpation. There are many of them, far too many to count. They were human beings, once. But not anymore."

Suddenly the words came tumbling out. "They lose their individual personalities and forms and become black-robed monks. There are ten thousand, but there is only one. There is only one, but there are ten thousand. They never stop pushing the wheels and will push them for eternity, as long as the Circle exists. And that means as long as the world exists.

"What are stories?" U-ri asked suddenly. She answered before Kotaro could. "Stories are lies. To lie is a sin, and where there are lies there must be penance. The nameless devout do penance for the sin of stories. Each was once a person who tried to live a story that obsessed him, instead of weaving a story for himself. Desire and craving and lust, anger and jealousy and revenge drove them. They found a story that fed those emotions, and they prized it more than their lives in the real world. They tried to bring a story into reality.

"And so they were condemned. They became the nameless devout, banished to the Nameless Land to bear the original sin of stories on behalf of humanity, forever. But there's one saving grace. The Nameless Land is also a timeless land. There is only the present. Eternity is a single moment."

Kotaro was completely lost, though he'd heard some of this before. For Shigenori it was gibberish. He sat motionless, as though turned to stone.

"Galla." Kotaro still held U-ri's hand. "Why do you have to go to such a place? Why do you have to vanquish the Sentinel?"

There was no answer.

U-ri grasped Kotaro's cheeks in both hands and turned his face toward her. "You mustn't ask that. It's something you don't want to know. You've got to stay out of it."

"I'm sorry." He gently grasped her wrists and pushed her hands away. "Galla stood by her end of the deal. Now it's my turn. I have to keep my word."

"Please!" U-ri's voice trembled and tears welled up in her eyes. Kotaro stroked her cheek gently.

"Thanks for worrying about me."

Though she'd seemed not to hear them, Galla spoke suddenly, her back still turned.

"I go to rescue my child."

U-ri, Kotaro and Shigenori stared at her openmouthed.

"Ouzo is my child, a guardian of the Tower. Someday, when my strength begins to ebb, he was to succeed me at the Third Pillar. But he violated the Law."

Galla has a son?

"For this he was banished to the Nameless Land. He too is a nameless devout."

Kotaro watched the blood drain from U-ri's face. "Is that why you're going?" she said in a tone of desperation. "You think you can rescue a nameless devout?"

"Yuriko-chan…"

"It can't be done! No one can do that! No one!"

"Perhaps *you* could not." Galla's averted gaze spoke volumes. Her voice was cold. "You failed, mere human that you were. And you would fail as the wolf you are now."

"I know that, Galla. So will you."

"We are different."

"Galla is right."

Another new voice, this time a male. A moment later, a dark shadow touched down lightly on the edge of the roof, facing Galla.

The figure was clothed in black and shod in the same tough boots as U-ri, though his boots were half-concealed by the cloak that reached his ankles. A hood concealed his face; only his chin was visible. Long white hair streaked with black fell to either side of his jaw.

"Ash," U-ri murmured. A single tear rolled down her cheek.

"I told you it was no use, U-ri. Give it up."

She stood in one smooth motion, as though pulled by a wire attached to the top of her head. From his perch atop the wall, the black-clad figure put a hand over his heart and bowed to Galla.

"I too am a wolf. My name is Dmitri, but I am known as the Man of Ash, Friend of the Dead. Mistress Galla, Guardian of the Third Pillar of the Tower of Inception, I am honored to meet you. I ask you to pardon my apprentice's foolishness."

His voice was deep and textured, with an aristocratic crispness and a slightly sinister edge. With his black cloak he looked, even more than Galla, like a harbinger of death. But this wolf named Ash was not armed with a scythe. When he placed his hand on his chest, his cloak fell open slightly, exposing the hilts of a pair of long swords.

"Somebody wake me up. This has to be a dream." Shigenori put his head in his hands. "Have I lost my mind?"

"I know what you mean, but this is no dream," Kotaro said.

Ash would've stood a head taller than the average man, but he had to stand on the wall to look into Galla's eyes.

"I know the limits of our discretion. I've tried to inculcate them into my apprentice. But as you can see, she's something of a handful." Ash's face was still half-concealed. He had a crooked smile. "I won't let her display more of her bad manners." He chuckled. "We shall not disturb you further, Guardian of the Third Pillar. However—"

Ash cocked his head slightly and shifted his gaze to Kotaro, who felt his eyes boring in. "Human beings are brethren to my apprentice, and it was humans who imagined me. The boy and the old man seem confused. I wish to leave them with a bit of counsel. May I?"

"As you will," Galla said.

Ash stepped down from the wall. From the sound they made on the concrete, his boots were hobnailed.

"What does he mean, 'humans imagined me'?" Kotaro asked.

U-ri leaned over and said in a low voice, "Ash is a character in a story that was woven by a person."

Kotaro looked at her blankly. "He's what?"

"An imaginary character. The hero of an imaginary world. But his world is still a region, though it's fiction."

"So he's real, but he doesn't exist..."

Ash came and stood beside U-ri. His shadow fell across Shigenori, who was still holding his head in his hands. At the touch of Ash's shadow, he looked up apprehensively.

Kotaro felt a chill of fear. *Why?* he wondered. The presence of death seemed to cling to this man in black who called himself the Friend of the Dead.

For the first time, Kotaro truly understood the meaning of revulsion. Though he cast a shadow, there was something about this man that felt like a ghost. That must be the source of the revulsion. An embodied wraith...

"This may be more of a lecture than a warning. I'll only say it once, so I ask you to listen closely," Ash said in a low rasp.

"The Nameless Land is a forbidden region. No one may enter it, other than those who go there for eternity as the inculpated. Most are taken there against their will, and they cannot escape."

Kotaro could feel the man's eyes, though they were hidden under his hood. *He's reading my story.*

"When I went there, I wasn't as I am now," U-ri said. "I was given special permission to go, and could only stay a short time. I don't have permission anymore, and I don't think I'll get it again."

The hooded man nodded. "That is best. The Nameless Land is a solitary place, far more isolated than an island in an empty sea. But there is another region, one only, that shares the loneliness of the Nameless Land: the region where the souls of words are born. The Nameless Land and the Tower of Inception, the wellspring of all words, are a dyad. They are inseparable; no one can say which came first and which after, which is the head and which the tail. They are as two facing mirrors, each existing to reflect the other.

"Now, one may travel from the Tower of Inception to the Nameless Land. There is a stairway that passes between them. That stairway ends at the gate to the Nameless Land."

"Is that where the Sentinel is?" Kotaro asked.

Ash nodded. "He guards the only gate in the Nameless Land that opens outward. That is Galla's destination."

U-ri began to say something, but Ash motioned for silence.

"What I have told you is, in fact, nearly all I know," Ash said to Kotaro. "We humble wolves are forbidden to enter the Nameless Land and the Tower of Inception. I know only one more thing: the name of that gate. It is called the Gate of Sorrows.

"Only a select few know what waits there, but to those who would confront it, the wise quote a line from a book published long ago: *Abandon all hope, ye who enter here*."

U-ri hung her head. A final tear fell from a corner of her eye. "Don't go with Galla, Kotaro. There are things right here, more important things, that you need to do," she said.

"You mean Mika?"

"Yes, but not only her. I'm talking about taking care of yourself. Kotaro, I'm worried about you. You're just like my brother. Don't lose sight of yourself. Don't forget the people who care about you, people who are by your side every day."

Kotaro was about to nod, but hesitated. Instead he said, "I made my deal with Galla because of someone I cared about."

"To avenge her?"

"That's right."

"Then you've achieved your goal. Mistress Galla isn't demanding that you do more than that. You don't have to help her find that serial killer."

"It's not just that I gave my word. I want this for myself, too. I want to catch him."

Shigenori looked relieved. He was finally hearing something that made sense.

"With Galla's help, I'm sure we can catch him," Kotaro said, nodding to Shigenori. "If I give up now, I'll spend the rest of my life regretting it. I'll mourn the victims, feel shame toward their families, and curse myself as a coward for turning my back instead of doing something when I had the chance.

"Anyway, it's your mission to go after dangerous books, right? What I'm doing is kind of like that. I just happen to be an ordinary guy who was given an opportunity."

"Wolves hunt books." Ash's answer came immediately. "We don't hunt the living. You should not confuse the two."

"I'm hunting someone very dangerous. If I don't find him, a lot more people could lose their lives. I don't know what I'm confusing with what, but I don't think I'm wrong."

U-ri shook her head once, twice. "Kotaro, you don't understand. My brother made the same mistake—"

Uoooon...

An eerie call resounded in the distance. Kotaro doubted his ears.

"What was that, a siren?" Shigenori said. Ash looked quickly around. U-ri's eyes were wide with surprise.

Uoooooon. It came again, closer now. But from which direction?

His face still hidden beneath his hood, Ash turned to U-ri. His hands had disappeared inside his cloak.

"You won't escape a lecture if you intend to just stand there with that silly look on your face."

"Forgive me, Ash. This is my fault," U-ri answered in a voice filled with tension. "I used a wounded book to open a path here."

"It was wounded, yet you used it?"

"I didn't know it was hurt so deeply. Kotaro!"

"What did I do?" Kotaro said, thoroughly anxious.

"Is that note still in Mika's book?"

"Yeah. I didn't want to leave it lying around."

Uooooooooon. The cry was very close. It was a chorus of like-sounding voices, savage howls from the pit of bestial stomachs.

"Why didn't you take it out?" U-ri shouted in irritation. "It's been eating away at the book all this time—"

The howling was almost on top of them. They could hear ceaseless panting.

"The Hounds of Tindalos are on the scent of your book," Ash said grimly. He strode to the center of the roof, threw off his cloak in a single motion and tossed it high in the air. "Get under there and keep your heads down!"

He swept his swords from their scabbards. Slowly, almost languidly, Galla grasped the handle of her scythe, drew it from her belt and assumed a battle stance. She stared intently at a point in space.

"They come."

Beneath his cloak, Ash was still clad in black. His swords were strangely shaped, with large hooks curving forward from the cross guards. Long, black hair streaked with silver fell below his shoulders.

That was the last thing Kotaro saw before the cloak fell on him and Shigenori, covering them neatly.

"What the hell?" Shigenori said.

"Don't move, old man!"

"Are you starting that again?"

"Just do what I said, okay?"

The Hounds of Tindalos came in a pack. Kotaro could hear their labored breathing and feel the pounding of their feet under the cover of Ash's cloak. He sensed something leap over their heads. Its howling and snapping sounded from inches away, and it stank of the beast. Shigenori huddled close to Kotaro.

"Sorry, kid. I've had just about enough for one day."

"Me too. Let's hunker down and wait."

From the tremors and deafening noise, they could sense if not see that all was pandemonium. The air was rent with the shrieks of hounds being slashed and stabbed. The stench was enough to make them nauseous.

Kotaro could hear U-ri chanting an incantation. The moment she stopped, there was a strangled, high-pitched yelp just outside the cloak. It sounded very much like a dog of this world.

A pair of paws pressed against Kotaro's back. His family had kept dogs and cats, and he knew what the footpads of these animals were like. This was different. The sensation was horrible; the paws seemed to be melting their way into his flesh. The claws would soon pierce his skin.

He felt something graze the top of the cloak, followed by a thud. Again there was a high-pitched yelp. Ash—or was it Galla?—had taken out another attacker. He hunched over and closed his eyes. An eternity seemed to pass as the battle continued.

"You can come out now!"

The instant he heard U-ri's voice, the cloak was swept away. When he looked up, Ash was already shrouded in it, with the hood over his head. He seemed to be going well out of his way to keep Kotaro and Shigenori from seeing his face.

Shigenori gagged and retched. Kotaro held his breath and fought the urge to do the same. The hounds were nowhere to be seen, but the air was thick with a sour, bestial stench. Kotaro realized that the mounds of shredded fluff scattered over the roof were hanks of fur.

"Give me a second, I'll cleanse everything." U-ri strode to the center of the roof, placed her palms together over her heart and bowed. In a clear, sweet voice, she began to chant an incantation in a strange tongue. Though the phrases repeated over and over, Kotaro couldn't remember them or tell where one word stopped and the next began.

"It is the language of an ancient people. They disappeared long ago."

Kotaro looked up to see Galla standing next to him.

"Some among the wolves fight their battles with sorcery. This girl is gifted for one so young."

"Is it her specialty?"

"Indeed. Sorcerer wolves guard their spells closely. Ordinary people might hear a scrap of an incantation and misuse it. To prevent this, wolves craft their spells with dead languages."

After each incantation, U-ri changed direction and began again. At first Kotaro assumed she was facing the points of the compass; then he noticed that she had faced five directions, not four.

When she returned to her original position, she placed her palms on either side of her head and gave a short call. A pattern of white light, like the luminosity of a million fireflies, began to glow on the roof around her.

A pentagram.

U-ri stood in the center, moving her arms in graceful arcs as though conducting an orchestra. The pentagram responded to her movements by glowing brighter. One by one, its individual lines grew thicker. Finally it began to rise into the air, transforming slowly into a giant, three-dimensional flower with five petals of light.

The flower was exquisite. Kotaro was awestruck. Shigenori seemed to have found his legs again; he stood next to Kotaro with a hand on his shoulder for support, watching with wonder as the spectacle unfolded.

The flower of light opened and closed as it floated gently upward. Each time the petals opened, they released a flood of life energy. Kotaro could feel it flowing over him. With each pulse, the bestial, frightening stench of the hounds was slowly purified away.

The flower began to rise faster, as if it were being drawn upward by space itself. Kotaro never took his eyes from it, even when he had to crane his neck as it faded from sight.

"Do you always have to put on a show?" Ash snorted with disdain as he rejoined U-ri. "Does everything have to be so elaborate? It's not a performance."

"It's not?" U-ri laughed. Her ponytail was blowsy from the fighting. "We take these things for granted, but if you're not a wolf, it's pretty amazing. May as well make it pretty, don't you think?"

Galla strode to the edge of the roof, reached down and grasped something embedded in the wall. As she pulled it out, a few fragments of concrete fell.

It was a shiny black dart, about six inches long, fired from her gauntlet. Kotaro was shocked, though he knew about the darts. *They're powerful enough to pierce concrete.* Galla had once aimed them at him and Shigenori. He was truly grateful she hadn't used them.

"I guess even a guardian of the Tower misses her target now and then," U-ri said with a mischievous smile.

"I did not miss. The dart passed through the hound."

Ash gave U-ri a gentle poke in the temple. "You should've known that. And see? The dart pierced the beast, yet it remains undefiled. Only a guardian of the Tower wields such weapons. Best mind your manners."

"I understand, Ash. I'm sorry."

As U-ri stuck the tip of her tongue out in vexation, her eyes met Kotaro's. He smiled, and she returned his smile with a hint of pride.

Galla spun on her heel and advanced quickly on U-ri with the dart in her grip. For a moment, Kotaro sensed danger. He swallowed with fear. But Galla held the dart out to U-ri and said, "This is for showing me that beautiful flower. I am sure you will find a use for it."

U-ri straightened and bowed, and accepted the dart with both hands.

"I thank you, Mistress Galla." She put the dart between her teeth and raised both hands to undo her ponytail. She smoothed out her hair and bundled it again quickly behind her head, using the dart as a hairpin.

"How do I look?" she asked Kotaro coquettishly. "More grown-up, don't you think?"

"Very." Kotaro chuckled.

Ash gave another snort of disgust. "Okay, I know," U-ri said. "It's time to go."

She gazed wistfully at Kotaro. She knew she had run out of words to make him change his mind. She turned and looked up once more at Galla, who towered beside her like a wall.

"If Kotaro decides he's had enough, please let him go."

Galla nodded. "Very well. I shall."

Maybe we can all be friends after all...?

"Now go, wolf."

Okay, guess not.

Ash put a foot on the wall. U-ri did the same. She looked at Kotaro and smiled. Once again she was just an ordinary teenager named Yuriko Morisaki. For a moment, Kotaro was moved—by the past, the sins, and the sense of loss that this girl was carrying.

"Please, Kotaro. Be careful."

The wolves launched themselves into space. Shigenori, who had been watching them nervously, called out “No! It’s crazy!” Then he muttered something to himself and fell silent.

Ash and U-ri plunged into the night and disappeared.

▼

“Are you serious about this, kid?”

For a long time Shigenori and Kotaro sat on the roof, exhausted. Finally, Shigenori broke the silence.

“Do you really think you can catch the Serial Amputator?”

Galla stood on the wall a short distance away with her back to them. The skyscrapers of Shinjuku rose beyond her, but somehow Kotaro doubted she was looking at them.

“I caught Keiko Tashiro.”

“That doesn’t prove a thing. She was part of the victim’s personal circle. She was physically within striking distance, just as you were to her. The other murders, that’s a different story.”

“Don’t you remember what you told me? You said it right here, when we were freezing our asses off waiting for the ‘giant bird’ to show up. Tomakomai, Akita, Mishima, Totsuka. All the victims were killed by someone close to them. From that angle, Keiko fits the pattern. We use the same approach, we find the amputator. At least it’s worth a try.”

“That’s not the only thing I said. Think back. Each victim knew his or her killer, but how could all of them have been killed by the same person? It doesn’t make sense. The murders took place too far apart. It’s crazy, it’s weird, and it’s just not logical.”

“Do you remember my answer? With the Internet, one person can make friends all over the place. It’s dead simple.”

“They murmur in their thousands,” Galla muttered.

“Huh?” Shigenori was brusque.

“The thousands who have committed crimes, or who know someone who did. Their voices are everywhere.”

Shigenori flushed with anger. “And how the hell do you know that?”

Galla turned and pointed to Kotaro. “I was with him when he stood by the river. I read the words that flowed there.”

She’s talking about the server room.

“The words and stories I read are everywhere. To me they are as the air you breathe. I have no need to search them out. But that...server. That was a great river of words and stories, a river of all the words in this world.”

"So you *did* read it," Kotaro said. He turned to Shigenori. "But it won't help us catch the amputator. There are too many voices. That's what she said. The voice of the amputator is there, but so are the voices of many other criminals."

"That is so, but..." Galla looked at Shigenori. "It is not that I cannot read them. No; the voices speak both truth and lies, but I cannot tell one from the other. Truth and lies both belong to the realm of words."

"Ah...okay." Shigenori rubbed the nape of his neck. He seemed suddenly tired again.

"Look, I figured it would go this way," Kotaro said. "We've got to hit the street and search for clues. It's the only way."

"You're asking me to help?"

"Can't I ask?"

Shigenori didn't reply. He just kept rubbing the back of his neck.

"Remember, if we can just come up with the tiniest clue, this eye Galla gave me will do the rest. We won't waste any time on false leads."

"I guess..." Shigenori sighed and let his hand fall. He looked up at Galla.

"I was hoping you could do something more for us. I don't know, something more impressive. Like remote viewing, maybe."

Galla said nothing. The blade of her scythe, curving above her right shoulder, shone dully.

"Come on, detective. Clairvoyance?"

"Look, kid—we can tell the difference between truth and lies. How come she can't? Are we superior? I guarantee you, no one ever got the best of me in the interrogation room. No one."

"That's not the point."

"Then what *is* the point?"

Galla stepped down from the wall. Like a cat, she made no sound as she moved. Her eyes were fixed on Shigenori.

"Galla, wait. Just wait a minute," Kotaro said anxiously. He stood up and put himself between the warrior and Shigenori.

"Galla, listen. Let's do this. Give Shigenori the same left eye you gave me. Or the right eye, either way. That will show him more than any explanation."

Galla didn't seem to be listening. She closed the distance to Shigenori in a few great strides.

Kotaro had had enough of quarrels between friends for one night. Friends? Maybe that wasn't the right word, but he wished everyone would chill out.

"Come on Galla, calm—" He reached out reflexively with both palms up. The warrior passed through him as if wasn't there.

She's real, but she doesn't exist...

Kotaro felt his heart leap into his throat. Shigenori didn't move a muscle.

Galla stopped and looked down at him. To Kotaro's relief, her tone was gentle.

"Listen, old gatherer of sins. I understand very well what you wish to say. But this is not a question of mastery. We see the world in different ways."

"Different how?"

"Human beings see truth and falsehood in the meanings of words. But for a guardian of the Tower, all words are truth, once spoken."

"But you just said the words on the web are a mix of truth and lies," Kotaro said.

"Yes—for you. For me, all words are truth. There is no other way to see them."

"Sorry, I don't get it. Everything anybody says is the truth, to you?"

"It is."

"Doesn't matter what words they use? Even if it's nonsense?"

"Yes. Once words are uttered, they exist, and they are truth."

"Well that's just great." Shigenori cocked his head in puzzlement. "It sounds scary, Galla."

She smiled. "Yes. You would do well to fear words. And to respect them."

Kotaro was about to give up trying to understand, when something Ayuko told him in the restaurant echoed in his memory. *No matter how carefully people choose their words, those words stay inside them. They don't disappear, and in the end their weight will change the person who said them.*

"Ayuko told me one time that words never disappear, they just accumulate," Kotaro said.

"Indeed. The person who said that saw with clear eyes," Galla said. "When I harvested her killer's cravings, you saw me as I truly am. You must have thought me a monster."

"Ah...Well, I mean, you did look, you know..."

"Yes. And in my eyes, human beings seem strange as well. But not only strange in appearance. Your world overflows with monsters that surpass me. You made them yourselves. Monsters of words. Your stored-up words of hatred, lust, and jealousy have birthed myriads of monsters. They await you wherever you turn. Monsters that do not exist but are real, like jealous ghosts and vengeful spirits."

"Will I be able to see them?" Kotaro asked.

"You will. You have learned much about the eye. But take care not to seek them out."

"Why?"

"Because you may lose your faith in people completely."

Shigenori clapped his hands suddenly. "Let's put this to bed—punk."

He rose slowly to his feet. He had the look of a man resigned to battle, buckling on his armor.

"We've got work to do."

6

Shigenori sat down at his laptop. For the first time since he began pursuing the gargoyle—the origin of everything—he threw himself into the search for clues with a vengeance.

"You seem quite recovered," Toshiko said. "What are you getting up to now?"

"I think I'm going on a trip." Shigenori almost said "assignment."

Toshiko had been married to a patrolman, then a detective, for too many years to be surprised. "Is there something you've got to find out that you can't with that computer of yours?"

"Um-hm."

She didn't say more. The silence began to feel awkward. Shigenori looked up from his laptop.

"It's nothing important."

"Oh? Is that so?" Toshiko was wearing an apron and holding a strainer full of broad beans. *Is it that season already?* Shigenori thought.

"Just don't push yourself too hard. I don't want you in the hospital again." She disappeared through the half curtain that hung in the kitchen door. "I never dreamed you'd have a woman somewhere," she called out.

What!

"It's not anything like that, is it?"

"No. It's not."

"Are you on a case?"

"You could say that."

"You're not a detective anymore."

"I'm an ex-detective, and I'll be one till I die."

You're right, Toshiko. I have recovered. I got my stolen mojo back. Detective Tsuzuki is on the case!

He was surprised to hear a lighthearted laugh from the kitchen. "So? Where are you going?"

"Tomakomai."

The first murder. Visit the crime scenes in chronological order. Standard police procedure.

Shiro Nakanome was the first victim. He'd been discovered the year before, on June 1, stuffed into a discarded refrigerator, his left big toe severed.

Nakanome ran a local izakaya named after himself—Naka-chan—in a building near Tomakomai Station. Since he was forty-one at the time of his death, he likely had a wife, maybe children.

Shigenori's point of departure would be the people and places closely connected to the victim. While scouring the net for information, he reserved a plane ticket and a room. Then he asked Toshiko to get out his Boston bag.

▼

Every day was Sunday for Shigenori, but university students don't have that luxury. Kotaro would have to do some serious schedule juggling to free up time from school and work if he hoped to investigate the murder of victim number four, Saeko Komiya.

You don't have the time or the money to look into more than one murder. Take care of Totsuka and leave the rest to me.

Kotaro had argued for an even split, but Shigenori hadn't given him the choice. It burned him to admit it, but the old man was right.

Cutting class was straightforward, but rejiggering his Kumar schedule had been a major pain. If Makoto had been helping out, that would've pretty much solved the problem. Unfortunately, once things settled down after Ayuko's funeral, he'd been drafted over to Black Box Island. Kotaro and Kaname were buddies again, which was a major complication.

Still, she'd been generous enough to accommodate his request. "If it's for school, it can't be helped, I guess. We're students. We've got to put our studies first." Her kindness pricked at his conscience.

He had another reason for wanting time away from Kumar, one that would've been unthinkable a month ago: Seigo Maki. Kotaro was constantly tempted to look up from his monitor and focus the Eye on his boss.

Galla had warned him. *You may lose your faith in people completely.*

Perhaps. But Seigo was different. *She's not infallible*, Kotaro kept telling himself. Yet because Seigo *was* different, Kotaro kept the Eye in check. He didn't have to prove to himself that Seigo could be trusted.

Still, his resolve sometimes wavered. He needed to get away for a while. His head told him that, but in his heart, the ex-detective's words—*Maybe he and Tashiro really were in a relationship*—echoed.

Was Seigo hiding something after all?

As if to reinforce the doubts Shigenori had planted in his mind, the police were still a presence at Kumar. Detectives kept dropping by. Sometimes Seigo had to leave the office to meet with the special investigation unit.

Because Keiko Tashiro was officially missing, the case remained open. Even if the police ignored everything else, the fact remained that a member of a university club had been murdered, and another had gone missing shortly afterward. Naturally the remaining club members would become persons of interest—not just Seigo, but all the people Kotaro had met at the wake.

But was that the only reason the police were spending so much time with Seigo? Could he be their prime suspect? Had they discovered that his relationship with Keiko went much further than he'd been willing to admit to Kotaro?

Was that why they were paying so much attention to him? Kotaro was ashamed to even think it.

He finally persuaded Maeda, his boss on Drug Island, to get someone to fill in for him. Tomorrow, July 1, would be the start of a ten-day vacation.

"When summer break comes, the net will get busy. Be sure to make it back before then," Maeda said.

"I will. I promise."

"And go tell Seigo yourself. Apologize, okay?"

Kotaro was anxious to avoid just that, but he went to Seigo's desk and told him what was happening. Seigo pulled up a shift schedule and peered at it, beetle-browed.

"There's this seminar I want to take. If I don't get in now, I'll miss my chance."

Seigo only looked more dubious at this extra bit of window dressing, but after a beat he said simply, "Okay. Fine."

That's all? No lecture? No questions about the seminar or why it's so important? Maybe he's shutting me out? Is it because I asked him out of the blue about Keiko, even though I'm not supposed to know the first thing about his college days?

Stop right there, Kotaro, he told himself. *Remember what Galla said.*

He went away from there in a hurry, not even waiting for the elevator. In the stairwell he ran into Makoto, weighed down by a bulging shoulder bag.

"Just getting off?" Kotaro asked.

"Yeah. You too?"

"Yep. I'll walk you to the station. Is BB Island getting to you?" Kotaro said as they walked down. Makoto looked tired and pale.

"Depends on the day, I guess."

"Is there more to deal with some days than others?"

"No, it's always the same. There's a ton of it. Sometimes it's just harder to handle. It can be a bit much."

I guess today is one of those days.

"I'm off for ten days, starting tomorrow. I feel bad that Kaname's gonna be by herself. If you could wrangle a transfer back to the island, you'd get a red-carpet welcome, squared."

"Mmm, I'll think about it."

Makoto said little during the walk to the station. If something was bothering him, he usually worked hard to act cheerful. That was how he chased away the blues. Makoto was the kind of guy that even guys thought of as a "good kid." He was unfailingly honest, open, and optimistic, the ideal young man.

Makoto should be okay, squared. Galla's not infallible.

And Makoto would be the perfect way to prove it. The station was three stoplights away. There was more than enough time.

Kotaro dropped back a few steps, dragging the heels of his beat-up sneakers to seem natural. Makoto's steps were heavy, not at all like his usual cheery self.

Kotaro closed his right eye and opened his left eye wide.

He stopped, stunned. Makoto drew away from him. Two steps. Three steps.

Kotaro was looking up at a giant.

Everything was close to pitch-black, but the giant was faintly illuminated by light coming somewhere from behind. The sky had been cloudy since morning, with the kind of humidity that seemed to drown you. The sun on this last day of June shone sluggishly through a thick wall of clouds and water vapor. That was where the light was coming from.

The giant looked like a mass of soot. No—it was full of something black, swirling in eddies. It was as though a huge inflatable doll had been pumped full of black smoke until it was close to bursting. That was the only way Kotaro could picture it.

The giant was a step or two ahead. It walked like Makoto. It was Makoto Miyama's Shadow, the aggregation of all the words he'd ever used. It was his story.

The Shadow didn't swirl around his feet the way Keiko's did. It didn't have the lifeless feel of a body bag. It walked under its own power, leaning forward slightly as if sheltering its owner, caring for him when he was tired and dispirited.

Kotaro felt the ground shake under the giant's steps. As though it sensed his gaze, it turned to look at him. It had no face, yet Kotaro had a feeling that their eyes met. It could see him.

The black smoke that was the giant's body swirled and pooled in constant motion. Kotaro heard a low buzzing sound.

Suddenly it hit him. The "smoke" was something else. What filled the giant were swarms of tiny black insects, flies or wasps, maybe horseflies. Kotaro tasted something sour rising in his throat.

"Kotaro?"

Makoto stopped and turned around. "Are you okay?" Kotaro saw the giant turn slowly away.

"Uhm, yeah, no problem." He hurried to catch up, but he stayed just behind Makoto. The giant was too strange. Like Galla, it probably wasn't a solid entity—if he touched it, his hand would pass right through—but he still didn't want to get near it. His knees were shaking.

You were warned.

A few short threads of silver crossed his sight and disappeared.

▼

Kotaro hunkered down at his PC. He had to gather every scrap of information he could find before tomorrow's sleuthing. Not surprisingly, he found a lot of information about Saeko Komiya. It was useful, but the fact that it was there troubled him.

Personal data about the Serial Amputator's victims—five, since everyone was still convinced that Ayuko was one of them—was easy to find. Job history, family makeup, personality. Customer opinions, if the victim had run a business. Even in the Akita case, where the murdered woman was unidentified, there was information on the condition of the body and about people who thought she might have been a relative or friend. The details were scattered, but they were there.

There was a blog post from a woman who thought the victim might have been her grandmother, missing for two years. She had traveled to Akita all the way from Kyushu, only to discover that the victim was someone else. She included lots of details, like the name of the supervising detective and how the body had looked in cold storage.

Every crime is surrounded by people with some relationship to the perpetrator or the victim. Even if they don't see the whole picture, they have pieces of it. If they, or the people they've spoken to—from journalists to the kid next door—put those pieces on the web, an aggregator can assemble them into a bigger picture and repackage them for others to consume.

Your world overflows with monsters that surpass me, Galla had said.

Not all those monsters are evil. They often have good intentions, even a kind of sincerity. They don't "leak," they "disclose." In a free-market, capitalist world, information wants to be free. Citizens have the right to know everything. Knowledge should be freely available. These are rights, not obligations.

But there are monsters waiting along the information highway.

A hideous monster may not necessarily have hideous intentions. A monster may look hideous because it comes bearing information that is horrible in itself. Information monsters are most often neutral, neither good nor bad. But among them are some that truly are evil. How do you tell them apart?

Right and wrong are not my concern. Galla didn't distinguish one from the other. That left Kotaro unable to judge whether Galla herself was good or evil. In that sense she was no different from the monsters on the Internet. They were all words personified.

All this concentrating left Kotaro nearly mute during dinner. For the first time in months, all four family members shared the table, but Kotaro hardly spoke even when spoken to. For the last few months, the only words he'd exchanged with his father were "Good morning." Now it seemed Takayuki had been transferred to a better position within the bank. Asako was in a very good mood. Kazumi, who typically had little friendly to say, always switched on the charm when both parents were around. Very calculating, in a teenage girl sort of way.

If, five minutes after he'd left the table, someone had asked Kotaro what he'd had to eat, he would've been hard pressed to answer. His head was so far away from the present moment that he forgot to ask Kazumi how Mika was doing. He also forget to tell her about the suspicious-looking young man he'd seen outside the Sonoi house after the trial of Keiko Tashiro. But seeing her did remind him of one important thing.

Upstairs, he rummaged in his backpack. He pulled out Mika's book, *Land of the Sun*, and extracted the hateful note inside the cover. He was about to rip it to shreds, but thought better of it. Yuriko Morisaki's prediction seemed off target, but if anything did happen, it might be valuable evidence.

He still had work to do. He sat down and stared at his laptop screen.

Makoto's giant. He wished he hadn't seen it, and it would be better not to mess with it. Still, it had been bothering him since he got home.

He gave up; it was no use. He opened his mail program. Transparency is a citizen's obligation. Access to information is a citizen's right.

Where are you, Kaname?

Kotaro here. Off work?

He entered the subject line and paused to think.

Im really sorry to put u out. I owe you. Treat u when I get back.

OBTW I walked Makoto to the station today. He seemed real down. I never saw him like that. Have u heard anything about problems with BB? M wouldn't tell, so I figured I better ask u. If u have 411, mail me.

He sent the message, closed the program quickly, as if running away, and went back to his research. When his mother yelled up the stairs for him to take his turn in the bath, he went right down.

When he came back, there was no response from Kaname.

7

The drug store in Kawasaki where Saeko Komiya had worked was called Sakura Pharmacy.

The neighborhood was a mix of residential and commercial. Sakura Pharmacy, which occupied the first floor of an old building, was one of several near a cluster of medical clinics. The only thing new about it was the wheelchair ramp to the entrance.

"I used to live in the neighborhood and got some prescriptions here. I wanted to offer my condolences." Kotaro knew how to turn on the courtesy when he needed to, the kind older people didn't expect from the young. The white-coated, middle-aged pharmacist who received him bowed politely.

"Thank you, we appreciate that." Kotaro noticed that the hair on the top of the man's head was thinning.

"Many of her patients have stopped by to pay their respects. Saeko started working here before she got married. She was one of our veterans, very friendly with a lot of people."

Kotaro knew that. He'd read it on the web.

I knew Ms. Komiya...

I got prescriptions from her for a chronic condition for many years...

She gave me an antipyretic after I had a reaction to Tamiflu...

She was very kind and always saw me off at the entrance...

"I hope they catch the killer soon," Kotaro said.

"Yes, it's something we pray for every day."

This was his first attempt to "read" a place, rather than a person, with his left eye. His first impression was one of solidified anxiety, with a faint shadow of fear. There were thin but distinctly visible threads of terror and fragments of sadness.

Hospitals and pharmacies are frequented by the sick and those who fear they may be sick, and their words leave a characteristic signature. The words in Sakura Pharmacy were not harsh or sharp. They didn't writhe violently or rush like knives at Kotaro's eye. A faint smell of sadness seemed to cling to the place. For the first time, he detected the odor of words.

There was no trace of the killer. He saw nothing that suggested the presence of a murderer, no Shadow like the one Keiko Tashiro had dragged around. The countless words about the murder had left behind only fear and sadness and regret. They were mixed with the remnants of words that predated the murder, or were only potent enough to persist for a short time before fading.

Whoever killed Saeko Komiya had no connection to this place. Even if the perpetrator had been here, his words could no longer be traced.

"Does the family still live in that condominium?" Kotaro asked.

"No. Mr. Komiya couldn't take care of their little boy on his own, so he sent him to live with his grandparents."

"I'd like to leave this." Kotaro held out a small bouquet. "If it's no trouble, maybe you could put these in some water and leave them on her desk."

"Thanks very much, I'll do that."

Kotaro left the pharmacy and traced the victim's route home. The buses she used to ride kept passing him, but he walked all the way.

Condominium complexes big enough to have their own nursery school are like small towns. There must have been five hundred residences.

Traces of words danced in the air, swirling and scattering as though blown by the wind, flowing, clustering, and disappearing. The sheer number was astonishing. This was another first for Kotaro, to see so many words in one place. There were so many that he had no idea where to start.

But one thing was certain: he saw nothing dangerous or evil, or mournful. Most of the words, when he tried to focus on them, were too old and faint to make out.

Like the others in the complex, the building where Saeko Komiya and her family had lived had no security lobby. Their condo was number 303, third floor, west side. Kotaro walked up to the door. The nameplate had been removed. There was nothing in the mail flap. A small bouquet of chrysanthemums was wilting in a milk bottle by the door.

There were no traces here either. The husband and son had moved out soon after the murder. Kotaro went back down the stairs, wishing he'd brought his bouquet here instead.

The nursery school occupied the northeast corner of the first floor. BLOSSOM SCHOOL was pasted to the inside of the big bay window in letters of colored felt. The door was glass too, with a colored frame.

Facilities that care for children almost always have tight security. Without being a good deal older or younger, it would be hard for Kotaro to get a look inside by posing as a family member. But in the end it wasn't necessary. As he sidled up to the entrance, using the big potted plant outside to keep out of sight, he saw it.

The frame around the safety-glass door was a cheerful green. Just inside the glass, next to the frame, was a frozen string of words.

Thoughts.

The nursery school was full of words, floating like dust motes. There were fewer here than outside, and most of them were colorless, faintly glowing fragments and broken threads. These must be the words of children, still learning to use language. Their words weren't dyed with mature emotions and intentions.

The black, slimy clot on the inner surface of the glass seemed to dominate everything else. The sight was so bizarre that Kotaro almost gasped with surprise. It reminded him of a fleck of vile, liquefied decay that had spurted from a puncture in a body bag.

The maggots in the clot writhed and crawled on the glass. Kotaro wanted to take a cloth and some disinfectant and expunge them on the spot.

Silver threads crossed his vision. *Defilement.*

"Do you think it's the killer's?"

That I cannot say, Galla's threads relayed.

True, the clot might have nothing to do with Saeko Komiya's murder. It might be a trace of some other conflict: a quarrel between parents or hostile feelings among the staff.

Still, Kotaro doubted it. There was something too awful about those words and the way they stuck to the glass like slime. Their vile color and the repulsive wriggling of the maggots almost burned themselves into his retina.

It was time to hit the crime scene—the gas station in Totsuka.

▼

"Hey, you okay, mister?"

A cracked voice called anxiously over his shoulder. Kotaro was in no shape to answer.

Everything about the gas station was old, from the building to its stained and rusting pumps and equipment. The only thing new was this portable outhouse in a corner of the lot. Kotaro was hunched over the bowl with the door wide open, retching his guts out while the attendant looked on anxiously.

The restroom where Saeko Komiya's body had been discovered was locked and cordoned off with yellow tape marked KANAGAWA PREFECTURAL POLICE.

"Yeah, it's too weird. Nobody's gonna go in there. Too scary. The boss figured leave it till they catch the guy, you know? So we got this thing—"

That was as much as Kotaro had heard before he lost his struggle with nausea and dashed into the outhouse.

There was no doubt. The spoor was clear and unmistakable. This time, what he saw *did* burn itself into his retina.

It was the nursery school all over again—black slime filled with wriggling black maggots. But here the slime had arms and legs, a torso and a head. It was an effigy of the killer himself, the dregs of his thoughts left behind in words, like fingerprints or footprints. But the writhing maggots made the effigy undulate sickeningly.

Like Makoto's giant, the effigy was faceless. Kotaro couldn't tell which way it was facing, which was a small blessing. If the thing had made eye contact, he wasn't certain he could've kept his sanity.

The killer had left a ferociously malevolent darkness. The effigy made no sound. Kotaro heard no voices. Like the words he saw at the nursery school, the traces here were fragmentary, but the stench of defilement and sexual frenzy was overpowering.

Kotaro recalled the snakelike appendage dangling from the effigy's crotch and was overcome by another storm of nausea. Trembling violently, he threw up everything he'd eaten since morning. When his stomach was empty, he tried to disgorge that as well.

"Should I phone for an ambulance?" The attendant rubbed Kotaro's back gingerly.

"No. I'm okay," he answered in a half gurgle.

"Are you, like, somebody who can see ghosts and stuff? Some people can. There's this girl that cries every time she comes round here. She says she saw a naked lady with a white face and a rope around her neck outside the restroom."

Kotaro flushed the toilet and stood up. "I'm not that type."

"Oh, okay."

"I knew the victim. I just wanted to stop by and say a prayer."

"Really? Sorry, didn't mean to be rude. Hey, why don't you come inside?"

They went into the office and the attendant handed him a moist towel. He had dyed red hair and a pierced ear—the picture of a delinquent, but he came across as a pretty nice guy.

"Thanks," Kotaro said. "Sorry to put you out. I'm not even a customer."

"Oh, it's all right. We practically don't have any customers anyway. I mean, since the thing happened."

"So you get mostly people who are curious?"

"I hear things were crazy right afterwards. These days it's people like yourself, who knew her or who're from around here. They leave flowers sometimes. There's the reporters, you know, and the TV people. There was even a big table out there for the flowers and candles. But the boss said it wasn't a good idea to have something like that around forever. So they got rid of it last week. I'm sure her spirit's gone to its reward by now."

Kotaro felt a sudden surge of affection for this openhearted stranger. "Have you worked here long?"

"Me? Oh, no. Started last week. Miyata and the boss, they keep getting called down to the station. They're too busy to take care of business." He laughed. "Course, we got no customers, so it doesn't really matter. But they need somebody to keep an eye on the place. That's me."

"The 'boss'—is that the owner?"

"Yep. Then there's Miyata. He's part time, but he says he's been pumping gas here ten years."

"The police are still talking to them? It's been a while since the murder."

"They're not suspects. They go down and look at photos. Most people pay cash here, but sometimes they use a card. We got a security camera too, 'cept the pictures aren't real clear." He pointed to the ceiling.

"This will sound kind of strange," Kotaro said, "but does either your boss or Miyata have young children?"

The attendant shook his head. His oversize earring glinted in the late morning sunlight. "Miyata's single. The boss has a son, but he's my age. We went to high school together. Well, for a year, anyway. Before I dropped out."

"I see. So that's why you're working here."

"Yeah. They asked me. Said I oughta work for 'em and keep an eye on the place if I didn't have anything better to do."

The owner and his part-time employee have nothing to do with the nursery school, then.

The slime at the school was on the inside of the door. Whoever left it there had some connection with the school—someone who worked there, family to one of the children, or maybe someone who would be in and out, handling deliveries or maintenance. In any case, some kind of insider. The owner and Miyata and this good-natured attendant were clean.

"You got good manners," the attendant said. His tone was utterly sincere. "You must be from a good family. Or are you with one of those religious groups?"

"Do you get religious people here too?"

"Yeah. They come to pray."

People were still looking for closure. The crime was horrendous, but there were no prospects of an arrest. Just rumors, with no clues to what was true or false.

"The Serial Amputator. You think they coulda thought up a better name," the attendant said. "What he does is a lot worse than slicing off a toe or two."

"I guess you're right."

"Feeling better?"

"Yes, thanks. Sorry to trouble you."

"Aw, it's okay."

Kotaro went around the back of the building on his way out. From there he could see the entrance to the restroom. He closed his right eye.

The effigy was real, but did not exist. Its head bobbed gently from side to side, but the wind wouldn't know it was there.

It looks like it's humming a tune.

Kotaro's stomach started to rebel again. His left retina was hot with anger.

As he turned the corner of the building, he saw the attendant carrying a broom and dustpan. He started sweeping up around the pumps. Kotaro hurriedly opened his right eye, but not before he'd caught a glimpse of the man with his left.

The attendant's Shadow was hazy and half-transparent, but it was no giant, and nothing like a body bag or a mass of slime. It was light and diaphanous. Neither his words nor his thoughts had much weight. But he'd been kind. Even if he was a fool, he was still a good guy.

Whoever had strangled Saeko Komiya, cut off her right leg at the knee, brought her body here, and dumped it in the restroom, was the antithesis of this attendant. The killer would present as a normal, well-socialized adult. No one at Blossom School would think him out of place.

But he was inhuman.

Galla? Can you trace him?

Silence.

Galla? Please answer.

A silver thread crossed his eye. *That is no ordinary spoor. It is excrement.*

What does that mean?

The doll is the killer's discharge, she explained.

Silence. The end of the silver thread fluttered.

To say it in a way you will understand—he gained release.

After strangling, mutilating, and dumping the corpse of Saeko Komiya, the killer had gone outside and shut the door. In that instant, he gained release. Whatever emotion it was he'd felt toward his victim—hate, anger, lust—had left him. Yes, the doll was his discharge.

That is why the spoor is clear at that place. But the link between doll and killer is severed. The doll is no longer part of his word body.

Are you saying you can't trace him? he asked.

I cannot. But if the one you seek is close, you shall know him.

Like comparing fingerprints. Or DNA.

Kotaro walked a few minutes down the road to a restaurant built over a parking lot. It was the middle of a weekday and the lot was nearly empty. He leaned against a pillar and tried to calm his breathing as he called Shigenori. The ex-detective picked up instantly.

"Where are you right now?" Kotaro asked.

"Haneda Airport."

Right. He's off to Tomakomai. "Do you remember the restroom where the Totsuka victim was found?"

"Unisex, one room. The manager has the key."

"Yeah. Would it be simple to copy a key like that? I saw something on

TV where they had this key, made an impression in soap or clay, and took it to a locksmith."

"You could do that. But you'd have to have a solid cover story. Otherwise no legitimate locksmith would help you."

"I think the person who killed Saeko Komiya was someone who could come up with a story that would convince any locksmith."

"Why do you say that?"

"Because whoever did it has some connection with the school her son went to."

Shigenori was silent. Kotaro could hear announcements coming over the PA system.

"What did you see?" he asked finally.

"I can't talk about it now. I'd probably barf again."

"Barf?" Shigenori's voice was high-pitched with surprise. "Then you'd better step away. I'll handle it."

"Is it hard to do a stakeout?"

"It's impossible for an amateur. What did you see? What's Galla's take?"

"Listen to the announcements, detective. You wouldn't want to miss your flight. Travel safely." Kotaro hung up. Shigenori didn't call back.

He squatted at the base of the pillar. His visit to the gas station had left him worn out.

If the killer was connected to the nursery school, he was probably familiar with the victim. If he was a parent of one of the children, he might've been good friends with Komiya. It would've been natural to approach her as she was heading home. Something like, *I'm on the way there myself. Can I give you a lift?*

The door opens. The victim gets in the car without the slightest sense of danger.

Kotaro remembered what Shigenori told him: that it had to have happened that way. It would be nigh impossible to forcibly abduct a young woman on a crowded street without drawing attention.

Had whoever picked her up committed the other murders?

Could someone unthreatening enough to pick up Saeko Komiya, abduct her, and murder her be traveling around Japan committing serial murder?

Kotaro shook his head and set that doubt aside. Right now the most important thing was to get close to the killer. Staking out the school seemed the best way to go; there was no telling when he might show up—

Wait a minute. What about the website? Kotaro pulled out his laptop and ran a search. Blossom School's site was colorful, framed by adorable illustrations. There was a photo of the director, a middle-aged woman, over a paragraph of text titled "Blossom School: History and Spirit."

Kotaro paged through the site. This Week's Activities. Parents Circle. Event Calendar. Gallery. Security was tight as a drum. Users needed two PIN codes and their child's ID number to log in.

If he could get behind the firewall, he could use the Eye to read the messages posted by parents and staff. It would be far more efficient than hanging around for hours or days outside the school, not knowing if the killer would even show up.

I'm an idiot, he thought, and hit himself lightly with his fist. *I'm supposed to be this web professional, but it's such a pose. This is way beyond me.*

He didn't have the chops to hack into anyone's website. Even if he made a crash effort to pick up the skills, he'd need someone to guide him. That could get sticky.

He got to his feet and set off for the station, walking faster as he went. It was like Shigenori's comment about locksmiths: he'd have to have a believable cover story, otherwise no one in Kumar would help him hack a site like that.

He bought a ticket from the machine at Totsuka Station and was walking through the concourse toward the Yokosuka Line platform when his phone buzzed. It was a voice call from Kaname.

"Hello?"

"Ko-chan? Oh, you're someplace noisy. Are you in a station?" Her voice sounded strange. Dark. "Can you find someplace quiet? This won't take long."

"Do we have to talk right now?"

"Yes. I have to get this off my mind." She sounded upset. Kotaro could picture her pouting. "I didn't send you a mail because I don't want to leave a record. It took courage for me to call you, Ko-chan. Just listen. I'll only tell you once. I'm mad at you."

"Me? What did I do?"

"Sending me a mail like that. Asking me about Makoto. Saying you were worried about him," Kaname said. "Did someone say something? Did you hear something? I know you. You're not the type to ask about stuff like that unless someone gave you the idea."

Kotaro moved anxiously to the edge of the concourse, away from the crowds.

"Listen, Kaname. I was worried about him, okay? I've never seen him look like that."

"Is that the only reason?"

No, that's not all. I got this magic eye from a demon named Galla, and I saw Makoto walking around with a giant full of black insects.

Kotaro didn't answer. Kaname was silent too. Finally she sighed.

"Okay. I guess I have to tell you, otherwise I'd be hiding something. I don't like that either."

There are lots of things you don't like, eh Kaname?

"You know Makoto is a really nice kid," she said.

He's a year younger than you. Does that make him a kid?

"But he wasn't always like that," she added.

"When are you talking about? When wasn't he like what?"

"He told me he's been a code jockey since middle school, maybe eighth or ninth grade. Like, almost a genius. And for a while he used his skills for stuff he's not proud of now. Defacing people's sites, hacking, things like that. He broke into a government website and uploaded nasty pictures. Another time he stole a client list from a health food company and published it." Kaname's voice tightened with fury. "He used to go into celebrity blogs, blogs by artists, famous people, and change their entries! Then he'd comment on the entry he changed and try to get people to fight about it! He thought it was hilarious. He couldn't stop."

Kotaro blinked as perspiration dripped into his eyes. The concourse was steaming in the rainy-season heat. He glanced nervously at people passing by as he held the phone to his ear.

"Makoto was on Kumar's blacklist until about six months before he got hired. But he was good enough to get on the list, right? So Seigo got in touch with him and convinced him to join us. He told him he ought to use his talents for something better."

Kotaro remembered the way Seigo had sold him on working at Kumar. He had a way of using your self-respect to convince you to reach for bigger things.

"Makoto decided Seigo was right. I don't think he's a bad guy. He's not faking it, he's showing us who he really is. The thing is..."

Kotaro could almost see Kaname pursing her lips.

"Some people in Kumar know what he used to do, and they don't trust him."

"BB people?" If anyone other than Seigo knew about Makoto's past, it would likely be someone on BB Island. Monitoring hackers like Makoto was part of what they did.

"I don't think his boss Inose knows. Otherwise I don't think he would've brought him over from our island."

"Probably not. He must have better skills than a lot of the people on BB," Kotaro said.

"That's another problem. Some of them might be envious that Inose recruited him. That would be reason enough to gossip."

"Maybe there's no point in worrying, but Makoto's down because of things on BB Island. It's not a friendly place for him to be."

"I wish he hadn't transferred." Kotaro sighed.

"Anyway, that's what's going on. I like Makoto. I'm not going to change my opinion."

"Hey, that goes for me too!"

"Thanks, Kotaro." The tension in Kaname's voice seemed to drop, finally. "You're a good guy too. See you."

Kotaro leaned against the wall in a daze, remembering the black giant stuck like glue to Makoto. It was his past, the embodiment of all the words he'd used during his hacker days.

On the Internet, words are actions. The net is a world where only words exist. Words are everything. They accumulate and become their speaker's past.

Ayuko's words echoed in his mind: *Whatever they say, the words people use stay inside them. They don't disappear. There's no way people can separate their words from themselves.*

Kotaro wondered how long Makoto would have to carry that giant around with him. If he spent enough time helping others, he'd probably work the burden off someday. The giant would wither away and finally disappear.

Or would it?

Galla had said that Ayuko understood the power embodied in words. Though he had no special insight, Kotaro had been given the capacity to see that power.

His vision blurred. The station was hot as hell. He couldn't stop sweating—

No. I'm not crying.

I need to see Ayuko. She'd understand. I need to tell her everything that's happened, everything I've experienced, all the stuff I've learned. She'd listen. She'd know what to do.

For the first time, Kotaro yearned for another person with every cell in his body.

8

Ten years prior, Shigenori had flown north to Tomakomai to investigate an armed robbery that ended in fatalities. Shoe prints at the scene had turned out to be from snow boots sold only in Hokkaido. The factory had been on the outskirts of Tomakomai. The boots in question were already long out of production, and Shigenori had had to wade through box after box of sales records in a corner of an office dominated by the glow from a well-fired potbelly stove.

Tomakomai had been a city of paper mills, and paper was the foundation of the local economy. Since then, Japan's economy had risen, fallen, and risen again. Paper producers moved their operations outside the country, and the industry was shaken up by mergers and acquisitions. Things had changed, and the changes ought to be visible, but Shigenori's memory of that long-ago visit was hazy. There did seem to be more and bigger buildings and more prosperous-looking residences. That vague impression was all he could summon up. But he did remember the sky, how it seemed somehow farther above his head than in Tokyo. That hadn't changed.

Above a certain size and level of prosperity, regional cities in Japan look alike. To discover what makes each one different, one has to sample the food and the sake, and stay long enough to see the patterns of life under the surface. Otherwise it can be hard to tell them apart. Wealth tends to smooth out the differences in the way people live. Life becomes standardized.

Only in nature, in the mountains and valleys beyond the hand of man, are the real differences, the real uniqueness, preserved. There is something about the air in Hokkaido, a kind of richness that will never change. For better or worse, the only thing that really changes is people.

Naka-chan was still open for business. Shiro Nakanome's izakaya was managed by his cousin now. This was another bit of information Shigenori found on the web, embedded in recollections about Nakanome that people had posted after his death. Shigenori was used to the fact that he could find anything on the web if he dug deep enough, but it still bothered him. Become a victim, and everything about your personal life is aired for the world to see.

The clearing where Nakanome's body had been found stuffed into a discarded refrigerator lay near a residential area among gently rolling hills northeast of the city. The clearing was in a slight depression, which made it easy to dump illegally without being seen.

The area wasn't exactly isolated. The multicolored roofs of nearby houses were visible through the trees. The hills seemed ideal for walking, but the clearing full of trash was an eyesore.

Shigenori had come straight from the hotel after dropping off his bag. He knew the way, even down to the landmarks to follow, from surfing the web. He was never close to getting lost.

He stood at the edge of the clearing and surveyed it with a slight scowl, calculating the lay of the land from there to Naka-chan. Only after considering this did he unfold the map he'd picked up at the airport.

A notice on a large sheet of plastic was nailed to a tree: ILLEGAL DUMPING PROHIBITED BY LAW. The wording was problematic but the message was clear. The sign was dirty and the foot of the tree it was nailed to was submerged in garbage. An old-fashioned twin-tub washing machine lay on its side a few feet away.

There were other signs around the clearing, stapled to trees or on stakes in the ground.

NO ENTRY AFTER DARK
FIRES STRICTLY PROHIBITED
RETRIEVE ALL CIGARETTE BUTTS!

The signs looked hastily erected, probably because of the waves of journalists and rubberneckers who thronged the site after the murder. Now they were tattered and weather-beaten.

What kind of person would kill a man, stuff his body into a refrigerator, and haul it all the way out here?

I wonder if Mishima could use Galla's power to see traces the killer left behind? No. That's no way to gather evidence.

Shigenori's slight scowl was shadowed by a rush of sadness. He gritted his teeth, turned his back on the clearing and walked down the hill.

Shiro Nakanome had once been married. There were no children. His ex-wife had remarried and was living in Tokyo. At the time of his death, he'd been seeing one of his regular customers. Neither of them had made a secret of it.

"We were more than friends, but that's all," she posted on the web. "Marriage wasn't on the table. We never fought about it. He was surprisingly popular with women, and for all I know he was seeing someone else, but we never talked about it. To be honest, I wouldn't have cared."

Nakanome might not have been pleased to hear his partner describe him as "surprisingly" popular, but Shigenori could believe it after watching him serve customers at Naka-chan in a video on the web. He was a large, rough-hewn man with a full beard. The beard made it hard to judge his expression; someone meeting him on a dark mountain road might mistake him for a bear.

But everything changed when he opened his mouth. He had a deep, soothing voice and was very good with customers. The video had been shot the September before his death, at a fifth anniversary party for Naka-chan. Shigenori wasn't sure whether to thank the person who posted it for saving him valuable time, or berate her for invading the privacy of the victim's next of kin. He just watched the video with a deepening frown.

He must've been quite a guy if he could run a watering hole and keep such a pleasant disposition.

Nakanome had gone to culinary school after graduating from the local high school. He'd married at twenty-two, but it ended after six years. Most of his years as a cook were spent in Otaru, in southeast Hokkaido. He'd returned to Tomakomai at thirty-four to start a small restaurant in a renovated wing of his parents' home. The restaurant prospered, and with new roots in the local community, he'd expanded into the evening trade with Naka-chan.

His parents were still alive and living in the same house. When he opened Naka-chan, Nakanome moved to a one-room apartment a few minutes away on foot, but he had still dined with his parents a few times a month. Sometimes his mother and father would spend an evening at the izakaya.

Nakanome was their only child. His ashes were in the family grave and coverage of his murder had stopped, but his parents were still in mourning. People in the neighborhood worried about them; on the rare occasions when they were seen outside the house, they looked thin and pale as ghosts.

Nakanome's childhood home was Shigenori's next destination after the clearing in the woods. The wing that had once been a restaurant still had a lonely-looking menu board and a few other fittings outside. The house was set well back from a broad public road in a neighborhood of fine-looking homes, but one of Japan's biggest delivery companies maintained a depot a short distance away. It was easy to imagine a restaurant offering cheap, tasty meals doing well here.

Naka-chan opened at five. With time to kill, Shigenori walked to Nakanome's high school, then his culinary school. He had no intention of talking to people. Even if he were to find someone willing to unload to a stranger who was neither detective nor reporter, the information wouldn't be reliable anyway.

The high school was crowded with students. Most of the people coming and going at the little culinary school along the main drag were young too, but there were a few men who were probably as old as Shigenori. Maybe they were planning to open their own restaurants as a second profession after retirement. If so, they were far more healthy and productive than Shigenori, who couldn't seem to put his inner detective out to pasture.

He saw little point in venturing inside either school. There would only be ordinary classrooms and ordinary people with nothing to hide. All he'd find would be peaceful daily life, with the usual backbiting and insecurities beneath the surface, just as there surely had been when Nakanome was here, when no one would've dreamt someone would take his life at the age of forty-one; when he couldn't have dreamt it himself.

Shigenori's feet ached. There was a donut shop not far from the culinary school, on the same street. He went inside, bought a donut and coffee, and sat down near the windows. The place was cavernous but there were few customers. The parking lot outside was big too. There were multiple shops from this chain in Shigenori's Tokyo neighborhood. The donuts were the same and the coffee was the same, but somehow this branch in Tomakomai felt totally different.

He finished his coffee, pulled out the laptop, and put on his reading glasses.

Shiro Nakanome's murder had entered the national spotlight after victim number two was discovered in Akita. The fact that both crimes involved mutilation had triggered a media frenzy. Partially because the murderer had taken pains to erase every trace of the second victim's identity, interest in both murders faded after a few weeks. But when Mama Masami's body was found, the media's attention returned, hotter than ever, and the specter of Toe-Cutter Bill was fixed firmly in the public mind. Shiro Nakanome became not just a murder victim, but the first in a series of grotesque killings and a subject of new interest.

Shigenori peered at his laptop. What was happening before Mama Masami was found? How was Nakanome's murder covered between June 1, when his body was found, and September 22, when the Akita victim's decaying body turned up in a Dumpster at a public housing complex? What aspects did the media see fit to cover? What did the public—the Internet society, the people who couldn't stop talking about the Serial Amputator—think when there was just one murder, with nothing to compare it to? How did they guess the case might eventually be solved?

As far as he could discern from the ocean of information spread before him, the main point of speculation just after Nakanome's murder revolved around whether the refrigerator had been there before the killing or had been brought there with the body in it. A few days after the victim was found, careful inspection proved that the refrigerator had been in the clearing before the murder. This was important, because if it had been brought to the site after Shiro was killed, there would have had to have been more than one perpetrator. The site showed no sign of tire tracks, and there was no way a single individual could have unloaded the refrigerator from a vehicle.

If the refrigerator was in the clearing before the murder, one person could conceivably have transported the body. Or perhaps the killer somehow lured his victim to the clearing and killed him there. Both scenarios were possible. The refrigerator was in relatively good condition, and the body was found soon after the murder because some unlucky individual had been curious about whether the fridge was still serviceable.

Still, something about the setup bothered Shigenori. Was this really the work of one person?

Several of the posts he'd read commented on the victim's muscular physique and above-average height. They also noted that the refrigerator was a popular home model from ten years ago, a compact but surprisingly deep design with ample storage space.

But piecing information together wasn't enough. No conclusions could be drawn without a visit to the scene. Someone had overpowered and strangled a heavy, well-built man on uneven terrain—or transported the dead weight of the corpse up the hill and into this depression in the woods—and manhandled it up and into the refrigerator. Could all that have been the work of one person? It hadn't occurred to him to doubt it until he saw the site.

I'm losing my touch. "One more time" Tsuzuki, huh? I'm a rusty old has-been.

Like most people, once the second murder hit the news, Shigenori had been infected with the assumption that the same individual committed both crimes. And because he'd swallowed that assumption from the outset, he hadn't bothered to go back to the beginning and consider the first murder in isolation.

Serial killers with strange predilections work alone, committing their crimes in pursuit of dark fantasies that are uniquely theirs. They almost never work in concert with others, even people with similar destructive urges. Toe-Cutter Bill—the Serial Amputator—*had* to be a solo operator. There was no other way to look at it. If that assumption was wrong, the whole structure of profiling in criminal investigations would collapse.

But murdering Shiro Nakanome and dumping his body up in those hills looked like a team effort. One person could have orchestrated things while the other, or others, assisted. An inner voice was telling Shigenori that was how it happened, and that voice was growing more insistent. Did that mean there were multiple Toe-Cutter Bills, multiple Serial Amputators, collaborating to kill people all over Japan? It would be unheard of in the annals of crime.

Or maybe the whole thing was a one-off. After four murders, it wasn't surprising to have a copycat killing: Ayuko Yamashina. Maybe the killing in Tomakomai was a one-off too—and the domino that sent the rest falling.

At his table in the huge, quiet donut shop, bathed in sweet aromas, Shigenori glumly drank his coffee, input more search terms, and stumbled across this post:

"The victim in Tomakomai was stuffed into a *refrigerator* in an illegal *garbage dump*. The Akita victim was found in a *municipal refuse bin*. The Mishima victim was left in a *clothes trunk*. The Totsuka victim was discovered in a *locked restroom*. The killings share common features, but they each encode a slightly different message. The fact that the killer amputated a different body part each time might also be some sort of code."

The moon is round. So is a turtle. Not the same, but they look similar.

And that is all. Each of the five killings came saturated with the smell of an overall sequence, the legend of the Serial Amputator. The post had been uploaded two days before Ayuko Yamashina's body had been found in a vacant lot in central Tokyo. Shigenori wondered how the poster would've explained that.

Ayuko was still considered by the public to be the fifth victim. The poster would probably feel compelled to shoehorn her murder into the same theoretical straightjacket, and that probably wouldn't require much work. That's the thing about stories: they're flexible enough to accommodate just about anything.

Is anyone looking at this without bias? Shigenori squinted at the monitor. Had anyone in this far-northern town taken a good long look at the unshakable facts of Nakanome's murder without being infected by the serial killer story?

▼

Someone in Naka-chan was charring the fish.

There was a run-down game center across the narrow street from the izakaya. All the machines had seen better times in some other amusement spot.

It was ten past six. Shigenori had been here since before five, feeding the slot machine with game tokens. He'd planned to check out the izakaya at six, but he'd had a clear sight line to the front door since it opened, and not a single customer had shown up. So here he was, still dropping tokens and killing time.

It looked like the new manager, Nakanome's cousin, was a distant second when it came to culinary skill. Nothing seemed to have changed from the outside. Maybe the clientele Nakanome had spent years building up didn't like his cousin's style.

The smell of burnt fish was pervasive. Shigenori didn't want to be the first customer; it would make him too conspicuous. The slot machine was the only one he could manage to play and still keep the entrance to Naka-chan in sight, so he was monopolizing it. It didn't matter; there were hardly any customers, and the part-timer behind the counter didn't seem to care.

Maybe he should just go back to the hotel and wait? Arriving later in the evening would give him a better chance of chatting up some of Nakanome's old customers. But he also wanted to talk to the cousin when he wasn't too busy serving. He wanted to be there when there were a few customers, but not too many.

What the hell is he cooking, anyway?

The stool was hard and his rear end was starting to ache. He decided to get on with it. He didn't have to go in right away. There was something he wanted to see first, next to the sliding front door. Something he wanted to examine up close.

It was a stand of miniature bamboo stalks in a big ceramic pot, their slender branches festooned with strips of paper, each inscribed with wishes for the summer Star Festival. A few minutes before five, a thirtyish man in jeans, a polo shirt and a white apron had emerged from Naka-chan and set the pot outside.

There was nothing unusual about the bamboo. It was that time of year. Many other businesses had pots just like it outside their doors. Some even had a supply of paper strips so anyone could jot down a wish and tie it to the bamboo.

The stalks next to the entrance of Naka-chan were heavy with wishes, a pretty rainbow of color. It lent a very pleasing effect to the shop. Shigenori wanted to read the wishes on those strips of paper.

The man in the polo shirt was likely Nakanome's cousin, the new manager. He'd only been outside for a few seconds—not enough to judge a family resemblance—but he wasn't as physically large as the deceased. Medium height and build, close-cropped hair, clean-shaven.

The burnt-fish smell was fading. Still no customers. Shigenori got up from the slot machine and stepped outside. The pounding music faded as the door closed behind him. The narrow street, lined with multitenant buildings, was wrapped in lengthening shadows. It was less than an hour before sunset.

Shigenori strolled causally across the street and stopped in front of Naka-chan, as though noticing it for the first time. He glanced up and down the block and approached the door. The bamboo stalks stood higher than his head. They seemed to be bowing toward him gently.

He pinched a paper strip between thumb and forefinger and examined it closely. The characters were large; he could read them without his glasses.

I hope they catch the person who did it soon. —Aiko

Shigenori read one strip after another. Some were in a masculine hand, some were written by women. A few were clearly left by children.

Naka-chan, are you having a cold one in heaven? —Kenta

I hope they arrest the guy. —Miki

Naka-chan, thanks for your great sake. Let's raise a glass again. —Natchan

I hope they catch him and give him the death penalty. —Sanae

Naka-chan is forever! The killer can go to hell! —Katsumi

Naka-chan, we miss you. Please come back. —Rie

Rest in peace, Shiro. —Reiji

Shigenori read every strip. He glanced at his watch. It was 6:44. Still no customers. He heard music coming faintly from inside, some unidentifiable genre.

All right, then. I'm from Tokyo, here on business. I hear you have some great sake. I don't know anything about the murder. Not a thing. I'm just a guy.

Shigenori turned his cover story over in his mind one more time. He was reaching for the door when he felt a heavy hand on his shoulder.

▼

Kotaro's message to Makoto said to meet him at nine at the tea caddy building.

The place is empty. It's dark, but don't worry, it's not weird or anything.

Kotaro had added "It's urgent" and Makoto had seemed to understand. He didn't ask what was up. He just did what Kotaro asked, as though resigned to his fate.

There's no power, so put a full charge on your laptop. I want to see some of that old technique of yours, so get that charged up!

When they met up in front of the building, Makoto's expression was darker than the night around them. There was no breeze. It was humid, and they were both sweating.

"So, this place is empty?" Makoto looked up at the building, but Kotaro had already started for the service entrance.

"Yeah, totally empty. There's rumors about a ghost, but I haven't seen it yet."

Kotaro was thankful he hadn't returned the key to Shigenori on their last visit. The old man hadn't asked. He probably knew it was pointless.

Or maybe he thought there was nothing worse I could do with it. In that case, you've got another think coming, old man. I'm about to do something a lot *worse.*

Kotaro led the way up the stairs, flashlight in hand, not pausing until he was on the fourth floor.

"From here we go up to the roof." He lowered the ladder and motioned Makoto to climb.

Makoto finally broke his silence. "Can't we stay here? Up there we'll be exposed."

"Why should you care?"

"You said you wanted to see my old technique. Are you sure you want to be seen with me?"

Makoto's dark expression wasn't sorrow or regret. It was a mixture of resignation, a bit of anger, and deadly self-assurance. His question had a hint of humor in it. Kotaro didn't answer.

Makoto smiled grimly. "How'd you hear about me? It's not like you to pay attention to rumors. I was pretty sure you stayed away from gossip."

"Ashiya told me." Kotaro didn't feel like saying "Kaname." "But she told me because I asked her. I was worried about you after that walk to the station. You seemed really down."

"I see. She would tell you, in that case."

The two stood facing each other in the dark, each with his laptop slung over his shoulder. Kotaro's flashlight lit a circle on the floor. In silhouette, they looked identical.

"I need you to do something for me, Miyama." Not Makoto, now. "A little hacking. I need information. I'm not going to steal anything or cause trouble for anybody. But this is the only way I can get what I need. You can do that for me, can't you?"

The silhouette facing him was silent.

"It's the website of a nursery school. There's data about the kids, so security's gonna be tight. I want to see what the parents and staff posted there. Images, too. I want to see everything, wall to wall."

Makoto was silent for a moment before answering. "So why are you asking me?"

"Come on, you're the guy with the mad skills."

"If all you want is to get into some nursery school site, you didn't have to come to me. You don't know how, but that doesn't mean it's hard."

Kotaro exhaled slowly. He felt strangely calm. There was no sense of tension. It was the darkness. The darkness in the tea caddy building was his friend now. How much terror, how much astonishment had he experienced here? How many secrets?

The darkness was warmth. It gave him strength.

"You're right. I don't know the first thing about hacking. That's why I need you."

"Why should that matter to me?"

"If you don't help me, things will change."

He'd stepped off the cliff. There was no turning back. Kotaro Mishima was about to become a bad guy.

"If things change, see, BB Island is gonna be the least of your problems. I can arrange that real easy. You were right about me and rumors, I don't bother to listen. But when I heard about your past, hey, it was like I couldn't help it, you know? It totally blew me away to find out you were hiding your hacker past this whole time. So if I can't trust you anymore, that's gotta bother me," Kotaro said. "If I'm bothered, Kaname'll pick up on it. We're your best friends. Everybody knows it. If we're uncomfortable working with you, that's a bad sign, right? And once it's all over Drug Island, it'll spill out to the rest of Kumar."

It would be simple. Kaname was such a straight arrow that planting the seeds of doubt in her mind would be easy.

"But if we keep showing everyone we're behind you, I bet your BB problems go away. Whoever it is that envies you or is spreading gossip about your past is gonna end up the odd one out. Wouldn't that be better?"

The darkness in the room seemed to amplify his voice and kick it back at them.

Wouldn't that be better...? Wouldn't that be better...? Wouldn't that be better...?

Makoto spoke slowly. "There's another way. A quicker way. I'll quit."

"That's the worst thing you can do." Kotaro smashed the ball back over the net. "If you leave Kumar because of that, you'll end up back where you started, but this time it'll be worse. You can try to go straight, but wherever you go, it'll follow you. Your attitude will go to hell, and you'll start hacking again just to get back at the sons of bitches. Except this time it won't be malicious pranks. If you're gonna go bad, may as well make a living at it. You'll end up a criminal."

"What makes you so sure?" Makoto was calm.

"Because that's how people are. If you try to go straight and people don't give you a chance, you'll go off the rails for good."

No. That's not what I want to say. I saw him, Makoto—the giant that follows you everywhere, full of poisonous insects, their sickening buzzing...always clinging to you, standing over you, stepping on your heels, waiting for you to stumble. And when you do, he's going to devour you and digest you. He wants to turn himself into you. He's waiting for his chance. He doesn't want you to whittle him down to nothing. He wants to absorb you.

"You can't quit Kumar," Kotaro murmured. Again the darkness threw the words back at them.

You can't...You can't...You can't...

"Stay with us, Makoto. You've got a mountain to climb. You'll have my full support."

"And to get that, I have to do what you say?"

"Yep. You help me, I help you. It's a transaction."

Makoto didn't answer. The darkness was just as silent. When he finally spoke, his voice was clear and pure, as if the sediment of doubt had been filtered out of it.

"As soon as I learned to use a PC, people were calling me a prodigy. My parents were the first to notice. My tutor—he was this college student who lived in the neighborhood—gave me my first real coaching. He was a very nice guy. Had a very positive outlook on life.

"Everything about coding seemed so effortless. Everything I learned I could apply right away, and the more I applied, the more I learned. My tutor always gave me great feedback. He said I was this genius."

Geniuses don't know they're geniuses, Kotaro thought.

"Even when I was messing up websites, there were people who thought I was some kind of wizard. I never really got it. Why? It was so easy to do. But Seigo understood. 'Defacing websites isn't challenging enough for you, is it? It'll never satisfy you. So—do something else.' That's what he said.

"His logic was simple, but it really knocked me back. I wonder why." The silhouette shook its head. "I guess he just knows how to persuade people."

Yeah, but I don't want to think about Seigo now.

"Then we're all set," Kotaro said. "Seigo convinced you, and I'm his sidekick. That should convince you too."

"You're not Seigo," Makoto said cuttingly. His answer hit like an arrow. "Mishima, look. I haven't changed. I'm a coding prodigy with not much understanding of a lot of things. But there's something very important that I do know."

Kotaro was getting impatient. *Come on, out with it.*

"You want to strike a deal with me. To get there, you went through a one-way door. I know exactly what that means, but I don't think you do." He laughed quietly and set his bag on the floor. "I came prepared. Let's get started. I haven't done this for a while. I'm actually a little nervous."

Kotaro didn't want to watch. He knew he was even guiltier than Makoto. He was the one pulling the strings.

He went down to the third floor. The air here seemed thicker, with a dustier smell. He leaned against a wall and slid down to the floor with his knees drawn up.

Kotaro had never examined this floor closely before. In fact, this was the first time he'd actually stepped into it. The beam from his flashlight showed an open door to what must have once been a private living space. There was a clothes closet. He could see a washbasin in a bathroom off the main room. The toilet was missing.

The darkness was quiet and cooler than upstairs. He killed the flashlight and set it on the floor. He rubbed his face and laid his head on his folded arms. For several minutes, he sat there without moving.

Someone was whispering.

It was a rustling that he felt rather than heard. He raised his head.

Darkness. Abandoned, forgotten darkness.

He closed his right eye.

She stood right next to him, a phantom spun from silver threads. Her graceful, diaphanous form undulated gently, unsteadily, like an image under windswept water.

Her body's silver threads were whispering. Kotaro could hear them with the Eye. Each was murmuring the same word, alone and in unison.

lonely lonely lonely lonelylonelylonelylonelylonelylonelylonely

Kotaro watched, entranced, as time seemed to stop.

I'm looking at a ghost. Come to think of it, Tsuzuki said something about a young woman...

Words that were spoken years ago, here, by a lost young woman. Thoughts in words, still wandering in search of acceptance.

The phantom turned away, as though satisfied that Kotaro understood its message. Still undulating gently, it drifted through a wall and disappeared.

Kotaro noticed other word traces in the room. These were fainter and less distinct than the ghost, as if they had been worn away. They writhed weakly, shapeless blobs of jelly that never quite assumed a distinct form.

They're crying...

Was it because they were forgotten? Were they bitter at being left behind?

I won't cry.

Yesterday, after talking to Kaname, he'd found himself crying. He was determined that that wouldn't happen again.

Lonely? No, I've shut that word away for good. I'm not going to leave a trace of my loneliness anywhere in this world.

Because I'm a hunter.

"Mishima?" Makoto called down the stairs. "We're good to go."

Kotaro opened his right eye and banished the lonely, fluttering phantoms. He stood up.

▼

The man who stopped Shigenori before he could open the door to Naka-chan—who led him without a word down an alley and bundled him into the back of a parked Corolla—was in his forties, not a big man, certainly not muscular. His eyebrows sloped downward, framing perpetually narrowed eyes. The way he'd blinked when Shigenori looked him in the face betrayed deep discomfort.

Another man waited behind the wheel. This one looked to be twenty-five or twenty-six at most, rail-thin, with a pale face and a nervous expression.

Shigenori didn't resist. He knew he was heading for an unmarked police car as soon as the older man flashed his badge. They took him to a corner conference room on the fourth floor of Tomakomai Police Station South.

Shigenori wondered how many hours he'd been here. He looked at the clock on the wall; the hands were about to touch nine.

The room had a long table with five chairs. More folding chairs leaned against the wall. The cream wallpaper was sun-faded. The calendar didn't offer anything to relieve the eye, just the dates.

Shigenori could see an ashtray on a stand outside, in a corner of the balcony. That must be the designated smoking area. Stuck in this room with no one to talk to, he suddenly felt a powerful urge for a cigarette.

He'd told them the truth: address, name, background, everything to the last detail. The only thing he'd fudged was his motivation for being here. He'd come through Tomakomai with his wife four or five years ago on a vacation. They'd dropped by Naka-chan and been impressed by the sake selection. The grilled mackerel and the scallop sashimi had been wonderful. After he heard of Nakanome's death, he'd waited for a chance to stop by his house or the izakaya and offer a prayer. That was all. That was really the only reason he was here. He was a civilian now.

Maybe he'd pushed the "civilian" thing a little too hard. It certainly hadn't worked as well as he'd hoped. Now the two detectives who were unlucky enough to cross his path were probably in a huddle with their superiors, planning their next move. No, they'd be finished with that; they'd be running a background check. He'd given them two references, former subordinates who could vouch for him. *Just trying to be helpful, detectives. Of course, these aren't people who just sit around waiting for someone to call. They'll be hard to reach, probably. More work, detectives.*

They hadn't even offered him a cup of tea. Every now and then the older one would stick his head in the door and mumble an apology for keeping him cooling his heels. Sometimes there'd be another face behind him. One of the brass, checking him out. Shigenori always waved a hand genially. *No problem, detective. Please get on with your work. Don't mind me, detective.*

But he really needed a cigarette. He was dying for one. He didn't care if he ended up going back to them after all these years—

The door opened and the two men came in.

"We're very sorry to keep you waiting, Mr. Tsuzuki."

The one with the drooping eyebrows apologized, pulled out a chair and sat down across from him. Fatigue had merged with the look of discomfort in his eyes. Shigenori half-expected him to complain about it. His nervous young partner stood next to him, leaning a hip against the backrest of the chair. He already needed a shave; his beard was starting to turn the pale skin around his mouth blue.

"That's quite all right," Shigenori said agreeably. He was enjoying the opportunity to talk, though he couldn't hide the fatigue in his voice. "I've just been sitting here. You two seem to be very busy. What is it that seems to be the problem?"

The younger man's cheek twitched. His eyes flashed with irritation and the corners of his mouth turned down. His partner chuckled uncomfortably, which made his eyebrows droop even further.

"It took us a little bit of time to check your bona fides. My boss—well, he said to make it thorough."

He reached inside his coat and extracted a card. "Torisu, Detective Section. My partner's Matsuyama."

Shigenori accepted the card politely. Torisu's rank was sergeant. Matsuyama didn't seem to have a card. He just stood there scowling.

"I'm sorry," Shigenori said. "I'm afraid I don't carry cards anymore. I'm unemployed at the moment."

Torisu waved a hand affably. "It's all right. We know. We spoke with Detective Imai at the Metro Police. He gave us an earful about you."

Shigenori made a mental note to drop by the station and thank Imai when he got back.

"Really? I'm afraid I've put you to a lot of trouble. But really all I wanted to do was say a prayer for Nakanome. That's all."

"Yes, yes." Torisu nodded. Without missing a beat, he added, "Is that why you were scoping out his parents' house earlier?"

Shigenori was startled. His reaction must've been obvious to both of them, but the angle of Torisu's eyebrows didn't budge. His squint showed no trace of acknowledgement.

"After that, you checked out his high school and the cooking school. Do I have that right?"

They tailed me. I really am over the hill. Didn't notice a thing.

"You're very thorough, detective. So you had me marked as soon as I arrived at his parents' place."

"Marked? Oh, I wouldn't put it that way."

Torisu was being slippery. Shigenori decided to go with the flow and play his next card.

"So you must have the house under surveillance. Do you think there's a chance the killer might come back?"

"That's none of your business," Matsuyama snapped, with a shrill edge to his voice. *He really is wet behind the ears*, Shigenori thought. He felt a stab of nostalgia. He'd once had men just like this under his wing.

"Watch your manners, now," Torisu said to his partner.

"But sergeant!"

Torisu ignored him and smiled grimly. "The killer issued a statement after the fifth murder, in Tokyo. We thought it might be better to stay alert, in case he decides to circle back."

"I see. But those letters were sent to the media. There wasn't any mention of the victim's family. As far as I know, the killer hasn't contacted the relatives of any other victims, either." Shigenori smiled thinly. "Of course, maybe he did and it just hasn't been announced."

Torisu blinked with surprise, as though the thought had never occurred to him. "We're foot soldiers. We just follow the policies laid down upstairs. They're the ones with the inside dope. We don't know the details. The case is being run out of Central."

Tomakomai Central Police Department. Interesting.

"Can I speak freely, Mr. Tsuzuki? Your eyes…they're a little too much on point, if you know what I mean. The way you walked your route today didn't exactly have 'citizen' written all over it. So you see, we had to have a chat with you."

"Is that so? Did I look that suspicious?"

"Not suspicious. Like a pro."

"I'm over the hill, detective. I'm retired."

"Are you, really?" Torisu leaned forward. His hand was on the rudder now. It was time to get down to cases.

"You were with the Metro Police, so I assume you know this even better than I do, but a gruesome killing brings a lot of different types out of the woodwork. Not only the media. Freelance journalists, so-called. Nonfiction authors, film producers, that sort."

Shigenori smiled to show he was enjoying the ride. "Yes, yes. Definitely."

"Just last week, this young kid, looks like a college boy, shows up at mom-and-pop Nakanome's with a video camera. He's badgering them at the door, trying to get an interview. So I invite myself to have a chat with him. He tells me he's an Internet journalist. I couldn't get a straight explanation of just what that meant."

"It means he goes around with a camera visiting crime scenes and accidents," Shigenori said in a helpful tone. "He shoots some footage, slaps a little commentary on it, uploads it to YouTube or wherever. Or maybe he has his own blog and fronts it there."

For an instant, Torisu's eyes opened almost to normal size. "That's right. That's what the kid told me. You know all about this stuff. Are you an expert on the Internet?"

To Shigenori, this detective on the cusp of middle age might as well be no older than his partner, but he enjoyed watching him play the clueless oldster.

"Every day is Sunday for me. I've got a lot of free time. Sometimes I fool around on the laptop, that's all."

"I see. I don't put any stock in all that cyber-whatever stuff. I guess I'm just a hick."

"So how did things end up with that journalist?"

"I got him to leave, finally, but only after a couple of hours getting tongue-lashed about press freedom and the citizen's right to know and police secrecy."

"You have my condolences." Shigenori smiled ironically. "So is that what the two of you do all day? Shoo people away from the house?"

Torisu nodded dejectedly. "That's exactly what we do. When I think about what his parents have gone through, I just can't let them be bothered."

"And then I showed up, and you decided you had a problem on your hands."

"Well, to be honest, we thought maybe the Nakanomes had gone and hired themselves a private detective. You certainly look the part. This case has been dragging on too long with nothing to show. We're losing credibility."

Maybe that's true, but you're playing it up, mister. I can smell it.

"But this is much bigger than just the one murder. You're dealing with the Serial Amputator," Shigenori said insistently. "His victims are all over Japan—well, maybe that's going too far. He hasn't killed anyone east of Kanagawa. But he gets around."

"He certainly does." Torisu nodded vigorously. "Joint investigations, now those are hard. It's not like law enforcement is always reaching out across jurisdictions. It's hard to get people in sync. I don't know how the guys upstairs see it, but to us foot soldiers on the front line, every local situation has its own logic."

"I think you're right."

"If we didn't have all this coordination to deal with, we'd go slow but steady, one step at a time. As it is, it's like we gotta go three steps forward and two back just to get a step ahead. The victim's relatives have a right to be frustrated."

Shovel away, detective.

"If all we had were newspaper and television reporters up our noses, we'd be in clover. No, we have people calling themselves Internet reporters or investigative journalists—who knows if they're the real deal or not—sniffing around all over the place, spreading their own theories about the case. Then we're on the spot and we end up having to rebut all their nonsense. It might even turn out that their poking around gives the suspect—the Serial Amputator—an idea of where we are on the case. I shudder to think about it," he growled.

"I understand completely," Shigenori said. "It was careless of me to blunder around like I did. I've wasted too much of your valuable time. Please accept my deepest apologies."

He straightened his spine, put both palms flat on the table, and bowed until his forehead touched the wood. Torisu was flustered, or at least pretended to be.

"No, we're the ones who should apologize, for dragging you in here and treating you like a suspect," he said, before pivoting casually. "Your wife isn't with you on this trip, is she?"

"No, she's not. She's busier than I am, making a home for us both. There's no retirement from that job. She's got a lot of women friends her age to keep up with too."

"She sounds fully occupied."

"I didn't mention this, but I had an operation at the beginning of the year. Have you heard of spinal stenosis?"

Torisu looked up questioningly at his partner. For the first time, Matsuyama's mask of irritation and discomfort changed. His new expression was derision.

"The lumbar spine presses on the nerves. Makes your legs hurt, or numbs them."

"Really?" Torisu said. "How do you know that?"

"My mother has it. It's a postmenopausal thing, sergeant. Men don't get it."

Tsuzuki looked him straight in the eye. "Orchestra conductors develop it quite often. It's pretty common among athletes too, of both genders. People who engage in a lot of strenuous physical activity when they're young develop it in middle age. If you're into sports, you should be careful."

Matsuyama retreated into glum silence, as if Shigenori had interrupted a private conversation he'd been having with his boss.

"Anyway, the operation was a success and I finally got the cast off. I'm so happy to be pain-free that I've been traveling all over Japan. My wife thinks I'm crazy. She says she can't keep up with me."

"Sounds great. I envy you," Torisu said. The atmosphere was almost bubbly.

"I won't be causing you any more trouble. As for Naka-chan, I'll pay my respects after you catch the killer. I'm heading back to Tokyo tomorrow."

"Sorry to spoil your trip, Mr. Tsuzuki." Detective Torisu stood up. "You need your driver's license. We don't want to keep you." He looked up at Matsuyama. The young detective strode out of the room. Even his footsteps sounded irritated.

"Detective, can I ask you something?" Shigenori leaned forward and lowered his voice. "I was just wondering..." He lifted two fingers to his lips.

"Sure, I got some." Torisu fumbled in his jacket pocket and brought out a half-crushed packet of Caster Milds and a hundred-yen lighter. He held them out to Shigenori.

"Appreciate it. Out there?" He motioned to the balcony with his jaw. "I quit a long time ago. Almost forgot about them completely, but for some reason I've been dying for a smoke since I got here."

"I'm cutting back, but I just can't quit," Torisu said. "Especially when I'm on edge, I end up reaching for a cigarette. Sorry about this. It's because we've been keeping you cooped up here. Please tell your wife that Tomakomai South is to blame for your going back to smoking."

"She won't find out. I'll just have one."

"Oh, no." Torisu shook his head. "They always find out."

He got up and opened the sliding glass door to the balcony. "Let me get you a cup of tea. We should've brought you one earlier. Relax and enjoy that cigarette."

He left the room. Shigenori went out on the balcony and closed the door. He leaned on the railing and lit a cigarette, took one pull and had a coughing fit. He hadn't really wanted to smoke. He'd just wanted to go through the motions of smoking.

The police station was surrounded by a scattering small office buildings. Most of the windows in the buildings were dark. There were no pedestrians in the street below, and no cars. A traffic light diligently changed colors for an audience of none.

Shigenori sensed something in the darkness. He didn't bother to turn around; he already knew.

"Well, this is a surprise."

"What are you doing, old man?"

The cigarette glowed red. Shigenori turned slowly. Galla was perched on the railing, wings outspread. Her long hair flowed in the evening breeze.

"That's right—you don't need to spend money on airplanes. But I'm surprised you found me."

"I can find you anywhere by following your words. Have you forgotten?"

"I've just been chatting with local law enforcement. Well, more like answering questions."

Either way, it doesn't matter. They told me what I needed to know.

The Tomakomai police didn't have the Serial Amputator anywhere on their radar screen. They'd already decided that "their" murder was a one-off. They were searching for the killer of one man, Shiro Nakanome. And they already had a suspect.

That was why they had Naka-chan and the Nakanome house under surveillance. When Tsuzuki showed up, looking as if he was there for a purpose, their suspicion was aroused and they tailed him. Maybe that talk about the Internet journalist and the rest wasn't made up. But no police force worth its salt stakes out a location just to keep pests away from a bereaved family.

They were probably on the verge of making an arrest. That would explain why they'd had to bring Shigenori in for questioning, not just chase him away; why they had run an identity check, and why the results had put them on edge.

Torisu stumbled when he referred to "the suspect." He'd quickly corrected himself and gone out of his way to make sure Shigenori thought he was talking about the Serial Amputator.

Because he wasn't.

Killer and victim knew each other well. The problem from a police standpoint was motive. It wouldn't be something straightforward, like money or a romantic conflict. That would've been easy to establish. It would be something under the surface, a problem that had been festering over years, something the killer and his victim might not even have recognized as a problem until just before the murder, when something pushed it over the edge.

Shigenori stepped over to the ashtray, stubbed out his cigarette and took a deep breath.

Shiro Nakanome's murder wasn't the beginning of anything. The Serial Amputator was never here.

But in that case, why couldn't the police in Tomakomai crack the case during the nearly four months between the discovery of Nakanome's body and the "second murder" in Akita on September 22? The anonymous victim had had the fourth toe on her right foot amputated, panicking the public into believing that a serial killer was at work, a killer dubbed Toe-Cutter Bill, a.k.a. the Serial Amputator. If the Nakanome case had been solved before then, things would have developed very differently.

Maybe they ran into a wall—a local wall, or a family wall, the bonds of silence connecting friends and relatives of victim and killer. Unraveling those bonds would take time and patience. It would be like draining a small, quiet marsh, cup by cup, until the tendrils of some poisonous plant hidden just below the surface came slowly into view.

If Shigenori was right, all of that buzz about the Serial Amputator was just a vexing wild card. The negative mania, the dark carnival that always follows in the wake of a series of shocking murders, would have had an alarming psychological effect, directly or indirectly, on the victim's family, the killer, and the people around them, with their half-formed doubts and suspicions. Their understanding of the truth could change. Each person's attitude toward the police and their response to the investigation could be influenced for the worse.

"Old man."

Shigenori came out of his reverie and looked up. Galla was now a silhouette, darker than the night sky, only faintly visible.

"Your hand is stained with sin."

Shigenori glanced at the hand that had just held a cigarette.

"You touched sin with that hand. Sin, embodied in words."

Shigenori was nonplussed. He frowned. Galla flicked a finger toward his face, as if throwing something small and light. Shigenori shielded his face reflexively and took a step back.

"What was that? What did you do?"

The conference room door opened. Torisu was back. Galla merged with the darkness and disappeared. Shigenori stepped inside, trying hard to conceal his bewilderment.

"Sorry to keep you waiting. I'll give you a lift to your hotel." Torisu held out Shigenori's license. The offer of a cup of tea was just for form's sake, apparently. Torisu would've been making sure it was all right to let Shigenori leave, either with his bosses or the special investigations unit. Or both.

Shigenori was about to demur, but some intuition changed his mind. Torisu was alone. His partner Matsuyama hadn't returned.

"Are you sure you don't mind?"

"Not at all. It's on the way home. I hope you won't mind the car. It's an old clunker."

"I'd appreciate it."

The car was parked in the big lot behind the station. Torisu was right; the white compact had seen a lot of years. Torisu likely used it to commute. When he wasn't buried in work, he'd use it to go shopping with his wife or take the kids to and from school.

If Shigenori's hunch was correct and the police were close to an arrest, Torisu's story about going home would be another smoke screen. He had to make sure he delivered this troublesome piece of Metro Police baggage to the hotel. He couldn't just see him to the sidewalk in front of the station and wave goodbye. He had to know that Shigenori wasn't going to go strolling around the neighborhood again. Sending him back in a patrol car would be too heavy-handed; it had to look like a personal favor.

But there was also a chance that he wasn't quite finished with Tsuzuki. Maybe there was something he wanted to talk about one-on-one. Shigenori decided to roll the dice. He wouldn't risk losing anything.

Torisu pulled the car out into the quiet of the night. His speed was rock steady just below the speed limit. Safe driving. Shigenori broke the silence first.

"Naka-chan doesn't seem to have any customers," he said in an offhand way. "It looks like it won't last long at this rate."

Torisu kept his eyes on the road and nodded. "Shiro was popular with the customers. I'd guess they're reluctant to go there now." His eyebrows twitched nervously. "But it fills up later in the evening," he added hastily. "You got there right after they opened."

The car was oddly free of clutter and personal items. The only hint of ownership was a little carved-wood cat dangling from the rearview mirror. Its long tail was jointed to wave back and forth with the movement of the car.

"Listen, detective." Shigenori kept his eyes on the cat's tail. "The only reason I'm here was to say a prayer for the deceased. But when I saw how empty Naka-chan is, I got this feeling I can't quite seem to shake."

Torisu didn't reply. Shigenori felt the car slow, almost imperceptibly.

"Maybe Shiro's old customers feel it too. How should I put it? That there's something behind all of this. Something very close."

"And just what would that be?"

"I'm a civilian now. I don't have the right to weigh in on these things. But I used to be a cop, and I still have some of that old sixth sense. That sense is buzzing now. Shiro Nakanome was murdered by someone he knew. In fact, I'd guess it was a relative. That's why the investigation is complicated. This wasn't the work of any Serial Amputator."

Torisu hit the brakes. The light ahead was yellow, but he could've made it easily.

Shigenori shifted in his seat to face him. "I'm willing to bet you agree with me. Maybe there's a different opinion at the top, but who cares? You have the same instincts I do. You slipped back there, you know. You called him 'the suspect.' "

That hit a nerve. Torisu's eyes flickered with surprise.

"I don't know," he said tightly. "It's hard to say." His eyebrows jumped up and down. "I'm a foot soldier. I do what I'm told. The Prefectural Police—

"The light's green, detective."

Torisu punched the accelerator.

"Sorry to ramble on, detective. I'm not trying to make your life harder. I don't want to stick my nose in your business. But you can't shake your uneasiness about what I'm really thinking. That's why you're taking the time to deliver me to the hotel. So I decided to level with you."

"Oh?" said Torisu quietly.

"A nice place like that with no customers. It's a waste, isn't it? It must make Shiro sad too. Maybe his cousin doesn't have a head for business. Was he helping out there before the murder?"

That might have been where the trouble lay, under the surface. It was a shot in the dark, but the shooter was a veteran.

"My understanding," Torisu said slowly, "is that Katsumi and Shiro got along just fine. They were more like brothers than cousins. Katsumi couldn't bear to close the place down, so he's keeping it going."

"But for how long, I wonder? It's a losing proposition. He'd make more money closed."

Shigenori's wheels were turning as he talked. *The cousin's name is Katsumi? Katsumi. That name is familiar. Why would that be? Wait—the bamboo, for the Star Festival. Strips of paper—*

The lightbulb over his head finally went on. Shigenori understood. He almost shouted in triumph.

Your hand is stained with sin.

He had touched the paper strips with their wishes. Galla had been trying to tell him. One of them was left by the killer.

Torisu opened his mouth to speak, but Shigenori held up a hand. "Detective," he said quickly, "I promise not to cause any more trouble. Please take me to Naka-chan. I won't go inside. I want to check something outside. Please."

Torisu must have seen a light in Shigenori's eyes that was not of this world. He pulled the car over and set the brake.

"What exactly do you plan to do?"

"There's some bamboo out front, for the Star Festival. You saw it, right? I've got to examine it. There's something I need to confirm."

Shigenori didn't have the power of Kotaro's eye. He wasn't sure what, if anything, he'd learn by looking at those strips of paper again. But he couldn't ignore Galla's hint and just go back to Tokyo.

"Mr. Tsuzuki." Torisu's face was pale in the darkness. His drooping eyelids spelled dilemma.

"The guys at Central...They figured you were from Metro Police. An advisor, or an observer maybe, sent here to check on us. This joint investigation stuff is hard to stomach. We're not in a strong position. If we say anything, we just get our teeth kicked in for not solving the case faster."

"Detective, get a grip. Advisor? You overestimate me. I'm retired."

So they thought I was a spy from the big city. If Torisu hadn't looked so uncomfortable, Shigenori would've laughed in his face.

"Yes, I understand that you're retired. Or at least you seem to be."

Shigenori burst out laughing. Torisu laughed awkwardly too. "That's why they wanted you out of here quick. I tried to be as polite as I could—"

"You've been nothing but decent to me, detective. In fact you've been very kind. That's why I'm asking for just one more favor. Take me to Naka-chan. All I need is one minute. That's all, and I promise never to go near it again."

Torisu was wavering. Shigenori shifted gears, to Bad Cop.

"Of course, if you're not willing, I can always change my mind. I could hang around until tomorrow, spend a leisurely evening sampling the sake at Naka-chan. Maybe have a nice long Q&A with the current management. I'm sure it would be very enlightening."

This line of attack sent the needle of Torisu's discomfort meter against the stop. He sighed and pulled away from the curb. Shigenori was watching him closely, and he saw something in Torisu's eyes that he couldn't conceal. Whatever it was that this over-the-hill ex-Metro detective thought he could discover by going to Naka-chan, Torisu wanted to know what it was.

Naka-chan's block was deserted. The bright lights along the street seemed to strengthen the atmosphere of solitude. Shigenori got out quickly, crossed the street and approached the miniature bamboo festooned with colored paper. Torisu stayed in the car, slumped behind the wheel. With Naka-chan under surveillance, he probably wasn't eager to be seen.

The long, slender stalks of bamboo bent diffidently under the weight of their Star Festival wishes. Music and the sound of a woman's voice drifted faintly out onto the sidewalk. Shigenori reached for the nearest strip, an inscribed ribbon of pink.

A spark seemed to leap between the paper and his fingertips. The glow expanded and spread, racing to the end of each stalk and the tip of each slender green leaf, almost as though it was scanning the bamboo. Then, just as quickly, the light disappeared.

Shigenori blinked with surprise. Everything was as before, except for one—no, two strips of paper. Not one, but two. Shigenori balled his hands into fists, trying to stop them from shaking.

Naka-chan is forever! The killer can go to hell! —Katsumi

Rest in peace, Shiro. —Reiji

Both strips were the color of blood.

A mastermind and his accomplice. One of them was named Katsumi.

Shigenori straightened up, put his palms together in prayer and bowed to the bamboo. He recrossed the street slowly, eyes downward in thought, and got into the car.

"Let's go. I did what I came here to do."

Torisu guided the car back to the main road and toward the hotel near the station. It was the same route Shigenori had walked earlier, not much of a distance by car.

"Detective, I'm going to sit here and chat with myself for a bit."

"Huh?"

"I don't know if Katsumi is a cousin on the victim's father's side or his mother's side, but I'm guessing that his father's name is Reiji."

Torisu's head swiveled to look at him. His eyes were wide. Shigenori plunged ahead.

"Katsumi and his father killed Shiro Nakanome. I don't know who played the main role, but judging from where the body was found, it took some planning. In my experience, it's usually the older perp who takes the lead. And since this didn't revolve around money problems or a romance gone bad, the motive would be some sort of family conflict, something that built up over time and ultimately became intolerable. This wasn't the result of some emotional blowup. It was planned, and planned carefully. That's typical of an older person."

Torisu broke out in a cold sweat.

"I only got a quick look at Katsumi. I'm not sure if he'd be able to lift a man as big as Nakanome into that refrigerator—"

"I'm sure he would be." It just came out. Torisu seemed as surprised as Shigenori.

"Katsumi Nakanome played rugby in middle school and high school. Football in college," Torisu said, "He dropped out in his sophomore year, so he didn't leave much on the field in the way of accomplishment. Not much in the classroom, either."

Shigenori nodded and said nothing. Torisu was probably relieved to talk about it. Or maybe he was just resigned to it. He took a deep breath.

"Reiji Nakanome is Shiro's uncle on his father's side. His father's younger brother, to be exact."

He braked smoothly for a traffic light. The lights of a taxi in the opposite lane shone in their eyes.

"Reiji is sixty-five. He's a frail old man with quite a few health problems. He can't do anything that requires strength."

"I'm almost as old," Shigenori said. He had to chuckle. "I was a frail old man too, before the operation."

"Do you have any children, Mr. Tsuzuki?"

"No. Just me and the wife."

"Katsumi is Reiji's only son. After he dropped out of college, he drifted from job to job. He's past thirty now, but he still lives at home."

It was a common scenario. Parents without the resources to raise their kids right, saddled in old age with adults who still need parenting.

"The victim's father and his uncle were not on good terms. It goes back a long way, but both of them were fathers to only sons. Let's just say one turned out quite a bit better than the other," Torisu said.

"That wouldn't make for harmony in the family."

"Not at all. Everyone knew about it, of course."

The light turned green. Torisu wiped the perspiration from his forehead before he pressed the accelerator.

"Reiji Nakanome spent most of his life working for a company in Sapporo.

He moved to Tomakomai after he retired, so he's a new face around here, but the Nakanomes have been living in this part of Hokkaido since before the war. The family has a lot branches and deep roots in the community, through marriage and otherwise. None of them wanted to see one of their own end up in the slammer."

Torisu was a generation younger than Shigenori, but for a moment he felt a professional kinship with the young cop.

"They're a very tight-lipped clan, very stubborn. We have to approach this carefully, or they'll clam up tight."

"I understand." Shigenori had now heard everything he needed to hear. Coming up with irrefutable proof and consolidating the circumstantial evidence was taking time. "Say no more, detective. You were just talking to yourself, right?" The hotel's lighted sign was visible down the street.

"Mr. Tsuzuki, are you really—"

"Yes, I'm a private citizen. Not an advisor or an observer or a spy. I came here on my own initiative. What I told you is my opinion alone."

He unbuckled his seat beat and was about to get out when something occurred to him.

"Why do you think the killer took one of the victim's toes?"

Torisu shook his head slowly. "We have no idea at this point."

"I see. Well, you'll get it out of them. But just talking to myself here—"

Layers of experience laid down over years were whispering to Shigenori. They had probably been whispering all this time, but he hadn't heard them over the clamor of the Serial Amputator story.

"They may have taken it as some kind of talisman."

"A talisman?"

"Yes. I've seen several cases like it, usually in robberies, but sometimes murderers do it too," Shigenori said. "There was one guy who always drove a three-inch nail into his victims' foreheads. He did it after they were dead, but it was still grotesque. I thought it must be a sign of hatred toward each of the victims, but after we arrested him, he turned out to be a penny-ante housebreaker who knew none of his victims personally. If the owner was unlucky enough to wake up and confront the thief, he or she ended up dead. The perp told us he took the trouble to drive a nail into their skulls because he was afraid they might come back to life and take revenge on him.

"There was another killer who blindfolded his victims after they were dead. He told us he didn't want them to see which way he went. If they couldn't see him, they couldn't tell anyone.

"If you kill someone, they're no longer a threat as a living person. But the dead aren't so harmless. People in this country have that kind of mentality.

Or if things go well when they do something specific, after that they do the same thing over and over, automatically.

"Sorry, it's just something that occurred to me. Don't take it too seriously. You can let me off here."

The hotel was still some distance down the street, but Shigenori got out of the car. He wouldn't be seeing Torisu again. The white compact drove away.

He didn't wait to go to his room. He stood by the road, took out his mobile and sent a mail to Kotaro.

Tomakomai was not the work of the Serial Amputator. It was a one-off.

He input the rest of the message quickly, paused to think, and added a final line.

Watch your back.

Watch your back for what? Am I getting superstitious too?

The murder of Shiro Nakanome was supposed to be the first in a series. Now it had disappeared. The killing of Ayuko Yamashina was a ham-fisted copycat crime.

Would the other murders turn out to be the same? Maybe all five were unrelated, and the Serial Amputator wasn't even real. Maybe everyone had just been trying too hard to see him.

▼

Kotaro didn't notice the mail from Shigenori. His eyes were glued to Makoto's laptop.

When Makoto found friends at Kumar, he'd promised himself he'd never touch this laptop again. All of his lovingly developed hacking tools were loaded into its hard drive. But he hadn't been able to bring himself to erase the drive. Instead he'd tossed it in a closet and tried to forget it.

Hacking Blossom School's website was simplicity itself. Kotaro watched as Makoto breached one layer of security after another and page after page of content scrolled up the screen—messages between staff and parents, chat pages, news and photos. Kotaro's left eye was filled with countless floating silver threads.

"Stop!"

A cluster of blood-red threads.

It was a post with a headshot. As Kotaro watched, the threads wriggled and rose out of the monitor into the air, like worms carrying an infectious disease. They curled and formed into clumps that divided like cells and came together again, slowly assuming a shape.

It was a humanoid shape, like the "excrement" that had stood, gently undulating, outside the restroom in Totsuka. But this one was red, the color of fresh-spattered blood.

Kotaro felt his gorge rising and clapped a hand over his mouth. Makoto peered at him doubtfully in the blue-white glow from the monitor. With his innocent face, Makoto looked like a child's ghost.

"Are you all right, Mishima?"

Kotaro was frozen. The minikin looked like a little blood bag. It advanced on him, shaking its head from side to side, swinging its tiny arms as it walked toward him relentlessly, suspended in space.

When Kotaro was very young, he'd had a horror of moths. If one flew into his room at night, attracted to a light, he would scream for help.

I hate you, I hate you! Go away! Don't touch me! No, get it off me!

He'd become that frightened child again. He had to restrain himself from flailing away at the little red monstrosity. Instead he opened his right eye. The miniature blood bag disappeared. He pointed at the monitor.

"That post—"

"It's from their gardener," Makoto said, peering even more curiously at Kotaro. "It's about the flowers he planted outside the school."

Why would Kotaro be so disturbed by an innocent post? Why was his face twitching like that? Makoto—Good Makoto—looked at him warily.

I can't help it. You can't see it, but I can. You can't even see the giant you're dragging around.

The school gardener.

The post listed the names and species of flowers planted, with information about each one and the human qualities each was said to represent, all in a gentle, approachable tone. The posted closed with this:

> *We hope you'll enjoy these little blossoms as you watch your own blossoms at play in the nursery school.*
>
> *Katsura Florist*
> *Flower Delivery, Garden*
> *Care and Yard Work*
> *Kosuke Nakasono, School Gardener*

The headshot showed a suntanned, smiling man with a square jaw and short hair. The corners of his eyes crinkled pleasantly. He wasn't young. Early forties, perhaps.

"Makoto, do a search on Katsura Florist."

Makoto went silently to work. A moment later the website filled the screen. Kotaro had to turn away from the gaily colored home page with its photos of flowers and smiling staff.

This time the blood oozing from the monitor was black. The numberless clusters of words were interspersed with screams. They came splattering from the screen and onto Kotaro.

It was too much. He slammed the laptop shut. His head was spinning. He started shivering uncontrollably.

Words, millions of words. Putrescent blood.

She's not his only victim.

"Kotaro!"

He came to his senses to find Makoto shaking him by the arm. With both eyes open, all he could see was reality: Makoto Miyama and his hacker's laptop.

"Sorry. I've seen enough. We're done."

Makoto packed his gear quickly between curious glances at Kotaro, who started down the stairs ahead of him.

"Was that really everything you needed?" Makoto called after him. Kotaro didn't answer. He just kept going. Makoto hurried to catch up.

"What did you find? I swore never to touch this laptop again, but you threatened me. I deserve an explanation at least."

"What are you talking about? I didn't threaten you."

"You sure did. You said things would change."

Makoto sounded almost lighthearted. He and Kotaro were partners in crime, though he wasn't sure just what the crime had been. He felt somehow as though things were back to normal. Kotaro was Kotaro, not Mishima, and he was Makoto again.

"Kotaro? Something's different about you."

They reached the second-floor landing. Kotaro turned and closed his right eye.

Makoto's giant towered over them almost protectively. It thrust its huge head slowly toward Kotaro. He could sense it examining him with curiosity and a kind of interest. It was buzzing even louder than before—the buzzing of insects bloated near to bursting with poison.

Friend…

The black giant was Makoto's past. It was his Shadow. Now it was Kotaro's confederate. Now they were in the same business.

Fine. Whatever it takes to catch that monster.

9

The next morning, half past nine. Kotaro was staring at the steel shutters over the front of Katsura Florist.

Opening time: now.

The florist occupied the first floor of a newish-looking, three-story building on a one-way street not far from Blossom School. The second and third floors would be where the owner, Kosuke Nakasono, and his family lived. The balcony and widows were profusely decorated with flower boxes and planters.

Other than the flower shop, the neighborhood was purely residential. Many of the houses had space for gardens. It was a prosperous-looking area. Katsura Florist probably did good business.

The street was in an elementary school zone. The children were in class and the street was quiet and empty. A misty, dew-like rain sluiced down from an overcast sky. Kotaro's hair was beaded with moisture.

He used the camcorder he'd brought from home to shoot the white van in the parking space to the left of the building. He checked to make sure the license plate was clear. He moved to the side of the van and took another photo. This time he captured the lettering on the side: KATSURA FLORIST—YOUR GOOD NEIGHBOR.

A metal stairway ran down the outside of the building from the second-floor entry to the parking space. A mailbox labeled NAKASONO was bolted to the foot of the railing. A little bicycle with training wheels and a larger one with cargo baskets fore and aft were parked in the lee of the building.

A man with a trademark smile, living with his family in a chic house in a chic neighborhood.

Why him?

The night before, after he'd gotten home, Kotaro had noticed Shigenori's mail.

Tomakomai was not the work of the Serial Amputator. It was a one-off. The local police will make arrests soon. There's nothing for us to do on this one.

The copycat killing of Ayuko Yamashina, complete with a cooked-up statement from the killer, wasn't the work of the Serial Amputator either. Could the other three killings—in Akita, Mishima, and Totsuka—be laid at his feet? And was Kosuke Nakasono that person?

Kotaro had seen blood gushing from Makoto's laptop—the blood of more than one victim.

The door on the second floor opened. A man in jeans and a white T-shirt, a denim apron and long rubber boots, started down the stairs. His hair was cropped close to the skull, much shorter than in the photo on the website.

Nakasono was dangling a key holder between the fingers of his right hand. Kotaro thought he might be heading for the van, but he walked past it and around to the front of the shop, where he unlocked the shutters and started rolling them up.

Without hesitation, Kotaro closed his right eye.

The hardworking florist was nowhere to be seen. Instead, Kotaro saw that the interior of the shop was filled with a red-black vapor. The vapor looked moist and solid, like a rain cloud, almost solid enough to grab.

Engulfed in these clouds billowing out of the shop was a humanoid figure with two heads planted on a grotesquely wide shoulder girdle. The creature was bringing out planters and buckets and putting them on the sidewalk.

Each head had mere dimples where the eyes would be, and a projecting bump of a nose. Kotaro was astonished to see that the right head seemed to notice him, while the left was facing the opposite direction. The creature's translucent skin was redder than the vapor, and its heads and body contained scores of black whorls that coiled and uncoiled restlessly, becoming more distinct as they moved closer to the surface of the skin and disappearing as they sank deeper inside. The whorls merged and separated, waxing thicker and thinner, distending the skin as they moved.

The creature had arms and legs, but instead of fingers, each hand had a dozen or more slender appendages like tentacles that busily extended, contracted and intertwined. The legs seemed to function like those of a human, but as the creature moved about, they sometimes changed grotesquely, with the knee flexing in the wrong direction, like the rear legs of a goat. Whenever they did, the feet morphed momentarily into hooves.

The creature also had a tail that dangled awkwardly almost to the ground, but the way it swung as the creature moved about was not quite like a tail. Kotaro peered at it, baffled, before realizing suddenly that he had the appendage on the wrong side.

It was a penis.

The creature was Kosuke Nakasono's word body, the repository of his experiences and memories. His true form. Kotaro closed his eyes and turned away. He took a deep breath and fought the urge to vomit.

The effigy outside the restroom in Totsuka and the tarlike slime stuck to the door of Blossom School came from the same source. The creature he was looking at had excreted them. It was just as Galla had said.

There was no time to lose. He had to stop this man before he committed another atrocity.

Kotaro turned and strode resolutely across the street. Nakasono was lining up planters and buckets of flowers in front of the shop. Water flowed over the pavement at his feet.

He turned just as Kotaro was almost on top of him. Their eyes met from a pace or two away. He took a step back, almost bending backward.

"Whoa, sorry..."

His tanned face was flushed with vitality. He had a firm, deep voice. The friendly, cheerful flower specialist. Katsura Florist, Your Good Neighbor.

Kotaro's voice wouldn't come. Nakasono looked at him with wide-eyed surprise.

"Um, is there something I can do for you?"

Someone watching them would've thought Kotaro was the strange one. He'd been loitering outside the shop since long before it opened, shivering in the summer heat. Now his face was pale as he fought the urge to vomit. Nakasono eyed him with concern.

"Are you feeling all right, sir? You don't look well."

Nakasono was a professional. He treated everyone as a customer, even "sir"-ing this young college kid.

What did you say to Saeko Komiya? What words did you use to lure her into your van? "I'm the gardener at Blossom School. Are you picking up your child? I'm on the way there myself. I'd be happy to take you."

And what did he say to her just before he killed her?

"Sir? Are you all right?"

Kotaro struggled to answer. It cost him a tremendous effort of will to find his voice, as though he had to draw it up a pipe drilled deep into the bed of an undersea trench.

"Are you Kosuke Nakasono?"

The man's eyes flickered in bewilderment. The whites of his eyes were pure. "Yes, that's right."

"You're the gardener for Blossom School. I saw it on their website."

Nakasono's expression relaxed instantly. It reminded Kotaro of the red-haired guy at the gas station. The corners of his eyes crinkled in friendly welcome.

"Thanks for your patronage! Yes, Katsura Florist is the designated garden expert for Blossom School. Let's see, you don't have a child there, do you sir? You're a little too young."

"My... sister. Her kid goes there."

"Is that so? It's a very nice school, isn't it? Your sister must feel safe with her child in their care."

Kotaro had worked out a script for this encounter. He had an older sister. Her son went to Blossom School. She was impressed by the well-tended planters in the yard. She'd mentioned them to Kotaro. Now he needed flowers to mark an important occasion, and wanted Katsura Florist to handle it. He needed them delivered at nine tonight to a certain location—

But the carefully prepared script had flown right out of his head. All he could think of was how to make this man squirm. He wanted to wipe that phony smile off his face.

"I know what you did."

"Thank you."

He doesn't even know what I'm talking about.

Kotaro came closer and lowered his voice. "I know all about you, Kosuke Nakasono."

The smile hardened into a mask.

"You killed Saeko Komiya. I know you did. I've got proof."

Nakasono's eyes twitched deep in the smiling mask. His pupils flashed for just an instant.

"Wha...what are you talking about?"

"You wouldn't want your wife and kid to find out." Kotaro lowered his voice to a whisper and rolled his eyes toward the second floor. "We'd better discuss this somewhere in private. Of course, if you refuse, it's fine by me. I'll just show the police what I've got."

Nakasono's nostrils started to tremble. The mask was beginning to crack.

"I'm not...I don't know...what..."

"Before I see the police, I'm going to upload proof of what you did to the web. Even if the cops don't believe me, the rest of the world will come after you."

Nakasono laughed. The sound was like air escaping from a balloon. "Hey, k-kid, kid. I've got no idea what you're talking about."

"You deny it? Suit yourself. I was just trying to give you a chance."

"A chance? To do what?"

"To run."

The two men stood facing each other. Looking at Nakasono's healthy, tanned mask, Kotaro couldn't help wondering which head was looking at him now. Did it have some kind of expression? Were the black whorls moving faster?

Nakasono lowered his voice. "Why should I run away?"

"You killed someone. When they arrest you, you're not going to talk your way out of it. You know that."

Nakasono's jaw moved as though he was chewing something. Maybe he was biting back words he'd thought better of.

"You don't want to lose your wife and child, do you?"

More chewing motions, and the trembling nostrils.

"You've got a nice situation here. Nice house, nice business. If they send you to prison, you lose everything. You'll get life at least. By the time they parole you, you'll be so old you can barely walk. Or maybe they'll just hang you." Kotaro snorted dismissively. "You've been busy for a while, haven't you? Japan has jury trials now. Kill more than once and you could get death, especially when the crimes are cruel and perverted. You sure fit the profile."

Nakasono wiped his face with a thick hand, the hand of a working man. His fingers were long. He was starting to sweat. His left hand came down over his mouth and paused there. He was wearing a wedding band.

"I am..."

The mask crumbled. Kotaro almost thought he could hear it cracking. Good and evil, reality and obsession in equal measure, sealed tight behind the mask of a friendly, fortyish man. Now the mask was bursting open.

This is what hides the two-headed monster. That's the real Kosuke Nakasono. But they're not just behind that face, they're mixed up in his head. This guy is deeply disturbed. He's got two people inside him.

The other head turned to face Kotaro. It gripped the mast from inside and tore it away.

"Whatcha got? Mmm? Come on, punk. Whatcha got?"

Somewhere behind the threatening tone was a peal of derision, like a sound of a triangle ringing faintly amid a clamoring orchestra.

"You think I'm going to stand around here and tell you?" Kotaro stood his ground and chuckled, returning the derision. "Let's meet tonight. We'll discuss this. Take our time."

"Is this about money? Is that what you want?"

"Sure, money is good. But what I really want is a full confession, straight from your mouth."

Nakasono's lips contorted in a scowl. Kotaro was struck by how genuine it looked. The smiling face of Your Good Neighbor was definitely a mask. It was probably the only thing his wife had ever seen. It was such a good mask that it could hardly be distinguished from the real thing, but it was bogus.

"My confession? What the hell good would *that* do you?"

"It goes straight to the net. I'm gonna scoop the world."

Nakasono didn't seem to know much about the Internet. He rolled his eyes, baffled. "You'll get yourself arrested if you do that."

"What makes you think people will know it's me?"

They faced each other silently. Kotaro's smile was fixed. It was his turn to wear the mask. Standing here looking at Nakasono's real face, he was afraid to show him what his own looked like.

"Tonight. At nine." Kotaro jerked a thumb over his shoulder. "In the parking lot, around the corner to the right." He had already scoped it out. It was open to the street, with a high fence on three sides. "Wait for me under the sign on the east side."

"Why should I do what you say?"

"Oh, you will. You don't have a choice. We both know that."

We're done here. Tonight Galla will take you to the place of judgment.

▼

Sometimes Kotaro woke with a start after nodding off on the train, or in one of the armchairs in the cafeteria. He'd feel as if he'd been asleep for a long time, but when he looked at his watch, only a few minutes would've passed.

He felt that way now. He'd lost consciousness momentarily. When he opened his eyes again, he was on the rooftop of the tea caddy building.

Someone had been here. The roof had been tidied up; the fragments of the gargoyle statue were gone. Oddly, the hatch leading to the fourth floor was gone. The expanse of concrete was unbroken.

He looked around. The lights of West Shinjuku seemed to press down on him, close enough to reach out and touch. Yet the lights from the skyscrapers on the far side of the district seemed oddly far away, like a distant star cluster.

He heard a thump and turned to see Nakasono sprawled on the roof. A moment later, Galla touched down alongside him.

Kotaro spoke first. "You sure didn't waste any time showing up."

He had intended to lure Nakasono into the shadows, as he had with Keiko Tashiro, but Galla was upon them as soon as Nakasono arrived at the appointed spot.

"Next time give me some warning, okay? My head's spinning."

Galla gazed at him. The blade of her scythe shone dully. "You have not left your house."

"Huh? What's that supposed to mean?"

"It is of no importance. What will you do with this one?"

Nakasono coughed painfully and sat up, holding his head. He gazed around in a daze, as though he'd just woken up. When he finally noticed Kotaro, he nearly jumped out of his skin.

"It's you!"

"Good evening."

Kotaro walked up to him and squatted down so he could look straight into his eyes. The man slid hurriedly away from him on the concrete, as if he was afraid Kotaro might infect him with something deadly. He was wearing the same jeans and white T-shirt. The apron and the rubber boots were gone. He had changed into sneakers.

Kotaro showed him a big grin. "Got anything with you, like a knife?

Some kind of weapon? I figure you wouldn't meet me in the dark without bringing a little protection."

If Nakasono had believed Kotaro's story, killing him would've been an option he would have considered, along with trying to befriend him, or feed him some kind of story.

Nakasono shook his head and glowered at Kotaro with indignation. "Where is this? What did you do to me?"

"You'll find out soon enough. You didn't bring any money with you? Don't you want to buy my silence?"

Something happened then, something that had never happened before. He saw the monster with both eyes open. Whorls of black tar eddied and pulsed beneath its skin. In a moment it was gone, replaced by its owner.

"What do you want from me? Who are you?" Nakasono's jaw was trembling so hard that his words sounded slurred.

"That's what I was going to ask you. Who are you? Are you the Serial Amputator?"

Again for a split second, he saw the monster. The head facing him had an expression this time. The two black knotholes that served it for eyes, and the larger hole below and between them, were round and dilated. It looked like a wailing ghost in a spirit photo.

"I'm not a criminal," Nakasono said doggedly. His human version was shaking so violently with panic and indecision—Should he threaten Kotaro? Try to get him on his side?—that he was about to lose control of his bladder. This made him furious, and he looked it.

"Liar. You murdered Saeko Komiya. I've got proof."

"No way. You've got nothing."

"So you think. People like you assume they're clever. But everything they do is screwed up."

Instead of reacting with more anger, Nakasono's face drained of color. His thoughts were easy to read. Maybe he really had left some clues behind. Where? Had he made a mistake? Fear fought the instinct to deny everything, and fear won out completely.

"It was…her fault," he said haltingly. "She got in the car. She should've said no. She made the decision. *He* took her away. I couldn't do anything about it."

Kotaro had to know if he was conscious of what he had done. "You said she got in the car. You invited her to get in, didn't you? 'Are you going to the nursery? I can give you a lift.' That's what you said, wasn't it?"

"Well, yeah. But—" Nakasono put a hand to his throat. His eyes jerked back and forth in their sockets. "I wasn't doing the talking."

Kotaro's left eye saw it again. He stepped back quickly. The face with the knothole eyes and mouth swiveled away and the other head turned to face him. It was blank and featureless, like the effigy at the gas station. Just below the surface of its skin, snakelike forms coiled and uncoiled ceaselessly.

"He...he likes that kind of thing. He's always made my life miserable. First it was animals, then he had to start in on people. He likes women. Women with beautiful legs. And if they look a little vulnerable, like they need a little help, so much the better."

Kotaro watched, fascinated, as Nakasono transformed into the monster and back again several times a second, like the animation in a flipbook. Man, monster. Fake, real. Outer, inner.

"I try to keep him from coming out. I'm a respectable citizen. He's not. Everything bad is his doing. I'm a good person."

It was like a scene from a bad psychodrama, complete with bizarre special effects. Nakasono couldn't stop his diarrhea of the mouth. He just kept repeating the mantra: He's evil, I'm good. Kotaro broke in cuttingly.

"This monster inside you—does he have a name?"

Nakasono's mouth snapped shut. Suddenly everything was quiet.

Kotaro wondered what Galla thought of all this. He could sense her somewhere behind him. She must be invisible to Nakasono, or maybe he was too preoccupied to notice her. He sat slumped over with his mouth half-open, looking slightly idiotic.

"I call him the Beast."

The monster with hooves.

"He says he's me. He says we're the same."

"I see. It must be hard."

Kotaro was shocked by his own words. *Why should I feel sorry for this piece of shit? He won't admit that everything is his responsibility. He just keeps crapping on about his split personality.*

Nakasono's face was wet. Kotaro thought it was perspiration before he realized it was tears. The man was crying.

Kotaro stood up and patted his pockets, searching for his mini camcorder. He hadn't brought it. He realized he was dressed as he would be at home. He'd even forgotten to bring his jacket.

After leaving Katsura Florist that morning, he'd returned to the gas station in Totsuka. The good-natured attendant wasn't there; the pumps were manned by Tomita, the ten-year part-timer he'd mentioned. As always, there were no customers. Tomita didn't have much to do, but he quickly recognized the pictures of the van that Kotaro showed him on his camera.

"Ah, right. The florist from Kawasaki. He comes by every couple months, maybe. He said he has a regular customer near here."

"I went to the gas station where you dumped the body," Kotaro said to Nakasono. "The attendant remembered you."

Nakasono looked up at him, eyes brimming with tears. "It wasn't me. I didn't do it."

"So the guy who gets gas there every couple of months isn't you? It wasn't you who lifted the key and made a copy? If the Beast inside you is doing all this, where are you when it's happening? Answer me that."

No reply. The man just sat there sobbing like a little girl. He didn't even try to run away.

"Are there other victims?"

Nakasono nodded dutifully.

"You're the Serial Amputator, aren't you?"

"No. That woman was the first time I ever killed anyone. I thought I'd get lucky. I could make it look like the serial killer did it. I never did that before."

The crybaby face was replaced by the two-headed monster. "I wanted to see what it was like." The voice of the Beast was a thick wet tongue moving in a wet maw.

"You thought people would blame it on the Serial Amputator?"

"Mm-hmm." Kosuke Nakasono was back. He nodded deeply, appealing for sympathy. "It seemed like the chance I was waiting for. If I cut off part of the body, everybody would think the Amputator did it. It worked, didn't it?"

Black thoughts eddied in whorls in Kotaro's head now too.

"Who else did you kill?"

"I told you, I didn't. I just...I cut them a little, with a knife. He likes women. He likes their blood." He wiped his nose. "It's their fault anyway—walking alone or riding their bikes through the park late at night. That's when the Beast goes hunting."

Blood pouring from a laptop screen. The image was burned on Kotaro's retina. *I just cut them a little. He likes their blood.*

It made a kind of sense. If Nakasono had attacked several women in his neighborhood, that would explain what Kotaro had seen on the website. A woman walking at night is slashed by an unknown attacker. It was outrageous, but the papers would only run a brief account, with no follow-up. You wouldn't know from the media whether or not the perpetrator was ever caught. That's just the kind of crime it was.

"How long have you been doing this?"

Nakasono had to think carefully before answering the question. He wiped his nose and eyes again. "The Beast does it. I can't remember."

"What about before the Beast? You must've been obsessed with something. Something that brought out the Beast and made it stronger."

"I collected women's shoes," he said without a trace of guile. It was as if he'd said he collected *Pokémon* cards as a child. "When I was a kid, there was a rooming house in our neighborhood. It was a dormitory for nurses. They always left their shoes and sandals in the entryway. I couldn't resist them."

This guy's a certified deviant. I'm listening to the diary of a pervert.

"I didn't care about underwear. I specialized in shoes. They're easy to steal, just sitting there in the entryway like that, so I had to make it more challenging. I'd snatch them right after the girl took them off."

"That's enough." Kotaro was tired of struggling with his nausea. "I'll ask you one more time. Answer truthfully. You killed Saeko Komiya, didn't you?"

"Y-yes."

"And no one else?"

"No, nobody. She was the first. Until I tried it, I wasn't sure I could do such a thing."

"Where did you kill her? You took her someplace."

"We have a warehouse. We rent it, near my parents' house. I'm a native of Totsuka."

Kotaro almost groaned with disgust. "What did you do with her leg?"

"It's in the warehouse. I wrapped it in plastic and put it in an oil drum. I'm not like the Beast. I didn't care about the leg."

The Beast was in hiding during this exchange. There was no flipbook effect from man to monster. But now it was back with its thick, wet voice. "Anyway, I kept her shoes."

The black tar whorls under the beast's translucent red skin revolved with dizzying speed. Kotaro knew it was aroused.

"So you didn't have anything to do with the murders in Akita and Mishima?"

"Not me, pal."

The fourth murder was another one-off. As Kotaro stood there dazed, Kosuke Nakasono returned and started muttering compulsively.

"All I care about is shoes. He's the one with the bad habits, not me. He wants women's blood. He wants to kill. It's a bad habit. It's his fault—"

The whining stopped abruptly. Kotaro realized that this nondescript, middle-aged man was staring at him in wonder.

"Are you a Beast too?"

What the hell? Why is he looking at me like that?

Nakasono looked slightly exasperated, as though waiting for a customer to settle a bill. "I mean, you've got huge fangs..."

Kotaro's eyes widened in surprise as an intense flash of light exploded behind Nakasono's neck.

It was Galla. She raised her scythe above her head and whipped the blade sideways.

The crescent hissed. Nakasono's head took flight as his body toppled forward slowly. There was no blood.

Out of the severed surfaces gushed a red-black liquid that was somehow light and insubstantial, like smoke. The streams spiraled around each other in midair before disappearing into the blade of the scythe.

It was a double helix, like a string of DNA.

Galla held the scythe over her head, twirling it like a baton, and began an elegant dance. The red-black torrent chased the blade. Its tip shone with a pure light as the torrents twisted in the air like a charmed snake, drawn to the scythe.

The torrent was powerful, inexhaustible. Galla's dance accelerated. She traveled the circumference of the roof, returned to where she'd been before and hurled the scythe straight upward. It rose into the air, turning end over end.

The red-black torrents chased the tip of the blade, plunging toward it with greater urgency. The spinning scythe blurred and became a pale disk high above Galla's head.

Two points of light flashed out from the disk. Galla extended both arms above her head as a scythe fell into each hand. Her long, gauntleted fingers gripped the handles triumphantly. An instant later, the pair of scythes were stowed behind her back.

Each one had a slightly smaller blade than the original, with a shorter handle, but the blades shone with an icy brilliance that waxed and waned like peaceful breathing. They were alive.

The physical manifestations of Keiko Tashiro and Kosuke Nakasono's cravings had been horrifying and grotesque. But with each new infusion, the beauty and power of Galla's weapons only grew.

There was a faint noise, like dry leaves rustling. Kosuke Nakasono's head and body, emptied of craving, crumbled into dust and blew away on a phantom wind.

"His body was little more than a vessel for his cravings," Galla said quietly. Kotaro nodded, remembering what she had said about Keiko Tashiro.

"Without its contents, the vessel can't maintain its existence."

Galla could return Keiko Tashiro's craving, but she could not be restored to her original state.

"Galla..." Kotaro found himself on his hands and knees. He looked up at the warrior. "I think something's happening to me. When I was talking to him, I could see his true form with both eyes open. He kept changing from human to monster and back again."

Maybe the power she lent me is growing and becoming part of me. Maybe the more I use it, the more I'll be able to possess it.

But Galla's answer was immediate. "It is not strange, in this place." She walked slowly to the edge of the roof. "We are on sacred ground, a sanctum of my making. My power is everywhere here. Anyone entering this space gains the power to see words. To see the Shadow."

"Are you saying this isn't the tea caddy building?"

"It is not."

Kotaro tried to get up, but his legs were so unsteady that he had to crawl to where Galla stood. He looked over the edge of the building.

Immediately beyond the rooftop was a void. The warren of streets and buildings that should have been below him was nowhere to be seen. That explained why the cityscape farther away looked so bizarre, as though seen through a lens that distorted spatial relationships. Buildings that were closer were too close; those farther away looked too distant.

"I can no longer use that building. I have been too long in your region. Its reality hinders me."

"But it's a special place for me." *That's why I made it a point to have Makoto meet me there.*

The tea caddy building had been the setting for Kotaro's transformation. It had shown him the way to things that were real but did not exist. It had changed his world. It was the birthplace of Kotaro, hunter of evil. His place of power.

"I cannot share your sentimentality," Galla said drily. "I also have no reason to stop you. But I warn you: you would do well to avoid that place from now on."

The twin blades glowed above her head. "My weapons are strong now."

"Are you finished here, then?"

"Not yet. There is more I must do before I can vanquish the Sentinel at the Gate of Sorrows."

"Then we should—" Kotaro caught himself midsentence.

Three of the murders were each committed by a different person. Each mutilation was carried out in imitation of another killer's work. The simplest conclusion was that the Serial Amputator never existed. He was a fantasy, an urban legend. Akita and Mishima would probably prove to be the work of different killers with different motives as well.

In the Tomakomai case, the victim's right toe was missing. That was the beginning. At first they called him Toe-Cutter Bill. As more people died, he became the Serial Amputator, and the legend took on a life of its own. To reveal the truth of the three killings would be to dismantle the legend.

"I'll solve the other murders. Shigenori will help me. We've come this far, we can't stop now. Whoever committed them is sure to have strong craving."

"No one compels you to do this," Galla said.

"It's not an obligation. I want to."

As he got to his feet, he had a vision of Ayuko's face, her ivory skin and jet-black pupils. The vision left a gentle warmth before it disappeared. He even felt the touch of her hand. He'd never actually touched her, yet he was sure what he felt was real.

The legend is evil. You must bring it down, but don't lose your bearings along the way. Your thirst for justice can blind you to the harm done by lies and violence. Don't yield to the craving, Kotaro.

Galla was saying something. Kotaro shook his head and shut his vision of Ayuko away in his heart. His eyes were brimming.

"Um...what?"

Galla stood there looking down at him. She swept her hair behind her back, turned, and walked away. The studs in her boots made a metallic sound. She stopped at the opposite edge of the roof, her back still turned.

"Of those I encountered here—the first whose craving I harvested—some wept with loneliness, some were wracked with shame for the blunders they committed. Some were filled with despair, others begged me for forgiveness. I took their cravings, and with them the source of their suffering. Their very bodies brought power to my blade and they ceased to exist in this world. This was their wish. And yet...their cravings seemed at first a trifle. However much I harvested, they ran like sand through my fingers. I thought I had erred in coming to this region. The source of the Circle!

"But I was wrong. I knew too little of this human world. Your will gave birth to the Circle and gives you the strength to turn the Great Wheels of Inculpation. It is a power beyond anything I dreamed of. The craving that rises from your will to live is great and mighty."

Kotaro felt the strength of Galla's emotion, yet her tone contained no hint of admiration.

"You humans are powerful, but you are also defiled." She turned to face him. "Were you not troubled?"

"By what?"

"His words. He spoke of your fangs. All who enter this place see with my eyes. That is why he saw your true face—the words that give form to your Shadow. That Shadow has fangs."

"Makoto's Shadow was a giant," Kotaro said. Galla nodded. "I wonder... is my Shadow a werewolf? Or a hound? They have fangs. I think it's perfect for me. I mean, Yuriko's a wolf too. 'Cause she's a hunter."

"Wolves pursue. They do not hunt. They seek to return to the Nameless Land those who have escaped, who have breached the seals meant to keep them there. Their task is eternal and it is fruitless. They are unbound by time and can cross the gap between regions. They are deathless, and they are everywhere. Yet they are also nowhere, for they do not exist, though they are real," Galla said. "The girl who appeared before you is already becoming a phantom. That is the fate of wolves. As they pursue, their existence slips away, little by little. Would you join them?"

Kotaro returned Galla's stare. "I'll tell you after I find the truth behind the last two murders. You can wait, can't you?"

Galla's reply was to spread her wings and rise into the air. She hovered over Kotaro's head, black wings beating, and dropped toward him like a stone. In his mind, she spoke.

You will regret this.

▼

Galla's voice was still ringing in his ears when Kotaro realized he was standing at the front door of his house, next to the mailbox. He felt like someone waking from an episode of sleepwalking, but he had his shoes on. The night was warm and stifling.

The front door was unlocked. He stepped inside. The sound of the TV came from the living room, and the voices of his father and mother. He raced upstairs. The clock in his room said five past nine.

So this was what it was like to travel to Galla's sanctum and return. There was a gap in his memory of the evening; he didn't remember actually going to Totsuka. His head felt stuffed with straw.

His pack with all his gear was in his room. Nothing was missing. His phone was where he had left it in one of the outside pockets. He was reaching for it when it started ringing. The display showed Shigenori's number.

"Hey, detective. Are you back in Tokyo?"

There was a pause followed by an explosion on the other end of the line.

"What the hell are you talking about? I've been calling you for hours. Where've you been?"

"Ah, um...that's hard to explain. Do you know what a sanctum is?"

They debriefed each other. Shigenori was still hot under the collar. He couldn't fathom why Kotaro had gone off on his own with another kangaroo court.

"Why didn't you force him to turn himself in?"

"There wasn't time for that! What if he ran away?"

Shigenori wasn't fazed by his description of Galla's sanctum. Instead, he had news that left Kotaro much more surprised.

"She let me use her power for just a moment. I could tell who the killers were by touching the wishes they wrote for the Star Festival. I didn't ask her. She just gave it to me. Let me tell you, I've had enough of this stuff."

"Why? She helped you."

"Whatever. I've still had enough. It's time for you to come to your senses. Get out of this mess. Go back to your studies."

"Sorry, can't. Two more killers to nail."

"There is no Serial Amputator!"

"I know. We've got to destroy the myth."

"No one even knows who the woman in Akita was. It's no job for an amateur."

"Then I'll tackle the Mishima case. You handle Akita."

As they were going back and forth, Kotaro's battery died. *Good timing.*

He booted up his PC. There were a few new mails. One was from Makoto. There was a large attachment. The subject line was "I had to check this out."

I also wanted to understand why you had me hack that site.

Makoto knew his way around the web. He'd used Katsura Florist's SNS blog to find the sites Kosuke Nakasono frequented, the people he shared information with, even his online payment history.

Turns out that the guy actually had a second IP address.

And walking back the traces from that address led to the two-headed monster.

This site is on BB's watch list. Your florist seems to have a thing for women's feet.

A site for foot fetishists. A place where they could exchange tips, stoke each other's fantasies, and share their thrills. Kotaro mailed back.

Thx Makoto. You can forget about this guy.

That was it. Kotaro leaned back in the chair and closed his eyes.

10

Kotaro's vacation was over, but he was still cutting classes. It wasn't helping his grades. He'd spent the rest of his ten days collecting and collating information about the last two cases, but time ran out before he had a chance to visit Mishima, much less Akita.

Ayuko's murder had left a void that could not be filled, but somehow Kumar limped along. It was like a twin-engined aircraft with one engine flamed out. The loss of its founder made planning for the long term impossible. The plane had to land somewhere for repairs. Closing the Tokyo office and moving to Sapporo would be the chance for a needed breather.

The police were leaving Seigo alone, but his time was taken up visiting

Kumar's banks and conferring with clients. He wasn't in the best of moods, and delegated most of the day-to-day management to his island chiefs.

Seigo wasn't the only one acting different. A handful of regular and part-time staff had already quit, and a few of the chiefs had announced they wouldn't be going north. The vibe was confused and unsettled. It had been like this for weeks, but Kotaro had been too preoccupied to pay much attention.

Without Ayuko, even Kotaro was losing his attachment to Kumar. Kaname planned to stay till the end, then concentrate on her studies.

"Hope things go well in Hokkaido," she said to Makoto.

"Thanks. Come visit anytime."

Kotaro and Makoto had made their peace since their "transaction" at the tea caddy building. Now they worked hard and competed to see who could make Kaname laugh.

Finally a day came that started out like any other. The three of them were on break in the lounge, shooting the breeze, when an employee staring at her tablet and munching on a sandwich gasped in surprise.

"Look at this—arrests in Tomakomai!"

Kaname and Makoto were shocked into silence. The three of them crowded around the tablet.

"It's the Serial Amputator!" Makoto said breathlessly.

"Well, I'm not sure. It doesn't say that," said the tablet owner. The news feed had a one-line headline.

ARRESTS IN MURDER OF TOMAKOMAI IZAKAYA OWNER:
UNCLE AND COUSIN

Things heated up quickly. The islands competed keenly to find the latest scraps of information. Everyone assumed that the arrest of suspects in this case almost certainly meant that Ayuko's killers had been found.

No, you're wrong. You're all wrong!

He wanted to shout it from the rooftops, but Kotaro thrust his hands into the pockets of his jeans, gave the tumult a cool gaze, closed his ears, and immersed himself in his monitoring.

Two hours later, Seigo sent everyone an email. The men arrested in Tomakomai had nothing to do with Ayuko's murder, or with the statement sent to the media. Tomakomai Central Police Department hadn't made an official announcement, but he had this information from the special investigation unit in Tokyo. Everyone should calm down and focus on their work.

It was seven by the time Kotaro got home. Asako—and Kazumi, who'd lately been even ruder than usual—were glued to the TV. Making dinner didn't look likely to happen anytime soon. Every network was running special coverage of the arrests.

"Hey guys. When's dinner?"

His mother and sister looked at him with astonishment.

"Kotaro, haven't you heard? They caught the Serial Amputators!" Kazumi said, pointing to the TV.

"They're the ones who did that awful thing to the president of your company," Asako added.

"Nah, it's not them. Don't jump to conclusions."

They gaped at him with total incomprehension. Kazumi's finger was frozen, pointed at the television.

"The guys in Tomakomai didn't kill Ayuko Yamashina," Kotaro added. "You ought to listen better. The police haven't said a single thing about the Serial Amputator, have they?"

"But, but..."

The networks reported that Shiro Nakanome's uncle and cousin had murdered him because of a conflict over the right to manage the izakaya. There were more details on the web that hadn't made it to television, but they were from established sites that didn't usually blow smoke.

"It was some kind of family conflict," Kotaro said.

"But they cut off his toe!" Asako insisted.

"So? They must've had a reason. Or maybe they didn't. It doesn't matter. I'm phoning for pizza."

The women turned back to the TV. Takayuki soon arrived home and joined them. When the pizzas came, they ate and channel-surfed the news. Kotaro had his fill and drifted quietly away from the table. Halfway up the stairs he heard his mother say, "Ko-chan's still in denial. He says they're not the ones who killed his boss."

There'd been a call from Shigenori ten minutes earlier. He hadn't left a message. Kotaro called back, but the line was busy. He was booting up his PC when Shigenori finally rang back.

"The Tomakomai police will hold a press conference at nine," he said without preamble. "If you've been watching the news, you pretty much know what they're going to say. But I've got something that won't be at the press conference."

Kotaro didn't ask what it was. He could tell Shigenori was excited. He was going to say it anyway.

"The uncle—Reiji Nakanome—confessed to cutting off the victim's toe. He said it was for luck. About thirty years back, there was a robbery-homicide in Sapporo. A shop owner was murdered and three million yen was stolen from his safe. The case was never solved and the statute of limitations eventually expired. The perp, or perps, got away clean," Shigenori said. "The owner was missing his left big toe. He lost it in an accident when he was young. It's hard to keep your balance and even harder to walk without a big toe. The victim was in his forties, but he was already using a cane."

Kotaro said nothing.

"Reiji Nakanome killed his nephew with his son's help. He cut off the victim's toe as a talisman, hoping that whatever good fortune let the killers in Sapporo get away scot-free would attach itself to the murder in Tomakomai. Sympathetic magic, in a way. That's not the sort of motivation the police could infer without a confession. Unfortunately for Reiji and his son, the statute of limitations on violent crimes has been abolished. No amount of luck can help them now."

"Are you sure about all this?" Kotaro asked.

"A hundred percent. I heard it from the detective who collared me there."

"But the robbery was in Sapporo. Tomakomai's pretty far away."

"Reiji Nakanome lived in Sapporo for years. Anyway, this wraps it up. The Serial Amputator's debut was nothing of the sort. He's a phantom. Are you convinced now?"

Detective, are you excited about this?

"You've been lying low recently, Kotaro. I was happy about that, to be honest."

"I'm busy with school. I don't have a lot of free time."

"Keep at it, then. Stick with your studies."

"If it was a family thing, how come the cops didn't arrest those guys sooner?"

"Crimes like that are actually harder to solve. Families protect their own. Not out of compassion. Out of shame."

Kotaro could sympathize with that motivation.

"Since there were no witnesses, it was hard to check people's alibis. If the crime takes place at night, everyone you talk to was home asleep, and it's usually true. It makes things harder to sort out."

You're not just excited. I think you're enjoying this.

"The police were walking on tiptoe until they had definite proof," Shigenori added.

"What did they find?"

"The body was abandoned in a place where people were dumping trash illegally. The area's full of discarded furniture and appliances with thousands of partial fingerprints and palm prints. But the police worked everything over for prints. It must've taken them weeks.

"Anyway, they got lucky. They found Reiji's fingerprints on a busted bicycle saddle, and half of a palm print from his son on the side of a filing cabinet.

That gave them the wedge they needed to make arrests. Reiji confessed to everything. He says it was all his doing. He forced his son to help him."

Kotaro was still doubtful. "Why did the detective give you all this, anyway? It sounds a little too kind. You must've threatened him or something."

"That's kind of a hard way to put it." Shigenori chuckled. "I had a hunch about why they took the toe, and it happened to pay off. I think he was just trying to thank me."

Kotaro could tell from his tone that he wasn't just pleased because his hunch had proved out. For the first time in a long time, he'd helped an investigation move forward.

"Today, when we saw the first news—"

Kotaro paused. *Am I really going to say this?*

"—everybody at Kumar totally freaked out. They were over the moon. They thought the Serial Amputators, the people who killed Ayuko, had been captured."

Shigenori sighed. "I'm sure they did. That's how everyone is reacting. Japan has been hypnotized by a phantom. People haven't woken up yet."

"Keiko Tashiro will never be arrested. No one will hear her confession, because I nailed her."

"You're right, kid."

"Even if they solve those other murders, people at Kumar will never get closure," Kotaro said. "They won't be able to hold on to that feeling of relief they had when they first heard the news today."

What Kotaro needed just now was someone to tell him to stop worrying about it, that it was over and done with and couldn't be helped. He needed someone to drill that into him and let him off the hook.

But Shigenori wouldn't play ball. "It's not just the people at Kumar. Saeko Komiya's family and relatives, her friends and the people she worked with—they'll never lose that knot in their chests."

The truth Kotaro had been running from was suddenly staring him in the face and wouldn't let him look away.

"You got involved with the dark side, kiddo. You took the law into your own hands. Now you see the result."

"But...I couldn't..."

"Let it go. You can't take back the past. Just don't make the same mistake again. That's all you can do."

A dressing down or some blistering criticism would've been easier to take than Shigenori's preaching. *I can't stand this guy.*

"I wanted retribution. I thought doing anything else would mean letting them off easy."

He didn't wait for an answer. He just hit END. The phone didn't ring again.

▼

In the morning, the news shows were still banging away at the break in the Tomakomai case. Every channel had its panel of experts trying to get a handle on what it meant if the "first" murder in the series wasn't the work of the Serial Amputator.

The textboards were in the same mode, with people vying to make sense of the news and rejiggering their profiling theories. Some insisted stubbornly that the arrests had been a mistake, that the two men had been falsely charged. All five murders could only be the work of one man—the Serial Amputator!

I call on the Serial Amputator to make a statement. To understand what you really want, we need more than that letter you sent to the media.

Comments like this were all over the boards, and they brought a response. "Yes, I am the Serial Amputator. I killed my first victim long before Tomakomai, and I'm planning my next even as we speak." This was what passed as humor for some.

Words. A torrent of words. Utterance upon utterance, piling up endlessly. But these mountains of words were invisible to ordinary people. They were invisible to upstanding citizens of the web and to those in the shadows waiting for a chance to do harm. No one felt them growing heavier with each passing moment.

No one can monitor them. That's why I had to—

Hanging from a strap on the train, Kotaro stared at his face reflected in the window. The face of Kotaro Mishima. He'd had it for nineteen years.

What would it look like through his left eye?

You've got huge fangs…

You betcha. Me and Makoto's giant, we're thick as thieves.

His phone vibrated. It was Asako. She hung up as soon as the message service connected and tried again.

He got off at the next station and called her. This wasn't normal. It had to be some kind of emergency.

"Hey Mom. What's going on?"

"I'm leaving for the hospital." She sounded relieved to hear his voice. Her own voice was trembling. "Mika's been injured."

"Mika? How? At school?"

"I don't know the details, but they say she fell down the stairs. She hit her head and they took her away in an ambulance."

▾

Takako Sonoi worked for an international trading company in the heart of Tokyo, near the Imperial Palace. It took Kotaro thirty minutes to get there. On the way he got a text from Asako.

Mika is alert and talking.

He walked into the steel and chrome lobby of a futuristic skyscraper, went to the reception desk, and demanded urgently to see Takako Sonoi. He waited impatiently for a few minutes, complained at the desk again, and steamed for another ten minutes before she emerged from one of the elevators.

"Ko-chan? What's going on?"

"Did you check your phone?"

"I was making a presentation," she said. "It was off."

She looked very much at home in a stylish black suit with black high heels and a white dress shirt. Her makeup was elegant. Kotaro had never seen her dressed for battle; to say she looked impressive would've been an understatement. But as he told her what had happened, the blood quickly drained from her face.

"Aunt Hanako is so upset that she's bouncing off the walls, so Mom's at the hospital. You better get going too. I sent you the address and phone number. I can take you there if you want."

Takako was still pale, but she pulled herself together quickly. "No, I'll be fine. I'll leave right away. You shouldn't miss class. I really appreciate your coming to tell me."

"Are you sure you'll be okay?"

"Don't worry, I'll text you as soon as I see how Mika's doing. Thank you," she said and gave his shoulder a firm squeeze. She turned and dashed back to the elevators.

Caught up in the moment, Kotaro gave in to temptation and closed his right eye.

So far everything he'd seen with his left eye had been ugly, if not horrible, but he was sure Takako's word body must be completely different.

The elevator opened. Takako got in, turned and waved to Kotaro.

Two pure white wings rose above her head. To Kotaro, they looked like the wings of Pegasus, folded behind her back. Their wingspan would probably be wider than she was tall. They sheltered her from harm and, with a good wind, could take her as far as she wanted to go. The edges of each feather sparkled. In motion, they would be sure to leave a powdery wake of light.

Those wings are protecting Mika too.

He wanted to tell Takako that she had beautiful wings. Maybe then she would use them to fly straight to Mika.

Kazumi had told him Takako was touchy about her inability to be there for Mika, the way Asako could for her own children. But if Asako had seen her today—even without her wings—she surely would've felt outclassed.

Kotaro's morning lecture was distilled boredom. As he sat there fighting drowsiness, he got a mail from Mika.

Ko-chan, I'm sorry you had to worry. I slipped and fell down the stairs. I've got a lump on my forehead!!

The message ended with a tearfully laughing emoji.

Mika wasn't excitable or impetuous. Kazumi, maybe. Mika was down-to-earth. Perhaps she'd been thinking about something, let her attention wander, and slipped.

U-ri the wolf. Kotaro stirred uneasily in his seat, remembering what Yukiko Morisaki had said that day in the park. *Mika's troubles aren't over.*

But Mika said she'd just slipped. It must've been a simple accident. There was no point in assuming the worst. That was a slippery slope.

Just before class ended, Kotaro got the grade on his latest report: C minus.

Stick to your studies.

He shook his head. Now Shigenori's words were echoing in his ears.

When he arrived for the evening shift, things at Kumar had settled down. Naturally, the atmosphere of calm was alloyed with disappointment and gloom. Seigo's desk was empty and only a few members of Drug Island were on duty. Kotaro took a seat next to Maeda and went to work.

After about an hour, Maeda said abruptly, "Narita's quitting at the end of the month."

It took Kotaro a few moments to digest this fresh serving of bad news. "I didn't know."

"I think he's the third chief to leave." Maeda stared at his monitor. "The move's been rescheduled. Have you heard?"

"No, nothing specific."

"It's not next March. We close at the end of this year. Too much bad stuff has happened. First Morinaga disappears, then we lose Ayuko. And we still don't know the truth."

Kotaro felt a stab of guilt.

"What do you think? Tomakomai was a one-off, but is the Serial Amputator real?" he asked.

"I don't know what to think," Maeda said. He put his hands behind his head and arched his back to get the kinks out. He turned to Kotaro and smiled ironically.

"I don't believe anything anymore. Now that I look back at it, that statement the media got smells like a hoax."

Kotaro wanted to smile ironically too, but something held him back. "I heard that a friend of Ayuko's and Seigo's from college disappeared right after the murder."

Maeda's eyes widened in surprise. "You *are* plugged in. Where did you hear that?"

"Someone talking."

Maeda leaned toward him. Kotaro did the same.

"I heard something myself. The police are treating her as a suspect."

"*Her*? The suspect is a woman?"

"Yeah." Maeda nodded and paused. He seemed to be sizing up Kotaro's reaction to this bit of information.

Playing dumb was easy, but it got on Kotaro's conscience. He looked away and said, "Just like Kenji. It's spooky."

"Yeah, but this woman has nothing to do with Morinaga. She has everything to do with Seigo, though." Maeda lowered his voice to a whisper. "Ayuko was seen with her the night before she was found. A security camera filmed them. They say she also called Ayuko before that, when she was in a taxi."

"Is she a suspect?" Kotaro fought to calm the pounding in his chest. He feared what he might hear next.

"Seigo had to meet with the cops again today. They're going to search her apartment."

So it had finally come to that. Kotaro wanted to clap hands with joy. He wanted to shout. Instead he clenched his fist under the table, fighting back the urge.

He was fighting back something else as well. The police were talking to Seigo again.

They're not finished with him.

"Seems like there was some kind of triangle, I guess you'd call it." Maeda scratched his head awkwardly. "They say you can't tell what happens between men and women behind closed doors. I don't have much experience in that area, so I couldn't say."

"Come on. You must be popular."

Maeda was muscular and manly, but he just guffawed. Another island member looked up curiously from his monitor.

"You can't attract women just by going to the gym, okay? Still, I don't have any problem shoveling snow. I was almost set to go to Sapporo myself, but I'm quitting. I'll be here to the end. After that I think I'll go back to my hometown and look for a job."

"Where's home?"

"Kobe. Great food. You should visit. Once I leave Tokyo, I don't think I'll be coming back."

Something seemed to occur to him suddenly. He sat up in his chair. "I must be getting senile. I'm babbling on and almost forgot to tell you the most important thing. Morinaga's father is coming to Tokyo. He says he wants to meet you. You and Kenji were friends, right? The guys on School Island say you knew him even better than they did. His father's been wanting to talk to you for a long time."

This was not good news. Kotaro didn't want to meet Kenji's father. He wanted to run away. *I know what happened to your son. I know, but I have to pretend I don't.*

"Oh...okay."

"How's your schedule?"

"I guess when I'm here in the afternoon would be best. Anytime is okay for me."

"Okay, I'll tell Scheduling to fix it up. Sorry, gotta hit the head." Maeda stood up and turned to go.

"Can I ask you something?" Kotaro said. "Did you decide not to follow Seigo because you lost respect for him?"

Maeda jerked back in surprise, as if he'd taken a slap to the cheek. "What's that supposed to mean?"

"Well, like you said...I mean, if Ayuko wasn't murdered by the Serial Amputator, if it wasn't the work of some crazy person, but happened because of some kind of romantic conflict, Seigo would be partially responsible, so—"

Maeda put a hard hand on the top of Kotaro's head. "That's enough." Kotaro's head was in a vice.

"Too many sad things have happened. I don't want to bring that baggage with me to Sapporo. Seigo's doing a stellar job of running Kumar. Of course I still respect him."

He turned and left the room.

▼

On the way home, Kotaro took the train from Ochanomizu to Akihabara and switched to the Yamanote Line, looking for a station he'd never gotten off at before and probably wouldn't use again.

He chose Sugamo, the old folks' Harajuku. He passed through the wicket and found a pay phone.

THE SPECIAL INVESTIGATIONS UNIT, TOTSUKA POLICE STATION, KANAGAWA PREFECTURAL POLICE, IS LOOKING FOR INFORMATION CONCERNING THE MURDER OF SAEKO KOMIYA. IF YOU HAVE DETAILS CONCERNING THIS CASE, PLEASE CALL—

Kotaro punched in the number on the printout. After two rings, a male voice came on the line.

"I have information on the case." The man started to talk, but Kotaro ignored him and plunged ahead. He wasn't calling to answer questions. He spoke quickly and crisply.

"The man you want is the gardener for her son's nursery school. He owns a flower shop. His name is Kosuke Nakasono. You'll find he's been missing for a few days. He has a warehouse near his parents' house in Totsuka. The victim's leg is in that warehouse, in an oil drum. Match the DNA. He's been slashing women around Totsuka too. You should be able to connect the dots."

He hung up. The man on the other end was shouting, but he didn't pay attention.

He'd thought the call would leave him feeling light and refreshed. Instead, he couldn't stop shaking. His breathing was shallow and ragged.

Please. You've got to help. I erased Kosuke Nakasono from this world, but if you trace the evidence, you'll be able to prove he did it, won't you? The truth will give the bereaved at least a little peace.

Won't it?

I meted out final justice, Kosuke thought. *He's not in the world anymore.*

By the time he got home, he was feeling a bit better. Asako and Kazumi gave him a detailed rundown on Mika's accident. Kazumi was furious about the slippers that students were required to wear in the classroom and corridors. They were old, and it was easy to slip in them. Mika was going to spend a night in the hospital under observation, but she'd be going home tomorrow.

"Hospital food is awful. I feel sorry for her," Kazumi added.

"But they calculate the calories for you. It's a good way to diet," Asako put in.

Their banter cheered Kotaro up. There was more to be cheerful about when he got a mail from Takako.

Ko-chan, many thanks for today. You're like a big brother to Mika. You helped us both.

He fell asleep buoyed by this feeling. The next day he woke refreshed and rested for the first time in months.

Downstairs, Asako was standing by the stove, eyes fixed on the TV in the living room. Smoke was pouring from the frying pan.

"Hey Mom, the eggs are burning!"

She hurriedly turned off the burner, waving the smoke away from her face.

"It looks like they solved the Akita murder too. The perpetrators came forward and confessed," she told Kotaro breathlessly.

The perpetrators were a woman in her mid-fifties and her second daughter, twenty-five. The victim was the eldest daughter, who was twenty-six when she was killed.

Mother and daughter had turned themselves in at a police box near their home—not in Akita, but in suburban Tokyo—and were being held at the nearest police station. Reporters from the news shows were clustered outside the station, microphones in hand.

Kazumi had already left for team practice. Takayuki, Kotaro and Asako ate breakfast and watched the news. The killers were apparently cooperating fully with the police, though the details were still unclear. They had turned themselves in at around eight the previous evening.

"It was supposed to be one of those Serial Amputator murders," Takayuki said through a mouthful of buttered toast.

"Right, the second murder. But I guess it's not him." Asako poked at her salad. "I'm starting to wonder if he even exists."

"But there are three other cases—" Takayuki broke off and looked sidelong at his son. "Are you all right, son?"

"Gotta go," Kotaro said and went upstairs.

The textboards were boiling, naturally. Comments like Asako's were all over. What the hell was going on? Was the killer's statement a hoax? Had someone done it for kicks? People were begging the Serial Amputator to come forward and say something.

Kotaro called Shigenori and got his answering service. He hung up without leaving a message and headed for Kumar.

He ran into Narita at the first-floor elevator. He was carrying a plastic shopping bag from a convenience store. It was probably his breakfast. He'd pulled a night shift; his face was covered with stubble.

"Hey, mornin', Kotaro."

"Is Seigo here yet?"

"Um, no, not yet." He gave Kotaro a slap on the shoulder. "I'm sure he'll let us know if he finds out anything about Akita from the cops."

"That's why I'm here."

Kotaro wasn't scheduled to work that day. Kaname wouldn't be around until the afternoon. Narita knew that, but he wasn't surprised to see Kotaro. "Just couldn't stay away, huh? Head for the lounge, you're not alone."

The lounge was crowded with off-duty employees glued to their devices. There was little talk, but people seemed to want company, like animals huddling together in the face of an approaching storm.

It wasn't long before Seigo arrived and asked everyone to report to the third floor. He was going to brief them in person this time.

He looked thin and tired, as though he'd been up all night. Maybe he'd been working, or he just hadn't been able to sleep. He was pale and unshaven. He didn't look healthy.

"Sorry to interrupt your day," he said to the room. His voice was weak. "As you know, the murder that everyone thought was the second by the Serial Amputator has been solved. The details haven't been reported yet, but the case is definitely closed. The victim was killed by her mother and sister.

"Apparently the murdered daughter was a wild child who'd been giving her mother and sister trouble for a long time. Of course, the deceased isn't here to defend herself, so I can't really say. Whatever the trouble was, it was enough to drive her mother and sister to kill her, mutilate her body, and dump it in Akita. The mother said they cut off one of her toes to make it look like the work of the Tomakomai killer."

The room started buzzing. Seigo must have gotten this from the special investigation unit, as he had with the inside information about the first murder.

"At the time, no one was talking about Toe-Cutter Bill or the Serial Amputator. The Tomakomai case was unsolved. But mother and daughter were alert to the possibility that mutilating the body might put the police off the scent. I guess they were right. They convinced me too. Pulled the wool over my eyes completely."

He attempted a wry smile, which only made him look more pitiful. Kotaro remembered how convinced Seigo had been that a serial killer was on the loose.

"Everything that might've been a clue to the victim's identity was removed. Apparently the daughter was the one who handled that."

One of the employees raised her hand. "Nozaki, from BB Island," she said. "I saw something on one of the boards that said the family used to live near where the body was found, maybe ten years ago."

Seigo nodded. "Interesting. That would explain why they chose that location. They were familiar with it."

"The husband—the victim's father—was posted all around Japan by his employer. This is according to someone who went to high school with the victim in Akita."

"Thanks for that. Does anyone else have something?"

Another person raised her hand. "The younger daughter's SNS page says she's a big fan of police procedurals. *CSI*, shows like that."

"TV's getting a little too instructive." Seigo smiled. Again, it just made him look more pathetic.

A veteran of BB Island spoke up. "The victim was pretty well-known around the neighborhood for being a problem child. Seems she was emotionally unstable. She got married three years before and divorced immediately. After she went back to live with her mother and sister, she hardly came out of her room, but sometimes the neighbors could hear her and the mother having screaming matches. Once she put her mother in the hospital.

"Early last year the father was killed in a traffic accident, and the family got a big insurance settlement. The fighting got worse after that."

"Where did you get that?" Seigo asked.

"From someone who says she lives in the neighborhood. She's been tweeting a lot of details."

"All right, that's enough." He held up a hand. "Concerning the murder of Ayuko Yamashina—"

Everyone fell silent. This was what they'd been waiting for.

"That had nothing to do with the Serial Amputator either. The statement sent by the killer was a hoax."

Someone sitting near Kotaro murmured, "I knew it."

"This is all I'm at liberty to say at the moment. I apologize." He dipped his head. Kotaro fought the urge to close his right eye, and somehow won out. *This isn't the time or place. I might scream.*

"We're forming another special team," Seigo continued. "Let's take a fresh look at all five cases, especially the two unsolved ones. We'll gather the latest information and organize everything chronologically from the beginning. I'd like one volunteer from each island. Let's dredge the textboards too. If you want to get in on that, let me know."

The meeting broke up. Someone tugged on Kotaro's sleeve. It was Makoto.

"They probably wanted to take the body all the way to Tomakomai." He was talking about the Akita case. He had a pained expression, almost as though he had a toothache. "But it was too far, and they didn't make it. They must've run out of emotional and physical energy. They would've taken the body up north in a car, which would've been horribly stressful."

As it happened, their choice of Akita to discard the body ended up complicating the investigation even more than if they'd gone as far as Hokkaido. Investigations across jurisdictional boundaries were never a strong point for Japan's police forces, and just taking the body out of Tokyo would've made it much harder for local law enforcement to get traction.

"It's almost like you feel sorry for them," Kotaro said.

"Not almost. I *do* feel sorry for them. Family strife is something I know firsthand. So will you be dredging?"

"Yeah, I'll volunteer."

"Good luck, then."

Kotaro wondered what kind of strife Makoto meant. Of course, he was aware that when it came to murder, the killer and victim usually knew each other. They were almost always relatives, friends, or coworkers. Still, how could he feel sorry for them? No way should a mother who killed her daughter, a sister who killed her sister and mutilated the body, be allowed to plead for leniency because the victim was driving them crazy. Seigo was right. The dead can't speak for themselves.

But that afternoon, more information came to light that gave Kotaro second thoughts.

The break in the Tomakomai case was one of the reasons mother and daughter had come forward. They'd begun to worry that it would be only a matter of time before their number came up. The unexpected resolution of the case hung heavy on their minds. But there was another reason, a more significant reason, for their confession.

The dead daughter's ghost was appearing to the mother, night after night. The daughter had tried to convince her it was just a bad dream, but eventually the mother reached the limits of her sanity.

Kotaro understood. He knew the fear and terror of seeing something that was not of this world.

In tears, the mother told her daughter she'd have to confess or commit suicide. This was why the pair had turned themselves in at eight in the evening. The weeping mother had told her daughter she couldn't spend another night in the house. If she didn't kill herself, her dead daughter would do it for her.

The daughter, who was also at the end of her rope, brought her mother by the hand to the nearest police box. The killers were unmasked not by the authorities, not by the media or citizens of the web, but by the victim herself.

lonelylonelylonelylonelylonelylonelylonely

In his mind's eye, Kotaro saw the apparition in white that he'd encountered in the tea caddy building. The ghost that stood by her mother's bed must have whispered something similar. *Lonely lonely lonely lonely.*

The two women had strangled the eldest daughter after she'd taken a sedative and was sound asleep. They had hidden the body in the house at first, wrapped in plastic sheeting, but after it began to decay, they knew they had to get rid it. As they were stripping the body of anything that would betray its identity, the daughter remembered the Tomakomai murder. If that case had been solved quickly, things would have played out differently.

Perhaps the other murders would've drawn hardly any attention. Perhaps Ayuko would even be alive now.

During the evening break, Kotaro checked his phone. There was a mail from Shigenori.

I'm heading to the scene of the crime in Mishima.

▼

It was past ten when he finally got home. Kazumi was just out of the evening bath. As soon as she saw him, she exploded. "Where've you been? Mika was here tonight. She wanted to apologize for putting you out. She even brought a cake."

"Is she all right?"

"Yeah. Well, she still has a Band-Aid on her forehead."

Kotaro went to his room and sent Mika a text. She answered instantly.

Welcome home. Put your head out the window.

He followed instructions. Across the street, the second-floor window of the Sonoi house opened. Mika put her head through the gap in the curtains and waved. She was still wearing her team jersey. Kotaro waved back. She didn't seem to have the Band-Aid now.

This time he wasn't tempted; he was worried. He closed his right eye.

Nothing much changed. Mika seemed slightly blurred, as if she were surrounded by a thin mist. Her word body hadn't had time to coalesce.

She disappeared behind the curtains, catching them in the sliding glass window as she closed it. She opened it again and pulled the curtains inside.

A black object the size of a baby's head silently scurried up the side of the house and disappeared inside before she shut the window.

Kotaro started with shock. For a moment he thought he was seeing something real—maybe a large rat.

No—it was words, and they were not Mika's. They were pursuing her, or at least trailing after her. And they were clearly malevolent. In fact, the object had moved like a huge spider. It had had six legs—no, maybe eight. Or ten?

He hurried downstairs, dashed outside in his bare feet, and crossed the street to the Sonoi house. The creature had gone into Mika's room, yet she wouldn't even know it.

"Galla!" He shouted out of fear before clapping a hand over his mouth. A silver thread crossed his left field of vision.

When you seek me, I am here.

He held his breath. He kept the Eye trained on Mika's window.

"I didn't just imagine that, did I?"

There was no answer.

"Come on Galla, help me out. What should I do? I can't let that thing hang out in Mika's room. How do I get rid of it?" The soles of his feet were getting cold.

She does not know.

"So what should I do?"

Ask her. That is what words are for.

The silver thread disappeared.

11

The events of the next seven days or so were like a dam giving way.

It was as if the break in the Tomakomai case had created a tiny hole from which water had begun to spurt. The confessions in the Akita murder widened the breach, causing cracks to form around it. Water started leaking from these cracks as well. The hole got bigger and bigger, and the stream turned into a gusher—

The gusher began with a wave of new developments in the murder of Saeko Komiya. The first brief announcement of the discovery of the victim's severed leg was soon followed by details at a press conference of the Kanagawa Police, timed to coincide with the evening news. Kosuke Nakasono, owner of a flower shop in Kawasaki, was wanted for murder. His whereabouts were unknown, and he was presumed to be a fugitive.

Two days later, the special investigation unit handling the Yamashina case announced that it was searching for a female acquaintance of the victim as a person of interest. Evidence also indicated that the same individual was responsible for the letters sent to television networks after the murder.

By coincidence, the press conference took place the same day that the national weather service announced the end of the unusually long rainy season. It was as though the clearing skies over Japan were a sign that the specter of the Serial Amputator had disappeared too, dissolved by torrents of truth.

Keiko Tashiro's whereabouts were unknown, but she was not wanted as a suspect, and the police didn't mention her by name. Instead, she was an important person of interest. Perhaps the police hadn't quite been able to dig up enough evidence to put her on the wanted list, or perhaps they were already planning it but the timing wasn't right.

"I wonder if they'll really find who did it," Kaname said, forlorn.

Kotaro was frustrated that he couldn't cheer her up. *Sorry, it's all my fault. I should've gotten the details out of her, like I did with Nakasono. Then I could've given them to the police. Security camera footage and phone records are just circumstantial evidence. But when I hunted her down, I was still new at it, you know?*

People at Kumar were lucky to be insanely busy. They had no time to think about anything unimportant, including Seigo's chronic absences and the unwelcome attention he was getting in the media. At least there was some hope of resolving the mystery of who had killed their founder, and they responded with genuine joy and relief, throwing themselves into their work. They needed to fight their way through to the light.

Now only the murder of Mama Masami remained unsolved. Kotaro waited for news from Shigenori, but it seemed he was lying low. When Kotaro ran out of patience and called the older man's cell, he discovered that he'd been to Mishima and returned days before.

Instead of information, Shigenori had a question. "What's the leading theory about Mama Masami on the net these days?"

"I can't tell you in a nutshell. There's too many theories and they keep changing all the time. You know something, don't you? Did you make friends with the detectives in Kanagawa this time?"

"I'm not that lucky, kid."

"So you came back empty-handed?"

Shigenori went quiet. Kotaro could sense a heavy vibe on the other end of the line.

He waited. He was sitting in an armchair in a corner of the cafeteria. It was summer break. Outside, the midday sun flooded the pathways that crisscrossed the campus. The only students here now were dedicated club members, serious people who were immersed in their schoolwork, and those like Kotaro, who had blown it the previous term and had to attend supplemental lectures and resubmit their term papers.

Shigenori broke the silence in a low voice. "There was a suicide."

It had happened soon after the murder, around the time when the public was going crazy over the Serial Amputator story.

"A guy she went to high school with. He dropped by Misty now and then. Unemployed, age thirty-five."

"Was he a suspect?"

"Totally off the radar screen."

"What about her customers? Did anyone notice something odd?"

"No one noticed him doing or saying anything out of the ordinary. But just past midnight, about ten days after she was killed, he ran right into a highway divider. His car was totaled. He must've been killed instantly."

"Maybe it was an accident?"

"A truck driver in the opposite lane saw the whole thing. The guy accelerated right into the divider. The airbag didn't deploy. It had been disabled, I assume deliberately."

"I bet he didn't leave a note."

"Not as far as I know."

"I'll go there myself," Kotaro said. "He must've left something behind I'll be able to see."

Shigenori didn't answer. Kotaro had an idea why.

"You got some help too, didn't you? You 'saw' something."

"I took care of this one myself. Galla didn't do anything to me."

Not "help me," but "do anything to me?" I guess there's no way to bridge that gap.

"It was intuition," Shigenori continued. "I've seen a few cases like this in my time. Right after a murder takes place, someone related to the deceased commits suicide. We didn't have any idea they might've been involved until they did away with themselves. It's rare, but it happens.

"You have someone who's committed murder, but no one suspects them, no one's checking up on them. Yet they end up caving to pressure from their conscience. They can't run away from what they've done, and it corners them. It's not so different from that ghost who wouldn't give her mother any peace."

"But what was the motive?"

Shigenori laughed briefly. "He owed Masami Tono money, it turns out. A little over twelve thousand yen. Unfortunately that's nowhere near enough to furnish a motive. He didn't have a bad relationship with her, either. He wasn't a regular at Misty, but he dropped by every couple of months. The other customers say he got along well with her. They spent a lot of time talking about their high school days."

"So why kill her?"

Shigenori snorted with derision. "When he wasn't at Misty, and wasn't around people who knew Masami, he spent a lot of time making fun of him—I mean, her—and generally criticizing her. He couldn't forgive her for transitioning."

Shigenori continued. "I poked around a bit and found out soon enough. He liked making her the butt of his jokes when he was out drinking with friends. Other guys thought it was hilarious. It's a common thing, I'm afraid. The people who listened to his Masami jokes never got the impression that he hated her enough to actually kill her. Maybe he didn't realize it himself.

"At the same time, he was watching her engage with her situation in a positive way, and he hated her for it. He never wasted an opportunity to heap scorn on her. He apparently felt compelled to visit Misty from time to time. His hatred made it impossible for him to stay away."

The opposite of love is not hate, but indifference. Kotaro remembered coming across this insight in one of his required readings, though he couldn't recall the author.

"Mama Masami was loved by her customers. Her bar was thriving. In that sense, there are parallels to the Tomakomai case. She had carved out a place for herself in the world and she was flourishing.

"The suicide worked for a well-known firm in Hamamatsu. Six months before the murder, he was laid off. Losing his job was the last straw for his wife. She took the kids to her parents' and was consulting a lawyer about divorce."

"Talk about adding insult to injury," Kotaro said. "Couldn't he find a new job?"

"He was a doing routine sales work. It's hard for someone like that to get hired these days."

"Maybe that's what pushed him over the edge."

"Stress factor. Yes, it's an element in a lot of criminal behavior. Unemployment, divorce, the death of someone close. Extreme experiences of loss."

"You sound like a profiler, detective."

"Tell me about it. Old cops like me never trained with the FBI. We learned it on the street. Oh, and by the way, my experience is telling me something else." He seemed to be making an effort to sound casual. "If one were so inclined, one might propose that this guy didn't commit suicide because his conscience was bothering him. Maybe he'd already decided to die, and the idea of his high school friend thriving and enjoying her life after he was dead was more than he could bear.

"His life is crashing down around him. He decides to end it. It's a lonely decision. Maybe to ease the loneliness, or out of the pain and rage he felt at being pushed off a cliff by life, he decided to take someone with him."

"That's a rotten thing to do," Kotaro said.

"Murder is always rotten. Naturally, severing one of the victim's toes was meant to make the killing look like the latest in a series. Suicide would put him beyond the reach of the police, but people want to escape blame even in death. The Serial Amputator would be the ideal cover. And so you get yet another murder by a serial killer who doesn't exist.

"As far as stuffing her body in a trunk and dumping it in the woods goes—not far from the home of parents who couldn't accept the way she was living—that was a final symbol of spite and contempt for her and what she represented."

It was a dark obsession. Kotaro couldn't help but wonder how the killer would have looked through Galla's Eye. What monstrous form must his word body have taken as it dogged his every step?

"Do the police suspect this guy?"

"I don't know. I didn't meet any nice detectives this time who were willing to take me down to the station and interrogate me until I found out what I needed to know."

Kotaro had to laugh.

"But it's already clear the whole Serial Amputator story is out the window, so they might be looking at this suicide in a different light after all. People are waking up from that dream and opening their eyes—not just the police, but people who knew him, and people who heard him insulting the victim over a mug of beer. Well, we'll find out before long, I'm sure. There's nothing to do but wait."

As Kotaro left the campus, he decided to drop by Kumar. He wasn't scheduled, but he felt the need to put in an appearance. He wasn't the only one who'd acquired this habit. Everyone was thirsting for news about Ayuko's murder, and they were drawn to Kumar if only as a place to scour the web and monitor the television for new developments. Somehow Kumar seemed the place to get news fast and accurately.

Kotaro climbed the stairs toward Drug Island. As long as he was here, he thought, he might as well see if there was anything the team needed help with. Seigo was talking to an older man in a suit who had pulled up a chair next to his desk. As Kotaro entered the office, Seigo waved him over. The man in the suit stood up.

He looked somehow familiar. Yes, the family resemblance was strong. Anyone would've recognized him.

"Ko-Prime?" Seigo gestured to the man. "This is Soji Morinaga. Kenji's father."

▼

Kotaro decided that the coffee shop where Kenji had initiated him into the world of underground sites would be the best place to talk. Luckily it wasn't crowded, just like the night he'd been there with Kenji, except it was the middle of the afternoon and the air conditioning was blasting.

Soji gave Kotaro a business card. He owned and managed a souvenir-cum-coffee shop named Tree Leaf in one of the tourist towns that faced the Sea of Japan.

Kenji's childhood had been filled with hardship after his father's company failed. Running a coffee shop for tourists was a big step down from managing a company, but for Soji it must've been an oasis of calm and a stable source of income, enough to send Kenji to university and on to graduate school in Tokyo. The Morinaga family had managed to pull their ship off the rocks.

Yet Kenji had disappeared from the world. It was enough to make Kotaro grind his teeth with frustration even now. *Kenji, why?*

"Thank you for meeting with me. I'm sorry to interrupt your holiday." Soji dipped his head politely. It made Kotaro uncomfortable, given the gap in their ages.

"It's all right, Mr. Morinaga. I've got work and summer classes. I'm not really on vacation anyway."

He was beginning to seethe with frustration. Soji's drooping shoulders and careworn, lonely appearance just seemed to raise the pressure inside him, pressure that had been building and building and now seemed ready to boil over.

He wanted to tell him everything—about Galla and where Kenji was. Tell him everything and ask him how to convince Kenji to come back to the world.

No, taking this sad-eyed father to Galla would be even better. If Kenji could look out of Galla's scythe and see his father, surely his heart would be moved?

"I asked to meet because I've been wanting to ask you something, Kotaro."

Kotaro sat up in his chair, beaten to the punch. "What was that?"

Soji blinked hesitantly. Kenji had his father's eyes.

"Mr. Maki tells me Kenji confided in you. He told you homeless people were disappearing and he wanted to investigate, that he couldn't bear to see needy people in trouble, and that he had a reason—not just a sense of justice, or the kind of curiosity a journalist might have, but something that made him feel their misfortune was his too."

Is that what you came here to ask me? Kotaro was baffled.

"Ah...yes, he did say something like that."

Soji's spirits seemed to lift a bit. "How did he put it, exactly?"

"When he was in the fifth grade—he told me—he and his parents had to drop out of sight to get away from their creditors."

Kotaro remembered what Kenji had said about how fragile people's situations could be—how a few minor misjudgments mixed with a bit of bad luck could be enough to make everything fall apart.

"Yes, my business went bankrupt. The banks were after me. So Kenji told you all about it. I see." He sighed. "You're probably the first person he ever opened up to about it—about the bankruptcy and the hard times afterward. He never had a word of complaint to me or his mother. I'm sure he never told his friends either. Somehow he acted as if it had never happened.

"He wanted to forget, I think. It was something one ought to forget. I think it's fortunate that he grew up to be the kind of person no one would guess had a difficult childhood."

That certainly included Kotaro. Kenji, with his ever-changing, colorful glasses, had always seemed like someone from a comfortable background, with the naïveté to prove it.

"But he told you about it," Soji added. "That shows how much he trusted you."

Kotaro was doubtful. Kenji was two years older, but had never looked down on him. He'd been a good workmate and a nice guy, but that was all. Their relationship had never reached the point where a heavy word like "trust" even applied.

"I think he told me because finding out why those people were disappearing was so important to him. He thought it was a tragedy."

Soji seemed to sag even more with disappointment. "Then if his investigation was so important to him, why would he disappear?"

"What do the police say?"

"They don't seem to have a specific theory. Maybe he got mixed up in some sort of trouble while he was among the homeless. But you would expect someone to have some information about him, something to lead us to him. The detective in charge thinks he most likely got depressed with his situation, or maybe with life, and decided to drop out of sight," Soji said. "It happens to people doing volunteer work with the disadvantaged, sometimes even to journalists writing stories about them. If they spend enough time with certain groups of people and get to know them well enough, sometimes they decide to cross over and join them. At least that's what the detective says."

"I doubt it was that simple," Kotaro said.

"I do too, but they do say someone with a psychological burden, or misgivings or doubts about their life, might suddenly decide to live on the streets. The detective told me he thought Kenji himself might have smashed his phone. It would be a symbol of his decision to be free."

Kotaro didn't know how to answer that. He would have to think about it.

I know what happened. Kenji found Galla near the tea caddy building and she took him to the roof. That's when he dropped his phone. On the roof, she told him why the homeless were vanishing, and he decided to follow them—

If that was the truth, the detective's theory still sounded plausible. In fact it was correct, in the sense that Kenji *was* trying to get away from reality.

One truth with two interpretations. An observer would give credence to both.

It's like a story. It all depends on how you tell it.

But both stories contained the same riddle. What was Kenji's motive? What was his real reason for dropping out of the world?

"Did Kenji give you any other... details?" Soji asked cautiously.

"What kind of details?"

"Well, that is... to borrow a phrase from the detective, did he seem as though something was tormenting him? Something to do with atonement?"

Kotaro stared uncomprehendingly.

"Did he seem to feel guilty about his life? Did he feel there was something he deserved to be punished for?"

Kotaro doubted his ears. Soji looked down in embarrassment.

"Are you saying Kenji did something that he *should* have been punished for?" Kotaro asked.

Soji Morinaga's face drained of color. "He... he didn't say anything to you?"

"All I heard was that the family had to run away in the middle of the night, that you moved from one place to another, that relatives and friends helped you out, and it took about two years to get back on your feet."

"It was mainly a friend of mine who helped us. Kenji didn't tell you about this?"

"Why? Did something happen?"

Soji peered at him and nodded slowly, as thought his head were heavy. "There was... an accident."

The air conditioner was blowing on them. *That's why I feel cold*, Kotaro thought.

"I have never asked Kenji about it," Soji continued. "He's never said anything himself. There was a time when I think he wanted to talk about it. But I didn't ask him. I was afraid.

"When I heard he was missing, the accident was the first thing I thought of. I never once asked him about it, never gave him a chance to unburden himself. That was my mistake. I'm sure he must've grown tired of carrying that burden alone," Soji said.

"Giving your creditors the slip means running away from society," he continued, matter-of-factly. "In a sense, you fall through the cracks. At first we moved from place to place, living with people who would take us in, but moving around like that meant Kenji couldn't go to school, so we left him with my parents, then my wife's parents, or with our siblings.

"That didn't go well either. Naturally my creditors quickly discovered who our relatives were and made trouble for them too, which forced Kenji to move again. Then a friend of mine from college offered to help us. He had a son Kenji's age, and he offered to take Kenji in until my wife and I were able to get back on our feet.

"Kenji had just started sixth grade. He transferred to the same school my friend's son was attending. He was registered to go on to middle school in the same district. My wife and I were relieved to have him settled. We focused on taking care of the loose ends after the bankruptcy and getting our lives in order.

"We spoke with him by phone from time to time. We were relieved that he seemed to be doing so well. But we were wrong. He was suffering. My son's friend was bullying him mercilessly.

"Kenji was in a weak position. In a sense, he was a freeloader. At first the son found it interesting to have someone his own age in the house, and he helped Kenji out. But when the son ridiculed me—his teacher told me this afterward—Kenji stood up to him. When the boy began playing silly pranks on Kenji, he ignored them, and him.

"Well, that sort of reaction probably grated on my friend's son. Pretty soon the boy enlisted a few of his friends, and together they started bullying Kenji. Apparently they were quite cruel, but somehow my son endured it."

The first term ended, summer vacation passed, and the second term began. On the surface, Kenji's school life was peaceful. But in mid-December, someone from the neighborhood found him sprawled in the middle of a farmer's field, midway between school and home. He was taken to the hospital.

"Apparently he'd been beaten by several boys at once. He spent three days in the hospital. This time the school really did sit up and take notice, and began an investigation. But before they were able to learn much, my son's friend was found dead. He'd fallen off a cliff.

"My friend lives in a housing development carved out of woods and hills. The house—it was quite large—sat on the edge of a cut in the hills. The backyard ended in a drop-off higher than a two-story house."

The son had fallen from the cliff, struck his head, and fractured his skull. He had no other injuries. He was dressed in a shirt, sweater and jacket, and sneakers. The control unit of a radio-control airplane was found smashed on the ground next to him.

There was no fence at the edge of the cliff. The view of the city spread out below was splendid. The boy had often flown his radio-control airplane out over the woods beyond the cliff. Apparently he had been doing that when he fell; the little airplane was found caught in the branches of a tree near the foot of the cliff.

A young boy, fascinated by his model airplane, slips and falls to his death. A tragic accident—

"But earlier, his mother heard him and Kenji shouting at each other in the backyard. She was in the front yard and saw nothing, but she heard snippets of what they were saying because they were shouting so loudly—'give it back,' 'idiot,' 'cheeky,' 'homeless,' things like that. She was worried that they were fighting again, but then things got quiet and she forgot about it. She was the first to find the body, later that afternoon.

"The police came and questioned Kenji. He said there'd been an argument because the boy refused to return some math notes Kenji had lent him. He told them…that he got tired of arguing, went in the house, and didn't see what happened afterward. He didn't know anything was amiss until the boy's mother told him."

Kotaro peered at Kenji's father in disbelief. Soji gazed back at him. They both shivered. The air conditioning was freezing.

▼

Kotaro still felt a chill when he got home that evening. It was as though the cold had sunk into his bones and was cooling the air around him.

He couldn't get Kenji out of his mind. His words, the look on his face at times—everything kept coming back. When the hands of the alarm clock he'd been using since elementary school touched midnight, he made up his mind.

"Galla. I've got to talk to Kenji."

He would convince him to return to the world of existence. What he was doing was just not right. It was too hard on his father.

And what would happen if he didn't leave Galla's scythe? What would happen to him and the other homeless people and their cravings when she fought her battle at the Gate of Sorrows? If she won, would they become part of the scythe forever, helping her guard the Tower of Inception? And what if she fell in battle? What if the scythe was broken? Galla would die… or maybe she wouldn't, but if she disappeared, wouldn't those in her scythe disappear with her?

He stood at the window. For a moment he felt pressure in his ears, as though he were diving into deep water.

He was in Galla's sanctum, on the roof of the tea caddy building. The lights of the West Shinjuku skyscrapers seemed as distant as the Milky Way. The buildings closer by seemed to press down on top of him, as though distorted by a fisheye lens.

Galla was nowhere to be seen. She was still wrapped in darkness.

Now you can talk to your friend.

He nodded and called into the darkness of the sanctum.

"Kenji?"

"You talked to my father."

The voice came from somewhere behind. Kenji sounded just as he had on that first visit to the coffee shop. It was his voice in the flesh. But when Kotaro spun around in surprise, he saw no one.

"Where are you?"

"That's a silly question. It's not like you, Ko-chan." Kenji chuckled. "I'm with Galla, always. I hear everything you say. But it's been a while since we talked like this, hasn't it, Ko-chan?"

Kotaro was on the verge of tears from joy and relief. Kenji was still his old self. There was still time.

"If you know I met your father, I don't have to waste time briefing you. Let's go home, Kenji."

Silence. He peered around, searching for his friend.

"You can't abandon him. You must've suffered, but he's suffering too, maybe much more now that he's lost you."

In Galla's sanctum, the human voice did not carry. Instead it seemed it disappear as soon as it left the speaker's mouth, as though carried away on a moving current.

At last Kenji answered quietly. "I don't have anything to atone for."

"What?"

"My father's wrong—though I guess it makes sense, since I was wrong for a long time myself."

No matter which direction Kotaro faced, his friend's voice seemed to come from behind him.

"I'm a murderer, you know."

"Your father told me what happened."

"He wasn't there. He doesn't know for sure. He said there was an accident. But I know what happened. I know what I did. I'm a child killer. I won't say I killed my friend. That kid was no friend of mine."

"That's right. You could just as easily have gotten killed yourself when he and his friends attacked you."

"So are you saying what I did was justified self-defense?"

Kotaro didn't hesitate. "Yeah, I am. All you did was fight back."

Silence again. The distorted cityscape seemed to press in even more. The reds and greens of traffic lights dazzled his eyes.

"That's what I thought too, at first. I thought my back was against the wall. I was afraid if I let him keep pushing me around, I'd end up getting killed. I couldn't stand the endless bullying. I was so angry and scared that I think I blacked out for a second. When I came to, he was at the bottom of the cliff. I thought I was free.

"But that feeling of being free from fear, of being liberated from a cage, didn't last long. After that, all I felt was horror. What had I done? I couldn't change what happened. That's why I was never able to confess. I had to pretend. I just kept saying I had nothing to do with it, that I didn't see him fall. I put a lid on the truth."

"But you were suffering, Kenji. Weren't you?" This feeling of always having Kenji somewhere behind him was getting more and more frustrating. Kotaro kept turning in place, looking this way and that. "You can't change the past, but you wanted to atone for what you did. Be of use to others, help needy people or people who'd been abandoned by society. That's why you couldn't ignore those missing homeless people—"

"You're wrong." Kenji's voice sounded right behind his ear. "That's not how I felt. I lied to you, Ko-chan."

Kenji was with Galla. Here in her sanctum, he was everywhere. Kotaro was enveloped in his thoughts, crystallized as words he could hear.

"True, I was worried about those missing people when I found out what was happening. If I didn't investigate, I thought no one would notice they were vanishing. I thought I had to do something."

"Of course you did." Kotaro spoke louder. "I saw the pain in your eyes. I remember even now. They weren't the eyes of a liar."

"Probably not. Because at the time, I was lying to myself."

"What does that mean?"

"As I walked the neighborhoods along the Seibu-Shinjuku Line, putting the pieces together and searching for Kozaburo Ino, I knew the stories about people going missing weren't rumors. They were true. People were vanishing. Someone was erasing people who had fallen through the cracks. I was convinced of it. That was when I realized that what I really wanted was justice.

"I wasn't worried about missing homeless people. I wasn't scared. I wasn't even interested in finding out *why* it was happening. I was angry. Who was doing this? Where was he? I wanted to see his face, hear his voice, listen to him try to justify himself, and then exterminate him.

"I wasn't out there trying to help people weaker than me to atone for what I did. I didn't feel that way at all, not really. That was just a story I made up for myself, a superficial motivation. In reality, I was enraged. Anyone who'd do this, I thought, isn't human at all. He has no right to live. *He has to be exterminated.*"

Kotaro gave up trying to turn toward Kenji's voice and stood still. He knew how Kenji felt. He'd felt that way himself. He understood the emotion and the eruption of energy it triggered. That's why he'd decided to become a hunter.

"That's when it hit me. When I pushed that kid off the cliff, I felt just the way I do now. I wasn't afraid of him or trying to get back at him. I was righteously angry, so I exterminated the bully.

"Since then I've never regretted what I did. I never thought I needed to atone for it. I was just pretending to myself that was what I wanted, because that's what good, honest kids are supposed to feel. But in my heart, I felt purified. I took it on myself to reduce the number of bullies in the world by one. What could be wrong with that? People like him don't change. In fact, they get worse as they get older. Poisonous seeds just grow into poisonous trees, with poisonous fruit that harms society. What's wrong with exterminating them?"

Kotaro knew exactly what Kenji meant. He knew it all too well.

"Galla showed me my true self. She revealed who I really am."

How, Kotaro wondered, but then he knew he didn't have to ask. Kenji would have encountered Galla as he searched for Kozaburo Ino. She'd probably taken him to the roof of the tea caddy building. There, she had shown him his Shadow.

"I want you to see it too. Turn around."

Kotaro closed his eyes, turned, and opened them slowly.

The darkness before him began to deepen and take shape, a human shape. It was larger than Kenji, with broad shoulders and thick, muscular legs. To Kotaro's relief, it was not a monster.

The darkness was fully congealed. Kenji's Shadow stood before him.

It was inky black and powerfully built. Its outstretched right arm grasped the long, stout handle of some sort of tool. It lifted the tool, which looked heavy. The head of it made a scraping noise on the roof. A real tool, but one that did not exist.

It was a huge ax. The Shadow would probably need both hands and all of its strength to wield it. It looked more suited to Makoto's giant.

But it belonged to Kenji. It was part of him, the embodiment of the words spoken in his heart, part of what he really was.

It was an executioner's ax.

This was Makoto's secret, a secret no one could ever have guessed, just as no one could have guessed that an extroverted female friend was secretly consumed by a jealousy powerful enough to drive her to murder, or that a kindly neighborhood florist was a pervert thirsting for blood.

The executioner took a step forward, dragging its ax. It moved closer to Kotaro in a jerky slow motion that sparked both drowsiness and nausea.

Kotaro was paralyzed. The black executioner drew closer until it was upon him, then passed through him, just as Galla once had. For less than a second, as Kenji's words passed through him, his heart reverberated with bellows of rage and screams of terror.

He felt compelled to turn and watch as the executioner melted into the darkness and disappeared. But before it was gone, he saw that its spine was paralleled by dense rows of razor-sharp spikes, like a dinosaur.

"If this is my real self, my true essence—"

Kenji spoke out of the enfolding darkness.

"—then I have no regrets. I have nothing to atone for. I would do it again if I had to, as many times as I had to."

Kotaro had a vision of Kenji at Kumar, eyes fixed on his monitor on School Island, tracking the text messages of young kids excitedly exchanging information about their "homeless hunting."

Kenji had gone from observer to hunter. He had awakened fully to his true self and would find it more than easy to do the same thing again, if he returned to Kumar.

All right, who's next? Whose evil head will this ax of mine send flying?

"But there's another part of me, the boy I was before I pushed the bully over the cliff, and it keeps murmuring in a small voice, 'I'm afraid.' " Kenji said. "I'm not a child anymore, but I'm also not clever enough to kill again and get away with it. If I keep executing people, it'll just be a matter of time before someone finds out. I won't be able to say it was an accident."

I'm afraid.

"Still, I wouldn't care. They could catch me and I wouldn't be sorry. But my father and mother would suffer. I can't do that to them."

That was why he'd sought refuge in Galla's scythe. He had offered up his craving to punish evil and root out those who would torment the weak, and turned his back on the world of existence.

"I wore that mask for my parents, the mask of the good kid." There was a smile in his voice now. "And I thank you for worrying about me, Ko-chan, but I'm not coming back. I can't."

Kotaro had lost his voice. He was too stunned to even nod.

"I think my father knows it wasn't an accident. My mom too. They took pity on me and suffered for me, and they both fear me. That's why my father's looking for me. My mother knows enough not to."

When Kotaro had parted with Kenji's father outside the coffee shop, Soji had said, "I think Kenji may already be dead."

"Goodbye, Ko-chan. I'm not going to die." As he faded away, Kenji called one last time. "I'll be with Galla for eternity. I won't exist, but I'll be real—forever."

Kotaro's legs turned to jelly. He sank to his knees. He covered his face with his hands.

All he could think of, all he could hear, were the words of a man facing extinction.

You've got huge fangs…

If what he'd just seen was the real Kenji, what did his own Shadow look like at this moment? Kotaro was engulfed in pure terror and immutable despair.

In Galla's sanctum, silence reigned.

BOOK V:

THE GATE OF SORROWS

1

"I'm thinking about washing my hands of this whole thing."

It was late August. The summer sun was still fierce, but there was a soft breeze. The bench under the trees at the edge of the quad was cool and pleasant.

Shigenori sat next to Kotaro, watching with a critical gaze as students walked past.

"Young ladies come to school dressed like that? What's with that chemise, or whatever you call it?" He sounded faintly lecherous. Kotaro hadn't encountered this side of him before.

"That's not a chemise, it's a camisole. And there are no classes now. They're here for club meetings. They can dress any way they want."

"You're taking classes."

"Just makeup lectures. Anyway, I'm finished."

For a week after his last encounter with Kenji, Kotaro had been sunk in a depression. His emotions had swung like a pendulum. He'd had trouble sleeping and his body felt like lead. He told his family it was just the summer heat.

He'd called Shigenori because the ex-detective was the only person who could understand what he was going through. Shigenori had agreed to meet right away. He hadn't even asked what it was about.

"Let's talk face-to-face," he'd said. "How about on campus. Will you be going there?"

Kotaro had been surprised to find him so up for a meeting, but here they were.

"Makeup lectures. Sounds like what they used to call staying after class, in my day. Will you have to repeat a year?"

"No, I dodged that bullet."

"Excellent. Don't forget that mom and dad are paying your tuition. Education is just about the most expensive thing around these days."

I didn't come here for a sermon.

Shigenori turned to see Kotaro making a sulky face.

"When people say they're thinking about washing their hands of something, they're not looking for advice, kid. All they want is someone to tell them they're right." He chuckled and looked out at the quad again. "You mean cutting things off with Galla, I guess. I'm all for that. I've been telling you to do it this whole time. So you finally saw the light. You sure took your time about it."

Kotaro was still sulking. "The timing wasn't right."

"What happened?"

"I said, the timing—"

"Out with it, kid."

He told Shigenori about Kenji. Soji's words were burned into his brain, and he played them back verbatim.

"What a tragedy," Shigenori said softly. He didn't seem to be paying attention to the girls anymore. "Then again, it's not unusual for a killer to look like he wouldn't hurt a fly."

"Come on, that's not fair to Kenji."

"Not talking about Kenji. I'm talking about you." Shigenori was suddenly the interrogator again. "You didn't pull the trigger yourself. But make no mistake—you used Galla as a weapon to take the lives of two people."

Don't you get it? That's why I want to stop.

"The string of murders that brought us together is finished. They've all been solved. Tomakomai and Akita, solved for the record. Nakasono and Tashiro will be fugitives forever, as far as the police are concerned, but the excitement's died down. And the suicide of one of Mama Masami's customers is finally getting some attention, according to the news.

"The only loose end is your next move. That's what worries me. If you've decided to wash your hands of Galla, great. Come back to the world of ordinary people—today, if you can. And forget what happened."

Kotaro didn't answer. *Detective, don't you know that pushing me to do what I'm saying I want to do is liable to make me change my mind?*

Perhaps Shigenori knew that, or perhaps he didn't, but he said suddenly, "What do *you* think?"

"Think about what?"

"Galla. Who do you think she is? Or what?"

"I don't want to talk about it now."

Shigenori looked at him closely. "Because she can hear you? Don't let that stop you. You shouldn't care what she thinks."

"And why is that?"

"Because she's not human. She doesn't think or feel the way we do."

"How can you say that?" Kotaro said with irritation. "Okay, she doesn't exist, but I don't see how you can say she doesn't feel anything."

"Why not?"

"Did you forget, detective? The reason she wants to get to the Nameless Land, or whatever they call it, is to find her son and bring him back from exile for whatever it was he did. She was powering up her scythe so she could take out the Sentinel."

"So what? Okay, she's a mother who loves her son. How does that make her just like us? She's a fundamentally different creature."

"Why does that make it wrong to think she's like us?"

Shigenori seemed about to disagree, but something stopped him. The corners of his mouth turned down in a thicket of wrinkles before he said evenly, "Why does she appear to us as half human, half bird?"

"That's a different question. Frankly I never gave it a moment's thought, but wouldn't that be because she doesn't want to scare us? Her true form is a horrible gargoyle. She actually told me we got our concept of gargoyles from the guardians of the Tower."

"Then why doesn't she just appear to us as a person?"

"Is it really important?"

"I think it's her way of warning us." Shigenori looked at him intently again. "It means, 'I'm dangerous. Don't trust me, and don't take me lightly.' That's the message she wants to send."

Kotaro remembered something suddenly, something Galla had said.

You will regret this.

She'd said it to him several times. A warning, to be sure.

"But she's a guardian of the Tower of Inception. According to U-ri—Yuriko Morisaki—Galla is a noble being." To Kotaro's mind, that meant she was close to the right and the just.

"Yes, she guards the birthplace of the souls of words," Shigenori said. "I've had some time to think about that, and the more I do, the more it bothers me." He peered steadily at Kotaro. "Mishima, what *are* words?"

Kotaro didn't know how to answer that one. It was like one of those Zen riddles.

"Words and language—they're not quite the same thing," Shigenori continued. "Language is culture. Words are not the way they're written, either. Writing systems are tools for keeping a record of words. Words can't be seen. They don't have form. They're real but they don't exist. Stories are the same. Words are woven into stories. Words and stories—you can't separate them. Now what do you call things like that?"

He didn't wait for an answer. "Concepts. Galla is a guardian of concepts. She's a concept herself. Real, but doesn't exist. Let me tell you something I learned when I was a cop: getting too deeply wrapped up in real but nonexistent concepts is a recipe for trouble."

"You mean stuff like religious cults and fundamentalism?"

Shigenori noticed his discomfort and chuckled ruefully. "Sorry. I wasn't trying to make things difficult." He scratched his close-cropped head. His hair was peppered with gray.

"The point is, Galla's form is a warning. I'm just saying we should've thought about that a little more carefully."

"But gargoyles are supposed to ward off evil. They have the power to keep evil at bay. That's why people put them in sacred places, like churches—to make sure only just and proper deeds take place in the sacred space."

"That's true. But do you know why the symbol of protection against evil is a monster? Because you need a monster to repel a monster. Evil against evil, venom against venom."

You've got huge fangs…

"You know, the gargoyles on Romanesque and Gothic buildings were also supposed to be symbols of the decadence and decline and corruption of humanity."

That's not Galla's fault.

"We were bewitched by a demon. A demon's black magic is pretty dramatic. Now it's time to wake up. The timing you were waiting for is here and now." He grasped Kotaro by the shoulder and gave it a shake.

"Give up the power of that left eye and get back to normal life. You've gotten too close to Galla. Fighting for justice against evil—you got too involved. Your intentions were good. Maybe Galla chose you because you're young, and exactly because your intentions are good. She has something that attracts you, doesn't she? But she's a demon. Humans and demons shouldn't get too close to each other.

"Maybe I'm just being pessimistic, but still—your word body, as you call it, all the accumulated words you carry around with you, it's a monster with fangs. Isn't it?"

Kotaro stared at his feet. Here in the shade of the trees, the two of them cast no shadows.

What if he were to walk out into the sunshine and found that his shadow was different? What if he saw fangs and horns? Or a misshapen third arm? Or a tail with spikes on each vertebra?

"I know. It's starting to scare me."

It was frightening to contemplate becoming a monster. Not knowing what kind of monster was frightening too.

"But Mika's still in danger. I think I might need my Eye to help her. I can't decide what to do."

Shigenori looked puzzled. "Mika. She's your sister's classmate. Did something happen?"

Kotaro told him about the enormous spider. Shigenori shivered with fear. "I've always been afraid of spiders."

"Well, luckily nothing's happened, but I'm worried about the future."

"I can't blame you. But think about it, Mishima. Will your Eye really help you solve the problem? All it did was show you things that were revolting, things that upset you. Maybe that left eye is hindering you instead of helping you."

He was right. Kotaro couldn't tell Mika what he'd seen. Naturally he couldn't tell Kazumi. She'd never believe him. He was just spinning his wheels. He wasn't sure he could get Mika to even tell him if there was a problem.

"Wouldn't it be better for you to be an ordinary person and a big brother to her, someone from the neighborhood she can consult whenever she needs to?"

Kotaro couldn't argue with that. Shigenori was right.

"Okay."

A group of students walked past. The girls were in their summer finery, the boys in studiedly casual jeans and T-shirts. All of them were thumbing their smartphones and laughing happily. Shigenori watched them pass. "You told me university life was boring."

Did I actually tell him that?

"You said everyone around you were idiots, like those guys."

"Hmm? I never said anything that negative." Even Kotaro thought his words sounded like sour grapes.

"You told me they were all leading trivial, pointless lives," Shigenori said. "In a word, idiots. But it's not like that, actually. If everyone here were an idiot, society wouldn't function. If you pull the camera back on society, it looks superficial and dysfunctional. Nothing positive about it. If you get your information from TV news, or a place like Kumar, society must look like a wholesale market for poisonous seeds and fruit. But that's an illusion, and an unfortunate one.

"You're not obliged to shoulder society's problems personally. Take a good look at this campus. Right now this is part of your life. It's not bad at all. A university is a great place. For an old, untutored man like me, just being here makes me feel smarter."

Kotaro wondered if Shigenori had wanted to meet here just to deliver this message. School was indeed part of his life. Shigenori was asking him to take a dispassionate look at it.

"Give the Eye back to Galla. You don't have to explain why. No excuses, no negotiation. Just tell her you're through. That's enough. You'll do that for me, won't you?"

Kotaro nodded. This time he felt completely sincere. He was ready to give up his power on the spot, now. The decision had been made. He could relax.

They parted ways. Shigenori went home and Kotaro left the campus and headed for the train station. As he waited on the platform, he saw a mother and her young daughter holding hands. They were wearing matching shorts and tank tops. They both looked so happy that Kotaro suddenly had a vision of Mana's face.

One thing left to do.

He wanted to do something positive with the Eye—for once.

▼

The crumbling apartment near Shinjuku Station yielded no secrets. Kotaro had expected to find little, but in fact he found nothing at all in the building and the surrounding neighborhood. There were too many people living there, and too much coming and going. It was like a word stew; he couldn't draw out anything specific connected with Mana.

In a way, he felt relieved. He saw no evidence of monsters like Kosuke Nakasono or Keiko Tashiro. It was clear that Mana and her mother had never been in danger from anyone here.

He called the Nagasaki mansion from the street in front of the apartment and learned that Mana was about to return from nursery school. It was quarter to four. He explored the neighborhood quickly, found a shop selling fancy cakes, and bought pudding topped with whipped cream.

His timing was perfect. As he rounded the corner and neared the front gate, he saw Hatsuko coming from the opposite direction, holding Mana by the hand. The girl was wearing a sunflower-yellow short-sleeved one-piece, and a straw hat with a ribbon of the same color.

"Oh, uncle!" Mana saw him first and smiled.

How long had it been? So many things had happened. He'd seen so much ugliness. It was as though he'd absorbed a nerve poison, and before he knew it, his heart was more than half paralyzed. One smile from Mana melted his frozen heart. He ran to greet her.

"Hello, Mana. It's been so long! Is school fun?"

"Mm-hmm!"

She had begun to talk. She was still smaller than most children her age, but her cheeks were plump. She was even suntanned. Hatsuko noticed his surprise and smiled.

"She loves to swim at the nursery school—so much, in fact, that we took her to a swimming school. The coach said she has natural talent. At the end of last month, Ms. Sato and I took her to the beach in Izu. I'm far too old for it, but I actually wore a swimsuit," she added shyly.

In Mana's room, they sat at her round table eating pudding with whipped cream. Kotaro learned that she was seeing her father regularly, and they had started to communicate. But his business wasn't thriving, and his life wasn't stable enough to allow him to take on the job of caring for his daughter. He had neither the confidence nor the desire to be a single father. He thought it would be best to find a family who was willing to adopt her, and he'd asked the Nagasakis to help him.

Perhaps this wasn't ideal behavior for a father, but at least he was clear about what he could and couldn't do. In the end, adoption would be better for Mana than for her father to try to care for her out of a sense of pride.

"So she'll be here from now on?" Kotaro asked.

"We'd like that, but adoption would be difficult. My brother and I are both getting on in years. If one of us were to fall ill, it would be hard to give Mana the care she deserves. We're working with Mr. Ohba from House of Light and the Children's Welfare Department to find the right couple to take care of her," Hatsuko said. "Of course, we'll always be ready to help her. We don't plan to change her situation right away in any case. Even if we find a good family, we'll go slowly so she has time to get to know them. She's finally settled in and used to living here. We can't make any major changes too soon. She'll be starting elementary school from here."

"That's next spring," Kotaro said.

"The days pass so fast. If you have time, please come see the matriculation ceremony."

Mana looked up at Kotaro and gave him a whipped-cream smile. "I'm go to school."

"So I hear. You'll be a student just like me, this coming spring." He returned the smile. It felt like his first heartfelt smile in a long time.

"Mr. Mishima..." Hatsuko looked slightly uneasy and lowered her voice. "I think we last saw you last in March, wasn't it? Have you been ill? You seem very thin. Maybe gaunt would be a better word. Your cheeks are hollow."

Kotaro anxiously rubbed his cheeks. "I've been too wrapped up in my job. I had to take a makeup class over the break to keep from repeating a year. My parents almost killed me."

"Oh, my. That must've been hard on you."

"It was, but it's over now."

"My brother is at a meeting over at House of Light. He'll be back by dinnertime with Mr. Ohba. Won't you stay for dinner with us?" Hatsuko asked.

Kotaro had a night shift at Kumar from ten to six. With people quitting left and right, Seigo was shorthanded.

"Thanks for the invitation, but—"

"Now please, don't be shy. We'd love to have you. My brother would be delighted too."

She left to go shopping, leaving Kotaro with Mana. "Let's draw!" Mana said, pulling out her sketchbook and crayons.

This was the moment Kotaro had been waiting for. He'd been making such an effort to resist the urge to close his right eye that he'd wondered if he might not have looked strange. He had to find out whether any of her mother's words—the thoughts of a mother who'd had to leave her child behind—were still here.

The Eye will tell.

He was sure that he'd see something bright and beautiful. Takako Sonoi, with her beautiful wings, had shown him what was possible.

I need to use this Eye for good, too.

The power Galla had given him was not only for hunting evil. It could recognize good in the world. He wanted to experience that before he gave it up.

"Look, uncle. I drawed them."

Mana turned the pages of the sketchbook. There were fields of sunflowers. A white beach with the ocean beyond. Memories of a happy summer.

"Very pretty. Mana, I think your pictures are even better than before."

He calmed his breathing, closed his eyes, and opened his left eye slowly.

He half-expected to see sparkling lights, or maybe a glowing, lacy pattern. Mana's mother was never here. If any of her words remained, they would be clinging to her daughter. By now they might be faded and indistinct.

But he was completely wrong.

Mana was already drawing—a big orange sun. She gripped the crayon and didn't notice as Kotaro gasped and flinched with surprise at the vision floating inches from his face.

A ring of light with the hue of a buttercup gleamed faintly behind Mana's head. It pulsed softly, a rhythm of respiration. The light deepened in color, then faded, over and over again, rippling as though waves were passing through it. It seemed to be hovering behind Mana and protecting her.

It's her mother.

The residue of a mother's love for her child, a legacy of accumulated words. Morning and night, it never slept. It was with her child on cold rainy mornings and during autumn sunsets when she felt her mother's absence most keenly.

A mother speaks to her child all day. She conveys her love through words, helps the child understand the world, assures it that Mother will always be in the world with the child, and promises that it will always be protected.

"Mana-chan?"

"Mmm?" Immersed in her drawing, the little girl didn't look up.

"What was your mother's name? I don't think you ever told me."

The crayon stopped. She looked up at Kotaro.

"Yuriko." The golden yellow ring undulated to the sound of her voice.

"Really? That's a nice name."

Yuriko. Mana was bathed in her warm light. Kotaro felt its warmth too.

Hello, Yuriko. You never left Mana's side and you never will. I should never have doubted it.

As Mana grew and her words began to reflect her true self, this ring of light would finally merge with them, become part of them, protecting her always.

She looked behind her, to where Kotaro was gazing. Her mother's gentle light caressed her daughter's cheek.

"What?" she asked Kotaro, puzzled. He stroked her head.

"Uncle's been studying very hard since he saw you last."

"Studying?"

"Yes. Do you remember? I promised to tell you if I found out where your mother went and when she's coming back. That's why I was studying, so I could tell you."

Her face lit up. "Did you find her?"

"I did. Your mother is right next to you. You can't see her now, but she didn't go anywhere. She's always by your side."

I've studied it, Mana. I know. The tuition was very expensive.

The little girl laughed happily. The ring rippled, as it if were laughing too. It would be Mana's forever.

I'm looking at an angel's halo, Kotaro thought.

▼

"Galla, you can have your eye back."

Dinner over, Kotaro walked toward Shinjuku Station. The narrow road paralleled the edge of the sprawling National Garden on his right. The elevated tracks of the Chuo Line blocked his view to the left.

"I'm finished with it. Anyway, I don't think I have the strength to use it anymore."

No one seemed to be on the street. It felt like the middle of the night, though it was just past eight.

"Galla?"

The warrior appeared in the darkness ahead. She descended slowly, just as she had the first time Kotaro encountered her on the roof of the tea caddy building. She touched down silently and folded her wings. The crescents above her head gleamed icily.

"Your hunting is at an end, then?"

He closed his right eye. There were no silver threads. Her voice reverberated deep in his ears, at it had before she'd given him the power.

The Eye was already gone.

"Then let there be an end."

He stopped a few yards from her and stood at attention. "I'm afraid I wasn't much use to you. I'm sorry."

Her eyes narrowed. She shook her head almost imperceptibly. Her hair streamed behind her, melting into darkness.

"But I took revenge for Ayuko. I can't thank you enough for that."

An express rumbled past on the elevated track. Kotaro was talking to the night.

Galla was gone.

2

Shigenori was right. With his power gone, Kotaro felt amazingly light and relaxed. He didn't wait to send Mika a text message.

How are you? I worry about you sometimes. Are you okay?

He got a response immediately.

You know people were saying stuff about me on that dark site. Gram told me. Let's talk. How about a date?

They rendezvoused for lunch at the McDonald's near the train station. Mika was just back from tennis camp. She was so tanned, Hanako had commented, that you couldn't find her face unless she smiled. She seemed energized and happy.

"What's Kazumi doing today?"

"She and Mom went to Shibuya. Shopping, supposedly."

"Oh." Mika seemed relieved.

"What, is this something you don't want her to know?"

"No, not really. But I haven't told her, or Mom either."

"Sensitive, huh?"

She paused. "It's about Gaku." She looked at him as if the name alone said it all, which it more or less did.

"The guy from your tennis team. The blockhead who doesn't have a sense of time or place. Is he still pestering you?"

"No, it's not that. He's not bothering me."

Hmm? She's defending him. Something's changed. Okay.

He stared at her questioningly. She started to fidget like one of those shy characters in a girl's manga. She was far more naïve than Kazumi.

"If you tell me to keep it secret, I will," Kotaro said.

"I know." Mika took a deep breath and a sip of coffee. "In April, just before the holidays, I got a mail from Gaku."

He'd written that he was settled into his new life as a high school freshman. He wanted to meet her and apologize for causing her trouble with his selfish behavior.

"I never gave him my email address, so I was kind of surprised."

"Someone's playing Cupid."

Mika had replied, telling Gaku she wasn't being bullied on the web anymore; that it had been rough at the time, but everything was okay now, and she didn't need him to apologize for anything.

"He wrote back and asked if it was okay with me if we...um..."

"Dated?"

She squirmed in her seat and nodded. In Kotaro's book, this was being a pest. Maybe girls didn't see it that way?

"I'm still only in second year..."

"So? Some first-year girls have boyfriends."

"I know, but my dad's not with us." She added hastily, "I don't mean Mom doesn't do a good job. She's done everything she could to raise me on her own."

"Your mom does a great job at home and at work."

"That's why I have to—" Her voice became small and timid. "I don't think it's the right time for me to have a boyfriend; it'd take my mind off my studies. I've really got to study hard and get into a good high school, and a good university."

Kotaro was impressed. "You're totally serious about this."

Her resolve was endearing, but it was hard to see having a boyfriend as that big a decision. He felt like telling her to relax and stop worrying about the future.

"Your mom would be happy to hear you've got someone special. She'd be sad if she thought you were giving up happiness just out of consideration for her."

"I don't know..."

"It's true. But I'm not saying you should date Gaku. I'm just saying you shouldn't deny yourself what you want out because of your mom. If you don't like Gaku, blow him off. If he keeps bothering you—just let me know!"

"Ko-chan, don't say that!" She seemed so anxious that Kotaro couldn't help laughing, which made her blush to the roots of her hair.

"So that's what you told Gaku, I guess. That you couldn't imagine dating someone right now."

"Mm-hmm."

"What did he say to that?"

"He said in that case would it be okay to send me mails sometimes? Like a friend."

The two began exchanging text messages. At first it was one-sided, with Gaku doing the sending and Mika mostly not replying. But—

"He wrote me about stuff happening in school, and what he was studying and books he was reading. It was interesting. After a while I started writing back to him. I started to feel different about him, like maybe he wasn't the kind of person I thought. He was always first in his class, and a tennis ace, and really popular, with all the girls swooning and stuff. I thought he was kind of a show-off. But it turned out he likes to spend time listening to music and reading books by himself. He said being around lots of people makes him tired."

"So you became mail buddies."

"Mm-hmm."

"And you haven't gotten together?"

Mike shrank into her chair. "We...did. I think that's why I fell down the stairs."

"You're kidding."

"I got a mail from him the day before. He said he was coming back from the library and he was, you know, in the neighborhood. So...I..."

"Went and met him."

"You know that little park on the corner, a couple of streets over? It takes about five minutes to walk there. I met him there. He lent me a book. It was a book he'd been telling me about. He was sure I'd like it a lot."

It had been a year since she'd seen him, and because she'd started to see him in a new light, he seemed much more attractive than before. Heart pounding, she'd felt as though her future were suddenly much brighter. Even after he was gone, the bells kept ringing inside her.

"I think I was kind of in a daze the next day."

"So when you slipped on the stairs, your head was in the clouds. Okay."

Kotaro sighed. "Mika, you know what that's called, don't you? A fixation. You're in love."

Kotaro listened as she told him her second-year middle school girl's story from start to finish—a love story, though she and Gaku had never been on a proper date. All they'd done so far was send mails back and forth and meet about once a week in the park, mostly to exchange books and talk about their favorite music, and movies they'd seen recently. That was the whole relationship, at least for now. Of course it would progress, but probably at a super-slow pace.

The more he heard about Gaku, the more Kotaro began to think he wasn't such a bad guy after all. Maybe blowing his chance to get into that school he'd been gunning for, and the disappearance of his fans and the collapse of his dream of popularity, had made him a better person.

His and Mika's long-distance relationship seemed like an anachronism. Gaku was proceeding with restraint in consideration of his girlfriend's age and tender feelings. When Kotaro first heard the story of his public love confession, he'd pictured a narcissist starring in his own romantic movie. But now it seemed likely that he'd been so naïve, he simply miscalculated.

If that was where things stood, it was no surprise that Mika would hesitate to tell her mother and Kazumi. Instead of disapproving of the relationship, they might accuse her of acting like a child.

Kotaro frowned for effect. "It seems weird that he has all those books. Are you sure he didn't steal them from some bookstore?"

Mika shook her head earnestly. "Of course not! He buys them with money from his part-time job. But I heard..." She lowered her voice. "I heard his family is really rich."

Gaku's father was a senior executive in a giant food company. Kotaro was impressed when Mika told him the name; you couldn't get away from their commercials on TV.

"So if his dad's such a big shot, how come he's not at a private high school?"

"He said it's his father's policy. He doesn't want Gaku to have special advantages, at least until he graduates from high school. His two older brothers were raised the same way. The oldest one is still looking for a job. His father won't help him. He says he had to climb the ladder without any help, and he wants his sons to do it too."

"Wow. Sounds like a pretty cool dad."

"But I can tell from the things Gaku says that his family has money. He's been on lots of trips abroad, from the time when he was little."

So that would make Gaku's family rich people from outside—not "aborigines."

"He can spend all his pocket money on books and CDs," Mika added. "He doesn't have to save money. I'm not like that."

"Do kids even buy CDs anymore?"

"Don't you know? People who love classical music collect them. Sometimes they have to have LPs, even."

"Classical. Okay. Sorry, I'm not that sophisticated."

They both laughed. But it was time for Kotaro to ask the question he'd been waiting to ask—about the spider.

"Listen, Mika. What's going on these days with Glitter Kitty? She was the ringleader, wasn't she?"

"Oh, her." Mika's smile disappeared. "She's a freshman at Gaku's high."

Kotaro's eyes widened. "Are you sure?"

"Mm-hmm."

"So you know who she is and where she lives—"

"Everybody's known since last year, at least on the tennis team."

Judging from the posts he'd seen, Kotaro had assumed that Glitter Kitty was a first-year student at the time, like Mika. Maybe she'd been trying to disguise her age. The web was tricky.

"She's a Gaku fan, right?"

"Mm-hmm. But it was like she thought he was her boyfriend." Unusually for Mika, she sounded suddenly scornful.

"So that's why she was bullying you. She was jealous."

"That's how she is, not just with Gaku. She's jealous of everybody and everything. She has to be first and best all the time."

Not a pretty picture. But Glitter Kitty had had a lot of followers who were up for tearing into Mika too. Maybe they were in first or second year and afraid to be seen anywhere other than on Kitty's side. That was the problem with girls—the clique thing. It was a real pain when it wasn't truly scary.

"If she's in the same school, do you think she knows about you and Gaku?"

"Of course she knows." Mika spat out the words. "She came to the tennis camp as an advisor. She told me to stay away from him."

Kotaro suddenly remembered the note he'd found in Mika's book.

If you touch Gaku, I'm going to kill you.

"What did you say?"

"I told her I didn't think it was any of her business," she said calmly.

She's got more guts than she lets on.

"What happened?"

"You mean since then? Nothing."

Kotaro furrowed his brow. "Are you sure you're not going to have any more trouble?"

"As soon as school started, Kiba-san asked him to be his boyfriend. He blew her off completely."

"Her last name is Kiba?"

Mika traced the two characters on the tabletop with a fingertip: "tree" and "garden." "Kiba" was one way to read them.

"But you can pronounce them 'ki-tei' too, right? She said that's been her nickname since kindergarten. It's what everyone calls her."

Her nickname was a personal brand. Kotaro slapped a hand over his eyes. "Say no more. I know exactly what she's like."

The spider dogging Mika would be the residue of Glitter Kitty's jealousy. It must have somehow split off from her word body. Maybe it didn't have the power to do much harm. Mika seemed healthy and happy.

"What I want to know is, why are they going to the same high school?"

"It's not his fault. She took the same set of entrance exams."

Kotaro found it hard to believe that a girl in her mid-teens would be so intent on capturing one particular guy.

"So, as far as Gaku goes—"

"He never liked her," Mika said. "He couldn't stand her. She was having this fantasy that she was his girlfriend and telling everyone and making trouble for him."

Kotaro felt both regret and relief. If he still had Galla's Eye, he would've used it on Glitter Kitty. At the same time, he was glad he couldn't do that anymore.

"Kitty's from around here, then?"

"Yeah. For a while she was waiting for Gaku to show up at the station every morning, so he started using the next one down the line."

A self-centered, insanely jealous type might respond to being cut dead by becoming even more attached to the object of her fantasy.

"And everything's cooled down now?"

"I haven't heard anything. Gaku hasn't said anything either."

"Be careful anyway," Kotaro was about to say, but thought better of it. Glitter Kitty was sixteen. If she were a guy, she'd be capable of violence, but there was a limit to how far girls would go. If Mika stayed away from her, Kitty would probably give up after a while and drift away.

Then there was Keiko Tashiro.

Cut it out, Kotaro. Stop picturing the worst case. It's like Shigenori says. I can't fix everything.

"Want another burger, Ko-chan?" Mika smiled.

Everything seems okay, he told himself.

▼

It was August 31, the last day of summer break.

Despite her high school entrance exams, Kazumi had taken part in the five-day tennis camp. Now she was nervous about her readiness, but she'd still spent the day at the living room PC, sorting through the photos she'd taken at camp. She became so absorbed that she missed another day of study. Asako was not pleased and made sure Kazumi knew it.

Kotaro was home all day too. He'd pulled a night shift at Kumar, and between that and the fatigue that had been building up since last year, he slept till early afternoon. He still felt sleepy when he woke up, so he went back to bed. His mother and sister couldn't believe it.

Kotaro's sleep was dreamless. That was a blessing.

By evening he was up and helping prepare the fixings for grilled meat. By seven thirty the three of them had gathered around the tabletop grill pan. They'd eaten their fill, and Kotaro was just opening the window to air out the kitchen, when the telephone rang. Asako took the call.

"Oh, hello." Her friendly tone changed quickly. "Mika? No, she's not visiting." She put a hand over the receiver. "Kazumi, have you seen Mika today?"

"No."

"What about email?"

"We haven't been in touch. What's wrong?"

"She's not home."

Kotaro glanced at the clock on the wall. It was five past eight.

Kazumi stood up. "She told me she had to spend yesterday and today working on a paper for lit class. She was worried she wouldn't finish it."

"What about the library?"

"No way. Not this late."

She took the phone. "Aunt Takako? It's Kazumi. Did Mika go out without telling you where she was going?"

"What about Aunt Hanako?" Kotaro said quietly to his mother. "She must be home."

"Takako says she's been in bed with a bit of a fever since last night. It's just a cold."

Kotaro studied his sister's profile as she nodded and said "Um-hmm, um-hmm," into the phone.

"She probably just went to the store," Asako said soothingly.

Kazumi had interrupted her photo project to have dinner. The PC was in sleep mode. Kotaro touched the mouse and the monitor lit up. Mika and Kazumi smiled back at him from the monitor, tennis rackets at the ready.

Kazumi slammed the receiver down. "Mom, what should we do?"

"I don't think you need to get so excited."

"No, I'm sure something's wrong!" She shook her head stubbornly. "First of all, she wouldn't have gone out and left Auntie Hanako in bed without telling her when she'd be back. When Takako got back, the porch light was out and the living room was dark. She didn't just go out for a minute. She's probably been gone for hours."

Kotaro stood up. "Come on, don't freak out. I'll go take a look."

"Thank you, Kotaro." Asako put a protective arm around Kazumi's shoulder.

He slipped his sneakers on and crossed the street to the Sonois'. Takako was on her smartphone as she opened the door. She hadn't even taken off her summer suit coat. Aunt Hanako was in the kitchen, slumped in a chair. She looked wiped out and suddenly very old.

"Oh, it's Kotaro," she said weakly. "I'm sorry, I've been in bed all day."

"If you have a fever, bed rest is the best thing. Auntie, when was the last time you talked to Mika?"

"Maybe ten this morning. She made me porridge. She seemed fine."

Takako ended her call. She had the same worried look as Kazumi. "She's not at her father's. I didn't think she would be, but I had to check. He hasn't seen her."

"I wouldn't worry, Aunt Takako. She probably went out to get something and ran into a friend and they got to talking."

Having said that much, Kotaro couldn't resist the pressure he felt. If he didn't say what he knew, things could end up a lot worse for Mika.

Mika, forgive me. I'll apologize once you're safe and sound.

"Look, I better tell you. Mika has a boyfriend. She's probably with him right now. They must be having fun and just forgot the time."

Takako didn't seem very surprised. "So that's it," she said and nodded. A mother's intuition.

"He was on the tennis team with Mika. His name is Gaku something, let's see..." Kotaro was so nervous, he couldn't remember the boy's full name at first. "Gaku Shimakawa. His family's pretty prosperous. He's a high school freshman."

Takako sat down heavily at the kitchen table, still holding her smartphone.

"They meet sometimes in the park near here," Kotaro added. "That's all, so far. They're being so old-fashioned, it's kind of adorable."

Mika's mother sighed. Hanako looked from one to the other, not quite grasping what was going on.

"We've never had a set curfew," Takako said.

"She still shouldn't be out late without telling anyone. It's not like her.

But they've got to be close by. I'll swing around the neighborhood and see if I can find them."

He rushed back to the house, leaped onto his bicycle and dashed at full speed toward the park.

Mika, where are you? You'd never worry your mother or Hanako. You must really be in love to do something stupid like this.

The most optimistic scenario was that he'd find Mika and Gaku deep in conversation on a park bench. He pictured her being surprised at hearing how late it was, and scolding her for being surprised.

It didn't take long for this scenario to fall by the wayside. The park was small, and a quick circuit showed it to be empty. Mika was nowhere to be seen.

Maybe they'd decided to head for a convenience store, or a bookstore or McDonald's. Summer days were long, and they might've thought there'd be no harm in staying out a bit later than usual. *But Mika, you should've at least told your grandmother—*

Then—though he couldn't explain why—Kotaro closed his right eye. Even without the power, he sensed a presence. Or maybe he was just used to closing his right eye when he was looking for something or someone, or trying to figure out what to do.

It was lucky he did.

He saw no trace of a happy couple, but he knew instantly which bench they'd been using. There was something there.

It was the spider, squatting in the center of the bench. He could see its eight legs with nauseating clarity. It had grown since he'd seen it scurry through Mika's window. It must be three times bigger—twice as big would be an underestimate. Its back rose to a rounded peak, mantled with a dense coat of fine black bristles, and its belly was swollen and pendulous. The spider sat motionless, as though it were digesting a meal. Its red eyes darted restlessly. The bench was dripping with red fluid—the residue of words that looked like blood.

Whose words? Whose blood?

He rushed the bench in a panic. He wanted to kick the monster off and stomp it to a pulp.

His sneaker crashed against the wood. Pain stabbed through his ankle. The bench existed, but the spider did not.

A silver thread crossed his left eye.

Fear is not your ally.

"Galla!" he cried out. "Why am I seeing this? I'm not supposed to be 'seeing' anymore!"

With his left eye he saw flecks of blood on his sneakers. The spider had skillfully evaded him by fleeing to the underside of the bench. Its upside-down eyes, almost the size of ping-pong balls, blazed red.

The power is already part of you. It is not something you can borrow and return as you please. When you have true need of it, it will be there.

The spider seemed to gaze at Kotaro with derision. It knew he was there. It was watching him with eyes that seemed to say, *Now do you understand? We're both monsters.*

"Don't fuck with me!"

Kotaro's yell seemed to shock the spider. It fled the shadow of the bench, legs pumping clumsily, yet moving almost too fast to follow with the eye. It left a gleaming trail of slime in its wake.

Shall we pursue?

Galla again. She had touched down behind him. Beneath a streetlamp swarmed by insects, she seemed to occupy a black void of her own.

A portal to darkness. A gate to other regions. Galla herself was the gate.

Why do you hesitate? Her "voice" came clearly this time. *Are you not curious to know why that insect waxes fat?*

Mika was in danger now, this very moment. It might not be too late. *It can't be too late*, he thought.

"Pursue. I've got to help Mika."

Galla spread her wings and the darkness swallowed him. The black torrents bore him away.

▼

What is this dump?

A house on a one-lane road. It was cheaply constructed but not very old. It also seemed completely untended. There were piles of trash, cardboard boxes and junk around the entrance, on the slab of concrete that doubled as parking spot and front yard, and even on the second-floor veranda. Some of the piles had toppled over, spilling their contents. Towels hung from a plastic pole that extended across the veranda; they looked as though they'd been there for days or weeks. A pair of sneakers with nearly worn-through soles perched on the railing.

Someone's actually living here.

This was not Galla's sanctum, nor another region. It was somewhere in Kotaro's world. He peered around; an ad for a medical clinic was pasted to a power pole. This was reality.

Yet for all that, he had no sensation of standing on solid ground. Even in Galla's sanctum, he had all his normal physical sensations, which made it hard to believe he wasn't really on the roof of the tea caddy building.

But not here. It wasn't that his body felt lighter. He had no body at all. He felt transparent.

The light's passing through me.

There was a porch light on the house behind him, and light coming from the windows, but he cast no shadow. As a small car passed, its headlights shone through him. He didn't bother to get out of the way. Sure enough, it passed through him and kept going. He was like Galla now: real, but nonexistent.

He tried to step forward. He couldn't see his body. He had no sensation of walking.

One moment he was in one location, and a moment later he was in a slightly different one. That was how he moved. It was like stop-motion, one frame at a time.

There was a nameplate nailed above the front door. IMAZAKI.

He passed through the door. The entryway was cluttered with so many pairs of men's and women's shoes and sandals that there was almost no space to stand.

The front hall was another maze of trash bags and assorted piles of junk. There were mounds of old magazines, including PC magazines. Some of them were far too specialized for the average user. Kotaro had seen one at Kumar.

I guess I'm still Kotaro Mishima if I can notice that.

The hall was dark, but light came from under a door to the right. Up-tempo music played softly.

Kotaro passed through the wall and into the room.

It was incredibly messy—large, but packed with junk. The center of the room was occupied by a long leather sofa facing the windows opposite the door. There were a few chairs with clothes draped over the back, and more clothes scattered around on the floor.

There were piles of magazines here too, but the most conspicuous object in the room was a large laptop PC on a desk under the windows. There were several windows open on the monitor. Some showed road maps. The window on the bottom was a news feed with text flowing from left to right.

Someone sighed. Kotaro's invisible body flinched with surprise.

The sofa was occupied.

He slowly "walked" around it. If something in the chaos of the room blocked his way, he just passed through it without making a sound. Even so, he stilled his breath and tried to walk softly out of habit.

A woman sat cross-legged on the sofa, settled deep into the leather back. A stylish shoulder bag lay open next to her.

She was putting on makeup. She had a kit open on her lap and was in the middle of applying eye shadow with a hand mirror.

No—not a woman. She's just a kid.

Her face was small under the makeup. She was slender as a wisp, fifteen or sixteen at most. She wore a backless one-piece dress, earrings and a necklace.

Kotaro felt an icy shock pass through his ghostlike body.

It's her.

She sniffled. The corners of her eyes were slightly red. She dug around in the kit and came up with an eye pencil.

There was a sound of footsteps. Someone was coming down a flight of stairs with a regular tread. A woman in an athletic jersey, with long hair carelessly gathered behind her head, walked through the door.

"Oh my god, are you *still* crying?"

Her voice was husky. She was mid-thirties to around forty, thin in an unhealthy way, without makeup. She had no eyebrows.

"I'm all right now," said the girl. She shut her makeup kit and looked up at the woman. "Are my lashes straight?"

"Very professional."

The woman went to the desk and picked up a pack of cigarettes and a lighter. She extracted a cigarette and lit it. "I don't think he's gonna come around," she said.

"I know."

"You ought to be satisfied."

The girl tossed the kit in her bag and frowned. "This is *not* what I wanted. I didn't ask you to grab him too."

The woman leaned against the edge of the desk and exhaled a long stream of smoke.

"We had to make a quick decision. It couldn't be helped. If we'd left him in the park, he would've called the cops."

"I mean, really..."

"What's the problem? You had a nice long talk."

"I guess." The girl bit her glossy lip. "I don't think he even heard me."

The woman laughed hoarsely. "What did you expect? If he was easy, you wouldn't have had to hire us."

Hire? The word didn't match the setting or the people.

The woman stubbed out her smoke and turned to the PC. She leaned forward with her left hand on the desk and began moving the mouse with her right. A new window opened, with icons and lines of text.

"Where's the final payment? You owe us half a million yen," the woman said crisply.

The girl narrowed her precisely drawn eyebrows. "I'm going to pay you."

"Mommy and Daddy aren't onto you?" the older woman asked.

"Don't worry. Mommy and Daddy don't know I've got the combination to the safe. They don't even know I know there *is* a safe."

The woman's shoulders shook with laughter.

"So please, let me take him with me," the girl said. "You can't get anything out of his parents anyway."

"But I hear they're loaded."

"His father's a pretty tough guy. If you kidnap his son, he'll go straight to the police."

"Are you nuts? We *already* kidnapped him." The woman glared at the girl over her shoulder. She had an expanse of white under each iris. "You're an accessory now, so clear off quietly, pay us and keep your mouth shut."

The girl pulled her head in obediently and looked up. "You'll keep me out of this, won't you? Erase my mails?"

"After you pay us."

"But will it really be okay? Getting arrested is the last thing I need."

"Same here. Hubby and I want to keep on being friendly Mama and Papa for Teen911.com. And you'll keep being a cute high school girl," she said with a very friendly smile. "Of course, we might ask you for a little help someday. This kind of relationship is forever, you know."

Kotaro felt something like the shiver he would have had if he'd had a body. He understood. Everything was clear enough to make him vomit.

Dear Teen911: I have a rival. She brainwashed my boyfriend and took him away from me. What can I do?

Glitter Kitty's spiteful posts to the dark website were burned into his brain. Each one had been a savage attack on Mika, full of fantasies of possessing Gaku. Full of egoism and ill will.

The woman and her husband were likely monitoring the school site as part of their business. Glitter Kitty's vitriol would not have gone unnoticed. Instead of giving her kind words of advice and support, Papa and Mama had sized her up—correctly—as needing a special service.

A revenge agency.

Kotaro had heard a lot about these websites and their services when he'd helped out on Black Box Island. The ones that made little effort to hide what they did offered relatively innocuous forms of revenge. The ones that provided more vicious services disguised themselves in various ways. Romance problems, conflicts with the boss, quarrels with in-laws—revenge agencies offered to help anyone who felt victimized. They offered counseling and helped clients troubleshoot ongoing disputes. Or so they said.

But their services were either illegal or just barely legal. Round-the-clock harassment, threats, even extortion. Sometimes they went straight to violence.

Clients paid these agencies via the Internet without knowing much about who they were. Satisfaction was all that mattered. If clients got satisfaction, they usually didn't consider the consequences.

The husband-wife team running Teen911.com presented themselves as kind and gentle Papa and Mama, but this was a snare for the unwary. When people like Glitter Kitty approached them for help, they reeled them in.

Doing business with teens wasn't a great way to make loads of money, but then again, the risk of being discovered was lower than with adults, who were harder to threaten and manipulate.

Now Glitter Kitty was tangled in their net. She'd given Papa and Mama a down payment to take care of her problem: make Mika Sonoi go away. Make sure she never gets close to Gaku again.

Today they'd carried out the assignment. They'd kidnapped Gaku and Mika from the park and brought them to this house—

"What do you mean, this relationship is forever?" Glitter Kitty was indignant. "I'm just a client."

The woman turned all the way around to look at her. She was grinning ironically.

"You know, you're *right*. We took care of that girl for you, just as you asked. *Just as you asked.*"

Kotaro felt himself disappear. When he reappeared, he was moving up the stairs.

The upstairs hall was dirty but bare. Dust bunnies nestled against the walls and in the corners.

Three doors: left, right, and straight ahead. The door straight ahead was half-open. Light fell into the hall. He heard a voice.

A tearful voice. "Can you . . . promise . . . me?"

He moved toward it.

A bedroom. There were two spring mattresses side by side on the floor. Each was covered with crumpled sheets and blankets.

Gaku Shimakawa slumped in a corner, wearing a white T-shirt and jeans. He was barefoot. There were flecks of blood on his chest. Otherwise he seemed unhurt, but his face was gaunt with fear and his jaw was trembling. His hands were confined in cheap-looking handcuffs. His ankles were bound with packing rope.

"If I go home . . . and come back . . . with my dad's ATM card . . . you'll let Mika . . . go?" The boy was sobbing and trying to be strong and negotiate at the same time.

A middle-aged, potbellied man sat cross-legged on the edge of the far mattress. *This must be Papa,* Kotaro thought. He was wearing a jersey that matched his wife's.

There was another man, a young man stripped to the waist, sitting diagonally across from Gaku on a clothes trunk. He was constantly jiggling one knee up and down. He sported flashy tattoos on both arms from shoulder to midbicep. His legs, sticking out of a pair of badly stained cutoff jeans, were similarly decorated to the ankles. Both ears were pierced with a row of small rings. He was chewing gum and smiling faintly, as though he were enjoying an amusing show.

"How many times are you gonna ask that?" Papa said to Gaku. He had fishlike pop eyes nestled in a fat, puffy face. "I told you, we promise. Just bring your dad or your mom's ATM card—"

"Best not forget the PIN code," said the young man. "You don't want to upset us." He sounded like he'd learned his gangster delivery from TV.

"All we need is some money," Papa added. "Then we let her go. Until then, we'll take good care of little Mika-chan."

The woman downstairs had said they'd "taken care" of Mika. Whatever that meant, Gaku hadn't been told.

"I want…to see her."

The young man lost his temper. "Cash card first, ya twit!"

Kotaro winked out. Two more rooms. Where was Mika?

Hallway. He passed through the wall into the room to the right. It looked like a storeroom. Cardboard boxes and clothes trunks were piled on top of each other. The curtains were closed.

One more.

This room was almost empty. There was a window opposite the door, but it was covered with a sheet of plywood. The edges were sealed with duct tape.

A cell. This is where they did the dirty work. The proof was on the floor next to the wall.

The ceiling light was off. A small nightlight in an outlet near the floor cast a faint yellow glow. Kotaro was not sure what he was looking at in the dimness. A rolled-up rug?

Someone was lying there, wrapped carelessly in a blue plastic sheet that covered the entire upper body, from the head to below the hips. The sheet was secured with duct tape, applied with equal carelessness.

Two bare legs protruded from the plastic.

The figure was facedown. The skin behind the knees was soft above muscled calves. Healthy legs, tanned from daily training. The soles of the feet were pure white.

What was this? There were streaks of something smeared down the thighs.

Dried blood.

He didn't have to check. He knew she was dead. She was rolled up tightly and bound in plastic, but she wasn't moving. She wasn't breathing.

He was too late.

Even without his body, Kotaro could cry out in anguish. He still had a heart.

He moved again, winking in and out. He felt it now vividly. Frame by frame, like a heartbeat. The sensation sharpened into crystal clarity as his pulse sped up, the pounding of a sinister drum.

Hunt, hunt, hunt—

Glitter Kitty came running up the stairs. She ran right through him just as he winked out. When he winked in again he was behind her, watching her rush into the room at the end of the hall.

"Mama just doesn't understand!" Her voice was shrill. "Gaku-chan, let's go. There's something wrong with these people."

"That's not very nice," Papa said.

"Why are you trying to get money out of him? We're not going to pay you more than you promised!"

Both men laughed.

"Very funny." The young man sneered. "You don't get how this works, do you?"

That just wound up Kitty more. "Why are you bullying him? You weren't supposed to touch him. Papa, you told me you wouldn't touch him."

Kotaro passed into the room. Kitty faced away from him. Her slender shoulders were heaving with rage.

She was just a girl. To look at her, she seemed completely harmless. No one would guess she was rearing a monstrous spider.

"Our software only tracks *his* smartphone. Haven't we been over this before?" The fat man's voice was calm, like a father admonishing a hair-splitting daughter.

"That's right," the second man chimed in. "Mikarin should've got herself the latest phone. It's not our fault."

Mikarin. He called her Mikarin. And the stains on his cutoffs.

That would be her blood.

What did he do to her?

"Come on, Gaku. Your nose is running. I can't believe you're so upset," Kitty said disdainfully. Gaku covered his face with his hands and shrank from her in fear. This couldn't be happening. It was a bad dream. Please be over, please let it be over.

"You're not nice to me, Gaku. That's the whole problem. Now do you understand? Come on, let's go home."

"We keep telling you, we've got business with him. I'll drive him home when everything's settled." The young man spoke as if addressing a simpleton. "Just go home. Get out of here while you can, for your safety."

"My *safety*? What does that mean?" She shrank back. Her voice had an edge of fear.

"By the way, it looks like he's blowing you off. If it'll cheer you up, I'll be your boyfriend."

"Are you crazy? Nobody in her right mind would be your girlfriend!"

Kotaro could feel his body flooding back. Hot blood surged to the tips of his fingers and toes.

Then he was there, complete, in a body that was his and not his. A body that was the sum of his words made real.

He heard a howl, the voice of a beast whose den had been destroyed, whose friend had been butchered. A howl of rage.

My *den.* My *friend. You devoured her. Now, I devour* you.

The girl is yours, Galla whispered.

He roared in answer.

He felt bared fangs. He raised his arms; they were not human. Dense obsidian fur covered powerful muscles. Claws curved from the ends of his fingers. They gleamed dully and clicked as they struck against each other.

He bayed with exultation and lunged at Glitter Kitty.

He encircled her neck with one hand as she turned toward him. Just then Galla flashed into being. She drew her blades and began to dance.

The blades flashed and sliced Papa, then the tattooed man, in two at the waist. Their torsos rose into the air, lifted by the whirlwind from her blades. Both were wide-eyed with astonishment. The young man still wore the shadow of an indecent smile. The blades flashed again, reducing both men to clouds of black dust that whirled around the room.

Galla danced. The dust spiraled into her scythes.

Kotaro lifted Kitty high into the air. Her head nearly touched the ceiling. He forced her to look at him. The girl was out of her mind with fear. She flailed her arms and legs frantically, trying to kick him.

He bellowed again and sank his fangs into her eye sockets. Blood gushed over her face. Her arms and legs still flailed, but in mindless spasms.

Kotaro pulled her head into his maw, bit through her neck, and spat her head out again in a shower of blood. The severed head hit the wall with a light thud and bounced off like a ball. Before it hit the floor, Galla's blade sliced it in two.

The blades shone with a dazzling light. In that light, Kotaro saw Glitter Kitty, her face distorted with horror. It was streaked with black blood. Her head dissolved into black dust from the crown downward as Galla's blades devoured her.

"What in the world is going on up there?!"

Mama's voice preceded her as she pounded up the stairs. She stopped in the middle of the hallway. Kotaro turned and hurled Kitty's headless body at her. She made an attempt to catch it but was bowled over onto the floor. When she realized she was holding a headless corpse, she screamed. She kept on shrieking as she shoved the limp body aside and tried desperately to crawl backward, too shocked even to stand.

Kotaro overtook her in a few huge strides and slammed a clawed foot onto her belly. The woman uttered a toadlike croak that turned into a gurgle. Her mouth flew open and she spewed a geyser of vomit.

He lifted his foot and the woman tried to run away again, clawing desperately at the floor.

Galla advanced silently down the hall, gripping a scythe in each hand just below the blade, touching the tips to the walls on either side. As she advanced, she carved a deep gash in each wall.

Those gashes were the dividing line between reality and Galla's world.

She passed through him and stood over Mama. She let the scythe in her right hand slide downward in her grip until she held the handle by the end. She put the flat of the blade against the side of Mama's head, against her left ear. She did the same with the other blade, pressing it against the right ear.

The blades shone with a cold phosphorescence. Dazzling, jewellike hues. The woman's twisted face seemed to levitate in the light.

"Help... Please, help me..."

Mika must have cried out just like that. Again, and again, and again.

Mama's head was pinned between the crossed scythes. Slowly, Galla lifted it off the floor.

"Help...help me..."

Galla's shoulders moved slightly. There was a dull crack as Mama's neck snapped.

"Now then." Galla lifted the woman's limp form by the scythes and brought her face level with her own. "I will take this one as well."

There was a flash as Mama's head separated from her body. Another flash, and she was transformed into black dust. Galla's blades fed again.

When the last particle was consumed, the air seemed to change. It smelled purified, refreshed.

Something else was different. Galla's blades were burning with a new light.

As Kotaro watched, the crescent blades grew longer. Each handle thickened, and a pattern emerged on the surface of each, an arabesque of lines that might have been intertwined hieroglyphs. Where the tang of the blade was embedded in the handle, a ring of petals emerged and swelled into a round object that was very much not a flower.

It was a skull, with its jaws wide open. Each icy crescent projected from the mouth of a screaming skull.

"Together they are one," Galla said, her back still to Kotaro. "They are the Skulls of Origin. One tells of the Circle as it was. The other, of what it will be. They speak with tongues of steel."

Galla deftly stowed first the right, then the left scythe behind her back. Even this much movement was enough to make the air hum with their power.

The scythes rose above Galla's head, each larger than the weapon she had originally carried. They had reached their final form. The blue-white light from each crescent pulsated with a rhythm of slow breathing.

"Your task is finished," Kotaro said.

Galla turned and nodded. "Now, I must go."

To the Gate of Sorrows.

Kotaro didn't think, and so he did not hesitate. "Take me with you."

Galla gazed at him in silence.

"I can't be in the world anymore. I hate it." He shook his head, to Galla and to himself. "I don't want to be here."

A world where a young girl like Mika could end up wrapped in plastic like a load of garbage. A world where a woman like Ayuko Yamashina could be strangled and mutilated and dumped like trash in an empty lot.

He had wanted to make that world just a little better. He'd wanted to help.

It made me a monster.

He could never go back. He could never forget the sensation of his fangs tearing into Glitter Kitty's neck. No matter how long he lived or how much happiness he experienced, it could never match the monstrous pleasure he'd felt at that moment.

His appearance was not the only thing that had been transformed. What he was inside—that was a monster now too.

"I don't care where you go. I'll follow. I want to witness your battle. I want...I want to see you reunited with your son. I want to be there when it happens." His eyes were brimming with tears. "That's all I can hope for now. After that I don't care where I go. I'll spend the rest of eternity wandering the gap between reality and the void."

A pack of creatures that roamed the gap between dimensions of time and space had attacked Yuriko Morisaki and her master, Ash, on the roof of the tea caddy building. Ash had called them the Hounds of Tindalos.

Maybe I'll turn into something like them. I only remember the horrible touch of their huge foot pads and claws, but now I feel like I have the power to see them.

Galla shook her head faintly. Her long, black hair flowed over her shoulders as if freshly combed and smoothed. For the first time, Kotaro could detect the sweet fragrance of it.

"You sought justice," said Galla. "Revenge was yours. In that there is no shame."

Craving for forgiveness. Craving for release. Craving for fulfillment of desire. Craving to devour. Galla had harvested them all. And that was what she had to say.

Kotaro wanted to believe she was right. But it was no use. His stomach rebelled—he could feel his gorge rising.

"I'm a monster. It happened. I don't even know if what I did was right or wrong. All I know is I was too late. I couldn't help her. And the violence I did after I realized that got me high. You warned me a long time ago. You said I'd regret it. I never even listened to you."

Yes, Shigenori had warned him too, several times. Yes, Yuriko Morisaki had begged him to return to everyday life. He'd ignored them both.

Galla motioned with her chin toward the open door behind them. "See to the boy."

It took Kotaro a moment to comprehend. Gaku Shimakawa! He rushed back into the room.

Gaku was out cold, curled up in a fetal position on the floor, still bound hand and foot.

"Do you think he saw?"

The room was torn apart. Clearly something very violent had taken place here. But there were no traces of Papa and Mama, or the tattooed man, or Glitter Kitty. There was no blood. They had simply vanished.

The only corpse in the house was Mika's.

Galla bent over the boy. She caressed his cheek, still hollow with terror. She put the tips of three fingers on his forehead and pressed hard. His eyelids, which had been screwed shut, fluttered for a moment.

"Now he will have no memory of us."

But he would remember Mika. He would remember what had happened to her and why. He would remember the horror he experienced. Unbearable fear, and even greater feelings of helplessness and guilt.

I'm sorry.

Why are our expressions of regret so short?

There was a window in the room. The double curtains were closed. Kotaro parted them an inch or two and peered out. All the lights were on in the house next door. Beyond it was a four-story condominium. All the lights seemed to be on there too, and an unusually large number of people were out on the balconies, looking straight at Kotaro. The neighborhood must have heard the screaming and howling.

"The police will be here soon."

Another uncanny case of disappearance—four at once this time, and all of them soon to become suspects in a murder-kidnapping. The survivor's story would sound made-up and hard to believe. He fainted, and when he woke up, the kidnappers had disappeared...

The only person who might be able to read the signs, other than the two wolves, was Shigenori. Doubtless he'd be furious with Kotaro. Again.

A siren wailed far off. It grew louder. Kotaro closed his eyes and listened.

It would be the last sound he ever heard in this world.

3

Where are we going?

Kotaro walked in darkness. How long had he been following Galla?

He heard his own footfalls. He wasn't treading on soil. The surface was hard and smooth, cool to the touch. With each step, his talons clicked faintly. They were curved, claws to pin the flesh of prey and never release it, like a carnivorous dinosaur.

He knew he had transformed into something strange. Fangs, claws, a huge body. The darkness was so complete that if someone had grasped the end of his nose he wouldn't have seen them, but he could feel his body. It was enormous. With each step, ponderous muscles slid and shifted in his back and shoulders, in his arms and calves.

Galla led the way. She was invisible, but he knew exactly where she was.

Something glowed, blue-white lights burning steadily but wavering with the rhythm of her tread. Flames. In the stygian darkness Kotaro walked on, guided by lights burning in the eye sockets of the Skulls of Origin like will-o'-the-wisps. The lights swayed up and down, leaving a trail on his retinae. Their graceful trajectory beckoned him on.

Out of nowhere, he remembered something that had happened ten years earlier, an overnight hiking trip with his family to the mountains near Tokyo. They'd spent the night at a famous hot spring inn.

Not far from the inn there was a creek where fireflies swarmed on summer nights. They'd stayed up late, and with the other guests had been guided by the inn owner to the creek to see the fireflies. Little Kazumi had been frightened by the dark mountain road, and Kotaro held her hand all the way.

The little waterway was alive with lights, as though a dipperful of stars had been scattered along the creek and the stars were alive and swarming, pulsating with a rhythm like breathing.

Asako and Takayuki were entranced. Kazumi was wide-eyed with wonder. Kotaro had been holding her hand firmly, but now she pulled away, overjoyed, reaching out gently for the dancing lights.

Kotaro's eyes were drawn from the clouds of fireflies by a solitary pair of lights—perhaps a male and female. As he watched, they floated away from the swarm and plunged deeper into the forest.

He had followed them, his steps quickening out of curiosity. He was convinced that he'd been chosen, that they wanted to show him something special, something even more beautiful. When he followed, they flew on; if he paused, they swooped back toward him, rising and falling, urging him onward. *Come. Come with us.*

At first the ground was uneven. He'd proceeded cautiously, but soon he stopped paying attention. As long as he was with his fireflies, he felt no fear. They were so kind; sometimes they almost flew against his cheek. *Yes, yes, come with us. Come.*

Suddenly they spiraled high into the air. He was about to bound after them, but a pair of strong arms bear-hugged him from behind.

"Watch out, son!"

It was the owner of the inn. He was wearing a hard hat with a light like a miner's helmet. His face was stern. "Look down."

Kotaro's eyes followed the beam of light. He'd been climbing a slope along the creek. At the top was a sheer drop into darkness. He was about to walk right over it.

"I was chasing fireflies," he said sheepishly.

"Those weren't fireflies. Real fireflies don't play tricks. The mountains are full of things that aren't what they seem."

Like the darkness.

Why had that memory come back to him just now? The fairy lights of the skulls rose and fell slowly ahead of him.

"Stop!"

A voice rang out, clear and strong. Kotaro stopped. His reverie popped like a soap bubble. Once more he felt the weight of his huge body.

"Kotaro Mishima, go no farther!"

Who was it? A man's voice. It was familiar. Someone had followed him along this road in the dark. The voice came from behind.

"This is your last warning. You must not go any farther."

Galla spoke. She sounded surprisingly close. "Leave us. The defiled have no place here."

The voice came back. "Guardian of the Tower! I call to the weak, to one whose place is in the Circle."

"Then you miss your mark. The weak do not walk this road. Only those with the strength of a Guardian can walk this road." Then, to Kotaro: "Come."

He stood indecisively, chewing his lip. He felt his fangs. *It's U-ri's master, Ash. The man in black with two swords. The wolf.*

"You remember," the voice said.

The road ahead and back was pure night. There was only the voice, calling him.

"That means you're still human," it said with a tone of relief. "Kotaro Mishima, I ask you to remember yourself."

He wavered.

"Remember U-ri."

U-ri. A mysterious girl, full of strange stories. Black hair. Petite. Beautiful.

"She told you about her brother. You remember, don't you? You're traveling the same path. That's why she's worried about you."

That story. I thought maybe it was phony. Now I know it was real.

"Is she there?" He finally found his voice.

"She's not strong enough to come this far. Even with my skills and knowledge, I can only go as far as the foothills of darkness. A wolf is no match for a Guardian of the Tower.

"That's why I can go no farther. Kotaro Mishima, remember! You are a person, raised by a mother and father, with friends and people who love you. A person, with a person's life."

He stood rooted, thinking. But something clearer and more vivid kept intruding, filling his mind: the sensation of biting through Glitter Kitty's neck.

I'm not a person anymore.

"I'm a killer, Ash." He turned to face down the road. "I'm a monster now."

Yes. I can feel my fangs in my mouth when I talk.

"What you see and feel," the voice answered, "may not be real. You've been bewitched by the greatest power in the Circle, so powerful and primal that it's beyond good and evil."

Bewitched. Someone else had said that to him once.

We were bewitched by a demon.

Kotaro swayed and almost lost his footing. His talons clacked on the stone. *This body is a pain in the butt.*

He lifted his hands in front of his face. He couldn't see a thing. All he knew was the weight of them. The mass of a giant body. A frightful smell, the stench of a beast. The reek of blood. His fur was steeped in it.

How can he say I'm still human?

Kenji had become a killer as well. Now Kotaro would take the same leap. He had a debt to pay. He would pay it without regret.

"I can't go back." He turned toward Galla. The skulls beckoned. "Say goodbye to U-ri. Thank her for worrying about me," he called over his shoulder.

"There's still time. Come back and tell her yourself."

"I'm not going back, Ash. I've made my choice."

"Kotaro Mishima!" The voice was breaking up, like someone on a radio with a fading signal. "Ko-taa-rooh Mi-shi-maa!"

The voice faded and disappeared. Absolute silence descended, a silence like gravity itself. As Kotaro closed his eyes and gave himself over to it, he felt a profound sense of peace.

He walked on, led by the skulls.

The road climbed slowly upward, became steeper. His talons scraped the stone. The path curved, became a clockwise spiral. He knew its cold, smooth surface now.

It dawned on him. He and Galla were ascending a gigantic spiral gallery. And he could see, but not because his eyes had adjusted to the darkness. They had merged with it.

To his left: a great void, a vast expanse of nothingness, of pure emptiness. Along the right margin of the gallery: a file of columns, each one immeasurably larger than the largest skyscraper. Kotaro looked up at them—it was like something seen through the multifaceted eyes of a moth.

He stood transfixed. His metamorphosis into a monster was complete, but he still had a heart capable of wonder.

This world was surpassingly beautiful, beyond the limits of mind. This was not scale that was meant to impress. It was not even scale that rendered an onlooker small and insignificant. It was scale beyond any human standard of reference.

Nor could the columns have been fashioned by human beings. At first they seemed to soar straight upward, but on closer inspection he saw that their surfaces followed complex, gently undulating curves. His eyes, now part of the darkness, saw how they glowed with the oily sheen of obsidian and the gleaming luster of marble.

The columns marked the edge of the gallery and the boundary with the world beyond. Galla and Kotaro were alone on the sloping road, but beyond the columns, the darkness was charged with a multitude of presences—the fluttering of wings, the murmuring of voices. A sharp shout of triumph. A cry of astonishment. There were no words, at least none that Kotaro could make out.

The voices were not human.

The chirping of birds, the snarling of beasts, the moaning of the wind, waves breaking on a distant shore. The voices of living creatures and of nature itself. Each voice seemed to contain both without being either.

Something scrutinized him from the darkness. It drew back, then the tip of a wing slashed the space just ahead. For a moment he saw a creature much like Galla in her true form.

That means, in the darkness beyond—

"These pillars support the Tower of Inception."

Galla spoke without turning her head. She kept walking at the same measured pace. "Beyond them lies my region."

The column alongside them erupted with a blinding light. As the light flashed from the base and hurtled upward, an enigmatic pattern seemed to levitate from its surface before sinking into darkness.

The light illuminated the column, yet nothing around it. The darkness beyond the pillars was impenetrable and vast, extending to untold distances. Doubt began to gnaw at Kotaro.

An abyss of endless night...?

A region so sacred, so noble, that even Ash and U-ri were barred from entering it. Yet it was a world of darkness. This was not the hazy image he had been imagining. The birthplace of the souls of words must surely be pure and bright, something like heaven.

"Darkness is the reason for our existence. We *are* darkness, so that there may be light. At the head of this gallery stands the Tower of Inception, one of the two regions that preside over the Circle. This place is its shadow."

Something sprinted across his path, treading on his foot as it sped away. Kotaro was astonished. Where had it come from? Where had it vanished to? And where had he felt that touch before?

That horrible foot pad. The cursed breath. It was a hound of Tindalos.

"Why are these monsters here?" he called to Galla.

"They come and go freely."

"Why do you let them run free just outside your region?"

"Fear not. They will not attack you. Not as you are."

"I guess you're right. I'm a monster too."

And he would spend eternity here, living alongside them. Would "living" even be the right word? Simply existing, perhaps?

What kind of existence did Galla have here? What about the other inhabitants of this region sealed in darkness? Was there some form of society? He turned the question over in his mind before he discarded it, shaking his head.

It was meaningless. How could entities that were real but did not exist form any sort of society? How could entities that were only real when someone in the Circle acknowledged them as real live as people lived?

But then again...

What about Galla's relationship with her son, Auzo? The one she had called her second self? Was it a relationship between mother and child, like human beings had? Like that between Kotaro and Asako? Or Takako and Mika? Did they share the same flesh and blood? The same sorrows and joys?

At the thought of Mika, the monster felt a sharp twinge in his chest. He gnashed his teeth and called up that memory—the sensation of Glitter Kitty's head nestled in his jaws, and how easily her spine had snapped. The gush of hot blood and her scream the instant before he bit her in two.

His heart was in an uproar. His thoughts came in snatches. *Galla and her precious offspring. Galla, who gathered raw craving to rescue her child who was banished to the Nameless Land. Her precious child.*

Even in a world of darkness, of countless monsters flapping their wings, there could be ties of love, of family—

Could there? If nonexistent beings couldn't form a society, could they love one another?

A world of darkness beyond the pillars. Galla's world. It was nothing like the image he had been nurturing in his heart.

Go back!

A voice that was not a voice. His heart beat wildly.

And there was light, everywhere.

▼

A bell.

Kotaro stepped from the solid darkness of the gallery into a world of light.

In the center of this world: a single tower.

A row of pristine white pillars circled its base. It rose into the sky, topped by a dome of pure crystal. Beneath the dome, a single titanic bell, majestic, beautiful, elegantly curved. The tower was white silver dusted with gold. No sculpture or inscription broke its water-smooth surface. The bell was without embellishment of any kind.

It revolved in a perfect circle. Anyone tarrying beneath that serene rotation would soon have grown intoxicated. The true circle traced by the bell's orbit was perfect beauty, perfect virtue, perfect truth.

The bell was silent.

Instead of sound, this sublime entity spawned words transparent to the eye and ear. It moved in its orbit without end.

"Is this really the birthplace of words?" Kotaro couldn't help asking. Galla didn't answer, nor did she slow her pace.

"Who's making it move?" He saw no sign of life.

The tower rose into a sky that seemed enormous and far away. Transparent golden shafts of light dropped from gaps in high, milky clouds. No birds cut through the shafts of light.

A world without life, without even the whisper of the wind. The stillness of absolute purity. As he followed Galla, entranced by the bell, Kotaro realized that it produced something else.

Darkness. The shadow cast by the bell as it moved cut through the light and fell at his feet, tracing out its perfect circle.

The shadow was inverted into light in the world below, enclosed by the columns that supported the Tower. The shadow cast by the bell gave life to Galla's world.

We are *darkness, so there may be light.*

Galla was a guardian of that darkness. Since their first encounter, Kotaro had conversed with her, exchanged opinions with her, and felt in his own way that he understood her. He'd spent a lot of time imagining what her world, the tower she guarded, must be like. The hazy image he'd formed was a child's dream. Someone else in the same situation, of the same generation, from the same culture, would probably have imagined something very similar: A colonnaded temple out of ancient Greece, but immeasurably larger, with the holy of holies, a stately bell tower, served by priests and acolytes. And to defend it, valiant, awe-inspiring warriors with multifarious weapons and armor.

But there was nothing like that here. This was something unimaginable, nothing someone might picture spontaneously. There was no link between the beauty of this place and the human imagination.

Stories.

There was no trace of narrative in this place.

That was why everything was so pure and undefiled, so untouched by any description. It simply was.

The words born here were ultimate emptiness, unsullied by meaning or narrative. Only people could bring meaning and life to the words that poured forth from the bell. That was why this region had to remain undefiled. That was why absolute silence reigned: where there is sound, the beginning of meaning follows.

This place was emptiness itself, the emptiness of undifferentiated potential. Yet how full of sound and life and overwhelming spectacle was the darkness beneath the tower! Even the Hounds of Tindalos possessed name and form there.

Confusion and bewilderment called faintly to Kotaro the monster.

People framed the meaning of life with words. Words allowed them to build societies. Could absolute emptiness spawn *words*?

No. It wouldn't do to question reality. He should be asking himself a question instead. Could he, Kotaro Mishima, believe that the words people used were born from pure emptiness?

It doesn't matter now.

He shook his head resolutely. Once, twice. He closed his eyes and clapped a hand to his forehead.

Accept it or not—it's not a choice I can make.

He was a monster, here in this place, because of the decisions he'd made. Now all he could do was accept it.

He opened his eyes, looked down at his feet. He was walking on air. There was no sensation of stone, or talons clicking on something hard.

He hesitated, peered around. He was hemmed in by white, faintly shining clouds. He hadn't noticed the tower go out of sight. They must be high above it now.

He saw Galla's black wings and streaming hair as she made her way upward amid the clouds. To his right and left and rear were only clouds and more clouds. They shone fresh, softly white, like untracked snow before dawn. They did not exist. They were eternally pure.

There was no road back, even if he'd wanted to return.

"You would only lose your way." Galla read his thoughts and barred the way home with her answer. "There is no road back, not to your region or anywhere else. We can go only forward, toward the Nameless Land. The Skulls of Origin guide us through this pure emptiness. And once one possesses the skulls, one *must* go to the Nameless Land."

Galla called the emptiness pure. Kotaro the monster blinked with surprise. "You think this place is emptiness itself?"

"I do not think. I know. We are ascending the Stairs of Emptiness. They link the Tower of Inception with the Nameless Land. Without the Skulls of Origin, even a guardian of the Tower would lose her way here. That would mean wandering in the void for eternity."

Kotaro was not so much walking as being pulled along. Galla's presence was the only thing keeping him from being swallowed up by this shimmering region of pure contingency.

He no longer had a choice, but he was not afraid. He did not call out in fear or try to run away. He no longer had the right to human reactions. Yet still there was an echo, a faint reverberation of the person he once had been. No, Kotaro Mishima would not have run away either.

He still knew who he was. He remembered. Ash had only been trying to help him, but Ash had missed the point. Kotaro was drifting like a buoy on an infinite ocean, drawn on by Galla's dark power, but only because that was what he wanted.

There was soft earth beneath his feet. The pure white emptiness drew back quickly on either side. A new world opened before him.

Terra firma and a breeze, heavy with the scent of dry grass, caressing his cheek. He reflexively lifted a hand and waved it toward his nostrils, hungry for the smell of it, the fragrant smell of dry spring grass and the moist air of an autumn night.

He was in grassland.

There was no moon, but he knew that the darkness here was the friendly darkness of night.

Countless lamps flickered and wavered far across the plain. People must be living there. A town?

The grassland spread from horizon to horizon. Here and there the ground rose and fell gently, but there was nothing to block the eye. The entire vista could be taken in with one sweeping glance. It was like having the sight of a god.

"What is this place?"

Galla planted her feet beside him, rose to her full height, and lifted her chin in triumph.

"This is the Nameless Land."

▾

Galla stood motionless, gazing at the lights. Kotaro stood beside her, shoulder to shoulder. Where once he had gazed up at her with fear and trepidation, Kotaro the monster was now as tall as she was.

The source of all stories, where they were born and to which they must return. The Nameless Land.

But for Kotaro, the gently rolling plain, the sky, the scent of the wind—everything was intimate and familiar. He knew the names of the things he saw. He could say their names. This was not a nameless place. After his journey past the darkness beyond the pillars, past that silent, shining bell and its massive shadow, through the faintly glowing emptiness between the regions, this place seemed to his eyes, to his ears and all his other senses, natural and welcoming. Even the touch of the night was gentle.

In the distance, a small galaxy of lights twinkled in the darkness, distant like the lights of the skyscrapers seen from Galla's sanctum, but without distortion. The sense of perspective was exactly what Kotaro was used to. The natural environment was compellingly real.

For a moment he forgot he was no longer human. He felt like a college student teleported to a mystery destination. Where was he? Europe? South America, maybe? Was this vast plain a nature preserve?

Where there are lights, there are people.

"That is the fortress." Galla raised a hand and pointed. "Its proper name is the Hall of All Books. It holds thousands of them, stories that cannot be allowed to leave this place."

"You mean, like a library?"

She smiled. "Just so."

"Then it must be the biggest library in the Circle." Judging from the number of lights and their size and distribution, the Hall of All Books had to be far larger than the Tower of Inception.

A pinpoint of light separated from the rest and moved flickeringly away. Then another and yet another began moving in the same direction, forming a string of lights.

"The nameless devout," Galla said. "They go to their labors."

"Labors? You mean they have to work?"

She turned to peer at him. "There is no work here."

He remembered what U-ri had told him, that the nameless devout had to turn the Great Wheels of Inculpation for eternity. Wasn't that work? But the nameless devout were confined here because of some sin they'd committed. Maybe if you were a prisoner, what you had to do every day wasn't considered work.

"The devout are not human," Galla said. "They were human once, but no longer." She paused. "Your wolf said U-ri's brother was a nameless devout."

She shook her head lightly, sending her hair floating behind her in the wind off the plain, and began to walk. Kotaro followed, pressing the grass beneath his feet. He too was a monster, no longer human. No longer Kotaro Mishima.

They moved side by side, neither of them human, treading the grass heavy with dew. Kotaro was quietly grateful for the compassion he felt in its touch. Because of the grass, he did not have to see his own footprints.

Galla had not drawn her weapons. She seemed utterly calm. Where was the gate, Kotaro wondered. Was it a long way from where they were?

As if in answer to his question, a light streaked across a corner of the sky. "A shooting star!" Kotaro was a child again, enchanted.

As though his cry of wonder were a trigger, one glowing trail followed another through the heavens, fainter and more ephemeral than the lights in the Hall of All Books, but like miniature jewels against the veil of night. The sight was beautiful—and to Kotaro, thoroughly familiar, no different from the world he called home.

Trees rose into view, dotted in far-off clumps, dense groves of trees and low hills. The trees were old and gnarled, spreading their branches close to the ground. They stood out against the sky like props on a grassy stage. Kotaro's eyes were those of a monster and of a child. Everything appeared new and wonderful to his sight.

But something cold and ominous reared into view that extinguished the pure curiosity and excitement of a boy discovering a new land. It was a black barricade, a barrier to those who would approach the Hall of All Books in the heart of the Nameless Land. With each step the barrier loomed higher, but Galla's pace did not slow. Kotaro's heart beat faster. He quickened his pace.

What from a distance had seemed to be a spaced line of iron palings turned out to be enormous pikes with their heads buried in the earth. They reached so high that their far ends were out of sight in the mist. At the foot of the pikes was a solid line of huge black shields, each inscribed with a pentagram that glowed a dull silver.

The shields were iron. The pentagrams were quicksilver. The night wind blowing through the barrier carried a faint trace of lead.

The barricade was not here to protect the castle. It was unlike anything one would erect to protect a town.

The barrier was a cage. The fortress was a prison.

"Halt."

Galla raised a hand. She stopped before the barrier.

4

Kotaro squinted into the darkness.

The lights of the Hall of All Books twinkled beyond the barrier, but seemed no closer than before. The endless line of pikes and shields seemed to have dropped from the sky, like the groves of ancient trees among the hills. Perhaps they were nothing more than visions conjured up from memory, in a place that was real but did not exist.

Then he saw that two shields in the line were missing their pentagrams. Their surfaces were smooth, unmarked black. Galla raised her right arm in one smooth motion, drew a scythe, and pointed it at the left shield.

"Here the Circle begins."

Was that Galla's voice? Kotaro didn't see her lips move. The voice was deep and resonant, like an incantation.

An eye opened in the shield, as though a giant were awakening. It was golden with a spindle-shaped obsidian iris, the eye of a demon, like Galla's when she assumed her true form.

She raised her left arm, drew the second scythe, and pointed it at the right shield.

"Here the Circle ends."

An eye opened in the second shield. The sclera was obsidian, the iris gold. Kotaro shied away instinctively. Some intuition told him it would be better not to face that penetrating gaze.

Holding her weapons lightly, still pointed at the shields, Galla called again. This time there was no mistake. It was her voice, clear and ringing.

"Sentinel of the Gate! The Skulls of Origin are with me. I would pass the barrier and enter the Hall of All Books. The duel is nigh!"

The eyes on the shields opened wider. A stronger light shone forth. A rumble began deep underground. Kotaro cowered in alarm. He stumbled and put a huge, brutish hand on the ground. The earth under his feet shuddered. Something huge beyond belief, sealed in silence and darkness for time beyond reckoning, was stirring.

A section of the barrier about twenty yards across, with the eyes at its center, started sinking into the earth. Some enormous power was pulling the barrier downward. As Kotaro watched, dumbfounded, the eyes on the central shields closed, as though returning to sleep, and sank out of sight.

Galla lowered her weapons and looked straight up. Kotaro followed her gaze. *So this is how it opens*, he thought.

No, it's not over. The ground was still quaking. The barrier was sinking quickly, but its upper limit was not yet in sight.

At last a deeper darkness appeared above their heads, entangled in the ends of the descending pikes. A giant chain? The shape was wrapped in layers around the barrier, or maybe entangled in it. As the pikes sank toward the ground, it came clearly into view.

It was not a chain, not a rope, not metal at all. It was not alive.

A stone dragon stared out across the plain, the guardian of the Nameless Land and the seal to the barrier that surrounded the Hall of All Books.

Kotaro sensed he was not looking at a statue. A dragon had perched on the barrier and turned to stone. Its fangs were savage. One wing was outstretched, the other folded. The claws of the left front leg clutched the barrier. The right was raised, ready to strike. The rear legs clasped the barrier, flexed powerfully, ready to spring into the air. With the dragon still high above their heads, the barrier stopped sinking. The gate was not yet open.

"Step away."

Kotaro looked uncertainly at Galla. Were her words meant for him?

"Get behind me. Now."

He found himself unable to move. He tried to speak, though he was not sure what he wanted to say.

"Galla..."

"The Sentinel is here." She peered at him steadily and nodded. "I will not fail."

He stepped backward stiffly, lost his footing and sat on the ground with a thump. With his eyes glued to the Sentinel, he could only retreat crabwise, pushing himself backward with his heels.

Galla adjusted her grip on the scythes and stepped forward. "Ill-starred Sentinel!" Her voice resounded. "Here the Circle—begins!"

She raised the scythe in her right hand, planted her feet, coiled her muscles and hurled the weapon upward with all her strength. The scythe flew, spiraling end over end like a boomerang.

There was a hard, metallic impact as the blade sank deep into the dragon's left shoulder. The long handle vibrated with a groaning hum. Kotaro was reminded suddenly of the poisonous insects of Makoto's giant.

"Ill-omened Sentinel!" she called again, more powerfully now, and hurled the scythe in her left hand.

"Here—the Circle ends!" The scythe sank deep into the dragon's right shoulder.

The blades were embedded nearly to the tang, as though the Skulls of Origin were sinking their teeth into the dragon's shoulders. Their eyes blazed forth with exultation, predators biting their prey.

Wild laughter. The skulls were laughing with joy!

Still rejoicing, teeth flashing, they began to dissolve. Their flaming eyes went out before they crumbled into fine black dust blown away in the wind. With the skulls gone, the handles of the scythes clattered down the dragon's flanks and fell at Galla's feet.

"You have your cravings," she called. "Rise and face me, defiled one!"

The surface of the stone began to fissure. Color and texture and life returned to the petrified monster.

This was why Galla had needed to gather craving. The gigantic Sentinel crouched atop the Gate of Sorrows was coming to life. Its eyes were the last to revive. The lids opened and the eyes moved in their sockets. Their pupils were black holes at the far reaches of the universe.

The dragon twisted on its perch. It raised its head high and flexed its wings. Its eyes found Galla and flashed with menace.

She's unarmed. How is she going to fight?

Galla gave a piercing war cry. The dragon answered with a howl that shook the ground and raised a swirling wind. Eyes locked on her foe, Galla spread her arms wide and began her transformation.

The shadow of her legs grew massive. Her silhouette blocked Kotaro's field of vision. He realized that what he'd seen when she harvested Keiko Tashiro had been a pale likeness of her true form. She was not just the model for humanity's gargoyles, demons whose power and appearance evoked fear and fascination. Her true form was far more frightening, far more powerful and repulsive. An entity greater than anything that ever lived, born of power and darkness and chaos, real yet nonexistent.

The dragon leaped from the barrier and plummeted toward her. Still supine with his hands on the ground behind him, Kotaro watched the duelists collide.

▼

Shigenori hunched his shoulders as a sudden chill ran up his spine.

It was 9:35 p.m. He and Shigeru Noro were standing at the service entrance of the tea caddy building. Aizawa from Labbra Technofusion, upbeat as ever, stood alongside them. A security technician sat on a stepladder with a laptop on his knees, verifying the operation of the new security system.

Aizawa had only informed Shigeru about the system the day before. Since late the previous year, the tea caddy building—still in legal limbo as far as ownership went—had seen a series of strange incidents and intrusions, though how people were getting in was unknown. Perhaps the rumors about the rooftop gargoyle had inspired people to break in. Aizawa's bosses had decided to install security cameras, and changed the locks for good measure. Now the cameras were up and running.

"We should've managed this property better," Aizawa said apologetically. "I'm sorry for any concern we might've caused the neighborhood association. I wanted to make sure you see the new system. If this puts your minds at ease, you won't have to do any more nighttime patrolling."

This little demonstration was probably his idea, not his bosses'. Shigeru wanted Shigenori to come along so he could give a presentation on the system at the next association meeting. "You'd better explain it to the board," he'd said. "I'm not a hardware kind of guy."

The hottest part of the summer was over, but the city nights were still tropical. The humidity had been unusually bad for the past few days, and in the concrete jungle of West Shinjuku, just standing around at half past nine at night was enough to leave everyone moist with perspiration.

So why am I feeling so cold? Shigenori wondered.

"Are you all right?" Shigeru asked. Shigenori's polo shirt was stuck to his back with sweat.

"I don't know, maybe it's a summer cold."

"Now that you say so, you look a little pale." Shigeru peered at him curiously. "Maybe it's just the street lights."

The security rep was explaining how the motion detectors worked. The LED above the back door was almost like a laser. Aizawa blinked as the technician triggered and disabled it over and over.

"Well Mr. Aizawa, that's enough light for the darkest night, I would think," Shigenori said and clapped the young man's broad back. He noticed that moving around made the chill weaker.

"Thank you, Mr. Tsuzuki." Aizawa smiled. "But are you sure you don't want to go inside and see more?"

"You don't want to get into more trouble with your boss." Aizawa had gotten a scolding for letting Shigenori and Shigeru into the tea caddy building in the first place without consulting his superiors.

"They won't find out," Aizawa said. "I'll keep my mouth shut this time."

Shigeru rolled his eyes. "You mean *you* told them before?"

"I said I had Mr. Tsuzuki come along because I've got this thing about ghosts. Everyone had a laugh except the head of our legal department. He threw a fit."

The three men chuckled. Even the taciturn security rep managed a thin smile. Shigenori was still distracted by his sudden chill; he rubbed the back of his neck and hunched his shoulders, trying to banish the sensation.

"So your legal guy has a fit, then sends you here again without an escort?" Shigeru shook his head. "Maybe he doesn't want to touch it," he said with a smile.

Aizawa took this utterly seriously. He lowered his voice. "You know, I think he's afraid of ghosts, too."

Shigeru burst out laughing. The sound echoed along the dark street a stone's throw from the restaurants and bars.

"I hope we unload this place soon," Aizawa added.

"That might be a good idea," Shigeru said.

The security rep turned his laptop to show them the video feeds from the cameras in and outside the building. The split screen let the user monitor four feeds at once.

"Looks like you spent a lot on this," said Shigenori. "I'll go around to the main entrance. Yell if you can see me."

"Will do!"

With Shigeru's cheery call echoing off the building, Shigenori left the men peering at the monitor and started toward the front entrance along the narrow space between the building and its surrounding wall. When he emerged on the other side, he stopped short in astonishment.

The entrance had been tidied up; the heavy chain and padlock were gone. A young woman in a bulky leather jacket and hobnailed boots was leaning against the double doors. Shigenori had seen that pale face and lissome silhouette before.

"You!"

The girl straightened up and motioned for silence.

He glanced behind him and hurried over to her. A smile showed at the corners of her mouth. "Don't worry, your friends can't see me. I'm still more real than my master, but people who can't see me, can't."

She was talking gibberish. He remembered that about her. This was the girl who'd appeared out of nowhere with her "master," a man in black, the second time Shigenori had met—interrogated—Galla on the roof of the building. She'd talked gibberish then too.

Yuriko, or U-ri. That was her name.

"Galla passed some of her power to you, I see. Not as much as she gave Kotaro, but that's why you can see me."

Shigenori felt a flicker of unease. "Who are you?" he said quietly.

"There's no time to go through all that again. Kotaro can tell you." She reached out and took him by the hand. Her slender fingers hid surprising strength.

"In fact, that's why I'm here. I want you to send your thoughts to him so he can come back and tell you himself. Please keep thinking about him. If you call to him in your heart, I think he'll hear you."

"What's going on?" Shigenori saw the urgency in the girl's eyes.

"He crossed over," she murmured. A tiny tear welled up in the corner of one eye. "I tried to stop him, but he went anyway. It's starting."

To Shigenori this was just more nonsense. He hadn't a clue as to what she meant. Then again, maybe he did understand, at least a little. And that scared him.

"Did he go somewhere with Galla?"

U-ri nodded. The tear ran down her cheek. Her mouth was set, solemn and brave.

"What's this about something starting?"

Shigeru called out cheerily from the rear of the building. "We can see you. Move around a little."

U-ri let go of his hand. Shigenori raised and dropped his arms as though he were doing calisthenics. He heard Aizawa laughing.

"Mistress Galla will defeat the Sentinel," U-ri said. "It's a rule of the Nameless Land. No one who gets as far as the Gate of Sorrows is ever defeated. That means..." She bit her lip. "It means Kotaro will never return."

Shigenori froze, hands in the air, and stared at her. Shigeru was laughing and telling him he could stop already.

"So pray for him. That's the only thing we can do for him now."

It was Shigenori's turn to grab for her hand, but his fingers closed on air. The wolf was gone.

He shivered with foreboding and fished his phone out of his back pocket. *Kotaro Mishima*...Flustered, he hit the call button. He got a ring signal. It rang three times before the synthetic voice of the message center came back.

On the last day of Kotaro's summer vacation, in a corner of West Shinjuku, Shigenori Tsuzuki stood rooted to the spot.

Mishima...

He had a vision of that face. A single-minded, cheeky punk who didn't listen to his elders.

What've you gotten yourself into?

▾

Mana opened her eyes. Something was calling her.

A little shaded lamp cast a soft glow in a corner of the room. Her friends—a colorful gathering of stuffed animals—surrounded her down pillow. She turned her head on the pillow and put a shoulder outside the light summer comforter to gaze at them, but she didn't think one of them had woken her up.

They're all go to sleep.

Aunt Hatsuko always put them to bed with Mana. She would address them in order. *Good night, Pepe-chan. Good night, Kuu-chan. Good night, Panda-chan.*

Before, whenever Mana had woken in the middle of the night, she'd begun to cry. Aunt Hatsuko would come and comfort her, but sometimes she'd be so sleepy, or cold, or worn out, that Mana learned to turn her face into the pillow and cry without making noise, because when she saw Aunt Hatsuko looking worn out and sleepy, she remembered how her mother had looked worn out and sleepy too, until one rainy night she went to bed and never woke up again. What would Mana do if Aunt Hatsuko didn't wake up?

But Mana didn't cry in the night anymore. Once she fell asleep, she slept soundly until morning, because she knew from Uncle Kotaro that Mama was always with her and would always be beside her.

What woke me up?

She sat up. The little light on the air conditioner glowed blue. Aunt Hatsuko had told her the air conditioner was always watching her with its little blue eye to make sure she didn't get too hot, but Mana knew it was just a light. Ms. Sato told her all about it. *That's just electricity.*

As the room came into focus, she started feeling thirsty. She put her arms around her knees and took a deep breath, and she knew.

The bodies and minds of very young children are connected by a direct circuit, one that parts naturally as they grow older. But Mana still had it, and it told her what she needed to know.

It's Uncle.

What's happen to him?

She felt like she did on the night her mother went to sleep forever. Something bad was happening.

Monster.

She threw off the comforter, knelt on the bed and gathered her friends —Pepe-chan and Kuu-chan and Panda-chan, with their soft round faces and gentle eyes—into her arms. She shared her nameless dread with them, and they comforted each other.

The summer sun would rise early. She would not sleep before it did.

▼

Two titanic bodies met head-on in battle.

Kotaro felt the staggering energy unleashed as they fought. This was not a clash of fang and claw. It was a hurricane. A tsunami. An eruption. A phenomenon of nature, something people can only watch with astonishment, waiting until it subsides.

Ancient people laid the blame for nature's ferocity at the feet of angry gods. Gods with ultimate destructive power were imagined as terrifying forms, giving rise in turn to purely malevolent deities that in turn spawned tales of numberless monsters.

All monsters are descendants of fallen gods. Now two of those descendants fought before Kotaro's awestruck sight. He was one of them, a beast with hooked talons and a terrible stench; he too was a walker in darkness, but he could not keep his footing in the presence of that terrible howling and the whirlwind and the quaking of the earth. It was hard to even keep his eyes open.

This was Galla's true form, the Guardian of the Third Pillar of the Tower of Inception. She had no need for puny blades. Her scythes were never really weapons. They were keys.

Fists like small mountains howled as they cut the air. The dragon's spine was a row of blades. It moved sinuously, taking her blows and hurling them back. Its long tail hammered the ground, raising clouds of dust and rending the earth.

But the gate beyond did not waver. The world it enclosed was quiet and serene. The distant lights in the Hall of All Books shone faint and clear, like stars in a galaxy beyond the Milky Way.

Galla's skin was obsidian. Her fangs and claws shone like drawn swords. Her whiplike tail was silhouetted against the sky as it lashed out and wrapped around the dragon's neck. Kotaro watched, transfixed, as she pressed the attack.

At first the duelists were evenly matched, but the balance was upended when Galla shattered her opponent's horn. The dragon had fought with spirit and power, using its torso as an undulating battering ram, but now it began to succumb to gravity. Its massive tail beat the ground erratically. Its jaws snapped, but the fangs closed on air. Galla seized her opening and tore off the dragon's other horn. Some of its hide came away, sending a spray of bright blood into the air. The dragon's howls turned to shrieks.

She seized her opponent by the nape of the neck. Her teeth gleamed in the darkness of the Nameless Land.

The memory was present again, as real as if Kotaro had been in that room watching, a scene he could not have witnessed in this way because he was part of it. He both saw and felt himself grasp Glitter Kitty in his claws, pull her close, and bite off her head.

Now Galla was about to dispatch the Sentinel the same way. She sank her fangs into its neck, grasped the neck with her claws and strained to tear the head from its body.

A ball rolls quickly along the grass in a park under a blue sky. It strikes a bump in the ground and vaults lightly into the air, just like Kitty's head. How small and light it was! How high it flew! One moment it was part of her body, and an instant later just a plaything soaring through the air.

Galla tore the dragon's head off and raised it high with a mighty cry of triumph. The decapitated corpse toppled slowly over onto its side with a shuddering crash. Galla bellowed as the crash reverberated. She was calling out, but Kotaro couldn't understand the words. Maybe they weren't words at all. Then he saw her howl with the Eye.

Hall of All Books, I have vanquished the Sentinel!

The lights seemed to quaver at the sound of her voice.

I am Galla, Guardian of the Third Pillar of the Tower of Inception, Mother of Auzo the Warrior. The Sentinel is fallen. Open the gate!

The Sentinel—its headless body and its head, still held high by Galla—returned to stone. The hide turned a cold ash gray as the head and body started to crumble. Thousands of years of weathering unfolded in seconds as the dragon collapsed into a pile of rubble.

Galla began to transform. As he watched, Kotaro noticed out of a corner of his eye that the shadow of her legs was shrinking. She became the Galla he knew best: long black hair, white face, inky wings, a strange and beautiful woman who was not quite human.

The lights in the fortress quavered in unison.

A stiff wind, cold and fresh as spring water, lifted Galla's hair and swirled around Kotaro as though purifying them both. He held up his hand. It was a human hand. He had human legs. A human body.

He felt his face. It was the face he'd lived with for nineteen years. His fangs were gone. The stench of blood had vanished. He was wearing the same T-shirt and jeans he'd had on when he raced to the park to look for Mika.

"Stay where you are." Galla spoke over her shoulder as she stood vigilant, eyes fixed on the Hall of All Books. "They will come quickly."

Kotaro's knees were like water. He had difficulty standing. He kept trying to get to his feet and falling over onto his hands and knees. *I have to get up. Galla brought me with her. I'm a guest in the Nameless Land. I've got to pull myself together.*

He managed somehow to crawl alongside her and come to a kneeling position. He looked toward the fortress and saw the same sight he'd witnessed when he arrived. One by one, lights separated from the Hall of All Books, gradually multiplying and forming a moving line. It was coming toward them.

"Are those guys nameless devouts too?"

Galla's eyes narrowed. "Only the devout live and move in this land. There are no others, human or animal," she explained. "The nameless devout are empty. There are tens of thousands, but only one. There is only one, but there are tens of thousands. That is what they say, but it is a figure of speech, and it is meaningless. Emptiness cannot be counted."

Kotaro finally struggled to his feet. He smoothed out the wrinkles in his T-shirt and brushed off his knees. The lights were getting closer.

There was a faint sound of squeaking metal. The ground vibrated faintly, then the rumbling grew louder.

A barrier of pikes linked by shields. With a rumble deep enough to shake the soul, the gate opened inward.

There was nothing between them and the nameless devout.

The lights of the snaking procession were torches held high by figures in simple black robes, with shaven heads and pallid faces. Their bare feet beat down the dried grass. They said nothing, and they made no noise as they walked. They almost seemed unreal.

The black wave lapped toward them. When the figures were close enough to tell apart, Kotaro gasped with surprise.

They had the same face, a face that was vaguely familiar, with symmetrical placement of nose and eyes. Kitty's cheeks. Makoto's eyebrows. Kazumi's mouth. U-ri's eyes. They looked like everyone and no one, approaching in three columns like a solemn funeral procession. The wings of the gate picked up the light from their torches, casting long, barred shadows.

Galla stood motionless, waiting. Kotaro followed her lead.

The marchers stopped. He wondered how so many people could walk in perfect formation. No matter how many there were, there was only one.

Three devout faced them, one at the head of each column. The one in the center came forward and bowed slowly.

"Mistress Galla, Guardian of the Third Pillar of the Tower of Inception."

A young man's voice. Kotaro looked up at Galla. Her pupils flickered almost imperceptibly.

"The Gate of Sorrows is open," the youth intoned. "Why have you come to the Hall of All Books in the Nameless Land? What is your purpose here?"

She took a long step forward. "I want my son."

"What is his name?"

"Auzo the Warrior. My only child."

"What was his sin?"

"He violated our Precept."

"And what would that be?"

"To be darkness." Her voice cracked like a whip. "Auzo wanted to flee our region in search of light. He betrayed our mission as guardians of the Tower."

Kotaro thought back to what he'd seen along that great gallery. The vastness beyond the pillars had been like the floor of an ocean, yet compared to the pure emptiness of the world of the Tower, how full of life and sound—how human, even—Galla's region had been.

What Kotaro sensed had been real. Something human did reside in that darkness, and precisely because it was human, it could tire of darkness and long for light. Auzo had sought only to spread his wings and seek other regions.

Is that a sin?

To search for other worlds? To rebel against confinement in darkness, against being forced to *be* darkness?

"We are darkness," Galla said. "We preserve the purity of the Tower where the souls of words are born. To accept darkness is our calling. To cast that calling aside is an unforgiveable sin. Auzo committed the great sin of exchanging his life for an obsession."

The wavering light from the torches reflected off the devout's pate as he bowed. "Yes. The one you speak of is confined in the Hall of All Books for that great sin."

"I ask you to release him." Galla's voice became suddenly menacing. "We are darkness. To continue as darkness, a guardian of the Tower may choose not to merge with emptiness. That is the law of the Circle."

"True," the devout answered. "But there is a price. Have you a scapegoat for the sin of Auzo's story?"

"To be sure. He is here."

Here. Kotaro froze. He couldn't grasp what he'd heard. *Here?*

Countless eyes turned toward him—Kotaro Mishima, a helpless skinny kid, marooned in a world that was real but did not exist.

The devout nodded. "Very well. We accept the scapegoat."

Several of his fellows stepped toward Kotaro. As they approached, their thin arms were already reaching for him.

"Hey, hold on a sec," Kotaro said nervously. "What's going on, Galla? What's this about a scapegoat?"

She studied the flickering lights of the castle. Her face was a mask. Her hair flowed in the wind.

The nameless devout grasped his arms and shoulders and propelled him forward through the Gate of Sorrows.

"Knock it off! What the hell is this?"

They had the same face, the same bodies and movements, the same voices.

"You are the inculpated."

"Inculpated for the sin of living a story."

"Time will pass for you no longer."

"You shall remain here for eternity."

"Come, sinner."

"You shall turn the Great Wheels of Inculpation."

"Stop! Let me go!" He struck out wildly, trying to break free. He was outnumbered and helpless. The devout were strong, yet trying to get a grip on them was like grasping at shadows. His flailing fists met only air. His kicks connected with nothing. The devout were emptiness personified. Behind that emptiness was a single powerful will.

"Galla, help me!"

He threw himself to the ground. His captors started dragging him along faceup by the nape of his neck and his arms and T-shirt. His heels beat the ground impotently. He clawed at the dry grass. It was useless. They dragged him faster and faster past the shadow of the gate cast by the torches.

This was the fate that had awaited him from the beginning.

"Galla, why are you doing this?" He could only cry out in desperation. The distance between them kept opening. She was a dark silhouette, blacker than the sky.

"I'm not a scapegoat! We never made a deal like this!" His vision was blurred with tears. Her answer seemed to come across a gulf of emptiness.

"I am sorry."

She'd said that at their first meeting. Then too, her tone was clipped and monotonic, because her apology was devoid of meaning.

"I told you you would regret it. You knew this would happen. This was the only thing that *could* happen. You sought to live a story instead of weaving your own life, Kotaro Mishima. You pursued an obsession, you wanted to hunt evil. The final chapter of stories like yours is always here, in the Nameless Land, where you and all those like you must finally go.

"I am sorry. I chose you in the beginning. But this? This you chose yourself."

You will regret this. She had warned him again and again. The guardian of the emptiness where words were born was the darkness of the void. The void has no need for meaning. It seeks no meaning, because the void has no heart.

He finally understood, though it was far too late. Shigenori was right. Galla was a concept. Human beings can't resist formless things. Instead, their concepts color them and finally consume them.

We were bewitched by a demon.

Galla the warrior was a concept that transformed people into something inhuman.

Kotaro kept kicking and punching futilely as they dragged him through the soft grass. His voice became a single wordless scream of rage and terror.

I wanted to do the right thing. I couldn't let evil go unpunished. I couldn't let murderers get away with it, that's all it was!

He was ready to become a monster, to spend the rest of eternity in darkness. The satisfaction of harvesting some measure of justice with his own hands would be enough, even if it meant gazing eternally at his hard-won justice, and the small measure of happiness he'd managed to salvage, as though it were a distant star.

But he didn't want to merge with emptiness, merge with the void and lose all emotion and feeling. *That* was a deal he never signed up for.

He'd been tricked. Conned. He, Kotaro Mishima, had been Galla's target from the beginning. She'd needed a scapegoat, one of the inculpated to barter for her child. And Kotaro had blundered into her flame like a summer moth.

A puny, fluttering insect that wouldn't even notice if someone crushed it.

I am sorry. Meaningless, empty words.

You will regret this. Galla's prophecy had baffled him, drawn him on.

Bait. Everything had been bait, and he'd pursued it, gobbled it up. What a fool he'd been. A hopeless halfwit.

"Liar!"

Galla was out of sight. He pleaded with his captors. "Wait—this is all a mistake—she lied to me!"

Yes, she'd deceived him, and he had *wanted* her to deceive him. He'd gotten drunk on the ecstasy of avenging evil, debauching himself with vengeance. He'd had chance after chance to run, and he turned away every time. People had warned him, and he'd ignored them all.

He was in love with the story he'd woven for himself, a story that became an obsession, about a young man with the power to weigh people on the scales of his personal vision of right and wrong. He'd believed with all his heart that living that story was the only thing that gave his life meaning and purpose—

No. I was tricked into believing it.

"You fucking liar! You're not a warrior! You're just a fucking fiend!" He wept and screamed and cursed Galla. He didn't even know if she could hear him. The nameless devout dragged him relentlessly on. The grass caressed his back. The stars twinkled in the sky above. The torches danced and flamed.

His captors began singing in unison, their voices low and subdued. The words ran together like an invocation in a dark, unfathomable language. Kotaro wished he could cover his ears. The singing had an ominous rhythm.

"Stop! Shut up! Let me go! Come on, leave me alone!" He cried and screamed, but no one heard him. No one came to help him.

He had arrived at the center of the Circle, and its furthest reach.

▼

If words must be born naked of meaning…

If they must be born pure and undefiled…

Why can't people live without them? Why do they keep creating them?

The Tower of Inception. The birthplace of the souls of words was beauty beyond description, a world of pure silence, yet it betrayed the very meaning of the existence of words.

A thing that seals darkness into its own shadow and tries to be free from defilement is by that very act filled with deceit. Words can never be pure and undefiled. They can never be born free of meaning.

That was the biggest lie in the Circle. It was also just another story.

Galla the Warrior waited beside the Gate of Sorrows. Its shadow overlapped her own on the ground—a shadow inmate in a fortress of shadow, a prisoner waiting for the moment of liberation.

The night wind swept over the sea of grass. The lights in the Hall of All Books shone brightly.

Galla pondered the shadows and waited. *A warrior must be where he belongs.*

In the region where words were born, words poured from the bell, bathed in light. For each word it bore, the bell sealed more darkness into the world beneath it.

We guard that darkness so that it may not encroach on the Circle. Be darkness. Embrace it, so that it cannot cause harm.

We shoulder the burden of darkness. As long as we are, the glory of the Circle will abide, even if that too is only a story.

Galla felt a word.

It was *Mother.*

She raised her eyes.

"My child, my son. Auzo the Warrior. Oh, how ghostly you are! Hardly more than a trembling shadow in the night, less substantial and solid than my own."

She released her human form. As a last gesture to the young man who would serve her son as scapegoat, she cast aside the appearance that had deceived him. She returned to her true form.

"Auzo, remember. This is what you truly are."

Mother.

It was not the voice of Auzo. It was only a word, an echo of his will. There is no time in the Nameless Land, yet those who are confined there quickly lose their real form.

"Auzo, you are free. You shall return to the Tower. You must fulfill your mission. From the inception of the Circle until its extinction, you must stand in darkness."

I cannot.

The two winged shadows faced each other beneath the gate. Of old, people knew them as demons.

Mother, I cannot. You practiced deceit to lure a child to the Nameless Land. That was an error. He cannot take my place. He is too pure, too weak. I shall remain here.

"Auzo, why?"

The dim presence wavered.

I saw the light that fills the Circle, if only for a moment. I glimpsed the world of light, and by so doing, Mother, I gained something you shall never have: a heart. To atone for my sin, I will remain here in emptiness.

Galla's eyes narrowed, but she was not perturbed. She felt no sadness. She was not surprised.

She had no heart. She only was. She was a mother and Auzo was her child because that was how it was, and that was all. The two shadows facing each other were mirror images. Ultimately they were the same reality.

I will become a nameless devout. I will bear the burden of my sin. The sin of seeking the world beyond, if only for a moment.

Mother, I must leave you now.

The presence receded toward the Hall of All Books.

Galla did not follow. She stood by the gate, a prisoner in its barred shadow. Darkness embodied as a demon, imprisoned in shadow.

She understood now. Auzo would not return.

She raised her eyes to the vault of the heavens above the Nameless Land.

The wind rose again, blowing from the Hall of All Books. Something light rolled along the ground and stopped against the demon's clawed foot.

It was a scythe handle. No blade, no Skull of Origin, just a simple length of wood. She reached for it and stopped. She would not need it anymore.

The handle burst into flame at both ends and was quickly consumed. The ashes blew away in the wind and disappeared.

The guardian was without her weapons. Her mission had vanished. She turned her back on the fortress and looked in the direction she had come. As though it had been waiting for this moment, the gate began to close behind her. The earth trembled.

The shadows cast by the pikes fell in stripes across the demon's face, flowing over it as the gate closed.

Abandon all hope, ye who enter here.

Galla faced the heavens and spread her arms wide. She spread her wings and flapped them powerfully—once, twice. The shadow of the Gate of Sorrows covered her completely.

My child, Auzo, will not return. There is no hope. There is no craving.

I must pay the price for opening the gate.

The black demon cried out and kicked off from the ground. It rose into the sky over the Nameless Land.

▾

An endless abyss.

Kotaro cried himself hoarse, fought and struggled until he almost blacked out from rage. But he remembered everything: being dragged for what seemed an eternity before the surface beneath him became something like cobblestones and his captors stopped their incessant singing.

Dragged faceup, all he could see was the flames of the torches. They had reached the fortress. Candles spaced along the walls cast their flickering light over shelf upon endless shelf of books. They went on forever, and between each book he saw a tiny gap, a sliver of darkness.

The ceiling drew back and became a gigantic dome. He could not see how far it extended; it was too high above the torches. They kept passing shelves and more shelves of books. The heavy pillars and beams along the walls were covered with complex patterns. Light mingled with darkness. There was a comforting smell of old bindings.

The floor became glassy smooth. The bare feet of the devout pattered on its surface. Somewhere along the way they had grown fewer. Two of them dragged him along the floor and another walked behind. His hands were clasped, fingers interlaced over his heart.

Three opponents. Maybe he could shake the front two off, kick aside the one behind, and escape.

His legs were paralyzed.

The corridor curved right, then left. Shelves, endless shelves of books. The walls were lined with them, lit by candles in sconces. They passed a row of slender decorative pillars carved with Japanese characters in relief.

It was time to fight back. This was the moment. He was ready to escape.

He couldn't move at all, couldn't feel his limbs. By now he experienced nothing more than a vague sensation of being manhandled along.

Somewhere ahead he heard a chain being reeled up, and the creaking of something heavy being lifted.

The end came abruptly. He was heaved into darkness, without stars or the light of torches. Impenetrable night. He realized he was in some sort of chamber and heard the unrolling of the chain and the sound of the trap door slamming shut. He looked up to see the silhouettes of the three devout disappear.

He was falling.

He fell slowly, drifting downward. No, he was sinking. He was still paralyzed, frozen in the posture he'd been in when they cast him into this void like a drowned corpse, arms and legs outspread, faceup.

He was in a vertical shaft that plunged downward without limit. The shaft was clogged with darkness, thicker than water or blood. He fell slowly, like silt drifting to the bottom of the ocean.

What's going to happen to me?

He could still think. He was paralyzed, but his eyes worked. His ears still heard.

He opened his mouth and tried to scream. His voice would not come. Darkness flooded his throat. He swallowed it reflexively. He took darkness into himself. He was becoming darkness.

He felt himself melting away.

Darkness seeped in through his eyes and ears and in the gaps between his skin and nails. As he sank, the pressure rose, driving it into him faster. It was neither cold nor hot. It was not painful. He was not afraid.

It kept filling him up. He was merging with it. When the darkness reached the center of his brain...

I will be pure emptiness.

He was becoming lighter. Disappearing. Everything he'd clung to desperately until now was vanishing along with the will to cling.

What am I? Who am I? What have I done with my life?

He crumbled silently, like a sugar cube in a cup of tea.

Who did I kill? What was I hunting? What is *hunting? Who did I hate? Whose blood did I shed?*

He sank faster and faster, down an immense distance. The surface of the darkness was far above his head.

It was so easy to let go, so comforting. To merge with emptiness was to gain supreme happiness. To feel nothing, remember nothing. To become empty meant overcoming all pain and suffering. He'd never dreamed that ceasing to be human could bring so much relief—

There was a deep tremor. He jerked to a stop, suspended in the abyss. He felt his half-melted face twitch with alarm.

Time ran backward. He was being reeled upward from the depths.

It was pure agony. *Who's doing this to me? Why? Don't send me back! I don't want to go back! I want to sink. Melt.*

He opened his mouth for a silent scream. He felt it opening. He couldn't breathe; he tore at his chest in desperation. He felt that, too.

The boundaries of his body, of Kotaro Mishima, were regenerating.

He moved his fingers, shook his head. He moved his legs. He was speeding upward. The darkness fell away quickly.

He flew through an opening in the floor of a corridor. He saw a kaleidoscope of dazzling torches and endless shelves. They raced past him, filling his sight—

He was flying. The wind hurt his eyeballs. He threw up his arms to protect his face as his body knifed through the air.

He rode the wind, swept along in the night sky. He felt the outlines of his body sharpening and filling in. The darkness that had eaten away at him streamed away as he hurtled onward.

He saw the Hall of All Books receding in the distance. There was a long line of torches like a fiery thread—the nameless devout. They were streaming toward the top of a hill; what was up there, anyway? A pair of enormous wheels lit by torches. The wheels were as large as a town. Hordes of devout seemed to be circling them. Maybe they were pushing them?

That must be the Great Wheels of Inculpation.

Two enormous wheels, sending stories out into the Circle and drawing them back again.

He felt tiny, fragile. He flew higher and higher, leaving the Hall of All Books and the great wheels of fire behind. At this rate he would soon reach the pike barrier. The Gate of Sorrows.

Child of the Circle.

The sheltering wind itself, carrying him through the sky, was calling to him.

I shall return you to your world.

Whose voice? It was very close. It was as though his ear were pressed against some giant object rumbling from within, sending pulsations throughout his body.

To return safely, you must call on your will. Remember. Think of the most wonderful thing in your life. The most beautiful, the most precious thing. Something you revere more than anything. It will guide you home.

Suddenly the wind fell away, and he was thrown headlong into the night sky. A pair of dark wings crossed the edge of his vision and vanished.

I am sorry.

The body of Kotaro Mishima, released from emptiness, traced out a parabola dictated by the law of gravity, the same parabola the moon would follow until morning in the Nameless Land.

A slug masquerading as a real coin. A proxy with no value. Something to toss aside without a second thought. The Gate of Sorrows was no barrier for something of no value in the Nameless Land. No strength was needed to open the gate, or close it.

Kotaro saw her. Echoes of the bond he and Galla had forged in their short time together in the real world let him see her.

The Gate of Sorrows had a new Sentinel, a petrified monster. An immovable seal so far above the plain that a visitor standing below would not even see it.

Galla the Guardian, turned to stone.

The price for opening the Gate…

Whoever vanquished the Sentinel became the Sentinel. Whether or not their hopes were fulfilled, whether or not they accomplished their aim, they would defeat the Sentinel and take its place.

Abandon all hope.

Galla…

She had betrayed and deceived him, but still he felt an upwelling of sorrow.

You knew all along it would come to this. You did it for your child. For your second self. What could that be, other than the workings of a heart? You had a heart after all.

"Galla!" He called to her with all his strength as he fell through the night.

He no longer knew where he was. He was simply falling, too fast to make anything out now. He didn't even know whether he was facing up or down.

To return safely, you must call upon your will.

"How do I do that?"

Remember the most wonderful thing in your life. Picture it, and it will guide you home.

"What in the hell is that?" Did something like that even exist? Every time he thought he'd found it, every time he'd dared believe in it, it had been taken from him. *Those* were the memories that were sharp and clear.

Ayuko had been murdered. His trust in Seigo had been undercut with doubt. He wouldn't believe in anyone or anything ever again, so who cared how things turned out for him? He'd threatened a friend, used him for his own purposes. He didn't deserve anyone's help or kindness.

He didn't trust anyone because he *wouldn't* trust anyone. And from there it had been a straight shot to bathing in someone's blood.

Something beautiful, something warm, something revered...

He'd tried to save Mika and failed. Now there was nothing left.

I've got no home to return to. There's nothing out there to guide me.

He longed to be a monster again, return to his real form, fall from the sky, and smash into a million pieces. *Yeah, that's it for me. Just let me die.*

Remember something you revere.

"There's nothing like that for me."

Help the world, at least a little.

Then he heard a new voice. *Uncle.*

He opened his eyes.

Your mother is right next to you. She's always by your side. That was his voice, a memory of it.

Always close to Mana, gently lighting up her daughter's smile.

His eyes filled with tears. *An angel's halo.*

It banished the darkness, engulfing him in radiance.

▼

"Come on, boy! Wake up!"

Kotaro stood up with a shock. Why was someone yelling at him?

No, he wasn't standing. He'd just lifted his head an inch or two. It was pounding. *Where am I? Why am I lying on the ground? What's all this stuff? Blood. My blood. My nose must be bleeding. Shit, it's all over the front of my T-shirt.*

There was something in his mouth. He spat it out. A broken tooth landed in his lap. Blood and saliva dribbled from a corner of his mouth.

Pain. His mouth was full of salty blood. His eyes wouldn't focus.

This was the real world. He was in the park near his house. Mika and Gaku's bench was a few feet away.

The spider was nowhere to be seen. The blood on the bench was gone.

His head hurt. His nose kept bleeding. This was no dream. It was real blood, his blood.

A dog was barking nearby like a metronome. He heard a shrill voice.

"Oh, my god! What happened to you?"

An old man looked down at him, wide-eyed with surprise. The man's Shiba dog was doing the barking. His bald head glowed under the street light. When Kotaro turned his head toward him, his expression changed from surprise to fear.

"You're covered in blood." The man ran to him and tried to help him up. Kotaro clutched at his arm. He didn't care about himself. Mika. Where was Mika?

"Did—did you see a teenage girl here? With her boyfriend? I think they might be in trouble."

The old man was baffled. "Trouble? You mean a fight?"

"No, not a fight..." Kotaro's head was spinning.

"How did you get hurt?"

"I don't know. I don't remember. But I've got to help them or something horrible will happen." Talking made him suddenly nauseous. He turned his head and vomited.

"This is bad. I'll call an ambulance," the man said in alarm.

His vision was blurred. The dog kept pacing back and forth nervously behind its master. It seemed to get bigger and smaller and bigger again. He felt an overwhelming vertigo.

Another voice. "There he is, officer!" A woman in a tracksuit. A policeman, too. They ran to Kotaro.

"Are you all right?" asked the cop.

"Don't move," the woman said. "Just stay put." He heard the squawk of a police radio. The trees against the sky seemed to be revolving, with him at the center.

"The medics will be here soon." The woman held his hand and spoke quickly, trying to comfort him. "I saw the license plate. The police are looking for them. Your friends will be all right. The police will find them soon."

My friends? License plate? What—

The dog kept barking. The cop was talking on his radio. *Getaway car—two teenagers—witness—one person injured.*

As he fought the vertigo, Kotaro slowly began to grasp what was happening. The jogger had seen Mika and Gaku being kidnapped and ran to a nearby police box. *Kidnapped by whom?* He was certain he knew the answer, but his memory had been wiped. His mind was a blank.

"Will the ambulance be much longer?" The jogger took the towel from her neck and wiped Kotaro's face gently. "He was just trying to help his friends, and those men hurt him. The one who hit him had something in his hand. I think it was a crowbar."

Her voice was quavering with shock. The old man tried to comfort her as he squatted next to his dog. "Don't worry. He's young. They were probably just drinking."

"No they weren't! There was a fat middle-aged guy and a young one, like a hooligan. They were taking this boy's friends away. He was hollering for help."

A fat, middle-aged man and a hooligan. Two people from the garbage emporium. They were with Kitty—

His memory was starting to return, but black waves of dizziness and nausea rose up, blotting it out.

"Hold on, kid! Help's on the way. You friends will be all right too!"

It was no use. He couldn't keep his eyes open. The black waves broke over him, but just before he lost consciousness, he saw the watch on the jogger's wrist, inches from his face.

PM 18:32

He'd returned before he left.

Mika—

We made it after all. I made it. I got to you in time. And I tried to help and they hit me and I fell—

Blackout.

▼

It was like watching an old TV on its last legs.

Sometimes the screen would come to life with ghostly, fragmentary images. The edges of the screen were blurred and distorted. Sometimes there was no picture, but the sound was clear and distinct.

"He's had a severe concussion. He was hit on the forehead, which caused a small amount of bleeding between his brain and the opposite side of his skull. It's called a traumatic subdural hematoma."

A burst of static cut off the voice, then it returned. "Anyway, he's going to survive, which is the only thing that matters."

That's Mom. Mom, I—

Suddenly a blinding brightness. He saw Kazumi's face distinctly.

"Kotaro? Are you awake?" She sounded surprised. He opened his mouth and tried to answer, but all he could produce was a rattling in his throat. Not the warm purring of a cat, but more like a wheezing pigeon.

"Don't worry, Mika's okay. Gaku too. They caught the kidnappers."

Something about a roadblock. Kazumi's face blurred and her voice faded. Kotaro took a deep breath, trying to clear his head. *Mika's okay. Mika's okay. Mika's okay.*

Head hurts. Nose hurts. Back hurts.

Caught the kidnappers? What was the name on that garbage dump?

Imazaki.

He must have said the name. "That's right," a voice said. "Imazaki, a husband and wife. Did you hear us talking about them? They're some really bad people. But the worst one is—"

Glitter Kitty. I know. I know. I know.

He fell back to sleep. It was like sinking into quicksand.

He opened his eyes. Seigo Maki and Kaname Ashiya stood side by side, peering down at him.

"Kotaro, it's Kaname. Do you recognize me?"

Yeah, but why are your eyes so puffy? Have you been crying?

"You're a hero, Ko-Prime." Seigo's eyes smiled gently. "I always knew you were on the side of justice."

No, Seigo. I'm the exact opposite. Or maybe I just went too far. Biting Kitty's head off, for example.

"Makoto wants to see you soon," Kaname said. "He's really worried about you."

"He's got his hands full digging into Teen911.com. We'd already seen some suspicious goings on with that site, but it wasn't on our watch list. After what happened, we're not leaving any stone unturned."

"Kotaro, can you hear us?"

Kotaro was struggling with more drowsiness than pain. He just wanted to sleep and escape reality. *Mika's okay. They caught the kidnappers. But I turned into a monster and bit someone's—*

No, I guess I didn't. I came back before it happened, which means it didn't happen. The cops rescued Mika and Gaku before they were taken to that house. That guy and his wife and the man with the tattoos and Kitty are all alive. They still exist. They're not missing.

But I don't remember doing anything. I don't remember what I did in the park.

And what about Galla?

Did none of that happen? Has reality experienced a total reset? Or was everything that happened after I went to the park and thought I saw a giant spider with burning coals for eyes, was all that just a dream I had while I've been lying here?

What you see and feel may not be real. He heard Ash's voice calling to him.

But was Galla unreal? Was she?

He heard a sudden, high-pitched beeping. The vital signs monitor was sounding a warning. His heart rate and blood pressure were spiking. It wasn't his body; it was his mind. His heart cried out in pain and sadness.

He would never meet the guardian demon again. Everything was finished. The worst had been avoided. He'd been saved just short of the point of no return.

But Galla was gone.

▼

"It's called retrograde amnesia."

Shigenori shifted uncomfortably on the hard hospital chair. "Hit your head hard enough and you can forget what happened just before and after that. So you don't remember what really happened—that you were trying to help Mika." The ex-detective snorted cynically and added quietly, "Some other things you still remember would be good to forget too."

A week after the incident, Kotaro was sitting on his bed in a private room. He head was wrapped in bandages and a hair net. The pain was mostly gone; he was feeling much better and could receive visitors like Shigenori. "Nothing like a fruit basket when you're laid up," he'd said as he set the huge basket at the foot of Kotaro's bed.

He told Shigenori everything that happened that night. He was the only one Kotaro could talk to about these things—seeing the Tower of Inception, traveling to the Nameless Land, looking up at the Gate of Sorrows, and Galla's fate.

"You don't really think it would be better for me to forget all that," he told Shigenori when the story was finished. "I sure don't."

Shigenori didn't seem surprised at this reaction.

"Those things are reality for me," Kotaro added. "They really happened."

Shigenori looked at him steadily and slowly shook his head. "No, you're wrong about that. This is reality, here and now."

The daily news shows were still focused on the Teen911 Incident. Toshiki Imazaki, forty-one, website administrator and self-styled systems engineer. Mieko Nakai, his common-law wife, age forty. She managed a small bar in the neighborhood. The man with the tattoos was a regular customer: Shinji Hino, thirty-one, unemployed. He had a record of sexual assault and not the faintest concept of PCs or the Internet, but when Teen911 had a revenge assignment, he supplied the muscle.

According to Seigo, Teen911.com had popped up on the web five years ago. In the beginning, it really did seem to be a site students could go for advice about romance and friendship, worries about their appearance, problems with their studies and so forth. The site was just what it claimed to be.

About a year ago, this had started to change. A student consulted the Imazakis about a bullying problem. They forced the leader of the students who were involved in the bullying to write a letter of apology, and they squeezed a "compensation" payment out of him. It was around this time that Shinji Hino fell in with them. His criminal record and appearance was more than effective for coercing and intimidating naïve young people. Teen911 quickly gained a reputation as the go-to site for local teens who wanted to get back at someone.

"School Island wasn't tracking them at all. We really screwed up," Seigo said regretfully.

The Imazakis' standard MO was to hustle the young person they'd been hired to deal with into their car, driving them around and berating them, or locking them up in the punishment room in their house for a few hours. Once the news broke, many past victims started coming forward. The media even speculated that the Imazakis might be involved in the disappearance of a male college student just after the beginning of the year.

Glitter Kitty, a 16-year-old high school student, was also in the spotlight. She'd paid to have Mika Sonoi kidnapped and beaten up, and because the Internet was the point of contact between her and the Imazakis, it was the perfect opportunity for the mainstream media to criticize web culture. At the same time, while the networks and newspapers were referring to Kitty as "Girl A," her face and home address, details about her parents and everything else concerning her were all over the web, a situation that fueled a fierce debate of its own.

Kitty had always insisted on winning at any cost. Many people weighed in with stories about her cruelty, her obsession with being first, and her unwillingness to take advice. As a fifth grader, she'd harassed her homeroom teacher so badly that the woman had been forced to take a leave of absence.

As Kotaro had heard himself that night at the Imazakis—an event that his reset had wiped from reality—Kitty's family was quite well-off, a fact she was stuck-up about. She was one of the wealthy who'd moved into the neighborhood after the farmland was turned into a residential area. She had a fierce superiority complex toward "aborigines" like Mika and Kazumi. It seemed that her hatred of Mika was partially fired by such prejudice.

That was reality on "this side." Kotaro was losing interest in the details. Mika was okay. The kidnappers had been caught. That was enough.

But he was not satisfied. He was extremely dissatisfied.

"I don't know how this 'law of the Circle' thing works, but if they were going to send me back in time, why didn't they send me back a lot further than just a few hours?"

Before Ayuko's murder. Before Kenji noticed that homeless people were going missing along the Seibu-Shinjuku Line. Kotaro would've been ready to have his whole life reset if it had meant saving those two people.

But Shigenori was having nothing of his disgruntled muttering. "You ought to be happy with getting just a few hours back. It was enough to save Mika, wasn't it?"

Kotaro hated to admit it, but Shigenori was right. He always was; that was why Kotaro felt driven to disagree with him.

"Mika's a cute girl. Your sister is more of a classic beauty. She takes after her mother."

When Shigenori had walked through the door, weighed down by his lavish fruit basket, he had run into two mother/daughter duos: Asako and Kazumi, and Takako and Mika. He'd casually introduced himself as a "colleague" of Kotaro's—Asako assumed he was from Kumar, someone even higher up the ladder than Seigo, and treated him with inflated politeness.

"I know it's none of my business, but I'm a bit worried about Takako Sonoi," Shigenori said. "When something like this happens to a child, it can be harder for the parents than for the child."

He was right. Mika had come out of her ordeal with barely a scratch, and she seemed buoyant and scrappy, but Kotaro thought Takako was looking haggard.

"I wouldn't say this to her, but I think she feels responsible for what happened to me too. Like, if she'd been more involved and a better mother, I wouldn't be sitting here."

Shigenori nodded. "You should make sure she knows that's not true. There wasn't anything she could've done to prevent it. Coming from you, I think she'll believe that. In less than ten months you've just about seen it all. You've been through hell."

"I don't think so," Kotaro said. Shigenori's eyebrows rose in surprise.

"Galla's eye didn't show me evil. It showed me words. Words created by people's thoughts."

The moment words are uttered, they are past. All words are residue. They gather like fallen leaves.

Shigenori looked at him intently. "I saw them once myself. At Naka-chan. Two paper strips for the Star Festival, turned blood red. I've thought a lot about that since then, and I've come to a conclusion. Words, and the residue they leave behind—what Galla showed you, what you experienced—people since ancient times have had a name for it.

"It's called karma. The karma each person carries with them. You accumulate it just by being alive. It's not good or bad in itself. But when it ripens, it can bring real misfortune. The monsters you saw, giants and two-headed beasts, are the personification of karma."

Kotaro was silent for a moment. Then: "Do you think Galla was evil?"

"I don't know. But I'm standing by my conclusion. She was a concept. That's how she could be real, yet not exist. Other than that, your guess is as good as mine. But she did deceive you. She used you—"

"Maybe she didn't. You know what she told me? That she chose me in the beginning, but in the end I was the one who chose. She was right. It wasn't her fault. I made the wrong choice, but her son Auzo ended up saving my neck."

"If you think that's what happened, then that's how it happened." Shigenori nodded, almost as if trying to convince himself. "By the way, it looks like the tea caddy building has a buyer." He shifted uncomfortably in the chair. "Things may be settled before you get out of here."

"If they put a shop in there, we can walk right in the front door," Kotaro said.

"They probably won't let us go up to the roof, though."

"That first floor looked like a good place for a restaurant. If they open one, let's have a party and celebrate my recovery."

"Sure, sure. Looking forward to it. By that time, you'll probably have a nice new implant to close that gap in your teeth. You'll be handsome again."

Shigenori's response was playful, but his eyes weren't smiling. Kotaro probably looked the same.

This is the end of the line.

It was better for both of them. They didn't have to say it to know it was true. This wasn't a sympathy visit. Shigenori had come to say goodbye.

The matter is closed. I'm going back to my life. You should do the same, kid.

That was how detectives said goodbye.

Fortunately for Kotaro, his hematoma wasn't so large that it required surgery. With time it would be reabsorbed naturally. Until then he'd have to be monitored closely, but that was all. Still, more than two weeks after that night in the park, he remained in the hospital.

Summer had hung on tenaciously but was finally gone. He climbed the stairs to the roof of his wing. As he strolled along the roof between the lines of flapping laundry and the high net fence, Seigo peeked around the door to the stairwell and stepped out onto the roof.

"I asked the nurse. She told me you were probably up here doing calisthenics."

"I'm not quite in shape for that yet," Kotaro said.

"It's nice up here on the roof."

"It's where they hang the laundry, but it's a paradise for secret smokers, too."

Seigo squinted against the breezy sunlight. "About five years ago, was it? Ayuko ended up in the hospital with meningitis. At the time, she was a smoker. As soon as she was up and around, she started sneaking around looking for a place to smoke. Another patient clued her in. And here I'd been telling her it was a good chance for her to quit."

Kotaro peered at him closely. The was the first time he'd heard Seigo talk about Ayuko since she died.

That was the end of the story. He turned his back to Kotaro, reached up and grabbed the wire mesh of the fence. "We're pretty high up here. It's making me dizzy."

The matter is closed. I'm going back to my life. Shigenori was gone, but for Kotaro, one loose end remained. Without an answer to that question—if he didn't at least try to get an answer—he couldn't go back to his own life.

"Seigo?" They were alone on the roof. He probably wouldn't have another chance like this.

"What?" Seigo glanced over his shoulder. From his expression, he seemed to have guessed what Kotaro was about to ask. He turned and looked off into the distance again.

"That woman, Keiko Tashiro—"

"Whereabouts unknown. Still."

"You two had a relationship, didn't you?"

Seigo had lost a lot of weight. Ayuko's death had deprived him of a vital part of his life. It was as if part of him had been cut away, leaving him small and diminished.

He'd never be the same again. The thought made Kotaro's throat tighten with grief, but he pushed on. "You weren't just friends, were you?"

It's yes or no. There are no other answers. You'll either face the challenge or run away. But Seigo didn't follow the script.

"I'm certain Ayuko didn't know. It was my fault. I never wanted to hurt her, though. I made sure she'd never find out. It was a one-time slip, it didn't last long. Afterward I felt like an idiot."

He finally turned around and made eye contact with Kotaro. "But that's no excuse. What she did was because of her relationship with me."

"The possibility occurred to me too."

"I see."

"But I don't see it that way now."

Seigo's mouth twitched for an instant. "Okay," he said. "But I'm not going to change how I feel. Once you lose something, it's gone forever."

"Sure. Sorry, that was a little rude."

"When did you notice? At the wake? She was there."

"I don't remember."

"You're not the only one. This kind of thing always gets out. I told the cops everything. I want you to know that."

"Okay," Kotaro said.

Seigo turned and headed toward the stairs. "I brought your pay slip," he called over his shoulder. "It's by your bed."

"Thanks, Seigo."

Seigo opened the door to the stairs. Another friend was leaving him, but this time Kotaro spoke up.

"Hey, Seigo! Okay if I come to work again?"

Seigo stuck his head around the door. "Tokyo office closes at the end of the year."

"Then I'll work till the end of the year."

"Got it. Give Maeda a ring. We'll get you a shift."

He disappeared down the stairs. Kotaro heard his footsteps dying away on the metal steps.

"Hey, dummy."

He turned toward the sound of a girl's voice. She stepped out from behind the line of white sheets fluttering in the wind on a clothesline.

"Did you really need to ask him about that? Why does it matter now?"

She was outfitted in her standard black, looking good as always. It was positively annoying.

"It doesn't matter now," Kotaro said. "That's why it was okay to ask. I doubt you'd understand, though, seeing as how you're still so green that Ash has to scold you all the time."

U-ri the wolf was not thrilled by this statement. She frowned. "That's not very nice."

"I hear you're not strong enough to go places like the ones I went with Galla."

"Well, it's not like you went there on your own, is it?"

He smiled. They leaned against the fence side by side. "I wonder if I saw your brother in the Nameless Land."

U-ri turned to look at him. She sighed softly. "My brother isn't there. Not as an individual person," she said with great gentleness. In a way, Kotaro felt her tone was meant for him as well as her brother. "You met the nameless devout. You only met emptiness. They aren't anybody specific."

"Oh. I see."

"It's great that you made it back."

"Thanks." Kotaro meant it, but U-ri shook her head.

"I didn't have anything to do with it. I couldn't do anything. The power of your story brought you back. That's where you should send your gratitude."

"Yeah. As soon as I'm out of here, I'll go see her."

When he was unconscious in the intensive care unit, dozens of voice messages and a mountain of mails had piled up on his mobile phone. The

Nagasaki siblings topped the list. As soon as he was able, Kotaro had gotten in touch with Hatsuko and apologized for causing her worry.

"My heart almost stopped when I saw the news," she said. "Mana is worried sick about you too."

"When I'm better, I'm going to bring the world's sweetest little girl the world's sweetest cream puffs," he said to U-ri.

U-ri giggled. "Head over heels, eh?"

Her cheerful response struck home. Something hard and unyielding seemed to give way in Kotaro's heart.

"I ignored your warning. I just made one mistake after another. I can't change anything. I can't go back and fix anything."

U-ri didn't answer. He felt her slipping away.

"If you're looking for somebody to comfort you and tell you things aren't that bad, you won't get it from me. Goodbye, Kotaro."

"Hey, wait!"

She was already gone. "Thanks a lot! Why did you bother to even come?"

He wanted her to tell him. It was something he couldn't ask anyone else. But he could ask her. He could cry like a wimp and cling to her and ask her.

"What do I do now?"

Just live. Live, live, live.

He looked out at the city spread below him. At reality. At the world.

This was the Circle, where stories never end, where the cycle of life rolls on, where prayers are answered, where cries of grief echoe.

You are a child of the Circle. Live.

He tarried on the roof for a long time. Finally—

"I am sorry."

He said it aloud. "I am sorry."

Somewhere inside and beneath the whisper of the wind, he thought he heard singing—or was it an incantation? The nameless devout. And on the wind, the scent of night dew and dry spring grass.

He gazed up at the Gate of Sorrows in that far-off land at the edge of the Circle. A gate guarded by something that once had been Galla.

I will live.

This is a work of fiction.

During the research for this book, I received valuable assistance from the staff of Pitcrew Co., Ltd. as well as the Social Affairs Desk of the Mainichi Newspapers, Tokyo Headquarters. To the extent that the events depicted herein reflect contemporary social conditions, it is thanks to the efforts of everyone who was kind enough to assist me. For this I would like to extend my sincere gratitude.

Miyuki Miyabe
January 2015

Apparitions: Ghosts of Old Edo

In old Edo, the past was never forgotten. It lived alongside the present in dark corners and in the shadows. In these tales, award-winning author Miyuki Miyabe explores the ghosts of early modern Japan and the spaces of the living world—workplaces, families, and the human soul—that they inhabit. Written with a journalistic eye and a fantasist's heart, *Apparitions* brings the restless dead, and those who encounter them, to life.

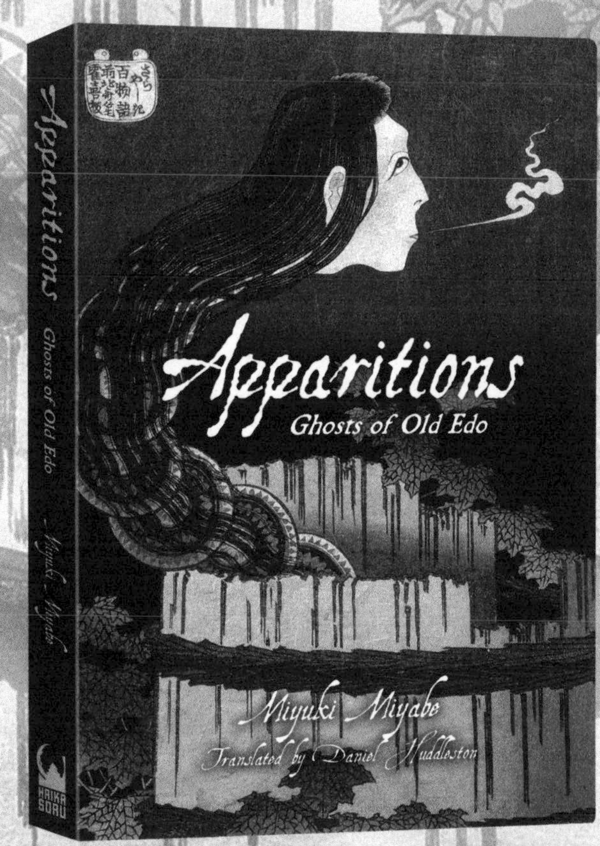

SRP: $14.99 USA / $16.99 CAN / £9.99 UK

ISBN: 978-1-4215-6742-6

At better bookstores everywhere and www.haikasoru.com